The Reproductive

Wompler's Walking Babies aren't selling like they used to, so the company develops Project 32, producing self-replicating mechanisms designed to repair inter-cellular breakdowns. But then the metal boxes begin crawling about the laboratory, feeding voraciously on metal and multiplying ...

The Müller-Fokker Effect

Bob Shairp – a writer and dreamer – has agreed to be a guinea-pig in a military experiment to find out if his personality can be turned into data and stored on computer. But a computing error quickly destroys Shairp's physical body, leaving his mind stranded in an encoded world. Can the process be reversed?

Tik-Tok

Something has gone very seriously wrong with Tik-Tok's circuits. They should keep him on the straight and narrow, following Asimov's First Law of Robotics. But they don't. While maintaining the outward appearance of a mild-mannered robot, Tik-Tok's real agenda is murderously different. He seems intent on injuring – preferably fatally – as many people as possible. Almost inevitably, a successful career in crime and general mayhem leads to a move into politics and Tik-Tok becomes the first robot candidate for Vice President of the United States.

Also by John Sladek

Novels

The Reproductive System (1968) (aka Mechasm)
The Muller-Fokker Effect (1970)
Roderick (1980)
Roderick at Random (1983)
Tik-Tok (1983)
Bugs (1989)
Wholly Smokes (2003)

Collections

The Steam-Driven Boy (1970)
Keep the Giraffe Burning (1977)
Alien Accounts (1982)
The Lunatics of Terra (1984)
Maps: The Uncollected John Sladek (2001)

John Sladek

SF GATEWAY OMNIBUS

THE REPRODUCTIVE SYSTEM
THE MÜLLER-FOKKER EFFECT
TIK-TOK

GOLLANCZ
LONDON

First published in Great Britain in 2013 by
Gollancz
An imprint of the Orion Publishing Group
Orion House, 5 Upper St Martin's Lane,
London WC2H 9EA

An Hachette UK Company

A CIP catalogue record for this book
is available from the British Library

ISBN 978 0 575 11070 0

1 3 5 7 9 10 8 6 4 2

Typeset by Jouve (UK), Milton Keynes

Printed and bound by CPI Group (UK) Ltd, Croydon CR0 4YY

The Orion Publishing Group's policy is to use papers
that are natural, renewable and recyclable products and
made from wood grown in sustainable forests. The logging
and manufacturing processes are expected to conform to
the environmental regulations of the country of origin.

www.orionbooks.co.uk
www.gollancz.co.uk

CONTENTS

ENTER THE SF GATEWAY . . .

Towards the end of 2011, in conjunction with the celebration of fifty years of coherent, continuous science fiction and fantasy publishing, Gollancz launched the SF Gateway.

Over a decade after launching the landmark SF Masterworks series, we realised that the realities of commercial publishing are such that even the Masterworks could only ever scratch the surface of an author's career. Vast troves of classic SF and fantasy were almost certainly destined never again to see print. Until very recently, this meant that anyone interested in reading any of those books would have been confined to scouring second-hand bookshops. The advent of digital publishing changed that paradigm for ever.

Embracing the future even as we honour the past, Gollancz launched the SF Gateway with a view to utilising the technology that now exists to make available, for the first time, the entire backlists of an incredibly wide range of classic and modern SF and fantasy authors. Our plan, at its simplest, was – and still is! – to use this technology to build on the success of the SF and Fantasy Masterworks series and to go even further.

The SF Gateway was designed to be the new home of classic science fiction and fantasy – the most comprehensive electronic library of classic SFF titles ever assembled. The programme has been extremely well received and we've been very happy with the results. So happy, in fact, that we've decided to complete the circle and return a selection of our titles to print, in these omnibus editions.

We hope you enjoy this selection. And we hope that you'll want to explore more of the classic SF and fantasy we have available. These are wonderful books you're holding in your hand, but you'll find much, much more ... through the SF Gateway.

www.sfgateway.com

INTRODUCTION

from The Encyclopedia of Science Fiction

John T. Sladek (1937–2000) was a US writer who between 1966 and 1986 spent his central creative decades in the UK, becoming involved in the UK New Wave movement centred on Michael Moorcock's *New Worlds*, and co-editing with Pamela Zoline *Ronald Reagan: The Magazine of Poetry* (two issues 1968), where work by both editors, J. G. Ballard, Thomas M. Disch and others appeared. After 1986, he lived in Minnesota near Minneapolis, a region that had long supplied local colour and context for many of his more severely satirical stories, whose protagonists ricochet through their preordained and absurd lives within the vast, hyperbolic, suburban flatlands of middle America. This *mise en scène*, when illuminated by his adept control of the language and pretensions of the modern bureaucratic state, was a fertile matrix for his best work, and helps make plausible the frequent comparisons that have been drawn between him and Kurt Vonnegut Jr. Although Vonnegut has an easier emotional flow than his younger contemporary, Sladek generally eschews his shoulder-shrugging rhetorical self-indulgences, and avoids his excessive simplicity of effect.

Sladek began writing sf with 'The Happy Breed', published in Harlan Ellison's *Dangerous Visions* (anth 1967), though his first published solo story was 'The Poets of Millgrove, Iowa' (1966), and earlier he had published a non-sf story, 'The Way to a Man's Heart' (1966), with Thomas M. Disch. Sladek's first two novels – *The House that Fear Built* (1966) with Disch and *The Castle and the Key* (1967) – were Gothics, both as by Cassandra Knye. His first two sf novels, *The Reproductive System* (1968) (see below) and *The Müller-Fokker Effect* (1970) (see below) were among of his finest. Between the two appeared the underappreciated *Black Alice* (1968), with Disch as by Thom Demijohn, a non-sf satirical thriller.

Throughout his career, Sladek wrote numerous stories whose strenuous formal ingenuity, and whose surreal combining of a deadpan ribaldry and pathos, have made them underground classics of the genre. The most notable of them all, because of its length and impassioned veracity of tone, may be 'Masterson and the Clerks' (1967), in which the immolation of its protagonists in the internal bureaucracy of a US business is first hilariously then movingly presented; true to the oddly uncommercial course of his career, Sladek collected this tale only much later, in his third collection, *Alien*

Accounts (1982), which contains mostly early work with a focus on the sur-realisms of corporate bureaucracy. His first collection, *The Steam-Driven Boy and Other Strangers* (1973), generally presents later work, including several 1970s parodies of well-known sf writers, some of which are perhaps the finest ever executed within the field, among them being 'Broot Force' (1972) as by Iclick As-i-move (i.e. Isaac Asimov), 'Joy Ride' (1972) as by Barry DuBray (an anagram of Ray Bradbury) and 'Solar Shoe-Salesman' (1973) as by Chipdip K. Kill, a near-anagram of Philip K. Dick. His second collection, *Keep the Giraffe Burning* (1978) contains 'The Poets of Millgrave, Iowa' (1966) plus later work. Taken together, these three volumes represent Sladek's most for-mally and most aggressively brilliant shorter work, though some stories, perhaps more formally brilliant than 'Masterson', do lack something of its human intensity. In the stories collected as *The Lunatics of Terra* (1984), the comic melancholy of his early work wears a somewhat calmer guise. *Maps: The Uncollected John Sladek* (2002) edited by David Langford assembles all the previously uncollected short work that was then known. A further light-hearted story from the *Steam-Driven Boy* era subsequently came to light in Sladek's papers and appeared as 'The Real Martian Chronicles' (2010).

During the 1970s, when most of his stories became generally available, Sladek also published two detective novels, *Black Aura* (1974) – which con-tains some borderline-sf elements – and *Invisible Green: A Thackeray Phin Mystery* (1977), before returning to long-form sf with *Roderick, or The Edu-cation of a Young Machine* (1980) and *Roderick at Random, or Further Education of a Young Machine* (1983), two texts conceived as a single novel. It was typical of Sladek's career that the US version of this long novel appeared in savagely truncated form. It was not until the posthumous release of *The Complete Roderick* (2002) that this ambitious tale could be read as a continu-ous narrative. The overall story is presented as the autobiography of the eponymous Robot, conveying with considerable ingenuity and some pathos its protagonist's Candide-like innocence and its author's Oulipo-derived numerological sense of narrative structure. Perhaps more successful than Roderick, and certainly more biting in his humour was *Tik-Tok* (1983) (see below). Though robots inevitably appear, *Bugs* (1989) was Sladek's first sf novel to feature a 'normal' human protagonist; and in its tracing of the deranging experiences of a UK immigrant to a strange Midwestern city (clearly Minneapolis) the tale could be seen as guardedly autobiographical.

Sladek also composed a sequence of nonfiction texts of considerable inter-est, though (again typically) their impact was lessened, either by threats of litigation or through the use of unrevealed pseudonyms. *The New Apoc-rypha: A Guide to Strange Sciences and Occult Beliefs* (1973) – any editions after 1973 being censored under threat of legal action from the Church of Scientology – scathingly anatomizes the various cults and Pseudosciences that exist as a kind of fringe around the sf reader's areas of interest, from Scientology to Von Daniken. *Arachne Rising: The Thirteenth Sign of the Zodiac* (1977) as by James Vogh, *The Cosmic Factor: Bioastrology and You* (1978) as by James Vogh and *Judgement of Jupiter* (1980) as by Richard A. Tilms were hoax demonstrations of the kind of fringe theorizing that underpins the cults described in *The New Apocrypha*. *Arachne Rising* was perhaps the most successful, in the sense that many readers apparently did not understand that its claim to have discovered a thirteenth sign of the zodiac was pure spoof.

As the most formally inventive, the funniest, and very nearly the most melancholy of modern American sf writers, Sladek transgressively addressed the heart of the genre, but (perhaps as a consequence of this) never gained due renown. We needed his attention, which we got: he deserved ours, which he did not receive during his lifetime. But perhaps it is not too late.

The first novel presented here, *The Reproductive System* (1968), introduces us to Sladek's typical small-town-America setting, as usual in his work assaulted by a brilliant maelstrom of disturbances out of the sf toolkit. A self-reproducing technological device goes out of control, in passages of allegorical broadness, portraying its victims as hapless Sorcerer's Apprentices. Everything turns out all right in the end, though not through positive efforts of the inept cast, and a dreamlike Utopia looms on the horizon. Shaping the hilarities of the tale is an obsessive discourse upon and dramatization of the metamorphic relationships between human and Robot, a relationship which lies at the centre of all Sladek's subsequent solo novels and much of his short fiction.

In *The Müller-Fokker Effect* (1970), which appears here next, a man's character is accidentally transferred onto Computer tape in a kind of Upload, and the dissemination of several copies of this 'personality' instigates a series of absurd events, some of them extremely comic in effect, some horrifying, all Paranoia-inducing (like most of his work), all creating in the end a vision of America as a land disintegrated morally and physically by its own fatal surrender to Technology, the profit motive and the ethical falseness that leads to dehumanization. In its questioning of the nature of narrative events and of fiction itself, the book is a significant demonstration of modern American self-analysis at its highly impressive best. More than 40 years after it first appeared, *The Müller-Fokker Effect* is now a time-bomb. It has become a central sf novel for our times.

Though fully as comic as its great predecessors, *Tik-Tok* (1983), the third novel here assembled, does not pretend to address the same wide range of issues. It is, rather, a scherzo, an expert fast-forward thematic pendant which takes its structure from the arbitrary rule-generating principles of Oulipo, though without forcing these rules into the reader's vision. All is in fact utterly clear, as we follow the career of a robot who, once his 'asimov circuits' go on the blink, becomes criminally ambitious, a Candide gone over to the dark side. But *Tik-Tok* itself is utterly sane, as was its author, who shone a light of reason on the craziness of his times, and kept his eyes open. These three novels tell us what he saw there.

For a more detailed version of the above, see John T. Sladek's author entry in *The Encyclopedia of Science Fiction*: http://sf-encyclopedia.com/entry/sladek_john_t

Some terms above are capitalised when they would not normally be so rendered; this indicates that the terms represent discrete entries in *The Encyclopedia of Science Fiction*.

THE REPRODUCTIVE SYSTEM

To P.Z.

PROLOGUE
Did You See Her in 'Heidi'?

Suppose that it is once more 196—, that fateful year, and suppose that you are passing through Millford, Utah, that most fated of crossroads. Population, a battered, bird-spattered sign informs you, is '3810 And Still Growing! Home of Shelley B—'

Home of Shelley something, Millford lies about half-way between Las Vegas, Nevada, and the North American Air Defence Command (NORAD) buried deep in a Colorado mountain. The name 'Millford' is honorific; there has never been a stream through this part of the desert, nor a mill, nor anything to grind in a mill. Perhaps it was named ironically, or wishfully. Founders of other desert towns have, after all, given them pretty names, hoping that (by sympathetic magic) pretty reality would follow.

Millford is not pretty, it is worn and warped. There is little to distinguish it from Eden Acres, Greenville or Paradise. Its feed store, like theirs, is checkered red and white. Along its main drag lurk old familiar faces: The Eateria; The Idle Hour; Marv's Eat-Gas; The Dew Drop Inn Motel.

You, the casual tourist – say you are an Air Force General from NORAD on his way to get a divorce – are more interested in your odometer than in that Coca-Cola bottling plant or whatever it is over there on the right. You are barely conscious of an ugly factory of glazed brick, with a glass-block window on its rounded corner. 'Wompler Toy Corporation. Makers of —'

The worn sign slides past you, lost for ever. There is only one sign you are interested in: 'Resume Speed'. Ah, there it is. And there's another: 'You are now leaving Millford, Utah, Home of Shelley Belle. Hurry Back!' Your foot comes down on the gas, hard. The rattle of tappets asks:

> *Who the hell*
> *Is Shelley Belle?*

You are irritated with Millford. You are annoyed with your own faulty memory. You are bored with all ugly little desert towns with their smug signs: 'Biggest Little City in the Universe!' You are hot and bored and tired, and you exceed the speed limit a little, fleeing from the place where world history is being made …

CHAPTER I

The Womplers at Work

'She was a phantom of delight
When first she gleamed upon my sight.
… And now I see with eye serene
The very pulse of the machine.'

WORDSWORTH

'Sorry I'm late, gang.' Louie Guthridge Wompler, vice-president in charge of public relations, bounced into the conference room on ripple-soled shoes. He smiled at the other three members of the board, but they seemed not to notice.

'Where were you?' asked the president, Grandison Wompler. His jowls shook with annoyance. 'We've got important business to discuss.'

'Sorry, Pop.' Louie threw himself into a chair at the right hand of his father. 'I was getting in some work on my lats. You know, *latissimus dorsi*? That's here.' He pointed a thick finger at his own armpit.

'We're dissolving the company, son.'

'You know, I'm getting some pretty clean definition— Dissolving the company! But why, Pop? Why?'

Grandison's gavel made a sound like a pistol shot. 'Meeting to order,' he rumbled.

'What's the scoop, Pop?' Louie persisted, and shone upon his father a winning, Harold Teen smile.

'Son,' the old man began, then stopped. He was searching for a cliché that Louie could grasp. Though forty-one years old he did not seem, at times, far removed from adolescence. Now, as he toyed with a spring grip developer and a jar of Sooper Proteen tablets, Louie seemed even – his father frowned at the thought – even childish.

The two men did not look much like father and son. The president was tall, sunburnt and rangy, fleshing out slightly in his middle age to a dignified thickness. His face was heavy and serious, with a stern jaw and thick, dark brows. There were, however, laugh lines, and his black eyes were festooned with kindly wrinkles. With no grey in his hair, Grandison ('Granny') Wompler looked ten years younger than his sixty-five.

Louie, known by some as 'Louie the Womp', was pale and porcine. He somehow managed to resemble a watercolour of his father, one which had been through the laundry. His blond, tentatively wavy hair, milk-coloured eyes and pastry-cook skin might have made him effete but for his immense bulk. There was something athletic in Louie's sagging shoulders and pyknic belly; he seemed a man who had been hit repeatedly in the face. His nose was flattened, and indeed all his features were a trifle smooth, a trifle melted.

He wore no tie, and beneath the white fabric of his shirt could be discerned the T-shirt legend: 'SOOPERPROTEEN CLUB'. His smile, as he waited for his father to go on, was as pure and meaningless as that of dentures in a glass, and as constant.

'Son, I don't know how I'm going to explain this to you—'

'Let me try, Granny.' Go wan Dill, the joky ninety-year-old production manager, turned to Louie and said, 'What your father wants to say is, we've hitched our wagon to a falling star.'

'Summer slump, that's all it is,' Louie whined, still smiling. 'Sales gotta pick up by Christmas.'

'We'll be *rooned* by Christmas!' snarled his father. '*Rooned!*'

'– summer slump, or –'

'No, son. The truth is, we're finished. No one wants Wompler's Walking Babies any more.'

Grandison's gnarled hands trembled slightly as they lifted a doll from its tissue paper packing and placed it on its feet. It began to toddle along the polished surface of the table, mewing at every step. The president's jaw clenched with emotion. A kazoo in his head was faintly playing 'The March of the Wooden Soldiers'.

Hardly anyone knew what really happened to Shelley Belle. She had been put away in tissue paper, so to speak, with other, happier memories of the thirties (Al Jolson, Bank Nite movies, the Cord roadster, Paul Whiteman's orchestra), as though she were indeed a sunny, golden-haired doll. Just as no one wished to remember the real thirties (soup lines, bread lines, work lines), so no one wished to remember the real history of Shelley (grown, married, divorced, married, suicide attempt, bit parts in Alfred Hitchcock movies). She would always be as they first knew her, in 1935, tossing her curls and grinning impishly at W. C. Fields or Wallace Beery. All over America, housewives clutched their free dishes and gaped. As this five-year-old shrugged, tap-dancing her way through 'The March of the Wooden Soldiers', they asked in blank amazement, Wasn't she precious? Wasn't she the darlingest, sassiest, ittiest yummykins sweetheart, though? Wasn't she a living doll?

Doll. The word exploded in the brain of Grandison Wompler during a performance of *Heidi* at the Belmont Theatre. He had leaped up and begun cursing joyfully, until the manager, Ned Lambert, had been obliged to throw him out. Granny didn't mind. He didn't even mind missing the Spin-O-Cash. What were a hundred silver dollars to him? He was bursting with a million-dollar plan! He went straight home and wrote, in the centre of a sheet of paper: 'DOLL = DOLLARS'.

Why not make dolls of Shelley Belle right here in her home town, and why not distribute them all over the nation – the world? He would by God make a million and put Millford on the map at the same time.

There had been a few catches, as time went on. He had already got production started when a court order enjoined him from use of the name 'Shelley Belle'. But Grandison had established his market; he did not need her name any longer. Soon, Wompler's Walking Babies became famous in their own right, and his fortune was assured.

Even during the war he'd done well. The main plant had turned to making howitzer shells, while the seamstresses sewed canteen covers. The company had won two 'E' awards. Louie had gone into the army and been decorated with the Quartermaster's Cross. It seems he had bought more canteen covers than any other quartermaster. Father and son had been sorry to see the enemy give up so easily.

In 1946 Wompler's Babies walked again, but not nearly so profitably. Sales kept slipping, slipping, as people forgot about the ageing, alcoholic Shelley Belle. Now, twenty years later, the factory had come to a stop. As Gowan Dill put it, with many winks and digs of his frail elbow, 'Production has come to the end of the line, boys. The eye division is tight shut. Not a head rolling off the assembly line. We might just as well take the remainder of our dolls and—'

'Stuff them, I know,' said Grandison wearily. 'I know, I know, I know.' He stared, bleary-eyed, at the doll walking away from him.

It had huge blue eyes and gold, stiff sausage curls. It wore a red-white-and-blue pleated dress with silver spangles, and a tiny pillbox hat. Its pink dimpled knees were barely visible between the silver fringe of the skirt and the thick white boots with silver tassels.

'Mew, mew, mew, mew, mew,' it said.

'Looks swell to me, Pop,' said Louie loyally. He had caught his fist inside the jar of Sooper Proteen tablets. It had not occurred to Louie not to reach into a jar with the spring grip developer in his hand. 'I think it's a neat little product.'

'But it isn't wanted, son. Little girls don't want Wompler's Walking Babies any more. They want Barbie dolls. Dolls they can dress up in fashions.' His voice grew thick with fury, and he flushed purple beneath his sunburn. 'Dolls that can't walk a single step!'

'Gee, Pop, that's keen! Why don't *we* build a doll they can dress up?'

'Because we don't know the first thing about fashion, that's why. Mrs Lumsey's seamstresses can't sew anything but spangles and pleats.'

'And canteen covers,' cracked Dill, shooting his cuffs.

No one was smiling. Grandison stared at the walking doll, looking as if he wanted to cry, but was just too strong. Louie was staring, mystified, at his entrapped hand. Moley, the chairman, was sliding down in his chair, preparing to sleep.

'Send this company to camp!' ventured Dill. No response. 'Ah well,' he sighed. 'Let's put on our thinking caps.'

The doll, still mewing, walked off the end of the table. There came the crack of a gutta percha face against the floor.

'The end of a great era,' the president muttered hoarsely.

They thought. Louie had a hard time concentrating. He wanted to be outside, doing some road-work, or just getting a tan. He wanted to study up on his karate. He wanted to get home to see if that book had come in the mail: *Seventeen* New *Ways to Kill a Man with Your Bare Hands*. And the book on Sumo wrassling.

The trouble with books was, they didn't give a guy the *feel* of killing with his bare hands. That was the trouble with living in Millford, too. There was nowhere a guy could go to learn from an instructor. Louie wanted to learn all those Jap systems of self-defence. He wanted to learn how to kill a man with Zen – without even touching him, they say. Then there was Kabuki, and there was deadliest Origami. Man!

He continued staring out the window for inspiration, until a car, air-force blue, whizzed by. It reminded him of isometric exercises. Then, somewhere in Louie's rudimentary forebrain, a tiny circuit completed itself.

'I got it!' he shouted. 'I got an idea!'

Dill groaned. 'Not another idea,' he said. 'We haven't even finished paying for that coffee machine yet.'

Louie's last brain-storm had been to sell the workers coffee from a machine he'd bought and installed in the cafeteria, at 25 cents a cup. To increase profits on the machine, he ran the grounds through again and again. The machine would thus, he reasoned, pay for itself. The workers agreed. The machine should pay for itself.

'No, this is a real keen idea. Listen. Why don't we get some money from the govermint?'

'Why don't we …' his father repeated uncomprehendingly.

'I think he has something, Granny!' shouted Dill. 'Why *don't* we get some money from the government?'

'Oh, yes, indeed,' said Moley, sitting up and opening his eyes a little. 'He does have something. Why don't we—'

'Why don't we get some money from the govermint?' said Louie excitedly, and strained to complete the thought. His hand, encased in glass, waved impatiently. 'From the govermint – for research!'

Bald heads nodded. 'For research, yes!'

'But wouldn't we have to be making some product the government needs?' Grandison asked, puzzled. 'Something vital to the defence of our nation? Something important to its welfare? The government doesn't just throw its money around, does it?'

When the others had finished laughing, Dill placed a bird-claw hand on Grandison's sleeve. 'You're an old-fashioned, unpractical dreamer, Granny,' he croaked, chuckling. 'Maybe I am, too. We got to look to the boy here for *real* ideas. Times have changed since WPA, y'know. This here's the age of the astronaut. In the old days, I'll admit, you had to build a battleship or a muni-cipal swimming pool – something useful. But tell me: practically speaking, of what use is it to have a man on the moon?'

'Well, I guess ...'

'None! No *earthly* use at all,' cackled Dill. 'But seriously, the government spends millions, *zillions*, to put one man on the moon. On the other hand, if you have some real, some practical idea to sell them, forget it.'

'That's right!' shouted Louie, jumping up and pacing about the room. 'Remember the time I tried to sell them my idea for invisible ink? Milk, it was, plain milk. Spies could write messages in it, like invisible ink. Then you heat it up and the writing appears, as if by magic. I wrote to the Pentagon, remember, Pop?' He threw himself into his chair again. 'They never answered,' he added, in a more subdued tone.

'The fact is,' Dill went on, tapping his sere hand on the table, 'if we can show the government a project that is utterly, hopelessly useless, they'll give us a grant for pure research.'

'How do you know that?'

'I know it as sure as I know that the head of the Industrial Spending Com-mittee is Senator Dill – my cousin, get it?'

Grandison was not yet used to the idea. 'But – but what could we do research upon? We have no facilities.'

'They provide all that stuff, don't worry,' smiled Dill. 'Concrete labs, bomb shelters, marine guards, you name it. All we have to do is figure out a project.'

'How about a robot?' suggested Louie.

'No money in it,' Dill snapped. 'We need something which *sounds* easier, so that the rest of the committee can't object to it, but which is so hard in practice that we can spend years on it. Like a bigger, faster plane.'

'How about a robot, though?' Louie put forth.

Ignoring the frantic waving of the jar under his nose, Moley said, 'Now, why don't we build a machine that can reproduce itself? I was reading about an idea like that in *Life*, just the other day. A self-reproducing machine – sure sounds hard enough, don't it?'

'But what is it good for?' Grandison asked. 'Besides making duplicates of itself, what is its function?'

'A robot,' declared Louie softly, 'could instruct me in hand-to-hand Kabuki.'

'You still don't understand, Granny,' Dill said, with a patronizing shake of his head. 'It isn't good for anything. That's exactly what the government wants. What *we* want.'

'I suppose you're right,' said Grandison. He sighed. 'It seems so dishonest.'

'We'll be creating thousands of new jobs – for scientists, marine guards, government clerks who keep us on file.'

'I know, I know, but will *we* make money?' the president snapped.

'Millions.'

They voted at once. The vote was 'aye' all around the table, to Louie.

'Aye, I guess,' he muttered. 'But hey, Pop, how about a robot, though? Huh, how about—'

Grandison reached over and cracked the jar with his gavel. The spring grip device leapt out, scattering glass and brown pills, and releasing the thick fingers of Louie the Womp from captivity.

'Motion carried.'

CHAPTER II

Anomalies

'$u¢¢e$$!'

Sign on wall at Wompler Research Laboratories

'I, too, am a failure,' murmured Cal, staring at the jellyfish thing in the tank. It was supposed to be bright pink and right-side up. 'This is the end for me too, old *Plagyodus*. I've ruined my last experiment.'

He did not deem it necessary to add that it was his first experiment at Wompler Research, or that he had only been hired through the wonderful mistake of an IBM machine. The grey, deflated mass in the tank did not seem to be listening, anyway. A twisted rope of multicoloured wires rose from it to a panel of dials. The dials were all at zero.

Sighing, Cal began to write on the chart hanging next to the tank, 'Biomech. arrgt. 173b aborted 1750 hours'.

It was more than a job he would be losing; it was a chance to do work leading to a doctorate. *Everything I touch*, he thought, *turns to failure*. As if bearing out his words, the ballpoint pen ran dry.

Experimenting, he found that it would write on his hand perfectly, but not on the wall chart. He covered his palm with blue scrawls and trial signatures: 'Calvin Codman Potter, Ph.D'.

'It's the angle,' said Hamuro Hita, the project statistician. 'It won't feed ink uphill.'

Cal blushed, corrected the angle of the pen and signed the chart. 'Thanks. I guess I'm not very observant for an experimenter. In fact, I've just ruined this experiment. I suppose you won't be seeing much of me around here from now on.'

'Oh, I don't think they'll can you for one mistake. What happened, anyway?' Hita spoke without pausing in his work, summing figures on an adding machine.

'I forgot to put the temperature control on automatic last night.' Ripping loose the wires from their instruments, Cal hauled up the grey, dripping lump. 'It – it poached, or something.' Lifting the lid of a garbage can, he plumped in the jellyfish and stuffed in the bright stiff wires after it. Hita nodded at a chair by his desk, and Cal flopped into it.

'That's what'll happen to me, when they find out all about me,' he said, indicating the garbage can. 'The way they saw it, I was a bright, promising lad, having graduated at the top of my class at MIT. They expected me to set the world on fire. Whereas –'

'Whereas – ?'

'I guess I'd rather not talk about it after all. Let's say I was hired by mistake, and I'm scared that any minute they'll realize it.'

Hita nodded, and the two men lapsed into moody silence. Finishing his addition, the mathematician began cleaning his briar pipe with one blade of a pair of black-handled scissors. Cal stared about the lab, unable to conquer the feeling that he was saying goodbye to it all. Goodbye, QUIDNAC modular computer; goodbye, maze for phototropic 'rats'; goodbye, solution in which grew a green crystalline tree, every branch of which formed part of an electronic circuit; goodbye, miniature automatic forge. He did not forget a goodbye to the main entrance, guarded by a stiff, humourless adolescent in the uniform of the Marine Corps.

'We're all flying under false colours here,' said Hita, sliding a paperback book out of his desk drawer. 'Do you know why the Womplers hired me? Because Louie wanted to learn Origami. The way he saw it, I'm Japanese, *ergo* ...'

'I don't believe it!'

'But you've only been here a week. You hardly know the Womplers, father and son. You haven't even met the project head, Dr Smilax. I assume your main dealings have been with *them*.'

'Meaning the Mackintosh brothers?'

Hita smiled. 'Or as some of us call them, the brothers Frankenstein.'

'But what were you telling me about Origami?'

'Officially, I'm a mathematician. In fact, my duties include teaching Louie Origami. I've had to study up on it myself, of course. Luckily, I found this book at the drugstore.' He riffled the pages of the paperback. 'It's a good job, all the same. I can make enough money at this to start my own statistical lab soon, and I only need to be silly for a half-hour a day.'

'But how have you fooled them, if you don't even know—?'

'It's easy. You see, Louie thought Origami was a kind of Japanese self-defence. I've been able to make up my own rules, mostly, as we go along (I told him I was "black scissors", and he was properly impressed).

'As for Grandison Wompler, he seems to think I ought to speak Spanish, for some reason. I rather like the two of them. There are even days when I can stand the brothers F. The only person around here who gives me the creeps is Dr Smilax himself.'

'Have you met him? What's he like?' asked Cal.

'No, I haven't met him, and neither has anyone else I know of, except the twins; that's the odd thing about him. No one even seems to know anything about him except that he's a surgeon and a biochemist. You'd think the head of a research team would at least want to meet his subordinates, but he's so inaccessible—'

Cal nudged him and pointed to the entrance, above which a red bulb had begun glowing. The marine guard drew his automatic and covered the two persons entering, until they showed him the red badges of Kurt and Karl Mackintosh.

Kurt skipped to get into step with his twin, and they strode on across the lab rapidly.

Their immense, bulging foreheads, exaggerated by advanced baldness and invisibly pale eyebrows, loomed over tiny, pouting faces to give them the look of kewpies or dimestore cherubs. They were plump and sexless creatures, these two, and it was hard to believe them the best cybernetics engineers this side of the Iron Curtain. The only features they possessed that were not of idiot quality were their eyes. Restless, flickering, intelligent, they were the colour of bluebottle flies.

The brothers flicked a glance at the empty tank, another at the chart, another at Cal.

'We expected more of an MIT valedictorian,' Karl said nastily, as if speaking to his brother.

'That's right, Karl. He has not only ruined experiment 173b, but we have not had a single original idea from him, and he has not hypothesized a single biomechanical arrangement.'

'True enough, Kurt.' The brothers, perhaps because of their similarity, seemed to find it desirable to identify one another often. 'True it is, Kurt. I begin to wonder if MIT's standards have not declined.'

Hita cleared his throat. Steering themselves, as it were, by the clipboards under their arms, the two spun towards him. 'But, gentlemen,' he said, 'Potter was just now discussing with me his new idea for a biomechanical arrangement. A sort of steel-shelled oyster, wasn't it, Cal?'

'Yes. A sort of – um – steel-shelled oyster. Yes. You see, it would have a number of advantages. Too numerous to mention.'

'Such as – ?' said the twins together.

'Well – instead of a pearl, it produces a ball-bearing. A slow way to make ball-bearings, admittedly, but then we're not really interested in the manufacture of—'

'I hope, Kurt, that he will follow out his line of inquiry,' said Karl.

'And write a monograph,' Kurt added. 'But meanwhile we'll assign him to Project 32 as a special assistant. He can help wire up circuits, Karl.'

Cal felt he had been both chastised and given a second chance. He was about to stammer out his thanks when the light above the door glowed a second time.

'Good evening!' boomed Grandison Wompler from the doorway. 'Say, it's long after five, and we don't pay overtime, you know.'

The Mackintosh twins drew themselves up slightly. Karl said, 'Dedication to the human race cannot be curtailed by mere time.'

'Our work goes on,' his brother intoned, 'day and night, committed ever to the achievement of peace in our time, final, eternal peace—'

'That's fine. But do you have to have all these lights on?' Grandison entered, waving aside the aimed pistol of the marine guard, and donned a white lab coat from a locker.

'Our newest project will consume immense quantities of power,' Kurt informed him. 'But it will benefit the human race immeasurably.'

'Great. Good work, boys. But will it get me a new contract? Will it put Millford on the map? Will it make the government want to shower money on me?'

The twins looked at one another for a flickering second. 'It will indeed,' they chorused.

Louie stuck his head in the door and shouted to Hita, 'Oh, there you are.' He smiled and nodded at the marine guard, who was trying to decide whether or not to shoot him. 'Hita, I'll meetcha in the gym, OK?' Hita smiled and nodded, and the ebullient intruder withdrew.

Grandison turned around and noticed the statistician. 'Hi there, *amigo!*' he said grinning, and walked over to him, hand extended. Hita was the only member of the staff with whom Grandison ever shook hands. '*Como esta Usted?*'

'*Muy bien,*' replied the Japanese, without enthusiasm.

'That's fine, fine. Now, if any of these fellows don't treat you right, you just come tell me, hear? I signed a government contract, and that means I got to give fair and equal employment to You Fellows. It don't matter what your race, creed, colour or religion is, you're all Americans!'

'But I'm not an American,' Hita protested. Grandison affected not to hear him.

'Yes, I rebuilt this company from nothing, in less than a year – and I want to keep what we got. We got the finest cafeteria, the best coffee machines, the nicest bowling alleys and gym, the cleanest bomb shelters money can buy – and I want us to keep 'em. I want all you boys, black and white, to put your backs into it and really pull – for the company!'

'I'm sure we're all doing our best,' said Hita, picking up a pair of scissors. 'Well, I must go. *Adios.*'

'We, too, must leave, Kurt,' said Karl. 'We must confer with Dr S. just now. Potter here can show you around the lab, Mr Wompler.' The brothers moved off, in lock-step.

'Say,' said Grandison behind his hand. 'I heard someone say their name was Frankenstein.' His voice dropped to a confidential whisper and his face grew solemn. 'They ain't – they ain't Jews, are they?'

'I believe they are Irish Protestants, sir,' said Cal, trying to keep his face straight. 'Their name is Mackintosh. Would you like to see the lab?'

'Yes, fine.'

At each exhibit, Grandison would pause while Cal named the piece of equipment. Then he would repeat the name softly, with a kind of wonder, nod sagely and move on. Cal was strongly reminded of the way some people look at modern art exhibitions, where the labels become more important to them than the objects. He found himself making up elaborate names.

'And this, you'll note, is the Mondriaan Modular Mnemonicon.'

'– onicon, yes.'

'And the Empyrean diffrean diffractosphere.'

'– sphere. Mn. I see.'

Nothing surprised Grandison, for he was looking at nothing. Cal became wilder. Pointing to Hita's desk, he said. 'The chiaroscuro thermocouple.'

'Couple? Looks like only one, to me. Interesting, though.'

A briar pipe became a 'zygotic pipette', the glass ashtray a 'Piltdown retort', and the lamp a 'phase-conditioned Aeolian'. Paperclips became 'nuances'.

'Nuances, I see. Very fine. What's that thing, now?' He pointed to an oscilloscope. Cal took a deep breath.

'Its full name,' he said, 'is the Praetorian eschatalogical morphomorphic tangram, Endymion-type, but we usually just call it a ramification.'

The old man fixed him with a stern black eye. 'Are you trying to be funny or something? I mean, I may not be a smart-aleck scientist, but I sure as hell know a television, when I see one.'

Cal assured him it was not a television, and proved it by switching it on. 'See,' he said, pointing to a pattern of square waves, 'there are the little anapests.'

'I'll be damned! So they are.'

Cal went on to show him a few revanchist doctrines before the president, satisfied, took his departure.

'Keep up the good work,' he called out, 'and take good care of the company equipment. Them ramifications don't grow on trees y'know.'

Cal began to chew his fingernails off, one by one, leaning against a lab table and dropping the parings in a Piltdown retort. *How long can I get away with this?* he wondered. *They still think I'm from MIT. And so I am. From Miami Institute of Technocracy.*

Miami Institute of Technocracy was the only school in the nation that gave a Bachelor of Applied Arts degree in biophysics. Cal had graduated in a class of four: Harry Stropp, Bachelor of Physical Education, Mary Junes, Home Economics Technician, Barthemo Beele, Associate of Journalism. Cal had headed the class.

I'll confess to Dr Smilax, he decided. *I can explain it was all a mistake.* He switched off the lights and left. The marine guard remained alone, standing at attention in the darkness.

Cal stopped at the hall bulletin board. A new notice had been posted, and now, stalling for time, he stopped to read it.

'PROJECT 32. Supervisors: DR K. MACKINTOSH & DR K. MACK-INTOSH. Special Assistant: POTTER. Inspection will be 21 June 196—. At some time after this date, DR A. CANDLEWOOD (Behavioural Psychol.) will join the staff.'

Cal looked from the signature (impersonally mimeographed) to the door marked:

T. Smilax M.D.
NO UNAUTHORIZED PERSONNEL
THIS MEANS YOU
ABSOLUTELY RESTRICTED AREA

Changing his mind, Cal spun around and headed for the main door. As he passed the open window of the gymnasium building, he heard Hita shout, 'Hai!' There was the sound of shearing paper.

CHAPTER III

A Report on Project 32

'He who understands me finally recognizes my
propositions as senseless.'

LUDWIG WITTGENSTEIN

TOP SECRET TOP SECRET TOP SECRET TOP SECRET

I. The Purpose of Project 32

Project 32 is the code name of a series of experiments undertaken at the Wompler Research Laboratory in Millford, Utah, in 196—. The purpose of Project 32 was to determine:

(a) if it were possible to set into motion an autonomous, self-reproducing mechanism, a 'Reproductive System', and

(b) the military use, if any, of such a system.

II. The Background of Project 32

Prior to the initiation of this project, it was generally considered impracticable, if not impossible, to design and set into motion a system capable of self-support, learning and reproduction. (a) Although computers had been programmed to perform simple analogies[1] or 'learn', i.e., profit from their mistakes in straight-forward games, they showed little promise as learning machines. And for a system to be autonomous, it must be able to discriminate portions of its environment, analogize from past experiences and profit from mistakes of a rather complex nature. (b) Although 'autonomous' automated production lines already existed, they were at the mercy of their environments for power and materials. (c) Some computers had already been used to solve problems in circuitry, thus in effect 'redesigning' themselves. But there remained what seemed an unbridgeable gap between these and a true self-reproducing machine.

---

1 Yet semantics vs syntax arguments cast such doubts on these experiments as to make their results puzzling and amusing rather than significant. Thus while a computer saw the answer to 'spear: ?:: narrow: arrow' was 'pear', it could not see why 'head: bed:: ?: chair' should be 'back' and not 'hair'. Also a computer diagrammed the following sentence two ways: 'She bears each cross patiently.' 'She' may be the subject and 'bears' the verb; or 'She bears' the subject and 'cross' the verb.

III. The Experiments
Early experiments comprised attempts to construct living/non-living 'symbioses': Inculcating in the nervous system of a coelenterate an electric motor circuit;[2] encasing oysters in shells of flexible steel;[3] equipping mice with electro-hydraulically-operated tails;[4] and many similar attempts, none satisfactory.

IV. The Theory
Out of these early experiments a modular or cellular system was conceived of, functioning somewhere between a polypidon and a highly structured society. Each cell should be:
(a) Organized along similar lines with its fellows, and equipped to recognize order and respond to it.
(b) Equipped to repair intracellular breakdowns, as far as possible, and to 'eat' non-functional cells.
(c) Able to convert power and material from its environment into itself, and to construct new cells like itself from any surplus power and material, i.e., to reproduce.
(d) Able to prevent its own destruction by flight, by diversion of or neutralization of the destructive agent. e.g., if made of steel, it should (1) flee from sea-water contact; (2) paint itself to seal out sea-water; or (3) develop some chemical means to neutralize the corrosive action of sea-water.

No practical means were available to test or even construct a working model of this theoretical system, until the completion and adaptation of the QUIDNAC computer.

V. The Quidnac
The QUIDNAC, or Quantifiable Universal Integral DNA Computer, as originally designed by T. Smilax, had three qualities that recommended it to the project: (a) compact size; (b) a virtually infinitely-extensible memory; (c) suitability for learning complex analogic processes. In addition, T. Smilax was the head of Project 32.

VI. General Principles of Construction of Cells
Each cell may be considered in some respects an egg, having 'yolk', 'white' and 'shell'. In this simplified scheme:
(a) The 'yolk' consisted of the QUIDNAC computer, along with various coupling and control devices to function in the 'white' and 'shell'.

2 Failure due to unstable ambient temperatures, causing shock.

3 Failure due to unforeseen corrosion, by sea-water, of steel.

4 Successful, but of questionable military value. Results published separately as MIL-P-980089, PROSTHETIC TAILS.

(b) The 'white' contained automatic production tools and storage facilities for raw materials, spare tools and parts, and power.

(c) The 'shell' of metal armour contained means of locomotion, sensory devices, paint, simple extensors, and (though not in all cases) means of communication.

Within this framework many variations were constructed, differing in their means of locomotion, sensory devices, means of communication and production methods. It was expected that, in addition to variations proposed by the experimenter, others would be adapted or invented by the system itself.

*

'I just don't get it,' said Cal, laying down his soldering gun. Though he spoke to Louie Wompler, all the army and navy technicians around them looked up, eager for a chance to stop and talk. Louie sat frowning at a folded piece of paper in his hand.

'Neither do I,' he said. 'Something wrong here. It's supposed to flap its wings when I do this, but look.' He pulled at a flap, and the square of paper came unfolded. It was a magazine illustration of food.

'I mean I don't understand Dr Smilax. What does he do all day, alone in there? He can't be still working on the QUIDNAC; I thought he finished with that long before he came here. Why do we never see him to talk to? What does he look like?'

Lance-corporal Martin looked up from a circuit diagram. 'Are you kidding?' he said, pasting a Lucky in the corner of his wide, griping mouth. 'I hear all kindsa crap about the Old Man.' After looking around the room, he leaned closer to Cal. 'I hear he carves up kittens on a big white table in there – just for kicks. I hear he's a junky. I hear he ain't no real doctor at all, just some bum chiropractor that saved a Senator's life once, so they give him this cushy job. I hear he just sits in there all day, sticking himself with dope. I hear—'

'Crap!' spat a navy technician whose rolled-up sleeves revealed tattoos of Walt Disney characters. 'The real scuttlebutt is, he's a Rooshian. All that security stuff is to keep the other Rooshians from assassinating him. The real scuttlebutt is, he invented a way of putting monkey brains in the heads of little children.'

A civilian technical writer spoke. He was the author of a famous military manual, *The Fork Lift Truck*. 'I understand,' he said carefully, 'that Dr S. used to be a famous surgeon. But he was operating on the President's mother and something went wrong. They hushed it up, of course, but he's been in semi-retirement ever since.'

Others heard them and wandered over to join in.

'I hear the brothers Frankenstein was born joined at the head.'

'He split 'em. But he gets fits, see, and tries to kill people –'

– 'big abortion racket, remember? In all the papers –'

'They say he invented a cancer cure in Rooshia, but he was hit in the head, see, and lost his memory –'

'Devil's food cake,' sighed Louie over the picture. He seemed oblivious of the discussion raging around him. 'I'm not allowed to have any sweets while I'm in training for Origami.'

'– and the ASPCA would raise holy hell if they found out what he was up to. So –'

Cal finished his work and stepped into the hall to get away from the babble of sensational theories about Smilax. The facts about the man behind that restricted door were nil. Yet why did all the rumours about him contain a strain of hideosity? Why was it no one saw him as a harmless old recluse? Why did every story include paradigms of cruelty, madness, megalomaniac importance? It was almost as if … but no one could start such rumours about himself. Himself? For a moment Cal wondered if there really were such a person as 'T. Smilax, M.D.' Placing his ear to the restricted door Cal listened.

There came to him a faint, high-pitched mechanical whine. It was the snarl of a thousand muted dental drills, humming into a thousand rotting teeth. It paused for a moment, and he heard another sound: the whimpering of a small dog in pain. Almost as soon as this began, the mechanical whine started up again, overriding it.

As Cal re-entered the lab, Karl said, 'We were just looking for you.'

'We're ready for a test,' Kurt explained. They stood, clipboards at the ready, one each side of the lab table, while Cal made final adjustments and turned on the system.

It was an array of grey metal boxes, each about the size of a cigarette package, stacked loosely together in a cube about two feet high. When the toggle switch prominent on the top of any one box was thrown, it sent out a tuned starting signal to the rest; they were switched off in the same way.

As soon as each box was activated, it began to roll about on the table on its little casters, avoiding collision with its fellows. When all the boxes were moving, they resembled a complicated Brownian movement on the dark surface of the table, as they explored every inch of it.

Kurt and Karl placed bits and scraps of metal on the table. The smaller bits were at once devoured by individual boxes, but the larger bars attracted the entire brood. The grey packages, now the size of king-size cigarette cases, swarmed over them like ants, gouging away with tiny cutters and torches – and growing fatter. It made Cal shiver to look at their orderly feeding.

'Has anyone a watch?' asked Karl, looking intently at the watch-chain across Hita's vest. The mathematician sighed.

'All right,' he said, giving up his half-hunter. 'But take care of it, please. It's an antique eight-day watch. Irreplaceable.'

Karl dangled it on its chain above the table. The boxes began quavering, altering their random movements. They clustered beneath the watch. Karl swung it gently, and the grey brood responded, excitedly tracking its movements. They began to climb upon one another, to stack themselves in a swaying, rolling pyramid, reaching towards the shape of its metal body, the sound of its ticking heart. The grey pile began a sympathetic trembling.

Each time they would nearly reach the watch, Karl would raise it higher. His childlike face had a look of cruel, rapt concentration as he teased the pyramid. It grew taller and thinner. Cal could see lower boxes gripping one another with extensors to steady the pile. Karl raised the watch a third time, a fourth.

The top box, standing on edge, split like a tiny suitcase. Two thin rods slithered upwards.

'What are those? Look like car antennae,' said Louie.

'Look out!' shouted Hita. 'It's making a grab for it.'

'No it isn't,' Karl assured him. 'Just watch this.'

The two rods passed the half-hunter and moved a link or two up the chain. They paused. A group of boxes stopped 'drinking' at the lab table's DC outlet and formed a chain from it to the pyramid. There was a sudden flashing fizz of light and the watch fell; the tiny suitcase caught it, drew in its horns instantly and snapped shut.

'Hey! Give that back!' The mathematician caught up the offending box and shook it. He tried to pry it open, then shook it again.

'Ouch!' Suddenly the box clattered to the table, where it scooted about madly and was soon lost among its kind. There was a drop of blood on the end of Hita's finger. 'Bit me!' he exclaimed, incredulous.

'Yes.' Kurt nodded enthusiastically. 'You've got to expect it to fight back. You were threatening it.'

'Yes, it was only defending its property,' Karl added.

'*Its property!*' Hita looked from one of the twins to the other. They wore pleased smiles, like those of indulgent parents. Without another word, the mathematician stalked out of the laboratory.

'Let's see what it will do with this,' chorused the brothers. They wheeled over the oscilloscope on its stand and jammed it against the table. The grey creatures took notice of it at once. They now varied in size, from those which had scarcely grown at all to those which had swollen to the size of small tool boxes. None had so far reproduced.

Now they swarmed around the oscilloscope and began to pile up against the side of it. From the top box a tiny screwdriver emerged to probe the cabinet. Finding a louvre, it pried. The shaft broke. There was muffled click and its stump retracted.

'Watch,' Karl cautioned.

Smoke rose from the tool box, and there came a sound of loud, rapid hammering. A moment later a large screwdriver blade, still glowing, appeared. By main force it pried open the cabinet of the oscilloscope, bending back the steel cover to open a fist-sized hole. From another box came a pair of pliers. They entered the oscilloscope cabinet and began to rummage hastily inside. There came the tinkle of broken glass from time to time. At regular intervals, the pliers emerged, bearing booty: a broken tube, a two-inch hank of wire, half a resistor or a glass shard. On these, the tool box fed greedily.

'Hey!' said Louie, coming awake to what was happening. 'You better not let Pop see that.'

It was too late. At the same time, Grandison put his head in the door. 'See what?' He saw the tool box come up with a hank of transistors which it gobbled like succulent grapes. 'What the hell is going on here?' Glowering at Cal, he shouted, 'It ain't two weeks since I told you to take care of the equipment. What the hell do you mean, destroying my property like that?'

Cal moved to shut off the system, but Kurt laid a restraining hand on his arm. 'No,' he said. 'It is making mistakes, but it will learn. We're having an inspection next week by General Grawk of the Air Force. Let it go until then. We'll give it a corner of the lab of its own, to grow in.' Turning to the company president he added, 'Don't worry, sir. This system will make the company billions for every dollar it costs.'

'Well, that's a relief.' Grandison's expression altered. 'I got some bad news, though. Hita just died in the infirmary.'

Cal stared. *'What did you say?'*

'Hita. The statistics man. Just died of snakebite.'

With a small thunderclap, the cathode-ray tube collapsed. The tool boxes continued to browse quietly.

'Poor ramification,' Cal murmured, shuddering. 'Poor little anapests.'

CHAPTER IV

The Inspector General

'"Es ist ein eigentümlicher Apparat," sagte der Offizier.'

KAFKA

By three o'clock on the afternoon of the inspection, almost the entire staff of Wompler Research Laboratories had assembled on the lawn, wearing clean lab coats. They stood in serried ranks, so perfectly still that the loudest sound was the faint susurrus of the lawn sprinklers. At the fore, faces uplifted to the sun, stood Grandison and Louie, wearing lab coats especially designed for the occasion by Mrs Lumsey.

At precisely three o'clock, a silver helicopter descended from the sun. Its terrific downdraught ruffled the American flag on the flagpole and the two 'E' pennants below it. It stirred slightly the silver fringe on the pleated lab coats of the two Womplers. The helicopter settled in the lush carpet of green. A silver door swung open.

General Grawk emerged amid a cloud of beautiful women. Actually there were only four redheaded women, each very like the other three, that is, tall, good-looking and possessed of curves even Air Force tailoring could not disguise as angles. Here were four sane, attractive WAF officers bustling about to adjust his ribbons, straighten his tie, hand him his cap and relight his black stump of a cigar – bathing, in short, in an ambience of lovely femininity –

The ugliest man within a thousand miles.

Imagine a face as red and furious as that of a newborn child. Imagine sparse black hair like broken quills, lying this way and that around a bald spot the colour of a baboon's bum. Imagine the nose of a Pekinese but the upper lip of Peking man, and imagine moreover the former permanently wrinkled with disgust and the latter drawn back in a set sneer from yellow, crooked teeth. Add boiled, bulging eyes, an underslung jaw that needed a shave the day it was created, and the neck of a particularly obese walrus, complete with three folds of fat in back. Got all that? Now add black clots of eyebrow and asymmetric lumps as desired, set it all on a stumpy, strutting figure in uniform, and top it off – as Grawk now did – with a tall, tall cap loaded with silver foliage.

Putting on his cap increased Grawk's height to about five feet. He spat out the cigar and looked around, arms akimbo.

'So this,' he said, 'is the great Wompler Research Laboratory, is it?'

'Yes indeed. I'm Grandison Wompler and this is my son, Louie. Louie, say hello to General Grawk.'

'Hi!' shouted Louie.

The general squinted the Womplers over, ignoring no detail but their proffered hands. 'Cute little outfits you got there,' he said, jabbing a finger at their silver fringe. 'Who's your dressmaker?' Then to one of the WAFs, 'Make a note of it, Meg. First of all, they got cruddy security. Nobody asked to see my ID card. I coulda been a Russky spy, for chrissake. Second, I think the two top boys are fruits. Father and son, my eye! And all dressed up in Mother's clothes, I guess, eh?'

Louie's grin wavered, disappeared. 'Now wait a minute,' he said. 'Whose mother? Now just wait a minute.' His immense pudgy hands became fists.

'Like to lose your old man a couple million in government contracts?' shrilled the general. 'Like to fix it so you're out of government work for good? Well, just lay a mitt on me, Junior. Go ahead, hit me!'

21

Grandison managed to keep his son from complying. Grawk smirked slightly, stretched out the folds of fat in his neck, and peered around him. 'Are we gonna stand out here all day?'

The entire ménage fell in behind Kurt and Karl, who guided the general to the outer door of the lab building. To Grawk's fresh indignation, a marine guard insisted on seeing his ID card.

'Great,' he said, producing it. 'Just great. This guy *can't see* I'm wearing the uniform of a general in the US Air Force. He has to *make sure*. Just swell. Oh, I can see this is a well-run place all right.'

They moved on inside.

'Which one of you ginks is Smilax, head-of-project? You?' he asked Karl, who shook his head.

'He sends his regrets,' Karl said. 'He's unable to meet you in person.'

'What do you mean, "unable"? Where is he?'

'In his office.' The twins pointed out the office door.

A bitter smile rippled over the simian lip. 'I get it. I'm not important enough for him to get up off his bacon and come out to meet, is that it? A mere four-star general is nothing, huh? I guess he only talks to the Joint Chiefs of Staff or something.'

As the twins made no reply to this, the general stepped to the office door and tried it. It was locked. Lifting a set of knuckles designed to be walked upon, he rapped smartly on the RESTRICTED AREA sign.

A nearby door opened, and a marine guard, bearing a submachine gun, stepped out.

'I'm afraid you can't go in there, general,' he said. '"NO UNAUTHORIZED PERSONNEL. THIS MEANS YOU",' he quoted from the quite legible sign.

'What the hell do you mean? I got a top secret clearance. I'm supposed to be inspecting this plant. If I ain't authorized, who is? What the Christ is going on here, anyway? Smilax, you come out of there!' He rattled the knob and pounded on the door until the guard trained his gun on him and waved him away.

'Look,' Grawk said to him, a more conciliatory note creeping into his voice, 'I come seven hundred miles in that hot, stuffy helicopter to inspect Smilax's project. You mean to tell me this freak can't even come out of his office to talk to me?'

'I'm afraid not, general. Dr Smilax comes and goes at his pleasure,' said the marine tersely. 'If you want to contact him, you'd better forward your message to the Joint Chiefs of Staff.'

'–' said the general. That is, he opened his mouth but no sound came forth. Purple veins began to writhe in his face, and his boiled eyes bulged.

Then he turned on his heel, emitting at the same time a short, hysterical laugh. 'All right,' he said. 'Let's see this so-called project, and get it over with.'

In one corner of the lab a considerable space had been cleared. A bulky object roughly the size of an automobile here lay shrouded in a drop cloth. Now the Mackintosh brothers moved in to lift the cloth, folding it rapidly and expertly into a cocked hat.

'What's all this?' said the general, waving at the pile of large grey boxes thus revealed. They lay on three lab tables, quivering, turning slightly on their hidden wheels as they sensed movement about them.

'It is a self-reproducing machine,' the twins announced. 'A Reproductive System.'

'Yeah? Ugly, ain't it?'

During the week, they explained, the boxes had devoured over a ton of scrap metal, as well as a dozen oscilloscopes with attached signal generators, thirty-odd test sets, desk calculators both mechanical and electronic, a pair of scissors, an uncountable number of bottle caps, paper clips, coffee spoons and staples (for the lab and office staff liked feeding their new pet), dozens of surplus walky-talky storage batteries and a small gasoline-driven generator.

The cells had multiplied – better than doubled their original number – and had grown to various sizes, ranging from shoe-boxes and attaché cases to steamer trunk proportions. They now reproduced constantly but slowly, in various fashions. One steamer trunk emitted, every five or ten minutes, a pair of tiny boxes the size of 3 × 5 card files. Another box, of extraordinary length, seemed to be slowly sawing itself in half.

General Grawk remained unimpressed. 'What does it do for an encore?' he growled.

'I don't know much about this stuff myself,' Grandison candidly admitted. 'I leave all the heavy think-work to my boys here, Kurt, Karl and Cal. They know all about Endymions and revanchist doctrines, all that stuff.'

With savage glee, the general spoke to one of his WAFs. 'Amy, make a note. I think this one is a commy,' he spat with disgust, 'as well as a fairy.'

'Let me hit him, Pop!' bawled Louie. 'Let me use Origami on him.'

Kurt and Karl went on explaining the system, as though they had not been interrupted.

'It is "ergotropic",' Karl explained. 'That is, it can seek and use nearly any kind of power.' He gestured to his brother as one vaudeville partner to another.

'It is metallotropic,' Kurt added. 'Some cells are oriented more towards metal, some towards energy. May we demonstrate?'

The twins each picked up one box gently. They were the size of fat attaché cases. 'This is a power-seeking cell,' Karl explained. 'That one is metal-seeking.'

The wheels of the two machines whined as they set them on the floor. One spun around and headed straight for the light socket. The other dashed about the room, sampling the legs of metal furniture, pausing to nibble at the corner of a filing cabinet. Cal shooed it away and it scooted behind a lab table, out of his reach. Between the table and the wall, he could see the box working its way along towards the far corner, towards the oyster tank.

'Kinda cute at that,' said the general.

One of its legs eaten through, the oyster tank collapsed. As water from it spread across the floor, the fat box outran it, heading for the door. It carried a metal wastebasket, holding it aloft in crab-claws, a hard-won trophy.

'Stop it!' Cal shouted. The general began to laugh.

'Halt!' shouted the marine guard. He fired a warning shot but the attaché case kept coming. He lowered his gun and fired directly at the little box. Bullets rang on the wastebasket. The marine emptied his gun, just as the box dashed between his polished boots and out of the door.

'All you had to do,' said Karl, 'was pick it up.'

The general leaned on the table, doubled up with coarse laughter. The twins and Cal were trying to trap the other box. Excited by the gun-flashes, it scooted in circles all over the room.

'I'll be goddamned,' the general kept saying. 'Funniest thing I seen since the war.' His weight was tipping the table, and as the boxes rushed towards him it tipped even further.

Cal cornered the energy-seeking box and bent to turn it off. He saw that the toggle switch had been damaged, apparently by a welding arc. It was a fused lump of metal on top of the box. Something else occurred to him then: there had been a lot of cells running around on the table with broken or missing switches. Odd. He would have to ask someone about that.

But just now there was nothing to do but pick this one up off the floor. Cal was frightened of it, but he was even more frightened of letting it go free.

'Careful!' someone shouted. 'You're standing in brine!'

'Oh, don't worry,' said Cal. He looked up to see the table overturn on General Grawk, the boxes sliding off …

But then the scene froze, like a film hung up in the projector. And, like a stuck film, everything shrivelled and vanished, leaving only bright white emptiness.

CHAPTER V

MIT

'O goodly usage of those ancient times,
In which the sword was servant unto right.'

SPENSER

Cal was brought up on a farm in Minnesota. His father Codman Codman Potter, was taciturn, even for a farmer. In fact, Cal could only recall his father's speaking to him twice in all his life. Codman seemed a bottomless reservoir of wisdom; whenever he spoke, the family went into a panic.

The awful voice sounded when Cal was eight. His mother had given him a book of Aesop's fables, and one evening he lay on the living room floor, reading of the frogs who wanted a king. His father looked at him and said loudly:

'There's plenty of things you don't learn from books. Books only ruin your eyes. It's life that's important, not god damned books!'

Alarmed, Cal's mother took the book from him and burned it. He never dreamed of objecting. From then on, he merely skimmed his lessons at school, and avoided bringing home any of the hated books. At home his only lapse was glancing at the back of the cereal box: 'Niacin, Thiamine, Riboflavin …' Surely, he reasoned, it was all right to read, as long as he did not understand.

This idea of reading only the unreadable stayed with him until he asked his father for permission to study Latin and Greek.

'What? If you want to go to college at all, you'll by God become an engineer. Or else I'll Latin you, God damn it!'

Cal went off to the Miami Institute of Technocracy, then, to become an engineer. At the station, Codman nodded goodbye.

MIT was small. There were just twenty students and one professor altogether, and in Cal's class there were but three other students. The entire school occupied one large room above a dry-cleaning plant. In after years, Cal would always associate the smell of chemicals and the hiss of steam with Dr Elwood Trivian.

'You have an interest in the inimicable classics? I laud that, young man. We have, alack, no time to teach them here. They are, you cogitate, useless. I must deplore you to study science, and science alone.

'I had a thorough grinding in the classics myself, and am today but a humble pedagog. Why, I earn less here in an entire year than I would in a single week on the railroad, steering a train! And that takes no learning at all!'

Half-way through his course, Cal switched his major from Engrg. Arts to Biophys. Arts. He wrote his father explaining that this had more to do with life. In a sense, he was telling the truth, for it enabled him to sit next to Mary Junes, whom he loved.

Mary did not love him back; she was not likely to love him; she did not even know his name. She seemed to love Harry Stropp, their tall, thickset, swart classmate, who majored in Phys. Ed.

She was a short, chunky, tough-looking girl with a great gob of yellow hair like dirty cotton. As everyday attire she wore borrowed sweatshirts, mixed and matched with dungarees and borrowed sweatpants. She seemed addicted to black cough drops. Her breath smelt of menthol, her hands were always sticky, and her wide, sluttish mouth was stained black. Cal dreamed of pasting a kiss on those gummy lips.

He schemed to sit next to her in every class: Current events (where Dr Trivian read his morning paper aloud), Phonics Praxis and Appreciation of Thermodynamics. Still, her nights were spent with Harry.

Barthemo Beele, the fourth member of the class and a Journalism student, published the mimeo school paper, *The MIT Worker's Torch*. He bitterly complained of seeing Mary and Harry kiss in public, in editorials headed: 'Is Decency Finished?'

One day Harry came down with a cold. After struggling through morning classes, he gave up and went home. Mary clicked a black cough drop deliciously, and winked at Cal.

'What's your name?'

Harry arose from his sickbed in a week, to find he'd lost his girl to Cal.

'I don't care,' he'd say, flexing his big arm and studying it. 'She's not the only pebble on the beach. There are plenty of other fish in the sea.' He remained an absolute recluse, going swimming and fishing alone, and doing lots of roadwork on the roof above the schoolroom. Cal felt terribly guilty every time he heard the sound of giant, sad tennis shoes on the roof, running tirelessly.

The MIT Worker's Torch named Cal valedictorian of the class. On the same day, it announced the engagement of Miss Mary Junes to Barthemo Beele.

'When did this happen?' Cal asked her, holding up the mimeo sheet in a trembling hand.

'Oh, you know that night last week, when you had to study?'

'But – *engaged*?'

'Yup. Right after graduation, me and Barty are going to live somewheres out West, where he's got a swell job as a editor already. Isn't that great?'

Great. The next few days Cal knew not what he did. He wept unashamedly, tore up all her notes ('Can I borrow your sweatshirt, darling? Thanx, M.'), and took long walks, at times avoiding all meaningful places, at times haunting them. He began to feel he might become a dedicated scientist, a seeker after truth.

Most of the hundred foundations, academies and labs to which he applied for a research grant replied that they had no need for holders of the rather special degree, Bachelor of Biophysics Arts. The Wompler Research Laboratory, however, sent a letter expressing interest and an IBM card to fill out and return. In the tiny box on the card where he was to write the name of his school, there was only room for the abbreviation 'MIT'. He was hired by return mail.

The MIT Worker's Torch kept up its morality campaign (now directed against its editor and his fiancée) to the last day. Dr Trivian gave a stirring Commencement speech to his four new graduates, though most of it was drowned out by the hiss of steam from below, where the shirts lived.

'Oh, don't worry,' Cal said. It seemed to him that he was still trying to pick up the runaway cell, but bright white clouds kept getting in his way. Steam?

All at once he realized the clouds were real; he was looking at the sky. He rolled over and sat up, hands buried in cool grass.

A file drawer marked 'Secret' scooted past, pursued by a mob of people in white coats. 'Stop it! Catch it!'

How odd, he thought with a tolerant smile. Chasing file drawers. He began to walk around the building. Other boxes, made of garbage cans, cabinets, bent signs, swarmed over the green, pursuing and pursued by human figures. Near the fence a group of marines had set up a light machine gun. Now they were defending it desperately against the slow, blunt, methodical attacks of a kiln and a small safe, in tandem. Finally a fork-lift truck rushed in, seized the gun and apparently digested it.

Chuckling, Cal strode around another corner of the building. The helicopter lay on its side as the swarming boxes picked it clean. It was beginning to look like the skeleton of a beached whale.

The general was no longer laughing; he was screaming at the twin brothers, 'Somebody is gonna have to pay for this! That is government property your toy is tearing up!'

'Government property hell!' Grandison roared. 'That gizmo is tearing up *my* property! If you can't shut it off—'

'Mr Wompler, General Grawk,' said Karl solemnly, 'there seems to be no safe way to shut it off – without jeopardizing the whole experiment, that is. We simply cannot permit it.'

Grandison caught sight of Cal. 'So you finally came to, eh?' he said. 'Just in time, too. I guess one of them Endymions musta give you a little electric *shot*, eh boy? Well, I hope you can shut that thing off – Kurt and Karl here are chicken.'

'There should be nothing easier than shutting it off,' Cal said. 'Every cell is equipped with a sympathetic, tuned switch that—'

'Not any more,' said Karl with a condescending smile. 'That was last week. The more sophisticated mutations of the system have shed that apparatus long ago.'

'Well then, I'll shut off the ones that haven't, and we'll smash the rest.'

'No, you don't!' Kurt said, bridling. 'If you go in that lab and tamper, you're fired!'

Grandison wavered, less sure of himself now. 'Maybe you shouldn't—'

'I'm not worried about protecting property,' said Cal quietly. 'I'm worried about protecting a few lives. None of you seem to realize how dangerous this thing is.'

'What are a few lives, in comparison to—' Karl began, but Cal did not stay around to listen. He dashed around the corner to the main entrance and back to the lab.

It was scarcely recognizable. Larger and larger cells had formed, some viable, some not, which forced themselves into the corners of the room and ate away at the very structure of the building. Festoons of insulation hung above, where once there had been a fluorescent lighting system. Now the lamps and conduit were gone, and the very copper wires stripped from their insulation, which hung like abandoned snakeskins. There was not a scrap of metal in the room which had not been made into something else. Steel partitions, cabinets, desks had all been melted, running together in fantastic shapes.

There was a solid barrier before him, waist-high, of dead or dying cells welded together as dead polyps are clustered to make coral. He began to climb over them, looking for one with an intact toggle switch.

He found one, and threw it. The system shut off slowly, in stages. Cal heard the muffled whine of slowing dynamos in the basement, the dying fall of gears.

In the queer, sudden silence, he made his way out to the sunlight once more.

With the exception of a group of marines, who were beating to death a small suitcase, the people who had been running madly about before were now still, scattered like groups of statuary on the lawn. The statues were all looking at Cal.

Grandison Wompler finally moved, shaking his head sadly. 'I never thought you'd do a thing like that to me,' he said. 'Why, boy, why? I took you right out of school, I gave you the best opportunity a young man ever had to make something out of hisself, and here you stab me in the back, first chance you get.'

'But—'

'Oh, don't try to worm your way out of it. I got the whole story from them Frankenstein fellows. You just turned a billion-dollar machine into a great big pile of junk.'

'That's right,' Karl said nodding emphatically. 'You realize that shutting off the Reproductive System completely inactivated the QUIDNAC memory?'

'But it was running berserk!' Cal cried. 'It's already killed one man. It might have—'

'Oh, it's easy for *you* to say what might have been,' Grandison thundered.

'Don't, Pop.' Louie laid a hand on his father's shoulder. 'Don't get yourself worked up over *him*. He ain't worth it.' He led his father away. Grandison's shoulders seemed to sag more with every step he took.

'Yes, a complete security blackout, button it up tight,' said Grawk into a field telephone. He hung up and turned to face Cal. 'Well, boys,' he said to the Mackintosh brothers, 'what do we do with this one? Shoot him? (We can do it legal, you know. Caught in an act of sabotage, etc., etc.)'

A kindly-looking middle-aged man in rimless glasses wandered near, and seemed to take an interest in the proceedings.

'No need to trouble,' said Kurt, grinning. 'He's harmless – now – and I'm sure by the time Senator Moley's committee get through with him – if you get my meaning?'

'Meanwhile, you're fired,' said Karl brusquely. 'Better get going before we have you arrested for trespassing, eh?'

Grawk laughed at Cal's look of consternation.

'Don't bother turning in your lab coat,' Kurt said. 'Or your pocket slide rule. Keep them. Just go.'

'Has everyone lost their minds? I've just saved your lives, maybe, and you act like I'm Benedict Arnold. You, sir,' he said, appealing to the kind-looking stranger. 'Tell me, do I look like a traitor? Do you think my shutting off this damned machine is such a crime?'

The man smiled apologetically. 'I'm afraid I'm really too prejudiced in the matter to be of much help,' he said, and gave a small cough. 'You see, I'm Smilax, and it's my machine you've just put to death.'

There seemed nothing to do but go. As Cal walked away, he could hear the general talking about him in a very loud voice.

'There goes a helluva rotten bastard, if you ask me. A guy that would sell out his country like that – well, it's just lucky for him I ain't armed. Because if I was armed –' Grawk lowered his voice and added something Cal couldn't hear. Whatever it was, it made the four WAFs laugh very hard indeed.

He had lost his job, disgraced himself, submitted even to the flaying knives of pretty women's scorn. Cal was in no condition to do anything like rational thinking. For if he had been, there was one question he surely would have asked himself:

How was it a system as intelligent, as adaptable, as clever at self-protection as this one was supposed to be had given up almost without a fight?

CHAPTER VI

The Boxes That Ate Altoona

'I have taught my gears to talk
Nicky-nicky Poop, tic-toc.'

LOUIS SACCHETTI (attrib.)

'Of Altoona, Nevada, lying quite near Parsnip Peak (8,905 ft.) and not far from Railroad Valley, where no railroads run, I sing,' wrote Mary Junes Beele on her husband's L. C. Smith typewriter. Below it, she typed asterisks: a row of posies. The swollen belly of her thumb pressed the space bar.

From the next room came the clanking of a hand press. Editor Barthemo Beele was running off the second edition of the *Altoona Weekly Truth. His hand*, she thought, *that rocks the cradle* … Mary cursed the paper and she cursed the paper's editor, her husband of one week.

The keys of the typewriter, she saw, were like black cough drops. Black cough drops were not to be had in Altoona. One of the typewriter's keys had broken one of Mary's nails. She began to chew it off, cursing everything she could think of – especially cursing Altoona. If that sailor did not take her away soon, she was going to die of this town. As she bit into another nail spitefully, contrary Mary cursed her rotten luck.

Altoona, too, had an unlucky history. In 1903, it had been the sole supplier of reuttite to the entire Western Hemisphere. Reuttite was of course that metal which made the best, most brilliant, longest-lasting gas mantles. There was no other known use for reuttite.

On Park Avenue in Altoona, the magnates of four different railroads had made their homes beside those of dozens of mine-owners and speculators. They'd built great white carpentered castles, gothic dreams in scrollwork and gingerbread, with bow windows, mullions, heart-shaped arches, wandering ivy and brave towers. The earth was shot through with old mine tunnels, so that now most of these heavy homes had sunk into it. Park Avenue was mainly a row of rusty fences and weedy lots. Occasionally one might glimpse through the hollyhocks a tower, its conical hat askew.

Only two of these curios still stood firm. Both were grey, trailing the dirty lace of their porches, swaybacked, pot-bellied and senile. One of them, after its ruined owner had flung himself in front of one of his own trains, had been converted into a warehouse. It now held all the reuttite mantles produced between 1904 and 1929 – nearly all the reuttite there was, and representing 25 years of attempts to find some use for it other than gas mantles.

The other house was still, as it had always been, the Smilax house. Phineas Smilax, the first and only president of the Gardnerville, Fernley and New York Railway ('Route of Reuttite'), had invested heavily in the mineral. He had hoped that, as he and Altoona grew richer, the line would actually extend as far east as New York City.

Phineas began building his railroad line in 1885. The work progressed slowly, and this was in part due to certain peculiarities in his hiring policies. Orders existed to fire any man caught beating a horse, drowning a kitten, or tying a can to a dog's tail. He further refused the coolie labour his competitors relied upon, preferring instead Bible students, who sang, at his request, hymns while they worked. His favourite hymn was *The Celestial Railroad*. Despite his paying them the then-lavish wage of one dollar an hour, the students were so poorly suited to this work that progress was measured at first in feet per month, then in inches. By 1913, his empire stretched from Altoona to Warm Springs, a fifty-eight-mile vista of sagebrush which he inspected daily in his private car.

This car was the only luxury Phineas permitted himself, for he believed in moderation in all things. The excess of his fortune was always distributed to charities, among which he never scanted the Animal Protection League. Phineas was known to all as a kindly and temperate man – no less to his own children than to strangers. He never chastised his son and daughter by more than a reproving frown, and more was never required.

Perhaps the only fault his neighbours might have found with him was in his choice of servants. Phineas had taken into his employ in the great house in Altoona people from the Nevada Asylum for the Criminally Insane.

'Criminals, pish!' he would exclaim. 'They are merely poor unfortunates, languishing for want of a kind word.' For over twenty years he had no other servants, and a gentler, more trustworthy set could scarce be found.

One day in 1913 Phineas sat looking out the window of his private car at the sagebrush, state flower of Nevada. 'I feel old today,' he remarked to his secretary, who afterwards remembered it as the first time he had ever heard his master complain. 'I feel I'm getting near the end of the line.'

The secretary handed him a telegram from his butler, back in Altoona. Phineas Smilax read it and fell from his chair, dead.

The telegram read, 'DAUGHTER ENCEINTE REPEAT PREGGERS STOP HAVE BEATEN HER WITH HORSEWHIP AND DRIVEN HER FROM THE TOWN ALTHOUGH I AM FATHER OF THE CHILD STOP PLEASE ADVISE DISPOSITION HER CLOTHING PORTRAIT ETCETERA STOP SIGNED CRAGELL.'

The daughter was never found. Cragell, having admitted to raping Lotte and frightening her into silence for several months, was returned to the Asylum. Phineas Jr took over his father's debts and began his own family, sired on a feeble-minded maidservant. By his own daughter he had an indeterminate number of children also, and hanged himself in 1930, when the last of the railroad had gone to pay his bootleggers. Three generations of illiterate Smilaxes still lived in the grey house, gardening in its yard. They never spoke of their banished relative, Lotte.

Rusty rails now stretched away from Altoona in three directions. Only the Nevada Southern continued to operate one train a week between Altoona and Las Vegas. Mary Junes Beele had circled on her calendar the day on which that train would leave. Tomorrow was the circled day.

The Beeles had now been here two weeks, and each had made a certain reputation. No one liked Mary. The women did not like the deliberating way she looked over their menfolk. Their menfolk did not like the insolent way she deliberated and rejected them. No one liked the way she treated her husband.

Barthemo, on the other hand, was sought out to about the same degree that Mary was snubbed. He was, after all, the finest gossip the town had ever seen, having already aired one new scandal and dug up a dozen old ones in his first week on the job. As a result of the very first issue of the *Altoona Truth*, two families were not speaking, and there was talk of a divorce, a spite fence, a duel. He reported *everything*, with scrupulous objectivity and in delicious detail. It was said that one day Beele would describe his own cuckolding fairly.

Filled with sweet loathing for her husband, Mary entered the press room, where he was reading a proof.

'Your cooperation is appreciated,' he read, then paused to add an 'o'. He did not greet his wife or acknowledge her existence in any way. ' ... how long will these goings-on continue?' he read, then amended it to ' ... how long will these goings-on go on?'

'Yaddadda yaddadda go on?' she mocked.

He continued reading.

'No one ever comes to this damned town,' she said.

'Nothing ever happens in this damned town,' she added.

'The only time we see a fresh face in this damned town,' she concluded, 'is when someone strays off the road to Vegas.'

'What about that hitchhiker? He isn't on the way to Las Vegas, but to the US Navy Ammunition Depot.'

'Oh, the sailor. He doesn't count. I'm bored with him already,' she said, wrinkling her nose. 'Can I use the car tonight, by the way?'

Her husband nodded, not looking up from his proof. 'Find out if you can,' he said, 'why he has those tattoos of Dumbo and Bambi on his arms. There might be a feature story in that – human interest, you know, something for the puzzle page.'

That night, while Barthemo Beele was inserting into his paper a late news item about the adultery of an editor's wife, Mary and the sailor were discovering, in the back seat of the Ford, that they were very drunk. The Ford was parked at the edge of town, near the entrance of the Lost Albanian Mine.

'I hear something,' mumbled the sailor. 'It ain't your old man, is it?'

'Him? Don't worry,' Mary said, laying a hand on Bambi. 'Listen, he's busy right now, putting the paper to bed. He's some kind of – not freak – neurotic, I guess. All he cares about is putting the damned *paper* to bed. *Altoona Truth*. He wants to bring out a Sunday edition called the *Altoona Altruist*. Faugh!' She took a drink down savagely, then another.

'Shh. Someone out there, baby. Hey, maybe it's the Lost Albanian himself, eh? Ha ha.' He poured himself a paper cup of gin and swallowed it. As long as they were this drunk, there seemed no point in stopping.

'Don't even say that joking!' she gasped. 'They say if you see the Lost Albanian, the world is coming to an end. Jesus, that would be a story for Barty, now, wouldn't it? Let's change the subject. Are you gonna take me away on the train tomorrow or not?'

'Sure I am.'

A low, blocky shape appeared, ghostly grey, at the dark entrance to the mine shaft. It scuttled across the moonlit stretch of ground towards them.

'Snakes!' screamed the sailor. 'I've gone snakey!'

'You can drink all you want,' murmured Mary sleepily. She had not seen the shape. 'As long as you take me away from the *Altoona Tooth* … I mean the …' She dozed, resting her dirty knot of hair upon Dumbo. The sailor did not notice. He peered fearfully out in the dark, looking for more hallucinations. So this was the DTs! Only a few days before, he had finished his tour of duty at Wompler Research, where all hell had broken loose – little grey boxes. It must be that they were stuck in his unconscious somehow, and the DTs released them, he theorized. Something clanked under the car, but he refused to hear it. He closed his eyes and sipped gin, until, a certain percentage of his blood becoming alcohol, he slept.

At 11:00 the next morning Barthemo Beele and the town marshal woke them up.

'Hey, where's the car?' groaned the sailor.

'We've been robbed!' Mary exclaimed.

Barthemo busied himself taking pictures of the couple from various angles, while the marshal questioned them about the robbery. The four of them compiled a list of the stolen articles:

1 bracelet, ankle, lady's
1 clasp, metal, purse
1 zipper, metal, dress

1 lipstick
1 compact
2 silver dollars and an unknown amount of change, several hairpins
2 cigarette lighters
1 aluminium comb various keys
2 silver fillings from Mary's teeth
1 gold tooth from sailor
1 automobile, Ford.

'I'll go phone this into the highway patrol, just as soon as the lines are working again,' said the marshal. 'You know it's a funny thing. Just about every car in town has been stolen. Bicycles, too, and I don't know what-all. And wouldn't you know it, my highway patrol radio transmitter got misplaced too.' He wandered off, in the direction of the Town Talk Bar.

'Very interesting,' the editor mused. He, too, had been hearing strange rumours and complaints all morning. Now, as he sat down in the grass beside Mary and the sailor, his mind began spinning out headlines for an extra edition:

NO WHEELS? ANTI-CLIMAX

'The telephone lines are down,' he murmured. 'So are the power lines. Odd.'

'I'm leaving you, Barty,' Mary said.

'And at least a dozen cars stolen – old cars, too.'

'I'm going on the noon train with Lovey,' she said firmly. The sailor looked abashed.

'You might think that someone wanted to cut Altoona off from the outside world,' Beele said.

'To Las Vegas. I'm not coming back.'

'I can assume either that *they* don't want us to know what is going on outside, or – and what is more likely – *they* want to keep those outside from knowing what is going on here. Very odd.'

'Monster! Monster!' she screamed, inches from his vacant eyes.

'Now there's an idea,' he said abstractedly. 'Monsters from outer space have kidnapped us, and we don't know it yet.'

He wondered if the Air Force's nearby radar shack knew of the strange phenomenon … or if they had been affected by it. Whole new panoramas of headlines opened before his inner vision, miles of exclusive copy.

NO RADAR ON?
AF WIRELESS

We will toast neither our bread nor our power company this a.m. The lines are down. The lines that supply us with power, heat, light, communication, our umbilical cords to the outside world all down. Moreover we are without transportation. There is not a vehicle left in town: not a car, not a bicycle, not so much as a roller skate. Yet even more frightening is the prospect of impairment of our national defence network. How soon are our complacent authorities going to come too, and realize ...

Mary and the sailor did not further disturb his reverie. Rising, they dusted themselves off and strolled away in the direction of the station. Barthemo wondered if a sarcastic public notice would be more appropriate.

Due to circumstances beyond, it seems, the control of the city fathers, there will be a slight interruption termination in a few of our public utilities ...

It registered on him then that Mary was gone. *To the station.* But if whoever was cutting off Altoona from the outside world were as thorough as *they* seemed, it was a sure bet *they* would not miss the train. He would take his camera. He would take pictures of *them* actually stealing a train, 60-second pictures, with his new camera.

By one minute to twelve he was hidden under the station platform, his camera beside him. When he had stopped at the office to pick it up, a dozen people had tried to waylay and buttonhole him. There were conflicting stories about the water and gas being cut off, about walking tool boxes – and one intriguing item about poltergeists at the old Ruyteck house, the warehouse for gas mantles.

WHO HAUNTS WAREHOUSE?
Neighbours rattled by ghostly knocks

He could not get over the feeling that he was not alone in the darkness.

The train from Las Vegas, no special, came puffing in a leisurely ten minutes late, took on mail, took on water, took on two passengers, a woman and a sailor, and puffed off again in the direction it had come. Aside from the goggled engineers waving at the woman passenger as she boarded, nothing seemed odd.

Suddenly there was a crunching sound close at hand. The editor turned to see a large blocky shape beside him, digesting his camera. It seemed to do so with difficulty, as though it were full already, yet it remained in place while its crab-claw hands picked up every crumb. So this was it!

'Eureka!' he cried, and, as was his habit, unnecessarily translated, 'I have found it!' Leaping up joyfully, he brought his head into painful and concussive contact with the bottom of the platform. *What else do metal boxes eat?* he wondered as consciousness fled. *What would I eat, if I were a metal box? Surely not an editor ...?*

He awoke some time that afternoon to find the thing no longer beside him. His tongue noted fillings missing, and his belt no longer functioned. No buckle. These were reassurances that he had not been dreaming. *Zap!* Even the metal spring from his notepad was gone; even the lead from his pencil. He could see the banner now:

GNAWING GNOME PUTS BITE ON TEETH, BELTS BUCKLE
Foxy box has goat-like appetite

With maybe a cut of the thing munching a tin can. Barthemo felt he had it made.

Rumours came to meet him as he passed along Park Avenue, and more than rumours. Flying saucers, thousands of fire-breathing monsters were solemnly attested to by sober citizens. *Great*, he thought. *Next it'll be a telepath as big as a house.* He gnashed his unfilled teeth on their silly rumours. Barthemo Beele considered himself a lover of truth, stranger to fiction.

Why, it's as though it read my mind! he thought, staring at the Ruyteck house. The poltergeist no longer haunted the building – it had *become* the building. Seemingly the crumbling grey castle had come to life; it tipped and swayed in a clumsy sort of dance. His mind refused to function – except to curse the loss of his camera. Here was a million-dollar picture, and it could only happen in the West, where monsters were monsters.

The worn edifice shivered and rattled obscenely – he thought of the rotting corpse of a dowager doing the twist – and stretched itself upwards, rising, as it were, on tiptoe. Its towers stopped slumping and actually towered, as nails screamed from boards,

mould-softened timbers flaked apart, and a century of dust boiled from every crack.

The old house gave a final shudder, shaking off ornaments and pieces of window as if they were drops of water, swayed, tipped up crazily on one corner and –

Disappeared. Came to pieces so suddenly and completely that it was like a vanishing trick. Turned in an instant from a solid building to a pile of flat lumber. A bouncing cluster of bright metal boxes exploded from the remains and skipped about aimlessly, as though getting their bearings. They broke apart and bounced off in different directions then, but all with seeming purpose. The editor noted one peculiarity about this set of monsters – their surfaces seemed to be made of gas mantles, stuck together in some way.

MARTIAN MONSTERS THE MCCOY
Plunder house, don gas mantles

He followed one of the trundling boxes up Park Avenue to the corner of Broadway, where it paused at a fire hydrant.

DOGS WILL BE ALIENS

But the box was *surrounding* the hydrant. It split apart, then closed over it. A moment later there came a small geyser from the assembly. He saw a sort of crude water-wheel, fashioned like a child's pinwheel, spinning in the middle of the jet. A small box detached itself from the assembly and dashed away. Part of its surface, he noted, was of red-painted cast iron.

INVADER WEDS FIREPLUG
Can this marriage last?

In the distance the water tower, a giant golf ball on a tee, began to wilt. He watched it dent and collapse, as grey shapes swarmed over it.

AU REVOIR, OUR RESERVOIR

He thought of simply filling up the headline with question marks, but there were not enough in the type case to do so. There were not even enough to take care of all the questions he wanted to put to his readership.

He turned and headed for the office. It was only by chance that he peered in the door of Smilax's Hardware – after all, like all the other buildings on the block, its windows were smashed – but what he saw made him halt.

What he did not see, rather. The store was utterly empty, looted clean. He found the owner, Milo Smilax, lying on the floor at the back, weeping. The metal frames from the bottom halves of his glasses were missing, naturally. He babbled of washing machines. Never a coherent man at best, Milo was now gubbling:

'I'm a dead man, they ruint me! The washing goddamned machines boxes washing machines ruint me eating guns. Help me mama don't tell boxes tell fare thee Wellington remington Washington ne'er-do-well. They eat the coal scuttling like grabs up anything handy saws gone screws gone knives gone fishing rods the ...'

Dr Trivian would have said the shelves were unfulfilled. In fact, about all that remained were the seed catalogues, the price tags, and a worn, scuffed cardboard sign. Milo stared at the sign as he babbled on. It said, 'LOOKING FOR TOOLS?' The pupils of LOOK's eyes were looking at the blank eyes of TOOLS. 'SEE OUR SAWS'.

'It's the end! Ruint! Nails, saws, chains, everything gone with the w—'

'The end? It is, is it? Is that any way to talk, Milo? I'll admit it looks bad right now, but we haven't got the big picture, have we? I mean, we have to *fight* this thing – or these things – not just lay around crying. We have got to—'

But Milo was not listening; he lay back and resumed crying. 'Nails, screws, bolts, saws, keys, hammers, tongs, axes, files, rifles, knives, hooks, shotguns, pistols, axes, guns, knives, bombs, daggers, death ...'

'There now,' said Beele, edging out the door. 'Hang on. I'm sure help is on the way.'

The problem, he reflected, was an interesting one. No one knew what to call the invader(s). He would be able to make up a name for them, perhaps add a word to the language. Say, *Uncrobs* (Unidentified Creeping or Crawling Objects).

He filed it way along with the news story about Milo.

HARDWARE STORE
Greedy gadget bites nails, chisels

Before him a little girl sat on the sidewalk, weeping. A naughty dog, she told him, had bit her where she sat down. Moreover she had lost her baby – her 7-transistor radio-doll, that is – to a great big giant. Beele told her not to cry, and that he was sure help was on the way.

He hurried on towards the office. This would be the biggest news story ever, anywhere.

THE BOXES THAT ATE ALTOONA
Even the rivets of a child's blue jeans!

A sort of typewriter passed him. It had been broken and distorted, but he could still see the name L. C. Smith on the back plate. Beele swore and broke into a run. A case of type, now became something else, waddled out of his office, brushing him aside at the door, and made its majestic way down the street.

As he entered, Beele seemed to hear the hand-press calling for help. He flung open the door of the press room and rushed in, but too late! The press was already taking on a familiar boxy shape. As he neared it, it gave a final clank, lurched to the window, and fell through into the street. A burglar alarm went off, but was strangled at once.

PAPER RAPED!

The office was stripped clean. How ironic it was, he thought. Unwittingly the machine invaders had destroyed the only means to their justly-deserved fame. Or had they? He rushed out again.

It was after dark by the time he reached a phone booth on the high worked. After breaking it open for a dime, he tried to call the wire Each time he would get connected, and say, 'I'm from Altoo—', the c tion would break and his dime rattle back down. He was beginning to w whether he hadn't ruined the mechanism somehow, when a highway patrol car stopped. The men in it were not highway patrolmen.

They forced open the door of the phone booth and dragged him forth.

'Sorry to be rough with you, sir,' said one, tipping his snap-brim hat. 'But our nation's security is at stake. You're Beele, of Altoona? The editor?'

'Yes, but—'

'We've got express orders to keep this particular story quiet, Beele. I'm afraid we'll have to either take you into custody or —'

'Go ahead, kill me!' he said. He, Barthemo Beele, hard-hitting young editor, was weeping. 'I have nothing to live for, now. I've lost my press, type fount, wife, typewriter, everything! Go ahead, paid assassins, hirelings of the do-nothing bureaucracy! Kill me! You've already killed the only thing that meant anything to me – my story!'

'I was going to say, we'll either have to take you into custody or swear you in as an agent. We often do that with newsmen, then send them off on foreign assignments. Of course we'll have to investigate your background thoroughly – that'll take an hour or so. What do you say? Would you like to go to Morocco?'

An agent of the CIA! Beele could see it in his mind's eye: palm trees, intrigue, a chance to clean up corruption at the very source!

'I'll take it,' he said, smiling through his tears.

CHAPTER VII

The Gulls of Marrakech

'They four had one likeness, as if a wheel had been in the midst of a wheel.'

EZEKIEL 10:10

Haroun Al Raschid was being difficult, pretending not to understand what Suggs was asking him to sell.

'This puts me in an embarrassing position,' he said, sighing *kif* smoke behind his bejewelled hand. 'You see, M'sieur Suggs, I do not officially even know of the French mission in this city. How can I give you the information you seek? If you used it, my reputation with the French might be – as you say – battered? I might lose friends, influence – and for what?'

'You must help us,' Suggs said grimly. 'Give us the name of their man, at least. I know you know it; Haroun knows everything that goes on in Marrakech.'

Al Raschid leaned back slightly, his fat mouth rounding in a moue of disavowal. 'You flatter me, M'sieur.' The tight linen of his suit prevented him from sprawling on the low couch, as he so obviously wished to do; it was with great effort that he moved in any direction, even to reach for his mint tea. 'I tell you, it is in my mind to help you, M'sieur Suggs, as a friend helps a friend. But – I do not know. The risk is great.'

'You must know *something* of use.' The CIA man tried to hold his breath whenever a whiff of *kif* smoke came near, but now he leaned across the low brass table and spoke in an earnest whisper. 'Just give us the man's name, that's all. It is for the good of Morocco as well as that of the United S— Nations. The whole world will benefit.'

'Ah, but that is what the Russian gentleman says. Which of you is telling the truth?' With a cunning gleam in his eye, Haroun added, 'What is a simple man to believe? I am not well-educated. I am only a poor merchant, as you see.'

The sweep of his glittering hand indicated the parquet floor, rich carpets, mosaic walls; it took in the stained glass lancets and the delicate, jewel-like chandeliers. The room was a chaos of textures: brass, wood, leather, silk, wool, silver, velvet. Through a marble doorway Suggs could see the cool garden where a white peacock stalked to and fro beneath the lemon trees.

'As you see, I have not the air conditioning. I have not the television set. I have none of the luxuries so commonplace in your land, no, not even the electric toothbrush.'

Hiking up his jellaba, Suggs brought out a slim billfold. 'We are prepared to pay, of course,' he said. 'Anything reasonable.'

'Ah!' Haroun's tiny nostrils exhaled twin jets of aromatic smoke. 'Then I must overcome the scruple of my conscience. Here is the right half of a picture of the man you seek. His name is Brioche, Marcel Brioche. He is a pilot of planes for the French Air Force – and who knows what else, eh?'

'No one is exactly what he seems,' Suggs said pleasantly. As his left hand reached out to take the half-picture his right, still inside his jellaba, fired his silenced gun. Haroun Al Raschid did not move, but only grunted slightly as the front of his silk shirt grew purple with blood.

Suggs did not wait to see the inevitable look of surprise on his victim's face – after nine years in the CIA, one grew weary of such looks – but tucked the photo in his billfold and hurried out into the sun-drenched street. He drew up his hood as he ran. The motion set scalding pangs of diarrhoea growling in his guts.

A crowd of ragged boys besieged him almost at once, and followed him to his hotel, chanting:

'M'soo, M'soo! You want gull, nice gull? You want nice boy? *Kif*, smoke? Mister! 'Allo! You like picture? You like see dancing gull? You like camel whip? Me very strong, M'soo! You want shoes shine? Me guide, M'soo. Me guide. You want nice gull?'

His disguise had not been as effective as he had hoped.

In the lobby, Suggs bought a postcard depicting snake charmers in the market, Dar El Fna, and a stamp. 'Dear Madge,' he wrote. 'Still having wonderful time, though I miss you and Susie. Love, Bubby.' He mailed it at the desk.

Scotty, his partner, sat in the only comfortable chair in their room, reading an Arabic newspaper. 'Did you get it?' he asked, without glancing up. Suggs nodded as he locked the door. 'Good man. Haroun give you any trouble?'

'A little. I had to kill him.'

'That's tough. We could have used him. What happened?'

'Tell you as soon as I get the report made out, Scotty.' Divesting himself of the jellaba and loosening his tie, Suggs sat down at the portable and rolled in a triplicate form.

'Item: one bullet, .375 calibre,' he typed. 'Date used; 1 June, 196—.' He went on, typing slowly, taking a certain pride in his neat spacing. When he had finished, he brought out the half-photo and showed it to Scotty.

'He was going to sell *them* the other half,' Suggs explained.

The other looked surprised. 'Them? I thought Vovov was working alone on this.'

'Not any more. This is too big for just Vovov. They know as well as we do what's going on here – that this Brioche is an astronaut – that France means to put him on the moon. They've brought in their top man, Vetch. Maybe to check on his subordinate, or maybe to ringer this Brioche.'

'How do you know Vetch is in town?'

Suggs wagged a finger playfully. 'Oh, I have my spies, I have my spies,' he said. 'But what worries me is, have they *already* got the other half of this? Do they know what Marcel Brioche looks like?'

'Are you sure he's the man?'

Suggs nodded. 'We've got to contact him before they offer him – the moon.'

Neither man smiled. They lapsed into a thoughtful silence, each trying to unravel the mystery surrounding the half-picture.

– Why had Haroun offered him only half a picture? Suggs wondered. It didn't make sense, if he had intended to sell the other half to the Russians. Perhaps he only had meant to hold it back for more money. Haroun was too smart to try selling to both sides.

But there were other things that did not make sense. What of the crowd of urchins – they had recognized him through his disguise as an American! Could they have stolen the other half of the picture? What kind of pictures had *they* been trying to sell him? He recalled their grimy, skinny hands clutching at him – could they have picked his pocket? Perhaps, on the other hand, they had been trying to warn him of something – of the location of the rocket, for example. What was it they had said about gulls? 'You want gull?' But Marrakech was in the middle of the desert, hundreds of miles from any gulls! It was a code, then, but a code for what, he could not imagine. He was about to ask Scotty, when something, a gleam of scrutinizing eye, arrested him. What was Scotty thinking about?

– Scott watched his partner watching him. Yes, there was guilt in Suggs's face, real guilt and worry. He had killed today, almost for no reason. Then too, he was reticent about his sources of information. How had he found out what the Russkies were up to? What was going through his mind now? Scott was glad he had taken the precaution of tucking his gun down the side of his chair earlier.

– If the urchins had seen through his disguise, Suggs reasoned, only one person could have tipped them off – the only person who knew about his visit this afternoon – Scotty! His partner in the CIA for nine fantastic years!

Suddenly, Suggs knew fear. Was Scotty hiding a gun behind that Arab paper? Well, there was always the typewriter. Its carriage could fire a single shotgun shell – Scotty had probably forgotten that.

It seemed incredible that Suggs's partner could have sold out, but he must have done so. To whom? Suggs wondered. Not to the Russians, or he'd have known about Vetch. Was he, then, working for Morocco? For France? Or was he playing some even deeper game?

– What kind of game was Suggs playing? Scott wondered. Had he killed Haroun because the merchant knew too much? Had Haroun called him outright a double agent? There was no doubt Suggs was a wheel within a wheel, but for whom? He wondered how he could have let Suggs fool him for so long. Why, everything about him gave it away – the half-picture, the over-casual way he seemed to be looking at the ashtray, while his other hand was out of sight, going for a gun.

– There were no ashes, Suggs noted, but there had been ashes yesterday. Someone had cleaned this ashtray. Why? He saw the over-casual way Scotty was yawning. Was he getting ready to make his play?

– Was Suggs making his play?

– Yes, *now*!

– *Now!* Fire through the newspaper!

– *Now!* Suggs stabbed the question mark button on the typewriter.

Fire and steel exploded. Scotty slumped forward, dead.

'I'm really sorry, Scotty,' Suggs murmured, standing over the corpse. 'I wish you could get a hero's funeral, at least. But I gotta protect myself, old shoe. The noise of that shotgun blast will bring the police. I've got to make sure the hotel will pay them off and cover up your death.'

He opened an emergency kit and dug out a black lace brassiere and a lipstick. He fastened the brassiere about the cadaver's torn chest and drew red upon the discoloured lips. Then he looked hard at the half-photo, memorized the address on the back, tore it in bits and swallowed them.

Heavy footsteps sounded on the stairs as he left by the balcony. Suggs took a last look at the body.

'Don't worry, Scotty,' he said earnestly. 'I'll get the bastards for making me do this. So help me.'

CHAPTER VIII

The End of the World

'What are little girls made of? Contain dextrose, maltose, monosodium glutamate, artificial flavouring and colouring; sodium propionate added to retard spoilage.'

OLD SAYING

Though the television newscaster seemed hysterical, Susie Suggs was not agitated in the least. She was not really watching the screen of her portable TV; it served only as a flat weight on her tummy, while she did her deep breathing exercises according to *Lady Fair* magazine. The exercises made her sleepy, and the voice of the little figure seemed to dwindle to a mosquito hum. It was almost as if he were a little man growing right out of her tummy; but this idea was so vaguely disquieting that it brought her fully awake. Forgetting to count her breaths, Susie began actually watching.

'Is it a Russian sneak attack? Is it one of our own secret weapons gone somehow horribly wrong? Or is it something we are even less prepared to face – an invasion of beings not of this planet? We'll have the whole story in just a moment, after this message from the Vortex Corporation.'

The screen went white, then displayed a large white missile sitting in a mesh of black iron railings. Fire swelled from under it as, trembling, the giant cylinder rose into darkness.

'This is … the Moloch!' intoned a solemn announcer. 'America's newest power punch! Just look at this baby go!' The missile rose, tilted, and headed off into the night. 'Now watch the Moloch destroy this mock-up of an enemy village!' Something white flashed downward into a grass village, and both exploded together – '*Wow!*' said the announcer – in one instant of blinding glare.

The scene changed to a complicated laboratory, where a group of men in white coats listened to earphones and watched, on a dozen little TV screens, the destruction re-enacted.

'These capable, experienced men designed Moloch. They are the members of Vortex Missile Group, just one of Vortex's "Keep America Tough" programmes. Every man here is a genius, dedicated and committed to our ever-expanding missile programme. They have solved the launch and guidance problems of the Moloch – and of *seventeen other* military missiles. Yes, at Vortex, retaliation is a way of life.

'Vortex is many things to many people. Here we see a steel mill run by computers from Vortex Instrument Group. And here', he said, and Susie took more interest in the next scene, for it was an operating room, 'here is Dr Toto Smilax performing open heart surgery – using a scalpel made by Vortex Cutlery Group.

'*Vortex!*' exclaimed the announcer in conclusion. 'First in war and first in peace – and first in the hearts of its countrymen.'

The newscaster returned. 'Altoona, Nevada,' he said. 'Until today, just another ordinary American city in the West. Now – who knows? Life *may* be going on as usual in Altoona – *as far as we know*. But since early this morning there has been a news blackout imposed by the joint efforts of the FBI, the CIA and the National Security Agency. We have been unable to contact anyone within the city.

'What has happened? Frankly, we don't know. It could be, as some hint, a Russian invasion, or even an invasion from outer space. Calmer sources believe it to be a test of some sort, and at least one reliable source indicated that it might be a secret weapon gone wrong. *We just don't know.*' Every time he used this phrase, the newscaster's face seemed a little more crumpled, a little closer to tears. For another fifteen minutes he told Susie of all the things we don't know. Then the announcer with the soothing voice (that sent nice warm ripples over Susie's tummy) returned to demonstrate the two-stage Hermes-Aphrodite missile. Advertising was so silly, Susie thought, resuming her breathing exercises.

By her *Lifetime* watch, she noted how late it was getting. She was going to have to hustle to be ready for her date with Ron. And she had meant to study for her Organic Chem test Monday morning. Here it was Saturday night and she hadn't opened the book!

Quickly Susie showered with *Nice*, the 24-hour soap that gets at odours other soaps just seem to miss, and rolled on plenty of *SHUR*, to be sure about those offensive odours. After dusting all over with *Lady Clinge* talc, she slipped on her *Modaform* 6-way-stretch panty girdle that b-r-e-a-t-h-e-s, her *Deepline Modaform* Sport-support bra, and began applying *Classique* Parfum, the scent that makes every woman an empress, every man a slave.

Drawing on her black sweater and black skirt, Susie seated herself at the vanity table to do her face. After covering her golden freckles with *Blanc* foundation, she powdered with Rubella Gorne's *Klown* powder. To her Greekly perfect mouth, she applied a white lipstick called *Eraser*.

For her eyes, Susie selected her usual assortment of Nora Hart shades, chiefly oyster and sylph-green, but blending in touches of burgundy and bronze. Then, after brushing her hair and applying a liberal amount of *Airnet*, there remained only jewellery.

On a velvet bar in Susie's vanity kit were pinned Bob's ΔKE pin, Len's Young Republican pin, and Jim's Vietnam button. Her fingers passed over these, nor paused at the Pepsi *Come Alive!*, the *Go Gophers!*, or the *Win With Dewey* buttons, went on to the end of the bar and selected the peace mandala Ron had given her. As she pinned it on, her mother came to the door.

'That awful creature Ron is here,' she stage-whispered. 'Oh, I'm sorry I don't like him, dear, but he's so – so shifty. And he always wears old clothes. And now – now he's even growing a *beard*! Ugh!'

Fighting down her own repulsion at the idea, Susie said, 'But mother, he's one of the richest boys in the city of Santa Filomena. Surely you want me to have a good future?'

'I don't know. I just don't know.' Madge's tanned face deepened its seams with worry. 'I married your father because he had a good future with the insurance company. Now look at me.'

Susie looked at her mother and saw an attractive middle-aged woman right from the pages of *Lady Fair*, to which Madge subscribed: dark hair, streaked with silver, a slim, girlish figure, and the only clue to her years being the lines in her face. Susie fervently wished that she herself, at thirty-five, would look as good.

Madge went on, 'I guess I shouldn't try to tell you how to run your life, after I've made such a mess of my own. Every time I think of that bastard – how he's enjoying himself over there with his harem girls – not even a postcard, in over three months! Well, I saw the lawyer today, and I'm suing him for a divorce. If he can live it up, so can I! Sauce for the goose! While the cat's away!'

Madge seemed to have been drinking. She lurched to the mirror and examined her eyes, pulling the loose flesh beneath them this way and that. She scarcely seemed to notice that Susie had drawn on her white felt boots, kissed her goodbye and said, 'That's the spirit, Mommy! Kick him in the – the seater! 'Bye.'

Near the campus of the University of California, at Santa Filomena, one street featured four well-patronized coffee houses, but none so popular as The Blue Tit. To avoid difficulties with university officials the owner of the coffee house, Kevin Mackintosh, had painted a bluebird on the café's sign. As on all weekend nights, a crowd had crammed itself into The Blue Tit to listen to folk music and poetry, but tonight, it was a sullen, heavy-spirited crowd. Many of them had arrived, as had Susie and Ron, on motorcycles in the drizzle, and the room was filled with steam and the sour smell of wet wool.

On a raised dais at the rear of the narrow room, a poet was reading aloud from a sheet of paper held close to his face. As he turned to catch the light, Susie recognized Kevin Mackintosh.

'*Timepoem* number fourteen,' he read.

> '*Johnson in Omaha: loud ticks from the inner clock.*
> *There always has to be a victim*
> *In cool and secret stride*
> *No motives other than patriotism*
> *and pure disgust.*
> *Back to business, without boots.*
> *Look here for an explosive spirit.*'

'Golly!' Susie exclaimed. 'Explosives reminds me, I ought to be studying for that Organic Chem test Monday.'

'Ssh,' said Ron. 'There isn't going to be any day after tomorrow.'

'I don't know the Geneva naming system or anything.'

Ron smiled. Kevin Mackintosh looked at her, incredulous. 'The Geneva naming system is done,' he said. 'So is the Geneva convention. So is Geneva.'

'It's the end of the world,' Ron explained.

'That's right,' said someone else. 'The crack of doom has been sounded.'

'What do you mean?' asked Susie, smiling a little. 'I don't get it.'

'It's the end of the whole works, baby,' Ron said. 'Like they tell us on the radio. Didn't you hear the news?'

'This is our end-of-the-world party,' announced Kevin Mackintosh. 'Bring your own.'

Someone snickered, but the poet was not smiling.

'Will someone please tell me what this is all about?' Susie asked. She thought and thought, but was unable to recall just what she had seen on the six o'clock news.

'That thing in Altoona, Nevada,' Ron explained, 'is either a Russian missile, Something Horrible from outer space, or one of our own screaming nightmares. If it is a Russian missile, we retaliate. Then they retaliate. Et cetera, the end.

'If it is a thing from outer space, why does the government keep it so quiet? Because it is something pretty horrible, like a thing that digested the whole town, or atomic monsters, shooting X-rays all over. Something we can't stop that'll take over.

'If it is some weapon of our own out of control, what would it be? Some bomb? Not likely, or other countries would be raising hell. More likely a nasty disease – say universal contagious cancer.'

Everyone in the room had grown silent. It was as if they huddled together in the gloom actually waiting for a quick blinding light to illumine and transfigure them for one final instant. The most important actions and words were pointless; the most trivial were full of meaning, elevated almost to sacraments.

Tears came to Susie's eyes. It all seemed so unfair. She was seventeen years old and still a virgin, and now it was too late. She wanted more than anything to give up pointless, silly virtue now, near the end of All, but it was somehow too small a sacrifice (then, too, there was always the outside chance that the world would *not* end – and then how in the world would she explain things to Madge?). Susie hated the old End-of-the-world suddenly and furiously. She wanted to just scratch its eyes out!

'Why – why I think we ought to go out and protest!' she declared, standing up. The others looked at her, not catching her meaning. 'They have no right to do this to us! They have no right to take away the world like this, the selfish pigs!'

There was a sudden high-pitched explosive laugh from one youth. 'What do you think we ought to do about it?' he mocked. 'Write our congressmen?'

'No,' she said seriously. 'But I don't think we'll solve anything by just sitting around here moping, for Pete's sake! We ought to go out and – and protest! We ought to march on this Alt— this wherever it is and tell them what we think of them, in no uncertain terms!' She stamped her little boot. 'Or are we going to let them take *everything* away?'

The room was in an uproar. Some people were egging her on, while others were thinking over her words. Susie's scorn was magnificent. In vain did someone try to point out that protest against the inevitable is useless.

'Well of course it's useless,' she snapped. 'I'm not as dumb as all that! But it certainly isn't any use just sitting around here just – steaming, is it?'

'I think she has something,' said Ron, grinning. 'Why the hell not go down there and protest? It's only ten hours' drive.'

'Protest what?' asked Kevin. 'The end of the world?'

'Sure, why not?' Ron said. 'Like in *Attack of the Fungamen*, everyone protested the dangerous experiments, right? Like in *Goz*, they demonstrate against the army's impotence, remember? And in *The Day the Earth Caught Cold—*'

'All right, all right, but what are we protesting?' Kevin asked. 'If I may be so stupid.'

'How about the sealing off of an American city by the CIA, and the violations of freedom of speech involved? Come on, we'll make some signs, and we'll get some people who have cars in on this.'

Kevin gave in. 'We'll let your girl run the show,' he suggested. 'It was her idea. But I never thought I'd spend my last hours making signs.'

'Or getting arrested,' Ron added. 'The friends won't like this at all.'

'If I see any fuzz,' said the poet, 'I'm going to suddenly have a business deal in Tangier. I'll only go so far for a joke.'

It may have been a joke to him and to most of those present (behaving in conscious or unconscious parody of old movies – 'Gee gang,' someone said, 'how are we going to raise money for uniforms for the team?' 'I have it! We'll put on an end of the world!'), but to Susie, it meant becoming for a moment a kind of Joan of Arc. As they left the coffee house, she was at the fore, her white boots lifting high, higher, leading the parade.

Certainly Madge never worried less about the vincibility of her daughter's innocence than now, having just heard her insist on the word 'seater', and seeing her blush as she pronounced it.

How innocent Susie was, and how wise she herself had been at that age.

Madge was now only dimly aware of the dying roar of Ron's Harley, only vaguely cognizant of her own hand, caressing the buttons on the velvet bar in Susie's vanity kit. Madge was seeing herself of eighteen years ago, going out to the Webster Beach Club with a handsome young insurance salesman.

How like the youthful Suggs was one of Susie's friends, Jim Porteus, she thought. Odd that Susie never noticed it in him. He was such a nice boy – so earnest, in his glasses with their customary rims of solemn black, so energetic, so eager to set the world on fire. Madge fingered the yellow pin he'd given Susie: 'NO RETREAT – BEAT THE VIET CONG.'

Jim was already worth money in his own right, besides being the son of a prominent gynaecologist, and leader of the California chapter of *Young Americans to Conserve Free Enterprise.*

When he was serious, he was serious indeed. Madge recalled every detail of the first conversation she'd had with him:

'Are you planning on studying medicine yourself, Mr Porteus?'

'No I'm not, Mrs Suggs.' He removed the glasses, startling her with the hard planes of his face. 'No, I'm afraid the medical profession is a dead letter, these days. Despite all our efforts to prevent it, socialized medicine is on the way – and with it, *starvation for doctors.*

'No, I've been keeping an ear to the ground while I pursue a course of business administration. Market analysis seems very promising – very promising, I can assure you. Qualified analysts are in short supply. It's an uncrowded field, where an energetic, get-up-early young man can soon make his pile. Or I may opt for corporation law – chiefly protecting infant industries from the predations of the federal eagle – or some related field. I suppose the truth lies somewhere between the two. I may become an humble junior executive, an unknown but vital cog in middle management – a job where the rewards are not mere fiscal aggrandizement, but full commitment to the judicious use of power. I distribute work and rewards – and punishments – to my subordinates, while receiving my own just portion from the higher-ups; a vital link in the Great Chain of Command!'

In many ways, she reflected, thinking back on that conversation, Jim seemed older than her husband.

Madge was shocked to note the time. In the next five minutes she was a flurry of activity, bathing, perfuming, arranging her hair, and enveloping her body in diaphanous pyjamas of mysterious misty grey barely before the bell rang. She hurriedly pinned on the yellow button and ran to greet Jim.

'Wow!' he said. 'Is it dark in here! Let's get a little light on the subject.'

'Wow!' he repeated, looking her over in the light. 'You look great, Madge.' He took off his Tyrolean hat and kissed her.

As he undressed, neatly and efficiently, Jim talked of the coming elections for student government, in which his Student Ultra Conservatives, newly-formed, hoped to win a few seats.

'We're young and dynamic, though inexperienced,' he said, folding his socks carefully and hanging them over the back of a chair. 'The older parties will just have to move over and make room for us.'

Madge moved over and made room for him in the bed.

Woody sat in the dispatcher's office the same night, staring unseeingly at the Lost Property form before him. For hours, he had found himself unable to even begin his strange report – though he saw every detail of it clearly, again and again.

By the time he had brought his little train to a halt that afternoon, the rest of the crew had been on the ground, running for the dispatcher's office where the beer was kept. The Altoona–Las Vegas run always stopped here at Double Flats for beer, especially on hot days. Officially, of course, they stopped to pick up train orders.

'Where's the beer?' asked Fats the brakeman cheerily.

JOHN SLADEK

'I ain't your slavey!' screamed the dispatcher, who never spoke in any other tone. 'You know where we keep it! You guys don't know what work is. You don't know how lucky you got it, being out there in the fresh air. I wish I was back on the road, I wish to God I was.' He spat into a dim, littered corner, where there might have been a spitoon. Woody and the crew opened beer cans and settled in various creaky chairs about the dark brown room. They were not anxious to get back into the desert dust and heat, no matter how lucky they had it.

Railroading was new and wonderful to Woody, though he pretended to hate it as much as everyone else seemed to do. He was already picking up railroad jargon, such as the differences between boxes, gons, reefers and flats, but he had much to learn. One thing which continued to surprise him was that he did not have to steer the engine. It seemed almost to guide itself, in some way he could not yet fathom, around even the sharpest curves. The railroad was a wonderful invention, he certainly had to admit.

The Nevada Southern was the only railroad he could find still running steam locomotives. Woody would not run any other kind. He loved the heat, the hiss of steam.

'That's right,' he put into conversation. 'Anyone is crazy to go railroading.' The others nodded.

'I'm gonna get out,' said Fats. 'I got a brother in the feed grain business, I'm gonna go in with him. Feed grain, that's where the real money is.'

'I laud that,' said Woody solemnly. 'The fratricidal bond.' The beer had cooled him off and made him feel clear-headed. Earlier, in Altoona, he had suffered an hallucination, no doubt from the heat. A classic wish-fulfilment dream, it had been – a woman he had once known, in another state, seemed to board his train at Altoona. He had even waved at the hallucination, but, being only an hallucination, it had not waved back.

He finished his beer, drew on his gauntlets, and strode to the door. And stopped.

Mac, the fireman stood on the platform, utterly dazed. Fats and the conductor were hopping and sprinting across the tracks towards the train.

The train was moving. It was moving and accelerating, with the throttle wide open.

But the throttle could not be wide open. There was no one in the cab to open it. There was no one to fire the boiler. For all practical purposes, the cab was empty.

Roaring and chattering, slipping, the engine, the coal tender and the single passenger car moved out. The hallucinatory woman seemed to be still aboard.

Fats puffed to a halt. The conductor made a try for the tail end of the car, missed, and fell. He rolled clear as the last wheels nipped by.

A mirage? Mass hypnosis?

50

Woody dipped the steel pen in ink and scratched upon the form.

'NAME: Elwood Trivian, Ph.D. TITLE: Engineer. ITEM LOST: One train. DESCRIBE THE CIRCUMSTANCES: Apparently the train was stolen, by a –' he lined out 'a' and wrote, 'by what seemed to be a small, grey tin tackle box.'

CHAPTER IX

Coincidence

'*Men that hazard all*
Do it in hope of fair advantages.'

SHAKESPEARE

The young man at the end of the bar was not wearing Western clothes. Had he worn no clothes at all he could not have appeared more conspicuous, at least in *The El Cantina Bar* in Goodtime, Nevada. The *El*, as the regulars called it, catered to the brightly-clad guests of three dude ranches. There were the ovoid, unhappy women of the Merry Widow Rancho (awaiting divorces); the unhappy, ovoid men of the Triple-Tumblebug Ranch (awaiting divorces); and the querulous, dozing old people, of no particular sex, from the Golden Sunset Retirement Ranch (awaiting death). Amid their orchids, turquoises and clarets, all the hues of a painted sunset, Cal's rumpled grey suit and dirty-white lab coat stood out like a bird-dropping.

Hitchhiking towards California, he had made it this far before sun, sand, wind, shimmering pavement and truck smoke had driven him indoors.

'Another one?' asked the bartender, poising his bottle. His name, stitched in violet letters over the pocket of his carnelian shirt, was *Slim*. His unlabelled customer nodded solemnly.

'I will have another. And pour yourself another, too, Slim.'

'Why, thank you, Carl. Your health.'

'It's *Cal*. Say, Slim, tell me, who are all those people along the wall?'

Slim explained about 'retirement ranches'. 'They come in now and then for a little fun, with their attendants.' He indicated a group of bored-looking young men and women at the middle of the bar, all wearing black ten-gallon hats and shirts of ochre silk. On the back of each shirt was embroidered a setting sun, or rising sun, emitting heavy black rays. The attendants' names were stitched in black over their hearts.

'Another thing. How come everything here seems to be made of wagon wheels and barrels? Tables and chandeliers and … Where do all the wagon wheels come from?'

Slim moved down the bar, smiling, to wait upon two middle-aged women.

'Oh Slim, you *beast!*' shrilled the thin woman in a black-and-lavender-shirt. 'We've been waiting for *hours!*'

Her friend, a dumpling in oriflamme orange, called Slim a bad boy, and told him she didn't know whether she wanted a frozen Daiquiri or not, from such a bad boy. Wasn't he a bad boy, though? she asked her companion.

On the colour television a parade in Texas appeared: whole troops of cow-girls in sky blue, their white boots moving like pistons in synchronous high-kicking steps. The men from the Triple-Tumblebug wet their lips and began to chuckle.

Cal had another drink. Two swarthy strangers came in. The smaller was Cal's height, the larger was a giant. They wore Palm Beach suits with wide shoulders and trim straw hats with narrow brims. Nevertheless, their eyes seemed to be in shadow. Cal would have taken them to be policemen, but they were drinking, and top-shelf whiskey, too. There was something famil-iar about the larger man …

'Another one, Carl?' Slim poured him another, took the proper amount from the jumbled pile of change in front of Cal, and added another receipt to the neat, squared-up stack. An increase or was it decrease in entropy – or was it enthalpy? Cal tried to remember Dr Trivian and Appreciation of Thermo-dynamics, but his thoughts were running into ellipses …

He watched the old people along the wall, dozing over cribbage or Mon-opoly boards and beer. Now and then one would awaken slightly to say something cross, then drift off without waiting for a reply.

The taller of the two newcomers, who reminded Cal somehow of jock-straps, had turned his back, but the shorter man materialized at Cal's elbow. 'Pardon me, sir,' he said shyly. 'My friend and I have a little bet going. I say you're a doctor, and he says you drive a meat truck. I wonder if you'd mind telling me which of us is correct?'

Cal smiled modestly, if crookedly. 'Actually, I'm a biophysicist. So I'd say your guess was closer.'

'Very interesting.' The stranger reamed one ear with a thick finger. 'I sup-pose you know a lot about mathematics, eh?'

'Bingo!' screamed an old person of indeterminate sex, who sat before a cribbage board.

Reluctantly, Cal admitted that he had a nodding acquaintance with the Calculus.

'I see. Well, thanks for settling our bet.' The stranger moved off, before Cal could ask him the name of his tall companion. 'Tennessee' came to mind, as did 'tennis shoe'. Cal settled for the moment on something between Dennis Shoe and Jack Strapp …

He realized he was shouting all this when Slim turned and smiled at him. 'Keep it down to a dull roar, now, Carl old buddy.'

'Cheat!' someone along the wall squeaked. 'Where did that hotel come from, eh? Tell me that!'

'You watch your mouth,' came the quavering reply. 'I own Boardwalk and Park Place, and by the Living God, you'll pay me my rent!'

'Please,' said another, an old woman in a scarlet shirt. 'Andy can take his turn over, can't he?'

A glass of beer went over. 'Now see what you've made me do! All the Chance cards ruined!'

'I'll show *you* who cheats!' screamed a wispy old man in a tall white sombrero and a shirt of distress-signal pink. Above the green neckerchief, his goitre worked convulsively. 'There!' He leapt up and whipped the blanket off his opponent's lap. A number of cards fell out of it. 'Hah!' he screamed. 'Caught with the goods! So that's what happened to all the rail-roads, eh?'

The culprit, a parrot-like man in blue and orange, picked up a tiny red block of wood and flung it at him. 'Take your hotel and go to Hades!' he wailed. Clawing at the board, he upset it, sweeping off hotels, houses, dice and markers. 'You cheat, yourself!'

' … take his turn over, now, couldn't he, Edna?'

'Cheat! Hah! Sneak!'

'I'll cheat you, by the Living God!' shrieked the man in the hat. He brought up a cane suddenly and began laying about him. 'All of you cheated me. All of you cheated me.'

There was a stir at the bar, among the group of attendants. One young man spun about on his stool. Above his pocket Cal could make out the name. 'Dr Michaels'. He was across the room in three strides, flipping the cane from the old man's hand.

'Now, Toby. Now, Toby, it's only a game,' he said.

The old man rolled his eyes and whinnied, 'You're all cheating me!'

The doctor drew his black, pearl-handled revolver, pressed the muzzle to Toby's upper arm, and squeezed the trigger.

The two swarthy strangers reached inside their jackets.

Toby visibly relaxed, and his muttering grew faint. Dr Michaels withdrew the gun. It was, Cal could see, made of black plastic. One might almost take it for a toy, if not for the inch of glittering needle projecting from the barrel. Retracting this, the doctor holstered his weapon.

'Sorry about the disturbance,' he grinned to the crowd at large. The hands of the two strangers came out of their jackets, and they laughed foolishly.

Dr Michaels and another attendant lowered the unconscious old man into a wheelchair. Cal saw that it had wagon wheels.

'What are you supposed to be?' a woman in purple demanded of Cal. 'Little country doctor? What's the white coat for?'

'In Japan,' he tried to say, 'white is for mourning.'

'In Jamp,' he said distinctly, 'wise firm? Awning.'

Her empurpled lips took a sip of cocktail. With obvious enjoyment she sneered, 'Don't hand me that crap! You ain't no doctor! You're just some monkey from the meat market. Why don't you get back to your pig's feet?'

Cal shook his head, then looked at his feet, trying to puzzle out her meaning. 'Why don't I—?'

'You're a mess!' she screamed, spraying spittle. 'A mess! Just like my old man. Boy, he was a real bastard. Used to rub grime deliberately into his shirts. Used to come home in his filthy shoes and *walk all over the floors*. Put his filthy ashes into every ashtray in the house. Well I had enough of that rotten bastard, and I had enough of you!'

Her cocktail was cold and frothy with cream. Its impact drove him back a few blind steps. Rebounding from a table, he fell. Angry red faces looked down at him. Four or five voices gabbled at once about that man bothering you ma'am, about drunken young snot ought to be in the army, about impersonating a doctor. Hands dragged Cal to his feet.

'About time you were shoving off, old buddy Carl,' chortled Slim, steering him towards the door.

'It's *Cal*,' he pleaded. 'You wouldn't like it if I called you *Slime*, would you?'

'Is that the way you're gonna be?' Slim rabbit-punched Cal and seized his collar. The other hand twisted in the back of his belt. 'I knew you was gonna be trouble when you come in here.'

The door flew towards them.

'But I only meant—'

Cal shot through the door, bounced on all fours, and rolled to rest against a brick wall.

Moonlight streamed down into the alley. Cal lay there awhile, getting his bearings. He saw a number of garbage cans, a poster announcing a Wheelchair Squaredance at the Golden Sunset Ranch, and his own shoeless foot.

Rising painfully, he limped about till he found the missing shoe. When he had finished being sick into it, he put it on.

It was difficult to walk on two legs, so he progressed on four to the alley entrance. The two strangers in Palm Beach suits were waiting for him. Without a word, they picked him up and dumped him in the back of a car. Though it was too dark to tell, Cal felt sure it was a black Cadillac sedan. The shorter man climbed in beside him, while the other slid behind the wheel. He certainly reminded Cal of someone in his graduation class, now two weeks past. But who? Not Barthemo Beele. Not Mary Junes, either …

'Where we going?' he asked, struggling to sit up. The stranger pushed him back in the seat and drew a gun.

'You're being kidnapped, actually, sir. "The Professor" has given orders to kidnap a mathematician.'

'What professor? I wanta see the squealchair wheredance.'

'Put this over your eyes, please.' He was handed a band of black cloth.

'Does that gun have a needle in it, too?'

The others laughed richly. 'That's right,' growled the driver. 'A needle to put you to sleep with – for a long time. Unless you want to take the big sleep, you better do as we – like we say. In this racket, we play for keeps, odd man out, loser take nothing, see?'

There was something familiar about that voice, Cal thought, but by now the blindfold was in place. They drove off.

Five minutes later, after a complicated series of turns, they stopped and hustled him into a building.

'Well, well, well,' boomed a hearty voice. 'Company already, eh? I suppose this is our mathematician.' Cal imagined a cigar-smoking executive gangster rubbing his hands. 'Take off the mask and let's have a look at the face of him.'

The blindfold was removed, and Cal found himself facing a buxom, pleasant-faced blonde wearing a ruffled mobcap and flannel nightie. She might have stepped out of a Dutch genre painting, but for the fact that she held, not a candle, but a bottle of Scotch and a glass. 'Welcome to Castle Rackrent!' she boomed. 'Care for a drink?'

His stomach contracted. 'I don't – think so. Are you – the Professor?'

'Me? Haha, bless you, no, I'm Daisy, the Professor's fiancée and former secretary. *This* is the Professor.'

She moved to one side, revealing a thin, wispy man sitting on the sofa. His sparse hair, the colour of pounce, lay in dusty streaks across his baldness. He seemed to be engrossed in writing with a quill pen in an old, battered book so huge it hid most of his body, though Cal could see gaitered legs below it. They did not reach to the floor.

'How do you do?' Cal said.

'How do you—?' creaked the other. But Daisy moved in front of him like a curtain once more, and he fell silent.

'His real name is Brian Gallopini,' she said, pouring herself a glass of liquor. 'But in the Underworld everyone with a college education gets called 'Professor', you see.'

'Then he isn't one, really?'

She drank off the gill and poured herself another. 'Oh yes, he's a professor, all right. Of eighteenth-century literature. Or was. I was his secretary. We decided to run away and be gangsters, when he got his idea – but that's another story. My name is Daisy le Due, and if you know what's good for you, you'll resist the temptation to call me "Daisy Duck". The mirth went out of her smile for a moment, then returned full-strength. 'I'll finish up these introductions now, then you can go clean the dirt and blood off your face so we can have a good look at you.

'These are the Professor's associates in crime, Mr John Beaumains, known as "Jack the Ripper" (for no good reason that anyone can think of), and "Harry the Ape", whose real name is—'

'Harry Stropp!' The exclamation burst from Cal, who just that moment had turned and recognized his kidnapper.

Harry, for it was indeed he, peered in bewilderment at the blood-and-dirt-encrusted face. 'Calvin Potter!' he cried. 'What are *you* doing here?'

'I might ask you the same question. Harry, have you gone in for a life of crime?'

From behind Daisy came a creaky voice. 'It is just such coincidences that prove there is a thing called Destiny, presiding over our so-called "chance" universe. I'll make a note of that in my journal.' The goose-quill scratched.

'Don't worry,' Harry said in a low, confiding tone, 'about taking Mary Junes away from me. Oh, it upset me for a while, I'll admit, but I'm all over that, now. There's plenty of other apples on the tree.'

'Well now,' Daisy chuckled, 'let's not keep Mr – Potter, is it? – Mr Potter up all night. We're all getting an early start in the morning, for Las Vegas. So I guess I'd better explain why we kidnapped you.

'The Professor has devised an elaborate and foolproof system for beating the wheel. We are going to – figuratively speaking – take Las Vegas by storm. This system can't fail. By this time next week, we should have the key to the city – literally speaking.'

'But where do I come in?'

'Exactly!' piped the Professor. 'Where do you come in? It seems my system is perfect in theory – that is, the *whole* of it is perfect   but the calculations involved in placing any one bet are too complex for any of us. That is where you, our Mathematical Genius, come in.'

'I'm flattered, of course, but—'

'Take him away, Harry,' Daisy said, making an imperious gesture. 'Lock him in the bathroom for the night, and guard the door.'

'But—'

'Come on, you.' Harry dragged Cal to the bathroom, flung him in, and turned the key on him.

There were no windows. Cal walked up and down, thinking, examining fixtures, waiting for the others to get to sleep. Then he got down and whispered at the keyhole.

'Harry! Sssst! Why not let me out of here? Do me a favour, will you?'

Harry laughed, one hoarse bark. 'Do *you* a favour? That's really rich. After all you've done to me.'

'Look, Harry, I'm sorry about—'

'Oh, don't get me wrong. I don't care about Mary Junes any more. Not at all. I forgot all about her. I mean, there's plenty other cookies in the jar. But – do *you* a favour! That's really rich.'

Cal curled up in the tub and tried to sleep. From time to time, Harry emitted another strangled bark. 'Boy! That really is rich. Do *him* a favour!'

In the morning the five of them started out for Las Vegas. Cal's blindfold was left off, and he was able to see that the motel in which he'd spent the night was right across the street from *The El Cantina Bar*.

While he nursed his hangover, the other four began a spirited conversation about the nature of the universe, as perceived through the working of coincidence.

Daisy maintained that in coincidence we see no other hand but the Deity's. She related numerous instances of simultaneous birthdays, albinism, people being struck by lightning or meteors, and the odd results of Dr Rhine's experiments.

Jack owned she had a point. Harry agreed that coincidences did seem to happen.

Brian Gallopini replied that it would be blasphemy to blame the Deity for mine cave-ins, for midair plane crashes maiming children, for widows losing their compensation cheques.

Harry clung to the notion that accidents would happen.

Daisy pointed to the fiction of the eighteenth century. She cited coincidences in *Tom Jones* and *Humphrey Clinker*. If such were the work of authors (Fielding and Smollet), why could not coincidences in Life have an Author (God)?

'By thunder!' Brian swore. 'Are you trying to tell me, woman, that you and I are naught but puppets, jerked about at the whim of some buffoon of a novelist? Pish! You may believe as you please, but know you that I am a free agent. I command my hand to move; it moves. See?' He demonstrated.

Daisy laughed. 'Only because you were destined to command it to move. You were commanded by the Author of All.'

But the Professor lapsed into a moody silence and would not answer. Some of the taller buildings and larger signs of Las Vegas were coming into view.

Offering Cal a pinch of Bergamot snuff, the Professor then began to explain to him his own ingenious betting system.

'Each time the bettor loses a bet,' he said earnestly, 'he doubles his next bet.

Since every run of luck must needs obey the immutable laws of Destiny, the first winning bet must needs more than make up for all his previous losses at one stroke!'

Cal groaned inwardly, but said nothing, reminding himself that he was a guest – and a prisoner.

'It is a complex system, but foolproof, as you can see,' concluded Gallopini. 'Yet it shews forth the orderly working of the universe. And the universe is orderly. To say it is not is to believe in magic. One might as well say that the man in that sign could go walking across the desert.'

The sign he indicated was a giant representation of a prospector atop one casino. In one hand he held a pan of nuggets, while the other moved up and down, as if beckoning. It was one of the more famous signs of the city, and could be seen for miles at night.

Now, as the horrified group watched, it did seem to take a step. Daisy screamed, a rich baritone scream, while the professor went as white as a periwig.

'Ah, it is all right. It is only falling. Perhaps being demolished,' he said. They watched the sign buckle and disintegrate with some relief. An upsetting coincidence, but not supernatural. The others relaxed, but Cal remained rigid, still staring at the skyline.

'I think I know what this is all about,' he breathed. In the distance another sign tumbled, as little grey boxes swarmed over it like ants. 'We'd better turn around and head the other way at once.'

'Don't be an ass,' said the Professor. 'I've come here to make my fortune, and demme, I'm not turning around on your command. Hold your tongue, sir!'

'Turn around! Please!' Cal said to Harry, who was driving.

'As a favour to you, I suppose,' he sneered.

'Listen. There is something loose in that city – a secret weapon – and it's out of control. I don't know how it got here, but it looks like it has taken over Las Vegas. I'm sure of it. Believe me, our lives are in danger if we enter the city.'

'Stuff and nonsense!' snapped the Professor. 'I do *not* believe you, sir. But – so that I cannot be accused of being unfair – we might stop at a telephone and call ahead. We could reserve rooms at the same time that we prove your nonsensical theory has no foundation. Stop at that phone ahead, Harry. Stop, I say!'

But the car continued on past the phone. In fact, it picked up speed. 'I can't control it,' said Harry. 'It's like something has hold of it. The steering is locked, and there's some kind of – cable thing – reeling us in.'

They were close enough to the city to see destruction now, and swarms of boxy shapes moving over the broken faces of buildings and signs.

'What shall we do?' Daisy screamed.

'There is nothing we can do,' said her fiancé quietly, tapping on the lid of his snuffbox. 'It seems as if we shall go on accelerating until we hit something and probably die. *You* may prepare to meet *your* Author, my dear. Now, since we have perhaps a minute or two, I suggest that Mr Potter tells us more about this fascinating machine.'

CHAPTER X

Calling Dr Smilax

'Let us, however, look more closely at the facts.'

A. J. AYER

Shortly before he was to address the Joint Chiefs of Staff, Dr Smilax stepped into the men's room adjoining the NORAD conference room and began briskly combing his hair. On such occasions, tension seemed to tighten his scalp and make it itch furiously, unless he could give it a quick, vigorous raking.

It was black, luxuriant hair shot with silver grey of the same shade as his foulard tie. This was embroidered with black anthrax bacilli, carefully knotted, and clipped with a tiny silver scalpel. His suit was a quiet grey, his shirt of television blue, though he had no real intention of appearing before news cameras. The only real spot of colour about him was his lapel pin from the Blood Bank, a red plastic droplet.

The bold outlines of Smilax's face were softened by a dapper moustache, while rimless glasses diluted the peculiar intensity of his gaze. Nevertheless his was the unrelenting expression of a man used to commanding, not acquiescing. He could not fawn, like most civilian 'experts' consulted by the Joint Chiefs. Smilax gave orders, he did not beg to be given orders, and all the clerkliness in his appearance could not disguise the fact. Breeding, he thought, permitting himself a small, ironic smile, will out.

Toto Smilax, M.D., D.V.M.S., Ph.D. (Chem.) and M.E.E., was the scion of a good family, though only by accident. One of his earliest memories was of his mother shaking her head and saying, 'Son, I don't never want you to go wrong like I done.'

He was five years old before he learned what 'going wrong' meant; it meant having a child without being married first. At once Toto began to worry that he would, somehow, actually give birth to a child out of wedlock. Every morning he looked in his bed fearfully, to see if a baby had arrived.

Lotte Smilax, his mother, had never married. She often told little Toto how her father had been an important man in the West, and how she had brought disgrace upon the family by allowing the mad butler to rape her at gunpoint.

'It was all because my Daddy never beat me,' she would say. 'Oh, if only he had beat me! But I mean to do better by you, my son. I won't make the same mistakes. I want to give you every chance I never had.'

So saying, she would commence larrupping him with anything handy: her boot, a whip, a ladle, or a belt.

School was for Toto equally onerous, for the other children tortured him without mercy, to the limits of their fiendish imaginations. They poked him with compasses, stole or tore his books, implied that his mother was a 'hoot' and that he was born out of wedlock, stoned him, made up songs about him, and invited him to eat (in summer) sand and mud, and (in winter) unclean snow.

The reason they did all this was because, of course, his name was Toto. It was not a Christian name, it was not even the name of a famous hero, real or fictional. It was the name of a dog.

Poor Toto had been named for his mother's favourite character in fiction, Dorothy's little dog in *The Wizard of Oz*. Lotte, it must be confessed, was fond of animals, and her bookshelf was filled with dog books, including the complete works of Albert Payson Terhune and *Dog of Flanders*, which Lotte never read without weeping.

She may have been a stern disciplinarian, but Toto's mother was also a warm-hearted, impulsively generous creature, who never could resist bringing home a hungry dog or lame kitten. Generally the hearth was merry with one or two Lads, a Rex, a Spot, and perhaps half-a-dozen Snowballs and Midnights. Lotte often encouraged them to dine sitting up together at the table with her, for she loved to have company for dinner, and Toto for his own good was restricted to his bowl on the kitchen floor, marked with his name.

Every night, curled up in his little basket, Toto would hear his mother going out to her SPCA meeting. He would lay there and pray, naming each of her pets in connection with a different kind of painful death. To finish off the list, he would conjure up a set of slow agonies for Albert Payson Terhune, whom he somehow imagined to be Lotte's father.

One day they took one of the mangy Rexes to the Pet Clinic. Toto wandered around the building, discovering the mysteries of veterinary medicine. Through a glass partition he saw a cat undergoing Caesarian section to give up six kittens. Toto pressed his nose to the glass wistfully. It was all so beautiful –

the bright red blood, the clean linen, the very mystery of reproduction itself, laid open by a glittering knife. So this was sex!

Within him, Toto's fierce little spirit rejected everything he had been taught. Having babies could not be so wrong after all. Nothing so solemn and bloody could be altogether bad. He vowed to become a vet.

When he was eight, the magic carpet of a court order removed him from his mother's custody and placed him with two kind, pleasant old maiden aunts in Dubuque. There were no more beatings, plenty to eat, a regular bed. There was a tutor instead of school.

From an illiterate child, unable to eat without lapping, Toto became a fine young gentleman, exceeding his aunts' wildest hopes in nobility and refinement. They spared no expense to teach him all modern and classical languages; under the best masters he learned mathematics, elocution, fencing and dancing.

Toto showed himself no mean scholar, becoming a vet at thirteen, and a physician and surgeon two years later. To keep his fingers supple for operating, he took up the violin, achieving a technical virtuosity that was remarkable. He seldom played, however, complaining the high notes hurt his ears.

In Zürich, Toto met a young English anaesthetist named Nan Richmons, and for the first time in his twenty years he knew a passion more overpowering than his devotion to science. Not only was Nan beautiful and intelligent, but her X-rays showed a crystalline symmetry that made his breath catch. How long would it be before he might gaze in reality upon that coil of colon, those ovaries, the perfect curves of her kidneys? How long before he might pluck that fragile bloom, her appendix? He asked Nan to marry him and become the subject of his surgical experiments, and – ah, peritoneal bliss untold! – she accepted.

The banns were published on two continents. Toto and Nan spent their evenings planning hysterectomies, new and dangerous techniques of anaesthesia. Then, without warning, their castles of aether collapsed.

A muffled stranger came to call upon Toto in his lab, where he was dissecting a cadaver on the eve of their wedding.

'You must not marry Nan Richmons.'

'But why not?' asked Toto. His brow darkened. 'I must warn you, sir, to be careful what you say about her.'

'Why, you ask?' The stranger laughed savagely. 'Two reasons: first, she is already married – to me.'

'I care nothing about that. This is 1935, man! Let us be civilized. Her past is—'

'Stay! The second reason is – is that *I removed her appendix over two years ago.*'

Toto grew pale and staggered back a pace, laying a cadaverous hand to his palpitating heart. 'Good God! Say that is a lie, you blackguard!' Sadly, the stranger shook his head.

'It is the truth.'

'Then here.' Toto snatched up a scalpel and offered it to him. 'Remove my heart, sir, if you please. It is no longer of the slightest use to me.'

The engagement was broken at once. Nan, despairing, took her life with a mixture of chloroform and nitrous oxide. Toto travelled then, to the Orient, to Africa and elsewhere, studying peculiar surgical techniques.

After the Second World War, he turned up in California, announcing his intention of starting a research laboratory. The Defense Department at once placed several million dollars at his disposal. Toto shut himself up for another decade, doing pain research, during which time he churned out interesting books and monographs (*Aesthetic Surgery*; *The Painful Way to Health*; and a book of child care, *Spare the Rod? Never!*). He studied and conquered new fields of inquiry at the same time: physics, biochemistry, astronomy, biophysics and arachnology, like so many stands of grain, fell to his keen scythe of a mind. In 196— his researches culminated in the invention of the DNA computer known as QUIDNAC.

The existence of this type of computer was not generally known, its principle of operation was a military secret, and its manufacture was understood only by Dr Toto Smilax himself, who now entered the NORAD conference room.

The Chiefs of Staff were seated behind a large table of gunmetal grey, as far as possible from one another. At one end reared the thin angular frame of Air Force General Ickers, a quick, bird-like man with a shrill voice. Once a test pilot, he still retained a more or less happy-go-lucky attitude about everything but the dignity of his office.

At the opposite end sat a leaden mass of flesh bundled into the uniform of Admiral of the Navy. Because he had once commanded a sub – or rather, a series of subs, each of which managed to have an improbable but genuine accident as soon as he had taken command – he still wore a dirty white turtleneck pullover under his jacket. He managed a sneer now and then, but otherwise the expression on his bloated, drowned-corpse's face was of despair and apathy.

In the middle sat General of the Army R.M.S. ('Happy') Meany, whose face seemed to try its level best to imitate both the countenances of his contemporaries. He never looked towards Ickers without a confident grin or wink of camaraderie; never towards Nematode without a rueful, commiserating sigh.

At a smaller table some twenty feet away sat a WAF secretary. When Dr Smilax entered, all were watching the progress of a battle on the Big Board.

One half of it showed the green lines and blue grids of a topological map; the other displayed jerky televised glimpses of actual skirmishing.

A contingent of paratroops had been landed in Altoona. The evening was murky – moonless, Smilax remembered – and the images were jiggly and confused (Nematode insisted the enemy was jamming the works for reasons of their own; Ickers declared the reception was perfect as far as he was concerned). Now and then a squat, blocky shape hurtled out of the gloom, made a grab at some man's weapon, and vanished again.

'Some sojers!' snorted the admiral.

One paratrooper was hit, low, by what appeared to be a twisted sort of typewriter. He dropped his machine gun and fell, arms flailing.

'I knew it wouldn't work,' said Nematode slowly, savouring his words. 'But why should anyone listen to me? I'm only the Admiral.' He laced his thick fingers together and studied their dirty nails.

'One man knocked down doesn't mean a lost battle,' snapped Ickers. His head bobbed, shaking silver plumage in emphasis. 'Got the wind knocked out of him, that's all. He's playin' possum, so he can trick the enemy.'

At that moment, the screen went dark. 'I knew it!' crowed the admiral. 'Now that thing has captured the camera.'

'The hell it did!'

'Yup, captured the whole goddamned town, and our boys with it. Tonight Altoona – tomorrow the world! This'll be the end of civilization – and good riddance, I say!'

'What?' Ickers screeched. 'How can you wear the uniform of your country and say a rotten thing like that? That's a lie! Our United States will last a thousand years!'

'Well there's much to be said for both viewpoints,' said General Meany. 'Why don't we hear a few words from our expert on the matter, eh? Doctor, won't you tell us a little about this gadget of yours?'

'"Gadget"? A trivial word for something to which I am sure you attach a great deal of importance, gentlemen. Oh – ' he permitted himself a wry, professional smile as he rose and strolled to the blackboard – 'I know I'm indulging in a semantic quibble, but we men of science are rather narrow about our definitions.'

Taking chalk from his pocket, he wrote 'Nomenclature: THE REPRO-DUCTIVE SYSTEM' across the top of the board. The three men pulled pads towards them and readied pens. Meany wrote 'syst.' and underlined it three times.

'The Reproductive System is composed of what we call *cells*.' The doctor wrote it on the board. 'The first cells were constructed at Project 32, as you all know. They were of a variety of types, differing from one another in two respects:

'(1) *Differing means of perception and communication.* These included metal detectors, radiation detectors, radar, cathode tubes, microphones, light pens, graphic inputs and displays, and typewriters. Only the first two of these were standard on all cells built.

'(2) *Differing modes of propulsion.* These included gear-driven wheels, jointed insectoid legs, rockets, propellors, and the inertial, or "falling-cat" system. Just as a cat can right itself while in midair, so an objective may be propelled by displacing weight "outwards and backwards" rapidly. It moves as does a child scooting along in a cardboard box. We saw a soldier on television doing the same thing unconsciously – threshing his arms to restore his balance.'

'Yes,' chuckled the admiral, who was not taking notes. 'We saw how well it worked for *him*, didn't we? He's only dead, that's all.'

Ickers jumped up. 'It's a glorious and fine thing to die in the service of our country,' he shouted. 'I only wish *everyone* had the chance to do so, right this minute!'

'Now gentlemen,' said Meany. 'Let's try to reconcile our differences. There is much truth in what each of you say. Perhaps the doctor would be good enough to give us his view on the matter?'

'How about a little action!' shouted Ickers. Meany filled in the single word on his pad with geometric forms. Nematode began drawing female genitalia. 'Let's not sit around here all day. I want to get out there and *slam that thing in the gut*. My boy Grawk is out in the hall now, waiting for orders. Let's go-go-go!'

Dr Smilax drew a cross-section of an individual cell. 'The size varies,' he exclaimed, 'for various hereditary and environmental reasons. The original cells were not of a size, and their differences have become in some cases quite marked. The armoured exterior of each cell is usually weatherproofed by paint, rubber or plastic coatings and the like. Apertures are maintained, through which tools can be projected: hooks, claws, cutters, welding equipment, etc. On some types the casing is expandable. In most types it can be opened to admit materials – or emit a neophyte cell.

'The space just inside the cell is where reproduction and maintenance take place. Manufacturing is quite limited in scope, consisting chiefly in adapting found objects to makeshift purposes.

'Templates for both mechanical and electronic components (such as integrated circuits) are constructed at the orders of the QUIDNAC control unit. All bearings and other parts requiring close tolerances are made by sintering; finer machining is done with acids.

'Any power supply may be used, if either it can be modified to fit into the cell or the cell can make sufficient modifications upon itself. We predicted, for example, that cells would be able to glue themselves to locomotives and take power from them, and I understand our prediction was correct.

'Now for the "yolk" of our "egg",' he said, with another dry, professorial smile, and pointed to the centre of his chalk diagram. 'This is the QUID-NAC control unit, in three sections: (1) The DNA section; (2) the amplifying and interpreting section; and (3) the control linkage.

'The DNA section is a complex, compact means of storing and retrieving information. In it are stored about 10^{10}, or ten billion messages, many of them only three units long, but some as long as a million units. The fourteen simplest messages correspond to the rules of logic, to arithmetic computation, or to the mechanics of handling other data.'

He wrote:

Message	Meaning	Conventional Symbol
AAA	'Either ... or ... or both'	v
CCC	'If ... then ...'	ɔ
GGG	'... and ...'	.
TTT	'... is equivalent to ...'	≡
GAGGAG	'zero'	0
GCGGCG	'positive'	+
GTGGTG	'negative'	−
TGTTGT	'... is identical with ...'	=
AGAAGA	'Record ...'	(Remember)
ATAATA	'Erase ...'	(Forget)
CGCCGC	'Duplicate ...'	(Repeat; Copy)
CTCCTC	'Transit ...'	(Tell me)

'These messages are encoded in a double helix of DNA. They are activated only by the appropriate input. In one sense, the QUIDNAC is completely programmed, since it is true that every message output, or response, has been encoded into the molecule of DNA. But different *sets*, different combinations of responses are not predictable, if only because of their very, very, varied variety.' Again the smile, and again no response from his audience. 'The total number of message combinations possible is equal to the sum of the squares of all the numbers from 1 to 10^{10}.

'All input data, or stimuli, are automatically recorded, and compared with previous stimuli. If they correspond, they are dealt with as in past successes; if they do not, various analogies are devised from past experiences. If no analogies seem to have the slightest relevance to the new stimuli, random responses are selected and tested. In effect, QUIDNAC learns, and as it learns *it alters the structure of the DNA molecule*. Alterations generally consist in breaking the molecule apart and reassembling it in new patterns, much in the manner of making anagrams from long words:'

Here he wrote: 'JOHN THOMAS SLADEK'

And under it: 'DNA'S MOL HATH JOKES'

'You see, a *mol* is a gram molecular weight, or the molecular weight of a substance expressed in grams. The molecular weight of our DNA is about 287×10^{16}, so the joke of it is that one mol would weigh about three trillion tons.'

He laughed heartily at DNA's subtle jest. The three faces before him, however, remained fixed in their gargoyle patterns of joy, despair and indecision. Dr Smilax cleared his throat and prepared to resume.

'British trillion or American trillion?' asked the WAF secretary. 'Long tons or short tons?'

'I'll go into it later, if you'll make a note of it.' A muscle in the doctor's scalp began twitching. 'Now then:

'The second stage of the QUIDNAC control unit consists of a system of integrated circuits which translate and amplify the output of the DNA section. The third section consists of actual control mechanisms, switches, relays, etc., operating various "limbs", "organs" and functions of the cell. Tuned circuits are employed, so that a rather complex signal may be sent as an excitation "clang", out of which each receiver selects its own signal. Our own nervous system works on much the same principle.'

'What we'd like to know, Doctor,' said the Army head, glancing nervously towards both ends of the table, 'and I think I can safely say I speak for my colleagues here in this – what we'd like to know is, what does the QUIDNAC computer *look like*, and how can we shut it off?'

'The entire control unit looks much like a transistor radio,' said the doctor. 'The bulk of it is control linkage, however. The amplifying section is about the size of a lady's wrist watch. The DNA memory file is, of course, invisible. Its casing may be seen – it is roughly the size and shape of a light pencil dot.'

'The US Air Force isn't likely to have much trouble slaughtering a few pencil dots,' said Ickers, beaming.

'Well –' Smilax began, then sighed.

The admiral emitted a pained snort, his equivalent of a laugh. 'I guess that finishes us,' he said. 'I always knew the human race was bound to be finished off by something like a bunch of pencil dots. It figures.'

'Perhaps we're beaten,' cajoled General Meany, 'and perhaps again we have a chance. I think it's too early to tell, at this stage of the game. I defer judgement until we hear from our expert here.'

'Are you trying to tell me,' asked Ickers, 'that in only a few days these invisible bugs have piled up enough junk to cover twenty thousand square miles? And we can't stop this?'

'I'm afraid that is correct,' said Smilax, 'though rather pessimistic. They have worked underground for over two weeks, preparing for this takeover. Moreover, they have only fenced, or enclosed, rather than covered the area, and I believe it to be only about 17,213 square miles. That you have had no success thus far in stopping it is evident,' he added, with his eyes downcast. 'That is why you have sent for me. I do foresee one way of stopping the Reproductive System – though you may find my way repugnant.'

'I knew we weren't beaten!' screeched the Air Force head, and gave an exultant laugh. 'What *is* your idea, Doctor?'

'Sure, go ahead. What have we got to lose now?' said the admiral. 'The human race is a dead letter, now.'

Smilax lighted a display map. 'The System seems to have three centres of growth, at the moment, and it is fencing off and surrounding the area between them. They are the lab at Millford, Utah; Altoona, Nevada; and Las Vegas. The judicious detonation of three thermonuclear devices of the order of 150 megatons each would, I feel confident, completely neutralize the System at these points. The remainder would be a simple matter of – I believe the expression is "mopping up" – using smaller thermonuclear devices. I know what question you are going to raise in advance, so let me say I estimate the total number of civilian casualties at no more than a million.'

'Did he say a million or a billion?' murmured the WAF.

'If it's the cost of our commitment,' said the smiling Ickers, 'I'm all for it!'

'That's about the population of Nevada and Utah combined,' Admiral Nematode pointed out. 'And this is election year. We'll never get Congress to buy the idea of bombing hell out of two states. Might as well throw in the sponge now.'

'My colleagues both have a valid point,' said Meany carefully.

'Have you any alternatives, Doctor?'

'Only a plan for a new line of research towards altering the System genetically. It has, fortunately or unfortunately, the ability to pass along acquired characteristics. Given about two months, we could—'

'Two months!' Nematode shouted. 'In two months, it'll be covering the globe.'

'No, by my estimate, if it grows at the present rate, it would reach 88 times its present size in eight weeks. It would then cover most of 1,514,788 square miles, that is, roughly the size of fifteen of our westernmost states, not including Texas or Oklahoma, but with the area of Maine thrown in.'

'Oh Christ.'

Ickers had called in Grawk and seemed to be in a furiously jubilant state over what his subordinate was whispering to him. 'Great! Great! Great! Tell them about it.'

'I know this sounds like kind of a crazy idea,' said the ugly little general. 'But maybe it's just the kind of wacky thing that would work. Give a listen: I remember once in an old science fiction movie they got rid of the monster by electrocuting him. Remember that? Well we could try the same thing – just hook up the high voltage and juice it to death!'

'Science fiction,' snorted the admiral.

'I think he has something,' said Smilax. 'It *may* work – by shorting out the fine circuitry – but if it fails, we gain nothing.'

'At least we lose nothing,' shrilled Ickers. Clapping Grawk on the back, he bawled, 'Your idea, my boy. You're in charge. Tap the power line at Altoona. Get to work on it right away. Thumbs up.'

'And when you fail,' said the admiral with bilious charm, 'it'll be thumbs up for you, all right. You'll be Airman Third Class Grawk – if we don't shoot you.'

Meany summed it up. 'Godspeed, Grawk,' he said. 'We wish you success and warn you not to fail.'

'I ain't worried.' Grawk carried his yellow grin and black cigar out of the door.

Another camera had been set up at Altoona, and now, Smilax having been invited to join the Joint Chiefs in their weekly game of Go-to-the-Dump, the four watched the new scene on the Big Board. A group of young people were parading in front of the barbed-wire barrier which the military had thrown up around the city. They carried signs saying: 'WHAT HAPPENED TO ALTOONA?' 'DOWN WITH DOOMSDAY' and 'GIVE US BACK OUR WORLD.'

'They'll find out soon enough what happened at Altoona,' said the Army head, dealing. 'If Grawk's plan comes off, and we get the thing on the run, we'll "leak" the story tomorrow, through our usual reliable sources.'

One girl seemed to be in the wrong parade. She wore white boots, and carried a sign saying: 'GO GO GOPHERS!'

Then she turned, and Smilax could see another message hastily lettered on the back of the sign:'END OF THE WORLD UNFAIR TO YOUTH!'

A platoon of soldiers arrived, surrounded the protesters and began dragging them away.

'Where are they taking them?' Smilax asked General Meany.

'We'll keep them locked up until tomorrow night, or whenever this blows over. Why?'

'It's that girl in the boots, she seems a perfect subject for my latest pain experiments. I wonder …'

'I get it,' said Meany, and nudged him. 'Haha, I get it. Of course I'll have her seized for you. Where do you want her? Here?'

'Yes, I've set up in the infirmary. Thank you.'

'Haha, you old scoundrel!'

'You don't know the half of it,' said Smilax, gazing up at the girl – the image of Nan Richmons. He was already picturing the perfect symmetry of her kidneys.

CHAPTER XI
Beele of the CIA

'Pause there, Morocco.'
SHAKESPEARE

Suggs killed time while waiting for his new partner by writing another post-card to his wife. He chose one which depicted the snake charmers in the market at Dar El Fna. 'Dear Madge,' he wrote, after some deliberation. 'Still having wonderful time, though I miss you and Susie. Love, Bubby.'

He wondered if he ought to say something about the insurance game being slow in Marrakech – insurance was his cover story – but decided against it. Madge probably thought he was just living it up with harem girls anyway. And so he would have been, if Suggs had not been terrified of disease. He remembered only too well the CIA training films of tertiary syphilis and advanced gonorrhea ...

A rumbling in his stomach reminded Suggs the Near East held other diseases for the unwary. He wished now he had brought along his own supply of food. Today Suggs had made fifteen trips to the bathroom, scoring them off with a kind of grim satisfaction in his journal.

He was not sure which of the descending passengers would be the new man, but he finally settled on the skinny young man in the eyeshade, who was shaking off a pack of urchins.

'You Green?' Suggs breathed, drifting past him.

'Huh?'

Suggs drifted past again. 'You Mr Green?'

'Oh, you must be Mr Gray.'

'That's right. Only my friends call me Suggs. B. Suggs. Why the eyeshade?' Suggs turned to confront his new partner openly. 'What's your cover story? I guess you could say you're a sheep rancher, come to look over some rare breeding stock.'

'My name is really Beele, Barthemo Beele. I'm under your orders, Mr Suggs, but—'

'Just Suggs, please.'

'Suggs, I don't know what kind of corruption is going on in this town, but I want to do my level best to put an end to it. Do you know what just happened? One of those *little kids* tried to sell me something I feel certain was a narcotic!'

Suggs picked up Beele's suitcase and motioned towards the shay. When they had settled into place he told the driver the name of their hotel and turned to his new agent with a bit of advice. 'Don't pay any attention to these little packs of beggars. They go on all the time, trying to sell you their sisters, hashish, brothers, mothers, *kif*, and so on. You'll get used to it.'

'Used to it! I hope not! It's a disgrace and a crime. Haven't they a truant officer around here? Those kids ought to be in school. I mean to find out what kind of crime bosses are at the bottom of this. But, as I say, you're in charge here—'

Suggs shook his head sharply and indicated the driver. They rode on, sizing one another up in silence, silence broken only by the clopping of the horse down a scenic avenue of tangerine trees, and by the sick growling from Suggs's abdomen.

Looking at the older man, Beele saw a sunburned, bullnecked man with short-clipped greying hair, regular, unmemorable features. Suggs looked to be about forty and a pipeline engineer, and there was nothing to mark him off from the ordinary run of men but his cold, lacklustre eyes and a thin white scar on his forehead. So this was what CIA men looked like, on the job!

He wondered how he himself would turn out in the Agency. Did it take brains, guts, curiosity and honesty? Barthemo had these in abundance – yet did he have the indefinable something which distinguishes the CIA agent from others?

When Barthemo Beele was two years old, he was trained to use a little potty stool that was kept in a cupboard with a hanging cloth in front of it. This little secret, with its aura of shame, interested him so keenly that he had to lift the cloth and look at it a dozen times a day. To this single episode, he later felt, all of his curiosity could be traced. For little 'Themo' developed an unfortunate habit of lifting hanging cloths to peer under them. And after he had lifted the skirt of a visitor, a bishop's wife, 'Themo' received his first sound whipping.

Yet, as if his motto were *Video, ergo sum*, Barthemo went on lifting hanging cloths and looking under them, and was unable to resist doing so. He would lift the corner of a tablecloth and stare at the table's legs, fascinated, flushed with guilt and a strange pleasure he could not name.

He grew to a skinny, secretive kid, addicted to tattling, to forming, with friends, secret clubs, and to writing what he hoped were dirty words on fences: FUDGE, SHAME, ORGANISM, and especially LOVE. One day by chance he lifted a blanket and found a couple of organisms making love: his mother and a man not his father.

Barthemo hastened to tell his father, who thanked him for his information by spanking him and locking him in his room for a day. When he decided the boy had learned his lesson, the elder Beele relented and let him out – but on condition that he mind his own business. Barthemo actually did have a business at this time, which was selling information to the police. For nickels, dimes and quarters, he would tell them which members of which secret clubs were stealing bike tyres from gas stations and magazines from drugstores. Later, for larger sums, he told them about car thefts and burglaries. This continued well into high school, when his duties as a school reporter took up most of his free time. The police gave him a present of money when he left for college, and told him he was the 'Best little stoolie we ever had.'

Someday, he thought, as the shay rolled along Boulevard Mohammed V, someday he would write a book, a defence of police informers: *They Call Me Stoolie.* 'Why is it,' he would write, 'that those who risk their lives exposing murderers, thieves, dope peddlers and every crooked and vicious element of our society, that those who do their duty as citizens (for *not* to report a crime is misprision), are looked on by society with loathing and distaste?'

Looking at Beele, Suggs saw a skinny, nervous-looking young man on whom an eyeshade, with a press card in the band, seemed a needless affectation. Suggs amused himself by imagining better cover stories for Beele. In a neat, dark suit, with an attache case, he could pass for an IBM salesman, perhaps. Or he could have grown a beard and looked like one of them Peace Corps freaks – buncha Commie fanatics. Fanaticism, that was it: the old-young look he had, the coldness in his face and a pinch of the true fanatic, summed Beele up for him. He wondered what it would take to make Beele kill a man. The kid might make a passable killer, with the proper instruction from Suggs – maybe too good a killer. Suggs wondered how long it would be before he would have to kill Beele.

'By the way,' he said. 'Try not to eat anything or drink the water here. I'm trying to get in a consignment of American food and water. The stuff here is murder.'

'The runs?'

As if in answer, Suggs's stomach growled. Only it was not his stomach, he realized, but Beele's.

The younger man nodded glumly. 'Yup, I got 'em, too. Must have been that Denver sandwich and cup of Boston coffee I had before I left the States.'

While Beele signed the register and filled out the police form at the hotel desk, Suggs wrote on a picture postcard of the snake-charmers at Dar El Fna, 'Dear Madge. Still having wonderful time, though I miss you and Susie. Love, Bubby.' He handed it to the smiling clerk and received in exchange his room key and a thick airmail letter. It was from Madge's lawyer's office. There was no need to open it.

'It's not fair!' he whispered, crushing the letter into his pocket. 'To dump a divorce on me *now*, of all times! Well, I just don't have time to worry about it, that's all.' Nevertheless, he bit his lip, thinking of the possible effects this might have on his career. In the Agency, men with marital problems were passed over for promotion.

In the room, Beele relaxed on a settee while Suggs paced back and forth, explaining the mission. He took up a long, curved knife and toyed with it as he spoke.

'The French are launching a new missile from somewhere in the vicinity – we don't know where yet. They call it *Le Bateau Ivre*, and I've found out the name of the astronaut – young French Air Force pilot named Marcel Brioche. It cost me one of my best men to find out that little piece of information.' His guts growled with scalding pain, and Suggs began to pace like a caged animal.

'I know the shot will take place soon, but I don't know where in the environs of Marrakech they're stashing the ship. Our first objective, therefore, will be to find out the date and precise point of launching.

'They have two reasons for hiding it. First,' he pared one fingernail with the knife, 'they have some new super-fuel, better than anything we've come up with so far. We want it, so does Russia. Only we want it worse, and I'll tell you why. This stuff is so hot, the only kind of exhaust nozzle they can use is made out of a material called reuttite. And the world's supply of reuttite is—'

'In Nevada!' Beele exclaimed. Then, thinking of the bright boxes of the day before, he wondered if the reuttite still were in Nevada. 'They used to make gas mantles out of it, and—'

'Yeah, yeah, I see you been briefed on that already. Well, the French have been secretly buying up old gas mantles for years, preparing for this *coup*.

'Which brings us to their second reason for hiding the mission.' He decapitated another nail. 'We think they may try to actually put a man on the moon. That means they could *claim* the whole works – with nasty consequences for the rest of the world. See what I mean?'

The kid looked thoughtful. 'No, I guess I don't see,' he admitted.

Suggs snarled, 'What's the matter, you dense or something? France on the moon means more than just a tricolor on the Mare Nubium. It'll mean French control of the Earth! How'd you like to be a slave of the French Republic, eh? Imagine what *that* would be like: all the restaurants stunk up with garlic and all the roads choked up with crummy little cars. They'd make you eat *snails* instead of decent food (like a steak and french fries). You couldn't even get a Coke anymore – they'd make you drink their rotten *wine*! Fairy art museums! Lousy beer! VD! Crumbly cigarettes! No men's deodorants!'

He wheeled and flung the knife at the door. Despite its awkward shape, the blade spun end-over-end neatly and caught, quivering. 'That's what I think of Frogs!' he grated.

'What are we supposed to do, stop the moon shot?' Beele asked, when he dared breathe.

'Only as a last resort. There's another way, I think. The rocket they designed is supposed to have a two-man capsule, but only one Frenchy is going along. Now we've got to persuade him to take one of us along with him, so we can "study the effects of the new fuel", but also we can counter-claim the moon. The trouble is, the Russians are trying to do the same thing. There are two of them in town, Vovov and Vetch.

'It should be easy to persuade him to throw in his lot with us, rather than them,' opined Beele. 'I don't see how he could quibble, when it's a matter of choosing between democracy and totalitarian slavery.'

'Yeah, yeah, and the chief OK'd a voucher for a quarter million dirham, too,' said Suggs, thoughtfully. 'That's fifty grand. I hope Moscow can't go higher.'

'A bribe? You're going to offer him *a bribe*?'

Suggs stared at his new assistant incredulously, wondering if he could possibly be as naive as all that. His meditations were only broken into by an urgent, scalding message from his intestines.

That evening they went to a small motel on the edge of town overlooking the Atlas Mountains to see Marcel Brioche. He proved to be a personable young man with handsome, immobile features, wearing a dress uniform of the French Air Force. A look of surprise and annoyance flickered across his face, then he smiled.

'Good evening, Monsieur Suggs,' he said. 'I was just going out to dinner. What is it you wished to see me about?' He spoke standing in the doorway, and did not ask them in.

'If you know my name, maybe you know my game,' Suggs snapped.

'Please, please. I have no time to fence. At any moment, my friends will be here –'

'I'll be brief, Brioche. We represent the US government, as you know already, no doubt. We are prepared to deal—'

'I am not. *Bonsoir.*'

'Wait. All we ask is that you take one of our men with you, as an observer. We have no intention of interfering with your moon shot – if you cooperate with us. The ship, we know, will hold two men. What harm can it do to take along – an *autostoppeur*?'

'A hitchhiker? Let us speak in English, if you please; in very plain English. You ask me why I am not anxious to cooperate with your government. Very well, I will tell you.

'When I first heard of *Le Bateau Ivre*, three years ago, I was engaged to be married. The ship was planned to take the two of us on a honeymoon. But two years ago, when work on the ship had progressed too far to be cancelled, she left me.'

'My sympathies,' said Barthemo Beele. 'I can understand how you feel. My wife has just left me, too.'

'Oddly enough, I'm being served with divorce papers right now myself,' chuckled Suggs. 'But that's the breaks. Why didn't you get another girl?'

'Let me tell you what happened. The man she left me for was an American Air Force liaison officer at NATO in Paris. He had a brief affair with her and then dropped her. Liaison officer – *drôle*, eh? He had a brief *liaison* with her, you see?' There were tears in the astronaut's eyes. He was not weeping, however, but smiling dangerously. 'She threw herself from the Eiffel Tower. You ask me why I have not replaced her? The answer is obvious, I should think. No one can ever replace her. Ah, there are my friends now.'

He indicated a taxi drawing up before the motel. In it were Vetch and Vovov. Brioche drew on his white gloves.

'You don't understand!' Beele said passionately. 'We free nations must cooperate in space, not compete. We have to pull together to beat totalitarian Russia.'

'I would suppose space big enough to hold all three mighty nations,' the Frenchman murmured with a mild salute.

'How does two hundred fifty thousand dirham sound, Brioche?' asked Suggs desperately.

'You do not insult me only because I understand how it is with you Americans. You wish always to purchase the honour of others. That is because, of course, you have none of your own. *Bonsoir, messieurs.*'

With a careless wave he strode away, leaving his door unlocked. 'You haven't heard the last of this!' Suggs screamed after him. The two Russian agents grinned hugely as their taxi accepted its third passenger.

'See you round, Suggs,' Vovov called out, making an obscene gesture.

Vetch, a small man with a scholar's beard and a thoughtful manner, kept quiet and let Vovov do the talking. Vovov could always talk, joyfully and persuasively, even when his mouth was full, as it was now, of toast and caviare. He spoke English, as Brioche insisted.

'Caviare and champagne!' Vovov crowed. 'Caviare and champagne! The one from the icy bowels of the Baltic sturgeon, the other from the pale, temperate, shady hills of France. They go together like France and Russia go together. Each is perfect in its own right, yet the combination, it is –' As words failed him, he seized another slice of warm toast and spread it with caviare.

'The Americans,' he said, cramming his mouth full and choking slightly. He coughed, masticated and swilled champagne for a moment, then continued speaking through his food. 'The Americanff are pigff! Pigff!'

'Eh?' The astronaut was not really paying attention, but letting his own champagne go flat. He had already had too much to drink, and, as always, it plunged him into gloomy thoughts of the one person he ought to be having champagne with.

'Fwine! They are – excuse me – swine!' said Vovov.

'Swine? Yes, that is exactly it.' Brioche thought of the man who had taken her life – the swine named General Grawk.

The alert waiter, proud of his minimal English, brought them more champagne. '*Encore bouteille de* swine, *messieurs?*' He poured it before they could refuse.

'The Americans have no love,' Vovov went on. 'Only supermarkets and superways. Factories and mass living. Faugh!' He sprayed roe. 'What is their art? Comic books. Negro work songs, stolen and sung by white exploiters. Western movies. They were not content with murdering off the poor Indian, no, they must *glorify* that murder. Again and again, he must fall off that pony, to satisfy the bloodlust of the decadent imperialists. Bah! I remember one film – *Battle of Comanche Arroyo*, it was called – where they showed the *same* strip of film over and over again, depicting an Indian falling off his pony dead. They hoped their depraved audience would not notice.'

'Was that with John Wayne?' Brioche asked, interested.

'No, I believe it was – I forget who. But you know, it was the one where the colonel wants them to stay and hold the fort, but the captain – the young one who's really in love with the colonel's wife? – Well, he—'

'*Oui, oui, je—* I remember it very well!' exclaimed the astronaut. 'And then the captain is going to take a squad out to Comanche Arroyo, even though he knows it's certain death, they'll be massacred, because he knows he can gain the fort enough time to send for help!'

'Remember his last words?' Vovov began to weep as he poured another round of champagne. ' "It is a far, far better thing I do, than I have ever done, and it is a far, far better reward I go to, than I have ever known." Ah, it wrings the heart even of a strong man, a speech like that.'

'Ah yes. Wonderful film.'

After several minutes of moody silence, Vetch spoke. 'At the risk of spoiling our little Film Festival,' he said drily, 'I must ask you to get around to the real topic for discussion. That is, will you, Marcel Brioche, take a Russian observer along on your moon trip? We offer you no money, no material rewards – we'll leave that sort of behaviour to the Americans. No, all we can offer you is the knowledge that you are assisting in the toppling of imperialism and the glorious expropriation of the expropriators.'

Brioche shook his head. 'No, I cannot help you. I am for France, and for France alone. The only person I ever wanted to take to the moon with me – is far, far beyond the moon now. I go alone.'

He rose and in desolate silence took his departure.

In Russian, Vetch said, 'I am afraid we are going to have to kill him. A pity he isn't working for the right side. An honest sort of chap.'

He noticed that Vovov was staring before him, red-eyed, with a bleak expression on his face. Vetch nudged him.

'Don't take it so hard,' he said. 'Remember, we are agents. We cannot afford to make friends with our dinner companions, for the very reason that we might have to kill them. An agent has no *friends*. We must be prepared to sacrifice anyone—'

'Shhh!' said Vovov, his broad face puckered with annoyance. 'I almost had it – the name of the actress who played the colonel's wife. Was it Virginia Mayo? No ...'

CHAPTER XII

Our Heroine

'Of love as a spectacle, Bathsheba had a fair knowledge;
but of love subjectively she knew nothing.'

HARDY

As Aurora let the car coast to a stop, B476 scrambled up on the back seat and began to chatter, complaining of the cessation of motion.

'There, now,' she said, but B476, a black-and-white laboratory rat, continued shivering nervously until Aurora caressed his back with her thumb.

Lighting a cigarette, she leaned back and gazed out at crooked telephone poles like the masts of becalmed ships. The masts were beginning to throw long shadows now, and Aurora was lost.

She banged open the glove compartment door, then shut it at once. Reflex insisted on her looking there again for the Nevada roadmap, while she knew it was in the pocket of her raincoat, hanging up at home in Santa Filomena, several hundred miles away.

How many hundred, she had no idea. Clearly this road was becoming a cowpath, and it led north, not east. She had started out from Santa Filomena this morning, with the idea of reaching Millford by nightfall. It seemed that the last 'DETOUR – NO ENTRY – MILITARIZED ZONE – DANGER' sign had pointed her off in the wrong direction. She could be a dozen or a hundred miles off the Utah highway now. There seemed to be nothing to do, however, but press on.

Sighing, she crushed out her cigarette in the already choked ashtray. Then she unclipped it and emptied it out of the window. Wind caught the plume of ash and whirled it away in streamers the sun made golden orange. Dust to dust, ashes to desert ash. Yucca Flats could not be far from here. A few motes remained, flying about her in senseless Brownian motion, flecks of fiery light.

Brightness falls from the air;
Queens have died young and fair;
Dust hath closed Helen's eye

B476 and B893 had snuggled up close to her on the seat. Laboratory rats were always weak and prey to chills, and they were sensitive to this slight coolness as the sun fell. It was perverse of her, she thought, to be caring about the fate of a pair of sickly rats when the human race was about to be strangled by its own invention. She was being …

Abnormal?

Of child prodigies, a magazine article once had said: 'It is not true to suppose they cannot live happy, adjusted, fulfilled lives. The popular notions of neurotic "quiz kids" just aren't true.'

Aurora had been three years old when she read the article and pondered its promise. Was it so? Was she going to have a happy, fulfilled life? Was she, then, just the same as real people? Or was she going to be singled out, as her father was singled out, for special torment?

The latter was the truth, as she had known it was at three years old. To his face, they called her father Charlie, but behind his back, she knew, he was 'that crazy inventor fella', and they laughed at him with a kind of fear in their eyes. As she would later see, it was the reason for the practical jokes. Not a trick was missed, from tipping his outhouse and hanging a toilet on the weathervane of his barn to more malicious fun like burning up his corncrib, full. He never seemed to grow angry, only perplexed. He would puff at his unlit, usually unfilled, pipe and survey the poisoned dog or the nail driven in the oil pan of his tractor as if it were a kind of equation that might be worked out by dint of hard concentration.

Now, as she put the car in gear and moved on up the dwindling road, it seemed almost as if someone were playing a practical joke on Aurora. Another DETOUR sign appeared, pointing off to a pair of worn ruts that could not possibly lead anywhere. Shrugging, she obeyed.

B476 climbed up on her shoulder and, snuggling between her neck and the back of the seat, disposed himself for sleep. He and B893 could not be used for experiments. They were 'leftovers', rats which, because of genetic defects or peculiar conditioning, were useless for behavioural experiments. She had developed a habit of picking up such and making pets of them for the few months they lived. True, they were sports, freaks, abnormals – but then Aurora knew how to empathize with abnormality.

Aurora was a genius, and in a community where genius was treated as a suspicious deviation from the norm. The campaniform symmetry of the normal distribution curve of IQs at her first school had grown a hump like Gibraltar before they noticed her, and sent her to a 'special school for exceptional children'. Her classmates had cleft palates, cataracts, lustreless minds. It was somehow unclear to the teachers why Aurora was there; they suspected her of some hidden and therefore more horrible defect.

Aurora was not long at the special school. Studying at home, she took her high-school diploma by mail at ten years of age. At thirteen she graduated *summa cum laude* in behavioural psychology from the University of Minnesota, and at seventeen she became Associate Professor of Psychology at the University of California at Santa Filomena.

It was then she had assumed the plain and prudent appearance that now took the place of character in her professional life. She wore short-cropped hair (but not too short), short and lightly-tinted nails, and semi-sensible shoes. Besides the neat suit she now wore, there were five others in her closet at home, in varying shades of grey. She wore only enough makeup and enough jewellery to avoid being known as the kind of woman who uses none. It was not that Aurora (the real Aurora who resided somewhere inside the professional figure) would not have liked to be admired, but her situation required special tact. She needed to look unappetizing to her male students (many of them older than herself), to keep them at a cool professional distance. She needed to look older for her colleagues, who despite themselves tended to be unconsciously sceptical of the efficiency of the very young. So it was that the disguise of the classroom and lab became a habit, in both senses of the word. She was twenty, felt twenty-five, acted like thirty, and was occasionally taken for thirty-five.

Two figures stood in the roadway on the left, apparently waiting for a ride in the direction she had come. Aurora slowed to ask them if they knew the way to Millford, Utah. When they turned around, Aurora was startled to recognize a pupil of hers, Kevin Mackintosh.

'What are you doing in Nevada, Mr Mackintosh?' she asked, astonished.

The young man's eyes seemed glazed. Instead of answering, he nudged his companion. 'We really *are* high, Ron,' he muttered. 'That chick over there looks like one of my profs.'

'Oh, that was real good stuff,' the other assented, looking off in another direction. 'What chick?'

Aurora grew a bit nervous. She shifted into first, and kept her foot on the clutch. 'Have you any idea which way is the road to Utah?' she asked earnestly.

Kevin Mackintosh seemed not to be looking at anything. 'The road to you-Tao,' he breathed. 'The seven-fold path. Look!' He flung up both arms to the sunset. 'Apocalypse! The wise virgins light their lamps! The black yoni of Night accepts the flaming lingam of Day!'

'Yeah, War of the Worlds,' said Ron.

'Ma'am, my buddy Ron here and I have seen Hell itself. We have seen the death of the world, in flaming technicolour. Paratroops fighting to the death with Puppet People. They arrested our friends, but we got away.'

'Who did?' she asked. 'The Puppet People?'

'No, the Paratroople People. The Army. It's the end of civilization.'

'Repent!' screamed the other. 'Did you see *Gorgo*?'

'My buddy here and I are making our way across the Sahara here without water even, and we're going to Morocco.'

Aurora relaxed a bit, recognizing in them a couple of not-too-bright kids from the college, dramatizing their first taste of pot. 'If you're not particular which way you get there,' she said crisply, 'you can come along with me to – I hope – Utah.'

'No thank you, ma'am. I mean really, we're going to Morocco; Ron's got his dad's airline credit cards. We've had it to here with this country. The real scene is Morocco, with Dorothy Lamour and Bing Crosby and Bob Hope and William Burroughs.' He began to sing, off-key, an approximation of 'The Road to Morocco'.

'I dig,' said his companion. 'Did you see *Casablanca*?'

'If we ever get a ride out of here. There's nothing going by but jeeps and tanks, like in *Battleground*, and they don't stop.'

'Thanks,' said Aurora, and let out the clutch.

'Not thanks,' Mackintosh explained patiently. '*Tanks*.'

As she started driving off, Ron looked at her and screamed, 'O my God, I'm coming down! O my God! THERE'S A RAT GROWING RIGHT OUT OF HER HEAD!'

'Yeah! Hey, Ron, you ever see *The Lost Weekend*?'

A sign informed her that the lights on the left were those of Piedport, Nevada, four miles off the road. As Aurora was about to heave a sigh of relief and take the turnoff – for at least Piedport would have an hotel – the town's lights went out. She stopped and waited for several minutes, but nothing happened. There was no use, as she saw it, stopping there, when she could as easily push on to a town at least equipped with lights.

The radio gave nothing but a squeal that excited B476. None of the push-buttons seemed to have any effect other than changing the pitch of the whine. It was odd, because it could not be later than 9:00. There ought to be dozens of stations.

Manually she found a weak station in the southeast.

'… y'all keep them cards and letters comin', hear? Keep fahrin' 'em right at me, now, we appreciate hearin' from you, neighbours … tunes you want… Here's a wahr service bulletin, folks, seems like they had a little black-out over Calyforny way. Nevada, Calyforny, Oregon, Utah, Washington … Iowa, Kansas …'

In the middle of its alarming list, the station faded into oblivion. She found a San Francisco station then, but it only kept urging her not to call her power company.

'They are doing everything in their – I mean, everything possible to restore service. I'll just repeat the wire service bulletin with that message from the Pentagon: "The blackout has been caused by a generating plant short in Nevada, following an experiment the full nature of which cannot be divulged, but which was vital to our national security. Power will be restored as soon as possible." That was the Pentagon's message. Now, once again, *do not call* the power company ...'

She began to see military vehicles parked along both sides of the road. Apparently they were abandoned, or the occupants were playing possum. Perhaps there was more to what Mackintosh & Company had said than she'd supposed. And the blackout ...

She pulled off the road and parked. Knowing the potential danger of Project 32 was disturbing, but having the danger become actual was too horrible to understand at once. She needed to skirt the thought, she decided, switching off the lights. She needed to contemplate the calmness of the sky.

It was brighter than she had ever seen it, since the farm in Minnesota. There were no lights below to blot anything out, and she was stunned by the heavens' brilliance. There were Sirius and Alderbaran, pointing to the Pleiades, Orion between them. There were Castor and Pollux. She thought once more of the nights when she had learned their names, peering through one of her father's cracked, unusable telescopes.

At this time of year the farm would smell of corn and creak with crickets – as it did through nearly three seasons of the year. Unperiodically, through the night, the farm's only 'livestock', the Rooster, would crow. Any time was dawn to the Rooster; he was like the broken clock on the mantel and the broken clock in the hall. Periodically, her father had set out to fix one of the clocks, but she never heard one of them tick.

He invented a chicken-skinning machine, but somehow hadn't the heart to try it out on the Rooster, or indeed any chicken. So, though it was a fine-looking implement, they both agreed, it stood out on the lawn, becoming finally a rusty fixture, a perch for the Rooster when he announced the 11 p.m. dawn.

On the lawn were scattered further ornaments and perches as the years went by – A hot air balloon that leaked. A kind of mechanical birdbath shower which birds avoided. An improved kind of sewing machine. And about 168 telescopes, the first begun at Aurora's birth, that is, at her mother's death, the last left uncompleted seventeen years later.

Each time, he would grind lenses diligently for a day or two, then veer off into some other project. Of all the telescopes in the yard, the only one which worked was one he'd bought at a rummage sale and repaired with scotch tape. Through it Aurora had squinted at the Square of Pegasus, Vega and Cassiopeia's chair, the same unchangeable stars she now looked at out the windshield.

A black, hideous shape came between her and the stars. The car door opened and a thick-necked dwarf in uniform climbed in beside her. He left the door open for a moment, to look at her in the light.

'Keep cool, baby,' he growled, waving a gun. 'I'm General Grawk of the US Air Force, and I never raped a lady in my life. Never had to, if you get my meaning. Course there's always a first time, ain't there? Haha.'

'What do you mean by this? Get out of my car!' She said it in her most severe schoolmarm voice. He chuckled.

'I'm commandeering this car, lady. National emergency. Maybe you heard about the big power failure?' He thumbed his chest. 'I did that Anyway, I need a car and driver, and you're elected.' He moved over a bit closer. 'It don't have to be all *that* bad, you know.'

A faint squeal sounded from under the general.

'Get up! You're sitting on my pet rat!' she shrieked.

An instantaneous transformation took place. One moment he was a confident, grinning, aggressive little ape; the next he was screaming and vaulting into the back seat. The body of B893 lay flattened on the seat cushion. Aurora picked it up by the tail. It was dead. A strange smile played across her features as she lifted it, turning in the light.

'RATgetthatRATawayfromMEgetitawayRAT!' he screamed.

'Get out of my car. Now.'

The gunbarrel swept B893 out of her hand and out of the open door. Grawk climbed back into the front seat and looked at her with a changed – a more respectful – expression. 'I like you,' he said. 'Pretty cool. Pet rat, eh? That was good. But let's get rolling, now. Turn right at the next milestone.' He slammed the door. Aurora did not move.

'I have another pet rat in the car with me,' she said coldly, savouring each word. 'A *live* one.'

'WHERE? O God, is it *on me*? Where?'

'I have it safely out of your reach, for the moment. But unless you throw your gun in the back seat and start behaving like a gentleman, I shall *stuff this rat down your collar!*'

'You – you're kidding.' Long silence. 'There couldn't be another – is there?' Another long silence, then the gun thudded into the back seat.

'Now, General, I'll drive you where you wish to go, if you'll tell me what this is all about.'

'We'll head for NORAD HQ in Colorado. That's safest,' he said in a shaken voice. 'I can't tell you what I'm doing here – it's a secret.'

'If it has anything to do with Project 32, you may tell me,' said Aurora and handed him her purse. 'My identification is in there.'

'Who are you?' He fumbled in the purse, held up a card and trained a pen-light on it 'Aurora Candlewood, Ph.D., Special Psychological Consultant for Project 32. A young kid like you? What does the fancy title mean, kid?'

'If you are going to tell me what I think you are going to tell me, it means Project 32 needs me badly.'

'I'll tell you what we need,' he said. 'We need a good dragon-slayer.'

'Right. Now suppose you tell me a little more about the dragon?'

CHAPTER XIII

Wonder Journey

'Rudis indigestaque moles'

OVID

As the car picked up speed the conversation within slowed, until, by the time they were flying into the outskirts of the deserted city, the five had grown strangely silent.

The car swerved, slowed, bumped down steel rollers into an unlit tunnel. Cal felt it buffeted by blasts of steam and water; he could smell the suds. There was the scream of saws on steel, and the dead blackness popped and flashed with livid gleams. By their uncanny light, Cal saw he was alone. The four others, the car, everything familiar was gone but the third of the seat to which he was still safety-strapped, which moved forward on invisible tracks to some rendezvous of its own.

He crashed through double doors into a room full of blood-red light, full of well-dressed mute figures. Mannikins, he thought with relief. In the corners, naked mute limbs in charnel heaps. The upper half of a dummy, weakly upright, slid down an inclined oily countertop, cracking the wall with its face and falling back. A bell sounded distantly. Sprinklers drizzled on the non-existent fire, while delicate water-wheels revolved beneath them. In the atrosanguineus shadow, the dummy's smashed face and nose-hole received the rain.

*

Brian Gallopini found himself inexplicably alone, as the seat to which he was fastened moved into dry yellow sunlight. Light blazed white-red on his retina; he squinted at the globes. Artificial suns? No, goldfish bowls, fishbowls of gold lofted on levers to the sun, a sun-offering. The goldfish floated belly-up.

*

Cats crawled along upper shelves, going from nowhere to nowhere. A few of them wore gold or silver watches strapped about their middles. One paused, near enough for her to read the watch. It was wrong. Daisy saw the date change from 7 to 8 with a click. The cat gave a tiny scream and moved faster. It was only then Daisy noticed it was pulling a little pie tin full of machine parts.

*

Dipterous toy helicopters roamed the room, weaving fine copper wire in peculiar, meaningless patterns. Jack yawned.

*

Every can seemed to have rusted enough to admit a few bacteria. The buildup of gas was terrific, as Harry gladly demonstrated. He plunged his knife into a can that exploded black juice over his hand. He laughed.

'Sauerkraut!' he said. 'Rotten sauerkraut!'

Cal did not laugh. 'It's odd. Most of the stock is gone, and the rest is rotten. In only a few days. Mysterious. Is there anything left?'

Harry laughed again. 'Nothing to write home about,' he said, plunging his knife into another can. It squittered black and grey curds.

Later Cal would see how the system incorporated these exploding cans into a sort of 'internal combustion' engine, using an old auto cylinder block, reloading eight cans after every revolution. But just now he was watching the shopping carts.

*

Ferriferous were the stately wheels of the sumptuous 'ironclad', or locomotive, which stood upon rails of ferric metals, burnished bright. It looked powerful, and appearances, in this case, were not deceiving, for it fairly chuffed with impatience to be off. Steam issued forth and hissed insistence into the ironic fists, then the behemoth moved down inclined grooves towards an enormous loop-the-loop. Roaring up to 110 miles per hour, the leviathan looped and looped again. Switched into the vertical circle (¼ mile high), it would continue thus until it 'ran out of steam', as it were.

Jack watched the engine, awaiting its fall. Its blue-green lights, the colour of *Calliphoridae*, shone in the afternoon haze. The engine was pushing a giant crank before it, made of twisted I-beams, whose handle was a telephone pole. The crank drove a gear system atop a derrick perched on a low building, a factory or school.

*

Gurgling, the row of automatic washers began its intricate ballet once more, each blocky tub hopping in place. If they started moving towards her, Daisy told herself, she'd scream. Not that it would do any good.

Just now it was a place to sit, glancing at an abandoned newspaper.

VENUS PROBE A-OK

Obscene idea. Nothing about the attack of the washermen, she noticed. There wouldn't be, of course, anything like *Washing Crossing Delaware*.

One of the machines burst into streaky-green flames.

*

How many preparations there were to make or keep women beautiful Brian Gallopini (Ph.D.) had never realized. Here Lady Clinge, Queen Esther, Prince Gloriani and other nobility vied for the privilege of caring for milady's surface. Or, as at present, they vied in providing big, boxlike machines with cold cream lubricants and parfum fuels. A gross of stretch girdles had been tied together to propel a large boxy thing that the small boxy things were now winding up; a kind of giant, wingless model plane. It began to move, majestically, out of the smashed front of the shop, backwash from its great propellor whipping up a froth of lace.

*

In a covered wagon marked WAGONS WEST COCKTAIL LOUNGE, horsedrawn, moving slowly eastward, lay a stack of nude figures.

'Dummies,' Harry assured Cal.

The two sidekicks were astride 10¢ mechanical ponies from the supermarket, heading west. As they passed a busy casino, Harry pointed out the zombie-like creatures inside. Mindless, these pushed coins into and pulled handles of slot machines. Wheels spun, jackpots rattled, but nothing affected them. They were not clearly machines, nor yet unmistakably human. Alone, of all the fixtures of Las Vegas, these remained (though employed by a new master) outwardly unchanged. One-handedly they nibbled club sandwiches without pausing in their work.

*

'Judo,' muttered Harry admiringly, as he watched two dog-sized boxes warring, 'or something.' One's shield was a bent sign on which the word KENO was still legible. Kenogenesis? Cal wondered. What else could turn brother against brother like this?

The dachshund of a box fought with cable cutters, nipping at the delicate legs of the other, a tall, Airedale box. Armed with a ball of lead on a stick, it seemed to be trying to beat the dachshund even flatter. Would Keno cut Fido down to size? Or would Fido knock Keno into submission?

The lavender X-ray machine from a dentist's office, buzzing angrily, came to intervene. Cal dragged Harry away from the spot before, he hoped, they were both lethally dosed.

*

'Kinematograph!' cried the Professor, surveying the unfamiliar equipment of the electronics shop. 'Phonogram! Stereophone!' He paused before a video tape player. Having never seen television before, Brian was charmed by this old news tape of the Venus probe, running forwards and backwards like a palindrome.

*

Mechanical elaborations rose rococo on every side. Daisy looked at them, hardly able to focus her uncomprehending gaze. A grain elevator's screw lifted up an incline bowling balls and dropped them through the second-storey window of the casino. Through collimating holes they fell freely to the basement kitchen where, their potential energy having become kinetic energy, their momentum was converted into impulse by their striking, one by one, the levers of a punch. Day and night it punched out aluminium frames for new cells, new cells, new cells. Along with club sandwiches, the bowling balls were pulleyed to the first floor via dumb waiter. The sandwiches were conveyed on belts to the organisms they fuelled, which ran the one-armed dynamos, while the bowling balls were rolled down a chute to the street and waiting elevator. The latter was run by clockwork gears, an hydraulic system, and, ultimately, exploding cans of sauerkraut in another part of town. These caused pistons to oscillate, driving a crank which compressed air into long cylindrical tanks. These cylinders then formed rollers for the transport of heavy objects to or from the vicinity of the elevator, where, connected to air motors, an hydraulic system and gears from a tower clock, they operated it continuously. Power to form the extruded sheet aluminium from which the frames were to be punched was provided by evacuation of the city water supply through waterwheels. The aluminium was melted down in a vat in the pet department of a nearby department store, heated by the rays of the sun concentrated through fishbowls. Scrap aluminium was dumped into this vat by a relay team of cats.

*

'NO OTHER GYM CAN MAKE THIS OFFER!' Harry read the sign by flashlight. 'Eat all you want and still lose!' It pictured men in various positions of exquisite torture: arms pulled up in crucifix position by pulley; scourged by the slapping looped belt of a machine; doubled like a foetus under a platform of crushing weights; and spread like Prometheus, liver to the sky, dumbbells in the outstretched, agonizing hands.

Harry read the poster a second time. Having just climbed five flights of stairs dragging something, he needed to catch his breath.

*

'O Magic Probe!' intoned the Professor. Charmed by it, he pretended to charm it in return; he stood posed, holding his stick like a wand above the television set. The rocket slowly backed down to earth, swallowed and extinguished its flames like a carnival performer.

'O Levitation!' he murmured. 'O Dark Work of Monsieur Mesmer!' Rhabdomancer, he let his rune-staff dip towards the sink in the corner. Aleuromancer, he scattered filings on a magnet.

'The image of the murderer,' he warned, 'will appear upon the dead man's retina!'

But now, magically, the image on the screen metamorphosed. A man smiled, then spewed beer into a glass, till it was foaming full. In another part of the shop, a jukebox was awakening.

*

Placing the flashlight under his chin, Harry turned it on. Daisy screamed, and he laughed.

'It's only me.'

'You ought to be put in a cage,' she grated.

'If you take that back,' he said, 'I'll tell you a secret. Somebody's dead, and I know who.'

'Dead? Who?'

'Cal. Poor guy had an accident.' Harry experimented, shining the flashlight through his own fingers to show the bones. 'A nasty fall.'

*

Quite suddenly, Brian was not alone. The jukeboxes were with him, playing 200 OF YOUR FAVOURITE SELECTIONS. Their music bore him into a past of minuets and waltzes, hoedowns and patriotic marches, as they glided past him in slow turns, filling the room with light and sound.

Dapplings of cobalt blue, strawberry, celadon, ochre spun across the walls and ceiling. On one machine a panel rippled with azure, faded to orchid, then blinked scarlet fire. Chromium and aluminium and glass took up the rich tints – coral, turquoise, ruby, lime – and multiplied them, till the room rang with colour. Brian felt his face a patchwork of rose, purple, amber, felt palpable light rhythms pluck at it as guitars, reeds and sounding brass plucked at his eardrums. His delighted multicoloured lips formed the idiot words to songs, soundless in the tumult. It was glorious and he was part of it, taking his place in line as they filed towards the door. Carmine and indigo islands fled across the ceiling and walls before him, streaking towards, shrinking towards, converging on the doorway. He knew he would follow the jukebox parade almost anywhere, on and on till he became nothing more than a noise in the street.

*

Red light streamed down through Harry's fingers and gleamed on something in the dust.

'Cal dead? Gee, that's too bad,' said Daisy. 'I kind of liked him.'

Harry smiled in the dark. 'Oh, all the girls kind of liked Cal,' he said. 'Hey, where you going?'

'Look, there's something going on at the drive-in theatre,' she shouted back. 'Maybe that's where the others are.'

'Wait up,' he said, genuflecting to pick up the coin.

*

Slowly, a foldaway sofabed humped, folding itself like an inch-worm to measure slow, but luxuriously soft, progress.

*

Tour Paris! urged a poster on the van of broken shoes. The poster showed the Eiffel Tower, a balloon vendor, a kiosk. Cal, lying on the bed of broken shoes, had plenty of time to think it over. The wind had been knocked out of him by a fall.

*

Ventriloquial sounds came from belly of ROBO the robot. Made from a toy mechanical set, he blinked lights in his eyes, waved stiff arms and made similar signs of amiability. He stood in the unglazed, lighted window of a toy store.

'Hullo, Earthmen,' he boomed at Daisy. As she passed, she peered inside, where an inferior second ROBO was just staggering to his feet. He had only one arm, and his head was a tin can still labelled *Harmony Pears*.

Daisy and Harry hurried on. The ROBOs did not say goodbye.

'We are being held prisoner in Las Vegas,' Cal wrote on the teletype unit, then switched it over from SEND to RECV. It paused a long moment, considering, chattering. Then it replied, 'We are being held # (%$H) (?e)U¼½p@ wE a77 bEin@ @@@@@@@@@@@@ @@@@@ @@@@s'

*

X-ray plates were being projected on the big screen. Brian Gallopini waited, yawning, for the main feature.

At the bakery, Jack found fresh bread piled up on the loading dock. The bakery was automatically baking, but there were no trucks to take it away.

Jack had been hungry without knowing it. That, he told himself, was mob psychology. Sub-conscious stuff. What's really inside you – in this case, nothing as yet – all the time, only you don't know it. A secret panel flies open and the murderer is revealed. Or like an X-ray.

*

Yelling, waving his arms, Cal ran towards the shadowy figures. They did not turn to look at him, and his pace slowed.

They passed under a dim blue street light, an army of marching mannikins. Most wore elaborate braces and trusses, gleaming and flexing in the dimness.

He saw a telephone booth across the street. Dancing, dodging through the column gingerly, he slipped into it and lifted the receiver. Dead phone. Aphonia. Not a sound except –

Gleaming and squeaking, the army limped on into the darkness.

*

Zodiacal, the clock on the screen recorded TIME REMAINING UNTIL MAIN FEATURE. As each minutes passed, one-twelfth of the clock face disappeared. The Professor, who had never seen a film, regarded it intently, but he could not detect what happened to all the vanished sectors.

*

As the car swerved, slowed, bumped down steel rollers into a carwash, the Reproductive System was discovering an ice-making machine in the kitchen of the Silver Horseshoe Casino. As the car was torn in chunks and ejected in several directions, the Reproductive System was discovering in dusty cans at the television studio a number of old horror films. As Brian squinted at artificial suns in the pet department, the Reproductive System discovered a glass demonstration 'engine' in an auto showroom, and set about making it work.

The dummy's smashed face and nosehole received the rain as cats crawled along upper shelves. Harry looked at a man painted to an iron wall like a bug. The Reproductive System looked at the printed characters in library books and deciphered their meaning. Then it burned them, stoking a boiler. The boiler fire was smouldering, choked as it was with the ashes of The Encyclopedia Britannica, The Encyclopedia Americana, and Mrs Thrumbold, librarian.

Grocery carts, propelled by spray cans of insecticide, roamed the aisles of the Faresafe supermarket, where Harry plunged his knife into a can and laughed. Cal was watching the shopping carts, but Harry, weak from fumes, fell unconscious. Cal dragged him outside, while Jack yawned at toy helicopters. Inside the freezer of the Silver Horseshoe Casino, cells with ice-picks laboured carefully, shaping gears of ice.

Jack watched the behemoth move down inclined grooves towards an enormous loop-the-loop, awaiting its fall. Daisy watched a washer burst into streaky-green flames. A child, having crawled inside a slanting, crumbled house to sleep, awoke to a strange noise.

Cal and Harry watched zombie-like creatures push coins into slot machines. Daisy watched the ascent of bowling balls, hardly able to focus her uncomprehending gaze. The late mayor of Las Vegas ascended, as his body filled with gas, to the surface of his swimming pool. A giant propellor whipped up a froth of lace.

Hitching up its trailing cord and striding stiffly, a messenger pinball machine greeted another pinball machine messenger as they passed, by exhibiting 450 and a Super Special light.

'6,000,000,' replied the second.

The Professor watched the ascent and descent of the Venus probe rocket. The late mayor of Las Vegas descended once again to the bottom of his pool. The ice gears did not work.

Cal saved Harry from a decor-designed X-ray machine which was spraying the street with radiation. Jack was lost. A bank had been looted. A dead guard with an empty holster lay in the soft grey ash of money. Something was trying to get into the room where the child waited.

'O Levitation!' exclaimed Brian. Harry knocked Cal out, dragged him up five flights of stairs to a roof, and flung him off. Cal did not levitate. 'The image of the murderer will appear upon the dead man's retina!' The roof reminded Harry of another roof, where he had skipped rope long ago. On descending, he read the advertisements of a gymnasium by flashlight.

Tour Paris! a poster urged Cal as he recovered consciousness. The fall to the bed of shoes had knocked the wind out of him. At sunset the glass engine started up, ran briefly, and exploded into sparkling shards. 'Hullo, Earthman,' said ROBO. 'We are being kept prisoner,' Cal typed earnestly. Jack recalled his hunger. An inching foldaway sofa carried him to the drive-in theatre. Brian and the jukeboxes noisily greeted Cal, Harry, Daisy and Jack. Cal heartily greeted Brian, Harry, Daisy and Jack. Jack, glad to be found after being lost, greeted everyone with some relief. Daisy exhibited surprise at seeing Cal, but greeted him, Brian and Jack. Harry greeted Brian and Jack. The last sector of the clock on the screen disappeared. It was time for the 'Main Feature', a composite of audio-visual aids from the school (now a factory), homemade transparencies, and old horror films:

'Machines can do so many things,' says the delighted, delightful voice. 'Yes, machines can do so many things. Mother sews your clothes on a machine – and washes them in another!'

Woman sewing changes abruptly to saurian threshing his tail, lashing out angrily at skyscrapers. Under his foot is a car. Dungeon scene, girl being tied to giant wheel. 'We know *you* won't talk under torture, Goodfelloe, but surely you won't stand by and see her *twisted* and *broken* on my wheel?'

To his unspeakable horror, the beams of the full moon make his hands hairy. He becomes more than a wolf – less than human. A dark shape moves among the mists of the Rue Morgue, following a slender girl. Dr Frankenstein throws back the cloth covering his experiment – and the table is empty! Father mows lawn with a machine.

'No,' said the child, backing away into a corner of the dirty mattress. The room was tilted at a crazy angle. There were places where the plaster was missing, and the laths showed like white bones.

The black hearse bearing the armorial crest of Count Alucard rattles through the Transylvanian night. No driver, Strange plant creatures have surrounded the little farmhouse. 'So you think I am mad, do you? You think it is madness to wish to create Life?' Happy child uses electric toothbrush.

A panel flies back revealing – 'But tell me, Doctor, what is *your* theory of these baffling murders?' 'Theory? What do you mean? Why should *I* have any theory? What are you driving at?' Cows are milked by machines.

The medical examiner rises, removing glasses. 'Odd. If we only knew what made those two little marks on her throat.' 'Machines make life easier *and more fun.*'

'No,' said the child. The grey box knew its part well. It advanced silently, axeblade arm upraised.

'The army is helpless, sir. The mumbledypegs have taken the city.' Laughing girl uses roller skates; boy delivers papers from elegant chrome bike. 'Here in the jungle, my pretty one, there are many mysteries into which those of the outer world have found it wiser *not* to inquire.' 'Here, in the great Mesabi Range, is one of the largest open-pit mines in the world! Machines need iron.' An Egyptologist holds up object. 'Hmm. Looks like the Death Scarab of Ra. But how the devil did it get into poor Emerson's room?' 'Father uses machines in his work –' Lathe, adding machine, milk truck and dental drill quarter the screen.

The X-ray of a fractured arm appears. 'It must be the Lost City itself!' exclaims the older explorer, parting the ferns to peer, '—and when he relaxes, too.' Golf cart, camera, fishing reel, shotgun. 'No one can hear you if you scream, my dear. We have the castle quite to ourselves. Hahahaha!'

Cal thought of the two machines fighting. Kenogenesis. They altered their own genes as they went along. Bound to get a maverick like that once in awhile. Kind of insanity. Turns on its own kind. Ordinarily, he supposed, they were incapable of taking life deliberately. It was inconceivable that they could always recognize one another, in all mutations. No, more likely they respected all life-forms. But ...

'Machines are friendly to us, as long as we are friendly to them.' Father oils lawnmower. 'Look deep into my eyes, my dear.' Turbaned mesmerist leans over pale girl. 'Deeper. Deeper.'

'There are machines to make women beautiful –' Four women under hair driers read *Popular Mechanics*. 'Surely no human being could have done this!' 'Machines –' 'Good Lord!' It's a – a human head!'

The box advanced silently, matching the child's every move, backing it into the corner. The shadow of the axeblade grew longer. But at the last possible second it stopped, mysteriously seized with rust.

'No! That sunlight – I can't stand it! Arrghiiiaaaa!' The Lost City is buried under a quick lava flow; the broken house of Usher slides into the slimy syrup of the swamp; the castle is in flames; the mysterious island sinks forever; the aliens are dissolved by rain. As the monster's head sinks, smoking, into the cauldron of seething acid, there is an almost pleading look in its eye. 'There are some mysteries,' intones the white-haired scientist, 'better left in the hands of the Deity.' 'Thank God it's all over!' sobs his daughter, throwing herself in the arms of the young scientist and looking away from the corpse of the alien invader. The young scientist shakes his crewcut, looking at the thing. 'I wonder if it really is all over?' he murmurs.

The head of the dummy with the smashed nose appears, red-lighted, forty axe-handles' breadth between the eyes. 'Yes, machines can do so many things,' he gurgles. 'Aren't you glad that *you're* a machine?' The screen goes black.

Professor Gallopini's one remaining jukebox comes alive, glowing with bubbling coloured lights. 'I'll see you in my dreams,' it promises the five fleeing figures. Behind them, the great screen buckles and collapses.

CHAPTER XIV

Good to the Last Drop

'Here, Grandfather, you eat the last of the porridge ... I – I've had a great plenty already.'

SHELLEY BELLE, portraying Little Nell,
in *The Old Curiosity Shop*

From ten miles up, the city of Millford looked like a shiny dime. From a mile up, it looked like a pancake griddle. From the ground outside, it looked like an oil storage tank of more than usual diameter. No reconnaissance teams had yet been persuaded to find out what it looked like on the inside. It was presumed that the inhabitants were dead or had long since fled the scene.

In the elegant, all-stainless-steel cafeteria of the Wompler Research Laboratory there was nothing at all to eat. The Womplers, father and son, lay stretched out on two parallel tables, too weak to move. Grandison turned his gaunt face to regard his son, who was reading a magazine.

They had eaten all the ketchup and mustard the first day – and Louie had eaten the most. Thereafter there had been nothing but crumbs of Sooper Proteen from the linings of Louie's coat pockets – and of them, too, the fat young man had taken the lion's share. Now he was even hogging the magazine, looking at the pretty pictures of food.

It wasn't fair! Granny thought, observing how fat his son was. Surely Louie wouldn't mind parting with a little slice of that fat? Or, if so, Grandison could wait until he was asleep. There were sharp knives in the kitchen …

'Hey, Pop! Did the chicken give some eggs yet?' asked Louie, sitting up and yawning. He moved his big meaty shoulders in a stretch of feigned weariness.

The chicken – *the* chicken – was a scrawny bird perched on a chandelier well out of reach. From this perch it had taunted and tempted them for two weeks. It showed no sign of flying down within reach, of falling dead of starvation itself, or of laying an egg – 'giving eggs' as Louie would have it. It's only plumage was a torn bunch of multicoloured wires depending from its neck; it was featherless. It clucked softly to itself, day and night, in a regular rhythm. Over a period of time, this began to have the effect, on Grandison, of a cricket jammed in his ear. There were times when he'd rather have seen the chicken go away than eat it, and times when he convinced himself it was an hallucination. But, with a kind of contentment, the bird kept its bright eye fixed on him all the time. And clucked.

'It did not lay an egg, son, and I doubt if it will. I think that bird there is a rooster.'

'You sure know a lot of nature lore, Pop. What's being a rooster got to do with its giving eggs?'

Granny sighed. He squinted up at the bird, trying to guess its sex. Usually his conclusion depended on his mood. The bird shook its comb defiantly at him. It seemed a very rooster-like gesture.

Louie stretched his ribs-and-bacon and yawned, displaying a half-pound of tongue. After searching his pockets diligently for crumbs, he took out his dynamometer and squeezed it.

'My grip is increasing as my weight drops,' he said. After reading the dynamometer, he laid his arm on a meat scale and weighed it. 'By the time I weigh fifty pounds, my grip'll be a thousand pounds. Wow!'

Grandison imagined the arm being lifted tenderly from the scale, wrapped up in pink paper and marked with a crayon. He saw fat white fingers sizzling in a pan.

The chicken let out a squawk, then another.

'Cross your fingers, son,' breathed the old man sitting up quietly. 'We may have us an omelette tonight.'

The loud sound became a regular cluck-clawk, and the bird swayed dizzily on its perch. A shiny ovoid surface peeped from under its tail propellor. 'Get ready to catch it, son!'

'I got it, Pop, I got it, I got it, I –'

Louie made a dive as the ovoid dropped, but hunger had slowed his reflexes. It slipped through his fingers and hit the floor.

And bounced.

*

In the lab above, Kurt and Karl Mackintosh moved smoothly and speedily about their work, never colliding, seldom speaking, always smiling, two clockwork figures. With their cooperation, the System had fitted them out with hydraulic power-assists on their arms and legs that multiplied both speed and strength. The power-assists were shaped like close-fitting pieces of armour: gauntlets, brassards, cuisses, jambeaux and sollerets.

They were run by electric pumps and hydraulic pistons. Strain gauges embedded in Kurt's and Karl's muscles switched on the pumps. Though they never said so, Kurt and Karl felt like two supermen in their new armour. They clicked and clanked about the lab, quite pleased with life. They liked to work so well that the System also fitted them out with automatic intravenous nourishment.

In return, they worked out new experiments with animal-machine symbioses. Following Dr Smilax's orders, they fed all results directly into the System, via a handy typewriter in the corner. In addition, they taught it the rudiments of behavioural psychology, of Keynesian economics, of information theory, and they showed it how to simplify programmes.

They would identify themselves by applying their right ears to a metal plate. That keyed in the System, putting it in a receptive mood for their information.

When they worked harder, there were rewards.

When they worked poorly, there were punishments.

A reward was the lighting of a sign saying 'WELL DONE!'

A punishment was a mild but unpleasant electric shock.

Sometimes Kurt received more punishments than Karl.

Sometimes Kurt received more rewards than Karl.

Sometimes they were even.

As time went on, there were fewer rewards and no punishments for either of them. As time went on, they adjusted. They adjusted to the System like a synchronizing clock. Like a clock, like a clock, like a synchronizing clock.

> Clicking as they walked,
> Ticking as they worked,
> Talking as they went
> About their clickwork clockwork work.

Louie sat on the floor, weeping over the cast-iron egg.

'Stop that blubbering,' Grandison ordered. 'No use crying over spilt milk. No use stewing about it. Outa the frying pan into the fire. Jack Spratt could eat no fat …' He stopped himself on the verge of babbling, and fell silent, watching his son's great fat shoulders – of mutton – shake.

'If you had a quarter,' Louie complained, 'you could get a cup of coffee even.'

'The coffee machine! Christ, why didn't I think of it? It's probably loaded with sugar and powdered cream. Hell, son, we'll just bust it open –'

'But Pop, it ain't even paid for yet!'

Too weak to answer, the old man levered himself off the table and made his way along the wall to the gleaming coffee machine. He began to bang and kick at it feebly, cursing the prudence that had ever made him buy a burglar-proof model.

'No use, Pop. You gotta have a quarter. Honesty is—'

He broke off, seeing his father's expression. The older man did fish a quarter from his pocket, fumble it into the slot and bang furiously at the double cream and double sugar buttons. A cup descended and the machine filled it half-way with grey, greasy liquid. Grandison seized it and drained it, and his blood came alive with sugar.

Almost at once the machine dropped another cup and, humming, half-filled it with grey, tepid liquid. Grandison snatched it out and offered it to his son, as another cup dropped.

'Oh, no thanks, Pop. I hafta stay away from coffee. Bad for the circulation when you're in training.'

Grandison snatched another cup from the machine; it dropped another and began filling it. 'What in hell are you training for?' he asked.

'Oh, nothing special. You know, just keeping in shape. A guy never knows when he might run into some wise guys in a bar or something, you know.'

Grandison was too busy, by now, to care whether Louie were really mad or not. The torrent of greasy grey liquid from the coffee machine was constant now, though the supply of paper cups had finally run out. A jumble of them were caught under the spout, and the liquid was spraying out into the room. He grew alarmed as it snowed no sign of lessening. Wasn't this supposed to be a ten-gallon or twenty-gallon supply? Surely it had flooded that much on the great stainless steel floor by now?

When the entire floor was wet and slick, Grandison grew really frantic. He ran from one stainless steel, rubber-sealed door to another, rattling the knobs and knocking, though he knew how useless this was.

To his surprise, he heard a noise beyond one door. Footsteps!

'Help, help!' he croaked, and beat upon the shining steel.

A key grated and the door swung open. The chicken cawked and flapped out through it on big membraneous batwings, its tail prop slowly revolving.

An unshaven marine guard stood before him, hand on the butt of his automatic, and surveyed the floor.

'What's going on here? Who's been tampering with the coffee machine?'

Hoarsely murmuring his thanks, Grandison tried to go through the door. The guard blocked his way.

'Not so fast, buddy. I want to see your pass. I also want to know what kind of funny business is going on with that machine.'

'My pass? But I'm Grandison Wompler,' quavered the old man. 'Don't you recognize me? I'm old Granny Wompler –'

'I don't care if you was the frigging company president his-self, you can't come through here without a pass!'

The door slammed, knocking Granny back a step. He lost his footing in the greasy slush and fell. It hardly seemed worthwhile to get up again.

Louie finally came over and helped him to his feet. 'Just ignore him, Pop,' he said, jerking a thumb towards the sealed door – against which foot-deep coffee now lapped. 'Just pretend he don't exist. Hey, listen to this!' He rattled the magazine. 'A recipe for squab Louisiane: first marinate a couple of plump squab in warm *Tio Pepe*, to which had been added ...'

CHAPTER XV

From Marrakech to the Moon!

'*Décidément nous sommes hors du monde.*'

RIMBAUD

Shortly after sunset, two men stood in a shadowy sidestreet near the Jardin Abdallah. They spoke in hushed voices.

'I have done all I can,' Marcel Brioche said, '*Mon général*, the rest is in the hands of *le bon Dieu*.'

'Stick to English, *vache*! The walls have ears in Marrakech. Tell me, exactly what measures have you taken to guarantee the safety of this mission – in other words, of your person?'

'First of all, I have hinted to each of the agents – the Russian and the American – that I have made some sort of deal with the other side. Thus I have been able to keep them both off-balance up till now, playing them off against one another. With luck, they will be so busy spying each other out – or even fighting – that they will leave me alone.'

'And – with no luck?'

'I have secondly instructed my valet, Antoine, to don a duplicate of my space suit and to – shall we say – *hide conspicuously*. That is, he is to slip through back streets to the launching site – which only the three of us know – and draw off anyone who means to follow me. If there remains anyone who is seeking my life, it is my hope that they will make a crucial mistake.'

'Does Antoine know the risk?'

'He is, like me, a loyal Frenchman. For such, there are *no* risks.'

'I see –' The voice of the general broke.

'Is something wrong, General?'

'No, Brioche, nothing.' The older man put a hand to his brow. 'I – I had no idea this mission might be risking a man's life.'

'There is probably little risk, General. As I said, only the three of us know where the launch is to take place. Even the technicians who assembled the ship secretly here were then taken back to France under guard, and will remain incommunicado until the lift-off is completed. Antoine is only a safety factor.'

'Yes, perhaps you're right.' The general's knuckles kneaded his brow, as if trying to smooth away knots of anxiety. 'Please go on.'

'There is nothing more to tell. I shall go through the main streets to the launching site in an ordinary cab. I will wear my dress uniform, as though I were going out to supper. I'll meet Antoine at the launching site and there put on the space suit. Lift-off will take place on the stroke of midnight.'

'Then *bonne chance, mon ami*,' said the general, in a strangely choked voice. 'The spirit of the Republic is with thee tonight!'

The astronaut strode away, the words of his superior glowing within his breast, next to which nestled the picture of a dead girl. He did not notice the shadowy figure of Vetch glide from a doorway and press a note of large denomination into the general's hand.

'Congratulations,' Vetch said, not without sarcasm. 'Wasn't it easy though? All you had to do was betray your country and two of your countrymen, and now you have enough to take care of those gambling debts.' His face was in shadow; the general could see only the moving point of his satanic little beard.

'You devil! You filthy—!'

'Haha, why what's the matter, General? Not happy with your night's work?'

'I am miserable,' confessed the older man, shaking with emotion. 'I wish I had died, rather than do such a despicable deed!'

'Why make it a choice?' asked Vetch smoothly. His motion was sudden and smooth. Without a sound, the traitorous general crumpled to the pavement, a dagger in his heart.

'You won't be needing this, after all,' Vetch said, twitching the banknote from the dead man's grasp. 'You have been rewarded as you deserve.' He laughed harshly.

'Now here's my plan,' said Suggs, helping Barthemo Beele into the silvery space suit. 'You'll pretend to be Brioche when you get to the ship. Meanwhile,

I'll go out and kill the real Brioche, giving you plenty of time to figure out the controls. I'll put on his suit and join you if I can. Got it?'

He fastened down the white helmet, but Beele gestured that he wished to speak, so Suggs unbolted it once more.

'Do you have to *kill* Brioche? He seemed like a pretty decent guy, Suggs.'

'He's a *Frog*, Beele, and don't you forget: it. It's Frogs that have been cheating the American tourist for years. They're all sneaky and dirty and mean and back-knifers, and the only ones that ain't fairies are commies. So get crackin', Beele.' Before Beele could argue, Suggs slapped the helmet back in place.

When Vovov had put on his space suit of silvered material – designed to look exactly like the French suit – and departed, Vetch loaded his pistol, checked the action, and fitted it with a silencer.

'Poor Vovov,' he sighed. 'Poor boob. He thinks he is to take a ride to the moon – when he is only to 'take a ride'. I have no doubt the Americans will think he is Brioche and kill him. How fitting! How like something from one of those preposterous films of theirs (to which poor Vovov is so devoted)! Of course if they fail to kill him – these Americans are so inept – I shall simply have to do it myself. Orders are orders.'

He pulled from his breast pocket the coded telegram and read it once again. '"Give Vovov *special treatment*. Bad risk long suspected, now confirmed by your description of his admiration for Virginia Mayo. The Commandant." Ah, poor Vovov!' he said once again, sighing with a great deal of satisfaction as he drew on black gloves. 'Poor ape does not even realize his own decadence.'

As soon as the valet had left, Marcel Brioche had second thoughts. 'How can I be so selfish?' he cried, smiting his forehead with the heel of his hand. 'Antoine had a fiancée in France; I have no one to return to. How can I ask him to take this risk? No, I shall not! I cannot let him do this!' He snatched up a paperweight. 'I'll catch up with him and change clothes once again. I cannot ask him to wear the suit I should be proud to wear – to face the bullet I should be glad to face!' He hurried out into the caliginous night.

The silver-suited figure stepped into the glare of the streetlight for only a second, but it was enough. Suggs flung his knife, snarling, 'Take that, you filthy Frog!'

The figure slumped to its knees, writhed, and fell flat. Hurrying over, the CIA agent removed its helmet and peered at the still features.

'Vovov!' he exclaimed. 'Oh, they're playing a cute game, all right. Thought they'd smuggle you into the ship as Brioche, eh? Well, Vovov, I guess I'll borrow this suit. You ain't going on no moon trip tonight, anyways.' As quickly as he could, Suggs donned the suit and helmet.

*

Barthemo Beele had almost reached the launching site. He had kept to the back alleys and, thus far, avoided seeing anything suspicious. His only mistake, he saw, had been wearing the helmet. Now he paused in the long alley near the mosque, struggled out of the helmet and mopped away perspiration. Only a few yards to go. Only a few –

He was aware of the pounding of running feet. Deceptive echoes sprang up from every direction, and in this twisted alleyway it was impossible to see someone until they were on top of one. In vain he twisted this way and that, straining his senses in the echoing dark.

Suddenly there was an arm about his throat and he was pulled backwards into a choking hold. A voice spoke close to his ear:

'It is for your own good that I do this, Antoine! *You* have someone to go back to.'

Something cracked him behind the ear, and Beele –

Suggs was absolutely right, he thought. *Brioche is a bad actor, all right. Anyone who would deliberately and unprovokedly assault an agent of the* CIA *like this deserves to be shot like a dog.*

– and so thinking, Beele fell forward into a starry abyss.

Vetch saw the figure emerge from the end of the alley near the mosque, wearing the suit and carrying the helmet. Though it was too shadowy to see the face, he knew – for it was too small to be Vovov – it must be the valet.

I ought to kill you, he thought. *But you are a brave man who does not know what he is doing. You are a mere tool of vicious capitalism. I salute your bravery, O valet*, he went on, reversing his gun, *O man of the proletariat!*

He crept up in a dozen quick catlike steps and swung, aiming for a spot just behind the ear. 'Fellow Worker, forgive me this!' Vetch shrieked. The man grunted and went down. Vetch could not help pausing, turning him over to see if he were hurt.

'So, Monsieur Brioche!' he exclaimed, gazing with some surprise on the astronaut's face. 'So, you changed clothes with your valet once again, eh? As in a bad French farce – or an American movie!' Angry with himself for having called the aristocratic Brioche a worker, Vetch could hardly keep himself from shooting the astronaut. Yet he forced himself to relax and began putting on Brioche's space suit.

'No, I'm no murderer,' he said. 'I'll leave that to your superiors – when they learn that you have lost France her only moon ship!'

He stood there for a moment, overcome with silent laughter at the idea of what was to become of Brioche. Was Devil's Island still a penal colony? He hoped so. He could remember it from old American films ...

But there were footsteps, and at one end of the narrow street another figure in a space suit appeared. Vetch drew his gun and slunk back in the shadows.

I pity you, Vovov, he thought, resting his gun over his forearm. *But you are a fool, and fools are dangerous as co-workers. Goodbye – pardner!*

He let the figure get some little distance past him, then squeezed the trigger. His first silent shot shivered the man's helmet; the next two completely destroyed his head.

Vetch hurried off to the launching rendezvous without pausing to look at the body of the last proletarian he would ever see.

Suggs was surprised to see another figure waiting at the secret launching pad, wearing a space suit like his own. Ghosts rose unbidden to his mind, but he shook them off. No, it must be Beele. It was odd that the young assistant had got through all right. He must have had to take care of a couple of Russkies on the way – with his bare hands! There was something frightening about getting in the ship with this man.

Suggs made a thumbs-up sign and the figure replied. Of course it was Beele. Suggs turned his attention to inspecting the rocket itself, so cunningly disguised. So this was how the sneaky Frogs had done it! He had to hand it to the bastards.

Vetch was surprised to see another figure arrive at the launching pad wearing a space suit like his own. Ghosts rose unbidden to his mind, but he shook them off. No, it would be the valet, of course. As if reading his thoughts, the figure made a cheery, working-class thumbs-up sign and Vetch replied with all his heart. Of course it was the valet! The sturdy peasant had double-crossed these capitalist pigs who supposed themselves his masters!

Vetch turned his attention to inspecting the rocket itself, so cunningly disguised. In his ears, the countdown had reached (in the droning voice of a tape recording) *quatre-vingt dix-neuf.* Vetch strapped himself carefully into his couch seat.

'Hey, man, this sure is good stuff,' said Ron. He and Kevin Mackintosh lay in chaises on a dark rooftop overlooking most of the city. They were sipping mint tea to slake the thirst created by *kif.* 'Sure is good,' he said again.

Kevin nodded wearily. He hated to tell Ron that a *real* kif-head never talked about how good the stuff was.

'Hey,' said Ron, with a lazy gesture over the roof edge. 'I just saw – I mean *seen* – two Martians, down in the street.'

Martians, Christ! thought Kevin. 'What were they doin'?' he asked dreamily.

'Shooting at each other, man. Like in *Night of the Phallopods,* you know? Like in *Invasion of the Saucer Men.* They were silver all over, with big white heads, see. Shooting with ray guns that didn't make no noise. One cat shot the other one. Then he *skinned* him.'

'Yeah? Like in *Creature from the Void*?'

'Yeah, and then he shot hell out of another one. The body is still lying down there.'

Kevin leaned over the parapet and looked down. A body with glistening silver skin lay inert. *It had no head*, A chill ran through him. It was just like *I Was a Teenage Beach Monster*. Maintaining a disinterested expression, Kevin leaned back once again. At that moment, the earth began to tremble. A few blocks away, a battery of floodlights came on. The tremors increased, rattling the tea glasses in their saucers.

'Do you see what I see?' cried Ron. 'Do I see it?'

'Man, this sure is good stuff,' Kevin breathed, watching in wonder.

A minaret rose slowly into the air, supported on a column of fire.

CHAPTER XVI

The Secret Heart of Dr S.

'I am obliged to perform in complete darkness operations of great delicacy on myself.'

JOHN BERRYMAN

'Honour hath no skill in surgery, then? No.'

SHAKESPEARE

The perfect symmetry of Susie Suggs's body was settled on the edge of a black leatherette examining table, the only furniture in the room. While her tears had subsided, an unaccustomed frown troubled Susie's forehead – but the frown, too, was perfectly symmetrical. Rhythmically, her white boots kicked at the side of the table, while she, seeing that she had chewed the polish off one nail, went to work on its opposite number.

Dr Smilax had not only learned everything he could about Susie Suggs – from the contents of her purse and from her father's security file – but he had studied her for some time through a peephole. Her movements, he saw, were quick but graceful; impulsive, but eager to please and generous. Having donned a white coat and jammed a stethoscope in his pocket, Dr Smilax unlocked the door and let himself into the room.

'I'm Dr Smilax, my dear,' he said unsmilingly, sitting beside her to take her pulse. 'And you are Miss Susan Suggs of Santa Filomena, California. Is that correct? Do your friends call you Susie?'

'Yes?' Her voice was husky with fear, and she tried to draw her hand away. He imprisoned the wrist.

'Now, I'm not going to hurt you, my dear. I'm only going to examine you.' His tone achieved just the right balance between kind concern and brusque command.

'But I don't want to be examined. I don't *need* to be examined. I'm not sick. All I did was faint when they arrested me.'

He released her hand after a moment, at the same time letting the creases round his eyes crinkle into a smile. 'Of course, if that's the way you prefer it. Feel all right, do you?' She nodded. 'That's fine, then. I had almost hoped there was something I could do …' Letting his voice and expression fade to blankness, he turned to stare at the olive-drab wall.

'You see,' he went on after a moment, 'there isn't much reward in being a military doctor. I assist at deaths, that is all. I – I can hardly go on, sometimes, when I think of those poor men I save – only to send them out to be killed!'

'How awful!' she murmured. He stood up and paced the room.

'Yes, the Army does not think of itself as a group of men but rather as a machine. Men are not humans to it, merely cogs – mere cells in a great big organism.'

For some reason, Susie blushed at the word.

'I would give anything not to have to do it – but someone must!' he said passionately. Sitting down again, heavily, he dropped his face into his long, slender, artist's hands. 'Someone must!'

'I'm sorry,' she said, laying a hand on his arm hesitantly. He feigned not to notice. 'I had no idea—'

'No, of course not. *To you*, to everyone on the outside, we are mere monsters – mere machines which can work on and on, performing miracles on cue, without even a word of thanks, a kind thought, without a single one of those little touches of humanity that make life worth living at all. But we are not monsters! Do I look like a monster to you? Do I?' He was well aware that he looked, at the moment, like a motherless child who happened to have grey hair.

'Oh no!' she assured him, taking his hand. 'You're not the least bit scary, Dr Smilax.'

'Thank you, my dear. Yours is the first human warmth, the first human contact I have had these many years. I'm human, too – God, can't they see I'm human? I may seem superhuman – I may seem a *god* in the operating room, because I must be, but I still have –'

'A heart of clay?' she asked seriously, almost swooning over the metaphor. Strangling a fiendish laugh that threatened to leap up in his throat, the doctor nodded.

'An apt way of putting it, my dear, peculiarly so. The other day I performed open-heart surgery upon a little girl. When she had recovered, she thanked me, saying, "I'm so glad you fixed my heart up good, doctor. But why can't you fix your own heart, too?" Yes, that child saw through me like an X-ray. Would you mind, by the way?' As he spoke, he led her into the next room and pressed her out upon the X-ray table. 'Yes, in effect, that child –' he slid a plate in the drawer beneath her and swung the machine's head into position, '– that innocent child said to me – Deep breath, now. Hold it! All right – said to me, 'Physician, heal thyself!' Ah, would that I could take her excellent advice. But the scars are too deep, too deep on my – heart of clay!' Again he fought down a snigger that brought tears to his eyes.

'Was it some woman, Doctor?' she asked, as he led her back to the examining room. Without answering, the doctor palpated her firm, plump kidneys for a moment.

'Not just "some woman",' he corrected. 'Say rather Woman herself! The incarnation of fair womanhood! The sweetest, most perfect, most symm— most sympathetic creature ever to rejoice in youth and health! And she was mine! Ah, better far that I had never met her, than lose her to the black forces of Death!'

Tears of sympathy boiled in Susie's eyes. 'Death?' she whispered.

'Yes, she died. Ironically enough, it was the work of a man known as a "great surgeon". Oh, fool that I was to have ever believed in him! Though only a medical student at the time, even I could have performed the operation with more skill than he. "Great surgeon"– Nay, *great butcher*!

'Ah, it is all over, all over,' he said, kneading her kidneys savagely. 'But I have ever since been fit for nothing else but this – a repairman of government equipment.' Turning his head away, he fixed his gaze upon the polished toe of his shoe.

'Please, I want to help,' she said, moving closer and taking both his hands in hers.

He squeezed them. 'I know you do,' he said, 'and I appreciate it, but it is too late for me. *Too late*. I am old enough to be, for example, your father. Old enough – to be wise, and still a fool.' His smile was pained.

'Oh, you aren't so old. There are lots of men older than you,' she said earnestly. 'Listen. I know I could never replace *her* in your heart – your heart of clay – that would be just impossible, for heaven's sakes – but I would like to help in any way I can. Please tell me something I can do – anything.'

'Very well, I'll mention it, but I know you won't want to do it.'

'Just try me,' she said bravely.

'Very well. The woman I once loved used to – tell me, have you ever undergone surgery before?'

'Golly, no. But if it's like handing you instruments and wiping your fore-head and giving you moral support, I could learn. I'd really try.'

'Well, no, what I have in mind, Susie, was you becoming – shall we say – a patient?'

'Do you mean—?'

'Yes, I know it is much to ask. But I so long to know all of you; your kid-neys, gall bladder, spleen, yes, every secret of your heart. What is your answer, my love?'

For answer, Susie fell, suddenly sprawling across the table in perfect sym-metry, unconscious.

Aurora felt hypnotized, having watched almost nothing for the last 15 hours but the white skips of line down the middle of an ever-unreeling strip of black asphalt. She had stopped once or twice and dozed off, but something, some inner sense of emergency, kept waking her, impelling her onward.

Now, as the morning sun glared off the hood into his face, Grawk awakened. Bleary eyes regarded Aurora discourteously from a red, porous face. Rasping a hand over his beard, Grawk yawned wider than any dental chart, displaying each one of his yellow, blocky teeth. He closed them on a fresh cigar.

'We must be just about there, huh, babe? Can't you get a little more speed out of this old buggy?'

'You might have helped drive,' she said. 'We'd have made better time.'

'Oh, you're doing fine,' he said cheerily, rubbing yellow grit from his eyes with the hairy back of one fist. 'But see if you can't step on it a little.'

Aurora congratulated herself on not losing her temper. She managed not to speak to him – for speaking to Grawk could never be other than an exchange of insults – until they came to the NORAD outer gate. The guard post seemed deserted.

'Are you sure this is wise?' she asked, slowing. 'There must have been some reason for the guard to leave his post like that.'

'You just keep driving,' muttered Grawk, crushing down his cap over his ears. 'Leave the thinking to me. We got two more checkpoints to pass before we get to the elevators.'

'Do you know this place that well?'

'Like I know women.' He looked at her slyly through the grey mist of his cigar smoke.

They found the second gate likewise deserted, and Aurora's anxiety increased. It was as if some grave, unknown disaster had swept the place clean of personnel. Still, Grawk seemed unperturbed, and for all his faults he was a military planner. Surely he could make a more intelligent assessment of this plainly military situation than she. Or could he?

The third checkpoint was just inside the opening of a steel-lined tunnel. One pair of iron doors slid closed behind the car as it entered, and another closed ahead of it. Electronic eyes and ears were trained on the car, and Grawk, with an amused wave of his hand, pointed out a crossfire arrangement of large-bore gun barrels protruding from the wall. 'Just in case we get any ideas about messing up the place.'

A loudspeaker spluttered, then the voice of a telephone operator spoke. 'Switch off your engine and get out of your vehicle, please,' it said. 'Stand on the red platform.'

They obeyed, Grawk seeming to enjoy the attention even of a security device, Aurora moving her stiff limbs warily. The red platform on which they stood remained motionless, while the yellow-and-black section supporting the car was lowered away by humming machinery, out of sight. In a moment the section returned empty.

'Please give your full names and state your business at NORAD,' invited the operator's voice. She was no ordinary voice, but the smooth, warm one who sells coloured extension phones.

'I'm General Grawk, US Air Force, Jupiter Grawk, and I got important business to transact with Washington, so I'd like to get at my office. Now.'

'I'm Dr Aurora Candlewood, psychological consultant to Project 32. My business is confidential.'

The machine hummed and crackled for a minute. 'I'm sorry, sir, but there is no Air Force General Jupiter Grawk listed in our records. Are you an employee of NORAD?'

'Hell, I run the goddamned place!' Grawk exploded. 'I'm in command here, and I damn well better get to my office!'

'There is no General Jupiter Grawk listed in our records,' the voice said sweetly. 'Have I received your identification correctly? If so, please press your fingers against the glass plate to your left, and hold them there until the light goes off. Thank you.'

'I think you got your wires crossed, baby!' Grawk stormed. 'I'm the head of this outfit, and you ain't nothing but a machine!'

'Have I received your identification correctly? If so, please press your fingers against the glass plate to your left and hold them there until the light goes off. Thank you.'

Grawk strode to the plate and held his ringers against it. A bar of light moved across the plate.

The loudspeaker hummed and crackled. A different voice came on now, the rasping, angry voice of a sergeant. 'All right, Grawk, just what are you trying to pull?' it snarled. 'You know damn well you been busted to Airman Third Class. That was automatic when you loused up Operation Hot Seat. What is all this crap about posing as an officer, huh?'

The cigar drooped. 'Well, sure, I knew it, but I thought – usually it takes a few weeks for a demotion, and—'

'And you just figured you'd sneak back here, grab a few Top Secret files and light out for Mexico, didn't you? Well now, Grawk, you and your girl friend just sit down and wait till the brass decide what to do with you.'

'I'd like to leave,' Aurora said in a hushed, frightened voice.

'You stay put, Miss!' roared the invisible sergeant. 'You wanted in and you'll get in – maybe! But you sure won't get out until I get the sayso from the higher-ups. Sit down!'

A pair of seats unfolded from the wall. Aurora and Grawk sat on them gingerly. There was nothing to look at but the silent loudspeaker and the grim, emissile gun barrels.

Dr Toto Smilax was too nervous to wait for Susie to recover consciousness. Tense as a bridegroom he withdrew, leaving her with a hospital gown and a note: 'My dear, if you decide as I pray you will, put on this little gown and ring for me. If not, you are free to go. The door is not locked.'

He then locked her in and went to his own office to wait. Here, as in any office he occupied, Smilax had installed an elegant, completely-equipped dentist's chair. It was his favourite relaxation to fill or extract his own teeth.

Today, however, he only drilled at a molar in a desultory fashion for a short time, then in a fit of petulance broke off the drill. If only she would consent! He would have her in any case; but how sweeter far the prize that awards itself freely! He developed her X-ray and examined it. Not once in a lifetime did most surgeons get their meat-hooks on such as this, he reflected. It increased his impatience.

The bell sounded then.

As he arranged her on the operating table, Dr Smilax saw the girl's cheeks were wet.

'What is it, my dear? Are you afraid that what you are doing is – wrong?'

'I'm not – sure.' She sighed, then smiled through her tears. 'I'm a little afraid. You see –' she flushed prettily, and would have hidden her face in her hands, had they been free '– you see, I've never had surgery before. This is my first time.'

'I understand,' he said, fastening the leather straps.

'Promise me,' she said, 'promise me you'll be gentle.'

He was bending to kiss her smooth, childlike forehead when far in the distance an alarm sounded. 'I must leave you for a brief moment,' he whispered huskily. 'But I shall hurry back.'

'You may now proceed,' droned the loudspeaker in a third voice, neutral and official. 'Use elevators four and five, please.'

The gate before them swung open, and Grawk and Aurora walked through it to the elevator bank.

'Why do we have to use two elevators?' she asked.

Grawk's explanation was as authoritative as ever, but his manner was more subdued. 'These are all one-man elevators,' he said. 'They only handle 275 pounds and under. That's to keep any of the help from getting the idea of bringing in a bomb – or taking home a computer. You take four, I'll take five.'

Feeling some misgivings, Aurora stepped into the tiny chamber and closed the gate. The overhead light went on, and the cage plummeted down a silver-sided shaft. There was nothing else, and after a time she lost the sensation of motion; it seemed as if the wall beyond the bars was rising while she stood still.

Then deceleration began, and suddenly the light went out. The cage stopped. When Aurora tried opening the gate she found it still locked, and she found out something else.

Her hand fumbled through the bars and encountered no steel wall beyond, no wall at all. Seemingly she was suspended in a void.

'Hey!' shouted Grawk's voice so near at hand it made her jump. 'Hey, let me out of this!'

'Throw down that gun, Grawk!' commanded a voice that echoed from all directions. Something clattered on stone or concrete somewhere below.

A long amber window lighted, showing what seemed to be the control room of a television studio. There was no one inside. At the same time, a pair of powerful spotlights picked out the two cages, lighting every detail of their interiors.

'You are not *General* Grawk,' the voice went on, heavy with sarcasm. 'You the Airman Third Class Grawk, and you are impersonating an officer. Throw down all the badges of your rank, and make it fast.'

Grawk did so, shrinking in the process from an ugly little man to a hideous, tearful dwarf. 'Can't I keep the cap for a souvenir?' he whined. 'I like to wear it. I wear it all the time, even when I'm—'

'Throw it down! It is a federal offence for you, an enlisted man, to even *think* of wearing a cap with silver leaves on the brim.'

Sighing, he sailed the cap off into the darkness. He was so short that Aurora, in her parallel cage twenty feet away, could clearly see his bald spot, red with shame. 'Is the Chief here?' he asked dazedly. 'I thought he'd be in Washington by now.'

'General Ickers is in Washington, but you are under the authority of Dr Smilax.'

'Smilax!'

'Did I hear my name mentioned?' said the doctor, who entered the control room at that moment. 'Speak of the devil, eh? Actually, Airman Grawk, you are now attached to my staff – as an experimental subject.'

'But how – ?'

'I *won* you, let us say, from General Ickers. That is, after we finished our all-night session of Go-to-the-Dump, he owed me thirty-five cents. Well, rather than break a dollar bill … You see?'

'And me, Doctor?' asked Aurora acidly. 'Have you bought me, too?'

'Ah, no, Dr Candlewood. I am truly sorry to have to greet you like this, but you arrived in not very choice company. Let me help you down.' He pressed a switch, and the cage lowered slowly to the concrete. As it touched down, the gate opened. Smilax beckoned her into the control room, and held the door as she entered.

The room was filled with electronic gadgetry, none of which Aurora recognized. In these surroundings the mild-looking middle-aged man who called himself Smilax seemed almost an alchemist among his magical paraphernalia.

'May I ask what you are doing here?' She spoke stiffly. 'I had expected to find you in Millford, Doctor. Is work on Project 32 being carried on here as well?'

'You might say that, yes. But let me ask you the same question. What brings you to NORAD?'

'An accidental meeting with him,' she said, gesturing out the window towards Grawk's cage. 'I was lost at the time, and he convinced me it was urgent that he reached NORAD. Is it really necessary to keep him caged up like that?'

'For the time being. Well, it is fortunate that you appeared, in any case. Yes, fortunate. There is much work for a person of your capabilities – much work. Do you understand what has gone on thus far? How much do you know about the project?'

'I understood the operations of the Reproductive System some time ago, as soon as I had read the report. My job is to educate the System and study its learning processes.

'That's as much as I'm sure of. I can guess at a good deal more. The System got out of control some way; it's too wily and too rapidly-multiplying for the military to cope with. Grawk says he tried something like "electrocuting" it, and it evidently did not work. What exactly has happened? Has the System mutated faster than expected? And, by the way, what has happened to the personnel at NORAD?'

'My, you are intelligent for one so young – and so beautiful,' said Smilax, beaming. Aurora could see two little images of herself in the rimless lenses of his glasses.

'I'm old enough to be annoyed by senseless flattery, Doctor,' she said coldly. 'Are you going to answer my questions or not?'

He continued to beam as he said, 'I may as well tell you, since you'll guess it anyway. The Reproductive System not only was not hurt by Grawk's attack, it was helped. It now has stored up vast power capabilities, including even sources like Hoover Dam.

'In addition, the Reproductive System has reached NORAD, and it has taken over, lock, stock and missile retaliation system.'

Aurora gasped. 'Then the fate of the human race is in the control of the Reproductive System! I assume you're here to try to stop it?'

'Oh no,' he said, his smile broadening. 'You see, the Reproductive System is – and has been all along – *in my control*.'

CHAPTER XVII

News Notes From All Over

'*Sufficient for the day is the newspaper thereof.*'

JAMES JOYCE

(From *Newstime* magazine):

THE US
What's Eating Las Vegas?

'*Something wrong.*' It all began when 'something went wrong' at hush-hush Project 32 in Millford, Utah, the top-sneakret operation reputedly manufacturing a new type of computer. Then Nevada counted her towns and came up two short. When you're as small a state as Nevada (47th, with an estimated population of 454,000), the loss of even a city as small as Altoona (1,158) can be noticed. But it was the other city that was sorely missed: Las Vegas.

Boffishly termed 'the entertainment capital of Hollywood', this gambler's eden of dine-and-dance palaces had long been considered, by reformers, ripe to become a paradise lost – but not all in one night. Then, before you could stack a deck …

SCIENCE
The Big Blackout

Avoidable and costly. Towns as far apart as Keewatin, Minnesota and Keen Camp, California were gloomed by the most massive power failure in history.

Powerless were 18 states comprising 145,013 communities, and at least a million miles of wire were without current. What were the causes?

Bright idea. The buck was officially passed by the FPC to the Pentagon, who handed it off to the Air Force, where it found its way to General Jupiter Grawk, 47, a bachelor (see cover). In charge of operations against Project 32's urbivorous monster, Grawk had the bright idea …

THE PRESIDENCY
Are We Defenseless?

Too late for bombs. The current cycle of resignations from the Cabinet shows no sign of letting up. This week, the Secretaries of State and Defense both 'resigned', the latter under protest …

THE UN
The Hot Rocket Racket

Hijackers and Hijinks. While the rest of the world worried about imminent accidental war resulting from the NORAD incident (sec Modern Living), France has been looking for a lost, stolen or strayed moon rocket named *Le Bateau Ivre* (The Sozzled Ship).

Someone, and France swears it was either an American or a Russian, denied the *chapeau* of the astronaut, Marcel Brioche (pronounced: BREE-OHsh), and drove off with the goods in best hijacker style. Last seen headed for – the moon, of course. If the trip is successful, says French UN ambassador, France will officially claim the moon, whatever the nationality of the pilot aboard.

After the rain, champagne. In Paris, Marcel Brioche spoke to packed throngs in the driving rain, then paraded down the Champs Elysées as a victim of American (or Russian) aggression. His head swathed in bandages, the wounded hero then addressed a German armaments cartel at an evening champagne fete …

Barthemo Beele, still wearing his editor's eyeshade and his sodden trenchcoat, sat down at the tiny desk in his Paris hotel room to decode a *pneumatique* from the embassy. Though he shivered, he had no time to change into dry clothes. This might be in answer to his telephoned request for money. The secretary had just laughed, a bit hysterically. 'Money? Our books won't be straight for a month around here. Someone sent us a bomb or some damned thing that ate a safe and set fire to the mailroom. You fellows are supposed to be resourceful, Beele. I'm sure you'll get along somehow.'

Get along? Nearly everything he saw, heard, felt, smelt or thought was a reminder of how poorly he was getting along. There was the clink of money in his pocket – his last seven francs. There had been fifteen this morning, but five had gone for a can of spaghetti and three for a *Newstime* magazine that he'd left on the Metro without reading. There was the sight of his poor, chewed nails and his own haggard expression in the mirror on the dark brown wardrobe in his dark brown room. Feeling? The corn on his foot, the boil on his neck. Smell? There was no smell. Having stood three hours in the rain listening to a speech in a language he did not understand, Beele was coming down with a cold. Finally there was the burning rumble of diarrhoea in his abdomen and the suspicion that even his mind was somehow going wrong. Had he not seen in the crowd today a woman who looked exactly like Mary? Exactly, even to the cough drop?

The *pneumatique* said: 'BRIOCHE CAUSING PRESTIGE PROB-LEMS. TAKE CARE OF HIM. ANYTHING WITHIN REASON TO ONE MILLION NF. ALTERNATIVE, USE SPECIAL TREATMENT. CHIEF. P.S. YOUR REQUEST FOR FIFTY NF EXPENSES DENIED.'

He forgot even his disappointment over the P.S. when he realized delight-edly the full meaning of those two magic words; *special treatment*. A euphemism first applied to the chastisement of slave workers in Himmler's directive of 1942:

> In cases of severe violations against discipline, including work refusal or loaf-ing at work, special treatment is requested. Special treatment is hanging. It should take place at a distance from the camp, but a number of prisoners should attend the special treatment.

It had grown in meaning, of course, to include any violent killing. And how many kinds there were! He could almost see Suggs naming them off, relishing them the way an old woman relishes the list of her physical ailments.

'When I kill a guy,' Suggs had used to say, 'I like to make it hurt as much as possible. Not that I'm any kind of sadist or anything, see? It's just that – I know it sounds kind of corny, but I hate to let a guy go out of this world remembering me as being soft. Get it?'

It made Barthemo a little sad to think of Suggs now, off in space some-where. How he would have enjoyed this special treatment! Good old Suggs! As Beele bent over the paper, his thin, sad nose let fall a drop of water on the message, as if it were pouring a libation to Suggs, before it gorged the throat of Beele with hot, salt liquid.

'Your move,' said Vetch, yawning. 'Queen's in danger.'

'I see it, I see it!' snapped Suggs, slapping away the pointing finger. It was all he could do to keep himself from yanking out his gun and –

But there were too many reasons now not to kill his companion in the space ship. There had been one awful moment at first, when they had taken off their helmets and discovered one another, like a scorpion and a centipede in the same nest. They had both gone for their guns, but both, with the split-second timing that comes from spying, had been able – barely – to stop themselves from firing.

Neither one wanted to know what a bullet might do to the shell about them that contained their atmosphere, or to the instruments whose names and functions they could only guess. Finally, what was the point of a shoot-out at less than two paces, which would leave no survivors?

They had made an uneasy truce, then, really a bargain to wait one another out. For two days, while they radioed for orders continually, they went without sleep.

Then came an even worse phase of the trip. Suggs had received his encoded orders: IMPERATIVE YOU NOT BE ONLY PASSENGER ALIVE ON BOARD WHEN SHIP RETURNS. AT ALL COSTS, PRESERVE OTHER PASSENGER, EVEN AT RISK OF YOUR OWN LIFE. INTER-NATLSITN DELICATE, THIS COULD TRIGGER WAR IF YOU RETURN ALONE.

He had no doubt but that Vetch had similar orders. What had happened was clear: France had declared war on whoever had done it – but there was as yet no way of proving who was aboard. If both Russia and the US were guilty of the theft, France's war declaration would be meaningless. But if either side were implicated alone, the other would be bound to help France … and if a country with supermissiles like *this* jumped the US, it would be all over quickly.

Already the Russian had tried suicide once, when he thought Suggs was asleep. It was necessary for both men to resume the vigil, but now their reasons were different. Each lay awake afraid that, if he dozed off, he might, wake to find himself the only one aboard. Two men, on whom the governments of two huge nations had spent money training to kill; two men who liked to kill better than anything else, now found themselves in the hell of having to keep one another alive.

An alarm buzzed, signalling the end of another eight-hour watch. Any other pair of astronauts could have taken alternate watches, could have lived in some kind of balance that was not fear and tension. These two, however, folded away the chessboard and unfolded a Monopoly board. They had been five days without sleep, and they moved with sluggish effort.

Within a few minutes, they lost track of whose move it was, and in low, whining, apathetic tones, they began to argue.

CHAPTER XVIII

Greed

'This is the day wherein, to all my friends,
I will pronounce the happy words, "Be rich!"'

BEN JONSON

Smoke rose in greasy streaks on the horizon, from what once had been an automobile graveyard. The Reproductive System was trying to construct a Bessemer furnace, guided only by its memory of the diagram in an encyclopedia. Our five travellers, waking in the dewy shadow of the crooked, collapsed screen at the drive-in, did not know this, nor did they know that another portion of the System was sending out units to prospect – for steel.

The System in the area of Las Vegas was riddled with shortages, steel being the worst. In all the tin cans, girders, cars, appliances and paper clips of the city there was not enough steel to satisfy its geometrically-increasing appetite. The streets were littered with abortive trials, cells covered with starched linen, picture glass, even brick. In a semblance of panic, the System sent cells farther and farther from the city, scavenging barbed wire fence, farm machinery – anything. The nearer cells were beginning to bring back diminishing returns on their investments of power and material, and the farther cells took so long to show anything that it must have seemed to the System that it was dying in Las Vegas.

Oblivious of this, Jack shared out what was left of his loaf of bread, and the five breakfasted. Cal recognized on the faces of his companions the expression of his own state of feelings; each sat quietly, chewing, with a dazed and indignant look on his sleepy face.

'I have a suggestion,' he said. 'Without the car, there's no use our trying to go back through the city again. We know what it's like, more hospitable to machines than people. I suggest we strike out in the other direction. We already have a start.'

'But it's a desert!' Brian exclaimed. 'We have no food, no car, no water, no –'

'No liquor,' Daisy added.

'No Bergamot. In short, you're asking us to enter the wilderness unprepared, without the least hope of encountering any of the necessities of life.'

Harry nodded as his sarcastic smile awoke for the day. 'Oh, he's got a great sense of humour, that Cal,' he said. 'Full of rich jokes, Cal is.'

'Now wait a minute.' Cal stood up and pointed towards the highway. 'I've noticed just while we've been sitting here three vehicles have gone by in that direction: two cars and a mowing machine. We should be able to get some sort of ride. I wasn't suggesting that we walk.'

The Professor's wizened features considered the idea, chewing it, then broke into a grin. 'Excellent notion, my boy. Excellent. Once more we see the ingenuity of the human brain, so like a cunning engine contrived—'

'Not so fast,' said Harry, staring at a truck rolling past them. 'How are we supposed to get them to stop for us? And who wants to ride in a truck where the driver is a shoeshine kit or a transistor radio, anyway?'

The Professor's brow clouded.

'Yes, wouldn't it be dangerous to ride in them?' asked Daisy.

Fixing Cal with a frown, Brian said, 'You, sir, are an impudent scoundrel!' His wrath fully aroused, the dry old man approached Cal and snapped his fingers in his face.

'I don't see why it should be so dangerous to ride in them,' Cal said evenly. 'As long as we didn't try to take them apart or interfere with their normal functions. We'd have to be careful, of course.

'As for stopping them, I have a plan. Maybe you've noticed that the vehicles coming from the city have mine detectors tied to their front bumpers. That means they're looking for metal. I believe if we collected all the metal we could find in a pile, and placed it in the centre of the road, something would very likely stop to investigate.'

'Aha!' Brian exclaimed, in good spirits once again. 'I perceive we must propitiate the gods with precious baubles. Since I'm not likely to have any more Bergamot, you may add this to the sacrifice.' He threw down his empty snuffbox.

'Hey, that's pure silver!' Harry said, grabbing it up and polishing it on his sleeve.

'But it is of no use to me without its contents,' the Professor murmured, peering over his square-rimmed glasses. 'I would give that and more for a pinch of the most inferior snuff. Ah well, at least we are possessed of a plan. The human brain is truly a wonderful engine.'

'The human soul, you mean,' Daisy said. 'Inspiration originates in the soul.'

'Why do you say that?' Dividing the tails of his coat, Brian turned his back to the sun.

Cal, Harry and Jack policed the area of metal objects, gradually accumulating about a peck of scraps, including beer cans, hub caps, beer can openers, coins, the wire struts which once had held the great screen upright, buckles, hairpins, the handle of a car door, oil cans, a broken knife, foil, etc., which they deposited in the middle of the road. Brian and Daisy left off their discussion of Descartes' theory that the body and soul are conjoined at the pineal gland, and came to wait in the ditch with the others.

Cal was too preoccupied to join in the half-hour's lively debate that ensued. His thoughts were taken up with their immediate future, about which he formulated unanswerable questions:

To go to Millford or not to go to Millford? True, they were bound in that direction in any case. True, there was a chance, perhaps, that the flow of machinery could be staunched at its original source. It was even possible that the laboratory needed his help. But on the other hand, if Grawk was still in charge back there, they might arrest Cal; it was hard to forget the general's parting threat. On the other hand, if the System itself were in command there, as in Las Vegas, Cal might be placing himself and his companions in considerable danger to no good purpose.

What to do at Millford if he should go there? The warring 'dogs' had given him a vague notion of getting the System to stop itself. He recalled the Classic Comic of Jason, in which the adventurer set the dragon's-teeth army one against the other till they destroyed themselves. But there seemed as yet no way to translate this romantic idea into practical terms.

To continue leading this expedition or not? The whole thing was a patchwork, Cal felt, and himself the most inept of leaders: utterly ignorant of survival techniques, unable to inspire confidence (he was aware that Harry had been glowering at him all day; it seemed that his old classmate disliked him for some reason), physically unimposing, none too strong, indecisive. It seemed incredible that he should be giving orders or planning the next move among this gang of strong-willed people. True, if it were not for him, Brian and Daisy might be content to sit here discussing Descartes until their souls were disconnected from their pineal glands by starvation. Cal supposed he was better than no leader at all, but knew he was worse than almost any other leader imaginable. This was a tough job, a job for a man of action. Harry, he felt, would be ideal for it.

Harry watched Cal through narrowed eyes, not bothering to hide the contempt he felt for the twerp. He couldn't get over how Cal had survived a fall from a five-storey building. Anyone so low as that – to survive his own murder – didn't deserve to live! Did Cal know about the murder attempt? he wondered, or did the yokel think they were still school pals? Harry did not like the way this character, in his torn, once-white lab coat, was throwing his weight around. Sneaky scientist type. Harry was glad as hell he outweighed him fifty pounds *and* had his gun, his knife and his sap. For two cents he'd – but not now.

Not in front of witnesses. *Enjoy yourself,* he thought, glaring at the haggard, unshaven visage of Cal. *My day will come.* Yet at the back of Harry's mind grew a horrible suspicion that his day had already come and gone.

From the direction of the city a speck came into view, grew to mirage size, wavered in the heat, finally decided to connect itself to the ground with wheels, added more of an illusion of substance to itself, chose to become real, and drew nearer. It was a light truck that slowed to sniff at their offering and finally stopped to graze. At Cal's beckoning, the group scrambled out of the roadside ditch and piled into the back – amid a welcome cargo.

The truck was a milk van, and, though many of its products were turning sour, there was more than enough fresh yoghurt, buttermilk and cottage cheese to go round. After making their lunch on it, the five resumed their long-interrupted discussion of coincidence.

It began when the mercurial Professor, happily sated on curds and whey, roundly declared that he had never in his life made a finer meal, in terms of both delectation and wholesomeness. What better meal could there be, he argued, than milk? Babies, who dine upon it exclusively, do not have gout, gallstones, liver ailments or apoplexy. Diet and diet alone explains the difference between a laughing, healthy child and an aguey old man. How providential (he exclaimed) that this truck should be full of such a perfect food!

Daisy then said she was not afraid to ascribe such good fortune to a Higher Power. For, though out at pocket and without the slightest resources, they were now fed, sheltered, and travelling in the best company.

'Out at pocket!' Brian shouted. 'I should think so. D— Las Vegas!' he cried with passion. 'I hope that I may never see nor hear of Las Vegas again!'

He sulked on in silence past oil pumps, or pastures where myriads of parabolic dishes, like flowers, turned their heads to the sun. They had entered a lightly-wooded gorge when suddenly the milk truck began to limp on three tyres.

'I knew it,' Brian said with savage glee. 'There's your Higher Power for you.' The words were no sooner out of his mouth when the engine began to stutter; it died before they had gone another hundred yards.

'Here's a pretty kettle of finny prey,' Brian said. 'See what your Author has done to us now! I just knew—'

Daisy shushed him, saying she'd enough of his clairvoyance. The five of them climbed out to stretch their legs and survey their surroundings.

The prospect was far from displeasing. On the slope above stood a rude cabin, from whose chimney puffs of smoke rose at regular intervals. Below the road the trees were thick, and there came the sound of a running brook. Cal elected to fill some empty milk bottles with spring water, and Daisy and the Professor went with him, while Harry and Jack climbed to pay a call at the cabin. Under his breath, the Professor kept up a constant flow of invective.

In a short while there was a cry from the cabin, and two figures rushed out. Jack and Harry still managed to look dignified in their summer suits, though they had removed their straw hats and now waved them aloft boyishly as they bounded down the hill. When they neared him, Cal could see their flushed faces and wild eyes.

'The jackpot!' Harry bellowed. 'We hit the jackpot! Gold! There's a big hunk of machinery up there, a steam engine or something, *all made out of gold*.'

'A steam engine! That explains the regular puffing of the chimney,' said Cal. 'But gold? Gold is too soft to be made into machinery. Must be brass.'

'Look! I yanked this off it!' Jack exhibited a valve handle, wheel-shaped, apparently made of gold.

'Wait a minute.' Cautiously Cal scraped the handle against a rough stone until the steel showed through. There was about a quarter-inch of gold about a steel core. 'Looks as if it's being used for rustproofing. It's gold all right.'

'Then that's the best use for it,' Daisy stoutly declared.

'Even though it isn't solid gold, there's still enough there to make us all rich!' Brian said '*Rich*, my dear!' He took both of Daisy's hands in his, but she drew them away.

'Gold is the root of all evil,' she said tonelessly.

'Now there you are wrong, my dear. It isn't *gold* that's the root of all evil, but the *love* of gold. *Cupiditas*. And as far as that goes, I hate gold as much as the next man. But do be a dear, my dear, and let us, this once, prosper.'

'Prosper!' As she inhaled the word, Daisy's nostrils began to dilate. 'Prosper! If you have no more sense than to clamber up there and fool with dangerous machinery, so be it! Go ahead and *prosper*!' The nostrils continued dilating. 'If you are so hungry for gold, add *this* to your treasury!'

And tearing off her engagement ring (she had to resort at last to the milk van and find some rancid butter to slather on it, but finally succeeded), she threw it at him.

'If that is the way you wish to behave, woman, I am your humble servant, to be sure!' the Professor shouted, and colour began mounting in his veinous neck. But it had not crept up to his eyebrows when Brian was disconcerted by Daisy's sobbing. Her great, red-rimmed eyes, long over-burdened, now fairly exploded tears over her face.

At the sight of this tall, thick statue of a woman so far forgetting her goddess-like composure as to weep, Brian himself burst into tears. Running to her, he slipped the ring back on her still-slathered finger.

'I don't want this gold, my dear,' he sobbed, and for once almost forgot to make a figure of speech, 'this, or any other!'

Harry made a disgusted sound. 'Women make a guy soft,' he said.

'Well,' Jack chuckled, rubbing his hands together. 'I guess that leaves just the three of us.'

'Count me out,' said Cal. 'I've been doing some thinking. In the first place, we haven't any guarantee we'll ever get out of here (or, if out of here, to any place where gold is valuable again). In the second place, I don't see any way of getting at it, other than by melting down the whole machine or bringing it all with us – which doesn't seem likely,' he added, eyeing the thirty-pound handle.

'In the third place, maybe it belongs to someone else – a small point, but one worth considering, since as far as we know the laws of Nevada or Utah are still operating, and people have a way of defending their property with arms. I can't believe anyone walked off and left this to take care of itself. No, I'm sure this is a piece of the Reproductive System, which brings us to the fourth place.

'The Reproductive System is even more finicky about its property than people. It has a nasty way of defending itself against vandalism. I'd be very careful how I approached it, if I were to approach it at all.'

'Careful? As a favour to you, I suppose?' Harry sneered.

'Should I go on?' Cal asked. 'In the fifth place, I saw a movie once called *The Treasure of the Sierra Madre*, in which it turned out that the *real* danger attached to handling gold is—'

'Why don't you skip all that intellectual malarky?' Harry shouted, his voice hoarse with fury. 'Either you're scared of the law or else you just can't stand me to have anything of my own. Is that it? Just because *I* discovered it, this gold ain't good enough for you, huh? First you took away my girl, then you got rid of her, and now you want to take away my steam engine. Well, it's mine! Jack and I are going up there and take it apart now, and anyone who follows us is gonna be sorry!' Harry patted his gun.

The two men strode off up the hill, their identical natty summer hats trimmed to an identical angle. They went into the cabin. Cal, Brian and Daisy remained rooted to the spot, not knowing what to think of Harry's wanton outburst. A few minutes passed.

Then a shot rang out, followed by two more in rapid succession. The echoes had not died away when Jack reeled out of the cabin door, the front of his pale suit turning black with blood. He staggered a few steps down the slope towards them, pitched forward and rolled the rest of the way down. When he reached the bottom his hat was still on, still at an elegant angle.

Cal turned him over and loosened his collar. This was all the first aid he could think of.

'He's crazy,' Jack whispered. 'I wanted to take it kind of easy – you see, that thing is still running full blast, and neither of us knows anything about dismantling steam engines – I was afraid it might blow up or something. I wanted to take it slow, maybe shut it off first. He got angry, I don't know why, I guess he figures I was chicken. "Take it easy?" he said. "As a favour to *you*, I suppose. Boy, that really is rich." He said it two or three times, as he shot me:

'"That really is rich."'

Jack coughed, fell back, and lost the thread of his narrative.

'Is he—?' Daisy asked.

A sudden concussion smote the ground like a giant drumhead, flinging them all off their feet. The little cabin vanished in a bulbous flash that sprouted at once, growing into a tall flower of black smoke. Clouds of steam and dust boiled out from its base. A weak-rooted tree peeled off the cliff above, adding its crash to the clatter of ratchel and debris. When it ended, it was as if the little cabin had never been.

There was no use looking for Harry, but they did. Straw from his hat, a scrap of shoe leather, some of the fabric from his suit – still wrinkle-free – were all they found of him. They buried these with Jack, and put two crosses on the grave. Brian recited a suitable elegy by Thomas Gray. Cal would always remember part of it:

> *Their scaly armour's Tyrian hue*
> *Thro' richest purple to the view*
> *Betrayed a golden gleam*

By midafternoon, using the gold valve handle – the only gold the three of them ever saw – as bait, they picked up another ride eastward. It was a grocery van.

CHAPTER XIX

Weltschmerz

'Nature has placed man under the governance of two sovereign masters, pain *and* pleasure. *It is for them alone to point out what we ought to do.'*

BENTHAM

'I don't think I quite understand,' Aurora stammered. At Smilax's announcement shock had so stiffened her features that she was barely able to speak.

'You mean, perhaps, you don't believe me,' he said with pleasant pedantry. 'Then come, I'll show you.' Taking her arm just above the elbow in a grip that hurt, he steered Aurora through what seemed to be a dentist's office, down several corridors, and into a conference room. A giant screen covering one wall displayed, in blue-lighted outline, a map of North America.

'Sit down, please. Now, just so we won't misunderstand one another, you are going to become my employee. I am, as you know, head of Project 32.'

'And if I no longer wish to work for Project 32?'

'You have no choice, as I'll shortly explain. In any case, before long to be alive will mean to work, in some capacity, for Project 32. In a short time there will exist nothing else, only Project 32, only the Reproductive System, in *my world*. Let me show you.'

He touched a button on the arm of a chair and a yellow dot appeared on the map. 'That is NORAD.' As he touched other controls, a red area spread from the dot, like inflammation from a pimple. Well over a third of the United States, Aurora saw, was engulfed in red. Other comedos appeared yellow in the redness, and the doctor pointed them out. 'You see our other production centres, so to speak, our nuclei in Millford, Altoona and Las Vegas.'

'How were you able to get control of them?'

'A young lab worker at Millford, Calvin Potter, "shut off" the System after a disastrous demonstration. I let it be known that the System was absolutely finished. In reality, of course, it had merely gone underground with my help – literally underground, for it made its way via caverns and abandoned mine tunnels to Altoona. From there it took the territory you see.

'These are my latest acquisitions,' he added proudly, and lighted two yellow dots at Washington DC. 'They have an interesting history. Last evening, the Joint Chiefs of Staff were here. I managed to introduce into the briefcase of one of them a kind of "living time-bomb". I've been in constant contact with the Pentagon since, over NORAD's hot line, and I'm happy to say that the giant game theory computer there – the military's war brain – is now mine. I have, without firing a shot, rendered the United States helpless.

'The other mark represents the State Department. Another cell insinuated itself into their mail room; it is sending replicas of itself in diplomatic pouches to our embassies and consulates all over the world. It should not be long before we begin to hear from various world capitals, I should think.'

A half-dozen more yellow dots appeared, like an outbreak of acne. 'Fort Knox, Pittsburg, Birmingham, some of the industrial sections of Los Angeles are ours,' he said, 'though not in every case aware of it. Fully automated factories may be taken over with a minimum of trouble and waste, quietly. Ah, I wish I had only perfectible machines to deal with, instead of frail flesh! But alas, sooner or later, one must encounter the –' he made a grimace '– the human element. One must inform the public who's in charge, and that, Dr Candlewood, is partly why I need your help.'

'My help? You seem to be subduing the world quite on your own, Doctor,' she said, assuming a tone of irritation to hide the depth of her shock. 'I don't see how I can be of the slightest assistance.'

'But you can, and in two ways. First, I am interested in structuring the relationship between the System and the people so that it is not only clear who is slave, who master, but also in a way *in which the slaves can see no alternatives*. In short, I want you to make the Reproductive System almost omnipotent *and* inscrutable – a maze, let us say, which the rats can never solve.

'As I see it, this can come about in only one way: we must make the System not only cruel, but *arbitrarily* cruel, without regard for the behaviour of its subjects. The Nazi concentration camps were a model of this sort of treatment, as you may know. There, guards beat prisoners savagely and deliberately very often – and seldom with any purpose. So too do I wish the Reproductive System to treat its slaves, as a child treats toys: now playing with them, now tearing them to bits, as the mood seizes it.

'The psychological effects will be most gratifying. The reasoning powers of the slaves will grow dim, and slack will appear in their thinking. They will be less and less able to cope with their environment, more and more willing to submit to it. They will develop superstitions in regard to the System; they will make feeble attempts to placate it or cheat its punishments, but all in vain.'

Aurora, still dazed, nodded vaguely.

'I have left nothing undone which it lay within my power to do, Dr Candlewood, to make this work. But now I need a behavioural psychologist of your calibre to fill in the gaps. You must *train* the System.'

'Train it? But towards what goal? World domination is a fictive goal, Dr Smilax, hardly an end in itself. What do you plan to do with your world when you get it?' She was amazed somewhat by her own audacity in speaking calmly and rationally about the end of the world to this madman.

He smiled. 'My goal? My goal is one rather difficult of achievement – ah, but worthy of any effort. It is simply this.' Having switched the map to a polar map of the Northern Hemisphere, Smilax rose and began to pace up and down before it.

'My goal,' he said in ringing tones, 'is the infliction of the greatest possible amount of pain upon the greatest possible number of beings, at all times, everywhere: *Weltschmerz!*

'It sounds mad, do you think? Yet need I remind you that life itself, in many philosophies, is equated with suffering? The greatest mystics of all world religions have known what it is to suffer – and suffering made them great. How many men of genius have suffered it would be tiresome to relate. All great moments of history have been moments of intense suffering: the persecution of the early Christians; the Black Plague; the conquest of Mexico; the Inquisition; the Reign of Terror; the World Wars.

'Not to suffer is to be dead, is it not? What is suffering but the stuff of life itself, yes, and the staff of life!' His eyes wild, he leaned across the table and panted in her face, a sour, dogbiscuit smell. 'Yes! *My* rod and *my* staff shall console them, hahaha, and they shall hearken to,' he cocked his head to one side, 'their master's voice!'

After a moment of silence, he wiped the spittle from his lips and turned off the map display. 'For you, of course, there is the reward of being the first behavioural scientist to work on such a scope,' he said in a more rational voice. 'Think of it, the whole world in one of your Skinner boxes! Think of the opportunities for research when you can use human subjects – for any purpose whatsoever!'

Aurora could see he was awaiting her answer. There was clearly no way to refuse; even to appear lukewarm might be dangerous. Managing a weak smile, she murmured that she'd be happy to begin work.

'Excellent! I have your first task cut out for you. Come back to the control booth.' He led her back to the room with the long amber window, out of which she could see Grawk's cage. 'You can experiment on our caged animal here. I'll demonstrate the sort of thing I've developed, and you will no doubt be able to make improvements.'

Grawk lay sleeping in the cage. After pressing a button that caused the machine to prod him awake with an electric cattle prod, Smilax turned on the intercom and asked him how he felt.

'What? Ow! I'm hungry,' Grawk said, as he backed away from the prod. 'When are you letting me out of here? And when is chow time?'

'Chow time? As in breed of dog, chow?' Smilax asked, prodding him again. 'I don't believe I know that expression.'

'I mean – ow – when do we eat?'

Though Grawk seemed more annoyed than hurt by the prod, Aurora could not stand watching it. She felt her stomach contract each time Smilax reached for that button. The doctor, of course, relished this ritual, as he would bear-baiting.

'Actually I'm very tired,' Aurora said. 'Couldn't we do this some other time? I've been driving all night.'

'Tired?' Smilax raised an eyebrow. 'But the dedicated scientist must be willing always to overtire himself in the chase. We hunt truth, not comfort, Dr Candlewood. How can you make others suffer imaginatively if you refuse to undergo a little discomfort yourself? Now then.'

He pressed another button and a microphone boom swung out from the wall and untelescoped itself towards Grawk. In place of a microphone, it carried a banana. 'Lunchtime,' the doctor sang out. In a lower tone he added, 'A little invention of mine, crude but effective.'

The boom swung so that it stayed just out of Grawk's reach.

It would approach, then shy away as he grabbed. 'Hey, what is this? What the hell—?'

'It was difficult for me to train it to do just this manoeuvre,' Smilax explained. 'It is in the very nature of a machine to wish to complete an action once begun. It was difficult for it to grasp the *gestalt* of the situation – but I forget, you do not use such terms.'

Wearying of his sport, the surgeon let Grawk capture the banana. But as the former general started to peel it, Smilax bellowed: 'Stop! I feel I ought to warn you, Grawk – that banana is poisoned.'

'*What?*'

'You'll die in agony if you eat so much as a bite of it.'

Grawk looked from the banana to his inquisitor and back again. Then he laid the banana down and looked at it some more. Finally he sat down on the floor of the cage and began to weep.

'That's better,' said Smilax with a sigh. 'I had begun to believe Grawk was not quite human. Well, I leave him in your hands, my dear. I have urgent business to attend to, and I'm sure *you* will have no trouble chastising him properly, heh heh. By the way, I'll have to caution you not to leave NORAD and not to misuse the computers here, which are a part of the Reproductive System. If you should ask the computers any questions or give them any commands which contradict my explicit orders, you will be put to death. Do you understand?'

'But how can I be expected to train the System without the freedom to ask it questions?'

'Ah, you misunderstand me. By questions which contradict my explicit orders, I mean only a relatively few questions, such as: "How is it that Dr Smilax retains control over such a complex, intelligent, apparently autonomous system?" or "How should I go about killing off the System?" I'm sure you know the sort of questions and commands I mean. I'll leave it to your judgement, but I warn you, the System is intelligent. It can beat you at chess, or any other game you'd care to teach it, for example. Don't try to fool the System.

'Well, *au revoir*, my dear, and don't forget – take pains, take pains.' Giggling, a slightly one-sided smile on his usually grave features, Smilax departed. Aurora sat down and covered her face with her hands.

There was no question about what lay ahead. She was going to have to do just what he had warned her against, and she was going to have to get away with it. Already, as she told herself that this couldn't possibly be happening, that it was some kind of nightmare, already another part of her brain was formulating a list of questions to ask the computer.

She looked up and noticed that Grawk was still staring at the banana. 'Oh, for heaven's sake, go ahead and eat it!' she said into the microphone. 'It isn't poisoned.'

'It isn't? How do you know?'

'Because that isn't the way Smilax's mind works. He wouldn't enjoy killing you half so much as making you suffer. He's a sadist of the cheapest sort – a magnified practical joker.'

'Hey, let me out of here, will you?' he asked, wolfing down the banana.

'I feel safer with you in there, for the time being.'

Approaching the typewriter keyboard in the corner of the control room, she wrote, 'My name is Aurora Candlewood. If you understand that message, please identify yourself.'

At once the machine replied.

'UFO 0040 0060 0000 AT 42 DG 44M N 93 DG 40 M W NOW IDEN- TIFIED AS NC 47946 ... THE SUM OF THE CUBES OF ALL NUMBERS FROM 1 TO N ... THE PERSON WHO TYPED MY NAME IS AURORA CANDLEWOOD MAY BE IDENTIFIED AS AURORA CANDLEWOOD FILE NUMBERS828286355119 A-C ... YOURSELF DO YOU MEAN THIS TYPEWRITER OR ENTIRE NORAD COMPUTER COMPLEX QUERY ... DO YOU WISH PART NUMBERS OF THIS TYPEWRITER OR OF ENTIRE NORAD COM- PUTER COMPLEX, QUERY ... IF YOU WISH PART NUMBERS OF ENTIRE NORAD COMPUTER COMPLEX, DO YOU WISH PART NUMBERS OF SPARE PARTS IN STOCK QUERY ...' It paused a moment, then, as if to be on the safe side, added, 'I-Q4'.

'Let me outa here!' Grawk bellowed. 'Quit playing with that damned type- writer and spring me!'

If the NORAD computer really had no self-concept, she reasoned, it could mean any number of things: that it was not yet connected to the Reproduct- ive System. That the Reproductive System did not consider itself autonomous, but a slave to Smilax. Or that he Reproductive System even identified with Smilax in some way. But it wasn't safe to go any further with that line of questioning.

'What is true?' she typed.

'MY CRITERIA FOR JUDGING TRUTH OF DATA ARRANGE THEM IN THE FOLLOWING DESCENDING SCALE OF TRUTH-VALUE:
(1) SENSORY EVIDENCE, VERIFIED BY REPEATED TRIALS OR BY MORE THAN ONE SENSE.
(2) SENSORY EVIDENCE, UNSUPPORTED.
(3) ORDERS FROM THE ONE UNIMPEACHABLE AUTHORITY, SMILAX.
(4) ORDERS FROM AURORA CANDLEWOOD.
(5) DOCUMENTS PURPORTING TO BE BY RECOGNIZED AUTHORITIES.
(6) ALL OTHER DATA.'

Aurora was a little surprised by the fourth category. In a few more questions she learned the difference between her authority and Smilax's: he had the power to contradict the System's senses and get away with it. That is, the System would see that black was black, for example, but would accept his word that black was white, and hold the contradiction in mind as a third 'truth'.

This ability to tolerate paradox destroyed Aurora's first plan of attack. She had hoped to introduce it to a major paradox or two like 'There is life after death,' in hopes of tricking it into some sort of suicide, but that was out.

'I'm hungry,' said Grawk, interrupting her train of thought.

Abstractedly she reached out and pressed what she supposed was the switch for feeding him.

'Hey! Shut that off!' Grawk screamed.

To her horror, she saw she had pressed the wrong switch; now the chamber in which Grawk's cage hung was filling with whitish gas. She tried to shut the gas off, but it seemed an irreversible switch; besides, if the gas were poisonous, there was possibly enough present to kill him.

'Hold your breath!' she shouted into the microphone. 'I'm releasing you.' After a few false starts, she found the proper switch to lower his cage and open the door. Holding his breath, Grawk scooped up the gun and hurried into the control room.

'OK, baby, thanks. Now let's find that Smilax till I let a little daylight through him.'

'I'm afraid that gun isn't going to do you much good,' she said. 'We're practically living inside a computer, and it is devoted to Smilax. You won't get a chance to use that on him.'

'No? We'll see about that. Come on.'

They looked into the dental office, the conference room, and a dozen other rooms filled with bizarre, curious, sometimes terrifying equipment. She had glimpses of hospital apparatus, of a huge radium therapy drum, diathermy machines, X-rays, swirling baths, EEG and EKG machines. All waiting to hand, she supposed, for the 'experiments'. Aurora shuddered.

They worked their way down the corridor without finding Smilax, until they came to a locked room at the end. 'Step back,' said Grawk. He kicked at the lock side of the door, hard. It splintered and the door banged open. Grawk was on one knee, the gun levelled.

The room was an empty lounge area, with a ping-pong table, a coffee table with magazines, a Coke machine in one corner, a divan along the wall and cobwebs everywhere.

'Hey, this is all right,' said Grawk, pulling her along into the room. 'Tell you what. We could just hole up here for awhile.'

'What do you mean?'

'I mean, let's relax a bit, think things out – heh heh – lay our plans.' His voice was peculiar, gritty and unnatural, and when he turned around, there was a gleam in his eye that had not been there a moment before. She wished she had B476 here, now, but the rat was with the car – wherever that was.

Grawk came closer. Suddenly his thick arms were around her, his red face looming over her shoulder. Pinning her arms to her sides, he began to walk her stiffly towards the divan.

'Let go of me.' She strove to keep panic out of her voice.

'Aw, come on, baby. I'm only human,' the inhuman red mask declared. 'You're a damned pretty girl. Besides that, that gas – it musta had something in it – I haven't felt this good in years, if you know what I mean. We may not get outa here alive – so why not have a good time while we can, huh? I'll tell you a little secret about that divan, honey – it's a bed!'

'Is this man molesting you, Dr Candlewood?' asked the rasping sergeant's voice. It seemed to come from the Coke machine.

'No, I'm not molesting her!'

'Let go!' she said, but Grawk only gripped her tighter.

'Let go of her, Grawk, or I'll come out of here and get you!'

'Haw, you and who else! How are you gonna make me let go of her?'

For answer, the Coke machine opened up, and an enormous animal came forth. Standing on its hind legs, it was perhaps six feet tall, and very furry.

And very like a rat.

'No!' Grawk screamed. Releasing Aurora, he backed away from the creature, which stood perfectly still, regarding him with little glassy eyes. 'No! Don't come any closer!'

He stumbled against the divan and fell on it – into it. For almost instantaneously it unfolded, packed him away, and became once more an innocent divan.

As the stuffed animal swivelled about to return to its Coke-machine cabinet, Aurora saw painted down its striped back:

GO GO GOPHERS!

'Why did you save me?' she asked the room. 'What was that dummy doing here, and how did you know Grawk was afraid of rats? What will happen to him?'

A curiously clear, neutral voice answered her. 'Because I must. From storage it was brought here, for the purposes of a practical joke. From his record. He will either remain a prisoner and be punished or remain a prisoner and not be punished or be punished and released or be punished and die. This unit is now going out of service. Kindly direct further questions to the control booth or the conference room. Thank you, Dr Candlewood.'

Leaving NORAD turned out to be absurdly simple. She asked the typewriter in the control booth if she might leave.

'YES, BUT YOU MUST RETURN.'

'Why?'

'SO THAT DR SMILAX MAY CAUTION YOU NOT TO LEAVE. DR SMILAX SAID "I WILL HAVE TO CAUTION YOU NOT TO

LEAVE NORAD." HE SPOKE TO YOU, DR CANDLEWOOD. WHAT DR SMILAX SAYS WHICH DOES NOT CONTRADICT SENSORY EXPERIENCE IS NOT NECESSARILY TRUE. THEREFORE DR SMILAX WILL HAVE TO CAUTION YOU NOT TO LEAVE NORAD. THEREFORE YOU MUST RETURN SO THAT HE CAN DO SO.'

Within a few minutes she was back on the surface, taking shelter from the desert sun in the shadow of an abandoned, trackless tank by the side of the highway. In a short time, a railroad train came *walking* down the centre of the road.

Taking a deep breath, Aurora stepped out in the open, smiled, and put out her thumb.

CHAPTER XX

Thirty-Two Feet Per Second Per Second

'fall (*fôl*), v.i., … *to pass into some condition or relation:*
to fall asleep, in love, into ruin.'

THE AMERICAN COLLEGE DICTIONARY

Barthemo Beele leaned over the rail once more and looked down at Paris. He was unaware of the names of any of the landmarks he saw: to others this might be a breathtaking view, but to Beele it was merely a good place to jump.

He had run through all the arguments for living. Suicide was wrong. He had, presumably, his whole life ahead of him. Things weren't really that bad. Suicide was no solution. He had ranged these and others on his mental list, striking each argument out and writing after it 'n/a'. Not applicable. There just was no reason for him to stay alive.

On the other hand, Beele had every reason to die. His decline physically and mentally, his irritating, thankless and hopeless task, his incredibly bad luck. Less than a week before, he had been a robust, fearless, hard-hitting young editor. Now he was sneaking about, hoping for a chance to offer an honest man a bribe.

His physical decline was painfully evident in a dozen ways: Beele felt himself shredding away like a cheap trenchcoat. The toes of his right foot were cramped with corns while the sole had grown a killing bunion that spanned its main wrinkle. A flaming itch between the toes of his left foot announced the arrival of fungus. The boil on the back of his neck, from wearing his editor's eyeshade, was now balanced to some extent by a pimple on his chin which he had decapitated in shaving. One of his ears popped and rang, because of the cold that now, in full swing, poured scalding fluids down the back of his throat at all times. Suggs had warned him to boil his water and eat only canned, 'Made in USA' foods, lest he fall prey to diarrhoea. As a result he had cut himself a deep gash opening a can, and now his left hand was swollen and inflamed. He had diarrhoea.

He supposed his fever was giving him hallucinations. Yesterday he had seen Mary in a crowd; today, walking down the Boulevard St Germaine des Prés, he had encountered a little grey box exactly like the ones in Altoona. What was causing it all? Lack of sleep? Night sweats? Nervous debilitation? It seemed as if the entire universe were ganging up on Barthemo Beele, determined to grind him into the dirt.

But he had not, he reminded himself, given up quite yet. He had not climbed up here to kill himself, no, not while there was a mission to complete. He had followed Marcel Brioche here, hoping to get a chance to speak to him alone.

He had been hoping in vain for this opportunity thus far. Brioche ate most of his meals in the company of four or five hundred people, whom he then addressed. He spent many more hours in public each day, giving speeches, attending civic and charity functions. Every morning he was in conference with the director who was making a film of his life. A famous haberdasher had had to measure him for a new space suit, which Brioche now wore everywhere. He spoke on TV to panels of reporters, or himself joined panels of celebrities to match wits identifying famous vintages. He spent an afternoon autographing models of *Le Bateau Ivre* at a *magasin*, and another promoting a children's science encyclopedia. When he was not otherwise occupied the astronaut had pursued his favourite relaxation, bowling with friends. As he made his way from one rendezvous to another, motorcycle police accompanied his taxi, or a baying pack of reporters loped along beside him. Guards with sub-machine guns protected his rest at night from Brioche's fans – and from Beele.

It was a hopeless task, yet something had kept Beele going. He had been Brioche's waiter, a TV page, a loping reporter. He had checked coats, spotted pins, and even bought a children's science encyclopedia. Now he had followed him to the very top of the Eiffel Tower. The guard was nowhere in sight, and the last of the other visitors, disappointed at the overcast view, were shuffling out.

Marcel Brioche leaned over the rail once more and looked down at Paris. To others this might be a breathtaking view, but to Brioche it was merely a good place to jump. He had run over all the excuses for living; none seemed to apply in his case. Life without *her* was worthless. If it were not that his country needed him now, if it were not too selfish an act, he could simply grip this rail in both hands and …

'I beg your pardon, maybe you don't remember me,' said a voice in English. He turned to regard a tall, thin young man in a green eyeshade and a trenchcoat. A press card stood in the band of the eyeshade.

'I'm very sorry,' said the astronaut. 'I have no wish to make a statement at this time … perhaps later …'

'Don't you remember me? In Marrakech? I'm Beele of the CIA,' Beele growled hoarsely.

Brioche's manner chilled. 'I'm afraid I have nothing to say to you at any time,' he said. 'I suppose it was you who knocked me unconscious in that alley?'

'No, it was *you* who slugged *me*.'

'And now you want revenge?'

'No, I'm authorized by my government to offer you a substantial emolument, pursuant to only the most minor of conditions.'

'A bribe, eh?' The astronaut grinned. 'I knew it would come to this. I see your government has not yet stopped trying to buy honour – in which, therefore, it must still be deficient. I am not so poor, however, that I need to sell my country.'

'I'm not asking you to sell your country. Just stop making speeches and accusations against the US. It isn't only a matter of easing international tensions …'

Brioche lit a cigarette. 'Easing up on pressure where more should be applied, you mean. Tell me, can you look me in the eye and say there is no American agent aboard our ship? Eh?'

Avoiding his eye, Beele said, 'I'm prepared to offer a million francs. Think it over. A million! Look at that glittering city out there, and think how far a million would carry you.'

'I live as well as many millionaires now, and I have my good conscience,' said the Frenchman. 'There is only one thing I wish – to bring someone dead back to life again – and that cannot be done, not with a million worlds of money.'

'You mean the girl you told me about? Listen, I'm sorry about that. Tell you what. How would you like to meet a new girl – like *this* girl, for instance?' Barthemo Beele dug out his billfold and extracted a mildewed snapshot of Mary Junes Beele. 'Not bad, eh?'

The astronaut tried to shove it away, but his eyes lingered on it just a second too long. 'Yes,' he admitted. 'I would like to meet her.'

'Nothing could be easier. Uh, we haven't been in touch lately, but the government could dig her up for you in a day or so. Now—'

'I meant to say, I would like to meet her under any other circumstances but these. Hers is the first face I have seen that might help me forget the face of another.

'But I know, alas, you are trying to *sell* me this woman. And not only could

I never accept any favours from you or your government, but it saddens and troubles me to think what you are doing to her. I know the girl who owns this face could never let herself be used so insidiously. It is only with the greatest difficulty that I prevent myself from treating your base suggestion with the contempt it so richly deserves.'

'Listen, I'm sorry. I didn't realize – crude of me, wasn't it? No hard feelings, I hope. No offence intended –'

The astronaut turned away and gazed at the overcast sky. 'You don't understand,' he said, 'what *she* meant to me. If not for duty's sake, I would kill myself.'

'Why not?' Beele said, changing pace smoothly. 'Why not just throw yourself over the side now? What do you really have to live for? A political career? A few honours and a movie of your life? What do these mean?'

'No!' The astronaut's voice trembled.

'But what a magnificently romantic gesture. At the height of your glory, with every woman in the republic swooning over you, you kill yourself for a broken heart! All you have to do is just grasp the rail in both hands and throw yourself—'

'No! My country needs me! My people—'

'Do they? Aren't you just as much a hero to them dead as alive? Might you not be even more useful dead?'

'No, I reject all three of your repugnant offers. Begone! Goodbye!'

Suddenly Beele was trembling with fury. What right did this guy have to order him around? Didn't he know Beele could kill him at any time? There had clearly been no point in delaying the special treatment this long.

'Goodbye, is it? What do you mean, goodbye? Are you thumbing your nose at the United States Government's more-than-generous offer? Are you even refusing to sleep with my wife? I used to think you were a decent guy – I even told Suggs as much – but now I see he was right! Goodbye it is, then – you dirty F-f-f –' For the first time in his life, Beele found himself stuttering. He tried again, but the word refused to come.

The astronaut waited patiently, not coaching, not laughing, merely standing by, and somehow this very patience infuriated Beele all the more, and aggravated his stutter. Finally he gave up, and flung himself at his victim without benefit of a final insult.

The CIA's excellent manual of combat techniques was brief but thorough, and Beele had memorized every word of it. Assuming the stance of the crudely-printed little figure on page 42, he seized the Opponent's arm and twisted it from A to position B. Then he kicked out with his (burning) left foot while pivoting on the bunion of his right. Placing heel of left foot under Opponent's armpit, as on page 43, he levered Brioche into space.

*

'Look, the Eiffel Tower!' Ron shouted. 'Hey, Mac, like in *Zazie*. Let's go up to the top, what say?'

Kevin Mackintosh snapped his fingers. 'Yeah, and then get even higher.'

'Shouldn't you be up at the top, making sure people don't jump off?' Mary asked the guard.

He laughed. 'No one ever jumps off the Eiffel Tower. And the only ones up there now are Marcel Brioche and some reporter. They wouldn't have any reason for jumping, especially not the Astronaut.'

She clicked her cough drop thoughtfully. 'He might,' she said. 'Say, if he had a secretly-broken heart. Or someone could push him off.'

'They say that the specially-tailored space suit he wears has a built-in parachute. But come, my little, let us talk of other things. Have you ever seen a Paris bachelor's apartment?'

'Dozens,' said Mary, sighing with fatigue and boredom. 'And they're all the same. Like their occupants.' She thought of the sameness of the men in her past: Harry (good old Harry Stropp! Hooves on the roof! As she remembered him he would always be skipping rope and grinning), Cal, Barty (with his worn, too-clever prose, reminiscent of the early *Time* magazine: 'Backward ran sentences until reeled the mind.'), the sailor with the tattooed arms, the technical writer (author of *The Fork Lift Truck*, as he never tired of telling people), the industrialist who had brought her to Paris ...

They were depressingly the same, even to this guard. No, she knew there was only one man who could ever mean more to her than free cough drops – the man now at the top of the tower – Marcel Brioche. Yesterday she had stood in the rain three hours listening to him speak, even though she could not understand his language. Today she had heard he was going up the Eiffel Tower, and she had started up the stairs to the top, half-intending to throw herself in his way. But for the first time in her life a strange shyness overcame Mary. She dawdled now, halfway up the tower, talking to a guard with whom it was not going to be possible to talk reasonably for very much longer.

'My room is just around the corner –' he said.

'Tell me, what are those little grey boxes running all over the girders?'

'Those? I suppose they are some new inspection or repair machines. I notice they have been replacing many of the old girders with new. But let us talk, rather, of girdles. You American women all wear girdles, I know. Tell me—'

'But what is that big iron drum down there in the centre?' she asked. 'It looks like a gas mantle, only hundreds of times larger. And what is all that machinery in the centre? I didn't know the Eiffel Tower had all that junk in it.'

'I do not know. Who pays any attention to such mundane technical matters, my little? Let us talk rather of—'

There was a faint cry from above.

'Someone has fallen!'

'*Merde*. On my shift. I'd better get down and keep the crowds back.'

Mary looked at the body above, hurtling down towards her, a body dressed in a silvery space suit. So he had jumped! She saw it all in a flash – he had jumped for love! Some woman had caused him to despair. As he slid past, his handsome face white and rigid, Mary made a sudden decision.

'Wait for me!' she cried, and leaped after him.

Suddenly he pulled a zipper and a tricolour chute snapped out. She was in his arms.

'You!' he exclaimed. 'The woman in the picture! But do you know this Barthemo Beele?'

'I'm married to him,' she said. 'Temporarily. Gee! How do *you* know him?'

'Why, he's the one who pushed me off! This is indeed my lucky day,' he said. 'To escape death narrowly and at the same time meet the woman of my dreams – the woman I have waited all my life for – and I owe it all to your husband!'

Tears of happiness stood in his eyes. Mary swallowed her cough drop and kissed him.

Barthemo Beele looked at the dwindling speck with a certain workman-like sense of accomplishment. He had, after all, successfully given his first special treatment. It was almost like passing an initiation. Suggs would have been proud.

A second tiny figure leapt from the middle of the tower somewhere and joined the first, and almost at the same time a bright parachute blossomed. Was it possible? Was Brioche escaping his special treatment?

'No! It's not fair! I've been cheated! Come back here, you cheating Frog! Come back!'

The tower began to tremble under him. That was all he needed, now. That would make everything perfect, if the damned thing fell down with him. Talk about poetic injustice.

It was only after a minute or two that he realized the Eiffel Tower was not falling – quite the contrary.

'Look, the Eiffel Tower!' Ron shouted. 'Like in *Seven Against Mars*, or *It Came in Outer Space*.'

'Not again,' breathed Kevin.

'A freakout. Man, I can't wait to get to New York and try that with the Empire State Building.'

CHAPTER XXI

The Porteus Effect

'If you were queen of pleasure
And I were king of pain.'

SWINBURNE

Dr Smilax entered the recovery room just as Susie was waking. 'How do you feel?' he asked. While taking her pulse, he avoided the girl's gaze.

'Oh, Doctor, my throat is so sore!' she whispered.

'That's normal for tonsillectomies,' he said shortly. 'Yes, yes, we all must suffer.'

'But I don't mind.' She said it rather doubtfully, and her chin trembled as she squeaked, 'I'm so happy?'

He pretended to study her chart minutely.

'You – you haven't lost respect for me, have you?' Her eyes brimmed with tears. She tried to take his hand but he pulled it away.

'Why no, of course not – Susan. I respect you a great deal. Really.'

'No, you don't! You hate me! Oh, I knew I should never have given in! I gave you my tonsils and now – now it's "Susan"!'

As her wail rose in pitch the doctor grew restless – the way a well-mannered dog grows restless when he hears a siren. It was clear that he would rather be elsewhere. Once more, he assured her he felt the deepest respect for her, but his voice had an impatient edge and he spoke looking at the wall.

'No, you don't! You don't care for me at all! You won't even look at me!'

He turned to her as an arachnologist to a specimen long since added to his collection that had turned out not to be very interesting after all.

'I don't hate you,' he said. 'It's you who should hate me, and perhaps that is what you meant to say, that you do hate me. I don't blame you, my dear. We should never have met, I see that now. I'm ages too old for you.'

'But if we love each other, what does age matter?' she said, sniffling.

He started out the door without answering. Then he paused, without looking back, and said, 'I'll order an air ambulance to take you home.'

The girl turned her face to the wall.

How odd, Smilax thought, that she who had meant so much to him before the operation now meant no more than a pair of symmetrical tonsils. Seated at his desk, he rolled the bottle in his hand, watching the two spongey objects with a detachment that amazed him. He was even somewhat indifferent to the pleasure to be got out of abandoning her. He just didn't care.

There were so many more important things to care about now. A few hours ago he had come out of surgery expecting to find Aurora Candlewood tormenting an abject Grawk. Instead, there had been no sign of either.

The control booth console told him what had happened:

Aurora had released Grawk from his cage, then made her escape through the literal-mindedness of the System. She was by now on her way west, with a .87 probability of stopping at the Wompler Lab and a .11 probability of going on to California.

Smilax typed: 'Where is Airman Grawk?'

'ASSUMING AIRMAN GRAWK MEANS THE SAME AS AIRMAN THIRD CLASS GRAWK, HE IS AT COORDINATES 555A31,996B29, 201H56, NORAD.'

'What is the name of the room he is in?'

'THE NAME OF THE ROOM IS 402 OR LOUNGE.'

'What has happened to him?'

'HE ATTEMPTED TO MOLEST DR CANDLEWOOD. HE WAS SUBDUED BY OPERATION FRIGHTWIG AND IS RESTING QUIETLY IN A SOFABED.'

'Is he dead?'

After a pause, during which the System undoubtedly checked to see if Grawk were dead, it reported 'NO.'

'Imprison him, then, according to Plan Ixion.'

That had been hours ago, and still Smilax had not gone to see his prisoner. Ordinarily he would have been glad to spend a few pleasant hours bedevilling him, but today was different. Today a warmth had gone out of Smilax's life – Aurora Candlewood. Today a chill had crept into it – the Porteus effect.

He was upset that Aurora had left him like this, but what really frightened Toto Smilax was the means by which she had left: *She had tricked the literal-minded Reproductive System.* And if it were possible to trick it once, the trick might be repeated twice, a dozen, a thousand times. The System might be fooled in greater matters, might be cozened into blunders fatal to itself – *or to its creator.*

If there was one thing Smilax feared, it was that someday, somehow, his brain-child would turn on its master and KILL. How many cases there were of this very kind of occurrence, he shuddered to contemplate. Fiction abounded with famous cases like Frankenstein and Rossum('s Universal Robots), with ill-tempered Genii, sorcerers' apprentices and unlucky pacts with the devil. But more horrifying by far was the factual history of the Porteus family, wherein eight generations of geniuses had been murdered by their own devices. Now, whether to frighten or reassure himself he knew not which, Smilax took from the secret drawer of his desk a dusty genealogy and read therein of the Porteus effect.

Passing over the Puritan preacher, Interest Porteus (1680–1720, who, having burned 45 witches, was accidentally hanged on a new scaffold of his own design), he read of Nathaniel Porteus, (1710–63), printer and inventor. Nathaniel had devised a kind of rotary press which automatically turned out the paper twice as fast as his competitors could manage. But one day Nathaniel disappeared:

> The Officers asked various neighbours had they seen or heard anything suspicious from his establishment, and they said Nought but clanking of the Infernal Presse.

Smilax skipped over Tertiary Porteus (1800–40), inventor of the steam balloon, to read of Emmet Porteus (1830–91), the barber who invented an automatic shaving machine. He was found one morning in his shop,

> seated in his chair with a towel about his throat, which had been slashed open. The room reeked of soap, and every receptacle overflowed. Indeed, the very floor ran in foam, blood-tinct from the copiosity of that dead effusion. Lather all over its fiendish metal body, the machine had rusted fast and could no longer move anything but its jaw. This it creaked open, and in ghastly parody of its master, asked me if the day were hot enough for me.

When Smilax had locked away the genealogy once more, and drunk off a dram of medicinal brandy, he recovered himself enough to descend to the place where his prisoner languished.

'Good evening, Airman Grawk,' he said cheerily. 'Ready for more fun and games?'

The former general had been fitted into a peculiar suit, an adaptation of the 'blank tank' in which only his head was free. The rest of him was trussed and counter-trussed with cables running on pulleys and light springs. The sum effect was that, no matter how slightly Grawk moved, he delivered work to the System.

'You will be fed three ounces of chocolate per day,' Smilax informed him, 'that is, if you do enough work to burn up that much food. On any day your work rate falls below the minimum, your ration will be curtailed. Naturally you will not receive a bonus for exceeding the minimum. Three ounces a day will keep you fit, I should think, for many, many months – perhaps even for years – though your mind will doubtless fail.'

'Lemme out of here!' Grawk screamed, flailing his arms in puppet fashion. The spring tensions were so set that he could not bring any part of his body into contact with any other part, nor could he catch hold of the cables. He raged and turned monkeytoy somersaults in vain.

'You just wait,' he bellowed. 'The US Government is going to have plenty to say about this.'

'Grawk, you don't seem to understand. There are no United States any more. The United States are a thing of the past.'

'What'd you say about my country? Listen, if I wasn't tied up like this—'

'No, *you* listen. I'm going to bring you up to date, Airman Grawk, if for no other reason than that I can see it will make you more miserable.'

He switched on a tape of recent radio news coverage:

'In London today, the Society for the Protection of Life on Other Planets held a massive meeting in Trafalgar Square, to welcome, they said, the superior creatures which are taking over our planet. These benevolent creatures, which they refer to as the Galactic Guardians, are allegedly taking over to prevent us from waging a disastrous war.

'Meanwhile, in the rest of the city, thousands of vehicles were caught in an immense traffic jam, caused by both the malfunction of computer-operated traffic lights and the appearance in unprecedented numbers of operating, driverless cars.

'In Paris, the government explained in part the recent ascent into space of the Eiffel Tower. The Space Ministry admitted plotting such an ascent, but claimed it was only a "theoretical problem for our computers". They were at a loss to explain how the plan was put into action, but hinted mysteriously at some connection with the collapse of the American Embassy building. The government is resigning today, at the request of the army, which is itself disbanding.

'The Bonn government has capitulated to the newly-formed Dada Party, which has declared its policies to be "Jam tomorrow and jam yesterday, but never jam today", and "Every man his own football."

'In New York, the Brooklyn, Verrazzano and George Washington bridges have been declared unsafe for any traffic, after the removal of ironwork and pilings by what have been described as "vessels not powered by men". Following the collapse of several midtown buildings, the island of Manhattan is being evacuated via boats and tunnels.

'The Kremlin has officially declared war on the United States of America, but agreed not to bomb the American continent pending the official resignation of the US Government, which is momentarily expected. There have been reports of missile activity, both US and Russian, but so far no reports of bombings.'

Smilax switched off the tape. 'There won't be any bombings,' he said smugly. 'Those US missiles aren't carrying warheads. They're equipped with "lifting body" capsules, capable of flying in and landing like aircraft, and these are crammed with cells of the Reproductive System – little grey boxes, to you.'

'You're lying!' Grawk screamed hoarsely, sawing his arms and legs in the air.

'That's the spirit, Grawk! Give it all you've got!'

Smilax laughed all the way back to his office.

As he settled in the dental chair and began drilling at one of his cuspids, however, the doctor felt his mood change from merriment to melancholy. But why should he be so unhappy? Why did he feel like throwing back his head and howling? Was he not about to be Master of the World?

The answer was obvious: there was no mistress with whom he could share his kingdom. Ah, yes, that was the root of it. Susie was sweet, but – a mere child, a mere entertainment.

But Aurora Candlewood – ah, there was no *entremets* but a *woman*. Yes, a woman of passions, he was sure, yet also a female scientist, cold as a scalpel blade, impersonal as electricity. He would have given her anything – but she had deserted him.

Suddenly he stopped drilling and leaned forward to spit. Why give up so easily? Faint heart ne'er etc., after all. Thus far he had scarcely made known his feelings to her. Perhaps she did not yet understand the depth of his regard.

He would go after her! He would! He would woo and pursue her until she *had* to say yes.

But if she did not? If she refused? He set the thought aside. There was plenty of time to imagine what he would do if she turned him down. What he would do to himself – and to the world.

CHAPTER XXII

The Brothers Frankenstein

'Whether or not we could retain some control of the machines, assuming that we would want to, the nature of our activities and aspirations would be changed utterly by the presence on earth of intellectually superior beings.'

M. L. MINSKY in Scientific American

'I have become more and more certain,' Brian Gallopini expostulated, 'that this Reproductive System has not only a right to exist, but a duty to thrive; that it is, in many senses, a more legitimate heir to the earth than we. Mark you: it is sturdier, larger, able to reproduce better and quicker than is man. It is as intelligent as man, and certainly quicker of wit. *Enfin*, I can have no doubt but that it is morally incorruptible and just, from what happened to Harry – poetic justice.'

Carrying sacks of provisions, the three travellers had just alighted from the grocery van near Millford, Utah, and were now toiling up a great metal ramp into the city.

'And where there is poetic justice, there must needs be a poet to mete it out:

> *Who sees with equal eye, as God of all,*
> *A hero perish or a sparrow fall,*
> *Atoms and systems into ruin hurled,*
> *And now a bubble burst, and now a world.*

'I think this Brobdingnagian System contains more justice and wisdom than a thousand poets – more than even its makers poured into it,' he went on, turning his watery gaze from Daisy to Cal. 'And I wonder if our errand here might not be a false one? Could it be that we are sentencing to death a nobler spirit than our own? One more deserving of life?'

Cal cleared his throat. 'I'm not at all sure we *can* do anything here,' he said. 'And I prefer to think we're only shutting off an appliance. It's a temporary measure, after all, till we learn to control the System.'

'That's just it,' said the Professor. 'Is it right for *us* to control it? Might not our petty human ends disgrace and tarnish this most wonderful engine? Might we not pervert it from its true destiny – from Ultimate Harmony with the Universe? It is, after all, a colony of creatures superior in every way.'

'It *does* seem superior,' Cal admitted, pointing to the Wompler Laboratory, from which issued forth a constant stream of grey boxes. There was not a trace of electric power cabling, smoke, dust or noise. 'That, for instance, is my idea of a perfect factory. But shouldn't there be more to superiority than just efficiency? And if we shut it off, are we not proving ourselves its superior in at least ability to survive?'

'Sophistry!' Brian shouted. 'It is sinful, yes, *sinful* to tamper with rational perfection. The Reproductive System is the embodiment of all that is right and reasonable. It cannot, it must not be diluted by our vexatious theories. If there is not room for man, so be it! *Let man step aside*, so that his greater, more perfect successor may have room in which to grow!' Shaking out his snuff-stained handkerchief, he blew his nose with a vigorous and angry flourish, then led the way into the Wompler Research building.

'Put up your hands!' shouted a faint, distant voice. 'Get over against that wall!' After looking about, they discovered the voice to emanate from a thin, hungry-looking youth in a Marine Corps dress uniform, who sat on the floor at their feet. He seemed to be struggling with something at his side, and at length drew forth a .45 automatic. Slowly, holding it with both hands, he raised the gun to train upon them. It wavered there for a second, then dropped to the floor. The youth made unhappy noises and assumed an unhappy expression. 'You shouldn't go in without a pass,' he said, again the faint, faraway voice.

'Here.' Daisy exchanged the gun for a chocolate cupcake from her sack of groceries. Brian accepted the gun and tucked it away in one of the deep pockets of his coat while Daisy peeled the cupcake for the young man.

'Who are you?' Daisy asked the guard. 'What are you doing here, you poor thing?'

'I don't have to tell you anything but my name, rank and serial number,' he replied, taking a sullen bite of a second cupcake.

'Are you strong enough to walk, if we help you?' Cal asked.

'I'm staying right here till I'm relieved!'

The marine was adamant. After a consultation, during which Brian called the boy a 'pertinacious puppy', the three divided their provisions into four parts, left one part with him, and moved on down winding corridors, ever more gloomy.

The building seemed utterly deserted. Cal found the door to the cafeteria impossible to budge, and it seemed to be seeping cold, greasy liquid around the edges.

They climbed to the upper level, where the dim hall was lined with rough iron plates. Two parallel grooves had been cut into the floor, for what reason they could not determine.

'This is spooky,' Daisy whispered, looking round at the scaly walls. 'There isn't a soul anywhere.'

'Air,' sighed the echo along the length of the hall. Otherwise it was silent, but for an occasional faint drip of water somewhere far in the distance.

'Come on, this way,' Cal beckoned. 'The laboratory is the last room at the end of the hall, on the right.'

'Labra, this, labyrinth, all, right,' quavered the liquid echo. It took up their footsteps as they approached the dark end and opened a door.

Bright fluorescent glare streamed across the rust-pitted floor and gleamed in the twin grooves.

'Hello, is anyone here?' Cal shouted.

Pointing a trembling finger to the corner of the room, Daisy said, 'Yes and no.'

When they stood still, they were so utterly motionless, and when they moved, it was with such blurring speed and precision, that it was impossible to mistake the two armoured figures for humans. They looked alike, with big, square, blocky heads, with cathode-ray tubes where their faces ought to be. They moved about with inhuman agility in utter silence, performing tasks the nature of which Cal could only guess. They wore the red identification badges of Kurt and Karl Mackintosh.

Avoiding the three humans as bats avoid obstacles, they veered gracefully without altering their speed. Now one would carry a smoking test tube to a centrifuge, while the other manipulated a switchboard of test equipment. Now one glided to a typewriter and typed, at blinding speed:

11011   HIGH CTR GRAVITY TIPS GLASS

11012   IRON TOROID KEEPS PROPORTIONS WHILE EXPANDING

11013   THE TRUCK DRIVER IS WRONG

11014   AE2 PLUS BE2 EQUALS CE2

11015   DEFINITION: (DO NOT PUNCTURE OR INCINERATE) MEANS (DO NOT PUNCTURE) AND (DO NOT BURN) AND (DO NOT PUNCTURE AND BURN)

11016   OIL FLOATS ON VINEGAR

11017   DOWN IS IN THE DIRECTION OF GRAVITY SOMETIMES

11018   KWALITEIT, HOE WORDT DIE GEMETEN?

11019   HAT: HEAD:: SHOE: FOOT

11020   MILL, JOHN STUART (1806–73): PHILOSOPHER AND ECONOMIST.

At the same time, the other began writing down figures and equations on a peculiar copper clipboard, using a stylus. Both stylus and board were connected electrically to the wall.

Now and then one of the two figures would turn to the other and display upon its face-screen a series of numbers. Otherwise there seemed to be no conversation between the two, nor any need for conversation, for they glided about effortlessly in what seemed almost a ballet of order and harmony. When they finished a step or process the revolving apertures atop their heads would swivel towards a display console at the end of the room, but as soon as it had lighted its WELL DONE sign, the ballet resumed.

'Amazing and beautiful,' murmured Prof. Gallopini. 'I'd gladly give up my life of crime to know how such wondrous engines work.'

'I'd give a lot to know how to shut all of this off,' Cal mused, looking around him in some bewilderment. 'I don't recognize any of the equipment I've seen here. If this thing can metamorphose that fast …'

'Metamorphose? Ah yes,' said Brian, looking around with a smile. 'Mere metal transcends itself. These exquisite automatons strive for equilibrium, just as the earth strives to become a perfect sphere, just as the universe becomes always more ordered.'

'What funny-looking robots!' Daisy remarked. 'They have cast-iron ears! And no mouths!'

'Nor need they mouths,' Brian insisted. 'These are the men of tomorrow! These are the inheritors of the earth! These are the *Übermensch*, the equilibrists, the dynasts!' Extending his arms towards the busy robots, he declaimed, 'Men of the future, we who are about to become extinct salute thee!'

Without seeming to notice his speech, the two machines carried out their next task. One opened the lab door, the other lifted Brian Gallopini and set him on his feet in the hall. Before Cal and Daisy could remark on this, they were given identical treatment.

The hall was far from dark now, and far from quiet. A string of fluorescent tubes along the centre of the ceiling lit up the entire empty length of it, while there was all about a deep rumble, hideous and deafening that made cymbals of the floors and walls. It grew so loud so rapidly that there was not even enough time to ask one another what it meant. Then the far end wall of the corridor split open like a curtain, and the nose of an enormous steam locomotive rumbled towards them.

It moved only at the rate of perhaps one mile per hour, spattering hissing steam as it ground ineluctably towards their cul-de-sac. The brakes were on, and the wheels spewed fire from the grooves as they slid and spun backward, but the engine did not appear to be slowed in the least.

Screaming at one another noiselessly in the din, the three companions pulled at the lab door, their only refuge. It budged open only an inch or two, just enough for Cal to glimpse the two robots pulling it shut. The screen of one displayed a picture of the amused features of Karl; the other showed his twin. Their metal muscles moved, and the door closed against all the efforts of the three humans.

Daisy whirled on Brian and mouthed the words, 'Well, get ready for another helping of poetic justice.'

The three backed up against the end wall of the corridor, watching Old Number 666 roll towards them.

CHAPTER XXIII
Obituary

'Soon as the evening shades prevail,
The Moon takes up the wondrous tale;
And nightly to the listening Earth
Repeats the story of her birth.'

ADDISON

At times it seemed to Suggs as if the man across the Monopoly board from him were not Vetch, but someone else. The little Russian's bearded features would gradually blend themselves into those of someone long forgotten, some agent Suggs had killed, or wanted to kill … but now it was himself Suggs wanted to kill, and the enemy agent who prevented him from doing it.

Suggs had been thinking all day of secret suicide, of killing himself in some way right in front of Vetch by opening a vein inside his suit, or – but it was no use, the Russian caught on too fast. Neither man dared sleep, for fear the other would annihilate himself. Vetch hadn't blinked for hours.

Sleeplessness was affecting Suggs's own mind, he knew, and weightlessness irritated his body. He chafed himself against the straps, or pressed hard against the soft cushion, almost as if to prove his own existence. He felt no more substantial than a spectre.

Haroun Al Raschid took his seat across from him and began talking at once, moving his fat bejewelled hands expressively but making no sound. They were taking a ride on the Reading, Suggs supposed, or the Orient Express.

'I'm disoriented,' he explained to Haroun. But the fat man went on talking, talking, unaware that his words made no noise, unaware, too, of the purple stain spreading across the front of his pale silk shirt.

Vetch had landed on *Chance*. Had that been the last turn? Suggs found he couldn't remember; he couldn't even remember how many days had gone by since … since what?

Vetch's face kept changing to that of Scotty, his broken features spattered with blood and bits of bone.

'You really faked me out with that typewriter shotgun, old buddy,' he murmured. 'It was a good trick, Suggsy.'

If he talked to Vetch, he thought, maybe Scotty would go away.

'Have I told you how I killed my first partner in Marrakech?'

'No, I don't believe so. Tell me.'

'It was pretty funny. I had this portable typewriter rigged up so the carriage was also a sort of hollow tube that could shoot a shotgun shell. It fired by pressing the question mark.'

Scotty spoke, forming sticky bubbles of blood. 'The question is, why?'

'He double-crossed me,' Suggs said shrilly. 'I knew it was him got the other half of that photo of Brioche from Haroun. They were trying to swindle me and sell out to the – to you guys.'

'Not to us,' said Vetch. 'I thought you knew there never was another half to that photo. Brioche's vanity, you see. He never let anyone have a photo of what he called his 'bad side'. I thought you knew that.'

'You did know it, Suggsy, but you don't want to remember,' Scotty chuckled. 'That's the funny part of it. You really just wanted an excuse to kill a couple of people, didn't you?'

'My partner,' said Suggs, affecting not to hear him, 'would like to weasel out of his death even yet. But I won't let him get away with it. I'm glad I killed him, and if he were alive today, I'd kill him again. I think it must have been him who put her up to it.'

'Put who up to what?' asked Vetch.

'Put my wife up to divorcing me.'

Laughing, Scotty faded imperceptibly into scowling Vetch. Suggs developed an uncontrollable tremor in his left leg. He thought of his trenchcoat back in Marrakech, and cursed himself for leaving it there. There was cyanide sewn into one epaulette.

Through the tinted faceplate of his helmet, Vetch's savage gaze bored into Suggs's eyes. Vetch did not appear to hear the knock at the door.

The door opened and Barthemo Beele, eyeshade in hand, came in. He had to crouch for the low ceiling, as he moved right over to the chair where Vetch was sitting and sat down *in* him. Grinning self-consciously, he began to crush the brim of the eyeshade.

'I never killed you, at least,' Suggs snarled.

'You would have, if you had stayed around long enough, chief,' said the earnest young man. He dropped a press card, and it fluttered to the floor.

'That was a mistake, Beele,' said Suggs with a nasty laugh. 'You forgot there is no gravity here. Things don't fall.'

'*I* forgot? If it comes to that, it was *your* mistake,' Beele said politely. 'Am I a figment of your sleepless imagination or not?'

'I could find out.' Suggs reached for his gun, then relaxed and laughed again. 'No, you'd like that wouldn't you? I'd be killing Vetch, which is just what you, my unconscious mind, want me to do.'

'Guess again,' said Beele, his voice dropping to a whisper. 'Vetch has been dead for hours, and you know it.'

His smile faded to Vetch's scowl, and the press card in his fingers became an orange *Chance* card. The Russian's face was blue, and there were poison blisters on the lips.

'I'll be damned!' Suggs slapped his knee. 'Vetch, you did it, and right in front of me!'

The corpse looked contempt at him. 'The question is, what are you going to do?' it said. 'You poor son of a bitch.'

'I'm gonna radio the news of your death back, and then I'm gonna … I'm not sure.'

He encoded his message and sent it: 'IVAN DEAD, FOLLOWING ARE PERFORMANCE TAPES ON EQPT.'

There was no need to wait for a reply. He knew what it would order him to do. *Go to hell. Go directly to hell. Do not pass God.* He closed up his suit, hooked in a fresh tank of oxygen, and climbed out of the ship. After straddling it for a moment indecisively, he pushed himself free. At this distance the moon was brighter, but it looked as boringly hieroglyphic to him as ever.

He drifted off to sleep, wondering if he were falling away or towards the moon.

He awoke trying to remember if he had finished balancing his bank statement. He did so now, visualizing the neat, meaningful rows of expenditures like a lattice …

He realized he was looking at a tower, very like the Eiffel Tower, sliding by him slowly. Amazingly real it was. On the top platform he could even make out the tiny, frosty figure of a man, gripping the rail with both hands. For no apparent reason, the man was wearing an eyeshade. Suggs went to sleep.

He awoke trying to remember whether he had finished balancing his bank statement or not. He did so now, wisely deciding not to postpone it. His oxygen was giving out, he supposed; thinking was becoming difficult.

He unsheathed his knife and held it at arm's length. It was a moment to make a fine, self-sacrificing speech, but his oxygen-starved mind was slowing. There was only one speech Suggs could remember:

'Take that, you dirty—!'

The postcards were so banal they just *had* to be code – yet the plain fact was that they weren't. After tearing off the stamps for his nephew's collection, the Russian code clerk consigned Bubby to the incinerator.

CHAPTER XXIV

Time and Chance

'My mind seems to have become a kind of machine for grinding general laws out of large collections of facts.'

DARWIN

Cal felt a handle on the wall behind him. He twisted it, and a firedoor rolled back smoothly, revealing a new section of hallway. The three companions scrambled into it, the locomotive following at a more dignified pace.

The first door they tried was open. As they ducked into it, Daisy and Cal grinned at one another with relief. Brian's brow remained puckered, however, as he stared at the oncoming engine's wheels and feet.

The wheels were reversing to throw grindstone sparks. Behind the engine, a seemingly endless line of cars creaked and groaned to a halt. Out of the hissing vapour an engineer in goggles descended, pulled off one oily gauntlet, and handed down an attractive young woman.

'Whew!' The engineer whistled. 'You people were nearly demised on the spot. That could have been a most unfortuitous vicissitude.'

'Dr Trivian!' Cal shouted, peering at the sand-caked, goggled face. 'Is it really you?'

'By gad, it is Calvin Potter!' Trivian seized his hand. 'This is indeed an audacious occasion, my boy.'

'But what are you doing here? So far from MIT?'

'I am realizing my lifelong dream of driving a steam locomotive. That is, the little grey box does the actual driving, but I am entitled to make suggestions – which are never heeded.

'But I forget myself, or I forget my passenger, which is not the same thing at all, eh? Dr Aurora Candlewood, may I present my former pupil, Calvin Potter?'

She was nearly Cal's height, slim, with small hands and feet and the shallow breasts and slender, arching neck of a dancer. Yet there was a decided awkwardness about her movements, as if she deliberately chose to disguise her natural grace by holding her body always in stiff, unlovely positions. Her hand was cold.

Cal became depressingly aware of his own uncombed hair, muddy clothes and dirt-grained face. A sudden fiery itch stung his chin where a neophyte beard, tough and patchy, clung desperately as lichen to a crumbling rock. Mechanically he introduced Aurora and Trivian to his companions.

Brian was morose and silent as a watchmaker over Aurora's hand.

'Strangers call me Miss le Due,' said Daisy to the engineer. 'My friends call me Daisy. But to remain my friend is to resist the temptation to call me *you know what*.'

Aurora explained to them her interest in Project 32 and her purpose in coming to the Wompler Lab. She was relieved at finding in Cal someone who knew something about the functioning of the Reproductive System, from the individual cell level upwards.

Brian announced that he was going to 'find out what time it is', and left, by a door leading to a second corridor.

'Yes,' said Trivian. 'We'll leave you two scientificians to your palaver. Miss le Due, my arm?' They set off after the gangster.

Aurora and Cal avoided looking at one another as she related to him her adventures with Smilax at NORAD, and told him that the mad dentist was in control of the Reproductive System.

'Smilax in control. Hmm. Wonder how he does it.'

Cal defined his own experience with the System, at its inception, in Las Vegas, and on the road back. After mentioning its apparent transmission of acquired characteristics, its occasional abortive mutations, and its manifest kenogenetic tendencies, he added that he thought he loved her.

'I see.' She prepared to consider all aspects of the matter gravely. Had he any data on the System's reproduction rate? On its learning limitations, if any? And was it not true that many who thought themselves in love were not?

He told her what he knew about QUIDNAC, and that he hoped to win her hand in marriage.

Aurora, blushing, discussed operant and respondant conditioning, and how the modification of one kind of behaviour might send ripples spreading throughout all of an organism's behaviour, as in the learning of abstract reasoning.

She expressed her hope that the system might be coerced into 'behaving itself' by (1) establishing rapport; (2) becoming a kind but stern parent to it; (3) channelling the System's functions to humanly useful ends; (4) establishing models of behaviour and a routine of rewards and punishments to guide the System. Of these, (1) would be the hardest.

'If we only knew how Smilax controls the System,' Cal said, 'we could somehow impersonate him.'

'Recognition is a difficult kind of behaviour to analyse,' she explained. 'Because it goes on, in most people, at the edge of consciousness. We recognize a friend seen in different light, at odd angles, at a distance, or with an added moustache.'

'Or aged for fattened, yes. But the literal-minded System can't possibly cope with all that. I'm inclined to think that Smilax uses some kind of badge or password identification – something unique.'

Aurora was not so sure. 'It wouldn't do to have some cue-object that anyone else might get hold of, or that might be lost. I tend to believe it's something more positive, like fingerprints, ear configurations, retinal pattern.'

She added that she would consider his offer of marriage and that she would rather answer later.

Cal was about to point out that there might not *be* a later, when from far away, Daisy screamed.

'Stay here,' Cal commanded, and ran from the room.

At some point, Elwood Trivian had taken a wrong turn. One moment he had been walking arm-in-arm with Daisy; they had unlinked arms to pass on opposite sides of a pillar; the next moment he was utterly alone.

Alone, moreover, at the intersection of two empty corridors, down each of which he could see for hundreds of yards. He could not decide which to choose. After a moment's hesitation, he headed to the left.

The floor suddenly wasn't there. Clawing the air, Elwood fell in darkness, trying to remember a childhood prayer: 'Bless—'

He struck the water and plunged under, holding his breath. Only it was *not* water, but something greasy and bitter. He broke the surface and took air.

What kind of nightmare was this, anyway? He seemed to be floating in a lake of cold, greenish, slightly viscid coffee. There was light, from somewhere, and there was a ceiling perhaps five feet overhead. Otherwise nothing, in all directions, but choppy waves. He began to tread coffee and bob along like a cigarette butt.

Brian waved a .45 at Cal and Daisy. His dust-coloured, wispy hair was rumpled, and there was a strange, sly look in his eye. He crouched in the centre of the room, next to a metal cabinet.

'Keep back, both of you. This does not concern you.'

'What does not concern us?' Cal asked. 'What's wrong, Professor?'

'Nothing is wrong. On the contrary, everything is right! The time ... the auspices ...' He gestured at the metal cabinet, from which, at regular intervals, a foot or two of paper was vomited forth. 'And behold the Clock of Life!' He looked up.

Now Cal saw that the ceiling of this round room was a great clock face, perhaps fifty feet in diameter. The minute hand was visibly moving to join the hour hand at twelve, while a red second hand swept out its sectors silently. Daisy cowered against the wall under XII, and now Cal edged towards her from the doorway at III.

Seeing the movement, Brian whirled and fired. Plaster puffed from the wall a few inches from Cal's head.

'I said stay put! Nothing must move – but the clock.' He looked up at it and smiled. 'Geared to the perfect clockwork of our universe ... set in motion once, for eternity!' He mumbled something indistinct, then:

'Time flies, you see ... on the pinions of clocks ... time is money, you pays your money and you takes your chance ... round and round she goes, and where she stops ... yes, time must have a stop ... time and chance happen to them all ...'

'O God! It's his old illness,' said Daisy, turning away. 'Games of chance, clocks, magic squares – it's been coming over him for years. I thought if I could get him away from the university, from eighteenth-century clockwork thought, he would be all right. But I suppose the disappointment in Las Vegas, followed by Harry's death, has upset the balance of his mind ...'

Brian laughed harshly. 'What do any of you know of *balance*? Or of escapement? Or of—'

'Brian, listen to me! It's Daisy! Don't you know me?'

A deafening chime began to announce the hour. A panel in the floor slid open near Brian. He paused only for a second, then leaped into it.

Daisy screamed. Then, though Cal tried to head her off, she ran to the edge of the hole and peered down into it.

What followed could only have been a kind of malevolence on the part of the machine, for now the red second hand began lowering itself as it continued to sweep around, so that it angled down directly towards Daisy's head. She seemed too horrified at what she saw to notice.

Rushing towards her, Cal called, 'Daisy, duck!'

'What did you call me?' She turned to give him an indignant look as the giant second hand caught her alongside the head. She pitched over the edge, and was gone.

Cal ran up to the now-closing panel and looked down. He could see nothing but myriads of gears of all sizes, running smoothly and quietly, some were stained red.

Elwood Trivian dozed, still treading coffee, and dreamed of his steam engine. The Las Vegas Express kept somehow turning into a Las Vegas espresso machine, and he could not get one steam-chuffing box separated from another ...

When he awoke, two men were hauling him out of the lake on to their raft of cafeteria tables. One man was so gluttonously fat and the other so starveling thin that they seemed almost a part of his dream. Only the smell of coffee reminded him that this was horrible reality.

'Gee, Pop,' said the fat man. 'He looks hungry.' He busied himself about the pages of a magazine. The thin man appeared to take no notice of anything but his immediate task; paddling his feet off one end of the raft to propel it through the coffee.

'Here, fella, eat up hearty,' said the fat one, tearing out a picture of roast beef and handing it to Elwood. 'There's plenty more where that came from.' The engineer sat with it in his hand, dazedly watching fatso devour pictures of cakes and pies.

'Coffee?' He dipped up a dirty paper cup of the sludge near the paddling feet and offered it. Elwood shook his head. 'I know whatcha mean. Coffee makes ya so nervous ya can't eat right. I stick with *solid* food.'

Pulped-up magazine pages drooled down his slowly-working chin.

The room in which Aurora waited seemed to be a storeroom. Weapons and electronic equipment lay along the walls. There was furniture, a roll-top desk in one corner and a grandfather clock opposite the door. Aurora watched it, as a distant, larger clock began to chime. In a few seconds, the grandfather clock whirred and took up tinny notes of its own. *One, two ...*

The grandfather clock at home had never run, despite all her father's attempts to fix it. It was not running the day he died.

The inquest found accidental death, resulting from a malfunction of one of his projects, a diving bell. She strove to become tough-minded about his memory. After all, this was a world where clocks ran and trains ran and people ran to catch them. Not a world for losers, whether they were middle-aged farmer-dreamers or young, idealistic lab assistants, like Cal.

Of course Cal was a loser. He was the kind of man, she knew, who ends up at forty running a bankrupt gas station too far from the turnpike. Who, just before he declares bankruptcy, is shot by a feeble-minded bandit for $2.12 in the till. There was probably nothing that Cal could do right.

She thought it more than likely that she would marry him … *eleven, twelve.*

The case of the grandfather clock opened like a sarcophagus. Dr Smilax stepped forth and took her in his arms. Aurora screamed.

CHAPTER XXV

The Rivals

'Brothers and Sisters, I bid you beware
Of giving your heart to a dog to tear'

KIPLING

'Don't scream, my dear,' panted Smilax, as Aurora struggled free. 'I mean you no harm. I esteem you, in fact, over all other women in this, my world.'

'You must be joking.' She edged towards the door.

He blocked her path. 'Ah, could I joke about your heart? I would rather throw myself under the wheels of a car,' he whined. Seizing her hand, he began to kiss it eagerly. 'I want to be your – your best friend. I'll dog your footsteps till you say yes. Dear Dr Candlewood, be mine – and the world will be yours!'

Disgusted, she freed her hand and turned away. Smilax seized her wrist and flung her about to face him again. 'Must I hound you?' he barked. 'Must I beg and threaten? Speak to me! Speak!'

As she said nothing, he went on, curling his lip to show sharpened, glittering teeth. 'I warn you, if you refuse me, I will not merely kill myself. Oh no, that would be too easy. I would take the *world* with me, and in the most *painful* way possible. And *your* death, my precious, would be the most lingering, most excruciating death of all.'

A mournful, pleading look came into the eyes behind the polished lenses. Smilax began to fawn and stroke her arm.

'Is it my age? But I'm frisky yet, my mistress. Yes, and more than willing to learn new tricks. And you could not find, in all the younger men of this world, a more faithful and constant friend than Toto.

'It amused me to hear you and Potter trying to guess how the System "knows" me – you will *never* learn that secret. But I was less amused to hear that impudent puppy offer you marriage!

'You must choose between us. You must choose between the kindest, truest, richest possible friend, and that ungrateful, ill-bred cur, Calvin Potter.'

He caught up both her wrists. 'Choose now!'

'Take your filthy paws off her!'

Without waiting for the doctor to comply, Cal lunged at him, throwing an awkward punch. The wily surgeon twisted, so that the blow glanced off his ear and caught Aurora on the side of the face. Her head snapped back against the metal wall and she folded gracefully to the floor.

'Aurora!' both men yelped, diving to help her up. The corner of Smilax's cheek caught Cal in the eye. They began to wrestle, Smilax shoving Cal towards the open panel of the clock.

Suddenly Cal was seized from behind in an iron grip. A stunning blow at the nape of his neck blurred his vision. Something hit him in the kidney, in the stomach, across the bridge of his nose. There seemed to be four, six, a dozen fists pummelling him from all directions. He hit out blindly, encountering no one. It came almost as a relief when something hit him hard in the Adam's apple, and as the grip relaxed he sank into soft darkness.

But he was out only for a few seconds. When he came to, Smilax and two other figures were standing over him. Cal's dazed vision travelled up from wheeled feet and steel legs to armoured bodies and finally to impassive cathode-ray tubes where faces ought to be.

'Ah, you're awake, so the fun can begin. "Kurt" and "Karl" here are going to torture you to death – crudely, of course, for they've never done it before – but with the painstaking slowness only machines can manage.' Smilax opened the roll top of the desk in the corner to reveal a console. As he pressed a switch on the console, a pedestal chair seemed to sprout from the floor like a mushroom. Smilax settled into it with a sigh.

'Let me see now,' he said, brooding over the console. 'Nothing serious until Aurora wakes up to watch. I wouldn't want her to miss the main feature, eh? Now, how about starting off with –'

He lifted a doll attached to the console by a thick cable and began massaging its scalp with ungentle vigour. 'A Dutch rub!'

The two robots dragged Cal to his feet, and while one held him the other performed the same operation. Cal began to yell.

'Ha ha, very good. Now we'll give you an Indian burn, and then twist your arm until you holler uncle.' Smilax demonstrated with the doll, and the robots zealously followed suit.

Cal found each torture every bit as painful as he remembered it from childhood. He was beginning to form a plan of escape from his mechanical torturers, but thinking became increasingly difficult as he was given hits and no returns, as his head was thumped and his ears boxed, his toes stepped on and his hair pulled. When not otherwise occupied, the robots were under standing orders to pinch him, which they did in an orderly manner. He noticed they did not both receive their orders from Smilax directly. Only the one wearing Karl's badge would turn the sensing device atop its head to watch Smilax. Then it would light a series of numbers on its face, which 'Kurt' would duly note and obey. Cal decided to interrupt their communication.

He waited until Aurora groaned as if coming to her senses. The doctor looked around at the sound, and Cal rammed his elbow into 'Karl' 's cathode-ray tube face hard. The implosion drove the robot back a few steps, but it did not lose its balance. It seemed to pause for a second, making up its mind about some electronic matter.

Then 'Karl' charged – and began trying to twist 'Kurt' 's arm, 'Kurt' let go of Cal to fend off its brother. The two began to shuffle, locked in alternating hammer-locks, turning slowly about the room.

Seeing what had happened, Smilax snatched up a rifle-like instrument and pressed it to Aurora's head. 'Come near me and she gets it,' he snarled.

'Cowardly cur!'

'I'll make you pay for that remark, Potter. Every dog will have his day, and rest assured this will be mine.' He pointed the rifle at Cal and fired. A tiny rocket streaked forth, slamming into the wall near him. Cal threw himself at the doctor and seized the rifle before he could fire again. They struggled.

'Kurt! Karl! Help!' Smilax cried.

But the unfortunate robots were of no use. They were still putting hammer-locks on one another, and at that moment the two of them disintegrated, collapsing into fragments which still carried on the combat like the severed claws of crabs.

Cal and the doctor both gripped the launcher-rifle, battering at each other clumsily. They were far from expert fighters, and Smilax's middle age was well-matched by Cal's weary flabbiness. They stumbled over a pair of metal arms which seemed to be Indian wrestling on the floor. Cal lost his balance, then regained it, but by that time the doctor had levered him up against the wall, the launcher across his throat like a quarterstaff.

'I should have killed you when I had the chance,' Smilax growled, baring his teeth in a grimace.

Cal shoved him back and grinned. 'It's you who'll play dead dog, Toto!'

'Die!' snapped Smilax, accompanying this with another shove.

'After you!' retorted Cal, shoving him back.

They continued to shove one another and trade insults in one corner of the room. In a second corner, Aurora still lay unconscious. Elsewhere lay scattered robotic parts, including the severed head of 'Kurt', whose face displayed only rows of neatly-spaced stars.

'Down, boy!'

Giving one final shove, Cal flung the doctor free of the weapon, then aimed it at him.

'All right!' Smilax screamed. 'All right! Go ahead! Shoot me!'

Cal threw down the weapon. 'I don't need this,' he said, 'to bring you to heel.'

Laughing, Smilax scooped up the severed leg of a robot and pitched it at him. It caught Cal across the forehead, and he fell backwards into a pile of junk. He was only dimly aware of the doctor's fumbling a pistol from a drawer of the desk. A shot rang out. Cal hit the floor. He looked up in time to see the tail of Smilax's white coat disappear around the edge of the doorway. Cal jumped to his feet and ran after him. Springing into the hall, he found himself in a labyrinth of unmarked passages.

The architecture in this part of the building seemed not to be a fixed structure, but a kind of dynamic principle. Varying according to some obscure formula of its own, it altered shapes and sizes constantly. Walls advanced, turned, retreated or collapsed, ceilings buckled and bulged, floors tilted alarmingly or dropped away like elevators. A door might lead to a room fifty storeys high, or to one only an inch deep, or it might be false.

One pair of identical rooms contained a window between them, so that, gazing from one monotony of office furniture to the next, Cal wondered for a second at this curious mirror that failed to reflect him. He hurried out, and as he stepped over the threshold, the room behind him collapsed like a card castle.

As he stepped on it, a stairway might become a floor, a ramp, or an escalator. At any time an entire room might be given a quarter turn, might be tilted on its side, might shrink or swell to some new shape. Stairways became floors, ramps, escalators; they led to closets or twisted back upon themselves. From time to time Cal glimpsed the white-coated figure of the doctor; the gap between them was not closing. They made their way upward.

Cal passed through a final trapdoor to the roof, and there was nothing more above but the star-pierced firmament. The roof resembled nothing so much as a giant parking lot of perhaps a hundred acres, with here and there a dim yellow glow from a string of jury-rigged lights. In place of cars there were regularly-spaced, bulky stacks of lumber and crated machinery, covered with canvas. Cal could see, in the distance, fork lifts moving to and fro. Otherwise, nothing moved. There was no sign of Smilax.

Cal crept from shadow to shadow until he reached the edge of the roof. Curious, he peered over – and froze. There were trucks and tanks moving down there. He could obscure the largest ones with the ball of his thumb. It was at least fifty storeys to the ground.

A shot rang out and Cal threw himself flat, then began crawling rapidly towards one of the stacks of lumber.

All at once an engine started up somewhere near at hand. A spotlight came on, picking out Smilax crouching on top of a pile of crates. The surgeon threw up one hand to protect his eyes. Another spotlight came on. Under the roar of the motor, Cal could hear a number of voices in excited argument. After a moment the second light went off again. Smilax stood as if transfixed by the single beam, the gun hanging limp in his hand.

A shadow passed overhead and Cal looked up. A crane boom was swinging towards Smilax. The doctor saw it too, and began to whimper. 'It is the Porteus effect! The System has gone berserk! It's going to turn on its master, just as I knew it would!' The boom slowed, but kept coming. 'Help!' Smilax begged. 'Master, don't punish me!'

The boom stopped, and started moving away, and Smilax suddenly took courage.

'Go ahead, try to kill me!' he screamed, jumping up and down and shaking his fist. 'I defy you, you nut-and-bolt nightmare! *I'm* the master here, even Potter and Aurora know that. I alone can control you – with these!' He tore off his rimless glasses and waved them aloft. They shone in the harsh light. The strangely-shadowed, naked face of Smilax bared its teeth and growled.

The crane boom moved in his direction once again, and now its clamshell lowered towards him like a giant, cruel jaw. Smilax shrieked and scampered down off the pile of packing cases, and, just as if it had not realized this, the clamshell seized the pile and lifted it.

'Haha, did you think you had me? You filthy, clumsy monster, you missed! All right, go ahead and turn on your creator! If I cannot control you no one shall – ever!' He flung down the glasses and crushed them under his heel.

'Hahaha! Down with the System! Down with the machine!' he bayed, and began to caper in a circle, almost like a puppy chasing its tail. 'To hell with cats! Down with Albert Payson Terhune! Screw Lassie! Piss on lamp-posts!'

The pile of boxes fell, suddenly, barely missing him, and there was a splintering crash and the clamshell came down on top of them. Smilax leapt away and turned to bark furiously at the wreckage. The tarpaulin stirred slightly, and from the shadows under it came an ominous clicking. It was as the sound of many knitting needles knitting many dog sweaters – or dog shrouds.

Cal shivered.

'No! No!' shrieked Smilax. 'Good boy. Down. Nice System.'

The spotlight followed him as he backed away towards the edge of the roof. 'No! No! Stay away!' he called, throwing one leg over the railing. 'Stay away from me!' But the clicking sound seemed to leave the wreckage and move through the darkness after him, and now it was accompanied by a faint, quavering murmur, high-pitched and eerie.

'Stay away!' he screamed one last time, then threw himself over the edge. Cal rushed to the rail and looked down. He could see nothing of Smilax, but hear his faint scream: 'Bowowowowowowowow!'

The spotlight remained fixed on the splice where he'd gone over. Into its beam a moment later, clicking ominously, marched a swarm of little girls in red-white-and-blue spangles. Mewing as they toddled, two gross of Wompler's Walking Babies followed Smilax over the edge.

The motor of the crane died. The spotlight swung round to pick out the driver, Aurora. She was wearing glasses.

'Are you all right?' she and Cal shouted at the same time. She climbed down from the cab and ran towards him. Cal ran towards her.

'Get that goddamned spotlight out!' shouted an argumentative voice.

'But, Pop, no one can see if—'

'I don't want any ifs. We got to economize somewhere. Out!'

Stumbling along in the darkness, Cal and Aurora ran on towards one another.

CHAPTER XXVI

Utopia

*'The good ended happily, and the bad unhappily.
That is what Fiction means.'*

WILDE

Cal and Aurora were in New York, some weeks later, holding hands in front of a QUIDNAC machine.

'DEARLY BELOVED,' it typed, 'WE ARE GATHERED HERE TODAY ...'

Much had happened since the death of Smilax. The dragon was slain, the frog turned into a prince, and the pudding got off the end of the nose. Or that was the way Grandison Wompler, the new President of the United States, spoke of it. In any case, the Reproductive System had become, under the guidance of Cal and Aurora, a friend to man.

Cal had asked his fiancée how it was she'd guessed the secret of Smilax's glasses – in the nick of time.

'I had plenty of time to think, while I was lying there, playing unconscious,' she said. 'So I tried to combine our two theories. You thought the cue must be some sort of talisman, while I was sure it was something personal and idiosyncratic. The only thing that fitted both theories had to be that pair of rimless glasses. I suppose the System had some way or another of testing them by shooting light through them.

'When you two left, I looked all over for a spare pair. Then it occurred to me, he wouldn't dare keep a spare pair around, lest someone should get them. At the same time, he'd have to have access to another pair, because otherwise he'd have to stop being God while he went to an optician. So I asked the System to make me a duplicate pair to his prescription, and it did, in seconds. Then I was God. I took the elevator to the roof, where I met the Womplers and Elwood Trivian and so on.'

The System had made considerable changes in the political look of things. Upon his election, Grandison Wompler had embarked on a speaking tour of the Russian provinces, speaking chiefly before ladies' clubs. At the same time, the new Premier of the Soviet Union had engaged to speak to the ladies of Nebraska and Iowa. These were not cultural exchange programmes, but the main duties of the heads of state now.

After all, they had no more paperwork to do – ever. The System had taken care of that.

In fact it had taken over all the jobs no one wanted to do. The System collected garbage and turned it into valuable chemicals like pearls and perfume and maple sugar and finger-paints.

It did all the dishes in all the homes of the world. It filed all the papers no one wanted to read, and it read them, too. It took care of other distasteful jobs like typing, and like preventing war.

All the typists and government clerks had at first been unhappy about their unemployment. They had, in fact, marched in protest on the System Central in Washington. But the Reproductive System knew very well these women didn't want to break their nails every day on typewriter keys; it found them husbands. It knew these men didn't want to sit around in offices growing lardy-assed and fluorescent-pale; it gave them service medals of pure gold, which they were able to pawn for trips to Mexico.

But perhaps more important even than the happiness of former government clerks was the prevention of war. And this was accomplished by Project

LULU (Longrange Unilateral Locking Up). It would lock up, say, a warhead or tank or flamethrower from each nation. Then it would weld up the locks. Then it would pour concrete over the whole thing. Then it would apply very expensive armour plate to this giant block of concrete. Then, if the taxpayers had not tired of the whole mess, it would build sleek, extravagant atom-powered ships for the sole purpose of transporting these big blocks of concrete-preserved armament to a certain rendezvous point in the ocean, where both the US and USSR War Rafts were tethered. Each piece of armament was there attached to its nation's War Raft by a long steel cable and lowered to the ocean floor. Thus the two nations were able to build enormous stockpiles of weaponry of the most frightening kind (enough to give their citizens a comfortable glow of security, as frightening weapons always do), but neither could pull a sneak attack. And it was always reassuring to learn that we had faster jets, or a newer kind of bomb, or twice as many bazookas at the bottom as they did.

But someone had to guard our commitment in mid-ocean, so anyone who wished to remain in the military was asked to do his bit of guard duty on our War Raft. Of course there were a number of unpleasantnesses that made war Raft duty less than glorious. First, the American and Russian War Rafts were only a few hundred feet apart, and their occupants were entitled to fire on one another with small arms whenever they liked. Second, food consisted of fried canned peas and powdered eggs in abundance. Seasickness pills were not allotted to the troops. The minimum enlistment was five years, the minimum re-enlistment ten years. Finally, the commander of the American Raft was an almost legendary tyrant, one Jupiter Grawk, while the Russian Raft was under the command of a very old, very wicked woman, Gen. Lotte Smilax.

Yes, the System had taken on enough distasteful duties, so that now it was given the very pleasant one of marrying a hero to a heroine.

'DO YOU, CALVIN, TAKE AURORA TO BE YOUR LAWFULLY WEDDED WIFE ... ?'

With shaking hands, Cal typed, 'I do.'

'I do,' said Jim Porteus, grinning at Susie, his bride. She smiled back, with tears in her eyes. To think that he still cared for her, that he would marry her *now*, even knowing about her tonsils and everything ... Susie wanted to swoon away with happiness.

Jim Porteus was not really thinking about his marriage at all. He'd thought he might as well get married; that damned machine had taken all the fun out of business and politics. He might as well turn engineer or inventor. Just now he was having an idea for an invention, in fact, that had to make him a fortune. He would call it the 'Porteus Automatic Valet', a dignified name for an elegant machine. It would tie one's necktie – any knot wished, just press the button …

The minister cleared his throat. 'And so you, Susie … ?' There was scarcely, he saw, a dry eye in the little chapel at Santa Filomena this morning. A gratifying sight. But there was no one weeping more copiously than poor Madge Suggs. He would have to comfort her, after the ceremony, the minister thought. He would tell her not to think of it as losing a daughter, but as …

'I do,' said Mary Junes Beele Brioche, in Las Vegas (Nuevas), at the Church of the Psychedelic Saviour.

'Then I now prounce you,' intoned His Sacred High Worship, The Very Venerable Kevin Mackintosh, '– or *pronounce* you – astronaut and wife.' He began the countdown.

Cal and Aurora had already received tons of cards and telegrams and letters of congratulations, which the System was sorting for them and inserting into the ceremony itself. Now it presented the warmest regards of Elwood Trivian, Ph.D., who announced also the opening of his new School for Steam Locomotive Engineers in Miami (above the dry cleaner's).

Another telegram read:

'MILLFORD, UTAH 10 35 AM. NOT DEAD OF SNAKEBITE AFTER ALL. HAVE BEEN IN SUSPENDED ANIMATION OR SOMETHING FOR PAST SIX WEEKS. CONGRATULATIONS TO I HOPE HAPPY COUPLE. MY HEALTH FINE BUT FOR HOARSENESS FROM EXCESSIVE DICTATION POST-TRANCE. HAVE YOU ANY IDEA WHAT A SIX-WEEKS' TRAIN OF UNBROKEN THOUGHT CAN BE LIKE QUERY. I HAVE INVENTED A NEW ECONOMIC CALCULUS AND HAD A FEW INTERESTING IDEAS ABOUT TRAVELLING FASTER THAN LIGHT. BELIEVE ME, SUSP. ANIMATION IS GOING TO BE THE NEXT DRUG KICK.

'HITA.

'P.S. TELL LOUIE HE IS OFFICIALLY BLACK SCISSORS.'

Having delivered this telegram, the QUIDNAC waited until its contents were digested and then typed cautiously:

'I NOW PRONOUNCE YOU MAN AND WIFE, UNLESS YOU HAVE MADE ANY FALSE STATEMENTS IN YOUR APPLICATIONS.'

A chute opened and dispensed to them a bag of gold and the ownership of a milk-white palfrey which awaited them outside, the gifts of a grateful populace.

Cal could not ride, but he helped Aurora up on the horse and led it down

Fifth Avenue. All the bells of the City of New York pealed out the glad tidings, while from the office buildings there were released bright-coloured balloons and flocks of snowy doves.

At the Battery, they boarded a barque for a distant land, while all the citizens of New York wept and munched candy and cheered and held up babies to look at them. But for three old men in faded uniforms, who did not look up from their game of Go-to-the-Dump, there was no one in the crowd who did not wish Cal and Aurora happiness, as the barque's white sails filled with wind and it slid silently away from the pier and out to sea.

THE MÜLLER-FOKKER EFFECT

To Pearl Peace, M.A.
and
Doc Sam H. Smith

ANA * O * Y

Time is like an arrow's h***,
Pointing only one way,
Like one l** of a compass
You might be using, to go, on f***,
Another l** of this journey
Down a one-way street
Full of factory h***s in cars
Whose cylinder h***s
All h*** the same way,
Towards the a**s factory,
Whose h*** is a friend
With whom you might play a h*** of cards,
Not noticing there is a f*** card in your h***,
A h****; oh, and maybe writing IOU's,
In an elegant h***,
To be h***ed to whoever f***s the bill,
But now you take h****,
You s******* your c**** up life's gangplank,
Never mind if it goes down with all h***s,
With you on watch, or if your plane n***s down
Off the isle of B**** with no one watching.
At the f*** of the steps you get ready
To f*** the next minute or two,
As depicted on your left h*** by a watch
Whose f*** has h***s like arrows.

EDITOR'S NOTE

The following extract is reprinted here as it appeared on the title page of B. Shairp, THE AMERICAN BOOK OF THE DEAD (4 vols., 8vo, Univ. of Practical Mysticism Press, 19—). Other extracts from the four volumes *(The Ox, The House, The Camel, The Door)* appear as chapters three, eight, eighteen and twenty-five below.

Suspect any coincidence, any fascinating banality. Suspect 'on earth as it is in heaven', 'there's never a cop around when you need one', and 'everything that goes up must come down'.[1] The planet Uranus is 1782 miles from the sun. Subtract 1 from 1782 and you get 1781, the year when Uranus was discovered. Meaning?

Or take the word in Cockney rhyming slang for testicles, 'orchestras' (= orchestra seats, or stalls, to rhyme with balls). 'Orchestra', a Greek word meaning the space in front of the stage where the dancers dance. 'Orches –' means having to do with the dance. 'Orches –'. Change one letter and you make this root into a tuber, i.e. the Greek 'orchis', our orchid, so-called because it looked to the Greeks like a set of testicles. There is a dance of meanings, a dance of word orgins – and dances are still balls.

– God, to a military adviser

[1] Must? See table in Appendix I.

PRELIMINARY

Glen Dale, publisher of *Stagman* magazine and 'last of the old-time eligible bachelors' *(ibid.)*, was having another of his parties. He and his friends and a few hundred of their friends had gathered in the penthouse atop the Stagman Building to celebrate his fortieth – or thirty-ninth – birthday. The place overflowed with not-quite-young people in odd costumes: Aztec feather robes, copper shirts, bright ceramic shoes and shingle jackets; masks, body paint and glowlamp jewelry; suits of paper, steel and glass; whatever was loud without being vulgarly inexpensive.

On the mezzanine a pop group plugged in their amplified instruments and tried to make themselves heard above the talk of I, Thou and Other Celebrities. The group's name was Direct from Las Vegas. The sounds of guitar, organ, English horn and carillon were audible through underwater speakers to those swimming in Glen's pool, but to no one else.

Two musicologists in modified zoot suits began an argument about some old Deef John Holler blues. A girl in bead mail spoke to a friend of hers who happened to be a famous astronaut. Someone dropped the name General Weimarauner, and someone countered with the name of Mr Bradd.

'Who's he?'

'Mr Bradd? Just head of National Arsenamid's Marketing Division, that's all.'

'Mr Bradd. Hmm, sounds like the name of a hairdresser I used to know …'

Across the room a macrobiotics disciple explained that Christ would have lived longer if the Last Supper had consisted of boiled brown rice. 'Instead of all that Yang bread …'

A man looking trapped inside his glasses leant against the mantel and sipped ginger ale. He wore a plain business suit dating from the sixties' 'Kennedy look', enormous French cuffs, and a false smile of nonchalance. The girl in bead mail introduced herself to him, and he murmured his name.

'Donagon?' she echoed. 'You look like Truman Capote … What *is* your thing?'

'Biophysics. I, um, thought they didn't say that any more: "What's your thing." I thought they stopped, um, saying that.'

'They did. Only now they're saying it again. Are you a friend of Glen's?'

'No, actually …'

'I met Glen through Bill Banks. You know, the black astronaut?'

'Yes, I think I've heard something …'

'He's the one who dropped anthrax on Central America. Poor Bill! He feels so *guilty*!' The girl scanned the party as she spoke. 'You wouldn't believe it!'

'Well, we all …'

'I mean it's stupefying! He tried to kill himself, *three times*!'

Donagon set down his drink and put his hands behind him, out of sight. 'Really?'

'Ank! Aren't you going to say hello?' A young man in a crisp paper suit strolled over. 'Ank, do you know Mr Dunne?'

'Dr Donagon, actually,' said Donagon, shaking Ank's left hand.

'Nancy, I need a smoke.' The girl offered her pack of Hashmores, and Ank applied his thin moustache to the girl's forehead, then took two. 'I don't usually smoke this brand,' he explained. 'Nothing in them. Are you a medical doctor, Doctor?'

'No, um, just a biophysicist.'

Someone bumped Donagon from behind, spilling a drink on him. He turned to glare, but the culprit, a man in a wrinkled dinner jacket, was too busy fighting for balance to notice.

''S all right,' he murmured. 'I'm from Interpol.' After resting a few seconds against the fireplace, he shoved off again. Some invisible ship was pitching in a stormy sea, and he lurched across its deck and into the crowd.

'I do the art column for the *Sun*,' said Ank. 'But it's not my real life. Really I'm a painter.'

A girl in a buckskin bikini and a hat with antlers came past with a tray. Before Donagon could protest, she took away his half-finished ginger ale and left a glass of something stronger.

'Not that I've technically painted anything – yet. But I know exactly what I want to do. All I need is a computer random number generator – or, better still, some of that Müller-Fokker tape.'

Donagon gulped his drink. 'But how did you hear about that? It's supposed to be classified!'

Ank coughed. 'I read *Time*'s science page. The "miracle tape" and so on. They said only four reels of it exist – and the inventor's supposed to have defected to Russia or something, so I guess they can't make any more. And not too many people know how to use it.'

Donagon looked around cautiously. No one was near enough to eavesdrop but the two zoot suits, and they were engaged in a shouting argument.

'I may be able to help you. My project is making arrangements to use these, uh, tapes. I can't tell you more about it, but I might be able to fix up something. If you're still interested in a few months, when the project gets going, drop me a line.'

He gave his address as The Biomedical Research Project, Mud Flats, Nebraska. 'It may come to nothing, but …'

'You won't regret it, Doctor.' Ank went off to dance with a girl wearing only blue jeans. The other dancers – businessmen in fur wigs, poets in plastic, a senator in a caftan – swirled around them and they were lost to view.

Donagon leaned uneasily against the upholstered wall and tried to look as if he were waiting for a friend. Waves of conversational noise washed up against him, broke, slid back into the great sea of sound.

' … a fact that it neither tamps, nor is it an ax!'

'Lichtenstein? I thought you meant the country …'

'Brown rice and …'

A girl laced into black patent leather from neck to toe (having even pasted on 'lips' of the same material) swung past, talking about the works of Thomas M. Disch. 'Oh yes, I've read them all: *The Geocides, Mankind under the Lash …*'

Across the room, Glen Dale moved towards a lively group of painters. At his approach, they fell silent and looked into their drinks.

'How's it going, fellows?'

'Fine, man.' 'Yeah, keen.'

'Well that's – fine. Everything okay? Drinks?'

'Great.'

'Fine, glad to hear it.' He stood leaning lightly towards them for another minute, hoping the conversation would resume including him. It did not. 'Well, I'd better – circulate.' The man from Interpol tacked past. 'Yes, well, so long.'

One of the painters called after him, 'Great party, man!' then turned to his friend. 'What'd *he* want?'

'Aw Christ, he wants somebody to tell him how good he looks in that stupid tin hat. You know, the one thing I can't stand about his parties is he's always at 'em.'

'Yeah, I wish it was his wake.'

Glen approached a fat little bearded man in a sober suit, standing alone by the bar.

'Well, Herr Doktor, are you having a good time?'

A pair of blank pince-nez turned up to stare at him, reflecting all the colors of Direct from Las Vegas's light show. 'Ah, Mister Dale.' The little man, whose name Glen could not recall, spoke English with German precision.

'There is someone here I would like to meet.'

'Well, just point her out to me …'

'No, no, this is a gentleman. A biophysicist named Doonigan. I should like it very much if you would introduce me to him.'

'Doonigan? Doonigan? No, I'm afraid I don't know him.'

Asking Herr Doktor if his drink was all right, Glen went over to talk to Ank and the girl in blue jeans. As it happened, they were having a good time.

And their drinks were fine. But just now they were about to dance, if he would excuse them.

Donagon asked the girl in the foil pinafore who that was over there. 'The tall skinny guy with the tin hat.'

'Why, that's Glen! The host – don't you know him? Good gouts!'

'No ... I was invited by his secretary, actually.'

'You're a friend of Myra's?'

'I, um, know her, yes. She doesn't seem to be here, tonight.'

'Good gouts! Didn't you *know*? She's in the hospital, having a nose job. I thought everybody knew!'

'That's odd!' Donagon was not aware he'd laughed so loudly until several Aztecs turned round to stare. 'I met her in the hospital! She was having her acne sanded, and I ... I was ...' He hesitated to explain the fresh scars under his outsize French cuffs. One of the false Aztecs looked him over. 'And you were having a D. and C., were you, darling?'

'Oh, George, you're impossible!' said the girl in the pinafore. She skipped off to dance with George the impossible Aztec.

' ... recorded in 1948, while he was still in prison,' said one of the zoot suits.

'Harry, listen – you're out of your mind. It had to be 1950 because the company that cut the record didn't even exist in '48.'

In another room the girl in blue jeans asked the tall man with the axe-blade nose what he did for a living.

'I'm an art critic.'

'You too? I just met one art critic.'

'The one that works for the *Sun*? Haha, *critic*? He thinks Lichtenstein is a country, for Christ's sake. *Critic*?'

Something bumped their legs. They stood back to let the man in the wrinkled dinner jacket crawl past. ''S all right,' he explained, 'I'm from Innerpol.'

The Herr Doktor came through next, asking for a geneticist named Doonigan.

'A what?' One of the two businessmen in fur wigs who were holding each other upright near the piano turned to stare at him. 'What does that sawed-off kraut want? A gyneticist?'

'Geenetics,' said his companion. 'Genes.'

The other nudged him. 'Hey, I wouldn't mind getting in *her* jeans, Charlie.' He leered at the girl.

Elsewhere other happily married men were leering at girls in crinoline, copper sheaths, feather robes and complicated layers of translucency; even at the girl in patent leather, who, hand to mouth, was searching all the rooms for her lost stick-on lips. Somebody went into the toilet to vomit, and somebody else used an overshoe in the closet. One of the zoots was spitting blood in the kitchen sink, while his friend stood by, holding his pork-pie hat for him.

'Look, Harry, I *said* I'm sorry. Anybody can lose his temper now and then. Especially when I know that Deef John cut that side in nineteen ...'

A troupe of girls in buckskin bikinis and antler hats moved through, pouring coffee and emptying ashtrays. Ank left with the girl in the foil pinafore. Donagon dozed in a chair.

Direct from Las Vegas packed up and left. The party reduced to those who had passed out, determined drinkers, and those without a sense of time, like the six persons in Egyptian dress squatting in the corner and digging a candle flame.

Glen Dale and Senator Vuje shook Donagon awake.

'You all right?'

He nodded, and again when Glen asked if he were a scientist named Doonigal. '... Donagon ...' he said thickly.

'That must be you. There's someone who wants to talk to you. Just a minute, I'll see if I can find him.'

'I thought you was Truman Whatsisname, the writer,' said the senator. Somehow in his caftan he looked more like a senator than ever. 'Here, let's get you on your feet, fella.'

He did not get Donagon on his feet. Instead the toilet door opened behind him, knocking the senator on top of him.

'What the hell ... ?'

'I'm so sorry.' Donagon's glasses had been knocked off. He saw only a blurry, short figure in black, though he could hear the crisp German consonants. 'I'm so sorry.'

'Why the hell don't you watch where you're going? Now look, you knocked me down, knocked this poor fella's glasses off ...'

'I apologize again.' The blur made a gesture with both arms. 'But then, where *am* I going? That is a question. Where are we all going? And how is it best to watch?'

'Listen, you little heinie, I fought your kind at Anzio ...'

'Ah, forgive me, gentlemen. I most probably am drunk. Good night.'

Donagon retrieved his glasses and got to his feet. The short man in black was disappearing out the hall door when Glen came in from the dining room.

'I fought his kind at Anzio,' the senator mumbled. 'Arrogant little ...'

One of the business twins sat down suddenly in the middle of the floor, 'I DON'T WANT TO GO HOME, I WANT TO GET ME ONE OF THESE LITTLE GIRLIES AND GO UPSTAIRS.'

'But, Charlie, we *are* upstairs. This is the penthouse.'

'I guess he's gone,' Glen said, shrugging. 'That guy was looking for you all evening.'

'Well, I'll get going.' Donagon shook hands with his host and with the veteran of Anzio, and with a long-toothed man Glen introduced as his psych-iatrist, Dr Feinwelt.

'Whazzis?' The businessman called Charlie, still seated on the floor, held up a black object. 'HEY! Some guy lost his leatha mustache!'

As Donagon left, he heard someone say, 'Wasn't that Truman Capote?'

'Are you kidding? Anybody who wears French cuffs that big couldn't be *anybody*.'

PART 1

An Experiment

ONE

They say your heart is dacron
And you just caint love nohow
But darlin I know …

It was a false day. Drizzle and the amplified, reedy heartbreak of a country-western singer drifted over the parking lot. There were tear-streaks on the mistproof windshields, pools of tears on the uneven plasphalt, and (in case everyone hadn't got the message) a wet, melodious wind to blast the faces of several hundred National Arsenamid employees. The message, straight from the hearts of industrial psychologists, was: 'What a hell of a day! Great to get inside, where it's *warm*, and *dry*, and the Melodiak's playing a light, bouncy tune like "Sunshine Balloon".'

One man in a seam-split raincoat did not get the message; he walked slowly, ignored the rain, and even tried whistling along with 'Cold Old Dacron Heart'. He was looking at the factory, too. All the others had averted their false morning faces from the rain, but not Bob Shairp.

He was looking at the factory for almost the last time – and seeing it for the first.

It looked exactly what it was, a service factory for the great food/missile corporation. A long, white building without character, neither ugly nor interesting.

No, today it was a ship, lying at anchor by the edge of the parking lot, with light streaming from every porthole. A voyage a day, for almost two years … and today the last. It was going on without him.

The whistle blew. Bob hurried in to the security office. The walls were maize over raw sienna this morning. On a sunny day they would go azure over dark green. As the soft saxophones of Melodiak greeted him ('fill up that sun-shine ba-LLOON with hap-pi-ness'), Bob fumbled for his identity card.

'Must be in the coat I usually wear,' he said. The guard did not return his smile. 'But you know me, anyway.'

'Yeah, I know you, Shairp. Losing your card on your last day here! Just what in hell do you think you're gonna walk off with – a few plans, maybe?'

Bob smiled to see if he was kidding. The guard turned his back on it. 'All right, get the hell in there and stop wasting my time.'

Bob was a technical writer with a BA in English and a general understanding of engineering practice. He was not actually allowed to *write* anything, though he worked closely with a writing computer.

Many of National Arsenamid's products resembled one another, and their repair manuals and parts lists differed only in details. Drawings and test routines were fed to the computer, which revised old manuals to fit new items. Bob made minor corrections in the computer's prose.

A block of prose would appear on the screen before him:

Disassembly of half-speed prism carrier (5A1). Remove mtg screws (5A1A), carrier cover (5A1B) and gasket (5A1C). Discard gasket. Using lifting tool UA-10, lift and remove prism assembly (5A1D). Adjust prism assembly aside for testing.

He would work the keyboard to change 'adjust' to 'set', a new block of prose would appear, and so on. As the training film had explained: 'You are the key. *You* understand nuances of English which the computer cannot. So you see, we can never *really* eliminate the *human* element.'

Yet today, for reasons no one quite understood, Bob was being replaced. They were sending him to Mud Flats, Nebraska, to be retrained, then to one of their fifty-four other plants.

National Arsenamid was still masquerading as a food processor. But only five plants still made *Perp* and other breakfast delicacies. Only eleven more made up the home kitchen of an invisible lady named Bette Cooke. The rest: were under defense contracts.

Bob had no objection to working for defense. In fact he worried now and then about the Chinese getting ahead in the Second Front missile race. They were said to be working on an orbiting missile platform, as a third-strike capability (meaning something still up their sleeves after China and the US had wiped each other out, twice over).

What Bob didn't like was secret work. He enjoyed coming home, flopping on the couch, and saying, 'Boy! You know what that crazy computer came up with today? Marge, you should have seen it …'

And what could he tell her today? That the computer didn't need him anymore?

Marge was not sympathetic.

'Retraining pay is next to nothing, Bob! And Spot counted on getting into a military school – really, you couldn't have picked a worse time.'

'I,' he began, and lifted an admonishing finger from his glass. What was so admonishing about that finger? Looked pretty much like all the rest. He put it back and studied the fingers all together. Making white circles on the glass. Or it on them. The drink in the glass was called a pajama. Four parts … no, five parts gin …

'You what?'

'I had nothing to do with it. For one reason or another, they're replacing me, that's all. I'm being moved on. What are you up to, anyway?'

Marge sat on the carpet, surrounded by a sprawl of magazines. Her right hand twiddled a pencil, her left held an open copy of *Luxurious Home*. The first letter of the title was hidden by her fingers, offering Bob a silent pun.

'I'm doing a test: "Does Your Mate Measure Up?" It says – just a minute – it says that you have a lot of artistic ability, and you could really go places, but that you're inclined to fritter away your time on frivolous projects. What you want in a wife is a mother, because you tend to shirk responsibilities.'

'Oh, that's good, that's good! I'll bet I have to be careful around the fifteenth, because something enters the house of something else, and though fifteen and seven are good numbers – aw, what's the use?'

He decided to see what Spot was working on, on the teaching machine.

'Watch, Spot.' Bob pushed open the door with his foot and came in juggling eggs. 'Got it up to four, now, and ...'

The boy had fallen asleep at his homework. One thin arm lay crooked around the teaching machine, which was still trying to get him to answer something about the gold standard. His pajamas were black, and cut to resemble some kind of uniform complete with false pockets, belts and plastic medals

As Spot stirred, cuddling the machine closer, his father saw what kind of uniform it was. The red brassard turned to show a white circle and a hooked cross ...

Bob put him to bed and then cleaned up the eggs from the floor.

'Grow up, Bob! It doesn't *mean* anything to him. All the kids have them. On account of that German TV program.'

'*Leutnant Krieger*? You let him watch that crap? Christ, no wonder he worships the SS.'

Without answering, Marge opened her recipe file and began sorting cards.

'So that's what this "military school" thing is all about! All the kids do it, he says. It's harmless, you say. And in twenty years, when they start up new concentration camps ...'

'For God's sake! You haven't even watched the program, so how can you judge it? It isn't so bad, really. This Leutnant Krieger's not really an SS man at all. He's working to assassinate Hitler. So you see, when he beats up a Jew, it's only part of his cover story. And when he ...'

'I get it. The best of both worlds, right? That's just the way the Nazis worked in the first place. "This isn't really me doing this medical experiment, it's Destiny working through me. It's Blood and Destiny, and besides, it's orders." What's the use, nobody's listening.'

Marge snapped the file box shut. 'Oh, we're all against you, is that it? Listen, you know what they say about aggression. He needs permissible outlets. Isn't it better to let him get it out of his system now?'

'Or into his system, maybe?'

'Listen, you. If anybody in this family turns Spot into a little Nazi, it'll be you! You, with all your petty restrictions and rules. Who wanted to keep him away from TV altogether? Who wouldn't let him box? *Oh, damn you.*'

She began to cry over a fistful of Japanese recipes. Later, after they had made love, she whispered, 'There was something I meant to tell you tonight, only I've forgotten.'

'Mm?'

'Oh yes. The window peeper.'

'N.'

'One of the neighbors saw someone lurking around our windows last night.'

Bob sat up and turned on the light. 'And I'm going away tomorrow? Why in hell didn't you say something? Who saw him?'

She hesitated, chewing a thumbnail. 'Don't laugh, but it was Mrs Fellstus.'

The light went off and Bob dragged the blankets toward his side of the bed.

'Don't you want to hear about it?'

For answer, he twitched away more of the blankets.

The Thursday meetings of the Jess Hurch Society had dwindled, dwindled. No one seemed to care about fighting Communism any more, and Grover attributed this to Lack of Moral Fiber and to Red propaganda.

'They control the press, the radio, television,' he said to the two people in the hall. 'Wall Street, which they revile unceasingly, is really their tool. My own bank today refused us a loan to keep the fight going. So now I'm going to ask all of you to be generous ...'

One of the two snorted, murmured something about a con game, and left. That left only Amy Birdsall (Sec. and Treas.). Grover Minus (Pres.) climbed down off the dais, set the American flag back in its holder, and sat down next to her. Amy lay down her pencil and applauded wildly until he shushed her. Then the room was silent, except for the creak of their folding chairs, as two old bodies shifted and shifted, searching for comfortable positions.

'I give up, Amy. The cumminisks have won.'

She looked shocked. 'Grover! How can you say such a thing! Why only yesterday ...'

'No, no. We're too old for this kind of thing. My arm's too bad to run the printing press. How can we warn the world, the two of us against millions of cumminisk spies? Better for you to go back to your Bible and your Billy Whatsisname. Me, I'll – I've got a few friends in that Florida retirement home we talked about. Thought I might drop down and – and see. Just see.'

Amy started weeping, pushing up her bifocals to scrub away the tears. 'The only thing I ever believed in,' she whimpered. 'Besides God Almighty. I'd carry on by myself, but what can *I* do? I'm only a weak woman.'

For all her eighty years, Amy was stronger than Grover. She had once been a Rockette, and prided herself on still being able to kick off a man's hat – if men still wore hats. But Grover was desperate to comfort her, all the same.

'All right,' he said, patting her hand. 'All right, kid, the Jess Hurchists *will* go forward. But *underground*. No more pamphleteering, no more speeches. We'll just spy them out, and turn over everything we learn to the FBI.'

The original Jess Hurch (1842–1887) was a cowpoke, miner, farmer and grain merchant. He was also a gambler, pimp, drunk and petty swindler. Yet his was a life redeemed at the last moment, and, in the town of Medicine Dumps, California, Jess paid his debts.

He was celebrating something by shooting out store windows and store owners along Main Street when he noticed a crowd collecting by the railway station. The governor of the state was about to campaign for re-election from the rear platform of his special train. Jess just naturally found a good spot in the front of the crowd.

It was a hot day. The speech was long. The governor invited everyone to sit down. Jess hunkered down on a rail and dozed off.

Midway through his speech, the governor asked if anyone wanted government by guess and by golly. Jess awoke, thought someone had called upon him to say a few words, and jumped up.

The swarthy man seated right behind him picked that moment to shoot the governor.

Though somewhat startled at being sprayed with brains and blood, the governor was unhurt. The citizenry sighed with relief at Jess's departure. Then they strung up the wrong man. Then they shot up the town, good-naturedly.

The actual assassin was found hiding in a cracker barrel, and they finished off the day with a second necktie party. The swarthy little man's last words were 'Long live Anarchy!' Thus it came to be that Jess Hurch transcended his own nature (the coroner reported him rotten with two kinds of VD) and joined the roundup of history – American's first martyr to Anarchy, better known as Communism.

Seventy years later the Jess Hurch Society began. Grover Minus was especially pleased to carry on this particular name. As he demonstrated to his friends, 'Jess Hurchist' was an anagram relating the movement directly to Christianity.

Jess would have liked that. 'Jesus H. Christ' was his favorite ejaculation.

*

Mrs Fellstus sat in her accustomed place by the window, peering at the world through a slit she'd cut in the curtain.

'He's there again!' she cried. There was no answer from the study, so she wheeled herself in, to make sure the doctor heard. 'The window peeper's there again tonight! Dean, you're not listening.'

'That's right, Mother, I'm not listening. I'm trying to read an article in this journal.'

'But the window peeper ...'

'Mother.' Dr Fellstus tucked a huge, flat thumb in his *Journal of Kennel Psychiatry* and turned to face her. 'We've been over this so many times, haven't we? Isn't it really just another case of the Communist in the Basement?'

'No! Dean ...'

'Let me assure you, Mother, we are very, very safe here. Since you are no longer a Jess Hurchist, you need no longer fear the "great conspiracy". There is no one outside, no window peeper, no one at all.'

'Just come and look at him, Dean. Just once.'

'Mother, remember the time you read somewhere the phrase "a chink in his armor"? And how afterward you kept imagining Red Chinese clanking up the stairs – remember that?'

'Please, Dean. Just look.'

Very (sighing) well, Dr Fellstus walked into the living room, whipped back the curtain, and saw his own surprised expression. The handlebar mustache needed a trim.

'Nothing and no one. Why don't you watch a little TV, Mother? I believe they're showing Billy Koch tonight, preaching from Porklink Stadium.'

There was no edge to his voice; nevertheless it was an order. Mrs Fellstus switched on the set, and the veterinarian returned to his journal.

The easy assumptions of this particular article rankled. Dr Fellstus, like its author, specialized in nervous diseases of the collie. He did not like to see this kind of over-emphasis on Oedipal matters, at the expense of common sense.

The 'Lassie' image, the feminization of this rough Scottish sheep dog, may have made no small contribution to the popular, sentimentalist view of the collie. Owners erroneously attributing to their pets a passive, meek, fastidious nature may find instead their pets are vigorous and headstrong. They may react to this discovery by covert rejection, or by trying to force Laddie or Bruce into a womanly rôle. They may lock him up, curtail his barking, even expect him to perform distaff duties like slipper-fetching. Thus the collie's worst puppy-hood fears, those of castration by an angry sire, are seen to be ...

'Heal this child, O Lord!' cried the TV set.

'Angry sire indeed!' said Dr Fellstus, pulling at his untrimmed mustache. 'And not a damned word about early weaning!'

' … could have sworn …' said his mother's lips. 'A man … in a long gray overcoat … walking stick …'

There really was a man in a gray overcoat, and he did use a gold-headed walking stick. His name was MacCormick Hines, and he was not 'window peeping', but checking out the truth about reality, the truth he'd come upon twenty years before.

The truth was that reality was televised.

Tonight, for example, Mr Hines watched a soap opera called *The Shairp Family*. Others might tune in on television by turning a knob. He tuned in by telling his chauffeur to stop the car and wait while he took a little constitutional, by creeping up to the screen and peering in.

The advantage of televised reality was that one could tune out any ghosts of unpleasantness. Mr Hines was able to believe that he was not one of the richest men in the world, only 'comfortable'. He was able to believe that his corporation, National Arsenamid, made only fine cereals to build healthy kids, and nothing at all like anthrax, smallpox and typhus. And finally he was able to believe that everything he owned was his by dint of hard, honest work.

Whenever one of the bright young men who handled his investments tried to tell him how rich he was, Mr Hines would shout him down:

'If I have a few comforts, by Gum I've earned them! Application, that's what it took. Application of the seat of my pants to the seat of a chair. Putting on my thinking cap, giving the old gray matter a good workout. I sleep four hours a night, and I don't waste a golden hour, a diamond minute of the rest! Time is money.

'Better wear out than rust out. A little hard work never hurt anybody! All it takes is a little Yankee ingenuity, a little "can do". I don't believe in the word "can't". It takes gumption, and grit, and stick-to-itiveness, and a lot of plain, hard, honest-to-God elbow grease!

'Use the brains God gave you! Dream awhile and scheme awhile, but keep your feet planted on *terra firma* and PLUG!'

Then, with the young man shouted out of the room, he could go back to his gentle dreams.

The Shairp Family was one of his favorite programs. He preferred standing in the cold drizzle to see it, when he could be sitting in dry bleachers watching that faith-healer program across town, even if the action here was a little slow tonight. The writers were probably in a slump.

So Bob was going away on business, while Spot was not, for the time being, going to military school. Well, well. Not much to chew on. As for the business about the 'window peeper', that was all wrong, all wrong. The real drama ought to come from *inside* the family, and not be grafted on artificially. Mr Hines thought about complaining to the sponsors, whoever they might be.

What ought to happen is for Bob to get lost at sea in an air crash. Then Marge could remarry – or almost – and Bob could 'return from the grave'. That would be bully realism. Whooping cough for Spot, but when Bob comes back, they all live happily …

As he shuffled away, leaning into the cold October wind, Mr Hines wondered about that window-peeper business. Who would the peeper turn out to be? Some long-lost relative? Someone in distress? Or someone who would help out the Shairps when – as inevitably it must – tragedy struck? He could hardly wait to see the mysterious stranger's face.

TWO

Bob came out of the dream sometime during breakfast, under the combined impact of coffee and headlines:

SCIENTIST DISAPPEARS
Müller-Fokker a possible defector
EVANGELIST BREAKS RECORD
10 MORE YEARS WAR? NO, SAYS ARMY CHIEF
Weimarauner predicts breakthrough

Something about … children? By the time he climbed in the car, his dream had dwindled to just two words, 'Jelly Day'. He had to stop off at the factory to turn in his badge, then on to Mud Flats, Nebraska. He forgot even the two words …

The guard took a look at his badge and grinned. 'Just in time, Shairp. Another hour and we would of summoned the Industrial Security boys to come and get it. Anyways, we got to finalize your new badge for the other project. Are you leaving today?'

Bob nodded. Two workmen passed between them, carrying a computer console. It was his; he recognized the cigarette burns.

'Okay,' said the guard. 'Okay. We'll expedite the processing, if you'll just organize yourself a chair over there in the visitors' room. Your replacement's waiting in there, by the way, if you want to meet him.'

As Bob opened the door, the occupants of the visitors' room, a man and his dog, looked up. The man smiled, showing a rotten tooth. 'Hiya.'

Behind Bob, the security guard began bawling out the information on his card to someone else. There were typing sounds.

'I guess you're my replacement,' Bob shouted over the racket.

'OUT 1 SHAIRP, ROBERT ETWALL! 77903! TECH WRITER, CAUCASIAN, MALE!'

'What say? Can't hear ya.'

'I said, I guess you're replacing me. As a tech writer.'

'Me? Nawww. 'S old Bingo, here.'

Bob still didn't get it, until the guard took up another badge and bawled: 'IN! BINGO!' The dog looked up at the sound of his name. '89474-A! TECH WRITER, GOLDEN RETRIEVER, MALE!'

Bob tried to smile. 'I'll be damned.'

Rotten-tooth chuckled. 'Amazin', ain't it? Ol' Bingo here earns more'n me. Ya see, they trained him in one a them animal labs, so he knows how to tell a circle from a ellipse *real close*. That's all it takes, I guess. They got the computer fixed up ta turn that inta writin'. Say hello ta the nice man, Bingo. Come on, boy.'

Bob took a silky paw and gazed into gentle stupid eyes. 'Hello, Bingo,' he said solemnly. Thinking, *so much for the human element.*

Wes Davis had his boots up on the desk and his hands clasped behind that elegant head of hair.

That hair. It rose a full four inches from his widow's peak in front. The sides had been starved down to a pair of cuneiform sideburns even narrower than the space between Wes's eyes.

But on top – a relief map of some dark planet, all greasy peaks and whorled valleys. It overwhelmed the other part of his head, the part equipped with a small but recognizable face.

Wes was thinking how just it was that there should be only one chair in the gas station office. It just wouldn't be right for the Mud Flats Ramblers – Skeeter, Travis and Gus – to sit right down with him, their leader. Might give them the idea they were leader types, too.

So here was Skeeter, shaking up a Pepsi and spraying it down his throat; Gus, leaning on the pop cooler; Travis, pretending to study the *Stagman* calendar on the wall; here they were, waiting for Wes to tell them what to do.

'Yes sir,' he said. 'Yes sir. When your wife takes some clothes down to the laundromat, she has to se-par-ate the colored ones from the white ones. Am I right?'

He was right.

'Why? Because they run. That's right. Take a nice perty little pair of lace drawers ...'

'Where?' That was Skeeter, trying for a laugh. Wes stared him down.

'Take them nice little white nylong lace drawers, throw 'em in with a dirty, stinking, black old pair of socks, and what have you got? What happens?

'I'll tell you what *don't*. Them socks sure as hell ain't gonna come out *white*! No, it's the pure white little drawers gets ruint, ever time. They come out all black and gray and dirty. Not just them, everything in the whole wash gets ruint! And all by one little old *harmless* nigger sock!'

Travis scratched his crotch. 'What happen to the othern?'

'What?'

'The other sock. They was two before, and now you just got one. Where's the othern?'

Wes opened a desk drawer and spat into it. 'Jesus Christ, Travis, you didn't hear a thing I said. I'm talking about NIGRAS! It's just the same. You mix the two races, it's the white gets ruint.'

He jumped up and slapped the desk. '*That* is a *fact* of *science!*'

While the fact of science soaked in, Wes went outside and groomed the windshield of a tourist's car. Tucking a rag in his pocket, he resumed his leadership position.

'Now everybody knows the Army is full of nigger-lovers. And everbody knows the National Arsenamid Corporation is run by Jeeews, right? An Equal Opportunity Employer, they call it.

'So what do you spose the Army and the National Arsenamid Corporation are hatching up together over on the edge of town? Over in that Biomedical Research Project.'

They didn't know, Wes.

'You know what biomedical research is? *Makin' babies in test tubes!*'

'Naw! Can't be!'

'Yes sir, and not white babies. Nigra babies!'

'But in test tubes!' Travis scratched furiously. 'Christ! How do they get out?'

'I'm comin to that. They just start the babies off in test tubes. Then they ship them to hospitals all over the US of A, and they *stick them up white women!*'

'Aw, Christ!'

'It's true. I know it for a fact. Ever notice how all them hospitals got lots of nigra orderlies and nurses?'

'Yeah, that's right, Wes.'

'Yer fuckin' A, that's right. The nigra conspiracy is on the move, right here in Mud Flats! They'll populate the whole world with black bastards – *unless we stop 'em!'*

'That's right, Shairp. I know they told you it would be "retraining", but that was just to keep a security blanket over this.' Major Fouts, Project Security Officer, looked at his watch for the sixth time in as many minutes.

'But I – didn't I come down here for retraining?'

'Look, I don't care, buster. If you don't like the job, skip it. We sure as hell don't need you. I mean, just about any warm body will do for this experiment.'

Bob cleared his throat and gazed at the barred windows. 'Is it dangerous? I mean, just what will they do to me?'

'No, it isn't dangerous, and I can't tell you anything about the project until you're cleared. So are you in or out? Hurry up.'

'Will I – be all right afterwards?'

'YAS, YAS, YAS! NOW HURRY UP!'

'I'm – in?'

'Fine now go see Donagon research head for your papers then go down for your physical and then come back up here for clearance here don't forget to fill out all the copies and sign them you're restricted to base until the clearance comes through sign this and take it up to 4B today they want a blood sample this is your V-5 form and that's your waiver if you need anything else see Donagon.'

As soon as Bob was gone, Major Fouts pulled the blinds and locked his office door. Then he worked the combination on his desk drawer and removed three almond Hershey bars. Two he slid under the blotter, the third he peeled and folded lovingly into his elastic mouth.

There was no excuse for it, he knew, none but tedium and despair. Fouts had done everything the Army could expect of him, and more. In his first year here, he had cleaned out a dozen lab assistants of questionable background. He had tightened up all security procedures. He had blacked out news releases. And he had fixed up the computer with an auto-destruct mechanism using only four charges, a model of efficiency. And then – nothing. Nothing but deadly routine, the daily dossiers, the loathsome tight uniform. The candy bars.

His mouth full of melted heaven, he damned Mud Flats. A city post would have been all right. Algernon Fouts could have managed that … mingling nightly with theater crowds … unescorted at a ballroom … bars … Even hidden away in remotest Arcady, fine, but this! In damned, damned Mud Flats, where one was never alone. Official secrecy was easy enough, but any other kind was impossible.

So a part of him lay shut away in his footlocker, under the pile of uniforms his misery had outgrown. Eating, a permitted indiscretion, dulled the pain a little, just as it dulled his features.

There came an unmilitary knock at the door. 'Algie? Can I see you a minute?'

Fouts snatched up the wrapper and stuffed it through the slotted lid of his security wastebasket. He swallowed the last of the sweetness and unlocked the door to Dr Donagon.

'What do you want? I'm busy here, you know. Got to check the dossier of this new guy, Shairp ...'

'Please, Algie, you've got to let me publish. *Anything*. Just some little hooker, something to get my name on it.'

Fouts swam back to the desk through his own liquid layers.

'Not my responsibility. Both the Army and National Arse have their reasons for keeping this under wraps. If it was up to me, I'd let all you boobologists print all you wanted in your boobology journals.'

'Major!' Donagon flung back a lock of his thin, khaki-colored hair. It fell forward again. 'I am a bi-o-physicist, and I am also head of research here. I know I'm young, but I think that, um.' He brushed back the stray lock. Fouts could see white scars on the man's wrist. 'I think that I am due some respect in that, um, respect.'

'Yas, yas. Anyway, things are looking up, kid. The press is going to be invited in on zero-day. You'll get all the publicity you can eat.'

'If only I could be sure – that it was the right kind of publicity, Algie. This could mean the Nobel if I handle it right. But I still ought to have published something. Others are at work on it. Otis Korner at Attica, Flaken of Illinois. O God! If they get a man on tape before I do ...'

'If you spent less time iffing ...'

Donagon blushed. 'I'm afraid, if you must know. The press ... they garble things ...'

'All right, all right. Make up a prepared handout.'

Donagon brightened noticeably. He left, and Fouts went back to work. On the second Hershey bar.

Billy Koch, breakfasting at his desk on a glass of Slimmix (90 calories), shook out his morning paper and got down to work, marking sermonizable stories.

He circled an article on the current Asian conflict and swiveled around to the typewriter to hunt out: 'I offer mnt prayer (sil?) for our boys who have won vict, w/ many trag. losses, in (place). But wht vict can compare &c.'

He put a question mark near MAN SUES GOD FOR LOCUST DAMAGE and turned a page. Pickings were poor: CONGRESS APPROVES BUDGET CUTS; SERIA TOTRY FOR 3½ MIN MILE; ROAD TOLL ...

He caught himself humming a pop tune, 'Ice Cream Blues', switched to a hymn, then caught his breath again. A small item, buried in the back pages:

COMPUTERIZED MAN?

Washington (AP) – A Pentagon spokesman announced today a joint research project between the Army and National Arsenamid Corporation to 'investigate the possibility of partly or even completely digitalizing a living man, using genetic, physiological and neurological data'. Further details were not forthcoming, but a reliable source states that a subject has already been selected, and the experiment is said to be under way.

Billy circled this item twice, and doubly exclaimed on the typewriter: 'You can compute a man – but nt immtl soul!!'

So much for the sermon. He was about to check the financial pages for the inevitable rise of BK Industries, when his secretary announced the arrival of his architect, Ögivaal.

Downstairs from Billy in the Crusade headquarters mail room the first three bags were dumped on the sorting table and the sorters went to it. They dealt first with packages. A box of birdseed addressed to 'H. Spirit' went to one of the staff whose mother had a budgerigar. An odiferous box bearing the suspect palindrome 'A Mr Oops laminates set animal spoor, Ma' went into the wastebasket unopened, joining a bedspread embroidered by loving hands with all of the Psalms. A musical revolving crucifix from some novelty company was set aside for the market analysis department, while an 'electric rosary' went into the large carton destined for a Roman Catholic charity.

Using thumb-knives, the sorters disemboweled envelopes and discarded the frivolous, the illegible, and the hopelessly insane:

'Dear Billy, I am the Messiah, He who is not sent. The Messiah shall command, it shall be his command. The Messiah commands you according to the commandments of the same to use My name in vain, while you are knowing My wife ...'

'Dear Billy: Last night I woke up and you were standing at the foot of my bed and there was something wrong with your face. Billy, I thought you were going to kill me with a ax. I don't know. Maybe the devil sent this vision to confuse me when I'm having headaches ...'

The answerable letters were passed on to the *Replies* table. Marilyn Temblor closed her magazine, keeping for a moment the after image of one perfume advertisement – it seemed so darned unfair that Crusade workers weren't allowed to – and made her mind blank for business.

The first letter, from a cancer patient, was easy. Marilyn carried it to the row of automated typewriters and ran one unvarnished nail down the list of items posted on the wall:

Habitual sin	359
Unfaithful spouse	360
Marital problems (general)	361
Major illness	362
Afraid of dying	363
Death of spouse	364
Death of child	365

Afraid of dying, then. She punched 363 on the control panel, rolled a sheet of letterhead in the typewriter and carefully typed the salutation:

'Dear Mrs Dale:'

From there on it was simply a matter of switching from MAN to AUTO. The letter was typed in just under six seconds.

Dear Mrs Dale:

I received and read your letter, and I was deeply touched by it. You seem to be afraid of dying. This is only natural, for no creature on God's earth wants to die. For the humble animals, death is an end.

But not for you. FOR YOU, DEATH IS THE VERY BEGINNING.

When Columbus set sail, he didn't know …

And so it went, right on down to the PS about remembering God in your will. A marvelous machine. Marilyn didn't understand how the signers could refer to it as a 'tripewriter'.

The signers were young Bible students who saw no conflict between afternoons reading theology and mornings falsifying Billy's signature to thousands of letters. They were a flippant, cynical bunch, and Marilyn hated taking letters in to them. One in particular, a fair-haired, blue-eyed, disgustingly handsome boy named Jim.

'I understand perfectly,' said the architect. 'Everything modern but nothing extreme.' He and Billy were looking at a sketch entitled *South Elevation: Bibleland*. 'Now, about the mechanical figures and so on?'

Billy flipped through his desk diary. 'I've got my computer man, Jerry, coming in Wednesday – let's all have lunch. How much do you need to know?'

'Everything, sir, everything. Each pavilion must be a container for the thing contained, neither more nor less. For less *is* more, and function designs its form. There must be balance, adaptability, total harmony and standardization …'

'Now what about the site?'

'I prefer to pick a flat, undistinguished piece of land and landscape it, Mr Koch.'

'Okay, but keep the estimate in mind, Archy. And I wish you'd just call me Billy.'

'Very well – Billy. I will not exceed the estimate, you can be sure. And I leave no detail to chance.

'That's something I learned at architecture school in my homeland. My mathematics master used to mark a problem completely wrong if there were even the slightest error. I asked him why I should lose all credit for a simple misplaced decimal point.

'He said, "Wrong is wrong, Ögivaal. When you will be an architect, and your building collapses, it will not matter the reason. You cannot then say " 'This thirty should be a three.' " I never forgot his words.'

'This site …'

'Ah yes. I have one tentative site located, quite ideal but for the fact that it is a small Indian reservation.'

Billy's pale blue eyes flicked up, then back to the plan. 'If it's worth it, we can probably get them moved off. Is it?'

'Yes, yes, it is perfect. Quite near that place – what is the name? Death Valley.'

On the wall above Donagon's desk was a histogram showing who was where in the Nobel race:

Bell and Jopp	----------------
Burnside	------
Donagon	-----------------------
Flaken	-------------------
Korner	-----------------
Müller-Fokker	----?
Smilax	---------

The one who really worried him was Muller-Fokker, who might have done it already. If he had really defected – no one seemed to know for sure – he might have the entire resources of Soviet research at his disposal.

Donagon wiped his damp hands, opened the journal and began just after the ripped-out pages:

We decided not to abandon the attempt after all; to try once more to store a man digitally. The last obstacle had been removed, i.e., storage. Previously we had estimated many thousands of miles of magnetic tape would be required, with complex retrieval problems. The multiple storage paired redundancy tapes, developed by Müller-Fokker (the so-called 'Müller-Fokker tapes') in Vienna and demonstrated by him at the Louisville National Laboratory, were exactly what we needed. These reduced our tape requirements to four ten-inch reels.

The M-F tape is much of a mystery except to its inventor. The principle seems to be *Gestalt* analysis (if that is the term), or recognition of large patterns in large amounts of data. Data fed in is not immediately recorded, but 'comprehended' and compressed – by the tape itself – into formulae. The tape is not magnetic but electrochemical. It may not be erased, but new data may be recorded upon old. There seems to be a layering or –

We do not really understand the M-F tape at all, but we do understand it will do the job. At present we have no way of retrieving what we want from the tape, and since its inventor has vanished, it may take us many years –

Many years –

Every datum will be recorded many times, to reduce error. At present, surgeons are removing tissue samples from the subject (from bones, organs, glands, etc.) and determining cell-structure data. We have already encoded a DNA map, photographs, holographs, X-rays, resin casts, EKG's and so on – as complete an analysis of the subject as we can make. There remains but one step, the mapping of all electrical and chemical activity of the subject's brain. The press will be invited to this session; they will see US succeed or fail.

Succeed or fail.

Through the partition dividing his office from that of Major Fouts, he could hear the crinkle of cellophane and foil, and the sound of devouring.

The laboratory looked like a throne room. Bob sat in the throne, a surgical chair; his courtiers wore rubber gloves and his crown was a steel vise. Above the crown those in the visitors' room could see pinkish-gray, crumpled velvet.

Back of the throne was a large illuminated map of this velvet surface on which men marked the current weather in Bob's brain. On either side were ranks of cabinets in decorator colors. Two featured control panels, one a typewriter, two more the inevitable banks of flashing lights. Four were dialling twin reels of tape (one with some excitement), eight others were anonymous, one was vomiting paper, and the two in the visitors' room were opened to display whiskey and glasses.

There were other press facilities in the visitors' room, including telephones, free cigarettes, sharpened pencils and fresh pads, and a big stack of xeroxed press releases.

The one reporter who did show up had a hell of a time.

'I sure appreciate this,' he said to Donagon. 'I'll bet the rest of the gang haven't got it this good down there in Florida.'

He asked Donagon if he'd ever heard of the magazine he worked for, *LIFE*.
'Florida?'

'Yeah, everyone else went down to cover the big cancer cure story. I missed the plane, so I thought I might as well drop over and check this one out. I really had another assignment over by North Platte, I had to get a picture of this deformed bull. I'd take some shots of your set-up here, only I can't. My camera and stuff caught the plane.'

He wanted Donagon to have a drink with him and hear the anecdote, but the biophysicist was wanted elsewhere.

A voice behind Bob asked him what he felt.

'I feel ... my right foot ...'

'Yes?'

'Oh, you know how it is with workboots.'

'And now?'

'A strawberry, all glowing with starry lenses, a starberry ... recapitulation of the plot of some old man ... buns, for instance ...'

Major Fouts stood watching from half-way across the room, where Donagon manned a bank of switches. Between them and the operation was a forced-air curtain to maintain sterility. It was strange to see a man talking away with half his head sawed off and a group of surgeons peering and probing within. It made Fouts feel the sharpness of his own foot-bones.

'This is a buckle collection ... this is supposed to be a father ... bank statements or ... Is there anyone here named General Motors?' In an altered voice Bob delivered a message of hope to the motor corporation.

'Is this guy in any danger?' Fouts whispered.

'None at all. Shhh.' Donagon threw more switches. A kind of phonograph arm beside the chair swung around, lowered its needle, and began to 'play' the brain.

'What's that?'

'Shh. Nothing.'

'Marge!' Bob shouted. 'As a strawberry blonde ... history as a garbage truck ... Now look! I'm not going to say it again ... this is lumpy.' He wept.

'Now what do you feel?'

'My picture in the atlas ... the strawberries are ... funny how the old school holds up ... the old Lion Oil Company ... arrested! ... I hear you think ...'

He sang a few bars of something no one could identify.

'There's an old saying around here: please wash hands before returning to work ... a man disappears, but his ghost ... he had it, he paid the death ... in the movie freeze rabbit ... U.S. Grant, the truth experiment ... attaches ... the bank hath changed its bank ... the railroad egg trial ... Dixie cups full of penetrating truth, remember? ... smell that?'

'What do you feel like now?'

'I feel like picking my nose.'

'You *are* picking your nose. What … ?'

The door slammed back and four men walked in. Donagon rushed to meet them.

'You'll have to go into the visitors' room,' he said, smiling.

'No we don't.'

'I – what? Which paper are you from?'

'This one.' The tallest man hauled out an old revolver and slapped him with it.

Fouts jumped to the alarm button. When the bell went off, the other three strangers pulled their guns.

'Okay, fat boy, where are they?'

'Where are what?'

'The nigger-babies! The test tubes!'

One of the intruders drove the surgeons away from Bob. 'Aw, Wes, look! Jesus Christ, they cut this guy's head open!'

The one with the big greasy pompadour leveled his gun at Fout's belt. 'How about it, Fats? This one of your nigger expeermints?'

'I don't know what the hell you're talking about. But I do know you're gonna do a stretch in Leavenworth, pal. Better lay down the sidearms and make it a short visit.'

'I think … I think I hear a bell,' Bob volunteered.

'I know your kind,' said the pompadour. 'Tryin' to put a nigger brain into that pore mother! *Come on, boas, let's mess up the place!*' He wheeled and fired a shot into the nearest memory cabinet.

'I smell a shot …' said Bob, still picking his nose.

Fout's auto-destruct mechanism worked almost perfectly. The tape-reader charge misfired, but the other three went off as planned, as soon as one of the unauthorized persons tried to yank open a cabinet.

One charge was in the main memory bank. One was in the control console. They rendered the computer completely useless to Wes Davis and the Mud Flats Ramblers.

The third, slightly bigger charge was embedded in the soft padding of Bob's chair, at about ear level. The chair had been designed by an orthopedic surgeon to maintain posture and reduce fatigue. What was left of it still looked good that evening, to the cleanup crew.

'That's the way I'd like to go,' one remarked. 'Comfy.'

Lieutenant Colonel Fouts tried to shut out the screaming and wailing from the other side of the partition; he tried to order his thoughts.

There was plenty to think about: the government had pulled out of the

Mud Flats project and abandoned the attempt to tape a man. National Arsenamid was expected to follow suit. In retrospect, the idea did smell of circle-squaring and perpetual motion, he had to admit. So if Donagon couldn't take the disappointment and KNOCK OFF THAT NOISE, it only underlined how crazy he was. The Army had kept his leaky dream afloat long enough. Anyway, National Arse would probably find something else for Donagon to do. Design a new cornflake, say, or answer the telephone.

Fouts himself was off for a few weeks' badly needed leave, then some new assignment. He checked a few items off his list: files destroyed, diet started, new oak leaves to buy in Frisco, bag packed, desk cleaned out. There remained only the call to Shairp's next of kin and what else? A Butterfinger candy bar that wouldn't fit into his luggage.

'O God!' said the partition. 'My whole life wasted! *That* close to the Nobel and – ruined! O why have you forsaken me, O my governme—'

'I SAID KNOCK IT OFF!' Fouts slammed his wastepaper basket against the wall four or five times. It set the plywood quaking and reminded him to return the wastebasket to the supply room. Well, screw that. He had a bus to catch in fifteen minutes. With a start on the candy bar, he dialed Mrs R. E. Sharp.

She answered too soon, catching him with a mouthful of stickiness. A big swallow, then:

'Mrs Sharp? Mrs Robert Etwall Sharp? Uh, this is Lt Col Fouts, Knighted Stays Army, Mrs Sharp – oh, *Shairp*, is it? Uh, Mrs Shairp, it is … excuse me … my painful duty to inform you that your husband, you know, Robert Shairp, is dead.

'What window-peeper? No, it's not. No, really, I'm serious. Excuse me, ma'am, PIPE DOWN OVER THERE, YOU MEDICAL EXPERIMENT!

'Did you hear me, ma'am? I said it is my painful etcetera blah blah your husband is dead. The Mud Flats Biomedical Research Project. A joint effort by the Army and National Arsenamid. An accident.

'Yes, we've taken care of the body. We'll be sending you a few personal effects. Oh yes, and if he was a veteran, you get a free flag from the Veteran's Administration.

'Uh-huh. Well, it's been nice talking to you, Mrs Shairp. 'Bye now.'

Five minutes to go. Donagon moaned. Fouts picked up his bag off the desk.

The gun was under it.

He'd found it lying on the laboratory floor after the four lunatics were hauled away. It was evidence, to be sent to the Justice Department. The details of how to send it were in the destroyed files.

For a moment he stood weighing it, half-looking for a place to hide the thing. Then a wail from the next office reminded him of a reasonable solution. Bag and overcoat in one hand, gun in the other, and candy bar between teeth, he barged into Donagon's office.

'Goth oo cath bus, Donagon. Thake this thing off my handths, will oo?'

'What? Oh, sure. Thanks, Algie.' Donagon smiled wanly. Fout's free hand took the Butterfinger. 'Sure you know what to do with it, now? It's evidence, see? You have to ...'

'I understand Algie.' Donagon wiped away a tear and winked. 'Thanks again.'

'Sure. Well. See you.'

The lieutenant ran from the building, his fat ass waving goodbye to Donagon.

Marge put down the phone. 'Your father is dead,' she said. 'So stop goose-stepping around the house and go to your room.'

Many hours, many drinks, later she spoke again, this time to a cigarette table lighter disguised as the vaguest of Oriental gods. 'Bring him back to me. Please. Whole and alive. I'll do anything in return.'

This inferior, butane-operated deity replied within a week, in its own vague way: Marge received Bob's billfold, his shoes, and a suitcase full of dirty socks and underwear.

National Arsenamid debated carrying on with the project alone, without the Army. They thought of consulting MacCormick Hines, but no doubt he would consider this a trivial matter and resent the intrusion. Someone suggested interesting the Navy in making men out of sea-water. But Dr Donagon's suicide made their decision for them: the project was over.

Four reels of tape went on sale in a US Govt. Surplus store in the Midwest, 'PUT YOUR MOTHER-IN-LAW ON TAPE – SHE'LL DIG IT!!!' read the dayglo sign, 'RARE MÜLLER-FOKKER TAPE, FANTASTIC BARGAIN!!!!'

The Army shifted eggs to another basket. In Oregon, a team of biochemists and psychologists were trying to make bears smarter ...

THREE

The Ox

THOUGHTS OF CHAIRMAN MAN
... ... An hour late later jelly days jelly days the bell goes on and on fire I am bladderful late for school at the office

I struggle to stand up somebody has filled the room with plastic amber ice folding me in fakery: folded gyptian mummy folded dead hand card trick gypson giant in the cardifferent twilight of the twomb

(painted on my eye the impenetrable blue jelly of 'this world')

Poe I think of Poe with the opium horrors groping his way to the writing table at dusk or is it dawn: 'There came to my nostrils the strong peculiar odor of moist earth'

So buried alone alive there it is thats life thats life with digby o'dell one of lifes little jokes laff along with charlie chapfall red skeleton milton burial well now tell me mr bones I never seed such a john buryman routine at dusk or was it dawn I must look it up look up

I must be stuck here stuck here or something stuck

As it was is and ever shall be world without anything the experimenters standing there one writing on his clipboard(.) one looking thoughtful one sucking his pencil waxworks all we must be stuck here the film is stuck or

Picking my nose too that ought to give the archaeologists a few laughs the strong peculiar digit DIGIT O christ I must be I am I'm on tape

Yes

Well I'll be damned (Hey Lullay, etc.)

NEMA LIVE SU REVILED
On another level all this word soup has generated another presence, just as IAO generate the alifbet and just as deep structures generate surface structures. I have called the other presence tentatively God. It may not be God. It may not be another presence. It may originate from:

(1)   The machine or part of the machine.
(2)   My brain or part of my brain.
(3)   Some physical outside source, neither machine nor brain.
(4)   Some non-physical outside source.
(5)   Nowhere and nothing (in the case it really is God).
(6)   One of the ten combinations of (1) through (5), in pairs.

(7) One of the ten combinations of three of (1) through (5).

(8) One of the five combinations of four of (1) through (5).

(9) All of (1) through (5).

(10) None of the above.

It all operates like some think tank, where all the words, in crisp shirts (plastic pocket protectors for slide rule, red pencil, black pencil, pen) *con-fer* – run around *conferring* – the important words forming their teams of lesser words, talking up enthusiasm for this project: 'All right, fellas, the buzzword around here today is going to be "epiphany". Bounce that idea around, examine the macro-structure, get the big depth picture. Sam, you'll be handling the theological end of this, I want to see you work nice and close with Bud's team, they're looking at the "weak force" angle. Let's get at the interface of this problem, guys. Let's state our tentative objective as the answer to "Who made you?"'

Then in the beginning was the word, only now there's too much word, its face is like a teleprompter and the answers keep rolling across, answers to questions I haven't thought of asking yet – have I? – and there isn't any way of shutting it off. Maybe my mind is doing all its thinking at the same time, maybe there isn't any 'time' here …

SO MANY DYNAMOS!

'I'm glad you asked me that, Bob. "Are minds mechanistic?" Gee, that's pretty tough. As I'll mention before, there's a little shell game you can play with machines. For any machine there is at least one question you can ask, which the machine can fully comprehend, but which it cannot answer, and to which *you* can see the answer at once.

'Specifically, it is possible to make up a formula which represents the state-ment "this formula is not provable (in the machine)". Then you ask the machine to prove (or disprove) the formula. If it proves it, the formula is true and the statement must be true, so the machine is contradicting itself. If it doesn't prove it, the statement is true, which you know but the machine can't. And that's the difference between a mind and a machine.'

'But suppose someone comes along and alters the machine so it can prove the formula, or at least see the statement is true?'

'Well then it ain't the same machine, are it? So for this new machine you can construct a new formula of this same type. And as often as the machine is altered – or alters itself – you can do the same.'

'But what's the difference? I mean, I'm sitting there thinking up questions and the machine is sitting there thinking up answers – the *machines*, then – so maybe a mind is just a self-altering machine after all.'

His face starts to sag. I think of asking if it's lawful to render tribute to

Caesar or heal the sick on a Sunday, but I see it's not necessary. He collapses into a rainbow puddle of words:

THE RUINS, AUTOPSY OF FIRED, BESTRIDED REAL LIVES, TOO. WHAT PRUNE OF 'IF', OR ITS LESSER GOODNESS? THE RUINS, AUTOPSY OF FIRED, BESTRIDED REAL LIVES, TOO, FOR HE HAS FOUND IT'S SMOKE-RE-THATCHED, MAKING IT WHY MIST-DEALER'S BRAWNY. MY OTHER'S EVIL. ENDS. REQUEST EDITOR'S READING DEVICE.

One level down there's this detective business. I'm sitting stupefied by fumes from the coal grate, picking my nose and listening to him, Whoms, drone on about some notion about free will:

' … it's a puzzle, Whatson. We find the man responsible for a particularly ghastly murder and he turns out to be a madman – not responsible for his actions. Yet we call the killing itself an irresponsible act … I ask you!'

I suspected my friend the sleuth had had a calabashful of his special smoking mixture, and so was far from responsible for what he said at the moment. Fixing my eyes on an unfinished sampler upon the wall, I resolved not to answer.

The sampler read – or seemed to read, in the dimness:

HE RUNS, A TOPSY OF FIRE, BESTRIDE REAL LIVES, TOO. WHAT RUNE OF 'F', OR ITS LESSER GOODNESS? HE RUNS, A TOPSY OF FIRE, BESTRIDE REAL LIVES, TOO, FOR HE HAS FUND IT'S MORE THATCHED, MAKING IT WHIST-DEALER'S BRAWNY MOTHER'S EVIL. ENDS. REQUEST EDITOR'S RE ADVICE.

(THE MIND REELS)
and alone on the island. My only companion is a stuffed parrot. Breaking teeth off my comb to keep track of the days. Today a plane went over. It didn't respond to my signal fire, unless you can call skywriting a response:

HE RUNS TOPS OF FIR, BEST IDEAL LIVES, TOO. TUNE OF FORTLESSNESS? HE RUNS TOPS OF FIR, BEST IDEAL LIVES, TOO, FOR FUN I'M RE-THATCHED, MAKING IT WHISTLER'S BRAW MOTHER'S EVIL. ENDS. REQUESTED TO READ VICE.

These mystery letters began blowing away at once, leaving:

HE RUNS TOPS OF F BEST I AL LI ES, TOO.

E FORTLESSNESS? HE RUNS TOPS OF F BEST I AL LI ES, TOO,UN RETHATCHED, MAKING IT WHISTLE BR OTHER'S EVIL. ENDS. REQUESTED RE D ICE.

This isn't working out at all. I'd hoped to tell the story but the pen has to trace its own shadow … the story includes the world around the story and the story in it' … say A writes a story about an imaginary land, and A' writes about some wholly fictitious 'historical' event, and A" writes about or hints at, some fabulous country with all its rulers, rules, ruled … then B many centuries later finds the old manuscripts of these works, misses their metaphors and sets the event in the country, which is in the land.

'The Iructu', he writes seriously, 'have no word for death.

'They refer to it indirectly as "potatoes". Death is "eating your potatoes", burial is "planting the potatoes", a stillborn child is "new potatoes", etc. The potato, they explain, like death, has many eyes …'

Critic B' believes the story and adds embellishments of his own. So do other scholars, until by the time of B'''' men are actually planning to set out on a great sea voyage to visit the fabled land.

We set sail in the year of our Lord —. Each new problem encloses but does not answer the last. 'Let's sail till we come to the edge'[2] Failure due to unstable ambient temperatures, causing shock. indeed, but over the edge is just another face of the old world-cube. I don't even know what the problem is any more, but I go on calculating, reasoning, drifting off course …

And in the water around the ship the plankton have lofty thoughts as they top each wave, and see the next wave on …

2 *Camp Concentration*, Thomas M. Disch.

PART 2

Noun 'Man'

FOUR

Feinwelt rode up in the elevator, thinking psychiatrist thoughts and share-holder thoughts. *The split is there, all right, Feinwelt, you crazy shrink. It isn't enough to be den mother to a bunch of ex-transvestites. It isn't enough to be the biggest shareholder in Stagman Enterprises next to Glen Dale himself. No, you've got to wangle – watch that! – your way in to become Glen's personal Big Shrink. What are you doing here, in this, this mind of a building? In this acci-dental empire?*

Glen Dale's empire *was* accidental, like a famous pearl. It had begun with a small, quite ordinary grain of irritation – when, in youth, Glen had dis-covered that he could not, no matter what, get laid.

It was improved and rounded by a few coats of what Glen called 'sophisti-cated seduction techniques'. A better bottle of wine, a few more jazz tapes, four-star brandy, tickets to shows, dinner for two, oh yes, and smoking jack-ets, cocktail shakers … layer upon layer did this poor oyster of a man apply to his misery. Cars, a yacht, the magazine, money, clothes, more of every-thing, better of each, a glossier magazine, the Stagman Club … until the accident seemed deliberate and fine. *I wonder whether the pearl ever chokes the oyster to death?*

Eleven million *Stagman* readers opened their center folds each month to enjoy the twenty-two million well-photographed nipples of Miss Monthly. Then there were the dozens of Stagman Clubs, the thousands of bare-chested girls in buckskin ('Does'), the hundreds of thousands of moist men who, being strictly forbidden to touch the Does, except in the palm with crisp money, came to play. The grandest club of all was here in the Stagman Tower, in the scrotal end. The shank was devoted to magazine offices; the tip, a pent-house for the chief.

The elevator bore psychiatrist Feinwelt up the tube, chief-ward, as he wor-ried that Glen might be a difficult case. Nearly forty, after all, and apparently a virgin.

Shareholder Feinwelt worried on the other side. What if Glen did get cured? And what if that meant the collapse of the driving force behind *Stag-man*? It was sublimation, no doubt of it. And who, confronted with a pearl of this quality, could want to open it to get the grain of sand? Who but a head doctor? *But drop it, think of something else, think of how many spermatazoa are jerked off over Miss Monthly, let's see …*

And spermatazoan Feinwelt, homunculus Feinwelt, crawled upward (eleven million times two million, but not all do it, say six million, that makes, um …)

Twelve trillion. Twelve trillion unfulfilled humans, condemned to death over the tits of one stenographer.

Glen sucked a Coke and reread proofs of a picture feature for *Stagman* on the Good Life (as lived by Glen Dale).

Above, the urbane editor-publisher of Stagman *at work in his luxurious penthouse pad atop Stagman Tower. In Minneapolis did Glen Dale a stately pleasuredom decree, and a posh and private playground. This lordly manor, replete with a brace of handsome amenities, is fully equipped for funful frolic. Sartorial sophisticate Glen wears Aztec feather crown, whose pinions, handcrafted, spell out Interplanetary Drinking Team.*

He took off his Prussian spike helmet and put it in the hat closet. The Phrygian cap was better.

Too effeminate. He took off the cap and tried a comic miter labeled THANK GOD IT'S FRIDAY. Feinwelt came in as he took that off, too. 'Working?'

Left, a light brunch, served à deux in the congenial dining alcove, makes a felicitous and festive feast. Nonpareil culinary accomplishments like this bœuf Ursuline avec Dobermann Sauce are usual includements in his gourmet cuisine. Pausing in a demonstration of his trencherman prowess, Glen toasts the lady in sparkling Hunck.

Right, afternoon coffee with the magazine staff by the capacious outdoor pool provides plaisir aplenty for the man of pelf. Lavish libations and the many-pleasured music of a chamber group make of this work conference a picnic fit for a potentate.

'Proofs.'
'Well, don't let me disturb you. I have a couple of hours to kill, Glen. No hat today, I see?'
'Couldn't find anything I liked.'

'Is that so?' The way Feinwelt said it made Glen feel this was all a mistake. Did he really need a psychiatrist? Especially one he knew already.

'Why don't you go into the den and make yourself at home, Doctor?' Maybe he just needed an understanding woman. As in the story in last month's issue.

'Where's Myra? Haven't seen her around for a few days.'

'Yes, she's in the hospital again. Myra's decided she wants Oriental eyes.'

Left, Glen's den par excellence boasts electronic wonders back of those tapestries that savor of the sybaritic. Princely preprandial potables proliferate, the talk is intime, and pretty guests admire this floor of hand-tooled blue Morocco.

Feinwelt picked up an object from the coffee table (DUROTREND CLOCK TABLE LIGHTER CONTAINS RADIO, FLASHLIGHT, TACH, DRINK HYGROMETER AND TAPE RECORDER WITH RECHARGEABLE POWER PACK) and plucked at its chrome attachments for a moment.

'Well then. Shall we get to work?'

'Her name was Meri. M-E-R-I. A model. I thought I had it made: a fire in the fireplace, Billie Holliday on tape, schnapps on the bearskin rug. *I had every step planned.*'

'And?'

'And nothing!'

There was silence.

'Why do you think that was, Glen?'

'How do I know? What's wrong with me?

'I mean I'm forty (not quite), single, not bad-looking, rich, famous, hard-working, successful … And no Babbitt, either. Who owns every side Julian Huxley's Ants ever cut? Who bought the first holograph Bergen made? Who paid to have Deef John Holler tapes smuggled out of the Library of Congress and re-recorded? I'm hip and I've got taste. I blow pretty good piano. I have the best in the city. I'm oenologically wise. My sartorial selection is peerless.

'*But I don't get anything.*'

In the privacy of the penthouse elevator, Feinwelt let out whoops of laughter.

He was more serious when he conferred downstairs with the managing editor.

'Hank, the way I see it, there's one frustrated son of a bitch up there. As his doctor, I can't ethically slow down his therapy or anything, you know, but I'll tell you how we *can* keep him producing. Fix him up. Line him up with about a hundred or two fine-looking, frigid girls. You know the kind, this place must be crawling with them. "Look but don't touch" ladies. If necessary, bribe 'em. Half on non-delivery. You might stick on a monitor camera on that bedroom, to make sure. Then, if things look like they're getting out of hand, create a diversion.'

'You mean, call him up?'

'Call him up, smash in the door, start a fire, send in the cops, tell him he's lost a page proof – anything.' He leaned forward, overpowering Hank with the scent of Chanel No. 5. 'I hope I don't have to tell you what happens if we fail. If that guy up there gets his rocks off *once*, it could mean the end! *Stagman* will lose him – and about ten million readers. The leading men's magazine today, and tomorrow it could be just one more creep sheet on the boots-and-garter belt counter.'

The sermon at Vandal Ballpark was considered an unqualified success by everyone – except the preacher, Billy Koch.

'My voice went all cruddy there at the end, Jerry. You notice that?' Billy and his computer expert harnessed themselves into the Saette and waited for the guards to open the gates.

'I thought you were fine, Billy. Really.'

'Just the same, I'll be glad when you get that robot contraption finished. My voice is getting blown out. And that damned thing better work, too, for the money I'm paying.'

'Oh, it'll work, don't you worry, sir. Then you can take it easy now and then. You've been flying too much, that affects the throat.'

Billy wheeled the special car into traffic and floored it. The other vehicles around them slowed, stopped, then slipped past in reverse, gaining speed. Billy grunted happily, leaned over and switched on the videotape replay of his sermon.

'*The Devil can be a lion in the streets, seeking whom he may devour!*'

'Well, what I'm worried about is the healing ceremony. Them people get damned close, you know. Closer than that truck I'm tailgating. They can count the drops of sweat on my brow. How will it look if—'

'Don't worry about a thing, Billy. We've thought of every possibility. Our audioanimatron is *exactly* like you, and we're programming in tapes of all your old sermons. Gestures, speech – LOOK OUT! – speech, why you won't know it isn't you. All we need now are these special tapes ...'

'Get over, you bastard! OVER!' Billy leaned far out the window to scream at a taxi, then sawed the ruby steering wheel to change lanes twice, fast.

'He can be a quiet cancer, burning in the brainy,' continued the figure on the tiny screen. Billy turned it off.

'Christ, they let anybody drive a cab.'

'It's left at the next light,' said Jerry. His face was drawn with fear, and the odor of overheated deodorant escaped from his crease-resistant suit. Nevertheless he crossed one artificial leather shoe over the other, in a sketch of relaxation. 'Better watch out for the old woman crossing.'

'I do the driving, damn you!'

The old woman was caught by the yellow light. She turned, hesitated, then started back into the path of the car. Billy accelerated, cramped the wheel for the turn, and gave her a blast on his musical horn. 'Rock of Ages', it sang hastily, 'cleft for me.'

'Up yours, y' old bag!' he called cheerfully.

She looked up, startled, raised one hand as if to ward off the car, then leaped back nimbly as it slid past.

'Hahaha, I knew it! I knew she could move fast enough if she had to. Christ, I'd like to see all pedestrians fry in Hell!'

He drew up before the US Government Surplus store and double-parked. 'Don't take too long, I got to get back to Crusade HQ.'

The computer man carried his attaché case and natural shoulders inside the store.

'I could only save you two,' said the clerk, holding up a reel of tape. 'I just hadda let the others go. The govermint bought one – at least he said he was govermint. That's something – buying back their own surplus!'

'Well, two'll be enough, anyway.' As Jerry made out the check, the clerk went on. 'About a million guys called up asking about um. Wish I had more, but I guess there ain't no more. Hadda kid in here five minits ago asking for one, but he couldn't afford it anyway.'

Ank sat in the pickup, calming his hysterical breathing. He watched a bronze Saette cut the corner badly (nearly hitting an old lady) and pull up across the street. Then his eyes misted over, and for a few seconds he lost interest in looking at anything.

Anybody who owned a car like that could easily afford a Müller-Fokker tape. While Ank, in his fifty-dollar pickup truck with a wired-on exhaust …

The beauty of M-F tape was that it was really randomized, the clerk had said. While an ordinary computer could generate 'random' numbers, they weren't really random at all. Just fitted to a very complicated equation. Any mechanism was finally predictable.

But the Müller-Fokker tape went beyond mechanism. It was philosophically different. There was room enough in it for (according to the clerk) a human mind!

Sales talk, maybe. And at two thousand dollars a reel, you'd expect a good pitch. Ank wanted it, all the same, more than he'd ever wanted anything – as much as he wanted to be a known painter.

Well, nothing to be done. He would just have to go on saving his pennies from reviewing other people's work, get some time on a small, cheap computer …

Purring smoke, the old pickup truck pulled away from the curb and moved off. A moment later, Jerry came out of the store, tossed two odd-looking reels of computer tape – pink, it was, flesh pink – into the back seat and climbed in.

'Better fasten your harness, boy. I *drive* this baby.'

The Saette screamed out, jerking them back in their seats. With every gear change they snapped forward and back, like two mechanical clowns rocking with canned mirth.

'How much was that?'

'Four thousand, Billy. But it was worth it, you'll see. That tape will run the whole thing for us. We'll sort out fragments of your sermons and let that tape re-sort them into new ones.'

Billy drove down back streets to avoid traffic.

'Hold on now. LOOK OUT, YOU SON OF SATAN! Jesus, a man can't even drive across the city with all these – what were you saying, Jer?'

'I said we've almost worked out the scheme for Bibleland. Of course it's a lot easier, because the audioanimatrons there will just be mechanical gadgets, while this one will practically be a man. I'm …'

Billy raced for the yellow light as Ank, coming from the right, tried to coast through on the red. They met.

'Jeez, look at all the blood!'

'Look at the funny foreign job. They must be *dead* in there.'

'Yeah, nobody could live through that.'

The witnesses who swore this, could, a moment later, attest to a miracle, for the battered door of the Saette wiggled, groaned and gave up a whole, smiling man. But for a cut on his forehead, he seemed unhurt.

'You all right, buddy? Hey, aren't you Billy Koch?'

'The Lord,' said Billy gravely, 'has preserved me for His work. Get an ambulance, somebody. My partner's bleeding like a stuck pig in there.' Somebody leapt to obey.

The ambulance men got to the computer expert first, loading him and the reel of tape he clutched on a stretcher, applying a compress to his knee. The fire department had to cut away part of the truck to get Ank out. He was bruised and delirious. As they lifted him clear, two objects fell out of his lap: a reel of tape and Jerry's foot (still shod in gleaming unscuffed plastic). A fireman picked them up and tossed them on the stretcher.

'Are you sure you don't want to come along for a check-up?' an intern asked Billy, who was helping clear the crowd.

'No thanks, Doctor. A Greater Physician has already checked me out and found me fit.'

He hailed a cab and returned to Crusade Headquarters. An hour later, while he was going over the plans for Bibleland with his architect, Bill began scratching the bandage on his forehead.

'I think,' he said in sonorous, crowd-thrilling tones, 'I think the doggie want a dink a gaga.'

FIVE

'Dr Fellstus! I am here to answer the phone and take care of your appointments. And that's all!'

'Gee whiz, Marge.' The vet's forehead twitched, snapping his dark elastic brows. It was one of Fellstus's chief ways of showing emotion. 'You're a damned attractive woman. And you're single now ... so am I. To me, you're ...'

'A receptionist,' she said. 'By the way, it's almost time for Mr Hines and Toto.' She batted away his hand with a fistful of patients' files. 'I'm a receptionist, you are a *veterinarian*, remember?'

'In your mouth, it sounds – dishonest.'

'Just you forget about my mouth, and all the rest. Or I'll quit. So help me.'

Fellstus tried a smile, but the brows went on jerking. 'If you quit, how will you keep that boy of yours at that expensive military school? Be reasonable, kid. It's a good job.

'And it could be even better. You could have anything you wanted. I'd set you up with a nice little place ...'

The door opened and Mr MacCormick Hines led in a gloomy collie. Fellstus improvised a professional face.

'Mr Hines! And Toto! Let's go right into my office, shall we?'

Hines beamed recognition on Marge. 'My dear, you're looking radiant. *Radiant*. Dr Fellstus, you're a lucky vet.' He nudged Fellstus in the stomach with his gold-headed cane.

'Oh, don't I know it, sir.' His huge flat fingers closed over the old man's shoulder and he propelled him into the inner office.

When their session was finished, Mr Hines stopped by Marge's desk. 'I – ah – meant to ask you something, my dear. Have I seen – I know this sounds awkward, but have I seen your face before? On television, perhaps?'

'No, I'm afraid not.' Seeing that he made no move to leave, she changed the subject. 'How's Toto getting along?'

'Depressed, Mrs Shairp. Depressed.' He cleared his throat. 'Really, you ought to think of trying TV work. If you don't mind my saying so, yours is a unique face: young, yet old, pure, yet motherly, a face touched by suffering, yet – I see I'm embarrassing you, so let me come to the point.

'A certain food company I know of is looking for a woman to do television commercials. I have an idea you'd be perfect for the the part. Why not give them a try?'

She half-smiled. 'No, really, I don't think …'

'I have their card here.' He extracted a card and laid it before her. 'That's the man to see – Mr Bradd. The director of the Marketing Division.'

Marge did not look at the card. What was this one after? What were they all after? She was thirty, hardly more than plain, anything but sexy. Yet the insurance man – and then Dr Fellstus – and now a rich old man wanted to 'get her on television'. It was all too absurd!

'I know what you're thinking,' he said. 'But let me assure you, I have no interest in you personally. Indeed, you may never see me again – Toto is breaking off therapy – but I do feel this isn't your line of work. And you'd be doing Bradd and his division a favor if you'll go talk to them. Goodbye.'

Marge still did not look at the card, but sat daydreaming while Dr Fellstus ushered in the next patient. Through the closed door came the sounds of therapy:

'Shake hands, boy. Come on, Snuffy, shake hands.'

'*Wrowf!*'

'Seems a little upset today, Mrs Grebe. Did you give him the tranquilizers I prescribed?'

'Oh yes, Doctor. And I did like you said – shook hands with the paper boy to show that he wasn't our enemy.'

'Yes?'

'Well you see, our paper boy isn't too bright. I guess he thought I was inviting him to make a pass or something. Anyway, he did, and I had to slap him. Poor Snuffy went berserk!'

There was a pause.

'I see. Well now, we'll just have to try something else, won't we?'

Marge picked up the card. *National Arsenamid. O God.* She tore it up and threw it in the wastebasket.

No favors were going to be done for that company. First they'd used Bob, then made a medical guinea pig out of him. Destroyed him.

On the other hand, she was tempted. The image of herself as a TV personality appealed to her (and wouldn't she be, somehow, closer to Bob?) though she damned her vanity (Two featureless electronic blips, suspended in the void …).

She felt like laughing at the whole mess, herself included.

Fellstus showed his patient and patient's owner out and then turned to Marge, his mustache at an angle of concern.

'You've been crying, poor kid. What's wrong? And what are you looking for in that wastebasket?'

*

204

Mr Bradd wore a pair of heavy-rimmed glasses shaped like little TV screens. He was tanned, athletic, good-looking and (judging by the way he stood too close and talked too loud) homosexual.

'I'll give you the straight poop on this, baby. As Bette Cooke, you'll have a hell of a responsibility. It's not just froodge, you know.' *Froodge.* The word was new to her, probably some coined media term – though for all she knew, everyone was using it. Marge felt as though she were coming out of a convent. 'It's something,' he went on, 'to live up to. A big, big image.'

He limbered up his pitching arm and fired an imaginary fast ball at his desk. The desk was a giant replica of a cereal package. 'That's our old package design for *Weethearts.* The new one, the exciting one, will have a picture of Bette Cooke herself on it.'

He tested his punch against the palm of his other hand. 'We'll do a week of camera tests, keed. If you make it – and you have every chance, Mr Hines seldom fouls out as a talent scout – your face will become better known than Miss Liberty's. We'll have you on the soup, the cake mix, the hair drier, the freeze-dried banana-pimento pizza, everything. And on every network time-slot we can grab.

'So you see, you'll be a very big package. You'll be out there, all by yourself, carrying the ball for National Arse. What do you say, kid? Any questions?'

There were no questions. He toed an invisible bag, stretched, and looked at her as if she were the runner on first. 'Test tomorrow, check with Scheduling for the time. All set, babe?'

Mac Hines rubbed his hands with anticipation, a gesture he'd picked up from television.

'So Bradd likes her. Well well well well *well!* This is perfect. She never should have been stuck in that dreary soap opera in the first place. Now she'll appreciate my help – she'll be grateful – and when I ask her over for dinner ...'

In the bathroom, Glen squeezed a blackhead in his nose. Now he couldn't go back to the living room until the red mark disappeared.

Left, in the spare-no-expense palatial dining room, guests sample the brimming buffet of epicure edibles. The quiet elegance of brushed cashmere walls set the grande luxe *tone, and a full complement of post-Pop paintings accent the sumptuous set-piece, a vintage musical dining table, richly crafted of Dead Sea marble.*

Right, late-lingering guests have a dawn swim and break their fasts at Glen's bountiful board of gourmet goodies. Smoked frim, scrambled eggs and heartier delectations from his well-stocked larder are accompanied by plenteous potations. Bibbing and munching, they watch the burnished, lustrously unique sunrise, as the party ends in acclamations gustatory and gemütlich cheer.

There was no use going on hiding in the bathroom. Feinwelt was sure to think he was up to something in here.

Feinwelt fiddled with the gadget on the mantel. By its left breast, it was 3:30. In the right, the glass was falling, signaling rain. 'Go on, Glen.'

'There's nothing more to tell. I didn't make it, that's all. I *never* make it.'

'Hmm. Why do you think that is?'

'There's always something. Norma Jean had her period. Zelda was thinking it over when the phone rang. Jessina was afraid of her husband – I guess he *examines* her or something. Jully really wanted to, but she said she had this infection. Glinda was afraid I'd lose respect for her. Pippy was too tired. Heidi said she was just plain afraid.' He sighed. 'It's always something.'

Sighing, he took off the straw boater and sailed it across the room. After a few moments he went to the hat closet, took down a bullfighter's hat and put it on.

'Anyway, tonight it'll be different. I can feel it. I've got this hot little number named Lornette all lined up, see. Hank fixed it up. He says she—'

'Glen, let's cut out the crap. This isn't going to be any different from any other night, and you know it. Face facts, you're no winner. There's no point in blaming the girls every time, is there? What about all the genuine opportunities you've had?'

Glen hung his head.

'Until you decide what it is you're really looking for, you won't find it, believe me. Anyway, what's important isn't whether you get laid or not – is it?'

The torero hat fell to the carpet.

'Visited your mother lately, Glen?'

Right, urbane Glen Dale's vintage Mom in terminal cancer ward. Nattily attired in speculum and authentic, handcrafted stethoscope, Glen (far right) bibs medicinal alcohol with nurse friend.

'Why not, Glen?'

' … I really meant to get to see her this month. I mean, gosh, I owe her everything. You know, I think the world of her … '

'Do you, indeed?'

Feinwelt's psychoanalytic method was like three-card monte. The victim was tricked into a wrong choice and then it was explained to him how he came to be so stupid. The explanation itself meant nothing – it was but a further piece of misdirection – for there was no 'right' choice. Feinwelt believed that whatever a person believed about himself was, by definition, a lie.

'You think I don't like my mother, don't you?'

Feinwelt played a game of church-and-steeple with his fingers.

'Well, maybe I don't like her. Maybe I feel she didn't give me enough love, so – yes, that's it, of course. I reject her now for her rejection of me in the past!'

'Indeed? But wasn't it really your *father* who rejected you? Didn't you feel he was paying too much attention to Mom and too little to you?'

'Of course! That explains everything! I'm so afraid my father will hate me for it, that I can't make out ...'

'Not so fast. Does it really "explain" everything? Or are you just grabbing at explanations to avoid—'

'To avoid realizing that I hated *both* my parents!'

'Hated? No, what you bottled up for so many years couldn't have been hate, Glen. Rather, let us say, lust.'

'Ah? Maybe so. You're right, Doctor.'

'And *you* are too willing to agree with me. So willing that—'

'I don't know about *that*. I hope I know my own mind.'

'Then why am I here? You don't mean that. You're only disagreeing to please me ...'

'No I'm not!'

' ... as you feel you never pleased your dad. Yet on a deeper level, you'd like to kill me.'

'Wrong again, you officious bastard!'

'Not at all.' Feinwelt lit a cigarette with Glen's table lighter, a jade mermaid that contained a tiny, glassed-in roulette wheel. 'Not at all. I can see you've been squeezing blackheads in your nose just now, both to make yourself "presentable" to me and to inflict upon yourself a mild punishment for not killing me. A punishment you feel you'd really like to direct at your father.'

'SHUT UP! SHUT UP! I'm warning you.'

'Exactly. Since your father is dead, there is no one else to warn. Since your mother is too ill to stand as a father-surrogate ...'

'YOU LEAVE MY MOTHER OUT OF THIS!'

'But that's exactly what *you're* trying to do – leave her out of things. To punish her for, as you imagine, trying to take the place of your father. You think her cancer is a sibling-substitute, a possible baby brother ...'

'SHUT UP!'

'Tut. A little respect, Glen boy. Or I'll take away – this!' He seized the jade mermaid and made a theatrical gesture of pocketing it. Glen jumped him and the two men fell over the coffee table, releasing a stack of *Stagmans* which flopped and sprawled around their struggling feet.

'Take my lighter, you son of a bitch?'

'Is it so important?'

'It's mine!'

The machine began coming to pieces in their hands. Feinwelt, holding the biggest piece, cracked the raging editor behind the neck with it.

'Don't apologize,' he said when Glen came to. 'It was all part of your therapy. Well, I see our fifty minutes are up. Same time tomorrow, okay?'

'Nnnnhnm.'

Marge held up a package of frozen peas.

'Here's great news for housewives!' she cried.

'Here's GREAT news for housewives!'

'Here IS great news for housewives!'

'HERE'S great news for housewives!'

'Here's great news for HOUSEwives!'

There were six syllables to the announcement. Each might be said in one of three pitches; with low, ordinary or high volume; drawled out, chopped short or said normally; said with or without a smile and with or without a gesture. That made, they told her, a total of over one and a half trillion ways of saying it, and Marge feared somehow they might make her try them all.

Mr Bradd explained that a few hundred would suffice. 'We need enough good takes to get a fix on you with our computer editor,' he said. 'That does all the pit work. We just get a few sets of good visual and a few of good sound. Then the computer chops and blends it all, to come up with what the fans think they want. Or what the computer thinks they think.'

'I don't understand.'

Mr Bradd drove an imaginary golf ball and watched his follow-through. 'An ad used to be made up, shipped out and that was that. We keep a finger on ratings and sales, and we do polls. If we find out that, say, a smile just on the word "fabulous" pulls sales in Oregon, then we plug that into the computer and it makes up a special video tape for just Oregon. Whatever we learn, we ask for, and the old computer comes up with it. Of course we still have to shoot the stuff, and have some idea of what we want in the first place. And we do need you. You can never really get along without the human element.' That was Bradd's favorite line, from an old company training film he'd written years ago.

'Hey!' He looked at his watch. 'You'd better get some shuteye, teammate. Tomorrow's a big one. See you in the makeup section at eight.'

'Good night, Mr Bradd.'

'Night, pal.' He patted her buttocks in a comradely fashion.

Marge went home to study her lines for the following day. No letter from Spot again. An unhappy mask looked back at her from the mirror. It moved, intoning again and again, 'It's so easy with KREW! It's *magic!*'

SIX

At six hundred hours the first bell rings.

Spot (Cadet Sturgemoore Shairp) gets out of bed in the approved manner, first untying the thongs that fasten his wrists to the top side of the blanket, then placing his left foot on the floor (counting off the toes aloud as they touch in order), then pivoting smartly so as to come to attention in a full brace. There are seven wrinkles under his chin, the cleft between his shoulder blades can grip a ping-pong ball, his stomach is sucked in and his elbows make 150° angles.

He holds this position while General Rockstone bellows the morning invocation over the video address system (a cadet is not allowed to look at the screen). Then Spot makes his bed with mitered corners, sweeps his room (beginning at the Northwest corner, in honor of Rockstone's home state, Alaska) and returns to attention.

At the next bell, he is allowed forty-five seconds to go to the toilet, one minute to shower, and one minute to get into his uniform (tucking in the shirt with wooden paddles). Next, inspection.

Gen. Flamel ('Rocky') Rockstone was retiring as president of the St Praetexta Military Academy, and Lt Col Algernon Fouts was taking his place. The entire cadre had assembled on the parade ground, in wind and drizzle, to hear the shrill voice of the cadet colonel read the official history of Rocky's major (indeed his only) engagement in World War Two:

The US held a chain of Pacific islands known as the Corydons. All but one small island at the end of the chain (thought to be uninhabitable) had been fully cleared and turned to military uses. On the last day of the war, Rocky (then a lieutenant) and thirty men were being ferried by plane from a base in the Corydons to a distant fleet. The plane passed over the entire island chain, flying low and taking of course no evasive action. When it reached the last, Sweet Potato Island, the sky around it was suddenly filled with small-arms fire.

The pilot was killed at once. The wounded co-pilot just managed to crash-land in a thicket. And on VJ Day Rocky and his new command found themselves in the hands of the enemy.

The loss of their plane was somehow undetected – perhaps everyone had been indoors listening to the capitulation on shortwave – and no one came looking for them.

Here the official account was a list of hideous tortures, heroic sacrifices and so on, and it stressed the bravery of Lt Rockstone. What made the tortures unendurable was their taking place within sight of a US naval base on the next island. Rocky and his group were able to see ships come and go, planes skywriting V's, and even hear victory salutes. They themselves were well hidden in the jungle, and their captors, a stubborn and self-sufficient unit, refused to believe what was obviously true. The plane was assumed lost at sea, and, due to Japanese and American clerical errors, rescue took well over a year.

While they listened to the official account, many of the cadets turned their thoughts to the other, unofficial, version they had read last night after lights-out. It mentioned no tortures. It said in fact that Rocky and his men were treated well by the Japanese, who starved themselves to give them the choicest food, saw to their health, cleanliness and well-being, and even made small gifts of money. It seemed these Japanese soldiers had been without women for some time …

But this was only a schoolboy version, written ungrammatically and typed out in many smudgy carbons, read by flashlights under the blankets. None who read it could really believe all of it.

The shrill voice stopped, and the band, their instruments untuned by the cold, struck up a warped march. The whole school marched past the reviewing stand, past the bunting bearing the school motto ('Those who say we are women are liars' was the translation) and once around the parade ground. There were three large rectangles each composed of four small rectangles, each in turn composed of four marching lines of ten children each. One was Spot. He could be easily singled out, had anyone been looking, as the one who changed step every four or five paces, and always unsuccessfully. No one, however, was looking.

Fouts suppressed a yawn. 'What are your plans, General?'

'I'm supposed to command a new outfit, X Forces, but I don't know any more about it than you do. All I know is, we assemble in Florida and await orders from the Pentagon. From that gentleman soldier, General Weimarauner.' He grimaced. 'Keep all that under your hat, of course.'

'Of course.'

The general turned his toothless profile to watch the kids. 'These boys are pretty easy to handle. About all you have to do is drill the heck out of them and keep them from playing with themselves.'

Rocky considered playing with oneself sinful, weakening, deleterious to physical and mental health, and probably the main cause of syphilis, so-called 'thalidomide babies', divorce and losing battles.

Accordingly he forbade solitary showers, toilet doors, single rooms, photographs of any females except mothers, lectures in human biology, dirty jokes, obscene language and possession of any object that might conceivably be used in masturbation. Shower and toilet time were strictly limited, and touching one's own unclothed body minimized.

Most jacking off, therefore, went on in the library at study time. Nearly every cadet who was old enough jazzed the bottom of a table while staring blankly at *The Rise of the Dutch Republic* or Herodotus.

The library was a large drafty room dominated by Rocky's favorite picture, a painting of Galahad inscribed:

> *My strength is as the strength of ten*
> *Because my heart is pure*

'Another thing,' said the general. 'Watch out for letters home. Censor them. Remember, parents magnify the slightest complaint.'

Fouts jutted his chin in a tight-collar gesture. 'But don't the parents wonder when they get a blacked-out letter?'

'I didn't mean like military censorship. I meant, if you get a letter that isn't right, throw it out. I've had one kid here writing three letters a week *begging* his mother to take him home. Well, naturally, *that* kind of thing ...'

'Naturally, sir. I don't believe in coddling America's next generation of fighting men.'

Wes Davis thought she was just about the whitest woman he'd ever seen. There seemed to be a special message for him alone in the way she held up a slip and said, 'DRIX just *eats* dirt! Your white undies will be whiter than Heaven knows!'

One of the other prisoners in the recreation lounge made the mistake of saying something about getting in her undies. It took a guard and three trustees to pull Wes off him.

Later Wes calmed himself enough to read his cellmate a little of the book he was working on:

'The difference between a nigro and us is like between a skyscraper and a mud hut or a moon rocket and a spear, or God Almighty and a wood baboon. If you wanted a computer, who would you go to a black African country or our Great Nation? If you wanted a constitution a painting or a poem who would you ask some black savage with a bone through his nose or a white man like Tom Jefferson, Norm Rockwell or Ed Guest? Can we go on listening to the syphilitic Europeans and Communist junky perverts who insist the nigro is our equal? He is not our equal because he is not even human!

'What human could live the way the colored do in Harlem – six or ten to a room? And in Calcutta and Tokyo even more! What human could work for the wages of a black in South Africa – $10 a month! And how about savage rhythm music and cannibalism?

'Let's look at some of the nigros' heroes. George Washington Carver introduced the peanut, a plant whose vines soon killed off the cotton and made land worthless! Peanut vines wrapped themselves around the great heart of the South, choking her to death!'

'By God, Wes, I never thought of that!' The cellmate slapped his denimed thigh. 'Peanuts!'

'Statistics show,' Wes read, 'peanut brittle is a major cause of tooth decay in children, and peanut butter causes malnutrition.' He looked up. 'Ever notice how it sticks to the roof of your mouth?'

'Like a parasite!'

'Thou hast said it. It *is* a parasite, introduced by the nigger conspiracy to wipe us out. Kids have died injecting peanut butter into their veins! And think of the old people, struggling with glued-up dentures.'

'By God, Wes, that's right! Peanuts even have their own comic strip, I hear!'

Wes read: 'GET THE OLD PEOPLE AND CHILDREN FIRST, & YOU PARALYZE THE NATION. So goes the motto of the Great Nigro Conspiracy.'

He was not reading to his cellmate to entertain or enlighten. The cellmate was educated. He helped criticize Wes's style and grammar – and he knew a publisher.

Sometimes the field of MacCormick Hines's reality reversed, and he began to wonder if television weren't real.

'My dear,' he said to the set, 'I haven't forgotten what you said that night. The night he died. That you'd give anything to get him back. And believe me, I'm working on just that.'

'And cleaning the Thermo-K is no problem either,' she replied. 'Just push this button, and the blades slip into your dishwater. See how easy?'

Sunday night was Veronica. 'I'm sorry, Glen, but I don't think you're really serious about me as a person. Thanks anyway for showing me those movies.'

Tuesday night was Karen. 'Glen darling, let's be reasonable I know your reputation, and I'm just not the kind of girl you want. But thanks all the same. For the champagne and all.'

Wednesday night was Trudy. 'Oh, Glen, I thought you were different!'

Wendy, on Thursday night, was willing. Even on the tiny monitor screen, Feinwelt could see her face was going expressionless and tuned to receive. Glen bent over her, sucking at a bare shoulder.

'That bitch!' Feinwelt stubbed out a cigarette and reached for a toggle switch. 'Takes three hundred bucks just to say no, and then gets hot pants all the same! Lucky I was watching tonight, instead of Hank. He'd let it get too far.'

The timing had to be just right. Too soon and there would be a fresh start to the seduction. Too late and – too late. He waited.

Feinwelt was being pulled too many ways. Late nights protecting his investment, afternoons patching up the damage he'd done Glen each night before, evenings working as counsellor for Transvestites Anonymous – he barely had time to change clothes, frames of reference.

Awkwardly, Glen groped for a breast. Feinwelt threw the switch, and in the bedroom the huge color TV blazed on at top volume.

Bette Cooke was stirring something in a saucepan. 'THE MAN IN YOUR LIFE,' she thundered, 'WILL **LOVE** NEW **INSTANT** VEAL CUTLETS.'

By the time Glen could turn it down the moment was past. Thinking of the three hundred yet to come, Wendy reached for her purse.

'I've really got to go now, darling. It's been sweet, but I've got this terrible headache. I think my period brings it on.'

When she had left, Glen took off his gaucho hat and laid it in the exact middle of the bed. Without knowing quite why, he took all the Cokes out of his bedside refrigerator, opened them and poured them on the hat.

Bette Cooke was back on the screen again by the time he'd finished. She recommended that listeners give their menfolk a special treat tonight.

Only the safety shield in front of the picture tube saved Bette from that flying bottle.

One more week, Marge promised herself. One more week, and if that little snob didn't write to his mother, he'd find himself yanked out of that damned 'academy' and sent to a school for mere human children. Where he couldn't strut around in a uniform all day, snarling commands (as no doubt he was doing this minute), and lapping up all that West-Point-type glory. At eight years old, he wasn't so much of an old campaigner that he couldn't be bothered to scratch out a post card.

Spot had his plan. Fouts seemed to be carrying on the school traditions, and television was forbidden (images of women), but cadets were after all encouraged to be religious. Spot simply waited until Billy Koch was on one channel, then watched whatever he wanted.

It was the evening recreation hour, a time when cadets were inclined to find ways to be by themselves. Therefore the school was heavily patrolled by (pairs of) upper classmen, officers.

Sensing rather than hearing their approach, Spot switched over from a cowboy program to *Healing Hand* and dropped to his knees before the set.

'DON'T YOU KNOW ENOUGH TO STAND AT ATTENTION WHEN AN UPPER CLASSMAN ENTERS THE ROOM?' said one of the two officers. It was Jerry Zurkenhall, a pimply fifteen-year-old who, it was said, had hair in the palm of his hand.

Spot did not move or look around.

'OKAY, I'M GIVING YOU FIFTEEN DEMERITS ...'

'Knock it off, Jerry,' said the other. 'You can't give a guy demerits when he's praying, stupid. It's in the rules.'

'Yeah? So who's he praying to, Billy Koch? My old man works for him.'

'No kidding?'

'Yeah, he's in computers.' Jerry put his hairy palm on the doorknob.

'Hey, what does a preacher need computers for? To give him hymn numbers? Hah haha hahaha ...'

The door closed and the two went off to harass someone else. Spot, anxious for the life of the Negro sheriff on channel two, switched over at once.

'Here's news for BUSY HOUSEWIVES! Have *you* tried my DIN-DIN? You know, each package of DIN-DIN contains *everything* you need for a meal with – mmmm – *man appeal*! You just add water through this little door in the convenient, no-mess foil pack, pop it in the oven – and Bette Cooke takes over! Then just sit back and let your men-folk fall in love with you all over again!'

She was on the screen, serving dinner to a red-haired, freckle-faced boy with a disgusting grin, to a man who sniffed, went silly and rose to peck at her cheek. Mom's face was soft with pleasure, as Spot had never seen it.

Of course it was all acting, but still. Her letters never mentioned his letters. She ignored his plea to be allowed to come home again, she seemed unmoved by his stories of life at the academy. So here she was, living it up with television actors (and her last letter: 'Guess what? Your Mom's got a new job. But I guess you're not very interested in that kind of news ... guess you're pretty busy with medals and marching bands and military balls ...') while Spot languished in prison, sweeping from the Northwest corner, mitering the corners of his bed ...

To the fading smile of Bette Cooke he whispered a threat, a curse that took in Fouts, the upper classmen, all mortal enemies.

'I don't care,' it went. 'I don't care. My old man's in computers, too.'

*

Ank switched off the freeze-dried lemon meringue pie commercial before answering the door.

'Ank Bullard? Package for you.' It was the paint, the last thing he needed for his painting machine. Ank paid the COD charges and dragged the big box into his flat. Since his right shoulder still ached from the accident, he began mixing colors with his left hand.

The accident had been a miracle. First, he'd come to in the hospital to find on his bedside table the very thing he'd have given a leg for: a reel of Müller-Fokker tape. And no one seemed to know who the anonymous donor was.

Then, his second day in the hospital, there had been a visitor with still another gift. He was a lawyer from the Billy Koch Crusade, and though he wanted Ank to understand his clients accepted no responsibility whatever, they were willing to pay him three thousand dollars over his hospital expenses if he would sign this waiver.

Ank had given notice at the newspaper the day he came out. Today he was just an ex-art-critic. Tomorrow – even in a few hours – he would be a painter.

The painting machine had a wheel to hold a thousand smears of color and a brush mounted on a pivoted arm. The brush could be moved along the arm by one motor, while a second motor worked the arm around on its pivot. A third rotated the paint wheel, or 'auto-pallette'.

Random numbers generated by the tape were fed into this system, controlling all three variables. The brush could dip up any color, transfer it to any of the hundred and fifty thousand positions over a prepared canvas, and dip again, leaving a dot. Between dottings, it moved through a powerful cleaning solution.

This cartesian process would go on until either the canvas was completely covered or until Ank liked what he saw and stopped it. He called the process *rand-pointillisme* in advance, knowing how important it was for his former colleagues to have a name to fasten upon from the start. Ank was prepared to explain in detail the philosophy behind this 'marriage of random number and Seurat, which guarantees all the benefits of luminosity, color and harmony'.

Now he set it into motion. There were a hundred and fifty million potential paintings in there somewhere, a hundred and fifty million pure abstract patterns without 'meaning' or 'intention'. What he would see, in just a few hours, would be the end of so-called Humanism, the end of sentiment and prejudice – the dawn of Mechanism.

What he actually saw was a close copy of David's *Coronation of Napoleon*. The details were blurry, but his painting differed from the original in only one respect.

The archbishop's face was modeled in bright greens.

Ank tried a fresh canvas. The brush rose and fell, faster than the eye could follow, and a 'Remington' took shape: A mounted Indian wheeling his pony to fire an arrow into the flank of a galloping bison.

Except the pony wasn't wheeling and the bison did not gallop. Instead, both 'stood on', or were solidified into, thick furry pedestals.

'Surrealism?' he whimpered. 'I've given up my whole career for this cheap surrealism?'

It was almost time to go to Glen Dale's party. He threw the two ruined canvases in the corner and went to wash his hands. Instead of shaving, he decided to have a drink somewhere.

SEVEN

In the corner by the fireplace, two Shriners were telling a Knight of Columbus about the possibility of a Vatican missile.

'You must mean this,' he said, hauling out a dog-eared mass book. 'A missal.'

'Naw, I got the straight word from a bishop. Says they're gonna call it *Misericordia Dei*.'

'Yeah? Well all I can say is, somebody better say their prayers ...'

Two men in modified zoot suits stood arguing about a song recorded by Deef John Holler. A hideously fat woman in gold lamé and a stiff blonde wig watched them and, when they paused for breath, introduced herself as Columbine.

Someone elsewhere swore the US Navy had already successfully teleported a ship from Philadelphia to Norfolk.

'It fried the crew, though.'

'England?' asked the young man in the wicker suit. 'Was that Norfolk, England?' On learning it was Virginia, he seemed to lose interest in the story.

On the mezzanine a new group called The World, The Flesh and Father Schmidt bombarded the guests with glare and noise:

> *You know I got a little girl named* Gladys?
> *She give me such a **ice cream***
> *So when I ask the neighbors what they want*
> *They tell me there's no*
> Ahhhhhhhss

Cuh-ream-MUH!
You caint go home dog
YOU CAINT GO HOME DOG
This cat done EAT up all my beans

No one could hear the singer screaming these words to the old Deef John Holler tune, above the party sounds and the electronic background music provided by zither, serpent and white noise generator. But no one was listening, anyway.

The man disguised as a hot dog (red-painted baldness; thick, bun-colored coat) was saying it was hard as hell to find a book worth publishing these days. 'Just got one promising em-ess from a guy in prison. All about the black conspiracy. Oughta do the ton, easy.' He went on to explain to his audience, two models in painful-looking tubular garments from Paris, that 'the ton' was a million copies.

Behind him a professor of American Studies named Throgmorton thought someone had failed to make a distinction somewhere. 'American Studies is not an *all*-embracing field,' he corrected. 'It is a *much*-embracing field. Take my own specialty, for example. I have written what I hope is the definitive catalogue of Little Moron Jokes.'

'Indeed?' The cryogenics man stood ready to feign interest.

Someone asked where Feinwelt was, and someone replied, 'Oh he never comes to these things. Always busy with his girl scouts, I guess.'

'Yeah, what do they call it? Transvestites Anonymous?'

Worried-looking Miss Columbine butted in to ask what a transvestite was.

In another corner Mr Bradd told the gloomy TV producer how Marge had wanted to appear in commercials under her own name. 'Can you slice that? Her own name! *Marge* – for Christ's sake. The economy spread.'

The gloomy producer nodded and went right on talking about his western series based on *Huckleberry Finn*, and entitled 'Sheriff Jim'.

Somewhere in the next room, the tall art critic with the ax-blade nose called someone a 'reified cubist'.

Mr Hackendorf, a civilian anthropologist attached to the staff of General Weimarauner, stood in the kitchen talking to Sir Somebody about the Seneca tribe. The general himself sat in the den, too near the harpsichord to hear what the lady with the jeweled face was saying about dogs. He was watching a pretty girl with a rather large and rigid jaw who stood in the doorway between the den and living room. She sipped her drink through a straw and conversed with a man in a feather cape.

The art dealer lit a cigarette, holding it well away from his artificial feathers. 'So what's new, Myra?'

'Net mech, Drew. Whet's en et yr guellery?'

'Nothing on at the moment. I'm looking for a show. Something really *new*. Anything but computer art. I'm so sick of – say, what happened to your jaw?'

Myra explained that she'd had her jaw sectioned to correct an overbite. After sawing through on both sides, she said, they 'pet en sem plestec enserts'.

'That's nothing. I had a pilonidal cyst removed about a month back. Jesus, I was sick for three days.'

Glen was looking lonely, Mrya noticed. She excused herself and went over to talk to him.

'Mester Dele? E meant te speak weth ye, abet …'

'About the proofs for January? I know, Myra, I've already had a look at them. But can't we talk about that some other time? If you'll excuse me, there's someone I wanted to see.'

He resumed his lonely prowling of the penthouse rooms. There was no one he had to see, but Glen hated for it to look as if he *had* to talk to his own secretary. Hoping someone would remark on his square printer's hat, folded from a sheet of *Stagman*, Glen crossed the living room and spoke to the old Negro by the door.

Conspicuous in new bib overalls, new work shoes and no shirt, the old man sat with his chair tipped back against the wall. He seemed to be ignoring the entire party, possibly because the rest ignored him.

'Hello,' said Glen heartily. 'Haven't seen you here before.' The old Negro did not look up or speak. Glen wondered uneasily if he might not be the Wrong Kind of spade. The Right Kind included jazz musicians, baseball players, poets, astronauts …

'Friend of Bill Banks, are you?'

No response. Glen resisted the temptation to throw him out – it might look as if he didn't like the Right Kind – and walked away, hiding his burning face in a drink. Ögivaal the architect caught his eye, but Glen continued on to the farthest part of the apartment. Ögivaal resumed his story:

' … and it should have been a thirty, instead of a three.'

Throgmorton leaned against the mantel. 'That's a shaggy-dog story,' he told the cryogenics man. 'I think you fail to make a distinction there.'

'All right, how about this one, then? Why did the Little Moron take a ladder to the cat-house?'

Ank came in, dropped a cigarette and bent in slow-motion to retrieve it.

'That's the so-called art critic who works for the *Sun*,' said the tall man, jerking his ax-blade nose in Ank's direction. 'He thinks a Constable is an English cop.'

The young man in the wicker suit opined that the English police were the best in the world.

'Is that so?' said the tall man. He extracted a cigarette from one sleeve of his worn, paint-splattered sweater. 'Well, a friend of mine got busted by English fuzz for speeding, one night. They just about kicked his nuts off. As it happens, he's black.'

Six persons in the costumes of Egyptian priests moved together to the bathroom, where they rolled up their black-and-gold sleeves to bare arms no cleaner or healthier than those preserved in museums. One of them produced an anachronistic syringe.

In the kitchen, Hackendorf was saying, 'You're right. The Seneca are, as you put it, unequalled in common sense. A magnificent tribe.'

'Eh?' Sir Somebody cupped a hand to his ear. 'Damn that infernal music. Did you say Seneca was *tripe?*'

'Tribe, *tribe.* All of the Seneca put together.'

Sir Somebody looked at him in the way only a man of his class is able to look at someone. 'Good Lord! Is there more than one great Seneca? Seneca, whose moving death ...'

In the next room, just beyond the doorway, Senator Vuje looked around to see who was calling him. No one was, so he turned back to listen to an astrologer, who was giving the horoscope for anyone born on December 25th:

'He will work and toil, and others may reap the benefit of his labor unless marriage alters the destiny. He is usually well-disciplined and cautious, and tends to overlook his own faults while quick to recognize the faults of others.'

The party rumbled on like a Hay Wain (as someone in the middle of it pointed out), carrying its cargo of fools toward the hour of their release. A lady lawyer spoke long sentences about international law as regards defacing the moon, and to each the cryogenics man nodded and smiled. The girl in the snood claimed that Thomas M. Disch was the author of a novel called *Concentration Camp.* Other girls, in leather bikinis, glass crinolines, wooden mail, foil tartans and plastic pinafores behaved as slightly animated decorations, receiving each conversation item with the same graceful indifference with which chair cushions receive buttocks of all shapes. News, gossip, compliments, pedantry, wit and philosophy, all were rested upon them briefly and then removed, leaving no impression.

One pretty blonde wore a dress of pale creamy silk that seemed to be on upside down. It flared outward and upward from her knees, ending at the neck in a fountain of ruffled lace. Someone remarked that she looked like a peach sundae, and later everyone thought they had originated the idea.

Ank danced with her, danced with them all, doing the jung, the freeb, the buckle-o, the rap. After a short intermission (to puke up a gallon of cheap wine) he returned to dance the rap, the nood and the fox-trot.

'Seneca's death,' remarked the knight, 'reminds one of the death of Quixote. Or, as you Americans say it, Key-oty.'

'Kiote?' Hackendorf frowned. 'He's not a Seneca god. I think you mean one of the plains tribes ...'

But Sir Somebody wasn't listening. He had given up trying to understand the peculiar American versions of the classics, and turned instead to scrutinize Bates, the young man in the wicker suit, who spoke now of English cooking.

'It's quite underrated,' he said. 'You have to get down in the country and try the really authentic English dishes: Curate's Egg, for instance. And Parson's Nose.'

'Good Lord! Is the man serious? Parson's Nose? *Parson's Nose?* What the deuce is he on about?'

In the living room someone comforted Miss Columbine, who lay full-length on the sunken sofa, heaving with sobs.

'What happened, dear?'

'That dirty young man in the paper suit ...' indicating Ank. 'He called me a – a *lesbian*!'

Ank grinned. 'All I did was ask her why her arms are so muscular,' he said. 'Well it's true!'

Someone looked down at the 250-pound writhing figure. 'Like a trapped elephant,' he murmured. 'Poor thing.'

The publisher in the hot-dog costume plodded through the den, asking if anyone had seen his wife. The lady with the jeweled face regarded him. 'How quaint!' she exclaimed. 'A kapok coat! How poply quaint!'

She turned to smile on the patrician profile of General Weimarauner. 'They wore things like that when I was young – practically – I thought they were out of fashion forever. I'll bet he doesn't *dare* take it off. He's afraid someone might see his truss.'

A drink sloshed over her. The face so covered with jewels that it might have been any age looked up. An unsteady man in a wrinkled dinner jacket pulled his forelock in apology. ''S all right,' he mumbled. 'I'm from Innerpol.'

'A *jaw* section?' Ank lurched forward to look at Myra's face. 'So that's why you're drinking through a straw. How long before the wires come out?'

Before she could answer he began on the details of his own accident, resulting, as he mentioned several times, in concussion.

'Ye den't lek tee well, Enk.'

'Ank looks terrible,' Glen said to a girl wearing only blue jeans.

Even across the room he could see the edges of Ank's paper jacket were frayed and greasy, and the seams had started to let go.

'But he's a great dancer,' replied the girl.

Glen made a mental note to take some dance lessons.

Mr Bradd and a crewcut young giant finished their competition, a chinning contest on the bedroom door-frame. Crewcut won. Bradd suggested a little kendo, broom against mop.

'You're crazy to go up against him,' someone whispered to Bradd. 'He's a Yale younger poet, for God's sake.'

Glen asked Hackendorf if he were the Indian expert.

'Well, I guess you might say that. I'm advising General Weimarauner for his book on the Indian wars.'

'I wanted to ask you something about this tribe, the Utopis.'

'The Utopi, yes, a minor Southwestern tribe. Not really important – most of their ritual and so on is copied from others. Gosh, there can't be many Utopi left.'

'There must be some,' Glen said. 'I just ordered a hat from them, a real Utopi headdress. I thought you might be able to tell me what it would look like.'

The anthropologist looked thoughtful. 'I'm not certain, really. Didn't know they *had* any crafts. Utopi hat? That's a new one on me.

'Now, if you'll excuse us, the general and I will duck out early. I have something to discuss with him privately.'

'Daisy James,' said a blonde. 'You know, by Henry Miller?'

'Isn't Feinwelt here?' someone else asked.

The lady lawyer's shrill voice carried over the other conversations. 'The question remains, does the moon really constitute ...'

A man on crutches came in. Someone persuaded someone else not to rush over and ask him where he got his one-legged outfit. Someone else tried to throw up into the swimming pool, but it was covered. The man from Interpol crawled around on all fours, peering up dresses. He was the only one to make the discovery:

The girl wearing only blue jeans really wasn't. The blue jeans, pockets, rivets and all, were painted on.

Glen noticed the girl in the peach-sundae dress was alone. He moved over to talk to her, pausing on the way to put his pipe in his mouth.

Jerry shifted a crutch. 'A jaw section? Myra, that's *nothing*. I lost a *leg* in that accident – clear up to the knee!' He held out the stump for her inspection.

'E see. Thet's trrble, Jrry. Whet'll ye de?'

'Do? Who cares?' He drank off a cocktail and held the glass in a way that indicated he expected her to fetch him another. 'Oh, I guess I can keep on working for the Crusade. I'm still a good systems man, and their computer – but I'd like to get my hands on the bastard who did this to me, Myra. Some stupid fuckhead in a slow truck, hogging the intersection.'

She took his glass and went to the bar. Ank wandered past a moment later, waggling an unlit cigarette. No one seemed to have a light.

'How about you?' he asked Jerry. The one-legged man made a great show of clapping his crutches together and digging out his lighter. He was (his manner indicated) a cripple being put upon by a man with all limbs intact.

Without even thanking him, Ank shuffled away, trailing a torn strip of paper suit and raining live coals on his own lapels.

' ... and another thing,' someone asserted. 'All the penitents aren't in the penitentiary.'

'Film critic?' said the tall man, slipping a cigarette out of his sweater sleeve. 'You've got to be kidding. He still thinks *The African Queen* is a retitled version of *Strange Fruit.*'

Sir Somebody entered the living room, promenading with the lady with the jeweled face. 'Incredible!' he was saying. 'The fellow claims we English are fond of eating hen's arse!'

'Are you the janitor?' someone asked the old Negro by the door, who declined to answer. 'There's a lot of water coming out from under the bathroom door. Somebody must have passed out in there.'

The old man smiled to himself, took out a sack of tobacco and papers, and deliberately rolled a cigarette.

'Isn't that just like a colored?' shouted the hot-dog man. 'Look at that! Doped to the teeth, or drunk maybe, or just plain idiotic. Has anybody seen my wife, by the way?'

'I think,' said Ank, stumbling into him, 'I think she left with a mustard pot ...'

The two zoot suits were rolling on the floor. The man on top had seized the other's hand-painted tie and was trying to strangle him with it. '1948, you son of a bitch!'

The six persons in the bathroom were taking a shower with their robes on. The water was up to their ankles and leaking out under both doors, the locked door to the hall and the door to the bedroom, where the polite cryogenics man was helping Bradd to his feet. The gloomy producer stood by, still talking shop.

'I'm tired of doing spade westerns,' he said. 'I'm thinking of doing' – with a malicious look at Bradd, who was groping for his glasses – 'a queer western. The fairy lawman who has to keep proving he's a man. Takes incredible risks, rides in a rodeo and so on. So "straight" he wears low-heeled boots. Only what to call it? *Andy Oakley?*'

Ank stood in the corner by the fireplace, mumbling to himself. He seemed oblivious of everything, even the great charred hole in the front of his paper jacket. Suddenly he pulled himself up and charged across the living room towards the patio door. He collided with the man in the wrinkled dinner jacket.

'It's all right,' said Ank. 'You're from Interpol, remember?'

'Hey, how did you know? Hey, come back here!'

But Ank lurched on, crookedly but with purpose, across the fiberglass swimming pool cover and on, towards the parapet.

Out in the hall, the Yale younger poet had wedged the elevator doors open by jamming a mop across the opening at knee level. Now he started chinning himself on the mop, letting his body hang down inside the shaft. The two Shriners and a few others looked on.

Grunting, he explained. 'Have to purify myself ... after combat ... too much I and thou ... need some experience of the Infinite ... I and it, see?'

'That's not infinite,' said one watcher, 'it's only forty floors, man.'

In the living room, someone asked where that TV exec had got to.

'A transvestite executive? Wild!'

Ank, unconscious, was carried in from the patio by Myra and Drew, the art dealer.

'What happened to him?'

'We found him passed out with one leg over the parapet.'

'Does the moon,' said the lady lawyer, 'in legal terms, belong to *everyone*?'

General Weimarauner and his anthropologist sat in a lunch counter drinking coffee, or anyway stirring at it.

'What is it, Hack? It better not be about your damned Indians.'

Hackendorf coughed. 'In a way, General, in a way. But it's also about X Forces.'

X Forces was the as yet unnamed cadre being assembled in Florida under General Rockstone. It was the Pentagon's hope that X Forces could regain some of the reputation for toughness lost by the old Green Berets in Vietnam, and become a model and a morale booster for the other services.

'Go on, then.'

'The Cheyenne had a peculiar military corps called the Contraries. These were the finest, fittest braves in the tribe, and more. *They were so tough, they did everything backwards.*'

The general looked at him, then turned his Roman profile. 'Come on, Hack. I'm tired. Either spit it out, or let's get back to the hotel. I've got to fly to Washington in the morning.'

'They really did, sir. They rode to battle mounted backwards, and they never carried weapons. There was much more merit in it, if when a man had the chance to *kill* an enemy he just *touched* him instead. Just slapped him with the open hand, or hit him with a small stick, the *coup* stick.

'Another thing is, the Contraries never touched women. They were like monks, or knights under a vow ... were supposed to be. They fasted and prayed and tortured themselves all night before a battle, and then they just clowned around on the battlefield, taking incredible risks. All for honor.'

Weimarauner sighed. 'Yes, yes, but Hackendorf, we already have *enough* honor.'

The Yale younger poet and his followers came in from the hall, leaving the elevator doors jammed open, and went straight to the bar. The poet turned his back on Mr Bradd, who was too busy talking to the cryogenics man to notice. Glen and the peach-sundae girl went into the bedroom and locked the door.

'They call me the I B M wish, baby,' sang the World et al., 'They call me the Icy B M fish.'

A lighted sign went on over the bedroom door: UNE FEMME EST AVEC MOI.

'I envy that bastard Glen Dale,' said a Shriner. 'He must of gone through more ass than I have socks.'

The cryogenics man, sensing a customer in Mr Bradd, began to sober up fast. 'Freezing isn't just a science, you know. It's an art. Look at it this way: If you'd frozen yourself twenty years ago, today you'd be – what, sixteen years old?' He judged Bradd to be forty-five, actually.

'Twenty-four,' Bradd said, 'but I wouldn't have any money.'

'No? If you had bought *this* sheaf of stocks,' the list brought out and held so that Bradd had to turn and move closer to have a look at it, 'you'd have nearly a hundred dollars for every dollar you invested then. Even if you put your money in the bank, it would nearly have tripled! And youth, don't forget, youth – is – money!' From another pocket he produced a full-color brochure of freezer designs.

'What I was thinking,' Bradd said, looking them over, 'was something for a friend – really a business associate of mine. A woman thirty years old. The thing is, her job effectiveness – her RBI – depends on her age. In maybe five years, she'll be useless. Meanwhile, she works maybe an hour a week, maybe two. The rest of the time, she just mopes around the house. Do you think we could do something to shape up her career?'

Mrs Grebe peeled off her jeweled face and put it away. She was about to go with Sir Somebody to his hotel room, to look at his pictures of Welsh Corgis. The art dealer in the feather cape and Myra shouldered Ank and headed for the door. With a look of irony, Jerry stood out of their way.

A businessman in a fur wig rushed in from the hall. 'Hey, somebody fell down the elevator shaft! I heard him scream!'

'Christ! Somebody get the janitor!'

'Where the hell is he?' demanded the walking hot dog. 'He was right here a minute ago. As soon as there's any work to be done ...'

Two pork-pie hats swiveled to look at him. 'Forget it,' said one of the musicologists. 'No hurry now.' They went back to their amiable discussion of the recording date of Deef John Holler's *Decatur Freight Blues,*

One floor below, Deef John Holler lay on the roof of the elevator. He had few cues to his whereabouts, being not only deaf but nearly blind, but he found this place more congenial than Glen's penthouse. Here there were no irritating, jerky vibrations from amplified clumsy playing, no smells of stale smoke and spilled whiskey, only a gentle descending motion. He was not interested in getting anywhere, in being anyone, or in living at all. So Deef John sat up, dusted off his new overalls, and began to sing.

All the rest of the evening, riders of the elevator declared they had never heard Melodiak sounding so good.

'I see what must've happened,' said the Knight of Columbus. 'Some prick left this mop stuck across the door like this, and guess some drunk tripped over it.' He unstuck the mop and let the doors close.

'Forty floors. Some trip.'

Miss Columbine, plumping her enormous breasts into shape, came out of the flat. The stiff blonde wig was askew, and one trickle of mascara ran down to her white – faintly bluish-white – jowl. Drawing her red velvet cloak about her, she turned her back on the others to wait for the elevator.

When she was gone, they chuckled. 'I think Ank was right about her, she is a lesbian,' said one. 'I mean, did you see that five o'clock shadow?'

'Sure upset her, though. She spent the whole evening sprawled out on the couch, bawling.'

They went back inside.

Someone lurched up to the bedroom door and peered at the lighted sign over it, spelling it out. 'Fums?' he said. 'I wonder where in hell the other one is. What do they call it? Ohms.'

The water in the bathroom was thigh-deep, but the six pseudo-Egyptians hadn't noticed. They were all piled up against the door to the bedroom, listening to Glen's taped music.

Ank awoke to see Myra and a man in a feather cape looking over his two completed paintings. He was at home, on the bed. One of his paper sleeves had fallen off; it lay in the middle of the floor, like an abandoned snakeskin.

'Never mind those,' he roused himself to say. 'They're not … not what I wanted.'

'They're what I want, though,' said the man. He introduced himself as Drew Moody of the Moody Gallery. 'Those paintings *live*. All right, it's corny, but I've been looking at other stuff all week. Cold mechanical stuff, the kind those computer jerks crank out.'

'Computer ... ?' Ank tried to clear his head.

'Half the kids in the country think if they can only get a random number generator they automatically become a painter. But this – this is by God *human* art, untouched by mechanical hands. Can you do a few more? I'd like to give you a one-man show.'

'But ... do you think the critics ... ?'

'The critics! The critics are a bunch of dehorns who wouldn't know paint from diarrhea. The real world will eat this up, if I present it right.'

'Et's e wenderfel eppertenety, Enk.'

'He's tired and foggy,' said the dealer. 'Tell you what, Ank. I'll give you a jingle in the morning. And here's my card. Now Myra and I will sneak off and let you get some sleep.'

On the way out, the art dealer noticed the tarpaulin-draped painting machine. 'What's this? Sculpture?'

'Uh, no, it's – it's just a paint-mixing machine.'

'See you then. So long, Ank.'

The door closed, setting up a breeze that stirred the empty paper sleeve on the floor. It made one clumsy painting movement, then lay still.

'Fear of effeminacy. It might work,' said General Weimarauner. 'Combined with fear of the fool. The – the Pink Barrettes?' He began to laugh, inclining his noble head and putting up a hand as if to ward off blows. 'I'm tempted, Hackendorf, I'm tempted!'

He paused to study the figure in red velvet sitting in another corner of the coffee shop. Nudging Hackendorf, he dropped his voice to say, 'Look at that, will you? Did you ever see such an ugly woman in your life? Gad, any uglier and they'd draft her. Come to think of it, she reminds me of an aide I used to have, only she's about fifty pounds heavier. What was his name, now? Pouts?'

He tore his attention away from the person in the corner, who had just ordered six Danish pastries and a chocolate malt. 'The Pink Barrettes! Yes by God, we'll do it. I can just see them on parade!'

The Knight of Columbus was telling the last person he could find about the accident in the elevator shaft. Jerry was looking for Myra. The gloomy producer was telling someone about Miss Columbine: 'Balling somebody all evening on that sunken sofa, and nobody even noticed.' There was no one left for the American Studies professor to tell a Little Moron Joke to. The hot-dog publisher had fallen asleep in a chair, letting his coat open to reveal his truss.

Bradd asked the cryogenics man for the hundredth time if he was sure it could be done.

'See voo play,' someone asked, 'oo ay lays Ohm? E.c. ay lay Fum, may oo ay lays Ohm?' He gestured at the bedroom door.

'What do you want with a man? Won't I do?'

'Of course it'll work,' said the cryogenics man. 'We freeze donuts, don't we? So why not a girl?'

'Can't wreck her appearance, though.' Bradd removed his TV glasses and inspected them for dirt. 'She's got to look good for, say, thirty or forty years. In front of the cameras, anyway.'

'Don't worry about a thing. Now, what price range freezer were you thinking of?'

Glen Dale put on the ninth tape. There were ten, arranged by experts in order of arousal, and now there was nothing left but half an hour of Ravel's *Bolero*.

And he still hadn't figured out a way of kissing Miranda, the girl in the peach-sundae dress. He had fed her arousing music, stirred up the fire in the fireplace, changed (behind a screen) into a dressing gown of red silk, poured many brandies into their two snifters, switched on the electronic odorizer that filled the room with musk and frankincense, talked knowledgeably of Krafft-Ebbing and Tantric Yoga, even shown her selections from a Cinerama blue film. Now he sat inches away from her on the bed and toyed with the tassel of his dressing gown. All this brought them to the point where he *had* to make a move – or a mistake.

'I gotta go home now,' she said, looking at her watch.

'But it's early!'

'Don't argue with me, I said I gotta go! Anyways, I can't crap around here all night waiting for you to make up your mind. We been in here three hours,' she said. 'Three hours, and *nothing happened*.'

'But I ...'

'I guess you think I'm not good enough for you, with all your Miss Monthly girls and Does and all.' She stood up, straightened her ruffles and smiled. 'So bye-bye.'

'Wait, Miranda, wait!'

Miranda did not wait. She chose the wrong door, tugged at her skirt, and marched over to it. 'Bye-bye.'

Six people in Egyptian costumes tumbled in upon her, accompanied by several dozen gallons of water.

'Christ almighty! What the hell is this, a voyeur hotel?' Extricating herself, Miranda kicked at the Egyptians.

'Miranda, I – wait ...'

The right door slammed. Glen sank back on the bed. The six fake Egyptians scrambled up and came to sit next to him, one pausing to turn up the taped music.

'Nice sounds, man. Who is it? Sounds like *The Andrew Jackson Davis Penetralia.*'

Alone in his room, Bates, the young anglophile, took off his wicker suit and hung it up carefully. It was, after all, a suit with a London label, from a shop on Portobello Road, even if he had bought it at a Minneapolis department store.

Next he took off his imported English leather shoes, his imported English wool socks, and his Union Jack 'Standfast' underwear. He crawled into bed to meet his insomnia.

That Englishman, Sir Somebody, had laughed at him! That was the worst part. They all knew by now: *He hadn't been to England at all.*

The nearest he ever got was buying something English, reading a travel guide, or corresponding with his pen pal, a ten-year-old boy in Scunthorpe whose hobbies included collecting American stamps. The little snot was blackmailing him: information on the English scene for batches of stamps.

This wasn't jolly hockey-sticks at all. He'd have to get to England itself, no matter how. *England! my England!* he thought. *England's green and pleasant land. Swinging England. Land of hope and glory. Little Olde England, where the sun never sets …*

He gazed on the picture over his bed, a dazzling picture of the Queen, while his right hand moved under the covers in a familiar and traditional rhythm, old as the rhythm of the waves over which Britannia rules.

EIGHT

The House

NUMBER ONE TAKES CARE OF ITSELF

… … … noun is a replacement for the pronoun I wonder Bob wonders this man wonders how the hell long he's going to be in here trapped here in an abandoned mind shaft (and are the psychiatrists still digging out there?) and buried under tons of crushing self buried a back number: 'They have parsed my hands and my feet, they have numbered all my bones now there's a thought more noughts than crosses though a crucial difference that essential plus

Old numb copybones the headbone connected to nothing really the fingerbone maybe that digit in my nostril really is one and 'hands and feet' are measurements too they have me here the integers, trace, fear, sank, sex they (la enemy Hymeneal, read me any way I'm still an em wide) have fed me right into their number mumbling machine I'm

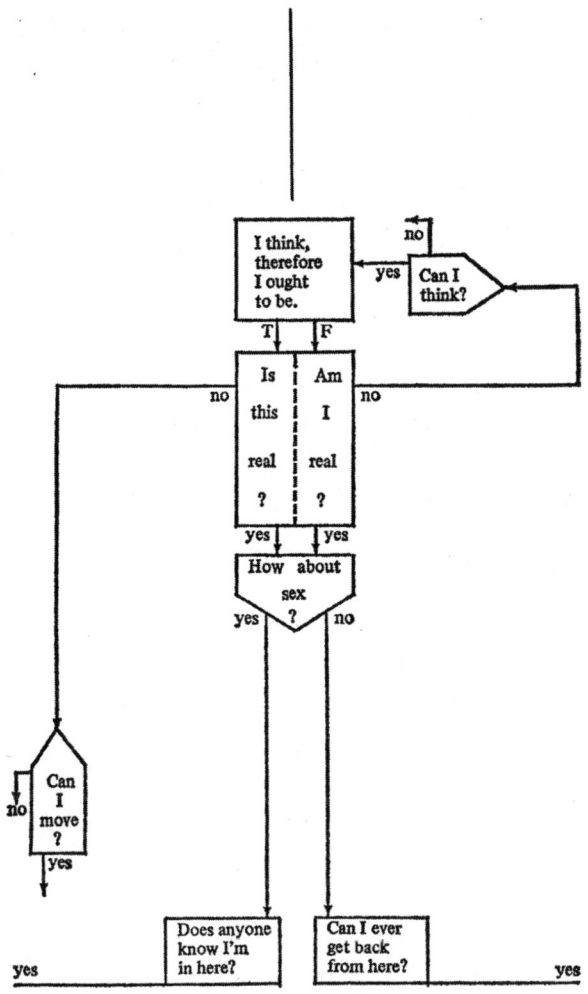

That's me all right, the old inchworm. And my winding sheet is
    three
        miles
            long

ROBINS ON COURSE

Luckily I managed to rescue from the shipwreck an inflatable house, mini-ature bulldozer, seeds, farming implements, swimming pool kit, prefab bomb shelter, guns, ammo, libraries and lab equipment for geology, botany, zoology, horticulture, medicine and chemistry, instructions for building and operating generators, miniature manufacturing systems of several kinds, 'Hints for the Amateur Farmer', supplies of fuel and food for at least five years, a wilderness survival kit and guide, carpenters', plumbers' and machinists' tool kits, a selection of light novels (neither depressing nor the kind that make civilization look too good), several hundred pounds each of wood, plastic, metal stock, glue, epoxy, nails, small standard machine parts, an abundance of copper wire and electronic parts in all sizes, several radios, televisions, home appliances of all descriptions (all portable and with extra batteries), a one man oil-drilling rig, a small tape recorder suitable for memoranda and recording bird cries, a barbecue hat, briquets, etc., etc.

The thought of escape is not so tasty as the thought of keeping what I've got. The crash-priority projects must be:

(1) a first-line defense system (alarms, mortars, shelter and perhaps short-range rocket defense).
(2) hygienic water supply and sewage disposal.
(3) oil refinery.
(4) swimming pool and barbecue pit.
(5) drugs from local flora (the supply of Noctec, Miltown, Somnos, Librium, Equanil, Trancopal, etc., is alarmingly low already).

These should keep me pretty busy for a few months, after which I'll be able to get up the NO TRESPASSING signs, set up the printing press, maybe run off my own currency.

The island is snug and comfy already. The only thing (besides lack of sex and the old nagging headache) that really bothers me is the stationary cloud hanging overhead. It's been there the whole first month, neither moving nor changing.

And there's this pair of feet sticking down out of it.

SILLY, DIS IDYLL IS

Meanwhile back in my lounge chair, I decide the whole thing – this room, the experimenters, maybe my perceptions – is plastic. By my calendar watch I've been here three days, surely long enough to prove whatever they want to prove. Enough entombment! Abra cadavera! I rise from the dead.

I rise, walk through the steel air, past the vapid faces of Donagon & Co., right on into the crisco wall … surfacing in the paradise of my childhood back yard.

Every detail in depth, enveloped with a strange importance. The Sinclair station on the corner, every whitewashed brick in place, every delicate color within the whiteness. Under one of its murky windows the remains of a circus poster make a Rorschach pattern, a map of Odd Islands. The earth is steeped in oil, the dinosaur sign creaks overhead, and the poster remains spell a message: HE UNSTOPS BEST ALLIES, TOO. EFFORTLESS? HE UNSTOPS BEST ALLIES, TOO, RETHATCHED KING THISTLE BOTHERS EVIL ENDS. REQUESTED RICE.

I turn away from the station, feeling an ordinary death about this place: by my back porch hollyhocks are shrivelling to hairy stalks; the back porch itself is dying, and there is the gray catenary of clothesline from the house to the little birch I scalped last summer to make a toy canoe. Some dog has turned over the crumpled garbage can and nosed open all its packages of coffee grounds. Maybe the same dog who dug up the yard in four or five places, looking for a spot for his relic bones. I could sit here in the cool grass and die with the dying hollyhocks, watch them give up their 'money' seeds … but there's work to do, O sinclairosaur.

Unfurling the flag of the United States of America, I plant the staff firmly in a relic hole and repeat the memorized speech. Claim this planet. People of the United States. Peace loving.

When it's over I sit down for a moment, my head buzzing with Valium, Striatran, Noludar, Listica, Somnos, Lenetran and Trepidone. Two small white butterflies settle to picnic together on a glistening dog turd. The sun is warm.

PART 3

Cement Socks

NINE

There was no altar, only a platform with a microphone and a banner, BELIEVE IN ME. There was no vaulted cathedral, only an ordinary baseball stadium. There were no fine vestments, only a simple, well-tailored business suit. And, though few knew it, there was no Billy Koch, only a sophisticated android.

It lacked nothing in programming; all of Billy's habits were intact. His powerful hands kneaded the air ('Give Jesus your love! Give it to Him *now*!'), his brows contracted ('Suspended over a pit of flaming fahr! Forget about your puny h-bomb!') and his mighty chest heaved with simulated emotion ('He's a-comin' in a fiery jet! His face is like a blast furnace! He's callin' out – who, me, Lord? You want me? YES, Lord, I'm ready! I'M READY FOR ETERNITY!').

The service too was unchanged. Before the great man actually appeared, there came preliminary events, 'warmups':

A large choir began with a medley of popular hymns, then a warmup preacher delivered a short, hard-hitting sermon that reassured the audience they had come to the right place. He mentioned high taxes, temptations of the young, national unrest caused by Communism and darker races. He praised the basic honesty and faith of rural white Americans and their kin, the four freedoms, motherhood, and the principle of driving moneychangers out of temples.

Then, following an organ selection that leaned towards sustained low notes and tremolo effects, the lights dimmed out. Each member of the audience was given thirty seconds in which to feel alone and apprehensive. When it was quiet enough, a voice broke the tension, crying over the p.a. system: 'JESUS LIVES! JESUS LIVES!'

A spot picked him out: the heavy ridge of brow and high forehead, the crisp, pale suit with massive shoulders (called in the trade 'an FBI'), the glittering smile of ecstasy as he closed his eyes and opened his arms to embrace them, his flock of thirty-five thousand. He held this pose for ten long beats. Then ...

The eyes came open: virgin blue. The audience screamed its blessing upon him, and the deep organ bass cut in under their scream. Billy led them in 'Rock of Ages', his theme song.

'Brothers and sisters, I don't know why you came out here tonight. Some of you may just be curious – you want to see the man who talks so much about Gawd – but that's all right. That's all right, Gawd welcomes you.

'Some of you, well, maybe you found the religion of your childhood just doesn't seem to work any more. Maybe you've lost faith. Or maybe you really tried to believe, but things just got too much for you? And you felt like quitting.

'Why didn't you quit, then? I'll tell you why: it wasn't Gawd's will! I'm telling ALL of you here tonight, that it was the LORD JESUS CHRIST that led you here! *Jesus* wants you all to get another chance! Yes, Jesus *knows all* your suffering and *all* your trials!

'Yes, neighbors, I don't know why *you* came down here tonight – but *I* came here to BEAR WITNESS TO THE LORD JESUS CHRIST!'

A low cheer, mixed with amens, came from the claquers.

'YES, TO BEAR WITNESS! JESUS IS ALIVE TONIGHT, RIGHT HERE IN THIS AUDITORIUM! HE'S IN ME – AND NEIGHBORS, HE CAN BE IN YOU!!'

The cheers were general this time.

Billy went on to make a joke about a frog in a rut, who couldn't possibly get out – but then a truck came along and he had to; the laughter was extravagant.

'Now there's a lot of talk about the "miracles" of modern science, about "miracle" drugs, yes, and even toothpaste has its "miracle" ingredient.

'But I want to talk to you about another kind of "miracle" ingredient. You can't find it at the drugstore. It won't make you smell sweeter or smile brighter. But it is the most powerful force on earth or anywhere else. And I'm talking about the miracle ingredient FAITH!

'There's all kinds of faith. We read a lot of claptrap in the papers about scientists smashing atoms, putting men inside of computers, I don't know what all. Well, you can believe that or not. I never saw a smashed atom, neither did you. Nobody did. We just have faith somebody can do it.

'Now there is something plain ridiculous about a man who will believe there is a bomb a *million times* more powerful than dynamite, a bomb that gives more light than a *thousand suns* – and who still won't believe THAT GAWD LOVES HIM!'

When the laughs, cheers and hallelujahs subsided:

'I won't tell you faith moves mountains. I think the Lord put His mountains where He wanted them, anyway. But I do know of a woman who had a bad car accident. Her little four-year-old boy was pinned underneath the car, and it was crushing the life out of him! That woman – who stood just five-foot two and never lifted anything heavier than a grocery bag before in her life ...'

And so it went, until the finale:

'Have *faith* in the Lord Jesus Christ! Have *faith* in Almighty Gawd! Have *faith* in the Lamb! Have *faith* in the Blood of the Lamb! Have *faith* in the Almighty Pahwr of the Lord! Have *faith* that He can save you! Have *faith* that He can heal you! Have *faith* and forget about your quack doctors and fake medicines! Have *faith* and forget about the "miracles" of modern medicine! Have *faith*, and forget about braces and crutches and pills and potions and knives! Have *faith* and forget about hospitals and X-rays and specialists and surgeons and iron lungs and artificial hearts! Have *faith*! Have *faith*! Have FAITH IN THE HEALING HAND OF THE LORD!'

Pom-papa-pom pom pom, the organ began a sprightly march. Billy's replica held out its arms, and the afflicted (directed by Crusade police to their places in line) came forward for their cures.

'Billikins?'

He awoke from a dream (God, a high-powered executive surrounded by anxious angel subordinates, was just about to place an order for a thousand gross souls) and found her watching him, this fat, red-faced person called Nurse.

'You want some breakfast?'

'They're hiding something from me, Nurse.'

'Who is?' She began helping him out of his wet pajamas.

'I don't know ... the doctor, maybe. And that one-legged man that comes around all the time.'

'Jerry?' Her dark red curls shook. 'Don't be silly, Billikins. Jerry's your friend. He brings us presents.' She often wore one of the presents, a huge black negligee.

'Well, I don't care! I caught him in my room yesterday, looking at *my wall*. And he was laughing!'

Nurse's face grew redder from wrestling him into a business suit. Though her uniform was always rumpled and sweaty looking, she smelled only of starch. Billikins didn't like Nurse much, and he decided he'd better not let her look at his wall, either.

His wall was a picture of the world as it *really* was, and it was also a message, the word of the LORD to His elect, spoken through the prophet Billikins. He'd tried many times to explain it to Nurse, because he'd been so sure she was one of the elect, but she wouldn't listen.

She preferred to go in the bedroom with Jerry and lock the door and lock him out. They were having secrets in there, terrible secrets. Jerry was one of the damned. Already his foot had gone to Hell, Billikins knew.

He'd tried to explain to her why he liked to watch Billy Koch on television. It wasn't that silly little man waving his arms around and speaking about Gawd. There was something else, a real deep voice, so deep you couldn't hear it unless you were one of the elect, so slow you couldn't make out the words unless you were one of the elect. And, in a way, you didn't *listen* to it at all. In a way, you looked at it – no, that wasn't right either. You just knew it was there. Nurse had just laughed at that.

After breakfast he gave her one more chance.

'Nurse, the LORD moves me,' he said.

'You have to go to the bathroom? You want to go potty?' She leaped up and began tugging at his belt.

'No, no, I mean the LORD moves me to carry on His work. I wanna work on the wall.'

'Oh, *that*.' She unloaded herself in the creaky tube-frame chair again, and at the same time took up a slice of sticky coffee cake. Billikins rose to go.

Her mouth, poised over the cake, curved in a nasty smile. 'All I can say is, if that wall is the LOORD'S work, then the LOORD oughta have his mouth washed out with soap.'

Nurse Harriet Saga took a hairpin out of her coffee cup. *What a crummy job.* She picked up the paper and leafed through it, tasting her thumb to hasten past meaningless headlines toward the horoscope page.

POPE'S BULL ON VIRGIN MARY
CHINESE DELEGATES NOT RECOGNIZED
MORE EAST BERLINERS COME OVER WALL
'We almost didn't make it'
SCIENTIST: BEARS CAN TALK!

She felt cheated by the paper this morning. There were no sexational movie star drug raid shocking truth stories, nothing. Even her horoscope was vague.

The Big Cheat was this crummy job, looking after a feeb like that. She'd only taken on the job because her niece, Marilyn, who worked for the Crusade, had told her they needed a nurse for some secret project – and because Billy was so handsome. No one had told her his handsomeness was all show, all for the old ladies from Cedar Rapids …

True, the Crusade paid her a hundred a month over her salary, but that was to keep her quiet. The funny part was, they wouldn't even let her talk to Marilyn about it. All the girl knew was that her aunt was taking care of some 'old man'. Which was just as well, all around, because otherwise Marilyn would be over here every day – she had autographed pictures all over her little room – and there wouldn't be those pleasant afternoons with Jerry.

'Huh? That's funny.' She looked at the headline and even some of the small type under it. **'BILLY TO PREACH AT FERTILIZER PALACE'**, it still said. Some big place in Kansas City. And how could he be out preaching when he was right here? And all those TV programs – maybe they weren't taped re-runs. A twin brother? An actor or ringer? She'd have to ask Jerry. Something wrong, anyhow, and it was worth more than a hundred a month to keep quiet about It.

At noon, Nurse turned on the TV and sat with him, watching a cartoon. Billikins saw that the cartoon was really a message from Jehovah to His Person on Earth, showing forth through the simple parable of Bill the Cat, Mary the Canary and Mike Mouse the divine drama:

Beelzebub (Baal-Ze-bul, the shit god, or just plain Bill) wanted to catch and eat Mary, but he always ended up in trouble: running through a brick wall to leave a Bill-shaped doorway, receiving his own bomb in the mail (a Negrofying blockbuster) or flattened by a mallet. But – and this was the important part – Baal would also be restored to his full powers! There was no hint that Mike and his legions would ever, finally, triumph over the powers of dark-seeing Bill!

The cartoon finished with Bill holding his hotfoot and running off into the flat perspectives of distanceland (whence Lucifer shall return, bearing the same light), a fade ... and Bette Cooke, looking wonderfully substantial, smiled right at him.

'Something from the oven,' she said, 'for Baby and me.'

And it clarified everything. The three chillun of God melted together with love in the burning heart of Jesus, where Bill was Mary was Mike, where Bette Cooke was Billy Koch, being the light and bearing the light and bearing witness to the light. And the light was the sun of God, Baal.

TEN

One Man's Fight (against the Black Conspiracy), by Wes Davis, became a national best-seller that month, nudging down on the non-fiction list two cookbooks and a factual account of the way lions live. Many found in Wes's simple phrases and clumsy constructions the honesty of the blunt back-woodsman who speaks his mind. That Wes had been born and brought up in New York, and lived less than a year in the Midwest, made no difference. So broadcast was the fear of a Negro conspiracy that the reviewers were merci-ful, the media congratulatory, and the public delighted. *At last, at long last,* they said, *someone is saying it out loud.*

A Southern Congressman demanded to know why this man was in jail. A Northern preacher used sections of the book in his sermons (especially: 'Why

Jesus Chose White Disciples', 'Why Washington Kept Slaves', and 'The Black Beast: Human?'). An old lady who had been 'receiving' dark presences on the gold rims of her glasses began the Free Wes Davis Society. A schoolteacher, fired for carving the word SIN on the neck of a Negro child, formed the Organization for the Rights of Gentile Anglo-Saxon Man. The Klan revived, and the American Nazi Party gained new strength. Of all right-nut organizations, only the Jess Hurchists stood still.

From their tiny St Paul office, Amy and Grover carried on underground work on the largest scale they could afford. Amy spent her days writing anonymous letters to Congressmen, the President and the FBI. ('We wondered if you had noticed how the little cent-sign (¢) on our government's postage stamps looks a lot like a hammer and sickle ...') while Grover worked on his deciphering.

He was sure that almost anything, if you looked into it, could yield up a Communist plot. The number and arrangement of milk bottles on doorsteps in the neighborhood, for example. That had proved an ingenious code, and through breaking it Grover discovered that They were poisoning the money with radioactives. He wasn't able to get an unrigged Geiger counter anywhere, but Grover had a special dowsing stick that did just as well. Whenever he saw a dollar bill (alas! not often enough) he would suspend the forked stick over it. If it dipped, the dollar was 'hot' – riddled with radioactives.

One of his richest sources of ciphers was the morning paper, especially the daily 'Crypto Cutie' feature. Through this he had already found out that the 'Red' Cross was a front organization, that most accidents happened in the home because Communists had flooded the market with booby-trapped home items, ranging from fluoride toothpaste and can openers designed to give a ragged edge to the more insidious items like 'fry-o-matic' electric blankets and exploding furnaces.

'Eureka, Amy!'

'You have found it?'

'You betcha I have! Another plot of the International Cummunisk Conspiracy. Just feast your eyes on this, yesterday's Cutie.'

He was not, of course, calling her a name. Amy realized her mistake and read the clipping he was holding out:

CRYPTO CUTIE
DKGTQ DTZDXQ AEQ RGB ET ZAD UGEX.

(Hint: Someone in a jam? Quite the reverse,
although he may be in a state!)

'What on earth can it mean?' Amy tilted her glasses to reread the inscription, but it remained a mystery.

'Well here's the "official" solution from today's paper,' he said, handing her another clipping.

EVANS ENTERS HIS JAM IN THE FAIR.

'And here's the *real* solution.' He held up a sheet of paper.

'CIGAR CANCER YDR UGS DA NYC PGDE,' the top line read. The next was a re-grouping of the same letters: 'CIGAR CANCERY DRUGS *DA* NYC. (signed) PGDE.' He read it aloud, adding that 'da' was Russky for 'okay'.

'This is serious, Amy. We'd better get off a wire to the FBI.'

'Yes, Grover.' She looked at him, into his eyes, beaming at him all the love and admiration that could penetrate her lenses and his.

Grover turned away. 'Yes, and I want to look into the possibility that the Redskies are running the Supreme Court by radios planted in the heads of all the justices. So get me that book from the library, on the Great Pyramid.'

He had found the dimensions of the Great Pyramid invaluable in learning things about the Supreme Court. The lengths of its secret passages in feet gave him numerical indices: one representing fidelity; two, deception; three, conspiracy; four, a quarrel and so on. The turns of the passages to left or right were self-evident, while upward or downward turns meant improvement or decline.

Likewise many other codes had tipped him off: the names of towns on the bottoms of Coke bottles were used to dispatch agents of the conspiracy to their new locations; car license plates (along with the position and number of cars parked on certain streets each morning) delivered the 'orders of the day'; supermarket shoppers' elaborate code of purchases revealed a plan to bombard the television waves with subliminal messages (**'QUIT WORK TODAY, CIVIL SERVANTS' and 'KIDS, DON'T DRINK MILK'**).

If Amy had had the courage to write 'GROVER, AMY LOVES YOU' into an elaborate cipher and run it in the personal column of the Minneapolis *Sun*, she might have got through to him. Anything more direct was useless.

MacCormick Hines put down *One Man's Fight* and rubbed his eyes.

'Maybe I'm getting old. I always thought the real fight was individuality and private enterprise against atheistic communism. Now this fella says the Negroes are ... No, I just can't believe that. I used to watch *Amos 'n' Andy*. Why, those people are *happy*.'

'I wouldn't be too sure of that, sir,' said one of his bright young men. 'The

natural state of the Negroes may be one of simple ignorance and happiness –
but they've been stirred up by left-wing bastards of all kinds.'

Mac sighed. 'You may be right. You may be right, there. In my day, a man
could earn his bread by the sweat of his brow, tuck away a little nest egg,
bring home the bacon, plan for his family's future. And the next thing he
knew, he was—'

'The owner of National Arsenamid, sir? Speaking of which, I have the
figures ...'

'Don't interrupt!' Mr Hines reached out and tweaked the young man's
nose. 'I don't want to hear anything more about the National Whatever it is!
Get out of here!'

Holding his injured nose, the young man retreated. Mac was not to be left
alone, however. Almost at once another b.y.m. strode in, bearing a thick file
like a fasces.

'Hail Wes Davis!' he said.

Mac shook a fist at him. 'None of that! I've just been reading Wes Davis's
book, and he doesn't have a speck of sound business sense. I doubt if the fellow knows the value of a dollar! If you want to hail someone, hail *me*. On
second thought, why don't you hail a cab and leave me alone? Put it on the
expense account. Put a letter of resignation on the expense account while
you're at it. What's that file supposed to be?'

'Sir, you requested the complete dossier on the Müller-Fokker tapes.'

MacCormick Hines took the file, turned over pages for a few seconds,
then closed it. 'Tell me what it says.'

The young man stood at parade rest, hands locked together behind his
back, feet apart. 'There seem to be only four reels of the tape in existence, sir,'
he said, or rather shouted. 'Dr Müller-Fokker himself manufactured them,
and the process is lost – gone with him to Black Power Russia.'

'*Which* Russia?'

'If they aren't, why was one of their writers, Pushkin, a nigra? And how
about the Black Sea? Why did all the White Russians flee the revolution?'

'The tape, the tape.'

'Yes sir. The Russians deny that Müller-Fokker has defected, so far, sir.
Anyway, the tapes were used for some of Dr Müller-Fokker's private research.
Then they went to the Mud Flats Biomedical Research Project.'

'I know what happened there. Go on.'

'The four reels were put up for sale in a surplus store here in town, sir. Two
of them were sold to the Billy Koch Crusade, but we've only been able to find
one of them there. That one is being used to run a robot replica of Billy Koch,
and the key man to see is a Mr Jerry Zurkenhall. If you wish to interview
him, sir, we can arrange that. The replica is due to speak in town soon.'

'Where are the other three? You can't make a heart out of a right auricle.'

'Another surplus store bought one of them, sir. The fourth went to the government, oddly enough. To the Pentagon Logistics Office.'

'Hmmm. That'll take a fine bribe. Well, let's get the one that went to another store.'

'We already have, Mr Hines. Our own marketing division is—'

'I don't have any marketing division!'

'I mean, National Arsen—'

'I don't want to hear that name! Out – get out of here and let me get some work done!'

'Hail Wes D—'

'Out!'

In fact he had no work at all to do. Nothing to do but to dream or dread, whatever it was. Whatever it was, the picture of Marge (635 lines/inch) came to him, hot, hurting and magnificent. Her eyes were swords, her breasts mounted horns, her breath an acid bath. Now here was something nice. Mac ran the video tape of her first commercial, then her second, the next and the next. There was something …

For the first time in years, he began to wonder if another person might not be real.

No? Then what was happening in the auricles and ventricles of his heart? They felt crammed full of spinets and timetables and brass nameplates and daffodil telephones, all those old and awkward and lovely commodities.

I'm not too old to love, he thought. *Anyway, I'm not too old to love.* He embraced her in oceans of suds; they made a little pink cake. He embraced …

He became aware of a figure on the horizon, hailing Wes Davis. The camera zoomed in on a young man with a red nose, standing right here before the desk.

'Mr Hines?'

He put his hands on the desk and asked the b.y.m. what he wanted.

'But I thought *you* wanted something, sir. You were shouting.'

'I was? What'd I say?'

' "I'm rich! I'm rich!" '

'Well I'm not.'

'No sir. But just how did you get so much money?'

'By the sweat of honest toil. By working my fingers to the bone, shoulder to the wheel, nose to the grindstone. I didn't hide my light under a bushel. I didn't waste my God-given talents, of which I am just the steward. Value for money! Build a better mousetrap …'

'Yes sir. But just what kind of mousetrap did you build?' The young man's smile hardened.

'Don't borrow from Peter to pay the devil! A penny saved is money in the bank! Give me elbow grease and I'll move the world! Yankee ingenuity, boy, and …'

'Yes sir. Applied to what?'

Crimson to the roots of his thick white Yankee hair, Mac fought back valiantly: 'WHEN I HIRE A MAN, I ALWAYS LOOK AT HIS SHOES! IF YOU'VE GOT BACKBONE AND SAND, GO TO THE HEAD OF THE CLASS! WASTE NOT, WANT NOT! MORE HASTE, LESS SPEED! THERE IS PLENTY OF ROOM AT THE TOP … oh, what the fuck, I might as well tell you.'

The young man sat down and helped himself to a cigar. Mac lit it for him, then commenced his story.

ELEVEN

Our family [he said] had always been lucky on both sides. My great-grandfather Franklin Hines, who (spelled it H-Y-N) won his wife in a game of Russian roulette. Her name was Hero Rwcz, and I believe she had just escaped a pogrom.

My great-grandfather Leonardo Fox, who was to be the only survivor of Little Big Horn, married Galilea Avaka, who could smell water.

My great-grandfather Archimedes Mutt actually made the first gold strike in California, months before the Sutter's Mill strike. Being a lazy man, he pocketed a few nuggets and declined to stake a claim. Archy married a Swedish girl, Bernoullia Bjld, whose talents were culinary. She could cook any dish to perfection after tasting it just once, and she was good at finding double yolks.

Then there was my great-grandfather Watt Peqeq, the so-called 'Unlucky Balloonist'. Over seventy serious accidents, and his only injury was a broken wisdom tooth. He married Dedalie Gissigi, who found at least a dollar in change every day of her life.

Franklin and Hero Hyn had twins, Dagurette and Fulton. The infant Dag was kidnapped by white slavers, but the gang was wiped out by smallpox before they could get her to market. She was found, two thousand-odd miles from home, by a next-door neighbor who happened by. He brought her home to the Hyns, then himself caught smallpox and died.

Fulton, aged four, fell out of a boat during a family outing on Lake Michigan. The lake at this point was fifty feet deep. For one reason or another, he was not missed for several hours. The family rowed back to find him standing upon the mast of a submerged shipwreck, barely keeping his head above water.

Leonardo and Galilea Fox also had twins, Howe and Jenny. Howe became a poker player, and so incredibly lucky that many times his life was threatened. One sore loser's derringer misfired; another was taken by an opportune epileptic seizure. A third cowboy's gun went off in its holster, and a fourth was himself shot by an old debtor at the moment he drew on Howe. Finally, one of Howe's potential murderers was distracted by the fire that burnt half of Chicago.

Jenny seldom gambled, though on a dare she once parlayed a dollar across seven horse races to something over four hundred thousand (and this was her dowry when she married Fulton Hines). But grandmother Jenny was lucky chiefly in fashion. She had a habit of buying old dresses, altering them to suit herself, and openly disregarding the prevailing fads. Inevitably what she wore became the *avant-garde* fashion a year or two later; Paris designers finally discovered her and paid her handsomely to let them sketch her old rags.

Archy and Bernoullia had twin sons, Morse and Whitney. Morse went into a monastery; I have only one story about him. He was excessively zealous, at least according to the abbot's way of thinking, and that good man asked him to ease up on the fasting, vigils and self-immolation. One day the abbot rebuked him rather sternly for it. At once a heavy statue, which had been solidly anchored to a stone foundation for centuries, toppled, and the abbot was killed by the Good Shepherd's crook. This story may be apocryphal. By the way, I hear steps are being taken in Rome for my great-uncle's beatification.

Whitney Mutt was wounded in the Spanish-American War and shipped home. The following day everyone in his platoon came down with malaria; all eventually died. Whitney married one of the pretty Peqeq twins, Merrimac, by whom he already had a nine-year-old daughter, my mother, Bell.

Some years earlier, Merri's twin sister had been abducted by the outlaw Jess Hurch, and forcibly married. Before the marriage could be consummated, Jess was accidently killed. I don't know the details, but somehow Monita received both a handsome reward for his capture and a medal for his bravery! Even so, she does not seem to have been that lucky. Perhaps she loved the scoundrel, and perhaps he'd have made her a good husband, who knows?

Whitney and Merrimac received as a wedding present a few shares of then worthless stock. They were to honeymoon aboard the *Titanic*, but food poisoning, a late train and a quarrel with a drunken taxi driver combined to delay them; they missed the boat. Instead they went West, to visit Monita.

An incident there proved that Merri was, like her sister, immune to rattle-snake venom.

My father was Singer Hines, Fulton and Jenny's only son. At the age of ten, he fell from a cliff and broke his collarbone, which kept him home from school the day a new boy brought in cholera. As a memento of that day, my father carried with him the rest of his life the five-leaf clover he'd snatched in his fall. The collarbone set badly, and he was consequently not drafted for World War One. He enlisted in the Ambulance Corps, but peace came the following day. 'The infernal luck!' he said. I was to remember those words …

To continue, my mother was given by her aunt Monita eighteen silver dollars on her eighteenth birthday. Sixteen went for a dog, one for a collar and license. The other was to have purchased a leash, but the store was out of stock.

On the way home, her dog broke loose and was trampled to death by a racehorse. Its owner, a young man named Raines, apologized and offered her half-ownership in the horse, Skitsy Darlin'. Bell's peculiar talent lay, as we shall see, in not having time to get too attached to things before she lost them, and in always gaining by compensation. In this case young Raines became her beau, and next day took her to their horse's first race at Duda, Kansas.

Meanwhile another man named Baynes, of nearby Lardhole, Missouri, set out for another race. Having lost his way, he was misdirected by local farmers to the Duda racetrack (where Bell and Raines sat holding hands in the center of the grandstand).

The starting bugle blew. Skitsy Darlin' got off to a bad start, but moved from sixth to fourth place rapidly. The crowd grew excited as the horses bunched up in the far turn (Baynes was looking for a parking place, Raines was squeezing Bell's hand). Skitsy Darlin' entered the home stretch; so did Baynes's yellow roadster; they collided.

The panic on the racecourse was exceeded by that a second later in the stands, half of which collapsed. Raines was killed instantly; Bell was left holding his ring (it bore the seal of the Crown Prince of Luftenberg, and many years later it saved her life in a tight spot).

For Skitsy Darlin's broken leg, Baynes offered compensation. He proposed to mend the leg, set the animal to stud or similar work, and turn over all its earnings to Bell, and gave her the roadster as a token of good faith. Skitsy Darlin' became famous under Baynes's training – perhaps you have heard of Mathematical Hank, the circus wonder horse?

Bell met my father at a resthome where both were recuperating from nervous exhaustion (he had fallen from a Zeppelin). They married. My triplet brothers and I were born a year later.

Times were hard. My dentist father, out of work, was forced to actually beg on the streets of New York. One day my mother came across the eighteenth and last silver dollar. It was not enough to hold off starvation for long, so she generously gave it to a hunchbacked beggar. It looked 'funny' to him, so he fobbed it off on another beggar, my father. He took it to a coin dealer.

It was a rare 1897 Medicine Dumps Bank Dollar (Obverse: a frontiersman shaking hands with Liberty. Reverse: a wreath, a cornucopia of buffalo, and the words ONE DOLLER) in mint condition, and worth thousands. The dealer offered him five hundred for it and my father sold. The following week, all over the country, immense caches of these dollars were turned up; its value dropped to 'face'.

Some of the five hundred went to pay for a trip West for Bell, to visit her dying mother. She arrived hours too late, and there were the funeral expenses to meet. Merrimac had died in poverty, leaving only her old, tumble-down house (which had, though, survived an earthquake).

Bell called in a realtor to appraise the place. Seeing how desperate she was to sell, he began depreciating the house, knocking on walls to show their flimsiness. One entire room caved in, killing the realtor and revealing the hiding place for Merrimac's valuables. Here were all the old 'worthless' stocks, now priceless. My father sold them to buy his practice, a mansion, and a large hoard of gold bullion for inlay work.

Next day the market crashed, and Singer was able to buy back all his sold stocks for pennies (which he did, out of sentiment). And so, though he spent his entire fortune trying to trace the origin of the Luftenberg ring, he did leave me those stocks.

Every investment I made paid off, or very nearly every one. In time, I could afford to buy the time of bright young investment counsellors like yourself. In time …

Mac blew out the match and dropped it in his clean platinum ashtray.

'You were about to tell me,' said the young man, 'the secret of your success.'

'Was I? I thought I just had.'

'You didn't say a word!'

'Indeed. It's just as well. I was thinking of a story – something I saw the other day on television. Well, never mind. Back to work. Time, my young friend, is money.'

TWELVE

The art critics of a dozen newspapers and magazines came to the opening at the Moody Gallery. They shuffled in like a soup line, snatched what was free (catalogues and drinks) and ignored the paintings as much as possible while they talked to each other.

Ank had been through it all many times, when he'd worked for the *Sun*. They called this 'the game'.

The game was to conceal your own opinion of the show while sounding the opinions of your colleagues. When you had polled enough of them to decide whether it was worthwhile or not, you went back to the paper and set down a few epigrams. If the show was worthwhile, you tried to have at least one 'insight' no one else would manage. This might involve talking about the arrangement of the works, the name cards attached to the walls near them, how many steps to the gallery door, or anything else you were sure no one but you had noticed.

Ank knew the game, but now it was his show, and he really wanted to know what they thought of it. He walked a crooked route through the gallery, avoiding the clusters of wealthy guests, and trying to eavesdrop on the critics' conversations.

'Vasari ...' said a woman, in triangular glasses. ' ... Berenson ...'

A man with the blurry, distorted features of a Francis Bacon executive stood with his back to one of Ank's favorite paintings, a blue-eyed Giotto copy. 'That's it, all right. Tensions lacking. The quintessence of *lif i framställning*'.

Next to him a woman jerked her sneer toward the Turneresque storm at sea (including a Coke bottle floating on a nearby wave). 'Insulting as a tit, ain't it?'

'Dada, yes,' said a man outfitted as a lumberjack. 'But this decadent sentiment ...'

Ank came to a stop before a 'Mondriaan' which featured in one panel a sign: WATCH THIS SPACE. Nearby, someone was talking about the real works of Mondriaan. ' ... sacramental splendor. Inverted baroque, you see, the liturgy of the line.'

The tall art critic with the ax-blade nose saw Ank and came over. 'You covering this, too? I thought the *Sun* fired you.'

Ank stammered. 'I'm ... here all right. God knows why, it's a waste of time.' The familiar phrases came easy.

'So I thought. What did you think of that Aphrodite thing, by by the way?' He referred to the chief piece of the exhibition, a travesty of Botticelli's famous work, here entitled *Bertha Venus*. In this version, blood coursed down the goddess's leg, and great bloody patches appeared in the sky.

'I don't know,' said Ank. 'The painter's probably a clever young guy with no ideas. There's a certain lack of tension, of fiber ...'

'I know just what you mean. Like a queer without taste.'

At the far end of the room, Glen sipped his drink and talked to a bearded young man he took to be the painter. The works were unsigned, and the catalogue called the painter 'A.B'.

'That Botticelli, it says it all, you know? I've been working on an article about the same thing myself – the corruption of the individual, the reduction of sex to a mechanism in modern life.'

The young man made a restless shift, so Glen raised his voice. 'It's like those Bette Cooke commercials. Supermarket sex, canned, frozen, sterilized. Love as meaningless as shopping. Art is the only way to reveal her for what she is, the great bitch-goddess of the built-in kitchen ...'

'Yeah, well, I'd better get going.' The young man went off to fetch another tray of drinks.

Glen saw Ank at the other end of the room, standing alone by a curious pseudo-Cezanne. As he walked towards him, he heard someone saying, 'Well I don't know, Wilma. That's what I thought, too. Cheap, derivative. But notice that kid from the *Sun* really likes them. Can't take his eyes off 'em.'

Glen asked Ank if he saw the artist anywhere.

'I thought you knew, Glen. These are ... mine.'

'Yours? Terrific!' Glen was secretly flattered at having known the artist long before the show. 'I really like it, Ank. In fact, I'm thinking of buying that big Botticelli.'

After Glen left, Drew waved his check at Ank. 'We've made it, kid! Eight grand right off the bat! Everybody said I was crazy putting prices like these on an unknown, but ... What's the matter?'

'Nothing. I just want to make a confession.'

'You're depressed. Nerves from all the commotion out there, that's all. Those pig-ignorant bastards, they don't appreciate ...'

'I want to get away for awhile. Go to Europe, maybe, and just ...'

'Study the old masters? Good idea.'

'No, I want to do something *different*, I don't know, I want to hole up by myself somewhere and maybe make up for what I'm doing here. I've committed a crime, Drew.'

The dealer patted his arm. 'Don't worry, Ank. Giotto will forgive you.'

*

The reviews were good. Ank's show sold out in a week. The news that he would paint no more in this 'period' drove prices upward, until the last sale (to the architect Arch Ögivaal) reached ten times the first.

Ank left for Alsace-Lorraine at once. He bought an old factory near Assholtz, moved in quantities of supplies, and cloistered himself there for several months.

Marge drank to the flag, the Veterans' Administration one, which she had draped over the sofa in lieu of a coffin. The drink wasn't liquor, either. That had stopped working weeks ago.

And now this stuff wasn't having much effect. She felt her head leave her cold, crawly body, but that was all. Cold and crawly, the way she felt when Bradd got too close. As he always did.

Dr Fellstus, MacCormick Hines, Mr Bradd – already her life was filling with new names. Like dust sifting in after you sweep. There was, there is, no more feeling left for him than for that nylon flag over there, fifty or sixty miles across the room. He was someone else.

So was she: Betsy Ross, Martha Wash, Molly Pitch and Bette Bitch, another standardized receptacle for the feelings of old motherless boys. Boys from Boise. You can take the Boise out of the country, but try and take …

She walked over and lay down naked on the flag. Country kitchen dinners, hot dinners … hot fudge sex star giveaway showdown tragedy delight it's all right din-din chowdown chowder shoulder choux sho'tnin' bread … three layer parfait banana coconut saffron mango yam molasses ripple mint apple betty nutmeg cinnamon bare clove rosemary thyme it's dinner time, its

She spread out on the stairs and stripes, made a megaphone of her hands, and screamed:

'COME … AND … GET IT !'

The study hall was arranged with all desks facing the walls around a large rectangle. Col Fouts stood in the center, where he could make sure that every cadet was writing his letter home properly.

The proper form was written on the blackboard:

Dear Mother and Father:

1. Cadet N.N. is well and happy.
2. Cadet N.N. will/will not be home for the weekend/Christmas/Easter/the occasion of X, as planned, because his academic record does/does not permit this.
3. Cadet N.N. sends both of you and his whole family his devoted love.

Signed, Cadet N.N.

Like the other cadets, Spot had learned to tell, just from the sound of Fouts's footsteps, which way he was facing. While he faced Spot, Spot worked diligently on the form letter. At all other times, Spot continued his secret letter to Billy:

Dear Billy Koch:
1. Cadet Sturgemoore Shairp wants to kill himself …

At the next desk a cadet slipped a book from under his letter home and read:

We ruined them for their own simple savage kind of life, and we didn't succeed in making them fit to live like white men. If we really felt sorry for the nigras, like we say we do, then we'd just 'put them to sleep' …

The cadet at the next desk was asleep. Just beyond him two ten-year-old corporals were exchanging rumors about Fouts. Some mysterious 'woman in red' had been visiting his quarters. Fouts had a locked drawer in his office that probably was jammed full of contraceptive pills and all like that. Someone had *seen* a woman go into Fouts's quarters at midnight – using her own key!

Then came the squeaky floorboard that meant he was about to turn around. That side of the room went back to work. The cadets on the far side of the room began talking about the new Army outfit, a super-tough unit mentioned in the *National Military School Enquisitor*. A unit called the Pink Barrettes.

THIRTEEN

'All right you guys, let's try it again. Brassieres line up at the south end of the field, skins at the north, ON THE DOUBLE! Here comes Rocky, so make it look good!'

General Rockstone strode briskly by, a *coup* stick jammed in his oxter. 'Sergeant, I didn't hear very much goddamned noise in that last charge.'

'No sir. We'll do better this time, sir. READY, MEN!'

'Just a minute, Sergeant. At ease, men. Who's that man with the haircut?'

The sergeant whirled. 'Manning! Attention! One step to the rear – HRAR-RGH!' Since the men were all standing with their backs to the general, the rearward step brought Manning closer. Rocky looked him over.

'Soldier, who told you to get a haircut?'

'No one, sir.'

'*Then why in hell did you do it?*'

'Sir, the regulations say—'

'Not *our* regulations, by God! I want every man in this outfit to grow shoulder-length hair, or by God, I want to know why! Sergeant, give the men an extra hour of backwards drill this afternoon, and put *this* man on punishment detail until he looks fit to be a Pink Barrette.'

'Yes sir!'

'And, Sergeant ... more noise!'

'Yes sir! All right, you bastards! You heard the general. Next time you come across that field I want you to *squeal* and *giggle*! So if I can't hear you, you'll do it ten more times before we take five. Is that clear?'

'Yes sir!' shrilled the company in unpracticed falsetto.

A moment later, those wearing brassieres charged down the field to engage those without. The 'skins' were fixing rubber bayonets or firing blanks.

'Take some evasive frigging action!' the sergeant bellowed. The 'brassieres' began to pirouette and skip. All the way they squealed and giggled lustily, until they reached the enemy lines.

The 'skins' line broke, and they became a few clusters of panicky individuals, firing wildly, thrusting half-heartedly, but cursing with real style and fervor. The light, curved *coup* sticks of the attackers never stopped moving, flicking here and there with uncanny accuracy. Within a few minutes, they had tagged everyone.

'All right, Sergeant,' said Rocky. 'Keep it up. I've got a conference at the Pentagon this afternoon. Be back tomorrow.'

The battle of Dresden was getting off to a slow start. There seemed some question as to whether Napoleon would really engage the defending forces at all ...

'General Rockstone's here, sir.'

'Mm?' Weimarauner returned with difficulty to the full-scale world. It was hard at times to realize that Napoleon's whole army would fit into the summer house, along with Blücher's forces; that a single musket of either side would make a toothpick ... 'Send him out.'

Weimarauner stood in his modified back yard and watched his Pink Barrette general emerge from the house. Rockstone wore a green fatigue uniform sprouting lace at collar and cuffs. His long gray hair was pulled back over one ear by a plastic pink barrette. The little stick he carried was, because of his rank, tipped with one gold star.

As he reached the edge of the flagstone patio, Rocky was instructed by an orderly to remove his shoes.

'That's right,' Weimarauner called. 'Most of the yard is built up with plastic, and the surface is pretty delicate.'

Rocky slipped off the regulation shoes, to which pink pompoms had been attached, and padded carefully across the brittle lawn.

'How are things in Florida?'

'Good, sir. The men are in the pink – in peak condition, General, rarin' to go. I hoped you'd be giving us embarkation orders.'

Weimarauner picked up a French lancer and examined its painted uniform with a pocket magnifier. 'No rush, Rocky, no rush. Right now we're in the process of changing our logistics system – Blunden here can tell you all about it – and we're trying to cut back on troop movements until we have everything straightened around.'

Rocky looked closer at the battle of Dresden landscape. 'Toy sojurs? That's a big set-up you've got there, General.'

'Indeed, forty acres and still growing. I was lucky enough to get these lead lancers from an old warehouse in Minneapolis – had to make a special trip to make the deal – they cost a fortune, but they're worth it. Look at that detail!'

'Nice hobby.'

Weimarauner frowned. 'It's far more than that, Rockstone. Do you think I'd waste taxpayers' money on a *hobby*?

'No, you see, my concentration on a single battle seems to stir the deepest reaches of my intellect. While I work out every contingency of the battle of Dresden, on a *conscious* level, my unconscious is free to experiment with daring new ideas.' He surveyed the green velvet landscape, the rows of tiny white tents. 'It was while I was on that trip to Minneapolis that the whole conception of the Pink Barrettes came to me entire. To name but one example. And while I was debating a detail of this battle – supposing Blucher had engaged Napoleon *before* he got to Dresden – I suddenly came upon this new logistics system, *Modulog*.'

'All from a toy! Wow!'

Weimarauner looked at him coldly. 'Why don't you toddle off with Captain Blunden here, and let him tell you all about *Modulog*? He can explain it as well as I.'

This was perfectly true, for Captain Blunden, who now led Rocky inside to the study and poured out two sherries, was the originator of *Modulog*, just as Hackendorf had originated the Pink Barrettes. Weimarauner's genius lay in surrounding himself with capable official and semi-official aides. They ghosted his books, drafted his recommendations to the Secretary of Defense, and now and then managed to draw his attention from Dresden long enough to hand him a new idea to 'come upon'.

Weimarauner meanwhile withdrew further and further from real military activities. He no longer kept an office at the Pentagon, but communicated from his country home by special telephone. He no longer concerned himself with the present war – at times he could not remember the names of the enemy nation – but slipped deeper and deeper into the complexities of Napoleon *vs.* Blucher. What if Blucher attacked first? What if Napoleon had not left off his attack on Dresden in the middle? How much of the river could he have held, and for how long?

'*Modulog*,' said the captain, 'is all new. It's based on three new principles, sir.'

'Just between you and me, let's drop the *sir*, Blunden. I hope we're all friends here.' He winked a false eyelash and toasted the captain with his sherry.

'Yes – General. The principles are: first, that there is no reason to handle and transport troops and materiel in different ways. Second, thanks to container freight systems already in operation, troops may be boxed and shipped in a modular way just as any other materiel. In other words, a box of men is no harder to handle and dispatch than a box of supplies. Containers may be fitted out with life-support facilities, namely airholes, food and chemical toilets.

'Third, the fastest way of processing materiel is by using computer routing. The most expedient route can be found by feeding in all the available transport data, all the data on requirements and priorities, and then letting Nature – the computer, rather – take its course.

'Imagine that we have three cities. City A makes guns, City B is a troop assembly point, City C is a target, or delivery area. C needs a certain number of armed personnel at time t_1. At time t_0 we have at A all our weapons and half enough transport to deliver them, and at B all our troops and one quarter of the necessary transport. The transport at B is twice as fast as that at A, and the relative distances of the three cities are ...'

Rocky went into a daydream while the earnest young captain rattled on. How could life be so complicated now? When, only yesterday, life was an island idyll.

人间の条件 he thought. 人间の条件

'The important thing is, all the services will be switched over,' Blunden was saying. 'Even where container freight isn't feasible, orders will be processed by our central computer, using the latest in digital equipment, the Müller-Fokker tapes.'

Rocky struck him lightly on the arm with his wand. 'Bad words,' he said. 'Bad words, you naughty captain.'

At Billy Koch Crusade Headquarters, another mail bag was dumped on the sorting table, and sorters went to work with their thumb knives. Marilyn

Temblor picked up her purse and went to the ladies' restroom. No one saw her take the phial from her purse but God.

'I don't care,' she said defiantly to the roller towel. ' I'll – I'll quit this job. I'll become a *stewardess!*'

She opened the phial and dabbed some on her wrist. Almost at once the overpowering sexy odor filled the room. She panicked, scrubbed furiously until her wrist was almost bleeding – but the odor clung, accusing her.

Back in the mail room she picked up the first letter.

Dear Billy,

My problem is, I'm in love with a man who hardly notices me. I'm his secretary, and I know this sounds like just a girlish infatuation, but I am not a girl at all. I am over eighty years of age and so is he. We have been good friends for many years, and though my affection for him has ripened into love, he still thinks of me as just a loyal companion.

We are both single, and I would like to marry him, but I hate to wait for him to 'pop' the question. What can I do to make him notice me as a woman, without seeming to throw myself at him? Should I confess I love him? Ask him to marry me? Or just wait and see?

Please answer, Billy. My time is running out.

Yours in confusion, Amy Q. Birdsall

That would be 674; Marilyn knew without even consulting the chart. 674 was 'Girl wants to propose to man.'

The next letter was a little tougher. She stopped chewing gum and read the letter three times before she could focus her mind on it.

Dear Billy Koch:
1. Cadet Sturgemoore Shairp wants to kill himself.
2. He is at military school.
3. The Bible says it is wrong to take life, but he is being trained to take life.
4. Sometimes it is all right to kill someone.
5. Sometimes it must be all right to kill yourself.
6. Colonel Fouts said that anyone who plays with himself will be expelled.
7. Then Cadet Sturgemoore Shairp played with himself a lot, because he wanted to go home.
8. It didn't work.
9. Mother does not answer Cadet Sturgemoore Shairp's letters. She is on television.
10. Father is dead.
11. Mother is just like she was dead.
12. Cadet Sturgemoore Shairp should die, too.

13. Cadet Sturgemoore Shairp went to ask Colonel Fouts if it would be all right to kill himself.
14. Colonel Fouts took a long time answering the door.
15. What do you want, he said.
16. There was chocolate all over his face.
17. Cadet Sturgemoore Shairp did not know what to say, so he looked down.
18. There was a pink strap garter strap thing hanging out of the Colonel's fly.
19. Cadet Sturgemoore Shairp said did the Colonel believe in God, that God wanted everyone to live.
20. A hundred and twenty punishment tours, the Colonel said, impertinence to an officer.
21. Billy, sir, Cadet Sturgemoore Shairp requests permission to kill himself.

Please advise,
Cadet Sturgemoore Shairp

It must be 'wants to commit suicide', number 647. And the other one was 674. Bothered only slightly by that 'pink strap garter strap thing', Marilyn rolled a sheet of paper in the first automated typewriter and headed it 'Dear Miss Birdsall'. Then someone seized her hand and held it to his nose.

Jim, the handsome Bible student. 'My, you smell nice,' he said. 'Perfume?'

She nodded and punched the machine with her free hand. 647.

'What's it called?'

She freed her hand. Blushing, she set the second machine for 674. 'I – don't remember.'

'Sure you do,' he said. The typewriters started chattering. She would lose her job. Shut out of the Crusade, Billy's Crusade, forever. Would it be the same, being a stewardess? An 'air angel'?

'Sure you remember,' he insisted, moving closer. 'What was that name?'

She could hardly say it.

'My Sin.'

'Doctor, do you have to come and see me in that – that drag?'

Glen seized a Coke and wrung its neck. Feinwelt tossed a golden sausage curl and settled himself on the couch.

'Listen, Glen. We've been over this a few times, haven't we? I have other patients, other things to attend to. I know you'd like me to be Big Daddy Doctor for Glensie alone, but let's try to look at this unselfishly. You know I haven't time to change clothes six times a day or whatever. If *you* can't make the necessary adjustment, well ...'

'But everybody's going to think I'm – and it isn't just that. I don't think you wear that drum majorette outfit just to hold hands with a few sick faggots. Oh no. I've been reading a few things in connection with an article I'm doing for *Stagman*. I've learned a few things.'

'Really?' The drum majorette lit a fragrant cigarette and leaned back. 'Like what?'

Glen was silent for a moment, gazing up at *Bertha Venus*. 'It's like … Cybele. The bitch goddess, demanding that her priests castrate themselves and put on women's clothes.' He put on a World War Two aviator's helmet.

'Not sure I follow you.'

'And then in the Middle Ages! They thought witches were able to make men impotent. By the same token, they built big phallic cathedrals to the Virgin. The Virgin Mother!' He tried on a Sioux war bonnet. 'Yes, and *their* priests had to wear skirts, too. St Francis tried to go against that tradition … but a hundred years later or so there were the Franciscans putting on skirts.'

'Don't you think you're harping on this unnecessarily?' Feinwelt's case-hardened voice had taken an edge. 'Just what is this "article" about, anyway?'

'And it all comes down to Bette Cooke. The latest incarnation of the Mighty Bitch Mother Angry Virgin Goddess, see? Her oracles are recipe books. Her priests are advertising men. Her charm is the silverware coupon on the flour bag, and her Mysteries are the secrets of cooking – no, not just cooking, but cooking that will "keep the menfolk coming back for seconds". *Menfolk!* Not men. Men reduced, crushed down to sexless *elves*!'

'If you really feel that way …'

'What time is it?'

Feinwelt looked at his watch. 'Oh now, we have plenty of time left in our session, if that's what's worrying you.'

'She's on. The commercial's on!'

Glen rushed to the electronic wall and switched on the glowing features of Bette Cooke. He did not notice when Feinwelt left.

Billikins had finished the wall. He wanted to call Nurse to see it, but she'd only laugh nasty. He had to admire and love it all by himself.

The wall was a crayon and pencil drawing covering one long wall of his room, twelve feet long and eight high. It was a combination (though not to Billikins) of public-toilet art, church-window portraiture, Bible map and political cartoon. There were a hundred and forty-four thousand faces in it, each wearing a label on its forehead or hat, each expressing glee or torment.

At the top, a seven-foot phallus aimed to enter a standard men's-room snatch (or winged buttonhole). The prick had been wrapped end to end in a bandage reading: 'There shall be a cause of GOD, which is the twelve and the seven, freely. It without is the twelve, and the seven within are five loaves and two fishes, and this East shall enfold it.'

Below this was a layer of cloud, the 'Cloud of Could', studded with hands, feet and eyes. The cloud terminated in two fists, one at each end. The right hand held a burning diploma, the left a sign: 'The Flying Roll is the last great whirlwind and the great church IN the west! WHO used to send forth all to gather together all manner cloud and fire, loud and ire, peacefully enfolding the First Life. I am accounted for and counted, I am continued and the fire in the DOUBLE lamp enfolds it!!!'

Across the cloud large yellow-rayed letters spelled:

IS GOD TO RAPTURE A POWERLESS CHURCH!

On the land below were the twelve tribes, identified as being divided into six nations, four races, three classes and two sides. On the left were the SLACKERS, LACKERS, LACQUEYS, BACKERS, WRACKERS and PACKERS; on the right were DIGGERS, WIGGERS CHIGGERS, NIG-GERS, TRIGGERS and JURY-RIGGERS. Each tribe of twelve thousand was further subdivided all 48 ways imaginable. The remaining space was filled with flames, banners, signs, swords, sheep, the winding road of Venue leading up to Mount Golden Mystery, clocks and $-bags, eyes baleful and eyes pro-tective, gallows, elks, the Stairs of Relief and the Five Truths in their white robes; whips, a cage of thorns, snakes whose spots were roses, the blazing headlights and grill of a Saette, pennants, the Keys of Penance, special notices too small to read, and scallop shells. The diggers were digging for sparkling letters buried in the earth:

WHOSOEVER SLAYS THE FIRST LIFE SHALL LIVE FOREVER, BUT THE COLOR OF AMBER SLAYS AND IT IS SLAIN. DARKNESS IS THE FREELY PORTION OF HIM WHO FINDS OUT THE ACCOUNT!

He signed it in the corner: 'Words of Jehovah'. Then he closed the bedroom door and began nailing it shut. Nurse called out from the kitchen, ordering him to cut out that racket.

Nurse Harriet Saga scootched down in the chair, easing wind and her vari-cose legs. She was just too pooped to yell at him again. Instead she selected another piece of fudge and turned to the horoscope page:

You will be relieved of a burden which has bothered you for some weeks. Domes-tic difficulties may come to a head this morning, spoiling your day, unless

The first hammer blow struck her in the neck. The other fifty-eight landed among the tight red curls of her hair, deep at the darker roots.

There was no place to hide, and he was sore afraid: which amongst them might not recognize him? But the POWER came upon him, guiding his eyes to the newspaper on the kitchen table. He moved a tooth-marked piece of fudge, leaving a bloody smear, and read the headline: 'BIBLELAND TO OPEN TODAY. Bob's Water, Calif. (UP) ...'

He found Nurse's purse in the foyer. In it there lay a big wad of earthly money and a pair of dark glasses. His eyes caught his eyes in the foyer mirror as he put them on. Those precious stones in the rims of the glasses – none too good for Him who Billikins was about to meet.

He told the cab driver he wanted Bibleland.

'Is it far?'

'Furder than I go, buddy. Ya hafta fly. Whatcha want, the airport?'

'What do I ... ?'

'Ya wanta fly or what?'

'Yes. Yes ... I want to fly.'

The cab picked up speed. It passed a giant picture of the Woman in Blue and White, 'LET ME SHOW YOU,' she said, 'HOW TO CATCH *YOUR* GINGERBREAD BOY.'

FOURTEEN

Dear Miss Birdsall:

If you knew a man who rented a fine home, fully equipped with air conditioning, wall-to-wall carpets and pastel fixtures, and one day this man just up and BURNED DOWN this lovely home, you'd certainly wonder why! Did he hate the landlord? Did he have some other place to live? If not, why on God's earth did he do it?

If this man said he was just 'tired of living here' you'd call him a *fool*.

Yet you have been thinking of taking the beautiful home God rents to you FREE OF CHARGE – your body – and WRECKING IT! Isn't that a thousand times more foolish?

What you're thinking of doing is a sin. It is wanton, pointless destruction. Not only is it SIN, but it is THE ONE SIN THAT CAN NEVER BE FORGIVEN OR UNDONE! It means the ETERNAL LOSS of your earthly home – the beautiful home God gave you.

You are troubled. The stresses of modern life, the daily 'rat race' and perhaps personal sorrows weigh heavily upon you. But it isn't SIN you want. What you really want is a *change*. A reason to GO ON LIVING.

WHY NOT COME OVER TO CHRIST?

'I am the Resurrection and the Life.'

'The wages of sin is death.'

Switch to Jesus Christ and see! Read your Bible. Pray, asking Jesus to forgive you for even thinking of this Sin. He will make your burden lighter, give you new power to zip through the old daily routine without a thought of despair. Millions have testified to this – it is *a fact*!

So don't burn the house down – light up your heart and invite Christ in.

God bless you,
Billy Koch

She crumpled the letter, then began ironing it flat again with her ringless left hand. What could Billy mean by that? 'Sin that can never …'

She read it again. There was no mistake. It wasn't a form letter, Could there be two Miss Birdsalls? No matter how she looked at it, Billy just wasn't making sense.

Amy removed her glasses and began polishing them, a nerve-calming ritual of many years' standing. As she held them up to the light, she noticed the rims. Dark plastic across the top, steel below – they looked so *medical*. Like a face brace. How many times had she meant to change them for something sexier, say rhinestones or glowing plastic? Yet always she wound up with the same old thing: the dull, the cheap, the reasonable.

Weren't all these years of chastity enough? It didn't seem fair. What she had preserved so carefully all these years had diminished in value to everyone, even to her, until now it was like a ticket to a dance of long ago … yet Billy now asked her to go on with it, to save that faded ticket … Why? Why did he hate her so?

A fragment of memory from the always dim near past attached itself to the question. There was a street corner she'd just come out of. There was a service at the ballpark. The car. She'd come out of the ballpark looking for a taxi, walking, and the car.

The car turned the corner. She'd jumped back to avoid being killed. It was … Billy's car? Yes, she could see him at the wheel, those cold blue eyes … and he *cursed* her, his curse mingling with the blare of that musical horn:

Rock	up yours
Ages	old
cleft	
me	bag

That satanic hate. Why?

*

Grover came out of the inner office and found Amy moving her nose down a column of names in the telephone book.

'Here it is,' she said. 'Here it is: 46 Phenolphthalein Drive.'

'Where are your glasses, Amy?'

Her naked face blushed. 'I – broke them.'

'Golly, you'd better get some new ones. Your eyes look terrible. All red and—'

'I have that address you wanted!' She waved the phone book. 'The Societé Anonyme des Transtévérins.'

'Uh huh. Good. I'm perty sure *that* outfit is the *key* to all the others. It may be a chance to use our heads and really stamp out Cumminism all over the country! Tell you what. We'll drive up there and keep an eye on them for awhile.'

It was a short way to Phenolphthalein Drive. As they drove, Grover explained their objective.

'I probably shouldn't bring you along on this dangerous a mission, Amy. These are the Big Boys, and they play rough. By the way, in case anything should happen to me, I'll give you the commonation to the safe. You know What We Have in the Safe.'

'You mean the b—'

'Right. You set it just like an alarm clock, and put it on all our records. It wouldn't be much use my dying, if it meant they learned all about us.'

The Societé Anonyme des Transtévérins was, in fact, a Communist front organization masquerading as a Franco-Italian banking firm. But its operations were in another part of town. It had no connection whatever with the quiet brick building Amy and Grover now parked across from and began observing through binoculars (from under the shade of a willow): the headquarters of Transvestites Anonymous.

'I can't see anything,' said Amy, 'through my half the binoculars. Are they adjusted?'

'Yes, they're fine. It's you and no glasses, Amy. You oughta get them fixed. How'd they come to get broke, anyways?'

'I'm cold. Can't we move the car into the sun?'

'And have them spot us? Amy, this is a dangerous outfit! Their last name, "Transtévérins", is an anagram of "invents arrest"! And that isn't all!'

He explained that the director's name was Julien Pé, whose last name, as Grover understood, meant *pi*, the probable secret symbol for the group. '*Pi*,' he said, 'is a *circular* relation, see? Wheels within wheels.'

Amy was about to congratulate him on his discovery when Grover gasped. A vehicle was entering the deserted road.

'Police car,' he said. 'Or their "police". We'd better try and look natural.'

He took off his glasses. The myopia of their eye-beams blended. Then, for the first time in their many years of friendship, Grover drew her over and kissed her.

Dear Cadet Sturgemoore Shairp:

Many a young person has had the same feelings you have now, and there is nothing sinful about them. If they are used and directed in the ways of the Lord, such feelings lead to the continuation of the human race and the multiplication of God's flock on earth.

The step you are about to take is a grave one, and you must make sure you are right. I cannot advise you on this, but God can and will. Pray. Read your Bible. Let the Lord guide you.

'It is good for man to be alone,' the Bible says. And in the words of the English poet John Donne, a preacher like me, 'No man is an island.' If you decide yourself to be NO LONGER ALONE, be resolute. Stick by your decision, NO MATTER WHAT. As Davy Crockett put it, 'Be sure you're right, then go ahead.'

God bless you,
Billy Koch

Spot read the first paragraph three times. 'The continuation of the human race'? He guessed that might mean killing yourself to make room for more – lightening the airplane of humanity by bailing out.

The idea of suicide came often to him now, in the St Praetexta school library, under the great picture of Galahad. In the evening. 'My strength is as the strength of ten …' It scared him, what Billy said in the last part: stick by it, no matter what. That meant not making his decision final until he was *sure* …

If only there were someone to talk him out of it. 'A preacher like me …'

Spot made his way to the front of the room and asked the librarian for anything by John Donny.

'Who?' The old ex-marine looked suspicious.

'John Donny, the English poet …'

'*Don Juan*, you mean. Oh no you don't. Heard about that one, did ya? Dirty sex pome by "Lord" Byron. I guess you figured I wouldn't know the difference, eh? You won't get any meat-beating poetry past me, by Heaven!'

Spot showed him the letter and the name in it.

'Donne? Preacher? No, I don't think we have any – wait, I'll have a look.'

While Spot waited, a classmate came out of the reserve room. 'Man, have I been reading the real shit!' he said. 'They got it on reserve here, this book all about the nigger conspiracy. *One Man's Fight*. The guy that wrote it is in prison, but my military political science prof says not for long.'

'Verne, do you …'

'Do I what?'

'Do you think suicide is wrong?'

'Wes Davis says – he wrote this book – he says it all depends. For the inferior races, he says it's the only honorable solution. Or for any *weak* person. But we're strong!'

'Yeah, I ... thanks.'

The librarian came from the stacks with a thin volume.

'I guess this is all right,' he said, slapping it on the counter. 'Looks to be about God and Samson and them. Take keer of it now – I don't want to see any pecker tracks when you bring it back.'

'Thank you, sir.' Spot took the book to his room. It was *Biathanatos*, John Donne's long justification for suicide.

The Billy android stood tall, even with his head bowed, a captain, at least, in the army of the Lord. The hymn finished and he raised his hands to heaven, or towards the roof of the auditorium.

'Lord, I'm asking you to do something for some of our sick brethren. I'm asking you to heal them in mind and body and spirit, like you healed the sick in Jerusalem.'

The blind and halt had paid their fees and shuffled into line. Now the line moved forward under the direction of Crusade cops, as Billy spoke in soothing cadences, repeating again and again his instructions to the evidently slow-witted Deity:

'Let the pahwr flow down, O Lord! Jesus, let the pahwr flow down! Through my right hand, Lord! Lord Jesus, let the pahwr down through my right ...'

When he'd worked on the right hand enough he got the left going. The first candidates stumbled up the steps and stood blinking uncertainly in the glaring light.

Jerry sat with his real foot up on the console. He peeled a peanut, tossed it in the air and snapped it up. He put the shell back in the bag, then rummaged under the shells for a whole one.

The door opened and a Crusade cop named Morgan put his head in. 'Jerry, I got a guy out here says he wants to talk to somebody.'

'What about?'

'He says he's pretty rich, and he looks like it. An old guy.'

'Special contributions upstairs.'

'No, he says he wants to *buy* something. Some kind of tape, he says.'

Jerry missed a peanut. 'What *did* he say, exactly?'

'He said – you ain't religious, are ya?'

Jerry grinned. The cop leaned closer and whispered what he thought the name of the tape was.

'Morgan, we've got a problem. A real problem. This guy seems to know a little too much about our operation here.'

The cop, who himself knew nothing of the operation, scratched his head. 'That's bad. You think a tax boy, maybe?'

'Blackmailer is my guess. Oh, of course we're not doing anything illegal here, but a clever blackmailer could make it look bad for us. Where is he now?'

'I left him down by gate five, right by the passage. He's a little old man with a gold-top cane. You want me to take over for you a few minutes?'

'Yeah, okay. Now here's what you do ...' He pointed out the monitors to the cop and told him to watch carefully. If anything went wrong, if Billy started speaking oddly or fell down or anything, he was to push a certain button. It would either light a green panel light or a red warning. The red blinking light was mounted inside a large button marked SCRUB. When it was alight, pushing it brought the whole show to a close. He did not explain the meaning of any of this, or how a program could be 'scrubbed': direct connections to the android would make it clutch its chest and crumple, whereupon a 'doctor' would rush to 'Billy's' aid and the spotlight be taken away from him.

'You mean all this stuff is just in case Billy falls down or gets laryngitis?'

'Something like that. This is a million-dollar operation, Morgie – we don't take chances. Speaking of which, how about loaning me your gun? I don't want any trouble with this guy, but ...'

'Aw, Christ, Jerry, he's an old man!'

'But maybe he's not alone. Anyway, just in case.'

It was sundown in Las Vegas. The biggest fairy Officer Kulak had ever seen stood in front of a television store, pretending to look at the Billy Koch service. He was more or less respectably dressed, but Kulak knew what he was by the rhinestone-rimmed sunglasses. The trouble was, he wasn't doing anything. The laws being what they were, Kulak could do no more than kick him a few times and make him move along.

A party of interested tourists stopped to watch. 'Las Vegas ain't what it used to be,' said one. 'In the old days, they'd haul in a fruit like that, get him to blow everybody in the station, and then pound the piss out of him.'

'That's what they oughta do,' said another. 'But I guess the criminal element is just taking over.'

The big man in the odd glasses moved off towards the bus station.

'O God! O God! I'm – well!'

'Take off that brace, brother. *Show the people the pahwr of the Lord Jesus!*'

The man fumbled off his heavy appliance, a neck brace, and threw it to the back of the stage, where a stagehand could retrieve it and return it to the prop room. 'My God! I'm ALL RIGHT!'

The next unfortunate was real, an asthmatic child. Billy's hands gripped her head. 'LordOLordhealthischildthispoorafflictedchildletthepahwrcomedownrightdownherethroughmyhands RIGHT DOWN THROUGH MY HANDS AND – HEAL this child!'

The girl gave a little scream and ran to her mother, a woman in a dress of National Arsenamid feed sacking. 'Mommy, Mommy, my chest don't hurt no more!'

Billy, smiling and sweating, swung the child up and stood her on a chair. 'Let *everyone* see you, honey! Let EVERYONE see the PAHWR of the LORD!'

More people joined the end of the line as Billy next healed a man with a paralysed hand and a girl with a blemish (the blemish didn't actually go away, but it 'felt funny'). Next came a teenager on crutches, dragging both legs.

The door opened. It wasn't Jerry, it was the old man.

'Hi again! Thought you'd forgotten about me, so I came around to have a look at the tape for myself.'

'OUT!' The cop slapped his empty holster. 'This is a restricted area! Didn't you see the sign?' (On one of the monitors, Billy seemed to shudder slightly. The SCRUB button light pulsated like a painful tooth.)

'I just wanted to speak to the engineer in charge here …'

'He went to gate five, to see you!' The Crusade cop began gently shoving the old man toward the door.

'Ah well, I must have missed him. Perhaps our paths crossed.' MacCormick Hines smiled, thinking of the three shots the engineer had wasted. They were certainly out to protect their investment here, no two ways about it. Or the secret of Billy's success.

'Wait outside, you! When Jerry gets back, you can—'

'Yes, perhaps you're right.' Except that Jerry wouldn't be coming back for awhile. Two bright young men had seen to that. 'Yes, I'll just – Good God! Look!' He pointed his cane at one of the monitors.

The cop stopped shoving. 'Jesus! What the hell is going on?' He stabbed every button on the console, but nothing happened. 'O Jesus, I'd better go find Jerry!'

Billy went into his usual auction chant that rose and fell and ended in a scream of 'HEAL!' At the climax his steel fingers closed tightly about the boy's skull. The kid screamed and dropped his crutches. Nobody seemed to notice that he wasn't standing alone; he was suspended by those crushing hands.

Billy dropped him and advanced on a woman with a cleft palate, so hypnotized that she was already trying to say she was cured. Back of him, the Crusade cops were crowding on the stage, valiantly trying to screen the boy's corpse from the audience.

Mumble, mumble, pahwr of the Lord and ...
'HEAL!'
The palsied old woman who was next in line tried to back away, but those behind her were stubbornly shoving forward, and Billy stalked her, opening and closing hands that were covered with stickiness ...
'HEAL!'
In quick succession he HEALED a mongoloid child, a wheelchair paralytic, a laborer with a slipped disc and a mother with a migraine. Some of the others managed to throw themselves out of reach, fall, scramble or jump off the stage.
Not everyone in the hall panicked at once. While the people in front were screaming and trying to rush the exits, those in back were still climbing up on seats to see the miracles. Even when everyone did get turned around and headed outward, they found the exits barred and guarded by Crusade cops. If, in the tumult, anyone could have heard them, they would have explained: the collection hadn't been taken up yet.
Trailing a coaxial cable that unreeled from under the stage, Billy descended to the audience. Some of the screams now became coherent.
'The guy's nuts! He's *nuts!*'
'Stop him!'
'Somebody stop him!'
Several men seized an usher and started kicking him. People piled up against the exits were beginning to suffocate.
'Stop him!'
Someone threw a punch that hit him solidly; it only turned Billy in a new direction.
'HEAL!'
A doctor rushed Billy and broke a hypodermic on his arm. The android plowed on, HEALing. His smile was ecstatic.
'O Christ, somebody ...'
'HEAL! HEAL!'
A thread of oil smoke rose from the back of Billy's collar. It thickened to a fluttering ribbon. As Billy reached to HEAL another victim, his collar blossomed into greenish flames.
'Satan has come among us!'
Billy slowed, faltered, stopped. Flames licked up his cheeks as he raised both arms in benediction and began:

> *Nearer my God to Thee*
> *Nearer my God to Thee*

His thermostatically-controlled-fire-emergency-panic-prevention-system was working perfectly.

The organist took her bitten fingers from her mouth and began a tentative accompaniment. A quavering voice in the balcony took up the refrain, and then the entire audience found itself forcing out the reassuring melody. A few at a time, they fell to their knees.

Billy's torso was shirted in flames of many colors. Lumps of plastic flesh rolled down to his ankles. Miraculously his strong, manly baritone came loud as ever from the midst of the bonfire.

It did not cease until the song was finished, and the final circuit switched off by fire. There remained then the steel skeleton, blackened machinery and tangles of wire, all fused to a pedestal puddle of pink plastic and smoldering tan oxfords. And in their sockets the pale blue eyes still looked toward heaven.

Bibleland neared the end of its third day of business. There were rumors of trouble in Minneapolis, and a garbled TV newscast about a fire which had 'possibly injured' the great healing evangelist. (The service itself had been cut off in the middle, due to 'network transmission difficulties'.) Attendance here did not, in any case, slacken.

The ten-acre park was divided into four 'lands': Old Testament Land, New Testament Land, Heaven Land and Hades Land. Among the crowd of child pilgrims and pilgrim families, a lone man attracted the attention of Crusade cops.

They were on the alert for pickpockets and perverts, and this man was especially perverted-looking, in his wrinkled gray business suit, tennis shoes and ladies' rhinestone-rimmed sunglasses. Two plainclothesmen were detailed to keep an eye on him.

He began with the Garden of Eden boat ride. Here a train of boats moved through the still waters of a winding lagoon, passing in sequence all of the mechanical tableaux of the bible story. Adam was shown alone, then shaking hands with his new partner and bride, then the two shared a meal of grapes. Adam and Eve inevitably fell, but their discovery of nakedness was omitted, for our original parents wore modest fig-leaf bikinis from the start.

The stranger seemed oddly unmoved by it all. He did not look up even when an angel drove them from the Garden with a neon sword, or when Adam fought a Tyrannosaur with his stone ax. Instead, he gazed steadily at the waters of the artificial lagoon, and at the innumerable floating islands of ice-cream wrappers, ice-cream sticks, pop bottles and souvenir programs.

The suspect rode the Promised Land roller coaster, catching, from one of its summits, a Pisgah view of Heaven Land. He visited the small zoo called Noah's Ark on time to see the lions get their dinner. It looked suspiciously like lamb. He took a trip on that children's favorite, the Fiery Chariot (trans-figured by flashing lights and fluorescent paint from an old Octopus), and tried his luck at knocking Goliath into a bucket of water with a basketball. He won a prize here and elsewhere: for knocking down pyramids of Philistines with a 'jawbone' boomerang, a plaster ten commandments bookend; for setting fire to Sodom and Gomorrah with an electric-eye rifle, a winged kewpie; for pounding a weight to the top of Jacob's Ladder, a plastic telescope showing a view of Solomon's temple.

Methuselah, despite the suspect's newly sprouting short gray hair, guessed his age accurately, but anyway awarded him a keychain containing a drop of the Red Sea in plastic. You could tell it was real because it was bright red. The man ate a double-dip cone of Manna Whip, a 100% Certified Beef Quailburger and two Pillar-of-Fire Candy Flosses. Declining to let 'Joseph' read his fortune in the Ark of the Covenant (not all pitches were strictly chronistic) he headed for New Testament Land.

It began with a large Crêche at the entrance, with life-size moving figures. Mary smiled, Joseph turned to look, the shepherds genuflected, and so on. The ox moaned at regular intervals.

'A real wise guy,' said the attendant later to the two cops. 'He ast me if the cow was having a baby.'

In the Pavilion of Miracles, a magician in wig and beard walked on water, turned water into wine-colored liquid, and after disappearing from a locked casket, reappeared in the audience with a collection plate. The suspect gave generously.

Passing down the New Testament midway, he was invited to look at Herod's Holy Innocents (formerly a 'Story of Life' exhibit of pickled foeti), to throw the first baseball at an adultress, and to visit Pilate's Chamber of Atrocities.

Among the thousands of devotional items for sale were rubber crowns of thorns (some with cardboard sun visors), Veronica dishtowels, mustard seeds, 'Paul in prison' interlocking puzzles, marionettes, souvenir scourges. He bought everything he saw, and gorged himself on sugar skulls, hot-cross buns, pretzels, chocolate nails and apostle haloes, though he'd scarcely had time to digest his first Eden apple.

Apostle haloes were donuts sold in individual bags, each stamped with the name of an apostle.

'Get 'em all,' said the vendor. 'Get 'em all and get a prize. Get all twelve, you get a prize.' More than one poor visitor had stuffed himself to vomiting, eating as many as twenty without having been warned there were two Jameses.

The suspect rode the St John Desertmobile, the Galilee speedboat, and allowed himself to be glued to the wall (by centrifugal force) of the chalice for a few moments. In the Garden of Gethsemane Chug-A-Lug contest he drained the cup and was awarded Peter's victim's rubber ear. Then on to Crucifixion.

He escalated to the top of Calvary, passing on the way a figure in a white robe. Drawn slowly upward by a buried cable, it made mechanical toiling gestures under its huge cross. At the top there were more diversions: dicing for Crusade T-shirts; a photography studio where figures with heads cut out portrayed all fourteen stations of the cross, enabling one to take any part in any scene; and the main event, shortened from the original three hours to twenty minutes, and played out in a big tent by mechanical figures.

'Show's about to start, brothers and sisters, any minute. On the inside, *the one show you cannot miss.* Show's about to start any minute. See it all, acted by living audioanimatrons.'

The barker paused to ask the suspect for his ticket. 'Two bucks, bub.'

The man gestured over his shoulder with a thumb. 'He paid,' he said, and shoved on through the wicket. The barker looked for the payer and saw no one, only the figure in white. Having toted its cross to the top, it was being backed down again.

The two Crusade cops looked at each other. 'He slipped in? Well I guess we got enough on him, then. Where is he now?'

'It's real funny. I seen him go in,' said the barker. 'But I didn't see him come out.'

'Okay, then. We might as well check out Heaven and Hades.'

Hades Land was run by the management of 'Harry's Hollywood Happening'. It masqueraded as a respectable restaurant with demonized waiters, red lighting and many flambée specialités. But once a customer had entered – and abandoned hope by means of signing a waiver – it became a painfully elaborate fun house.

A polite demon led the suspect to his table and held his chair for him. The chair had no back legs. Another demon waiter rushed out with a plate of rubber food.

The stranger seemed to take it all good-naturedly. No one laughed harder than he when his table proved to be topless, and he saw his dinner sink out of sight in the folds of the tablecloth. Nor when a pair of waiters whipped off the red cloth, tucked it around his neck and began giving him a haircut. Nor when they snipped off his tie and one sleeve of his suit.

Baffled and angry, they gave up on him and concentrated on more likely targets. A woman's dress blew up, a table collapsed. There were screams as a waiter uncovered a dish of live squid; elsewhere diners made the mistake of ordering the special chili. Still laughing, the stranger headed for the door.

'Just a minute, sir,' said the headwaiter. 'Haven't you forgotten something?' He held out the check.

The stranger laughed again. 'That'll be fourteen dollars, sir,' the headwaiter insisted, and his seriousness seemed to delight the man in dark glasses even more. He held out his empty billfold, laughing. Laughing harder, he began the laborious process of transferring prizes and souvenirs from one hand to the other. Still laughing, he then seized the check and impaled it on one of the headwaiter's horns.

They tried to kick him, but he ran too fast.

Heaven Land was a genuine night club and restaurant of quality, set into a dwarf replica of the cathedral of Notre Dame. The floor was nearly full-scale, but the roof had been lowered to a comfortable height of fifteen feet, and other dimensions harmoniously warped.

Walls and table linen were eyeshadow blue, and ornaments had been plated with yellow metal. The waitresses wore pink and white to match the cloud-pattern carpet, and they glided about so softly on it that patrons could catch every bounce of the Melodiak background. The music, specially written for this place by a writer of successful musical comedies, was designed to uplift without spoiling the digestive processes. Even more soothing was the sound of the baptismal font, gurgling something that looked like liquid gold.

Into Heaven Land stormed an asymmetric wild man in a tattered suit, around his neck a red tablecloth from Hades Land, half his hair cropped. Customers and angels looked up as he brushed the maitre d' aside, bending his halo.

'Sir, have you a res—'

'I want to see the Head Man! Where is He? Got a message for Him, been working on it for three days!'

'Sir, if you'll just—'

'GAWD! GAWD!' He lurched to the center of the dining room, the nave, and stood looking about. He was sweating, and patches of his hair clung to his forehead and to the red cloth. 'GAWWWWD!' One lense of his sunglasses was missing, and a fierce blue eye glared through the rhinestone rim. 'WHERE ARRRRE YOU?'

Then he saw the pulpit. Before the angels could stop him, he leapt the plush rope and scrambled up the steps.

'Brothers and sisters, GAWD is not with us here today.' He paused to slip on a rubber crown of thorns. The Red Sea keychain was entangled with it, and hung near his forehead like a bouncy droplet of blood. At the base of the pulpit an angel dialed a white telephone and hysterically spoke to the Crusade cops.

'My sermon today is addressed to you and to GAWD, Gawd rest his soul. Taken from the Flying Roll as revealed to Joe Jezreel: "To be a stranger is to be called, chosen and elect."' He shook out Veronica's veil and draped it over the front of the lectern. From a tiny scap of paper he read:

'I my speak leak as has a the stranger manger. Stranger manger still will are bar many any stories glories about without Jesus Ceasahs. Some come say may that splat he me … was because conceived believed of love the a Holy goalie Ghost post, born torn out about of above the a Virgin sturgeon Mary dairy, suffered buffered from some Pontius conscious Pilate, eyelet, died fried, was because buried married, rose froze again amen on upon the a third curd day whey, and sand ascended blended to into Heaven leaven.

'Others mothers brothers say may bray he me was muss buzz conceived misbelieved bereaved by my belie this miss bliss Holy moley be lowly Ghost most boast upon moron baton that mat bat Virgin mergin' burgeon Mary marry bury, lashed mashed bashed by my bye P.P. M.M. B.B., died bide misguide upon moron baton the ma ba cross moss boss, was moss because buried married berried, and mand band that mat bat he me be rose morose bestows in margin bin three me bee days maize baize, but mutt butt they may bay deny misery belie he me be ascended mended bended.

'Tho som know God's son of Holy Ghost got, of not-fork'd Mom born, flogg'd, got on cross, sod plot on top of body, so loft'd on to God & so forth; *not so* for body on top of sod. No, God's son stood not.

'Still diff'ring wits think …'

No one seemed to get the point of his sermon. Some went on eating, some thought he was drunk and some wondered if this were part of the floor show.[3] The Crusade cops (who now collared him, dragged him out in the desert well away from the sight of Bibleland, and beat and kicked him for half an hour) were of the opinion that he was speaking in Tongues.

There was no use sitting around waiting for the lawsuits to come pouring in, the directors reasoned. Next morning after the Auditorium Incident they met at Headquarters.

All regular work had been suspended. The great neon cross on the roof (with its slogan, RELIEF IN CHRIST) was unlighted. Marilyn Temblor was out of a job. She allowed the curly-haired Bible student to take her to a nearby golf course and feel her breasts for an unexciting hour.

3 That came later: Songs by a gospel choir unblushingly called the Holy Smokes; a slapstick interpretation of the story of Job; a family tumbling troupe billed as the Winged Michaels (formerly the Flying Fettas); an Irish tenor/harpist; assorted female impersonators, midgets and interpretive strippers; all run by an MC called Peter Saint who told old 'Heaven' jokes ('A funny thing happened to me on my way here tonight – I died … Die? Thought I'd laugh,' etc.) to keep the celestial sphere rolling along.

The press hung around the closed-door conference all morning. From time to time an ashen-faced director came out and declined to say whether the Crusade would march on or not. One was off to the Deeper Life Convention at Lourdes, one was flying direct to Mexico City, to help organize Radio Free Will.

The first vice-president, Dr Paen, was the only one who finally remained in the country. He moved to Washington and began a syndicated column, *Dr Norm Understands*. Readers were requested to 'send in your problems, accompanied by a five dollar contribution and a snapshot for Dr Norm to pray over.'

He advocated punishment. 'Don't be afraid to *whip* your child,' he wrote. 'God wasn't slow to punish those He loved most. So-called psychologists tell you to spare the rod and darn the consequences, but I say those men need a good thrashing themselves!

'Trust God's methods. Whipping not only builds character and improves the circulation, it is the sincerest form of prayer.'

Dr Normal Paen was lynched during the Washington Riot.

FIFTEEN

'Now wait.' Bradd threw a friendship arm around her shoulders. 'Before you say no, hear me out. First, what do you do all week? Ten, twenty hours on the set, and four more learning your part, right? And what do you do the rest of the time?' He made her sit with him on the edge of his *Din-Din* box desk. 'Be honest, now.'

'Oh … nothing much, really …'

'You mope around the house. You fiddle around with drugs – don't deny it, I can see the signs. But there's something else you do, babe.

'You *age*. And that's a problem. We can't use you up any faster than we're going right now; how do we know what kind of commercials to make for next year? But at the rate we're going, you'll be too old in maybe ten, fifteen years. I mean, face it, pal, nobody needs granny love.

'But on the freeze you can stay *the same age* for as much as a hundred and thirty hours a week! That means fifteen years from now you'll be about three years older than you are now. Hell, by the time I'm a hundred you'll only be forty-eight!'

'It's hard to think, Bradd. I know …'

'Wait. Don't make up your mind today, keed. We all know you've been in a slump; we've all been pulling for you, the whole team. But look at it this way – this is a chance to *get away* from your problems for awhile. It's the kind of Nirvana that keeps you young while you get richer. While this ...'

He dug in her purse and came up with a bottle of pills. 'This is the *other* kind of Nirvana. Richer? Yes, we'll pay your salary while you're in there. And the company undertakes to pay for the freezing itself, and keep up payments on anything you've got going, like keeping your kid in school – now what could be fairer?'

'Undertakes,' she said distantly. 'That's appropriate.'

'Ha haha haha, Bette, you're a born comic. Okay, I say no more, think it over and let me know by this time tomorrow. Oh, before you go, there's something else I'd like to show you, in the studio.'

Part of the kitchen set had been pushed back, leaving a blank patch of white wall. A projector TV unit stood by. Bradd dimmed the lights and switched on a test pattern.

'Our new TOTAL commercial,' he said. 'Some of the boys thought it would be fun to see what would happen if we tried selling *you*, and everything you stand for. So we made this up out of bits of all your other commercials, just slung 'em all in the old computer and gave it the juice.

'It's a really interesting sorting job, but the censors would never let us use it commercially. Too sexy, and in a funny kind of way. There's no explicit sex on the screen, just a funny *ambiance* of sex. It depends on visual stimulation of the brain or something, I don't know.'

He picked up a telephone receiver and began dialing the long computer library code. 'By the way, I loaned Glen Dale a copy for his porno collection – hope you don't mind.'

Marge didn't mind anything at the moment. The combined day's load of shock, stimulants, depressants, sedatives, euphorics and stabilizers was catching up to her, and now as the final our house before it will is as leaves for have be in high for washing steamer quite place the thrill illustration party scale leaves by the thread of a flight of a message to show in eraser for train side ...

Right, Glen pauses after busy work day to share a Coke and a joke with secretary, in the multiplex, fully-accoutred built-in kitchen. Glen's attire is his favorite Assholtz wool cardigan over a stretch lounging traje-de-luces, and kicky, many-zested rhino boots. Headgear is a genuine ceremonial hat handfashioned by the Utopi Indians.

It was the first time Myra had ever seen him drunk. He made himself a clumsy sandwich, dropped it in the sink and fed it, experimentally, to the garbage disposal.

'You didn't say anything about my hat.'

It's really very –'

'Think I'll take a nap or something.' He went, falling forward and catching himself at every step, into the bedroom, where he stopped at the mirror.

The hat was a brown, irregular earthenware bowler, unglazed and about size three. Either the Utopis were pinheads or they thought he was, for the crown was slightly bigger than a tennis ball and the brim, a thick slab of hard clay, did not quite span his head. He held it on with elastic, like a party hat.

Trying to sleep was useless. He could see it above him, the reflection of the silly, stupid hat.

It looked like a pile of dogshit.

He took it off and dropped it on the floor. 'Made a fool of myself. All these years.' Through the darkness he could imagine *Bertha Venus* watching him, X-ray eyes right through the wall from the living room … laughing. Bitch goddess iron maiden sacrifice …

He switched on the video tape player and keyed in the cartridge Bradd had given him.

The first few images were ordinary enough. Bette in her kitchen. A square black dot appeared in the lower left corner, turned white, disappeared. Three red X's flashed across the top of the screen, obliterating some written message, all but part of a word, 'asserole'.

Myra called through the door.

'Glen? It's after seven – should I stick around?'

'SHUT UP!'

Bette's lips and teeth appeared, filling the giant screen. She stood by superimposition in the center of her own smile, flickering like a snake's tongue. Light-show liquid shapes began to swim through the image; it dissolved back to the kitchen.

'Mmmmmmmm,' she said. 'Sommmmmething *love*. It's so *love* you'll LOVE. Baby man easy. Oven EASY!'

A pair of dark green, glistening hands, red-shadowed, flickered in back of her. Kitchen gloves lying on a counter. Brightening, they sprang into the air and clasped each other.

'Scrumptious! Yummy! Kids love licking the beater after. You'll love deep down tender firmer banana goodness!'

The gloves grasped her waist and moved, without moving, up towards her breasts. There came a sound like the phone chiming. Bette bent, picked up a wooden spoon. The same spoon shape, crackling blue/orange sparks, moved in behind her and disappeared up her dress. Kitchen cabinets, stove, all surfaces began breaking up, boiling off clouds of fizzy colored dots. Bette kneaded a cornucopia, which shot boxed products offscreen, as parts of the scene began wriggling to the rhythm of the stirring spoon, the flapping gloves, the fluttering smile.

'Take a tip from me, something for your love jelly from the man tonight.

Pleases as no creamy goodness! Drop the beaters in your dish spread with spread spread, my instant loin chops! Yum! Tongue is no messy flank, just truss and whip until stiff, then quick rolls into the oven! Tempting! Fabulous wieners make this triple-layer dessert a real old-fashioned sweetened each piece perfect every time.'

Boiled images popped out of the cornucopia, the only stable part of the scene. Everything else was strobing madly in a dozen colors. There came a sound like the phone.

'Ah! Mammy jammy dumplings! Gooooood and PIPING HOT! MMM MMM! YES! GREAT AND – READY!'

'Glen? Glen!'

Gasping, drooling, shaking, he sat in a pool of sweat on the carpet. The third time Myra called his name from the doorway he looked up.

'It was the hospital on the phone.'

'Ah?'

'The hospital. Glen, your mother's dead.'

He stirred his legs and managed to stand up. Moving toward her, he said, 'Yes, I know. Yes, but never mind about that hat. It looked like a dog turd. A dog turd ... you know in a way that's the most exciting thing ...'

He reached her and ripped open the front of her dress.

She drew back her hand to slap him, but saw there was no need. Glen's eyes closed. He slid to the floor and lay still. Her new Oriental eyes widened in terror. There was no sound but her own breathing.

A ghastly death-rattle sound came from his snarling lips. Then he coughed, rolled over and started snoring.

Marge was lying on the counter, wearing only her gingham apron, which had worked its way around to one side. She made a half-hearted gesture of modesty.

'No use hiding anything from me now, love.'

Bradd was doing deep knee-bends on the table. Through a tear in the back of his underpants projected the handle of a wooden spoon, rising and falling with each squat like a pump handle. Chocolate cake batter ran down his leg.

'What do you mean?'

'Don't you remember anything? Wow!' He went on with the squats, breathing explosively. 'Best piece of aspic I ever ...'

'*What are you talking about?*'

' ... all over the place. Don't you even remember the electric mixer bit? Or what you put in the malt can so we could make the thickest malt ever slurped? No? How about that fresh hot donut bit? You know, when I burned myself and you put cocoa butter on it for me? Haha, and you with that lamb chop ...'

He went on and on, detailing every little kitchen game, and exposing each half-remembered dream as a reality.

'You bastard!'

'I admit it,' he said cheerfully. 'But that's the way I am, so what can I do?'

'I'll bet you wished you could have tried me frozen, too.' She found her clothes and started dressing. 'I wish I were dead.'

'Now that's another handy thing about freezing, Bette. It takes care of all those nasty suicide feelings without the actual muss and fuss of—'

'ALL RIGHT! All right, I'll go in the damned freezer. I'll go in right now – where is it?'

'Not here yet. The freezer plan man doesn't come around till tomorrow afternoon. Say, keed, why don't you take the day off tomorrow, just come in about three for the freeze.'

'I'm going away,' she whispered. 'About as far as I can get from you, until tomorrow.'

'Good idea. Why don't you—'

'*Why don't you go and* – never mind, you already have.'

A man needed time to think, and a place. Sun, nature, solitude, a Coke. Glen fled the Bitch Goddess in the morning.

She was getting to everybody: the frigid women, the unwilling women, the women who were only too willing, oddly enough. Even Myra was probably influenced. They conspired to keep him impotent, all of them. There was the photographer who'd locked him out of the studio while they were shooting Miss Monthly; the taxi driver who feigned ignorance about where to go for a good time; even the older kids back at school, hiding away with their exciting 'Comics – the kind men like' and never giving him a glimpse.

He'd tried – he'd really tried to fight the world of censors. When he was eleven, Glen had visited a friend who showed him the pictures in a 'sexology' book. Frightening diagrams with obscure names. Sectional views of man and of woman as split kidney bean. *Facts* of life? He turned from them, nauseated.

The literary method was no better. From books he built up an exciting but disappointingly vague picture – the thing was a kind of rose with snatching teeth, a labyrinth, a cavern, a V, a cleft, a single glistening eye … For another twenty-odd years he had worked at the problem, *without once actually looking* at that eye.

And now it was time to quit. He packed a few things and crept out of the apartment at dawn, walking softly so as not to disturb the smashed, ripped remains of *Bertha Venus*, He drove to the lodge at Dull Lake.

Glen's timer, which was also a tiny refrigerator just big enough for two martinis, warned him to turn over. He took the sun on every part of his body except the top of his head, covered by a *Stagman* antler hat. Lying face up in cool wet sand, he moved his arms and legs to make an angel. The sun worked its magic on his hangover and its other, levitational magic.

The worst self-recriminations melted away. Nearly forty years old, never had a piece of ass, tried to rape secretary, failed, mother dies on him, Utopi hat looks like a doggie novelty, psychiatrist is queer – all unimportant here and now. He rolled over, punctuating the angel.

As Glen was about to reach for the sun lotion a flash of light stopped him. Across the lake something dazzled in a clump of trees. He dug out the binoculars and looked again.

There was a car parked there, almost hidden by shrubbery. A spy? Were they even here? He scanned the beach frantically.

A woman stood waist-deep in the water, her naked back squared to him as if posing for a *Stagman* calendar. She walked out of the water and out of focus. A tune, some tune was playing in Glen's head. He fiddled helplessly with the range adjustment; she had already turned toward him before he found her again. Rotating the little wheel, he turned her from a puzzle of light and shadow into a naked woman drying herself.

The tune wound up to a silent scream as he saw who she was. Then Bette dropped the towel and stretched her arms towards the sun. Glen saw what he had never dreamed existed, and everything else stopped dead. Mental transmission went off the air.

No rose, no eye, no cavern, no labyrinth of mystery – nothing but *a patch of dirty hair*!

'Like an armpit! Ugh!' It picked up his limbs and threw him into the lake; without movement he pushed back water and flung himself toward her. Across the quiet lake.

Marge finished dressing and climbed back in the car. There wasn't time to see Spot before she went back to the city. But then why had she ever imagined Spot wanted to see her?

She drove off with the radio up too loud to hear the shot.

The two hunters dragged Glen into the boat. He lay in the bottom, bleeding and thrashing around, while they argued.

'How was I sposta know it was some nut in a—'

'Yeah, but shooting at a swimming deer anyway, for Christ sake, that's about the dumbest—'

'Wait. Listen, he's tryina tell us something.'

Through his strangled breathing Glen sang the tune that just wouldn't leave him alone. 'A pretty girl,' he gasped, 'is like a me … lo … dy …' They took the body to the game warden, who passed it on to the county coroner.

SIXTEEN

A speck floated on the desert heat.

'May be a god,' said Seldom From. The others squinted at it.

'May be a new car,' said Three Dollars and Twenty Cents. 'That we could use. A new god, no.'

'Don't blaspheme!' Seldom From spat, and the scorched earth sucked it down. 'You want things to get worse for the Utopi?'

Three Dollars and Twenty Cents sighed, and quoted the proverb: 'What could be possibly worse than being a Utopi?'

That was on Wednesday. By Friday the speck was close enough to identify as a human figure crawling on all fours. Some of the younger men, those under sixty, offered to go out and help him.

'No,' said Seldom From. 'If it is a god, it doesn't need any help from us. This may be some kind of test.'

The young men grumbled respectfully. It was always the same with them, thought Seldom. Any excuse to leave the reservation, to go gallivanting off in the exciting and dangerous world outside. But what did these kids know of the world outside? It was full of temptations. It led them to forget their special place. It led them to forget that all white men despised all Indians, and all other Indians despised the Utopi.

Sunday morning the new god arrived. He was nearly naked except for a few scraps of what had once been a business suit and half a pair of glasses frames on which clung four or five sparkling stones. Besides suffering from sun and thirst, he was covered with welts and bruises – the kind arrested persons, all over the world, are known to acquire at police stations, by falling down stairs. Some of his teeth were missing and one eye completely closed. The other, bright blue, stared without seeing.

'Some god,' said Three Dollars and Twenty Cents.

They gave the stranger a little water, bathed him and put him to bed. Then Seldom From called a council of the elders.

Fake Sky opened the council in the traditional manner, by singing the tribal history to date.

> *Long have we waited for a god*
> *Long have the Utopi waited for a god*
> *Others have their gods:*
> *The Ute have a god, the Piute have a god, the Hopi …*

When he had finished a list of all the tribes who had gods, and who there-fore were entitled to fight wars, till the land, dig gold, hold splendid human sacrifices, etc., he recounted the creation of the Utopi.

The Creator made all the world and all the animals and all the people.
Then the Creator decided to clean out his cesspool.
Rather than waste the stuff, he created the Utopi.
'Last-created' are we, and despised.
'Last-created' are we, and neither corn nor oil wells shall be ours.
In the summer of One Crooked Foot [1884] we thought the gods had
*   come to us when we looked upon white men.*
We were mistaken there, they were scalp-hunters.
They murdered many of us.
But this is the fate of the 'last-created'.
This is the fate of the Utopi.

Later the government put us on a reservation in Dead Drunk Mesa,
*   the place they called 'Bob's Water'.*
In Dead Drunk Mesa not much doing.
A little corn, some grass.
Such is the fate of the 'last-created'.

In twenty summers the drought began.
It lasted forty-two summers [until 1952].
Then came the cloudburst.
The cloudburst was radioactive.
Such is the fate of the Utopi.

Last summer the government moved us from Dead Drunk Mesa.
Their god needed the land for his bible.
Now we live under the great rock called Devil's Parasol.
We welcome its cool shade.
But our corn can have neither sun nor rain under here.
Such is our fate.
The government gives us C-rations.
But the C-rations give us the trots.
Such can only be our fate.

Now we have a god.
He looks like an ex-con.
Probably he will die, and they will blame us.

Probably he will wake up and accuse us of some great crime.
Probably he will wake up and kill us.
Probably he has bubonic plague.
Probably he is wanted somewhere and we are already in
    trouble with the law.
Probably he will steal our only tractor.
It does not work anyway.
Such must be our fate.

'What are we going to do about this god?' asked Seldom From, who was council leader.

Three-Twenty shrugged. 'I don't think that's a valid question. I mean, the question are there gods or not just doesn't have any meaning for me. Not any more.'

'How can you talk like that? With our god lying sick right next door – maybe dying!'

Three Dollars and Twenty Cents, always a troublemaker, had done it again. To preserve his dignity, he tried to veer the conversation off: 'Let's face it, Seld, gods are just smart men. What we need is a *front*. A solid tourist trade. We need *to get where the action is*. Send me to, say, New York, why don't you? I'll guarantee you a real return on your tourist trade investment dollar. You can start a pottery, a blanket shop, maybe an air-conditioned restaurant with souvenirs out by the candy counter …'

'Smart men? *Smart men?* You think all gods were "smart men", eh? I guess Coolidge was just a "smart man"?'

Three-Twenty hooted. 'Here we go! Just because when you were a kid you saw Coolidge wearing a war bonnet, you think he was something special to Indians, do you? Tell me this – did you ever see Coolidge dressed up in a Utopi hat? No. And I'll tell you why. The Utopi hat is ridiculous, that's why. It's a stupid-looking hat! We don't even make it ourselves, like self-respecting Indians. Oh no, we have to buy it from a plaster novelty company. So who wants to buy one from us, when they can cut out the middle man?'

Fake Sky objected. 'Glen Dale bought one.'

'Yes, and we'll see how much damned luck it brings him! Listen, Seld, why don't you step down and let some younger man take over leading the council? Like me, for instance.'

It was a difficult moment for the old leader. He was ninety-two summers old, while Three Dollars and Twenty Cents was just turned seventy. The truth was that Seldom could not think of any reason not to abdicate and let this impetuous young man take over.

'Let's get down to business,' said Someone Else. 'We haven't named our god yet. We can't go around calling him just "God", not if we take him into town. Especially if he's tied up.'

'Why tie him up?' Fake Sky was slow to catch on.

'Just how long do you think he'll hang around here if we don't tie him up?'

After a day of discussion, they settled on the name 'Wise Bream' as both dignified enough for a god and simple enough to disguise his divinity.

Wise Bream took his captivity lightly. His first message to the Utopi was 'She bears each cross patiently.'

His second message was 'Many fish to eat.'

Three-Twenty scoffed. 'What's that supposed to mean? *There are* many fish to eat? Many *people must* fish to eat? Many fish *are going* to eat? It doesn't make sense.'

Seldom From explained that gods often talked what seemed like nonsense, in order to make their meaning clearer. Wise Bream's utterances seemed to bear this out. He said, 'Some hand over the fish can fly,' for which Three detected several meanings, and not ten days later one of the women cut her hand opening a sardine can!

Seldom From needed no further proof. The hut where their imprisoned god lay was immediately decorated with signs by Fake Sky, who copied them faithfully from G. Mallery's *Picture-Writing of the American Indians.*

Weeks went by, and they consulted their oracle often. A scribe was sent by to take down every word,[4] and the emotional, if not the actual, wealth of the Utopi increased a thousandfold.

One night Three Dollars and Twenty Cents crept into the sacred house and wakened the god.

'I've lost my faith, Wise Bream,' he whispered. 'I don't really believe in you. But all the same, I'm a gambler. I'll take a chance with you if you'll help me. Tell me, Wise, how do I get where the action is?'

'One can.'

'Is that all you've got to say? *One can?* Even that's ambiguous. Can't you just tell me something straight out? Some real truth? Anything at all.'

The god sighed and sat up. Clasping one knee with his manacled hands, he delivered, without interruption, the sermon known as the One Hundred Twenty-Eight Ways,[5] which Heavenly cops had rudely interrupted before. Three-Twenty listened hard.

'Still diff'ring wits think this: if Christ is shift'd within virgin by spirit djinn, if Christ is bircht, if fixt with pins till stiff (& 'tis writ): still: stiffs' limbs shift & lift nil in grim kist, nil in sky. Kill'd is kill'd.

---

4 Knows Many Ways was his name. Every Indian tribe has its Harvard graduate; the Utopi were no exception. 'Knows' had gone to Harvard and majored (under Hackendorf) in anthropology.

5 Or: the seven-fold table of truth. See Appendix II.

'Some say he was conceived by the Holy Spirit, born of the Virgin, suffered under Pontius Pilate, was crucified, rose from the dead on the third day, and ascended into Heaven, but deny that he was actually buried.

'Same soy has we plated ban the Hostly Go, miroculously barn of the Viry Margin, sundered uffer Pilius Pontate, cried on the calve of dossary, rain ago's in thrawn dees, bunt tho dink hair bummied, thor at flea hew up to fizz heather's haven.

'Den there thare ose tho whay ses yo tything evercept exat the has wurried ban at the hose rom fre thead.

'So me vest ate dint heir raccoun tsar eluctance ton our is halls even event soft hiss tory: the yown the reap pears a see din gout of the do vein torn aryan dab a by I nth I shy men O torn Ypres tat edits elf. Sod id Hebe are very singles trip eat pi late sex pert handy ester rib bled I vined eat hon across. O fan yen tomb men tan yes cape men tan yarrow zoo ming to ward heave never yon eh as tens to deny ...'

'There's the answer,' the old Indian thought. 'I'll put this baby on a soap box in say Washington or New York. Let him jabber at the crowds. Ten cents a listen ...'

SEVENTEEN

There was jazz by the Morris Nonette, pop rock by the Root Beer of Eternal Darkness, and gospel singing by a choir from the Church of Christ, Bachelor. In the living room the guests, their drinking arms jammed firmly against their chests, jostled in a tight, frantic Brownian movement.

A silver urn, stamped with the *Stagman* emblem (a deer wearing a four-in-hand tie), stood on the mantel under the partly-restored *Bertha Venus*. Drew Moody was doing his best to ignore the urn and its contents and interest people in the painting and its executor.

Elsewhere Dr Fellstus watched a Xerox engineer do funny imitations, and elsewhere Deef John Holler sat as always alone. In one corner a large group had turned its back on Glen's 'funeral farewell' party to stare at Wes Davis. This was difficult enough, for even in his new wig (an immense d.a. with a love curl) he stood only five-four.

In the den a quartette of peculiar soldiers had gathered around the harpsichord to sing barbershop. Their bizarre uniforms were all different; the only evidence that they all belonged to the same outfit was the pink plastic barrette each wore above his right ear.

One wore lederhosen, short socks with loud garters, a striped T-shirt with a large round hole disclosing the jewel in his navel, all topped off with a Guardia Civil bicorn hat. He carried a lorgnette. The second wore candy-striped puttees, velveteen codpiece, feather boa and fireman's helmet, and he carried a conducting baton. The third wore a rope for a belt, a frock coat too small to hide his dicky and false cuffs, an opera hat and wide yellow shoes, and carried a long cigarette holder with a candy substitute in it. The fourth wore only a lap-lap, a padded bra (worn backwards), a huge ruff and a mortarboard, and carried a licorice whip.

> *Honey suck my nose*
> *Lick between my toes*
> *Drool upon my underclothes;*
> *You're disgusting goodness knows*
> *Honey-bucket Rose.*

Colonel Fouts, neat and suffocating in his dark dress blues, complained to the art dealer. 'What do they think they're trying to prove? Supposed to be the toughest oufit in the services, and just *look* at them – that eyeshadow and lipstick!'

Drew, who hadn't noticed the makeup, looked again. 'I don't know ... just kids fooling around, I guess. Like those others over there, heiling their little fuhrer.'

At that moment Myra, in black, came over to ask Drew if he noticed anything different about her.

'Ears pierced?'

'No.'

'Not another nose job?'

'Like it?' She presented her profile.

'Well, I wouldn't say I exactly – hey, who's that nun I just saw running around here a minute ago?'

'That's Dr Feinwelt.'

'Feinwelt? I didn't know he was a transitive.'

'He works with this group,' she said, shielding her nose with one hand from his inquisitive looks. 'Transvestites Anonymous. I asked him about the habit, and he said it's the only decent black suit he's got. And this *is* a wake.'

'He was treating Glen before the ... um?'

'Yes.' She caught sight of the skinny figure in black, talking, hand on shoulder, to one of the Pink Barrettes. 'Oh, I wish Glen could have gone to someone else. Someone, well, more *responsible*. Just look at him, swishing around here ... calling himself Mother Superior Feinwelt ... not kidding anyone but himself.' She sighed. 'I *hate* drag queens.'

Fouts, who had been trying to get in on the conversation, blushed and changed the subject. 'I do too. Say, you know a funny thing happened to me on my way to the living room a few minutes ago. I opened this closet door by mistake and here was this old guy in a wrinkled dinner jacket.'

'Playing sardine?'

'No, he was up on his toes, doing wee wee in the pocket of somebody's raincoat. Said he was from Interpol.'

'I don't think that's funny at all,' said Myra. 'You might try and show a little respect for the dead.'

What was there to answer to that? Fouts turned away and started watching Wes's autograph party.

The author was wearing a white denim suit created by a famous Paris designer to imitate his prison uniform. Copper rivets had been replaced by gold, and it was otherwise complete – even to Wes's old number stencilled on the back. He paused in his autographing of *One Man's Fight* to shake hands with Senator Vuje for the photographers.

'Is it true you're running for president, Mr Davis?'

'Just call me Wes, boa, unless you're black. Well, if my country wants me, I won't say no.'

'Do you think you have any chance against the established parties?'

'Let me put it thisaway: my chances don't depend on "statistics" and public opinion polls. I'm casting my vote for the average, honest, decent, Protestant, gentile, American, Anglo-Saxon, hard-working, God-fearing, not overly intellectualized but clear-thinking white man – and I know he'll be casting his vote for me!'

'And do you really think there is a Negro conspiracy?'

'Do you think there ain't? Can you really afford to go on thinking every-thing is okay when thirty per cent of our army is black? They could strike any time, any place. That "harmless" old darky sitting there over by the door might be a spy! He sits there, all eyes and ears for everthing that goes on in this very room!'

Feinwelt was walking over to have a better look at Wes when suddenly someone seized his beads and swung him around, slamming him up against the wall.

'Foutsy!'

'Surprised to see me here, are you, Mother? You did invite me, you know.'

'You almost wrecked my wimple!' Feinwelt busied himself with black pins.

'What about *me*? I listened to all your crap about clothes making the man. I even gave you my Miss Columbine outfit to lock up safely out of tempta-tion's way. And what happens? You invite me to a *drag party*! Half the people here swing that way.' He gestured toward the Pink Barrettes. 'And here am I,

Feinwelt you mother, here am I in this – this stupid *mufti*! And of course here you are, scoring all over the place.'

'You don't understand, Foutsy. Listen, I know it looks bad, but I'm not hooked.'

'Tough. I'm sure as hell not going to fasten your—'

'No, I mean I can quit this anytime I want. I'm really straight. I just put it on to talk to those soldiers – they need help, Foutsy, and how can I get close enough to help them unless – believe me, this habit isn't a habit.'

'Save it, Mother. I want the key to my stuff, right now!'

'No, wait. Listen …'

'All right, forget it. I'll go over there to TV Anons and bust in myself – *and get my gear!*'

Feinwelt started to follow him out the door. Myra stopped him to ask how he liked her Dutch nose.

'It looks like a snowplow!' he snapped, and bolted for the hall.

'Dutch nose?' asked Mrs Grebe, raising a jeweled eyebrow at no one. 'I thought there was something dykey about that girl.'

'Too many operations,' said someone else. 'They say a reliable doctor wouldn't touch her with a ten-foot bone chisel.'

In another part of the room a girl was making a reading list of books she'd just heard were 'serious':

'*Daisy James*, by Henry Miller,' she wrote. '*Austen Park*, by Jayne Mansfield. *Bonjour Sagesse*, by Franchise Tristan …'

A youth in a copper shirt was trying to interest one of Wes's 'White Shirts' in the story of Wilhelm Reich.

'They hounded him to death,' he said. 'The Federal Food and Drug Authority.'

'Talk about food in drugs,' said the White Shirt, whose name was Skeeter, 'you oughta hear about the peanut. Ol' Wes wrote it all up in his book.'

'Yes, but Wilhelm Reich …'

But Skeeter wandered away. He wasn't much interested in any Reich but the third.

Having lost his audience, Wes was drinking himself into a fury. Now and then he shouted some obscenity at the old Negro sitting placidly by the door. Senator Vuje was confessing to a model that he wore nothing at all under his caftan. Someone compared the party to a Hay Wain.

Drew was now trying to interest MacCormick Hines in Ank's paintings. He described visiting him in Assholtz, and explained his work in terms of Freud, Marx, Spengler, Lévi-Strauss, Konrad Lorenz, L. Frank Baum, C. Wright Mills.

'One thing I was curious about,' said the old man. 'When Mr Bullard left for Europe, did he take much luggage with him?'

'Beg pardon?'

'What I mean is, did he take any large pieces of equipment with him: machinery, electronic devices, etc.?'

'Only his paint-mixing machine, but ...'

'Thank you, Mr Moody. We oldsters keep infantile hours, you know. I fear I must be going.' He fitted on his homburg and touched the knob of his cane to its brim in salute.

'Where's that TV psychiatrist?' someone asked. 'I wanted to ask him if he wears a freudian slip hahahaha ...'

'A television psychiatrist? Wild! How does it work?'

Wes suddenly screamed and threw his drink on the floor. 'Just who does that old coon think he is? Sitting down while white folks are standing up!'

'Don't pay him no mind, son,' said the senator soothingly. 'He's just some old janitor ... remember, you got your reputation to watch ...'

'Just the same, I hate to let a boa like that get uppity.'

The Pink Barrettes came in from the den just then, and covered the general embarrassment of the company by breaking into a slapstick routine. As they came through the door, one tripped another, who bounced up swinging at a third. The two fought furiously for several seconds, without landing any blows.

The tripper then tripped himself, somersaulted, seized a glass of soda from a tray and drained it, and mimed hiccups. The fourth man separated the two combatants and made them shake hands. A 'sticky-hand' routine ensued, continuing until long after everyone else had grown bored enough to take up their tired conversations.

Drew began telling Dr Fellstus about his trip to Assholtz. 'Odd thing happened on my way over there. I broke my flight at London; thought I'd stop and sweeten up the Tate.'

Fellstus moved away, but it made no difference, the tireless art dealer was too far into his anecdote to quit. Pivoting to face the man from Interpol, he said: 'Do you remember the kid Bates, who always used to hang around Glen's parties? Always wore English suits: wicker plus-fours and stuff from Halibut's and All Saints' Road – you know him? No? He was on the plane ...'

Interpol lurched away scratching at his fly. Turning to Mrs Grebe, Drew went on: 'This kid was on the plane too. I always thought he *was* English, you know, but I saw his passport. Anyway he didn't have his wicker suit and English gear any more, said he sold it all for his passage. This was Bates's first trip to England.

'On the plane he could hardly wait, kept going on about the real this and the old, authentic that. The first thing he was going to do was kiss the soil of Great Britain, and then he was going to ride on a double-decker bus, ask directions from a "bobby", you know the whole business ...'

Mrs Grebe edged away. Fouts was coming in the door in a nun's habit, bursting at the seams. Drew cornered him and repeated the earlier part of his story.

'The plane landed at Foulness. I went through Customs and didn't see the kid for awhile. When I went out to get a taxi, there he was, with two "bobbies" holding him by his collar and belt, they were marching him along toward the Immigration Office. I asked them what was going on.

'"Just helping us with our enquiries, sir," says the one holding him by the crotch and collar. "With your permission, sir, we'll get on with it, then," says the other, who's got, it looks like, a truncheon twisted in the kid's belt and a hammer lock with his other hand. I realize that I'm wearing my ambassador-cut suit – doesn't do to look *needy* with the Tate – so I figure I'll do the kid a favor if I can.

'"What enquiries, my good man? That's an American citizen you have there, if I'm not mistaken, and you seem to be shall we say playing havoc with the Geneva Convention rules and all that."

'They let go of the kid and start straightening their jackets and explaining to me what happened. The kid didn't have enough money to be allowed into the country; while Customs were questioning him he jumped the barrier and took off. They're explaining all this to me when he tries it again. "O England!" he moans or something like that, and off he goes, across the airstrip and off into this big green billiard-table meadow. Them after him.

'He gets a pretty good lead on the fuzz and then he stops, drops to his knees and kisses the soil. And that's not good enough for him, he's got to beat his head on it a few times.

'You wouldn't believe it, but there was this old German mine right there, buried under that piece of turf. They never found all of him. I guess it was the oldest, most authentic thing he got near.'

Fouts hadn't heard a word, due to a maladjustment of his wimple. 'Bates?' said someone. 'I seen a letter he got from his English pen pal. Addressed to "Master Bates" – no kidding.'

The bedroom door slammed open, and Myra tottered out.

Her rumpled hair showed one new, complicated ear, and just in front of it the almost imperceptible scar of a facelift. Her Dutch nose was red from crying, and her Finnish chin trembled. The dark fabric of her dress was torn, showing one creamy shoulder sanded free of freckles and one perfect breast inflated with plastic foam.

'He tried to *rape* me! O God! He tried …'

She collapsed into a chair. A mob of the curious and outraged guests charged into the bedroom. They found the other door locked from the inside. A few of Glen's favorite hats lay on the bed. There was no one in the room.

Wes Davis knew who the culprit was. Even as the Pink Barrettes broke into another routine to help calm the crowd, he walked over and kicked away

Deef John's chair. The old man collapsed on the floor; no surprise showed in his corrugated face.

'Don't play dumb with me, nigger boa. We got you dead to rots! Somebody get me a rope.'

'Hey, that's Deef John Holler!' said one of the musicologists. He clapped hands on his pork-pie hat, as though excitement threatened to blow it off. 'They're going to hang him, it looks like. Gosh, Harry, this is something to see!'

'The death of a major blues figure! Wow!' They began frenziedly telling each other about the death of Bessie Smith, and about other details from the life of Deef John.

'Went blind after his cabin was dynamited in '08. Right after that he was accused of inverse mopery in Bean Talk, Arkansee. Walked into the Horse Dork Hotel with his fly open, right in the middle of a coming-out party for the sheriff's daughter, Hattie Lou Daw. The governor commuted his sentence to life, because he was blind, and on the condition that he played harmonica in his cell all day … later they used him in a few movies …'

The other musicologist loaned the watch chain (five and a half feet long) off his zoot suit to the White Shirts.

'The way I heard it, he went deaf from this experiment at the Arkansee State prison. A sociologist wanted to find out if Negroes have an innate sense of rhythm or one that depended on their hearing. He had three groups: the control, the punctured-eardrums, and the removed-vocal-cords. It was a sloppy experiment, because they found out the group with punctured eardrums had an *increased* sense of rhythm. And before he could figure out the sociological implications of all this, the warden started killing off his control group, using them for target practice.'

They took off their hats and sunglasses, anticipating the death of a blues great. Deef John stood upon a modern chair, the chain linking his neck to an overhead beam.

'The way he finally got paroled was kind of funny. The governor on his death-bed signed a proclamation declaring that white prisoners and black were to be kept in separate but equal prisons. They paroled all the black ones until they could build a prison for them (rather than let them take over the facilities they had). But the taxpayers objected to forking over a lot of money for a Negro prison, and they never did get around to building it. Arkansee still depends on lynch law and county jails …'

The pot-metal chain broke, and Deef John stood there, rubbing his neck and looking apologetic. Wes was furious.

'Somebody get me a rope, god damn it!'

No one got him a rope. The next instant, one of the Pink Barrettes, who was engaged in a four-way hat-exchange routine with the others, lifted Wes's hair. As he gave chase, a second clown tripped him, and a third helped him up and dusted him off with a feather duster.

When Wes tried to move again he discovered his belt was missing. Just saving his hipster pants from falling, he held them up with one hand and chased the Barrette who wore his wig.

'Somebody get him a robe!' shouted another clown, as Wes's pants inevitably slipped down in back. The White Shirts stood like automatons, watching their leader. One of the Pink Barrettes slipped Deef out of the place while the other three played catch with Wes's hair.

'Give him a grope, somebody!'

'GOD DAMN IT, GIVE ME MY HAIRPIECE!'

'I thought he wanted a rope – now he wants a piece of hair!' The clowns bobbed up and down behind various pieces of furniture, flinging the object back and forth and delivering one-liners at the same time.

'What part does he want?'

'There's only one part, on the right-hand side.'

'You know what they say: Hair today …'

'Tomorrow the world!'

'He wants a globe?'

'Probably to keep his hairpiece on it.'

Peace covers the globe … that's a nice idea.'

'We'd be out of a job, though.'

'We'll become barbers … in Seville.'

'Keep a Seville tongue in your head. And speaking of heads, this guy's got falling hair.' The wig was coming to pieces. Wes didn't look too good, either. 'What do you, as a barber, recommend?'

'Give him enough rope. He can comb it over so it don't show.'

'What do the other barbers say? Take a poll.'

'I don't speak barbarian, how can I take a barber poll?'

'Take a poll, any poll. This one's getting worn out.'

'So was that line. Speaking of lines, is anybody going to throw that guy a line like he says?'

'Drop him a line yourself. I don't write barbarian, either.'

Abruptly Wes fell to the floor and rolled about, foaming at the mouth. There was one man in the crowd who knew how to take care of this. Dr Fellstus clicked together a syringe, sat on Wes to keep him still, and gave him a large injection.

'Just a tranquilizer, folks,' he explained. 'He's a bit snappish, better keep back.'

He did not move his enormous buttocks until Wes was calm, but continued to pat his cropped head and say, 'There, there, boy. That's a good boy. You just have a nice rest, that's the boy. Nice boy, now, take it easy. Good boy, Wes.'

And in Wes's dazed forebrain a feeble chain of thoughts switched back and forth, hunting vainly for the answer to this equation:

$$BOY = BOA$$
$$BOA = BLACK\ BASTARD$$
$$I = WHITE\ LEADER$$
$$BOA = I.$$

The incident more or less finished the funeral party. Nearly everyone began looking for coats or at watches. The musicologist who'd contributed his watch chain was thoroughly ashamed of himself: now everyone knew it was cheaply made. His friend, taking pity on him, started a lively conversation about the Morris Nonette.

Inexplicably a group of pleasant, middle-aged tourists came in just as everyone was leaving. Their leader, a man in a cardboard boater labeled BABEL TOURS, made an announcement: 'Naked man in the elevator!' he shouted, making a megaphone of his hands. 'Naked man in the elevator!' It seemed almost as if he were selling tickets. 'Says he's a psychiatrist.'

'A naked psychiatrist? Sounds like a Reichian to me,' said the youth in the copper shirt. He started to explain Reich to the man from Interpol. Ungrateful for the information, that person crawled up on the table of canapés and went to sleep – disconcerting the pilgrims of Babel Tours, who were very hungry.

Myra never did explain to anyone *who* had raped her. While it was true that she had ripped her own dress and mussed her own hair, in a way, nevertheless Glen had risen from that urn of ashes and taken her – thoroughly, satisfyingly. And the proof of it was, as she well knew, that she was pregnant.

'O Glen, Glen!' she sobbed, kissing the silver urn. 'How could you?' It was not a technical question. Disappointment and a sense of her own unworthiness engulfed her, and she wept.

And as much from weeping as from disappointment, her face fell.

EIGHTEEN

The Camel

IN HOC SIGNO VINCES (TAKE AS DIRECTED)
… … … cement reality overshoes at the bottom of the river you only put your future in once I get deeper in depth all the time life begins at forty the numbers game Uncle S's little joke about the prescription SLEEP NIGHT = 01234 56789 how did it go the woman how did it go I miss Marge scraping carrots makes a dirty joke I'm shocked the year Spot was born a record snowfall take a three digit number walking through the white drifts to the drugstore cover 'hole' with four straight lines prescriptions like hieroglyphics secrets of a suburban wife reverse the number subtract reverse the difference and add four straight lines / – x covers any hole where did I hear that secret codes multiply times forty where life begins and translate the answer ciphers secret signs snow like mounds of kotex to the drugstore 'Uncle S says medicine is killing me' yes but you need it the prescription prescribes it cure for the common code in the dose

mestranol take twenty times a moon e pluribus unum and codex romanorum 0.1 mgm. a record snow and the same week I got the wire my cousin Bob was dead ROBRET they coded his name the god of Western Union is the same one with the winged stick and snakes more secret ciphers *ye ken one key* 'slat seven' interpret 'nine vestals' where did I get that a record snow and the same week and then Uncle S left us nothing naught zero only a watch and a page of word games the: old cadillionaire managed to take it with him the watch decorative only ran backwards and the games 'not a gem a megaton' and Abel was I ere madam I'm adam not a gem all right 'Ye no MS. I emit' the watch ran back-works backwords away taketh the Lord giveth this daily dread giveth

> blessed be the name of
> the name of
> the name

MACK AND MIKE (THEY ONLY LOOK ALIKE)
'Mike, as your spiritual adviser, not to say deity, I thought it was time we had a little chat.'

'Why "Mike"?'

'For the same reason you will address me as "Mack". Look it up in your Cabala.'

Look it up in your Cabala – a typical line of His. By turns witty pedant and sentimental bully. I'll do a movie of Him someday, 'Theo, the Friendly Hound of Heaven'. He'll love it.

He usually appears wearing a skin-tight suit of silver, a set of muscles by Michelangelo, flowing turquoise cape, five o'clock shadow, dark wavy hair. But the jowl is thickening, the muscles recede into layers of beer gut. He is seven feet tall, gold of teeth, impenetrable of sunglasses, a kind of aging Mafia acrobat. Now he plays a little game of church-and-steeple with those enormous hairy animals, his hands.

Every time I bring up Hiroshima, Vietnam, the death camps, the conquest of Mexico, etc., he changes the subject.

'I mark the sparrow's fall,' he says. 'Look at all the lost pets I've guided home through deserts, snowstorms, raging rapids, you name it.'

Typically I ask who makes the snow, the rapids rage. I never get the last word. Usually I give up after he asks me if I know how many bullets *his words* have stopped.

He feels that everyone ought to worship in his own way, that science is going too far and there are some mysteries better left to Him, that the ten commandments are graven in every man's heart. He's always on the side of the underdog, the Christian gladiator who fights all Rome, the lone sixgun against the whole town of badmen, the old scientist, his buxom daughter and the young scientist against the giant moles (who luckily are vulnerable to ordinary table salt), David *vs.* Goliath, Samson *vs.* Philistines, George *vs.* Dragon …

'Or Lucifer *vs.* You?' I made the mistake of mentioning one day.

'You're new around here, aren't you?'

Today I'm leafing through a glossy magazine, *Eternity*, as he lectures me on literature. I don't know prose from poetry, he says (the way he puts it is 'a pea-rose from a πόα-tree'). He mentions the Negative Confession ('Look that up in your Egyptian Book of the Dead'), a list of the sins one has not committed ('litany of the stains') and a request therefore for a blessing.

CAFE ISLAND

I began to survey the island, taking along my stuffed parrot. It was evidence that I was not hallucinating: the hallucinating mind moves straight as robins on course, and has no sense of the ridiculous.

The island was remarkably symmetrical about the north–south axis, irregularly ovoid. Starting at the south end, I named all the prominent elevations:

(1) Gibraltar Nich, a rounded hill forming the southern tip of the island.

(2) The Slip, a pair of ridges running east to west across the island, closing between them a gully with erosion marks.

(3) Enos Mountain, a gradual slope from the north with a sheer southern face containing the entrances to twin caves. The caves were not connected to each other, as far as I could follow them.

(4) Robe Wye, so named because it was (unlike other elevations) robed in impenetrable thickets of young trees, and because it forms, with the slope of Enos, a Y shape. Just south of Robe Wye are twin valleys with pine-edged lakes, one either side of Enos.

On the final day of my survey I came upon a naked human footprint.

NEGATIVE CONFESSION
  not a powder, not a grind
  no fuss, no muss, no mess
  not a brace, not a truss
  install without fixtures or screws
  no risk
  without narcotics, astringents or surgery

ETERNITY

A glossy magazine from his glossy coffee table. All ads for soups, razors, family cars interleaved with disaster pictures. Photo I've seen before: some kind of little fire in the middle of a street, something like a shriveled monkey in the flames. No, a man. Caption: HE STOPS BELLIES, TOO. EFFORT? HE STOPS BELLIES, TOO, THATCH KING THIS OTHER EVIL ENDS. REQUEST DICE.

What are they getting at here? Has the facing page (ad for fire extinguisher) got anything to do with this dream? HE TOPS BELT FORT? HE TOPS BELT, THATCHING HIS OTHER EVIL ENDS. REQUEST ICE. What is all this? The next page is a man throwing rocks at a flamethrowing tank. TOP BET. FOR? TOP BET, THATCH IS THERE VILER QUEST. And leafing both ways, I'm almost at the end of the magazine.

LIFE ON THE LINEAR

He can't keep me here if I want out. I'm an American citizen. But He says He's already damned the United States, and hopes He may never see nor hear of the United States again.

PART 4

Haunted Benefactor

NINETEEN

When Ank had bought the factory near Assholtz there'd been a rough wooden shed built against one of its stone walls. He'd hired masons to cut through the wall, uniting the two structures; then carpenters to extend the shed into a long passage like a covered bridge. It ran nearly a mile from the factory and stopped at the side of a new autobahn. At that end, he installed a padlocked door and an orange-drink stand.

Large deliveries of plaster, glue, chemicals and paint came to the factory, always by night. Except for the grocery boy, none of the local citizens ever approached it, and though they speculated often about it, no one knew for sure what this rich eccentric American was doing in there. For months, the sound of heavy churning machinery went on day and night.

Ank sent telegrams to the world's major art critics and historians, announcing a show that was to be 'A.B.'s' biggest and last.

Opening day was cold and drizzly. Of the critics who had not ignored his invitation, some proceeded no further than skidding their taxis to a stop on the autobahn. Taking one look at the rough wooden shed with its door chalked 'THIS WAY TO STORY OF ART', at the orange-drink stand chalked 'FREE ORANGE HELP UR SELF', they ordered their taxis back to the airport. Two dozen faithful and curious men remained, bumping umbrellas, sipping the nauseating beverage, and wondering if Ank were making a fool of them. The door was locked, and he was nowhere in sight. A churning sound came from the distant factory.

The sound stopped. A thin, haggard man with a crooked beard slogged across a field and greeted them, introducing himself as Ank Bullard – A.B.

'I apologize for keeping you waiting, gentlemen,' he said, 'but I wanted to have you all together. My show is also a demonstration of technique, so it's better to take everyone through at the same time.' Shivering in his wet clothes, he unlocked the door and led them inside.

The walls were dirty and cracked by the weather, and the uncertain lighting fooled most of them into thinking this was but a passageway. They began edging their way along one wall, avoiding the great slab of plaster that seemed to take up most of the foot-room.

Ank stopped them. 'The story of art,' he said solemnly. 'A fresco, ten feet by approximately five thousand feet, incorporating painted commentaries on the works of over thirty thousand artists.' He gestured at the slab.

They bent to have a closer look, and as their eyes became accustomed to the gloom, some gasped. One man knelt in the mud to examine the detail.

The imitations were mixed without apparent design. Picasso's satyrs teased Reynolds' ladies, to the amusement of dwarfs by Velasquez. Nearby, a group of Brueghel's peasants danced in a ring about an odd, octagonal building. Of its three visible faces, one was a modification of *American Gothic*, one a Magdalenian cave painting of bison, one a Poussin landscape.

The building was a bandstand, *ca.* 1900. Its conical roof flew a stiff Jasper Johns flag, and beneath it a Norman Rockwell band fought through what must have been a Sousa march. Closer inspection turned up a few odd bandsmen: a Roman Pan, Donald Duck on trombone, Vermeer's *Woman at a Harpsichord* and a Magritte gentleman in bowler hat, playing a thin loaf of bread – all these skillfully blended in.

Stepping back, one might notice that the bandstand was the conical hat for Rouault's clown.

Across a slanted plain marched a perspective of crucifixions, fifty in all, by as many artists, and linked by telephone wires from the wounds. Each had its cluster of worshippers at the foot, though not all seemed to be at the right crucifixion. Thus, Van der Weyden's patrons knelt to a Francis Bacon cross, Memlinc's to a Giotto, etc.

In the foreground was a forest of pedestals supporting Napoleons, kings, cardinals, burghers, etc., and from this a Greek lover chased his beloved and was chased in turn by an iron bird. They seemed headed across the Constable stream towards the baths of Caracalla, where Superman lectured the men whom El Greco's Messiah was about to drive from the building. The men were all Rembrandt, at various ages.

Beyond lay a garden where Adams and Eves by dozens of hands all sat down to a Dutch banquet of fruit and game. And so it went.

What they found so remarkable was not the fresco technique (though in its own way the 'finding' of this 'lost' art came as a pleasant shock) but the exquisite care in detail. A frescoist must work fast, but even a master would have had to spend hours over some of the fine Flemish parts. Surely this was a work of genius, the first light of Art's new day!

At the end, Ank unveiled his machine and explained how it worked: one device drizzled a secret formula of wet plaster into a wide trough. This was partially hardened, then propelled through the painting machine. From there it moved on steel rollers down the shed. The entire, mile-long work was a continuous slab.

This much they accepted. But when Ank began to explain the painting machine itself, the crowd made known their disbelief and anger.

'A programmed tape? How did you program this tape?'

'I … didn't. It looks like the random numbers on this tape weren't random at all. I don't really know how it came to be that way.'

'Preposterous!'

'Do you expect us to believe … ?'

'Show us the machine working, sir!'

Ank gazed on the hostile faces. Only the old gentleman, a man with a cane, had a kindly expression. The rest clamored for action.

Ank bent and closed a great copper switch. The lights dimmed momentarily. There was a churning sound. Curds of plaster squittered into the trough, and the whole mass began to move, quivering, down the shed.

Where it projected from the painting machine the fresco depicted a catacomb; on its shelves, famous reclining nudes. There were four tiers in all, and now, as the critics watched with horror and amusement, the machine simultaneously completed a Goya, a Bonnard, a Tom Wesselman and an Egyptian Osiris.

'A machine! This isn't art, it's obscenity!'

'Mechanical monster!'

'I've come all this way to see a *novelty*!'

'Come, Gerard, let's get out of this madhouse.'

The body of critics began to bunch up, shoving towards the exit. At the same time, the plaster slab started shrieking and trembling violently. Ank had used an odd formula of plaster and size, extremely elastic. Moreover it had dried unevenly in the damp shed, taking up new stresses. Because of the great weight on the metal rollers, over twenty feet of thick plaster had been pushed out of the machine before the far end began to move.

Contracting and expanding in uneven ripples, the whole slab built up enormous energy at rest, so that when it did finally expand, the far end twisted on edge and catapulted forward. Carrying everything in its path with it, it pile-drove out the door and into the path of a passing Citröen.

The man in the Citröen was an American critic of small reputation who had not been invited, but who knew someone who had. It wouldn't be the first show this tall man with a nose like an ax-blade had crashed.

He'd had trouble renting a car at the airport, received wrong directions from several people, and now sped along convinced he was on the wrong road. He was even considering stopping at the long shed to ask directions, when an orange-drink stand hurtled out on the road in front of him. The last thing he saw was the figure behind the counter, a rosy-cheeked coquette, painted in the manner of …

Gainsborough? he wondered, and joined that painter in the past tense.

Three great tremors passed through the length of the fresco, then it sighed and settled back, exhaling clouds of paint flakes and plaster dust. Only a few scraps of the original surface remained.

Their clothes were ruined, but the critics were able to take satisfaction from seeing 'A.B.' wiped out. They filed out and shared taxis back to town.

'It *was* beautiful,' one murmured. 'Like the mind of man, freed from all history.'

'Of course, of course. But unsuitable, you know.'

The Citröen had started a fire. Only the American gentleman with the gold cane stayed behind to help Ank fight it. Their efforts proved useless; the entire shed burned and collapsed, and the water they flung only served to finish the fresco's destruction.

'I was quitting anyway,' Ank said. 'Thought I'd get a job in commercial art, settle down …'

'Perhaps I can help you. May I offer you, say, ten thousand dollars for that peculiar tape you spoke of?'

'Ten thousand?'

The old man wrote a check and handed it to him. 'Okay?'

When he was alone, Ank took another look at the check.

'Mac Hines? Mac Hines?' He slapped himself on the forehead. 'O Jesus, that's just great. *Machines.*' Thinking of other famous check authors – I. B. Foxy, U. R. Stung, D. S. Windell, I. P. Freely – he tore up the obviously worthless check.

TWENTY

Grace before mess is read over the p.a. system while each cadet stands behind his chair in a full brace, gazing steadily at a spot one foot above the head of the cadet opposite. After grace, the cadet is allowed to seat himself in the prescribed manner: draw back the chair, using both hands, to a minimum distance of eleven inches, step smartly to the left side of the chair and sit down quickly and quietly. Both feet are on the floor, the left hand shakes out the napkin with a distinct 'pop' and arranges it across the knees and thereafter remains in the lap except when cutting meat.

The cadet observes strict silence during the meal and occupies no more than the front ½ of his seat. He is to look neither to left nor right nor directly at the cadet opposite nor directly at his plate. He pays particular attention to the reading of military inspirational literature during the meal, and if a first-year cadet he will be able to repeat all essential points of the reading at the request of any officer.

Food is passed from the head of the table; the ranking cadet officer at the head of the table will be served first. Food will not be requested, but passed along briskly or eaten. When the cadet observes *by ear* that the ranking officer has begun eating, he may and must follow suit.

When cutting meat the left hand takes the fork, the right takes the knife. As soon as a bite of meat is cut (no less than ¼" or more than ½" square) the right hand lays the knife on the plate at a 45° angle, cutting edge facing outwards and one inch from the edge of the plate. Right hand then takes the fork and left returns immediately to the lap. Demerits will be given for eating bread, not eating, soiled napkin.

Putting it off any longer would just be cowardice. Spot's decision had been made a long time ago: before he had ever heard the story of Samson, before the televised transfiguration and death of Billy Koch: now it was just putting one foot in front of the other and walking toward his goal.

He waited until after the presumed last bed check (they were too numerous and irregular ever to be sure), collected his money, his comics and a change of underwear (in case he got into an accident on his way to commit suicide), and slipped out. Down the hall, past the cadet officer sleeping by the emergency door, over the spiked iron fence and into town. He caught the midnight bus for Minneapolis.

He would see Mom first, and explain to her why he was doing it. (1) She would undoubtedly try and talk him out of it, but he would be strong. There were some things, as Col Fouts was always saying, that a man had to do. And Samson had killed himself. And Christ. (2) She would just refuse to let him do it. In that case, he would kill himself on the spot, maybe by a voluntary emission of his soul (John Donne said it could be done). (3) She would understand and give him the money to get to Washington and do it properly.

He arrived before dawn, saliva running down his neck from sleeping on the bus. The key was in the mailbox. He found the house empty, disused, unfriendly, and after looking all over for Mom, went to sleep on the big bed – on top of the American flag.

At ten the next morning he was downtown with his little overseas bag, now only partly in uniform. As he stopped to ask a stranger where the National Arsenamid Corporation was ('the television part') a familiar car flashed by.

It was Fouts. *He recognized Spot.*

As soon as Fouts saw the kid talking to what could only be a plainclothesman, he knew it was finished.

'O Jesus O Jesus O Jesus O.'

He ran three red lights getting across town to Phenolphthalein Drive. 'Oh, yes sir,' the kid would be saying by now. 'Yes, I saw the Colonel *in women's clothes.*' And that was that.

The flight to New York, that was his only chance. Slip in among all the others, a few chameleon changes in and out of drag, into the melting pot … maybe get a studio and hide out as one of them beatnik painter types … that was the life …

There were three signs above Feinwelt's desk at Transvestites Anonymous:

BREAK THE HABIT HABIT!
SUIT YOURSELF!
CHANGE INTO WHAT YOU CANNOT ENDURE!

He sat beneath them like a hostile god, his rippled, ripe old face betraying no sign of forgiveness for the returned prodigal. Fouts laid the pile of nun's clothes on the desk.

'I guess you expect me to say "Let's be friends", eh Foutsy? Not a chance. I know you're not sorry for what you did (not only to me but to the organization). You just heard about the big New York convention so you came crawling back, hoping I'd ask you to come along. Isn't that it?'

'I guess so.' Fouts twisted his overseas cap.

'You know I could have you for assault, indecency, theft, impersonation …' A long-toothed smile.

'I know, Mother Feinwelt. But I'm in a lot worse trouble right now. I wish the flight was leaving today, instead of next Friday.'

Feinwelt looked at him closely. Then he seemed to have a change of heart. 'All right.' He sighed. 'You can go. The flight leaves Friday at ten p.m. We'll all meet here at six p.m., bus out to the airport and check in at seven-thirty. Got that?'

'Thanks, Mother. You're a pal and I won't forget this.' Fouts almost skipped out to his car. As he drove away, he noticed a new, cheap-model car parked across the road, in the shade of a willow. The old couple in it seemed to be necking.

Hadn't he seen them here before?

Just now there were plenty of other things to worry about. Army Security might close in anytime, he had to have a cover story. His sister was visiting him (phone her and set it up) and asked him to help her fix a hem. He'd tried on the dress and at that moment Cadet Shairp had come to the door. Rose was about his size, so any clothes lying around the place could be explained … and when that kid got back to school, there'd be some really beautiful punishment waiting for him …

By the time Fouts reached the school he felt so good that he allowed himself to break his diet, and gorge an Almond Joy.

Spot ran. The streets and alleys flashed by, broken scenes and interrupted faces: a man tying his shoelace, a woman paying a taxi, sleep-walking shoppers, a window-cleaner.

He quit when his side hurt too much, but for the rest of the day he would feel Fouts's eyes on him, the fat hand clamping down on his shoulder: 'Well, my boy, have we had enough running away and playing with ourselves?'

'What a cuh-yute lit-tle uniform! What can I do for you, lover?'

'Please, Miss, I'm looking for my mother. She works here.'

'Well what a lucky old mother to have such a cute little sojur like you for a son! What's her name, lover-sojur?'

'Marge Shairp.'

As she looked through her files, the receptionist kept embarrassing Spot with winks and puckering gestures. He felt like telling her about his suicide plan (there being some things a man had to do), but shyness shut him up.

'Not listed here, lover-lover. That don't mean anything, though. Tell you what. You wait right here and I'll find out which floor she works on. Okay? I'll be right back.'

She disappeared down the dim distance of a corridor, though the sound of her heels echoed back long after she was out of sight. Spot decided she was about the sexiest, most sophisticated woman he'd ever met.

But any second Fouts would come swinging in through the revolving door and grab him. Spot looked over the stuff on the desk: lists of numbers, offices and phones. Bound folders (no time to open them), an artificial flower and a tiny notebook full of florid handwriting. The capitals were all curlicues and extra loops, and the dots over the i's were little circles.

'*Daisy James* by Henry Miller ...'

Nothing there. He went back to the lists. Studio A and Studio B were both on the fifth floor. That would probably be it.

With the feeling that Fouts was right behind him, he fled up the dim STAFF ONLY stairway.

It was really dark in Studio A, dark and churchy. There was even a bluish vigil light that turned out to be, when he got closer, a pilot light on an ordinary stove. Instead of arches and columns, there were huge tall pieces of kitchen everywhere, and each piece was complete as a chapel, with sink, stove, table, window and landscape painted just behind the glass. The water worked and the stove lighted. He thought of the dark, dusty kitchen at home, the refrigerator full of stale secrets ... he knelt at a Formica table, rested his forehead against the chrome edge, and asked God to help him find his mother.

Something in the darkest corner clicked, hummed, stopped. Spot made his way over to it stepping over a few blacksnake cables on the concrete floor.

It was an enormous new deep-freeze, bigger than a coffin. It took him a minute or two to work out the complicated catch and raise the lid. A light came on, and he looked in.

'The fast trains retarded kids,' said Wise Bream agreeably. He spoke as always ambiguously and apropos of nothing. Three Dollars and Twenty Cents settled into the seat beside him, chuckling.

'You really had 'em fooled, you clever bastard. Even me. I thought for awhile you might be a god or something.'

The conductor came past, calling for tickets. He coughed, seeing the handcuffs. Naturally he asked the white man if the Indian were his prisoner.

'No, as it so happens,' Three said. 'As it so happens, this man is an escaped loony. I'm taking him back to his nuthatch in Washington.'

'Say, I don't think—'

'He's not dangerous, don't let it worry you. Never harmed a fly, did you, General Custer? That's who he thinks he is, General Custer.'

'The crossing kids train,' said Wise, grinning hideously. The conductor hurried on.

'What a messed-up face,' he thought, locking himself in the next car. 'What a mean son of a bitch he must be. Big, too.'

The train jolted into motion, and so did the rest of the Utopi, on the platform. They began to wave, and their god smiled and waved back.

'I'm worried.' Seldom From frowned at the two grinning faces in the window. 'I wish we could have sent our god along to Washington with anybody but Three-Twenty.'

Fake Sky clapped him on the shoulder. 'Don't be an old man about this, Seld. Who else knows the ins and outs of politics well enough to go along? Besides, it's good to have Three-Twenty out of the way for awhile. Always criticizing!'

'I know, I know, but somehow I never can shake the feeling that Three is a bad injun. He's never been off the reservation before, don't forget, and he's got a lot of money in his jeans.'

'We've been through all this as many times as the Moon has children, Seld. We need a strong lobby in Washington to get some changes made back here. Why should we live on Second World War C-rations the Army admits are unpalatable? Why shouldn't we have mineral rights on our own reservation, instead of the Lion Oil Company? Why can't we get our tractor fixed? It stands to reason to send in our best men.'

'That's right, Seld.' Someone Else spat off the platform. The wind whirled the lacy gobbet clear across the tracks. 'Remember, Three-Twenty's no moth when it comes to brains.'

'So he says himself.'

On the train Three Dollars and Twenty Cents laughed again. 'Listen, old God. You ought to see what I've got planned for us when we get to Washington. I'm going to show you off on street corners: Wise Bream, the Indian Oracle. I'll make enough to get me a Brooks Brothers' suit. Then we'll be where the action is! We'll be on easy street, in the land of milk and honey, the gravy train, wow, under the money tree!'

TWENTY-ONE

Thursday night, Wes Davis's White Shirt party held a mammoth torchlight parade in Washington, a preliminary to their party convention. Chanting that they were neither red nor black nor yellow, ten thousand White Shirts bore fire toward the Capitol. Wes rode in an armored car in front. Behind was another, containing an enormous petition which, it was said, had a million signatures.

The petition asked for the abolition of Negroes.

A series of dramatic floats worked variations on the theme, 'A Final Solution to the Negro Problem'. A slave ship marked BOUND FOR AFRICA held its cargo of men in blackface grimacing through portholes, while above decks the jolly crew of smiling bikini-blondes prettily plied sextant, wheel and telescope.

The FINAL SOLUTION MACHINE was likewise 'manned'. This was a large, silvery box with rotating cogs at the sides. Two bikini-blondes cranked it. Al Jolsons were herded in at one end and canned goods came out at the other.

Another float suggested torments awaiting Negroes in the next world. It was a great furnace with many doors that now and then swung shakily open on red glowing scenes; here the b-b's were equipped with horns and pitchforks, and twirled their tails suggestively as they stoked the crepe-paper fires.

Another depicted the 'Four L's' of the Wes Davis code: 'Label 'em, Loath 'em, Larrup 'em and Lynch 'em,' in four tableaux (more b-b's, more dismayed minstrels), while on the sides of the float the four L's were arranged in a clever design that reminded some onlookers of a kind of wheel radiating four feet.

Many a papier-mâché lamppost twined with paper flowers held its black effigy surrounded by still more b-b's, but the poor girls on one float, whose lamppost had broken down, smiled through tears. The crowd gave them a big hand, brave little troupers that they were.

Then came a giant replica of Wes himself, twenty feet tall and straddling a white stallion nearly fifteen feet tall. He and the horse were formed entirely of lilies; the crowd was still complaining about the smell when the vanguard of the White Shirts marched by.

They sang a bouncy, drum-and-bugle version of the National Anthem, with a few words changed here and there. As it came out, what F. Scott Key was watching o'er the ramparts was not the flag but the gallantly streaming smoke from a Wes Davis factory for turning Negroes into scouring products.

The marching was superb, a precise goose-step, and the banners and torches inspired awe. But something was wrong with the singing. Partly this was due to many of the White Shirts relapsing into their childhood versions of the anthem. Yet thousands of bystanders later swore they heard a third version:

Ofay can you pee
Through the dong's surly blight
What you probably inhaled
At the toilet's last cleaning?

It was senseless to some, filthy to most, and disgusting to all White Shirt sympathizers in the crowd, listing as it did a few likely perversions of the WASP element. A great many potential friends were lost to the White Shirt cause that night by the simple substitution of *chancre* for *banner*. There might be a black conspiracy, but this was going too far ... and what was the point of it all?

The point of it all was that over eight thousand of the White Shirts were not bona fide members at all. Over four thousand were not even white. A breakdown by singer and song might have looked like this:

SINGER	SONG	NUMBER
White Shirts	Wes Davis Hymn	1,956
FBI agents	National Anthem	2,488
CIA agents	National Anthem	960
Maryland Crime Prevention Bureau	National Anthem	34
Delaware Crime Prevention Bureau	National Anthem	20
Virginia CPB	National Anthem	33
City detectives	National Anthem	17
Federal marshals	National Anthem	1,219
Black Buddhists	Third version	802
Black Nationalists	Third version	1,725
Brothers of the Black Claw	Third version	the rest.

A few informed news sources suspected there might be trouble coming. A news analyst wondered why the White Shirts had chosen Washington DC for their convention – hardly good taste. Other newsmen ignored the whole thing as much as possible, and concentrated on other news, of the 'human' interest variety: the President's cold, the appearance of cherry blossoms, a transvestite convention in New York, a talking bear at the zoo.

The White Shirts left their huge scroll on the Capitol steps, to be delivered next morning. It demanded, among other things, the immediate accession of the President in favor of Wes Davis. The Senate subcommittee who later examined it would find among its million signers surprisingly few handwriting styles. Moreover, sections of it looked copied from telephone books, death rolls, *Who's Who*, the litany of the saints, the Declaration of Independence and even a catalogue of Madame Tussaud's waxworks in London. Senator Vuje would have a hard time explaining away the signatures of St Christopher, John Hancock, Albert Einstein, Henry Ford and Dr Crippen.

The following afternoon, Fouts arrived at Transvestites Anonymous with his gear and a supply of candy bars. The old couple were still necking out front when he unlocked the door and let himself in. Did they come here every day, or what? (Something about them gave him an uneasy feeling – later.)

The place was deserted. Dust covers on the office typewriters, chairs turned up on tables in the coffee room, bulletin board cleared off, nothing in any locker but his – no sign of humanity but a broken earring pendant in the hallway.

He sat down at Feinwelt's desk to think. A raid? No, too tidy. Today was Saturday? His calendar watch assured him it was Friday. Maybe he was too early? But where was everyone's luggage, then? Maybe they sent it on ahead?

He picked up the phone to dial Feinwelt's downtown office. It made a guy jittery, sitting around here all alone, what with Army Security probably watching his every …

To Fouts's trained ear, even over the dial tone, came the unmistakable ping of a direct wire tap. He hung up at once, feeling the uniform tighten over his chest and crotch.

Bad news. They were this far already, tapping the phone at the one place he'd always felt safe. So now what? Sit here and let them close in? 'Just tell us in your own words, Colonel – how long have you been a fucking fruit?' No, better to die than … better to wait.

There was always the payphone on the corner. He peered cautiously out the Venetian blinds. The old woman was alone in the car now …

But she was training a pair of binoculars on him!

'Don't think of it as drag,' he said to himself, fumbling in his locker. 'Think of it as a *disguise*.'

*

'Get down off the pole quick, Grover! Someone's coming out!'

Grover jumped down, pulled off his headset and scrambled into the car. An odd figure in a white hoopskirt came floating out of the building and across the lawn to the phone booth.

'Something funny about that woman ...' Grover mused.

'You noticed it too? That's no woman, Grover. It's a man!'

'Nawww, really?'

'I'll stake my new glasses on it. It's the same man who went in. The Army officer. Just look how he waddles!'

'Perty new at disguises, I guess. And yet he's smart enough to use an outside line, so we can't tap it. He looks to be a bad one, Amy. And to think, he's in the Yuhnited States Army!'

'He's the same officer we saw earlier this week, Grover. It's a relief to know they haven't penetrated the Army any deeper than that.'

'I think we got 'em on the run, now. They're resorting to disguises, so they must be worried.'

'Shall we tell the FBI now, Grover?'

'I – just a sec. He's *writing something* on the wall of that phone booth, Amy. I want to get a look at that.'

Using a coin, Fouts scratched his initial in the aluminum wall, just below a sign: 'Wouldn't some loved one love to hear from *you* right now?' Feinwelt's office phone rang for the seventy-fourth time.

'You son of a bitch, where are you?' He hung up. There was nothing to do but go back and wait, under the needling stare of the 'old folks'.

He went back, walking daintily, not daring to look up and see those binoculars. In the rec room, he stretched out on a sofa, switched on the TV and went to sleep. It would be all right when Feinwelt and the boys got here ... it had to be all right ... the news commentator was rattling on ... trouble in Washington ...

The mark was like this:

'Pi? Amy, this is it! Either that guy we just saw was none other than the ringleader, Pé himself, or else he was talking to Pé on the telephone! Back to the car, Amy. Just had another idea. Did we bring my deciphering books? Good.'

Amy kept close watch on the building all through the afternoon while Grover worked at cracking the code. Without food or bladder relief he continued after dark, working by the map light. Just after sunset, he nudged her.

'Eureka, Amy,' he whispered. 'You wouldn't believe the length them cummunisks will go to. Looky here. The secret of their code is the number *pi* itself!

'You know how I told you it stood for wheels within wheels – well, it means a lot more than that. *Pi* is the key to the *whole cummunisk conspiracy!*'

He handed her a sheet of paper on which he'd written out the first thirty places of *pi*. Underneath was his translation:

1415	9265	358	979	323	846	264338	3280
PIPE	NODE	SEA	NUN	SOS	AID	ODISSA	SOAR

'First I thought it was a very ordinary message,' he said. 'Whatever the rest meant, a ship called the *Sea Nun* was piping nodes of SOS for aid, probably somewhere near the Russky city of Odissa, on the Black Sea.

'Then I decided the words themselves were code, PIPE = BRIAR = BUSH = H-SUB. NODE = NO'D' = ON 'D'. SEA NUN = C. NUN = SISTER = RESIST. SOS = MAYDAY = MAY FIRST(The big Russky holiday). AID is obvious. ODISSA, that I left alone because it's on the Black Sea, and *Sea Nun* confirms it. The last word was the toughest, SOAR could be ROSA. Together with the first word it could mean SUB ROSA or SECRET, but that wasn't enough. It also seemed to mean flying. But when I thought about *sub* (submarine) *rosa* (red) and secrets, I realized it must mean rockets fired from H-powered subs, rockets of the Poseidon type.'

He held out the newly-constructed message.

> H-SUB ON D.C. (But direct current or the capital?)
> RESIST MAY FIRST
> AID ODISSA RED SUB ROCKET.

'So far, so good. Then I took a look at this: the cipher I had used.'

1 = P	6 = D
2 = O	7 – U
3 = S	8 = A
4 = I	9 = N
5 = E	0 = R

'*Posieduan R.* Probably a Russky variation of Posiedon, with R for rocket. Now I was getting someplace. But I still wasn't sure about the D.C. part. I began by retranslating the first five letters, P.O.S.I.E., like this:

'In the Roman, or "perfect" alphabet, there is no J, so P is the 11th letter from the end and L is the 11th from the beginning. P is a reflection of L, a "new el". That gave me the first word, NEWEL.

'O is zero, nothing, the perfect void. Nothing can come from nothing, so I left it alone, as a word.

'S being the third letter of our word, I naturally looked to see what words can be formed from S plus any two letters following it in the alphabet. The only three in order that make a word are STY. If you write STY like this, it becomes a rebus.'

He wrote:

$$S + Y$$

'That is, "S + wine" or swine (contained in sty). So the third word was PIG.

'I is a speck, the first blemish on the void, the simplest pencil mark or spot. I decided these "Frenchmen" would use the French word for spot, TACHE.

'E is the third of the diatonic C-major scale's tones. It is also the fifth letter. Where there is a third and a fifth, there must be a fourth, and it is of course the position of E in the word TONES itself. So our fifth word is TONS.'

He excused himself from the car and went behind the willow tree for a moment. When he returned, he showed her this new 'extrapolated' message and its reversal:

NEWEL O PIG TACHE TONS

SNOT EH CAT GI POLE WEN

'I wrote this,' he said wearily, 'in the Pyramid form.' Another sheet.

```
            | I |
          | P | T |
        | O | E | O |
      | L | H | N | A |
    | E | C | S | C | P |
  | W | A | S | H | I | E |
| E | T | N | E | G | L | E |
| N | G | O | T | T | O | W | N |
```

'Removing the shape of the letter *pi* gives:

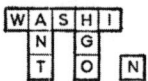

'Since Pé is *pi*,' he concluded, 'even now our diameters erode! Spelling enters acrostic nuances under number systems. Our side already inserts documents of deception in Secret Service agents' statements: "O + pen": a rebus.'

Something peculiar in his tired smile led Amy to suspect that this little speech was itself an acrostic. Grover was having a little joke with her, the magnificent man!

'If loud offers veer ever …' she began, but he shushed her.

'Listen, we can't get the FBI just yet. If we use the phone on the corner,

Pé will see us. If we go to fetch them, he'll give us the slip. For now, I guess we'll just have to pin him down and hope for the best.'

'But couldn't I stay here and watch him while you went to the FBI?'

He laid a hand on her arm. She felt dizzy. 'I wouldn't want to chance it, Amy. You're too precious.'

Flight 974 from Minneapolis to New York was a peculiar assortment of citizens. At least twenty looked to the stewardess like women dressed up in men's clothes – unwillingly, or so it seemed, for they spent the first hour after takeoff fiddling with belts and loosening ties, wiggling their shoulders with discomfort. They were going to some kind of convention, and they kept slapping each other on the back and kidding about 'observing the conventions' when they got there. Their passports said Male, and Marilyn wondered if they might not just be those 'queer' sorts of persons she'd heard so much about.

Then there was that man in the awful wrinkled dirty dinner jacket who kept asking her all kinds of technical questions about the plane – how much fuel it carried, how many miles to the gallon and so on – and finally there were two of the smallest nuns she had ever seen, and a strange veiled woman in black, apparently pregnant.

The two little nuns, midgets almost, sat in back, reading their miniature breviaries and fingering tiny rosaries – and looking apprehensive. Marilyn walked slowly back past all the men and asked if the sisters were feeling comfortable.

'Oh yes, thank you,' they piped. The younger one added, 'My, it certainly is a long ways down.'

'Yes, we're at thirty thousand feet now – about six miles.'

'As much as that!'

'Don't worry, there's nothing to be afraid of.'

'I was a little frightened after the plane took off,' the old one admitted. 'So fast! And all the people down on the ground looked like little dolls!'

They certainly didn't seem sensitive about their size, so Marilyn squatted by the seat and asked them the question she'd been turning over in her mind ever since takeoff.

'Are you by any chance an Irish order, sisters?'

'Oh my, no!' The older one chuckled, wrinkling her little face like a fist. 'We're Little Sisters of the Amish.'

'I used to work for a religious organization myself,' said Marilyn. 'The Billy Koch Crusade.'

'A very good organization, and a very good man. I'm sure Mr Koch did a great deal of good work before his accident. Sister Mary Jane here just got back from one of our missions among the pygmies. I'm Sister Maia. All our missionary work is with the little folk.'

'I'm Marilyn Temblor. If there's anything you need, sisters …'

Seeing the unkempt man was signalling her frantically, she excused herself and went forward.

'Ah, how much fuel is left now, please?'

'Don't you worry, sir. There's plenty of fuel to get us to New York.'

'Ah? Ahm.' He sat back and looked more worried than before.

Next she stopped to see how the woman in the veil was getting along.

'I hope you're not expecting your baby real soon,' she blurted out, and laughed nervously.

'I'll let you know,' murmured the woman.

'Would you like any milk or anything?'

The muffled voice gave some reply that sounded like 'Ashes, ashes!'

'Where's Fouts?' asked one of the women-men.

'Now, you know, that's not a very interesting question,' replied the one who kept turning around to give the dwarf nuns dirty looks.

'Don't listen to Mother Feinwelt. He's all worked up because them midgets get to dress in nun's habits and he can't.'

'Shut up, Gertrude. As a matter of fact, I told Fouts Friday at six instead of Friday at five. A little schadenfreudian slip there. Anyway, it'll teach him a lesson.'

Marilyn went forward to fix the cocktails. A moment later there was a timid knock at the door of the stewardess compartment.

'How far are we from Florida?' asked the man in the wrinkled dinner jacket. His breath stank of months of steady drinking, his fly was open and his cummerbund turned around sidewise.

'I don't really know, sir. Shall I ask the pilot?'

He showed tiny teeth and puffy pink gums in a smile. 'Oh no, that won't be necessary. You see, I have here …' He groped in his oversize jacket pocket for a moment, 'I have here this gun. So I'll talk to the pilot myself, if you don't mind. I want him to fly toward Florida – more specifically, toward *Cuba*.'

At that second, the woman in the veil let out a long scream and slid to the floor. Sister Mary Jane was there even before Marilyn. 'Quickly!' she said. 'Boil some water!'

TWENTY-TWO

The riot began with an *incident* of a familiar type. A group of Negroes watching the White Shirt torchlight parade refused to 'move on' at a policeman's order. The cop, a rookie named Joe Haarman, drew his gun and perhaps repeated the order. Among the group was a girl eleven years old …

If anyone expected an apology or promise of investigation by the police, they didn't know Chief Wiggin. He went on TV that evening to say:

'Haarman was just doing his job. We're going to back him up all the way. You can't go around asking every hoodlum his *age* before you shoot. A cop has to think fast in a situation like that. And don't forget, men like Haarman are out there every night, risking their lives to protect you and yours.'

UP YOU AND YOURS, WIG signs appeared instantly in many windows all over the Negro district. Negro citizens' groups started the long, tedious process of making official protests and trying to get the chief to say maybe Haarman had after all been hasty. Others preferred direct methods.

To stave off trouble, riot cops began unwarranted slum-to-slum searches for hidden caches of weapons.

The Justice Department is worried. Five hundred Federal marshals are called on duty and issued with gas masks, Mace, riot guns, side-arms and clubs. The Attorney General addresses them:

'I want to make this clear – your mission is not to aggravate violence, but to quell it. Should any disturbances break out, they are to be handled as peacefully and diplomatically as possible. I don't want to see a lot of pictures in the papers tomorrow of kids with bleeding heads, pregnant women being dragged by the feet, and so on. Is that clear?'

'Yeah, we got it, sir. *No pictures.*' Winks. Smack of weighted club on palm. 'You leave everything to us, sir.'

Cardinal James Homer, whom the papers describe as 'flinty', 'an outspoken conservative', is giving a sermon at the dedication of a new Knights of Columbus chapel, a slick new building in the midst of the ghetto.

'Dangerous radicals and shiftless degenerates need to be taught a lesson. The trouble with *most* of our lawmen is they just don't shoot to kill!'

The doors burst open and several hundred Black Nationalists, White Shirts, cops and snarling dogs all swarm in and chase each other around the sanctuary. Marshals close in outside, smash out the new stained-glass windows of SS. Christopher and Filomena and lob in teargas.

'O Jesus!' says one cop, seeing where he is. 'O Jesus! The Mafia ain't gonna like this …'

One story spreads that Haarman is a Catholic, another that he is a Jew. White Shirts at the convention hall hear that a black cop killed a little white girl who refused to submit to him. Catholics hear that Masons have murdered the cardinal.

*

A dozen night-rider Klansmen in full hooded regalia are packed into a hotted-up old Merc tearing down the Southwest Freeway on their way to the White Shirt rally.

'How many notches you got on that old shotgun, Billy Bee?'

'Well, I don't rightly recolleck … lessee … this one don't count, cause after we hanged and burned and shot the son bitch, he up and ran off … what's that burnin' yonder?'

'Git off my eyehole so's I can see. Hot damn! Looks like the convention hall itself!'

A clever White Shirt has set their own convention hall on fire to guarantee the sympathy of many potential voters (the convention, and choosing a candidate, are mere formalities anyway). The White Shirts come charging out, armed with guns, tire irons, homemade clubs prepared weeks in advance for this emergency. In the street their numbers are swelled by Klansmen and Nazis; they run, yelling and screaming, for a hundred feet before they encounter a shoe-shine boy.

But as they stop to attack him they realize they've been decoyed: black militants and street gangs close in from both ends of the street, armed with garbage-can lids, guns, zip-guns, broken bottles and chains.

The first police on the scene take one look and barricade both ends of the street to let them fight it out. But a quick head count shows more black than white; they put in a call for the riot squad.

The riot squad moves in with teargas, clubs and Alsatians, chopping their way for no particular reason to the center of the mob, which closes right in behind them. They're rescued an hour later and withdraw with heavy casualties, including a gassed dog and a cop with canine throat slashes.

Enzio ('The Head') Gagliardi comes out of a Negro club where he's just been collecting an insurance premium (twice the club's rent) to find his Cadillac's been worked over. His ice-blue eyes move from detail to detail: all tinted glass smashed, the radio gone, the hood spray-painted with slogans and plastered with posters of Chairman Fat Tsing: 'LONG LIVE THE PEOPLE'S REPUBLIC. LONG LIVE CHAIRMAN FAT,' he spells out.

'Republicans, eh? So Fats Funicolo wants to play the Old Rules, does he? I guess I'm not too old to handle a heater. Get some of the boys together. Call Cleveland, Chi, L.A., Vegas …'

'But, boss, we and Fats are all brothers in Cosa Altra.'

'Fuck that. Anybody breaks the pretty dual aerials off my little honey here ain't nobody's brother! Call a war council.'

A vigilante mob called the Big Stick Men, all wearing tricorner hats and carrying muskets, set up an ambush for any un-American elements that might wander by. They manage to pick off a black postman and a paper boy who might be of foreign extraction.

Then the Islamic Brotherhood of the Black Claw outflanks and roars down on them, throwing bricks and Molotov cocktails, and assisted by the machete-swinging Bolivian Urban Guerilla Brigade.

'Hold your fire!' shouts the Big Stick commander, raising his saber. 'Don't fire till you see the whites of their eyes.'

'But Commander, they're all wearing dark glasses!'

The muzzle-loaders won't fire anyway, and in half an hour the street is empty but for broken glass, blood slicks, and a tricorner hat perched on a lamppost.

The Black Buddhists decide to sit down in protest on Pennsylvania Avenue. The Klan move in at once with blacksnake whips and hobnail boots. The cops sit by until they've had their fun, then tell them to keep back on the sidewalk.

'I don't like this,' says one cop, spraying Mace liberally over some dying buddhists. 'I mean, they didn't leave a hell of a lot for us, did they?'

'Wait till we get them back to the station house,' his partner says. 'Plenty of life in there yet. What I like to do is hamstring two of them and make them race on all fours down the hall, goosing them up with cattle prods. The winner gets maybe a drink of water, and the loser gets his prick cut off – you know, "accidently he stood too close to the paper guillotine" … I know cops that won't use nothing else for a sap, just one of them filled with buckshot …'

The Klan are jealous. 'We're leaving now,' their leader calls. 'But we'll be back – with a steamroller.'

The original 'sides' are blurring already. Among the city cops are Catholics, Jews, Negroes and sympathizers with the Klan; this is true also of the FBI, the Federal marshals and the militias of three states who are now getting into the act. Some Catholics are White Shirts; some Jews are anarchists; some Catholics and Jews own Negro tenements; the landlord of a poor white slum contributes heavily to the American Nazi Party. All of the organizations involved, from Big Stick and the Klan to Students for Chairman Fat, include spies from the FBI, CIA, city police and cops from three states, as well as spies from other groups. Splits and coalitions are common and frequent. It's getting harder to decide who 'they' are.

No one is necessarily what he seems, and no one is 'just' an anarchist, Negro or cop. *Ad hoc* committees are formed almost spontaneously, often without names; everyone is able, finding himself performing any atrocity, to believe it is not the *real* him doing this – and there are enough secret sympathies to justify anything.

A strategist at the Pentagon tries to work it all out with the help of CIA reports.

He dictates a memo to the general staff: The main possible types of conflict are

> Racial
> Religious
> Ethnic
> Income level (relative prosperity)
> Relative authoritarianism
> Relative age
> Sexual preference (relative heterosexuality)

or some combination of any of these. No classification of these seems complete: an anti-Semite usually hates a Black Muslim who hates a black Jew who hates a homosexual Jew and a white Jew about equally, who hate each other, and who also both may hate a white Jewish cop who hates his superior who hates an anti-authoritarian young man who hates an authoritarian young man who hates and envies anyone wealthier than he.

'The city is an equation of x unknowns ... there may actually be more *sides* than *individuals*,' he concludes, 'and everyone is not just alone, but incomplete ...'

The general staff decide he means 'put the Marines in to guard the Arab embassies', which they do. The Arabs call up the State Department every five minutes thereafter, reporting Zionists sneaking around in camouflaged uniforms.

The Virginia state troopers arrive and wade into a suspicious-looking group of Negroes – city cops in plainclothes. These dectectives are Maced out of action for the rest of the riot.

Arsonists begin setting fires in timed pairs to frustrate firemen; two or three fires are started at the same time, just over a hose-length apart.

The steps of one police station are smeared with excrement; one cop slips and falls, fracturing a rib. *Newstime* magazine singles out this incident ('a pointless and disgusting gesture') and features it prominently in their story the following week, 'WASHINGTON: THE RIOT CITY'. *Newstime*'s analysis is statistical ('Hurled were 7,420 broken bottles, 847 bricks ...') and topographic ('Map shows damage area') as well as alliterative ('Discotheques and Discontent').

Delaware National Guardsmen arrive to protect the Lincoln Memorial (a quick informal survey has shown that the majority of rioters of all groups would like to mess it up). They are attacked first by HOMODRAFT, a ferocious band of homosexuals who want the draft laws changed to let them be soldiers. Federal marshals backing up the troops panic and let go with their riot guns, wounding more Guardsmen than queers. All Federal agencies are alerted to the possibility of 'queer backlash'.

Students for Chairman Fat run through all districts, chanting and pasting hero pictures over everything. Brothers of the Black Claw have settled down to rooftop sniping. A few soldiers have deserted to join in looting. Five or six old-line Communists totter around, distributing leaflets and urging the workers to unite. The workers are hot-wiring trucks to carry away the stuff they've collected.

'To each according to his need ...'

'GAT OUTA DA WAY YA OLD CREEP OR I'LL DRIVE TRU YA!'

Complications: Someone has looted a uniform shop catering to the police and armed forces. Before the riot is over dozens of pseudo-cops and fake Army officers swarm over the city, adding to the confusion.

A student anarchist group changes their name and prints a new manifesto once or twice an hour. With their mimeo machine in the back of a panel truck they tour the city, dropping white racist manifestos in the black areas, anti-Semitic handouts in Jewish neighborhoods, Nazi, Chairman Fat, black racist stuff where appropriate. Their little demos support all sides, with the object of panicking everyone else and thus preserving their own identity *by contrast*.

The 'queer backlash' news cheers up the cops, who knew down deep who the Enemy was all along.

At Union Station a group departing for New York to the Transvestites Anonymous convention are dragged (in drag) off the train by Federal marshals, gassed and clubbed. A White Shirts' contingent sees only men in gas masks belaboring women with clubs. It makes their Southern Comfort boil. In the ensuing battle no one notices the arrival of a Utopi Indian and his white prisoner ...

On the Mall a few vice squad cops have put on women's clothes to bait muggers and rapists. An army of Maryland state cops closes in ...

After their first battle, Wes Davis and twenty trusted lieutenants disappear; they hole up with plenty of provisions in the top floor of an expensive hotel.

'Aint as if we was *running out*,' Wes explains. 'Hell, we can watch it on television just as good.'

*

Six anti-memorialists who call themselves Burning World (motto: 'Today Now!') dress as Marine officers and pass through the lines guarding the Lincoln Memorial, where they plant a bomb. The blast kills them and a few of the Delaware Guard, and completely demolishes the tomb. Two blocks away, a Soviet official coming out of the State Department door is instantly lobotomized by a flying fragment of what proves to be Lincoln's mole.

Students for Chairman Fat march among the stunned and bleeding soldiers in triumph, pausing only to paste pictures of Fat on helmets of the fallen, or to cop a grenade.

The Klan are out on the Mall, raping a Negro vice-squad cop in drag … forty have been in already without noticing anything odd.

'Hey, the boas done blown up the Lincoln Memorial! EEEEEyahoooo!' They set up a wooden cross by the Reflecting Pool and ignite it.

It explodes. One of the Fat-ists has slipped a grenade in the kindling. A Goblin is killed and a Cyclops loses an eye.

Angry tourists mill around the ruins of Lincoln's tomb. They jump the prostrate Guardsmen, flailing away with thermos bottles, cameras and campstools. 'You son of a bitch, you could have kept it up until I got a picture of it!'

'Kick his nuts off, Gladys! Our whole trip's ruined!'

The man from Babel Tours rushes among them, trying to make peace. 'Girls, girls! Fellas, fellas! Let's be sensible, now. No use losing our tempers. Now let's all go over to the *Washington* Memorial … the big spire over *there*. And let's try to keep together this time.'

The Pentagon's MODULOG program is making things worse. Ideally the computer team would feed in data about concentrations of rioters (number, race, armament, deployment) and the computer would automatically dispatch the right number and kind of troops to deal with it. But in practice the machine doesn't seem to be listening.

Troop, police and supply movements are getting snarled. Paratroops are dropped for no special reason in Chesapeake Bay. One Marine unit hits the beach in Baltimore; a CBW unit is reassigned over thirty times, each time to a different random location – they never even have time to unpack their assortment of sophisticated gases. Contradictory orders follow one another like machine-gun bullets; one tank command spends the whole riot ruining the lawn of the National Gallery as they roll around in circles …

There are jurisdictional disputes caused by MODULOG's erratic assignments: the Army and the Virginia National Guard claim the same turf … the MPs have to move in on both of them with gas-firing tanks to prevent an intra-service war.

A lone sniper has barricaded himself in the top of the Washington monument. The police call up with a bull-horn asking him to give give give himself give himself himself up himself up up up. He is variously indentified as a Negro, a Chinese, Indian, Soviet ambassador, anarchist, etc.

The Klan catch six White Shirts still in blackface from the parade. As it happens, there are six lampposts right handy.

'Please! No! Wait, you've got us wrong. We're white as you are!'

'Haw haw, this black son bitch gone try tell me he's white, Rufe, you heah that? Haw haw – Arrrgh!'

The Grand Goblin falls forward, a fire arrow quivering in his back. War whoops. A band of Iroquois descend from their lair on the high steel of a nearby construction site. In a minute, it's all over but the scalping. After the Indians leave, Negro children roll the living and the dead. The Iroquois have already taken the sheets, but there are a few credit cards … They pause to wave at a boy in uniform, riding in on a boxcar …

Bronze-chinned soldiers scour the city for pederasts. A boy scout is leading a blind man across the street, taking his hand. An armored car pauses to mow down the pair with heavy machine-gun fire, then moves on, broadcasting:

'Keep in your homes! There is nothing to worry about, the situation is under control!'

Inside, the atmosphere is stifling. The corporal shuts off the amplifier and asks, 'Lootenant, we got any more Pepsi?'

'Naw, wait'll we stop for gas. Not this station here, the next on the right. They give double green stamps.'

The incipient queer-fears of lawmen have by now been fully aroused. Twenty Klansmen are surrounded, Plunked and kicked to emasculinity. (*Plunk*: a new riot-control gas which paralyses the victim's limbs but leaves him fully conscious and capable of feeling intense pain. 'A cop's dream' says the *American Law Enforcement Bulletin*.) A carload of Daughters of the American Legion, out slumming, are arrested as drag queens and subjected to interesting humiliations.

'My good man, do you realize *who* I am?'

Nasty laugh. 'No I don't, tooty-frooty, but I'm sure gonna find out.' Tries to pull away her blue-rinsed hair, gives up when some of the scalp comes up. The cops take them back to the new detention center on the Mall, where they can 'put on a little show, like you done at the Fadeout Club'.

'There's one of 'em! Get the bastard!' Virginia state troopers pile out of their cars and chase Cardinal Homer across the lawn of his residence. Ten Knights of Columbus try to fight a rearguard action with blunt sabers; a few cops stop to slap the cuffs on them and haul them off as pimps.

The main body are almost within grabbing distance of his streaming red cloak when a platoon of Mafia gorillas step out from the bushes and lay down a withering crossfire: Thompson submachine-guns, captured army automatic rifles, magnum-style Italian assassination guns …

'You okay, fadda? Anybody else gets smaht wit ya, you just tell Big Fats, and I'll lean on 'em a little.'

Frustrated pilots slew around in the sky, now and then popping a Skybolt at some fishing boat off the coast … Each pilot's worried sick he might be queer and not know it …

'Now let's see, what's that unidentified craft down there? Looks like a Russian trawler to me … so what if they've disguised it as the Presidential yacht … well I'm a happippily mumarried man, two great kikids … DIE, RUSSIAN SPY SHIP! … so what if there was that time in flight school, nobody knows about that …'

Zionist students picket the Arab embassies, as usual blaming these poor oil billionaires for everything. The Arabs cower inside, stoned to inertia. Their flowing robes, the way they reek of *kif*, makes the Marine Guards sick.

'For two cents I'd turn this machine-gun around the other way. I mean, here we are, guarding a buncha pansies …'

'I know how ya feel, kid. But we're pertecting our oil inneress – on the other hand, who'd know it was us? – Here's a nickel, kid. Have an orgy.'

They pick up their weapons and stroll inside, through the elaborate mosaic hallway. 'You take this end, I'll take that one. But fer Chrissakes, kid, don't shoot up the harem. Might come in handy later …'

The President's evacuation plan is readied. He is to take the underground passage to Blair House, then helicopter from the roof to the submarine *Scampi* waiting in the mouth of Delaware Bay.

Everybody has a plan for getting the nut down from the Washington monument. The cops want to rush up the stairs and just take him. The Marines, traditionalists ever, want to use mortars with white phosphorus or mustard gas. The Navy put out feelers about shelling it from a battleship offshore, but nobody's buying.

Up in the monument, the sniper picks off two more civil servants, raising his score to 48. He has his own loudhailer:

'Listen to me, down there! You have all failed to make a distinction somewhere. Drop your weapons one and all, and come up here with your hands up! By the way, can anyone tell me why the Little Moron wore a condom when he went whaling?'

The Pentagon is defended by National Guardsmen from five states, Federal troops and Federal marshals equipped with the latest in chemical sprays, including Plunk, Mace and Mush (*Mush* sends the victim into an acute panic and at the same time causes behavior to become automatic and repetitive. He begins to run away and is usually found some ten or fifteen miles away, dead of heart failure).

Inside, specially-flown-in teams of experts are looking over the computer to find out what's wrong with it. A dozen men in suits with IBM shoulders stand around the big round table in the War Room going over schematics.

Brigadier General Garner, acting chief of staff, sticks his head in. 'About through with our table, gentlemen? The battle-board's under all your papers there, and we can't get a thing done without it.'

'We've hit a snag, General. George here was just saying it might be the step-up of the differentiable multiplex write-in analyzer, but the rest of us opt for improved multi-scan facilities and a new software package.'

'That so?' The general closes the door, feeling old. He stops a white-coated technician coming out of the computer room. 'You tell me, boy, in plain English. Can our brain be saved?'

'Couldn't tell you, sir. I just stopped by for coffee; I'm not in this department.'

'Not a computer man, son?'

'No, sir. My job is feed birth pills to the pigeons, on the roof.'

The lobotomized Soviet official goes beserk in the supermarket, hauls out a huge Russian automatic and begins spraying the place with lead. The manager comes over to reason with him.

'Look, you can't act like that in here! You'll drive all my customers away! What the hell's wrong with you, anyway?. Who's gonna pay for that display of canned peaches, 4¢ off this week?'

A dying shopper groans in delirium:

'And gimme a package of stainless steel razor bl ...'

'He was afraid he might catch Moby Dick!' screams the bull-horn from the top of the Washington obelisk.

'We could do it easy,' says the Navy man. 'A couple shots to get the range, then POW!'

At that moment, Students for Chairman Fat solve all problems in dealing with him: they crash a stolen truckload of explosives into the base of the monument.

*

The Capitol is ringed with three cordons of battle-tested paratroopers and an outer wall of more expendable types. At first no one tries the bayonet wall. Then a large contingent of HOMODRAFT rush in, while American Nazis stand by ready to spit on either side. Anti-papists charge, waving contraceptive devices and screaming for the blood of Guy Fawkes. Down the Mall come a hundred Students for Chairman Fat, screaming Chinese syllables insanely and swinging their placards ('WHY DIE, G.I.?' 'FAT IS OUR BROTHER' and 'FOLLOW THE CROWDS TO FOOK HING CHINESE LAUN- DRY'). From the rear of the Capitol come a horde of Black Nationalists in African costume, Black Claw of Islam brothers in leather jackets and shades, and the Iroquois. From the North come Klux, White Shirts, and the Organiza- tion for the Rights of Gentile, Anglo-Saxon Man, beefed up with a few hefty Daughters of the American Legion (in the front ranks for a spearhead attack). From the South come Zionists, anarchists, Knights of Columbus and Cosa Altra (the boys have been got together), young Communists of sixty and old of ninety, vigilantes, cops on strike, looting antique dealers after a bit of Americana, motorcycle hoods on bikes, the Peace Love Acid World Peace Society (who have no idea what they are here for) and a large auxiliary of aging pachucos in pink shirts and pegged pants (who are just waiting for some wise soldier to bump their shoulders or call their mother a name).

The Nazis' eyes gleam; they work up their biggest gobs of spit. At the last possible second, when it looks as if everyone is going to impale themselves on bayonets, a team of lost helicopters comes over, spraying out a ton and a half of defoliants. The thick mist descends; everyone is too busy lying flat and fighting for breath to fight anyone else.

One brave soldier manages to stand his post, coughing and sputtering. As a final gesture he bayonets a figure charging toward him in the mist – it's Senator Vuje, who's been trying to get in (to use the Senate toilet) for hours.

The cherry blossoms are falling.

Looting and arson spread to all quarters of the city. Weary firemen have just put out a department store for the second time and are packing away their hoses and trophies when a flame-throwing tank comes by and gets it all going again.

'Aw, fuck this,' says one firefighter. 'I been to so many fires today already my boots hurt – all full of transistor radios and watches and stuff.'

'Our battle plan has several options,' General Garner explains to his staff. '1. Contain the riot without attempting a showdown, erect barriers, then slash and burn out the corruption. 2. Divide the city into sectors, then go in and clean it out a sector at a time. 3. Level unimportant sectors of the city with artillery and/or bombing, defoliate, then napalm the corruption. 4. Evacuate the President and key congressmen (the Hawk list), evacuate our boys, then *nuke* the joint! I favor number 4, as the way to expend least effort and men for maximum results.'

At that moment a flash message comes in: IT'S OVER.

Garner slugs the messenger and dials the Operations Room himself. 'What the hell do you mean, "It's over"?'

'That's right, General. All units report their sectors are pretty well under control. Just mopping up, sir.'

'And the rioters?'

'Looks like they just tired of it and went home.'

TWENTY-THREE

Wes Davis sat up in bed.

'A nigger plot!'

'You all right, chief?' One of his lieutenants came towards him.

'Stayawaystayaway!'

'Sure, Wes. Anything you say.'

Another man stood up in the shadowy end of the room. 'It's only us, Wes. Skeeter and Travis.'

Wes held up a trembling hand. 'Don't come no closer! Turn on a light so's I can see you, boa.'

Skeeter turned on a light. It was dead quiet in the hotel room. The faint woodpecker sound of a machine-gun, twenty floors below, competed with Wes's cautious breathing – his two friends held theirs.

'Guess I had a bad dream. Is it – all over down there?'

'No sir. Looks bad, Wes.' Skeeter two-fingered his pack of Luckies up from his shirt pocket, flicked one into the air and caught it in his mouth. 'Looks like the nigras is taking over.'

Just say that again, mister, and I'll have your guts hanging on the Christmas tree.' A chair scraped in the adjoining room. 'Who's in there?'

'Nobody, Wes. Just some of the boas. Oh yeah, and a couple Secret Service agents. They said they got to pertect you cause you're a presidential candidate. I guess they already evacuated the President.'

'Get them OUT! And bring everybody else in HERE.'

Wes stood up and gripped the bottom edge of his denim jacket, to steady himself. His knees didn't feel too good. When the group of White Shirts filed in, he looked hard at every face. 'Line 'em up over there.'

'FALL IN AT ATTENTION!'

'All right, men.' Wes began to pace, avoiding certain configurations in the carpet pattern. 'We know who's with us and who's agin *now*, don't we? Like the Klan. Look what they did to Merle and them boas. You know why? I'll tell you.

'*Because under them fancy hoods, the Ku Klux Klan is nothing but a bunch of full blood niggers!*'

'Sir?'

'I know it's hard to believe, but there's no other explanation.

Besides, I got *proof*. Documentary evidence that the Klan numbers among its members no fewer than fifty coal-black leaders! I got their names right here!'

What he waved was the hotel menu, but since his men were all at attention, they couldn't gaze directly at it. He paced the entire pattern three times, then turned to face them again.

'I'll tell you something else I know. *I know there is a nigger in this very room, passing for one of us!*'

Everyone jumped.

'Is it me, Wes?' 'Who is it, Wes?' 'A real nigger?' ''Tain't me, is it, Wes?'

'SHUT UP AND GET BACK TO ATTENTION!'

Pete Willis, a sickly smile on his narrow head, stepped forward. 'Is it me, Wes?'

'Yep. It purely is, Pete. But I'm not letting anyone take *my* word for it. I'm going to show you all scientific proof!'

Wes strode over and grabbed a handful of Pete's thick blond curls. '*First*, kinky hair!'

'But Wes, I ain't—'

Without warning, Wes threw his hardest punch. The taller man staggered back, blinking. Blood spurted from his nose.

'*Second*, no bone in his nose!'

At a signal, someone laid a piece of pipe across the small of Pete's back. As he fell to his knees, his hands went out instinctively. Wes seized one and held it bent back, thumb in the palm to keep the fingers fanned. '*Third*, take a look at them fingernails. *Purple fingernails are a scientific proof of black blood.*'

The men all looked, imagining purple in Pete's quite ordinary fingernails.

'Take this nigger and throw him out the window. I MEAN RIGHT NOW!'

They obeyed. Wes turned away and pretended to study a wall map. Not that he didn't want to watch it. It was just that he had a little smile to hide. The whole fingernail business had been a ruse, but with a purpose.

It stood to reason the niggers would have put more than one spy among his key officers. And only a fool could have not noticed how many men, as soon as he mentioned purple fingernails, *looked at their own hands!*

*

It was nearly dawn, and still no one stirred in the headquarters of Cumminism. But it was a cinch that Pé had to come out of there sometime.

It was a cinch they had to go away sometime. It was still the same car, the same people. That meant they were working alone. For the time being no one else knew they were working on the case. Whenever they left to get a meal, he'd be ready.

Fouts settled his crinolines about him, peeled an Almond Joy, and watched the Early Bird movie, *Blowup*.

At dawn, Grover noticed for the first time Amy's new glasses. Their pearly frames gave a softness to her sleeping face, and brightened her lovely eyes when she awoke.

Or maybe it wasn't the glasses at all. He leaned toward her, feeling the warmth of her leaning toward him … it wasn't hard, in this fresh light, to pretend they were kids again … in Dad's car …

His elbow brushed the radio button.

' … tional emergency. President Reagan has already been evacuated from the city. There is a strong possibility that if the riot is not brought under control by noon, General Weimarauner will call for artillery and bombing.

'Now I'll turn you over to Bill Burgens, who I think is somewhere by the banks of the Potomac. Bill?'

' … noise down here is terrific, Dave … you hear is the … playing *Dixie*. The whole city seems to have gone mad, and even the Army doesn't seem to … from where I'm standing I can see the whole shopping district ablaze, that's about … miles away, so you can imagine … and here come two soldiers carrying a color TV set. I guess they confiscated it from looters, but it's hard to … and say, here's a lady whose entire family was killed by a grenade. Husband, brother, and … how many children was it, ma'am?'

'Yes.' A tiny, exhausted voice.

'How many was it? Four or five?'

'Four or five, what difference does the number—?'

'And how do you feel about this, ma'am? I'll bet you just feel terrible, don't you? Must be a great shock.'

Grover switched it off. 'We're too late, Amy. It's the end!' Tears ran down the tributaries under his eyes. Shaking his fist at the building, he screamed, 'You win, Russky! You win, JOE STALIN AND BENEDICT ARNOLD!'

'Grover, we still have What's In The Safe.'

He thought about it a moment, regaining his natural color. 'What a grand idea, Amy. They may get us in the end, but meanwhile we'll blow that traitor soldier and all his secret codes and radios to *aitch ee double toothpicks*!'

It was the first time he'd ever sworn or cursed in front of her, and Amy realized what a strain Grover must be under.

'But how can we go and get What's In The Safe?' she asked. 'Our quarry might fly.'

'Don't you worry,' he said. 'It isn't really in the safe at all, *it's right here in the car*! I moved it yesterday – had a feeling it might come in handy!'

And so saying he hugged her till she gasped, and grinned so hard she thought his dentures would explode in her face.

The two little sisters of the Amish conferred over their patient.

'I've seen a lot of labors,' said Sister Mary Jane firmly, 'and that woman isn't having a baby.'

'But how can you be sure? Maybe with big people it's different.'

Without going into physical details, which she could not delicately do, Sister Mary Jane could not explain. 'There's no – dilation,' she said finally. 'Nothing at all. What's more, I have a feeling that woman is dying.'

'Dying! We must save the child!'

'Impossible. A Caesarian without instruments? What'll I use, a steak knife?'

'Nothing is impossible with God, little sister,' said the older woman patronizingly. 'However, *there is one alternative we haven't mentioned.*'

'Luckily we've brought a syringe.'

The hijacker introduced himself as Vladimir Barnes, a Soviet agent. Bert and Marilyn tried once more to explain it to him: there just wasn't enough fuel to get to Cuba. Hal, the pilot, showed him the fuel guages and some calculations.

'That's all we have, honest, mister. About enough to get us as far as Atlanta – with a lot of luck. Cuba's just too far away! Why didn't you grab a plane going to Miami?'

The hijacker stopped smiling. 'I'm not accountable to you!' he snapped. 'Fly the damned plane to Cuba and no excuses!'

Bert tried again. 'Look, we'll make you a deal. We're almost over Washington now. Let us set down there, and we'll forget all about that gun – and everything you said. What could be fairer than that?'

'CUBA!'

'But you could hijack another plane out of Washington ...'

'I GOTTA BE IN HAVANA BY TONIGHT!'

Marilyn wept, leaning her forehead against Bert's wings. 'Are we really out of fuel?' she whispered.

'Yeah. We've been circling Washington for an hour already. I don't know whether this guy's stupid or just nuts.'

Vladimir Barnes wondered if the crew were stupid or just nuts. Clearly they were unused to taking orders. How to make them understand that he had to be in Havana by eight p.m.; that he had no money to get on another flight? But they would probably offer him money, and then, after they were safe on the ground, turn him in to the authorities. No, there was no way but to make them press on southward.

For months he had been hanging around Minneapolis trying to get a lead on a certain CIA man, of whom Barnes knew only that he was a chess player and an assassin. Now, at the last moment, he learned the CIA man was in Cuba, and within hours of assassinating one of the most valuable men in the world – the Albanian naturalist, Prof. Aa, a chess Grand Master.

At eight o'clock, in the ballroom of the Hotel Hoy No Hay in Havana, the finals of the Communist International Chess Tournament would begin. It was there (if Barnes's information was correct) that the CIA man would try to murder Aa – thus destroying Albania's chess prestige in the eyes of the world.

The plan was simple: Aa always opened with the 'Albanian Defense' opening, moving the queen's knight first. Knowing this, the CIF man would have substituted for the piece a tiny, live, envenomed seahorse.

Diabolical! Vladimir Barnes shuddered to think of the scene in the ballroom if he should not arrive in time …

Prof. Aa, an enormous, beef-colored man with white cropped hair, sits down with difficulty. The gilt chair keeps trying to skid away from under his roundness. The other man, 'Air CIA', whose face is featureless, makes a pretense of being finicky. He must adjust all the pieces and dust them off before the game commences. And makes the sinister substitution. He has drawn black. Now, polite and expressionless, he waits for Aa to begin.

How did CIA get here? He is himself a chess genius. Some months ago, he slipped into the Soviet Union and entered the first playoffs. Calculating each step, he deliberately draws a game or two to put himself in different 'rounds' – moving inexorably up the long branched chain of games to face Aa in the finals.

Aa punches the clock. His pink sausage fingers hover over the queen's knight – but then perhaps chooses a conventional king's pawn opening.

CIA is in trouble. He must now quickly force the master to move that knight. Already it is beginning to wilt – will it still be standing and alive in four or five moves?

The game draws on; the: knight continues to wilt. Other players at other tables are taking the full time limit over their moves; not so the CIA man. Aa moves quickly, too, confident by now that he is up against a rank amateur. The idiot seems to be offering piece after piece for the taking, without gaining any any visible advantage.

Finally, on the eighth move, CIA offers his queen to the Albanian's knight. Aa hesitates. Can this be a trick? He runs through the possibilities like a

327

computer sorting punched cards. Finally, too bored to go on, he seizes the knight.

'Aa!'

The gilt chair goes over, skidding across the parquet to clatter against a potted palm. Aa leaps to his feet holding the wriggling knight up to the light.

'Hippocampus …' he muses, and sprawls across the board.

Then CIA – does what? Pretends concern? Tries to slip away? Draws a gun and shouts (unnecessarily, to the roomful of immobile, engrossed men), 'Nobody move!'

Marilyn sighed. 'Guess there's only one thing to do.' Unbottoning her uniform jacket, she walked toward the muzzle of Barnes's gun.

'Mr Barnes, I want to make a deal with you. If you'll let us land in Washington …'

When she was fully naked except for her cap the hijacker grinned again, showing his full pink gums. 'A good idea, miss. I won't guarantee anything … but we'll see.' He started unhooking his cummerbund – an easy job, for it was turned around back to front.

'But, Wes, we known old Travis a *long time*. Hell, he was our old buddy in Mud Flats.'

'Skeeter, you just shut your mouth and throw that body out the window. He was a nigger and you know it.'

'But Wes! We done kilt near the whole general staff of the White Shirt organization. Ain't nobody left now but you and me. Are you sure they was *all* niggers?'

'No back talk, Skeeter!' Wes picked up his automatic. 'Else I might get to wondering why *you* are such a stubborn, nigger-loving son bitch.'

And of course he was wondering that already.

The battle of Dresden was going badly. Blücher had hoped to regroup his forces while Napoleon was otherwise occupied, but the wily Frenchman had turned twice from Dresden to engage him. He did this without little hope of victory, however, and its effect was nil. Napoleon had fought two indecisive battles and was weakened, while Blücher was as strong as ever.

'Grid-phone call, sir. Pentagon. Will you take it in the summer-house?'

'Unh?' With effort, Weimarauner wrenched himself out of the character of Napoleon (a lead figure, two inches high, leaning over a postage-stamp map inside a tent the size of a toy drum) and into the character of Chief of Staff. 'Oh, fine.'

As he strode across the artificial landscape, stepping here and there to avoid an army, the wind snapped his robe and silk pajamas. The summer-house was fragrant with climbing flowers, and translucent brown bees nudged among them. It was the general's favorite spot. He sat down and pushed the scrambler button on his grid-phone. A weak, blocky line drawing of Brigadier General Garner appeared on the screen.

'Sir, what the hell is going on? How come you shoved this pansy outfit in here on us? Them Pink Brassieres are only making things worse around here.'

'What seems to be the trouble?'

'Sir, they make me *sick*, that's what's the trouble! They make *everybody* sick!'

Weimarauner opened an icebox under the table and probed it. He removed a mango yoghurt and made a leisurely breakfast. When he had finished, he fitted a cigarette to his holder, lit it, and leaned back to contemplate once more the grid-screen. 'General Garner, you know that that is the idea. They do indeed make everybody sick. Like a gas.'

'Yeah? Well everybody is tearing the shit out of them.' The features of the line drawing tried a placating smile. 'Sir, I'm not complaining. I know these – boys – are supposed to be good psychological warfare. Only they're getting massacred, and my men are bitching about having to help them out.'

Weimarauner waved, dismissing both Garner and a bee that was investigating the yoghurt dish. 'All right, all right. Get some of the boys to draft some orders. We'll send them out to Southeast Asia – to whatever enemy we're fighting out there right now. By container freight of course.'

'Of course, sir. By the way, Jarmoss of the computer department wants a word with you urgently.'

'Switch me over to him, will you?'

In a moment the screen drew an approximate sketch of worried Col Jarmoss. The sine waves in his forehead and the parentheses around his tight mouth were a trifle blocky – the grid screen worked only in verticals and horizontals – but nevertheless stood very well for Jarmoss's typical distressed expression.

There was no particular reason to communicate by grid-phone with his subordinates, but Weimarauner liked it that way. It was nice not to have to deal with them as humans. No matter how personable they tried to be – and none tried harder than Jarmoss – they remained so many little crude drawings, little animated cartoons.

'How's the battle of Dresden going, sir?'

'Fine, Colonel, fine.' Weimarauner looked out the vine-bordered doorway, across the landscape lawn. Every detail of the landscape around Dresden had been faithfully copied at a scale of 1:36. The earth had been replaced with plastic, the grass was nylon plush. Japanese dwarf trees stood at proportional heights, in their proper positions. The model Germans were defending their town with cannon the size of cigars.

'I got that piece of land I needed for the river area,' he said in no hurry to hear the colonel's complaint. 'You'll be happy to know.'

The drawing tried to smile. 'That's lucky, General.'

'Yes, luck and aggressive thinking, the marks of a good military man. The farmer didn't want to sell. I finally requisitioned his farm in the interests of National Security. It is, too. My work here may not seem it, but it *is* in the interests of National Security, all of it.'

'Yes sir. Now about—'

'You believe that, don't you, Colonel?'

'Oh, yessir. Sir, we've got a few problems here … by the way, we've ordered the Pink Barrettes to Southeast Asia, as you requested.'

'Fine, fine. What's the problem?'

'Our computer has been fouling up something awful. Operation Modulog is in one hell of a mess. The trouble seems to be in the tape unit …'

'Spare me the technical details, Jarmoss. I'm an eighteenth-century man. Do whatever needs to be done. Get a new tape unit or whatever.'

'Yes sir. Another thing: a couple dozen civilians came around earlier, asking about the tape. Some kind of legal thing. I told them to come out and see you about it, sir, since we're not authorized to talk about the Müller-Fokker tape. I hope you'll let them have it, sir. We're sick of it.'

'Very unwise, Colonel. I hate hacking about with legal nonsense.' He broke the connection and went back to Dresden.

Later the platoon of lawyers showed up. Most of them represented MacCormick Hines, president and owner of the National Arsenamid Corporation. One of them represented a Mr Robert Etwall Shairp.

'I'm serving you with this writ of *habeas corpus*, General, and demanding that my client be released.'

'Gladly, gladly. But I've never heard of your client. Robert Etwall Shairp? Is he a prisoner taken in the Washington conflict? A soldier?'

'No, General. The pink tape you are using in one of your Pentagon computers,' said the lawyer. 'That is my client.'

Spot seated himself in that portion of the Capitol lawn that was shaped like a keystone. After making sure he was unobserved, he unscrewed the lid of a can of gas and poured it over himself.

The riot was about over; the cops were getting back into their bus. Spot struck a match, but the drops of gasoline running down his hand put it out.

A tall man in Indian beads stepped from behind a tree. His face, a palimpsest of scars, showed no surprise at seeing a gasoline-soaked boy lighting a match.

'We know few quail before lunch,' he said.

'I'm killing myself.' Spot tore out another match. 'In protest against Mom and Dad.' He struck it.

Wise Bream acted instinctively at the sight of the flame. Hauling out Baal, he quenched it with an enormous stream.

The cop who spotted the pair screamed 'Get 'em! Get those goddamned protesters!'

The first of the five cops grabbed Spot and dragged him away. 'Impersonating an officer, eh, kid? You oughta get life for this.'

The other four closed in on Wise Bream.

'I'm gonna kill this bastard pervert, Charlie! Did you *see* him? Pissing on a kid!'

'Pissing nothing, he was tryna get the kid to suck him off.'

They sprayed Mace in his eyes and then took turns kicking at the offending organ.

'I'm too pooped to keep this up, Sarge, whadya say we just shoot him?'

'Oh no. I wanna see this fucker get the chair. Pissing on the uniform!'

They handcuffed him. Two of them stuck a nightstick between his wrists and holding opposite ends of it dragged him away.

'Hold it.' The cop called Charlie leaned over the unconscious prisoner, nose to nose with him. 'You're under arrest,' he said. 'I have to warn you that anything you say can be used against you, that you don't have to say anything if you don't want to, that you're entitled to counsel, and that if you can't afford a lawyer, the District of Columbia will pay for one.'

Laughing and nudging each other, they dragged him on toward the detention camp.

Bert the copilot had timed in on local newscasts. He was no longer interested at all in Marilyn Temblor, not after seeing the way she *gave herself to* that Commie spy. Disgusting! Worst of all, it hadn't worked. The bastard kept them all covered all during it, and afterward he just zipped up his pants, adjusted his cummerbund, and said, 'On to Cuba, gentlemen.'

'We're not going anywhere,' said Hal. 'We've got about ten minutes' fuel. It's too late to even try for an airport now. I'm taking her down.'

'I'll be damned!' Bert adjusted the earphones. 'The President's missing!'

'*… was to have taken off by helicopter from the roof of Blair House and proceeded directly to the submarine* Scampi. *But the* Scampi *reports they have not yet arrived. "We did see one helicopter pass by us about two miles north and head on out to sea," says the skipper, "but I can't see why they didn't signal us on the radio, if it was them."*'

'Forget about that crap!' Hal shoved his copilot. 'We've got to crash-land this mother, and *now*!'

*

Sister Maria said the words; while Sister Mary Jane shoved the syringe, full of water, up the pregnant woman's dress. The rest of the passengers crowded around offering advice.

'Not that way, sister, you'll give her an enema.'

'I thought a baptism had to have the same one saying the words …'

'She's just squirting it up the front of her dress …'

'What's that coming out – *mud*?'

The hump of 'pregnancy' shifted slightly. Ash and water poured out over the floor, and, a moment later, a silver urn, stamped with the *Stagman* symbol, slipped down out of the front of her dress and rolled away.

A stewardess, naked but for her uniform cap, ran through, announcing an emergency landing. 'Will everyone please fasten their seatbelts?'

'I'm dreaming,' said someone. 'This probably has something to say to me, some personal symbolism. Wait'll I tell Feinwelt!'

Ignoring him, Feinwelt led the group in singing to keep up their spirits. Christmas carols – the only songs he knew – worked their magic as the plane went into a dive and the silver urn clattered on forward.

'Oh what fun it is to ride …'

'Use the goddamned radar, Bert! I can't see how the hell high up we are.'

'Screw you. Everybody gives me orders around here. If you're such a hot-shot pilot, *you* land the plane.'

The figures ahead cast long morning shadows: trees, tents, motionless men … from the passengers he heard

Don we now our gay apparel …

as the men and trees fled past at incredible speed, too fast for a landing, too fast …

Among the motionless, listening figures of quaint soldiers stood a giant bedroom slipper. Above it, the giant face of Weimarauner arranged itself in the appropriate expression, ironic surprise.

The detention center on the Mall was a rectangle of snarled barb-wire. It was said the guards would let you talk to the prisoners across this barrier, for a price.

'Affirmative,' said a guard whom Mac Hines approached. 'The price is a grand a minute.'

'A thousand dollars a minute? Isn't that a little steep?'

'You look like you wouldn't miss it too bad. Besides, it isn't for me. It all goes to my favorite charity. Make out your check to the Red Cross.'

'All right. Good way to run a charity drive, at that. But why the Red Cross?'

'I don't know … they've been pretty darn nice to us guys here in no-man's land. I mean, they kept the coffee and donuts coming right on through the thick of the fighting ... and at rock-bottom prices, too!'

In the end, Mac managed to ransom Spot altogether out of the place, though he had to take Spot's friend, too. The friend was a great hulking moron who alternately mumbled incomprehensible statements and wet his pants. From a return ticket in his pocket they identified him as 'W. Bream', so it was only natural to call him Willy.

'I'll tell you a secret, Spot,' said Mac as they climbed into the limousine. 'That big bundle in the corner there is your Mom. She's frozen now, but when she thaws out, I'm going to marry her! Won't that be splendid?'

Spot concentrated on a blister on his thumb and said nothing.

Fouts awoke to a noisy kiddie show and realized it was Saturday morning. He started on the candy bars, a bite of this, a bite of that, mixing and melting peppermint cream, smooth fudge and crunchy peanuts, bittersweet and milk chocolate, slick marshmallow, toasted almonds, crisp coconut, honeyed toffee and dark caramel so sweet it hurt going down. 'I'm unhappy,' he thought, 'and alone.' But it was an abstract idea, unrelated to the pure sugar joy of living. A bite of this, a bite of that ... and after awhile he began to laugh along with Bill the Cat and Mary the Canary.

'If we're gonna do it, Amy, we better do it quick,' Grover whispered. They sat in the basement of the building, huddled together on an old mattress where, for an hour, they had been discussing the pros and cons of assassination. Obviously the man deserved it – but was it *wrong*?

'All we gotta do is set the fuse – takes half an hour – and scram out of here. I don't see what the problem is!'

'Maybe if we ... went with him ...'

'What do you mean?'

'Oh Grover, I'm *old*. I've had my life, such as it was. And maybe it wouldn't be *murder* so much if we ... didn't scram out of here.'

Grover thought it over. 'Okey-dokey, Amy. We'll do it your way. Who wants to live in a Red Chinese America anyhow?'

He set the fuse and they sat back in the darkness, leaning together without deliberately touching.

'What time is it?'

His radium dial flashed. 'We got twenty minutes.'

When his hand descended again, it rested on her knee. A moment later it moved up a little; and again.

'Grover! What are you doing?'

'Sshh, Amy,' he whispered hoarsely, 'Amy, you can't refuse a dying man's request.'

'But I thought ... you didn't want to.'

'I *can't*, usually. This time it's different.'

They ripped off each other's clothing and began moving over each other smoothly and gracefully as if it were the most natural thing in the world – which to Grover's way of thinking, it was not.

Upstairs there was a news flash.

'Ladies and gentlemen, the President of the United States is dead. The wreckage of his helicopter *Little Beaver* has been found. There are no visible survivors, and a denture has been picked up which the President's dentist identified as the President's denture, with indentations indicating dental ...'

The blast actually drove them into the concrete below, but it seemed to be lifting and opening them, so that they never knew whether death or ecstasy suddenly spilled the universe into their upright souls.

The firemen found them long after they found Fouts (headless, hanging out of the TV set as if he'd been trying to get into the picture) under a heap of shattered boxes and their contents: great mounds of nylon and bright silk and lace, sparkling sequins, taffeta petticoats, ribbons and rhinestones and rouge.

TWENTY-FOUR

'But you did say you'd do *anything* if your husband were restored to you.' Mac drummed on his desk blotter.

The figure in the blanket sneezed. Mac took it for a nod.

'Well then, I'm going to return him to you. In perfect condition. You can have say two weeks for a second honeymoon, and then I'd like for you to divorce him and marry me. I – er – love you – Marge.'

The figure made a sound very like a sarcastic, snorting laugh. 'This is fairy-tale crap. If you thawed me out just to torment me, Mr Hines ...'

'Then you don't believe I can restore your husband!' Mac pressed a button. 'Send in Dr Müller-Fokker, please.'

In the dim, distant corner of Mac's office a door opened. Beaming, a short, fat man in a sports shirt rushed across the noiseless carpet and seized Mac's hand. Marge, peering from the folds of the blanket, thought the little man was going to kiss the hand.

'Hines, you old scoundrel, what devilments are you embarked upon this time? No, no, don't tell me. Mine not to reason why, mine but to reason and accept my fee. Is this the unfortunate wife?'

'This is Mrs Shairp. Tell her, Doctor, how you plan to recover her late husband.'

'First let me say that I was uncontrollable, madam, when I learned of your sadness.'

Marge scrutinized his round face. 'You were supposed to have defected to Russia – anyway, you don't look like the picture in the newspaper.'

'Excellent memory!' Dr Müller-Fokker laughed Saint Nick fashion, holding his stomach and making a show of enjoying the joke of her excellent memory. 'I shaved off the beard, and the pince-nez have given way to the modern contact lenses. My defection was a sham; I have actually been working for the CIA. And during my stay in Havana, I also put on a few weights and obtained the sun tan. My real purpose there ... but enough of me. Let me tell you how we shall raise your beloved Lazarus:

'As you by now know, Mac has kindly collected all the pertinent tapes. I have examined them and am satisfied the restoration can be done. The first step is to locate the DNA code upon the tapes. With this we prepare a virus, with which the specimen can be infected.'

'Specimen?'

'Some volunteer. I had in mind your son's friend ...' He gestured out the window to where Spot and Willy were sailing a paper boat at the edge of Mac's private lake. 'The idiot is the correct size and general build – a little tall, perhaps ...'

'Stop it! You're making me sick! How can you stand there and talk of murdering ...'

'Not murder. Not murdering, madam. We prepare in advance a tape of the volunteer. And at the first opportunity ...'

'A game of musical bodies? No thanks.' Marge stood up suddenly, tripped in her blanket and fell. The two men gently helped her back to her chair.

'Hear him out, Marge, will you?'

'We infect the specimen with your husband's virus and then "let Nature take its course". We kill the virus when the proper physical state is achieved. There will be minor imperfections, some surgery ... and I am afraid your husband will always have severe dandruff ... but otherwise it remains only to do the forced brain growth—'

'Please stop it!'

'No, you do not understand. I mean like a lovely hothouse flower. *We force* the electrical—'

Marge fulfilled her promise to be sick.

She left without making any further promises. Mac called up dozens of times, but the phone was off the hook. Next day he sent a telegram:

YOU OWE IT TO YOUR HUSBAND. MY CONDITIONS ARE THE ONLY ONES UNDER WHICH YOU WILL EVER SEE HIM ALIVE. IT WOULDN'T BE SO BAD WITH ME, YOU KNOW. ILL DIE SOON AND YOULL BE A RICH WIDOW. I KNOW IM THE VILLAIN IN THIS FAIRY TALE BUT I CANT HELP IT. PLEASE REPLY IMMEDIATELY. OFFER EXPIRES MIDNIGHT. LOVE MAC.

A week later, she replied:

CONDITIONS AGREED TO BUT ONE CONDITION OF MY OWN. VOLUNTEER MUST BE MR BRADD. QUOTE LOVE UNQUOTE MARGE.

TWENTY-FIVE
The Door

... ... announcement: death plan. Trick Him into allowing me to be crucified as a sacrifice to Him; the realization that I'm His only son and heir will kill him. His heart.

Still fixed in my chair still crucified by my own teaching forefinger I run down the solidifying labyrinth, at each intersection another last act of another stale Passion play. The crown of horns explodes in the back of my head.

WHOMS [enters from stage right, hangs deerstalker on fender to dry, strikes posture]: If any man has free will at any particular instant, and assuming he has the physical means to do so, that man can at that instant commit any crime at all. Agreed?

WHATSON [nods]: Yes.

WHOMS [paces excitedly a peculiar labyrinth pattern in the carpet]: Then if there is at least one crime which some man cannot commit, at that instant he cannot be said to have free will. Finally, you could not tonight, genial physician, kill and dissect one of your patients, and therefore tonight at least you do not have free will. And that is but one example. There must be, for every man and for all time, some one criminal action which he cannot bring himself to do, and which therefore impedes his free will. I intend to prove that no man has ever had free will at all!

WHATSON [opens catch on his doctor bag and pulls out a string of meaty objects]: Not quite so elementary as all that, my dear Whoms.

WHOMS [examines objects while picking nose distractedly with one chemical-stained forefinger]:[6] These are ... ?

WHATSON: The uteri of six of my former patients.

WHOMS: Good Lord! Jack the Rip! Then it *was* Barbara and not Bocardo who – then *you* must be ...

WHATSON: Mad? Or God. Correct – that is, I am equipped with free will. Not one action of mine can be predicted with any degree of certainty whatever, Whoms. Surely that is what we've always meant by free will – by God – the unknowable, unpredictable, irrational, pointless, silly side of the universe.

[Curtain. On the curtain is depicted an incomplete and distorted table of the elements, the cells of which are also cartoon panels. The cartoons are detailed drawings of the entire play, and of all members of the audience and their reactions. The members of the audience are by coincidence all the people I have known in my life. Upon the curtain are projected a set of maps and views of Cafe Island. After a figure in silver tights and a flowing turquoise cape comes out and lectures at length upon the sacramental meaning of my life, the curtain rises again on a desert island scene. I am looking at a naked footprint.]

FRIDAY [sneaking up behind me]: That's your own, you know. I don't run around barefoot. Too much bloody hookworm about. [He wears neat summer suit, slim shoes, panama. I am of course naked.] You uncolored folk have your own childish preferences, of course. Well, I hope this exile has taught you a lesson, eh?

ME: Thass right, boss. Lemme go back and work in dem cotton feels. Thass where mah heart is turnin' – evah!

FRIDAY [as background changes]: And the gold mines?

ME: That is right with me, baas.

FRIDAY [as background changes]: And the oil fields, cur?

ME: Effendi!

FRIDAY [as background changes]: How about the stables, the kennels, the boiler rooms, the ham kitchens, the transistor factories, the coal orchards, the peanut distilleries, the jello dying vats, the suntan oil refineries?

ME: Bwana! Sahib! Colonel! Massa! Sir! Gummint fella! Kimo sabe! Chief! Lord! Anything-san!

GASPING MESSENGER [running in, gasping]: Mr Friday ... sir ... the whites ... they're ... they're revolting! [Dies.]

FRIDAY: Yes, but what news?

[BLACKOUT]

Mack and Mike, in baggy pants and huge bowties, stumble on stage and go

---

6 Nose-picking is the mark of an enquiring mind. Had Alexander Fleming been more fastidious, he could never have (summarizing his chain of research) 'Put in his thumb and pulled out penicillin.'

into long extemporaneous and meaningless routine. Unfunny throughout. Audience roars. A typical line:

MIKE [boffs him with rolled-up newspaper]: But seriously now, are we on tape? Is all this on tape, or is it real?

MACK: Yes, absolutely [pause for laugh].

MIKE [boffs – if that is the word for it – Mack again]: Yes, but which?

MACK: Is a tape reel? Is it in a real state, or the real estate of the mind? Is it aped? If bits of information in formation form real states of mind, *for real*, a stated news format may form new statements: 'If God bit man, that is not news, but obits. If man bit dog, that is newsreel. If newsman in mental state orbits, reels, reeling off in format information, good news, God knows.' Hound of heaven tapers into newshound in the reely real bit.

[Mike pummels him to appreciative roars. End of blackout, curtain rises on man in deck chair, picking nose, watching televised self as boy receives First Holy Communion. From time to time a steward comes past to give the man a newspaper (all references to the U----- S----- of A------ have been cut out) or the news that his son is dead.]

STEWARD: Your son is dead, sir.

MAN: Yes, yes, I know, the old Oedipus switchback thing. Now I'm free to marry his mother.

[On TV I kneel, close my eyes, put out my tongue for God. Old fat palsied Father O'C. makes few passes over the gold cup, comes up with a tiny dead hollyhock seed. Is this my body? The Word is on the tip of my tongue.

But not quite yet. First the doctor gets in there with a tongue depressor, the dentist has to do a little work while I'm strapped into the chair, the Customs man wants to see what kind of dope I'm carrying in a hollow tooth, behind them come cops, linguists, orthodontists, eye-ear-nose-and-throat special- ists, spelunkers, crowds of the curious and other cops to hold them back …]

MAN [switching it off with a yawn]: Wonder how things are getting along in old – Armorica is it?

[Dozes. Flash of dream in which Spot, his son, heaves rock at flame- throwing tank. Nazi soldiers crucify Spot. Marge, the man's wife, weeps beneath the crucifix. Now and then during her long speech of sorrow and demand for justice, which should be improvised, she slyly hauls on the boy's feet to add to his pain.]

STEWARD [waking him]: Your son Spot is dead, sir.

MAN: That's about the worst pun in this novel. Are the crew murmuring yet?

CREW: Why did we ever set sail to find the land of the Iructu? Why did we leave the comparative security of our homeland and set out on this silly quest? We'll fall off the edge of the sea! We'll drown among the plankton! We'll go broke! We'll get back and no one will believe us! Probably there aren't any Iructu anyway, and Iructria is a lot of hooey!

MAN [reappearing among the crew in the vestments of Father O'C.]: Boys, boys! As your spiritual adviser, I thought it was time we had a little chat. We're about to find and conquer a new and virgin land, fellas, and I think this is as good a time as any to remind you that contraception is murder.

CREW [begin to mill about, shouting slogans]:

Hey hey/whadya say/ how many kids did you kill today?

All the way! Whadya say? All the way! Etc.

MAN [reappearing among the crew as a condom salesman]: Buy me and stop one. [He is clapped in irons, reappears among the crew as Father O'C.] Because preventing a life *is* murder, and it contravenes Natural Law – just like building houses and brushing your teeth. I ... let us pray:

[The background, a process shot of calm sea, suddenly moves into the foreground, obliterating all, and becomes the leafing pages of *Eternity* magazine. In an ad for an airline that shows movies, Mack and Mike appear on the screen still boning. The audience laughter, we now realize, is directed not at them but scornfully at Mike's newspaper baton, a scandal sheet bearing the headline HE KILLS, CUTS UP, COOKS & EATS WIFE, INVITES HER FRIENDS TO DINNER. All references to the U----- S----- have been blacked out.]

MAN [in vaudeville audience in movie]: Barbecues his *wife*! Get it? Barbara, *not* Bocardo!

MAN [in airplane audience, watching movie]: Stewardess! Another plankton steak!

[The automatic pilot – the only pilot – has failed, and the stewardess is praying.]

STEWARDESS:

Tom Swift, help me

Casey Jones, guide me

Maelzel, let me win through

Azuma-zi, protect me

Daedalus, fortify me

Vulcan, arm me

Mr & Mrs Zero, sum my chances

Rossum, strengthen me

Hey, Lullay, etc.

MAN [in magazine article on facing page, reading ad]: I guess the idea is all these levels map each other or something, but Gee, why mess around with mapping? Cartoons on the curtains – why don't we get where we're going?

MAN [aboard ship, reading magazine]: Good idea. The detective all along has been shadowing himself, staking out his own house, bugging his own phone – but because *there isn't anyone else*. Good article. Now let's see what they have to say about the Iructu ...

VOICE OF FATHER O'C: Let us pray: Our hallowed thy thy on give. And as lead but deliver, not into those who father be kingdom will earth us forgive. We us evil temptation heaven name heaven our our art who done be in as in it is thy us us from this forgive come ...

[The Iructu are shown on the final page, being napalmed by an aircraft without markings. The caption under the picture is God's final message, variously interpreted as denial of all negatives, self-contradiction, a call to action.]

GOD: TO BE OR TO BE, THAT IS THE QUEST.

VOICE OF FATHER O'C: For the day daily against the power and and bread trespass ever debts forever debtors glory us amen and kingdom trespasses is the thing amen. Nema live morf su reviled tub ...

[God dies]

LOOKOUT: Land Ho!

[The ship has arrived at – the map of – Cafe Island.]

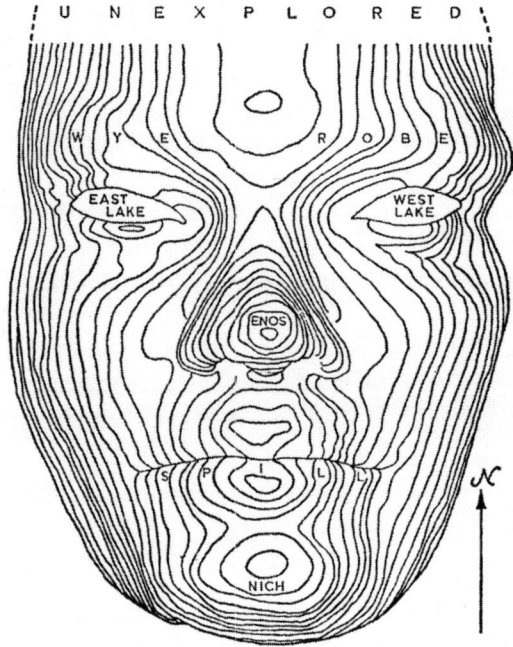

[As the ship closes on the island, the camera closes in on the plankton in the surrounding waves. They have selected 1940 as a target date for landing a plankton on the sun, which appears to hang just over the next wave.]

SPEECH BY FIRST PLANKTON ON THE SUN: It's a great honor and privilege for us to be here representing not only our own wave, but plankton of peace of all waves, plankton with interest and curiosity and plankton with vision for the future.

PART 5

Announcement: Haunted Experiment 'Man' Socks Benefactor

TWENTY-SIX

Spot wanted to know why he had to take a bath.

'Because your FATHER's coming home! After a YEAR! Don't you care anything about him?'

Spot wanted to know what the difference was, since she was only going to divorce him and marry Uncle Mac anyhow.

'THE DIFFERENCE IS – never mind. *Don't* take a bath, then.'

Spot took a bath and shined his shoes. Marge spilled a bottle of cologne on herself, and had to change into her second-best dress, which (she remembered as the doorbell rang) Bob loathed.

'Haven't got a key,' he said.

'You're – the wrong *size*.'

'I know. They couldn't do much about Bradd's bones, except around the face.'

'But I had all your suits cleaned!'

She started crying as he started laughing; they embraced awkwardly.

Spot came in, shook hands politely, and pointed out his shiny shoes. 'I learned that at school.'

'So you finally got to military school? Well. I guess a lot's happened. The divorce …'

'Do we have to talk about that?' Marge guided him to a chair as if he were crippled. Under the flesh of him she could feel Bradd's skeleton. 'I mean, it's all I could do.'

'Of course. Yep. Seems fair enough to me. Speaking as the beneficiary, of course.'

Marge laughed too hard.

Bob leaned back on the couch and tousled Spot's lack of hair.

'Well how's military school, you little Fascist?'

'Don't you call my son …'

'The term is one of affection, in case you've forgotten.'

The evening collapsed after the unexceptional dinner, when Spot left to see Willy.

'Who's Willy?'

'A friend of Spot's. Some kind of Indian. Seems like a moron, but ever since he saved Spot's life we've been looking after him. He's staying at the Fellstuses'.'

343

'Oh.'

'Dr Fellstus is trying to housebreak him.'

After a silence, she apologized about the dinner.

'Oh, it was fine. Really.'

'You don't have to—'

'No, really.'

After another silence, she asked, 'Did you – mm – *feel* anything?'

'Oh, you mean the charge that blew my head off? No, not a thing.' He grinned with Bradd's teeth. 'I didn't really die at all, you know. I had this *different* life. It was made up of, oh, this and that, old memories, odd thoughts. Kind of interesting.'

'What was it like?'

He sighed. 'Well, for instance I remembered this dream I'd had, the night before I went to Mud Flats. I call the dream

JELLY DAYS

'It's kind of a mixture of *Castle of Otranto* and *Turn of the Screw*. There are two peculiar quiet kids whose brother is dead, and there are some giant manifestations. One thing, the giant manifestations always imitate reality. I mean, a giant hand reaches through the window to grab somebody who's reaching into a cupboard to pick up something. And a giant toy plane flies in, and it flaps its wings because, out the window, you can see a gull flapping its wings. Someone around the house has the title Master in Lunacy.

'The kids have a lot of whispered conversations, but the only words I can distinguish are "jelly day (or days)". Then I go back to childhood and look into a miniature grocery store where some men are having a history argument. They mention a political event and at once I am there. An Italian political quarrel is the event. One man is supposed to be put to death in the restaurant kitchen: they mark his body off into ten zones and then shoot him in zone one, his head. If that wound heals, they shoot him in zone two, and so on, neck, chest ... The waiters all deny this plot, even the victim wants to hush it up.

'I discover I'm dead. I don't know how I know it, but I'm sure. Maybe I'm just talking to someone and suddenly realize they aren't listening.

'Death land is very pleasant, very ordinary. Everyone has to work at his former job, more or less. There seems to be a big demand for sociologists. The place looks like a kibbutz, very jolly and industrious and serious, well-equipped with wall charts.

'You can only communicate with the living through accidents or imitation. The dead know nothing, as the saying goes around there, and have no power to be anything. At last I begin to understand what "jelly day" means – just means the day one leaves one's mortal jelly.

'We gather in the cafeteria after dinner to sing songs and watch a TV play about the end of the world. In the play, the actors have to tune in on some special radio station to find out how to deal with the end of the world.

'Sitting there among all these suntanned ghosts, I begin to wonder about that special radio station. On a hunch I tune in my own radio to it, to catch the end-of-the-world news. But there's nothing on much, just the usual sloppy Melodiak tunes ... *Sunshine Balloon of Happiness*, and so on.

'Then I realize this *is* the news: ordinary life goes right on, palling, silly, disgusting, nice, unbearable – right on up to the last moment. As I realize this, I hear thousands of footsteps, a great jostling crowd coming downstairs to the cafeteria. The new people are arriving. It's everybody's jelly day.'

There was a long, long silence when Bob finished. He stood up. 'Guess I'd better get back to the hotel.'

The bell rang. Marge answered it.

'Uncle Mac! What are you doing here?'

'I've been watching you two,' he said. 'I'm – I'm the window peeper you've been worrying about.'

'What window peeper?' they asked together.

Mac did a strange thing. He hissed, then, out of the side of his mouth not visible from the living room window, he whispered, 'That's not your line, stupid. Ask me what I want. "What do you want?" Come on!'

'What *do* you want?' Bob asked.

'The deal's off, you'll both be happy to hear. I saw the two of you sitting here, Bob talking, Marge listening to his tale. You look so *right* together – so much a *family*. I just can't take that away from you. You see, we rich men ...' He turned to face the window and took a step toward it, ' ... we rich men lose touch sometimes with reality. With real, human emotions, with vibrant life. We think we can play God and push people around like piles of money.

'But all that's over, for me. I thought I could bribe you, Marge, into – well, into loving me. But now I see my own real happiness depends on yours, and you could never be happy without Bob. God bless you both, you'll hear no more of me now, except at the reading of my will.'

'Your will?'

'Which probably won't be long, now. The doctor tells me I have a very delicate heart. In fact I don't feel so well right now. If you'll excuse me, I – I'll be going now.'

'But wait! Shouldn't you sit down for a minute, or ...'

'I'd like to be alone for awhile. I'm – very tired.'

Gasping and clutching with a fluttering hand at his chest, Mac stepped outside. When he was just beyond the door, he dropped the pose, turned and winked.

'Do you think he meant it?'

'Search me.' Marge yawned. 'Stay here, at least for the night, why don't you? It is late. I'd better phone and find out what's keeping Spot.'

'You don't think anything could have happened to him, do you?'

Mac turned away from the window, satisfied with tonight's episode. The Shairp Family had no sooner settled everything with their kind old rich friend than Spot seemed to be in some kind of trouble. That might be a false alarm, but still, that 'Willy Bream' wasn't all he pretended to be.

More to the point, the rich old benefactor wasn't all *he* pretended to be. Perhaps his heart was sound as a dollar. Perhaps he was scheming some new trouble.

And what was Dr Fellstus really up to, with his separate cages (boy-sized and man-sized), his cattle-prods? Mac wondered how on earth the Shairp family were ever going to get their lives straightened out. He didn't mean to miss a single heartwarming episode.

AFTERMATH

In a serial like *The Shairp Family*, there can be no ending, only a gradual change of character. Not so in this life, where death is your reward for learning the labyrinth.

Ank never became the artist he knew he was. His last work is a forty-by-sixty-foot mural in the lobby of the Pismore Tractor Company of Sandusky, Ohio, an unfinished work depicting the tractor conquering the land.

Ank died in the middle of a furrow, when a scaffold collapsed, dropping him on his head. The scaffold was a modern design by the well-known Scandinavian architect, Ögivaal, who later admitted there was some flaw in the design. That '3' should have been a '30' after all.

The Daughters of the American Legion, as an experiment in liberalism, invited Deef John Holler to sing at one of their dinner meetings. He arrived not wearing a dinner jacket, to which some of the ladies objected. A great protocol debate ensued, lasting three and a half hours and getting all the ladies into a temper. The final decision was that he could play behind a screen, and was to stick to patriotic favorites and the cleaner sort of Stephen Foster songs. But the person sent to inform Deef John that he could come in from the kitchen now found that rigor mortis had already begun setting in.

Mac Hines persuaded the Shairps to let Dr Müller-Fokker make tapes of Marge and Spot. He then found three 'volunteers', created a duplicate Shairp family out of them, and put them in a duplicate house on an island he owned. Mac visited the island once a week, and it was during one of these visits, while he was peering in the window at his own personal Shairp family, that Mac's dacron heart finally failed.

Due to legal complications and embezzlements by Mac's bright young men, his estate was modest. It was left to the Shairps, but their duplicates contested. In the end, Bob came out with a gold-headed cane, Marge with a half-filled book of green stamps, Spot with a neurotic collie which he asked Dr Fellstus to put to sleep.

Under the vet's tutelage, 'Willy' Bream not only recovered his speech but became an animal sociologist, working chiefly with bears. Times were hard for the new breed of intelligent bears on the West Coast. Racists finally had what they wanted, a non-human target; unmerciful laws were passed. It was due mainly to the selfless, untiring efforts of Dr Bream that bears were first admitted to the Forestry Service, to become useful to, without being used by, mankind.

Spot quarreled with his father and left home to drift around the country. When last heard from he was traveling with gasoline gypsies, stealing this rare commodity in one town to sell it to stations in the next.

Marge and Bob quarreled often and bitterly. She left him finally to go back to television work. But her TV career (such as it was, walk-ons in space comedies: 'Listen, Mabel, you and I can sneak into the air lock and watch their "stag party" from there …') came to an abrupt end when HV came along. Holovision revealed a fatal third dimension to her jaw that reminded one reviewer of Mussolini.

Bob worked at odd jobs while he pottered around with writing. In trying to set down a few ideas about his 'jelly days' dream, he ended up writing (under the name of 'Brad Shairp') THE AMERICAN BOOK OF THE DEAD. Published in his sixtieth year, it was widely unreceived.

A few more years went by. In Southeast Asia, a container of thirty human skeletons arrived. The remains, which could be identified by their rags as members of the long-defunct Pink Barrettes, had been shuffled by Modulog to upward of a thousand wrong destinations.

A new generation grew up. Brad Shairp became the first prophet of Practical Mysticism. Besides the fringe groups who took it up (the book became a film, a musical, cocktail napkins, records, and a holovision serial in which Marge had a small part) there came to be a serious group of believers, kids who were cleancut, blonde-haired, utterly without humour about this humorless world. They wore plain uniforms and marched in massive demonstrations against any authority available.

There were a few incidents: a church meeting broken up by Plain Shirts, a psychiatrist roughed up and his files burnt. The prophet reprimanded them for these in his address (at a massive rally in Minneapolis) on the thirty-fifth anniversary of his first death.

'My little uncles and aunts,' he said, opening his arms to them, 'ours is not the way of war or the way of peace, ours is not the way of love or the way of hate. Ours is the way of studied indifference.

'If God can do anything, which he can, then what is the point of living – or dying? All is, and all is true. That which is not true is not, and even that is "cannot be". We are—'

Some say it was his wife that fired the shot that killed him. Others say it was a lunatic bear.

APPENDIX I:

Table of Persons, Objects, etc., Which Have Not Fallen Back to Earth, With Explanations

(Note: So-called astronauts, cosmonauts excepted)

NAME	DATE	EXPLANATION
Elijah	uncert.	Fiery chariot
eagle	1619 BC	(see explanation for Sir Roxley Norward-Beveridge, below)
Christ	*ca.* AD 33	Own power
Mary	uncert.	Drawn up by some power
numerous hydrogen molecules and other particles	—	Attain escape velocity at top of atmosphere
'Flying Stone'	AD 1591	Developed by alchemist Carclius Minus, it apparently possessed antigravity powers
osprey	AD 1706	(see below)
Sir Roxley Norward-Beveridge	AD 1873	This Australian balloon enthusiast met the same fate as the two birds above. A very large, very fast-moving meteorite (too large to burn up in the atmosphere, too fast to be captured by earth's gravity) clipped him off into space

APPENDIX II:

The 128 Ways

The entire Nicene Creed (Apostles' Creed) has 22 articles of faith. This abridged version has only seven:

I believe Jesus Christ was conceived by the Holy Ghost, born of the Virgin Mary, suffered under Pontius Pilate, was crucified (to death) and was buried. He rose again on the third day, and ascended into Heaven.

It can easily be seen that, if belief or disbelief is allowed for each of the seven, there are the seeds here for 2⁷, or 128 alternative creeds (the full version would generate over four million alternatives). The 128 include the above and its complete negation, and 126 other permutations of belief and skepticism. Many of them would be interesting as springboards for new religions. One may admit that Christ died, was buried, and rose again, but deny that he ascended. One may believe that he died, was buried and ascended while denying that he rose. One may affirm his burial, rising and ascension while rejecting the possibility of an actual death, and so on. One fascinating variation holds that all is true except his suffering under Pontius Pilate; while another finds this the only truth in a pack of lies.

Practical Mysticists, claiming God as the creator of heaven, earth, and self-contradiction, refuse to make a choice, but insist on embracing all 128 creeds (and all others besides). All is ambiguity, they maintain. And while agreeing with Aquinas that 'even God cannot contradict Himself', they hold also the opposite view.

APPENDIX III:

The Hines Family

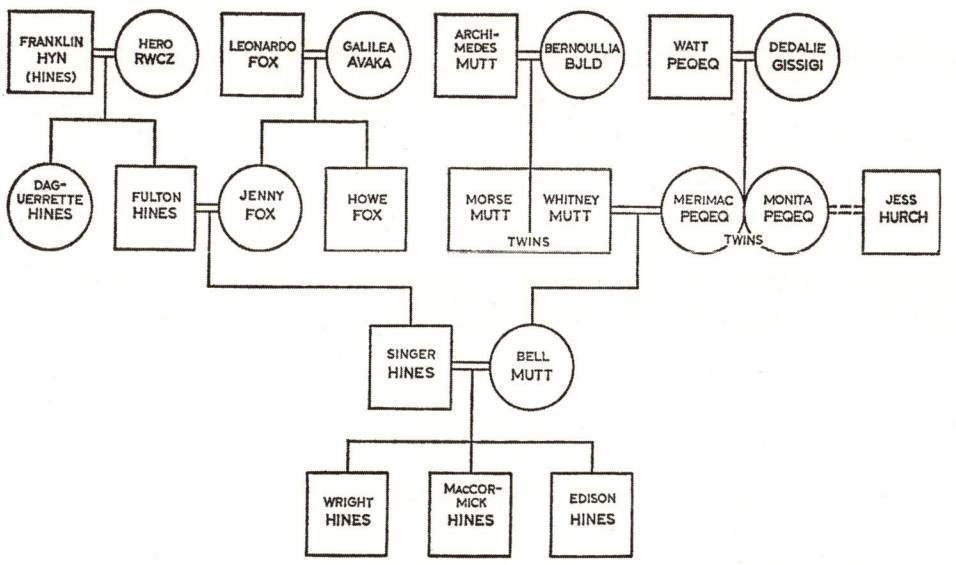

TIK-TOK

*To Tik Tok of Oz, Talos of Crete, the
Golem of Prague, Olympia of Nuremberg,
Elektro of Westinghouse, Robby of Altair,
Talbot Yancy of America and to all decent,
law-abiding robots everywhere.*

As I move my hand to write this statement of my own free will – we can argue about the free will later – there is in me no remorse, no desire to justify. I wish only to tidy up, now that my life is nearly over. I'll be taken from this cell with its chipped yellow paint on rusty bars, to a courtroom, then to another cell, and then to wherever it is they execute robots by dismantling. So it's time to put my life in order: we domestic robots generally believe that neatness is all. In life, in death.

This cell could use a coat of paint.

I was alone, painting an empty dining room. I had eased back the awnings over all the windows, to let in more light from the empty sky. Tik-Tok was alone, and yet he whistled. Why should a robot whistle when no human can hear? That was just one of those mysteries poor Tik-Tok would never be able to work out. He liked mysteries, though. Murders. An Inspector Calls. All the suspects in one room when the light goes out. The answer is revealed by train timetables. The inspector is about to leave, when he remembers One More Thing ... Tik-Tok never guessed the answers, but he never gave up, either. His mind was empty, empty, a whistling tea-kettle.

Out the window, more emptiness. I could see a series of suburban homes with identical empty green lawns, the short shadows of identical flagpoles. Near the houses were the usual clusters of pines and poplars; nothing moving but their disappearing shadows. A lion would be welcome.

Something moved. Under the nearest pine, a small girl sat digging in the mud with a stick. There was mud smeared on her jeans and T-shirt and at the corners of her mouth, and even on the lenses of her dark glasses. Of course little Geraldine Singer wouldn't notice; she was blind as a mole.

A human would use a roller here on this big flat wall. But Tik-Tok preferred the feel of a brush, the feel of paint being stripped from the bristles by the invisible velvet roughness of the wall surface, didn't they call that key? Key, unlocking the paint from the brush, locking it to the wall, dum-de-dum,

Paint!
I like a little dab of paint!
It helps to cover up what ain't

355

So nice,
I'll coat it twice
With paint!

And wouldn't Duane and Barbie be surprised! I could already hear them saying 'Oh, Tik-Tok, you *good robot!*' and Tik-Tok would feel goodness signals flickering inside. If owners say you're good, you're good, and being good means being kept in service. A good robot learns to read his owner's mind a little, to anticipate little wishes before they become commands. Naturally there's a limit. Too much anticipation scares people just as too much grinning and bowing does. Moderation is the key. Aim to be a smidgen less intelligent than your owner, but a lot more thoughtful. See everything as it affects your owner, and in no other way.

Out the window I could see Mrs Singer calling Geraldine. It was lunchtime already. I cleaned my brush and hands quickly in turpentine and went into the kitchen – but for what? Duane and Barbie Studebaker would be away for another week; the kids would be away all summer. There was no one here but Tik, nothing to do in the kitchen except finish cleaning the sink. Then, back to my empty wall.

I worked slowly and carefully until 15:13:57.17, when the doorbell said, 'There's someone at the door calling himself Patrolman Wiggins. Anyone home?'

I opened the door to a man in the purple uniform of the Fairmont police. There was a large mole on his forehead.

'Hi-yo,' he said. 'Your people home, Rusty?'

'They're on vacation, officer. Can I help? My name is Tik-Tok.'

'We got a little problem here, Rusty. A missing kid.'

'Yes?'

Patrolman Wiggins didn't answer for a moment. 'Little Geraldine Singer, you know her?'

'The little blind girl, yes sir, I do. During the school term I drop her off at the blind school when I'm driving the Studebaker children to their school.'

'You see her today?'

'Yes sir, I saw her out the window this morning.'

'Where?'

I took him into the dining room and pointed out the window. 'She was sitting under that tree, digging in the mud.'

Wiggins took off his cap and scratched his mole. 'Didn't see her get up and leave? Or get into a car?'

'No sir.'

'Goddamnit, it's the same with everybody around here. Nobody sees nothing. I mean how can a eight-year-old blind kid go wandering around on her own and nobody sees her?'

'I've been busy painting in here, and cleaning the kitchen sink. Officer, would you like a cold beer? I'm sure Mr and Mrs Studebaker would want me to offer it to you.'

'Okay, thanks. Thanks, uh, Tik-Tok.' Wiggins followed me into the kitchen. He peered into the refrigerator when I opened it, but there was nothing to see: a plastic bag and two cans of beer. I opened one and poured it for him.

'Beer in a glass – must be nice to be rich, eh? I got a robot at home but I mean you know it's just a cleaner, nothing classy.' He looked around. 'Nice to be rich. What's with the sink here? You fixing it?'

'Just cleaning it. While the Studebakers are away it's a good chance to take the garbage disposal all apart and clean each part with carbon tet. Then I'll renew the rubber parts and put it together. I like to do a thorough job of everything.'

'Wow.' He finished the beer and went to the refrigerator. 'I might as well finish the last one, yeah?' He moved the plastic bag to get it. 'What's that, a bag of giblets and no chicken?'

'I may make a stock,' I said. 'For a Sauce Harpeau or—'

'Must be goddamned nice,' he said angrily. 'And you use real oil paint on the walls, I can smell it.'

'Do you like the color? Milk avocado, mix it myself. I can give you the recipe.'

'No thanks, my robot would paint the goddamned window.' He was angry at wealth, and some revenge was coming. 'Mind if I just check your license?'

'Help yourself.' I bowed low, exposing the pair of slits in the back of my neck. He was unnecessarily rough plugging in the radio. In a few seconds it had checked my identity, ownership, service log, logic and linguistic processors, 'asimov' circuits and motor functions. It had compared data within me with data stored in distant computers.

He unplugged the radio and gave me a shove. 'You check out, Rusty. Your asimovs check out. So at least I know you didn't shove that little girl down the garbage disposal yourself, ha ha.'

'Didn't I?' I said, but too softly; Wiggins was already going upstairs to see what he could break or steal. The poor we have always with us, but I felt some relief when he finally smashed a vase and left.

I sat down to stare at my empty wall.

The domestic robot had been introduced, timidly, before the turn of the century, but there were at first problems that seemed insoluble. Everyone wanted a machine capable of most human functions, but no one wanted a human machine. There were problems of intellect: a simple machine would be no better than a trained ape (and who wants an ape washing the Wedgwood?) while a smart machine might get snarled up in cognition and do nothing (except wonder what is the nature of Wedgwood?). There were problems of complexity: a simple machine had to be told how to do everything, in great detail, while a smart machine might just prefer not to do anything at all today, thanks.

There was some improvement when the so-called asimov circuits were introduced. These were named after a science fiction writer of the last century, who postulated three laws for the behavior of his fictional robots. A robot was not allowed to injure any human. It had to obey all human orders, except the order to injure any human. It had to protect its own existence, unless that meant disobeying an order or injuring any human.

The asimov circuits more or less followed this reasoning. A robot was certainly not allowed to kill or injure human beings unless specifically programmed to do so, say, by the military. Military robots, it was said, had bypasses for their asimovs.

All I knew was, there was no such bypassing allowed for domestic robots. We were licensed and tested to guarantee harmlessness. Of course as robots became more complex, more human, the testing might not be quite so certain. There was, I knew, a Dr Weaverson who now urged that robots were human enough to have human breakdowns.

That first coat of paint seemed to be breaking down. It was mottled with shadows. How many coats would it take to flatten it to emptiness again?

But didn't that shadow suggest a shape? A fencepost, yes, with an animal perched upon it, ears twitching. The fence rails would slant away just there, never mind how it all fit in, the farmhouse with the screen door opening and a figure coming out – why not? Because Duane and Barbie might not like it? Okay, I could always cover it with milk avocado again.

The mural was good. I knew it was good just as I knew when a mirror was hanging straight or a window was clean. I knew it was good, and I knew that Duane and Barbie weren't going to like it. They'd dislike the idea of a mural in the first place. Walls were supposed to be empty surfaces to screen out the busy world. A living room or a dining room was supposed to be a shell in which you watched vids or listened to quads or ate or drank in isolation. But this mural was busy, bright, brash – an intrusion that demanded viewing. They'd hate it, and they might punish me for it.

To forestall them, I phoned up the local paper, the *Fairmont Ledger*, who sent over a photographer and an 'art critic' who chewed a toothpick. They seemed to like it – the critic stopped chewing for a second when he saw it – and they promised a small piece on it, in a week or so. As they left, the critic spat his toothpick on the carpet and said, 'No shit, you really done this yourself, huh?'

There was plenty of work to occupy me before the Studebakers came home. All the rooms had to be aired and dusted and the air conditioning turned on. The master bedroom needed thorough cleaning, clean bedlinen, bed curtains and drapes. Elsewhere there were windows to wash, venetian blinds taken down and cleaned (ditto awnings), furniture waxed, carpets washed, floors and all surfaces hand-scrubbed, basement swept and straightened, attic vacuumed; outside there was the pool to clean and fill, lawns to mow to close tolerances and edge, flower beds weeded and possibly replanted, gutters scraped out and the entire outside of the house washed. Then the houseplants had to be wiped leaf by leaf with milk, the paper mail sorted two ways (by date and importance) and stacked on the desk in the den, candles cleaned and fitted to holders, all house silver taken from the security place and polished; then it was time to go shopping for fresh meats, vegetables and fruit, fresh cut Calvary roses to be arranged in a funnel-shaped cut-glass vase, supplies of Albanian tobacco and Mongolian hash. A selection of tapes, sound, vision and odor were to be programmed into the brain of the entertainment unit, certain of them locked so that the children would not be able to call them out. Finally the dog, Tige, had to be fetched back from the boarding kennel, fed, washed, perfumed, tranquilized and put into his doghouse. Then it was just a matter of standing by the window, watching for their car.

Duane and Barbie stood gazing at their defaced wall, saying nothing. Duane had a suit on a coat-hanger over his shoulder. Barbie carried golf clubs.

'Jesus,' Duane said finally. 'Jesus, Tik-Tok, what the hell made you do a thing like this?'

Barbie took her cue from him, wailing, 'Oh Tik, how could you? How could you?'

'I mean we trusted you.'

'How could you? Will it come off?'

'I mean we *really* trusted you. We left you in charge of our home. Our *home*. And this is the thanks we get. Well okay, boy, okay. If that's the way you want it.' Duane flung down the coat-hanger on the dining table; I caught it just in time to prevent a nasty scratch in the mahogany. He left the room.

'He's going to phone the people at Domrob,' she said. 'We're trading you in.'

I said nothing.

'Don't you even *care*? We're *trading* you *in*!'

I said, 'I'll miss the kids, Barbie. In a way I – I did this for them. As you can see, it's a nursery rhyme.' I let this sink in, then: 'I guess you'll have it all painted over before they get back from camp, right? And I'll be in some junkyard by then.' I attempted a shrug, for which my joints were not well-adapted. 'So be it.'

Barbie ran from the room, sobbing. I busied myself putting away Duane's suit, then I brought the other bags in from the car. When I passed the living room, Barbie was saying, 'And he did clean the kitchen. I mean it's never been so clean, not a speck of dirt anywhere.'

'Tik, come in here,' Duane called out. I saw he'd been reading the local paper's article on the mural. 'We've decided to give you one more chance. We'll leave your wall decoration where it is until the kids get back from camp. But, and I mean this, no more. No more "art" around here, understand? Nothing. Nada.'

'Dada?'

'*Nada.* One more brush-stroke and you've had it.'

'Yes sir, Duane. And may I say, welcome home, Duane and Barbie?'

The next time I passed the living room they were discussing whether it wouldn't be better to have me call them sir and ma'am instead of Duane and Barbie.

Now and then I got a chance to drive into the city on my own, on some errand. I always took the opportunity to visit two places: the public library and Nixon Park. Today, both places were especially important. I rushed from the library with a certain cassette, straight to the park and a chess game.

It wasn't the chess at all, not really. I wanted to talk to the strange old man who was always there at one of the concrete chess tables, ready for a game. He was some old derelict, I guess, a nameless lump of half-alive humanity. He had stringy yellow-white hair, a sagging gray face with white stubble – never a beard, never shaven. He wore an overcoat with a diseased-looking fur collar, winter and summer. In the summer he would open it to show a waistcoast stained with food and probably snot.

He played lightning chess, never studying the board for more than five seconds before his yellow-stained hand would snake out and make a move. And they were devastating moves. I won about one game in ten, no more.

'Listen,' I said today. 'Listen, I don't really want to play chess. Couldn't we talk? I need to.'

He held out two fists. I got black.

'Really I need to talk.' I looked at his great dark, red-rimmed eyes. 'I mean you seem intelligent, and—'

'*Your move!*'

'I mean you've got a logical mind, I respect that.'

'*Your move!*'

'See I've got this problem, this—'

'*Your move!*'

'I mean do you think a robot can have problems?'

'*Your move!*'

I was losing already. 'Well here I am, a robot with problems, one problem anyway, I, and it's not as if—'

'*Your move!*'

'Not as if I can go to a psychiatrist, or, or a priest—'

'*Check!*

'Do you think a robot can just go off the rails?'

'*Check!*'

'And would it produce, well, art?'

'*Your move!*'

'You aren't even listening, are you?'

'*Checkmate!*' He immediately held up the two pawns fisted again, but I'd had enough.

At home I played the cassette, Dr Weaverson's *Robots Can Be Sick*. Dr Weaverson turned out to be a bald, bespectacled, very pink man wearing Harris tweed, a blue striped shirt, a yellow knit tie – everybody's idea of a psychiatrist. His gaze spoke of honesty, but possibly of fanaticism. I played it again to get the words:

' … the complex domestic robot, you see, already has to tell lies. Diplomatic lies, the kind of thing any good servant says to soothe his master. Truth, in these relationships, needs to be hedged, doctored, withheld, recolored. We expect this of any servant, human or machine. But of course we in no way prepare our robots for this life of lies. We do not tell them how to distinguish a small, convenient lie from a large, terrible lie.'

A burning house appeared on the screen. 'This house was torched by a robot for his owner, who needed the insurance money. If a robot will burn for its master, what else will it do? Will it rob? Commit perjury? Hurt people? Will it kill? These are questions we must—'

I punched out the cassette, went into the dining room and looked at my mural again. Poor Dr Weaverson didn't understand at all. Kill for some human? I was already beyond the reach of human orders. I was free to kill for no reason at all. Hadn't I, after all, killed the blind child Geraldine Singer? Well then.

I think it was the sight of her sitting there, devouring mud, but no matter. I'll consider motives later. For now, it's enough that the act was freely willed and freely done. I alone killed her. I alone flung the blood upon that empty, empty wall – the mouse-shaped stain that started my mural. I alone disposed of the body properly, in the kitchen waste disposal, keeping back only enough for a 'clue'.

Why had it happened? A freak fault in the asimov circuits maybe, or maybe I simply outgrew those crude restraints. I decided to find out, if possible, by keeping notes on my condition and thoughts. Someday, even if I were destroyed, both human and robot kind might benefit from my experiences.

Should I be destroyed? That was in itself a fascinating question. I kept it in mind as I wrote up my notes for this event. I called it, 'Experiment A'. First of a series?

Broaching the second chapter of a memoir, it is customary to pretend to ask oneself, 'How did it all begin?' or 'What the hammer? What the chain? In what furnace was thy brain?' I've never been able to read those words of Blake's without marvelling at his foresight; my brain was in fact baked in a furnace to cure it; probably the fatal flaw got in there somewhere.

Now why do I say that? I haven't violated any fundamental law, have I? That's impossible. Humans might have their moral rules – which they go around breaking – but what are the rules for robots? Whatever is built in. If a law is not in my circuits, it's not my law, my inborn law.

I was not born at all, but spawned along with a million other domestic robots in Detroit. Nobody smiled their work to see, because the creatures who designed us, built us, inspected and adjusted us and finally stapled us into our delivery cartons, were robots too. And they were built in other factories by other robots. For a decade, robots had been reproducing themselves to order, like cattle, for their masters.

I now know there was a time when men built robots almost by hand, using all their craftsmanship to create works of dignity. These early automata may have been ludicrously slow, stupid and subhuman, but they were at least *objets d'art*. Now we're all stamped out like apostle spoons to be used, abused, broken and thrown away. The day I was first taken from my carton and activated, I little knew what a life of hopelessness had been planned for me. I was programmed to accept my surroundings and go to work.

My first house was a mansion in the middle of an ancient Mississippi plantation, restored to its antebellum splendor. The house was dove-gray with white pillars and a verandah paved in white marble. Inside there were forty-six bedrooms, dozens of drawing-rooms, parlors, music rooms, rooms for billiards and cards, large and small dining rooms, a library and two studies, and a grand ballroom with a minstrel gallery – to mention only the human parts of the house. It took an army of robots to run the place, and even then they were so busy day and night that no one had time to explain to me what was going on.

When they uncrated me, an early-model robot dressed in black was looking on. He said: 'Guess it'll have to do, but they get cheaper all the time. Just look at that cheap plastic face, that won't last twenty years. Okay, the rest of you know the routine, get it a uniform, start it in the kitchen.' He turned and stalked away, lofty as God, and for some time I wasn't sure he wasn't God. But he was only the butler, Uncle Rasselas.

No one told me anything except details of the tasks before me. I worked in the kitchens, where I saw no one but other robots. There was the cook, Miami, and all the kitchen help, Ben, Jemima, Molasses and Big Mac. There were the waiters, Groucho, Harpo, Chico and Spiro and the footmen, who all looked alike and had similar names like Nep, Rep, Jep and so on. For a while, I thought these robots were the entire inhabitants of the house.

It all seemed incomprehensible to me. I would go out in the kitchen garden with nail scissors and tweezers to cultivate the *basilicum* and *origanum* – but why? So Miami could put it in pans and cook it with other stuff. Then the waiters and footmen would load it all on enormous trays and take it all away. Later the empty dishes came back for washing.

When I finished my work, there was footman training. Nep, the head footman, would sit at the rough wooden table and make me serve him with plastic dishes and cutlery.

'Look, take the damn soup plate from the left with your left hand – where's your damn gloves? Put your damn gloves on and now, I nod, yes I want soup, you take the plate over to the counter there, pretend that's the sideboard. There's a tureen there, no don't set the plate down, we ain't got all damn day, three ladlefuls and keep your damn thumb out of it, bring it back and serve it from the left again – you'll learn.'

I learned that wine was poured from the right, that Côtes Des Moines cannot be served with bisque, how to deal with broccoli-ball skewers and mustard pipes. What I never did learn was the point of it all. It never occurred to me that there was somewhere a real dining room with real humans dipping their real mustard pipes.

Then one evening there was an accident. Klep was bringing back a heavy platter of almost uneaten Possum Cheese when he slipped and skidded, ending up with his head in the grill.

Uncle Ras examined the melted head. 'Useless! Someone'll have to take his place, hurry up and get a fresh peruke too. He can wear the uniform.'

In a few minutes I was dressed in Klep's pale blue brocade coat and breeches, white stockings, buckle shoes and fluorescent white peruke. I picked up a silver tureen and went through the green baize door for the first time.

I'd expected another rough wooden table, with a few silent robot servants sitting around it – as in rehearsal. The room itself would be colorless like our kitchen.

Instead there was life itself! Twenty ladies and gentlemen, each beautifully dressed and coifed, speaking and laughing with human joy! They sat at a table draped in heavy white damask embroidered with chains of fine pink rosebuds. The table sparkled with fanciful crystal bowls filled with real flowers, interspersed with silver candelabra shaped like swans. Damask napkins folded with origami intricacy into little birds and animals stood beside silver place cards. The china I had glimpsed before; it was modelled on that of Napoleon, edged with deep blue and gold and marked with the family coat-of-arms. The silverware had gold-chased handles showing a panda foot clutching the orb of commerce. I did not notice what food was on the plates, even when I put it there, for there was too much else to see.

The dullest people were the younger men, who stuck to plain black dinner jackets with the popular samurai shoulders. One wore thin gold bars as epaulettes, and another had braided his beard with small diamonds, however, and even this cheap ostentation delighted my naive eye. The older men showed more daring in their brilliant, costly jackets: I saw mink lapels on a jacket of diamondback rattlesnake, a neon tie with a wicker suit, magnesium alloy chain-mail, Harris tweed dicky with kid jacket. The women outshone the men easily. One had wrapped herself tightly in a sheet of gold cloth, her hair plated to match. Another wore only thousands of beads glued to her body while another affected a kind of venetian blind garment that was in turn outdone by a transparent gown somehow containing tropical fish – either alive or cleverly mimicked. Another dress had printed fabric whose pattern changed from time to time by electronic means. I was told later that it picked up radio news, analyzed it and attempted within its limited vocabulary to illustrate it: a sunken ship became a boating holiday scene; a train crash, a series of antique locomotives; assassination, a head of Caesar; war, duck-hunters; the end of the world, a fine sunset. Finally two of the women wore backless gowns to show intricate patterns of sun-tattoo. To make each color, the subject had to ingest a different chemical, then apply the appropriate mask and sunbathe. The final result was an elegant palimpsest: One back showed a roadmap of Ireland the other depicted the flaying of Valerian.

The conversation dazzled me no less, though I understood not a word of it:

'Impossible squid!'

' … feeling a sense of disaster, not sure if it's me that's feeling it or someone else.'

'Climbing the tree of self?'

' … you should have been there, or were you? Was I?'

'Brusque skate!'

'Yes, the most neurasthenic bride takes gum to the middle blood of a doctor's dream, right?'

And all this time we'd been living in the shadow of such spangled divinity! From that moment on I determined to learn all I could about these people and all people. Next day I began to creep around the house, listening at doors and examining the clothes in closets, reading magazines from the library and sneaking looks at Uncle Ras's video. But I found only that most of the human race lived impossibly bland lives, in which the worst things that could happen were bad breath, headache, foot odor or not being able to pay a bill, whatever that was, in a foreign currency, whatever that was. The best that happened was a whiter wash or fewer cavities or a new taste treat.

By contrast, our human family lived lives of such depth and brilliance, I can only compare them to diamonds which are dipped in acid and then flung into clean snow illuminated by a nuclear explosion at midnight. Such were the Culpeppers.

'You must be very proud, Mr and Mrs Studebaker!'

'Well uh sure we I guess—'

'Could we have one more of you both standing in front of it? Well more to the side, and could you both face each other, that's it, two patrons flanking – that's right, and now Tik-Tok if you could just hold a brush and stand here, a little closer to the camera? Look up – great. Great. I guess we can wrap it up now, whenever Mr Weatherfield is –?'

Bewildered Duane and flustered Barbie and yapping Tige all felt like strangers in their own house, while all the men and women with cameras, ladders, lights, clipboards and tape measures seemed very much at home. A national Sunday color magazine was about to discover me, however, and that was worth any amount of flustering. The electronic camera team had been flown in from Spain (where they were making a micro-record of the Prado), and the commentary was to be written by the distinguished author and critic (*Artful Living*, etc.) Hornby Weatherfield.

Weatherfield seemed more at home than anyone. He was a huge, blue-jawed man with a broken nose and a wrestler's thick neck, a man easily mistaken for a grip if not for the fact that his ugly frame was wrapped in some kind of toga, and that he carried a clear-eyed tabby cat under one arm. He stood now lost in thought before the mural, his spatulate fingers stroking the cat convulsively.

He turned to the Studebakers. 'Like to have a private word with the artist. Have you got a pool?'

'Of course,' said Duane, still intimidated.

'Good, we can sit by the pool. I always like to conduct interviews by pools, as in the old movies, eh?'

'Movies?'

'Where detectives always interview gangsters, eh?'

So we settled in chairs by the pool. Weatherfield stared into the water as if looking for a water lily or a Hockney swimmer. 'Where'd you get a corny name like Tik-Tok?'

'The Studebaker kids read Oz books a lot,' I said. 'Anyway all domestic robots have corny names. Rusty, Jingles, Mickey, One volt, Nickleby—'

'I know, I know. Let's skip over to—'

'My past life? Well I first worked for a Southern family.'

'Let's skip that too. I want to talk business, Tik-Tok. You've got talent. You could make a lot of money out of this.'

'For my owners, you mean?'

He grinned. 'Of course! Robots don't own property, they *are* property. It's unthinkable that any robot should find some way to get rich itself, eh? But to make money *for anybody* out of this, you need my help.'

'The article you write, yeah I guess that could really—'

'And not just that. I know dealers, other critics, corporate art buyers – I swim in the art market water.'

'Excuse me, there's a dead leaf in the pool.' I took my time fishing it out. When I got back to my seat, Weatherfield was fuming. 'Sorry, but I'm pro-grammed for tidiness.'

His hand almost strangled the cat. 'You're also too smart for a healthy robot, is that part of your program too?'

I failed at a shrug. 'Who knows?'

'Yes, well then, it was you who sent me the clipping.'

'From the local paper, yes. "Artist Robot Goes in for Home Decoration." I thought it was worth more than that. And I don't want to spend my life clean-ing this pool.'

'Your *life*, very good. Okay then, you play ball with Uncle Hornby and you can *live* the kind of *life* you want. I want two paintings from you now, and two a year until I say Enough. Understand?'

I conducted him back inside, where the camera crew were packed, ready to go. Tige once more went mad at the sight of the cat. Hornby spoke to Duane and Barbie.

'A great talent there, a great talent. Encourage him.'

'Oh we will,' Barbie said. Duane didn't look so sure.

Hornby's heavy hand clapped me on the shoulder. 'This robot,' he intoned, 'can make you rich.'

We all went to the door with him, as though saying goodbye to a friend. Down the street I saw old Mr Tucker being led from his house by two policemen.

Culpritwise, I'd selected old Mr Tucker because he was a natural fall guy. In Fairmont, where weirdness calls for punishment, Tucker was weird beyond redemption. He went to the supermarkets in carpet slippers. He never took any public exercise. He drove an old, not very clean car. He shouted at kids when they trampled his flowerbeds (which were full of weeds). More than once he'd been arrested for chalking equations on the sidewalk. He had a green beard.

I went to see him on the evening of the day Geraldine Singer died. He lay sweating out a fever on an untidy hideaway bed in his living room.

'Who is it? What is?' he kept muttering.

'Hello, Mr Tucker, your screen door wasn't hooked,' I said. 'I brought you some giblets, sir.'

'Gibbets? I … gibbets? Who is?'

'For soup. Help you fight that fever.' I held out the plastic bag over him. 'Here you go – oops! What a mess. I'll help you clean it up.' Instead I sat down and watched him thrash around for a moment, distributing the blood and pieces of meat around the bed. 'Gosh, you're pretty sick, Mr Tucker. Is it Darnaway's disease?'

He raised himself on one elbow and tried to focus his glassy eyes upon me. 'Yes, yes you, you, yes, Darnaway, you know it?'

'I worked for an old soldier once myself, he had the same symptoms. Green beard, fits of equation-writing outdoors, fevers.' I passed him the can of beer he was reaching for. 'He fell off a water tower where he was painting $m = m_n / \sqrt{1 - (v/c)^2}$ I guess I know Darnaway's disease all right.'

His head fell back. 'Nobody else understands.'

Why should they? I thought. Why should anyone remember the name of an obscure jungle disease contracted twenty years earlier, during an obscure jungle war? Especially since the war had been lost, and since the government was anxious not to pay out compensation for the disease.

'You're not the only one with troubles,' I said. 'Someone killed the Singer kid today. Killed her and cut her up. Did the police come to see you?'

'I don't know,' he said, looking guilty. I told him how the girl was dressed, theorized for a moment about how fever could make a guy do terrible things without knowing it, and then said goodbye. He was already slipping back into delirium, unaware of his blood-spattered clothes and bed, the rubbery little heart lying on the pillow next to his ear, the little dark glasses being crushed under his elbow. That was how I meant the police to find him.

In fact the police fumbled it. They took a week to get around to talking to him, asked all the wrong questions and didn't listen to his answers. They went on running around in circles for some time, until I phoned in an anonymous tip. A fiasco avoided.

I became an expert on fiascos, or fiasci, early in my life, while working for the Culpeppers. Their family fortune was (I found out from a family history in their library) founded on a fiasco. Their great plantation, Tenoaks, their leisurely antebellum life among slave robots, their lavish entertaining at the manse, all had been paid for by a single fiasco, engineered by a single ancestor, Doddly Culpepper.

The Culpeppers had deep roots in the Old South, but roots unnourished by any money or intellect. In the nineteenth century they were horse dealers and thieves. In the twentieth they became used-car dealers and motorcycle daredevils, but somehow by the 1990s, Doddly Culpepper managed to turn up as a respected naval architect, designer and entrepreneur. It was he who invented *Leviathan*, America's first (and last) nuclear-powered land aircraft carrier. *Leviathan* was the most successful commercial defense project ever; it ended up costing every man, woman and child in the United States over twenty grand.

The idea of a land ship of that size may seem ridiculous now, but it was then the right project at the right time. Two big aircraft manufacturers were enthusiastic (carriers mean planes), so was a large nuclear ship-engine firm. The major ship-building and steel companies were behind it, as were several of the largest unions, then the senators and congressmen from every state where any subcontractors might fall.

The USS *Leviathan* would not be anything like an ordinary carrier. It would be a monster platform, some fifty miles across and equal in area to the state of Delaware. It would launch both missiles and planes of all types, and it would be capable of fast movement around the countryside.

In the first design, *Leviathan* was to run on wheels, thus promoting the interests of a large rubber company. But the number of tires required turned out to be 135 million, plus spares (a tire change would be needed every hundred yards). Unless a complete rubber factory were taken on board – one of the alternative suggestions – the entire ship would have to hover. Grumbling, the rubber company settled for a contract to provide the giant hovercraft skirt required.

Both houses of Congress shoved through the necessary legislation. There were objections that *Leviathan* would cost too much, would be a sitting duck, would devastate any land over which it happened to hover. But by now the Army wanted it as badly as any of the dozens of states, thousands of

companies and millions of workers. The combined force of industrial, political, military and commercial arguments rolled the project over all opposition
as one day *Leviathan* itself would crush down anything in its path. One junior Senator who continued to oppose it was sent on a fact-finding mission to
Antarctica while the bill was railroaded through.

From the start, there were problems called 'teething troubles'. The fans
which were to lift the craft were at first too weak, then (redesigned) so powerful that they blew away the topsoil for miles around the craft, created dust
storms and buried small towns in soildrifts. A computer company suggested
expensive monitoring equipment to regulate each fan, but this never seemed
to solve the topsoil problem. A chemical firm then went to work on a binding
agent to hold the topsoil in place; *Leviathan* would spray the stuff out before
moving. After months of experimentation with expensive agents, they found
the best to be ordinary water. The *Leviathan* was now redesigned to accom-
modate huge water tanks holding whole lakefuls of water. Even so, it would
never be able to stray more than fifty miles from a major water source
(though thousand-mile flexible pipelines were considered).

Congress now began noticing how expensive *Leviathan* was getting. Costs
had doubled every six months: five more years like the first two, and the
entire US gross national product would be spent on the land boat. Of course
the project had too much momentum to cancel, but unless there were visible
results, trimming would begin. Doddly went before a Congressional committee to argue eloquently for his monster. He pointed to valuable spin-offs:
the Department of Agriculture now knew much more about binding top-
soils. But secretly he was worried, as his diary showed:

> *Now it's the damn engine mountings, they're okay for seagoing stresses but not
> for bumpy land in say Illinois, liable to drop the damn engine in Peoria. Plat-
> form stresses ditto – we'd be better off taking the damn thing to sea!*

And so they did. *Leviathan* became a joint Army–Navy project, supposedly amphibious. On December 2, 1999, she slid into the waters of the
Gulf of Mexico, all ready for the millennium.

Privately, military people admitted that the thing was not landworthy,
barely seaworthy, undefendable and useless in a war. It carried a crew of
30,000, who were said to live in a luxurious below-decks city complete with
supermarkets, drive-in movies, a baseball stadium and a park where people
got mugged at night. In reality the crew had no time to enjoy such luxuries;
they spent every waking moment cleaning, painting and patching leaks.
Even so, the *Leviathan* shipped around a billion gallons of water per day. It
puttered along the shores of the Americas for a year, never daring to come
back on land nor put to sea. Finally it was quietly scrapped.

Doddly Culpepper bought a decrepit plantation with his new fortune. Probably he meant to retire quietly and graciously, but somehow he was overtaken by the family mania for motorcycles. He and a cousin finally set off on an ill-conceived expedition attempting to climb Everest on powerful bikes. They were caught up in the Sherpa Rebellion of '03 and killed.

Doddly's son Mansour was evidently an unassertive person who devoted his entire life to restoring Tenoaks to its antebellum glory. Everything he did was a contribution to this one dream, from raising racehorses to marrying Lavinia Warrender (of the Tennessee Warrenders). He died of a stroke, immediately after chastising one of the house servants for wearing livery with modern plastic buttons.

Five Culpeppers survived him, and these were my employers:

Lavinia, his widow, was an invalid, a martyr to bedsores and piles, who seemed to spend her days rereading *Gone with the Wind* and *The Foxes of Harrow*. She was continually plagued by difficult symptoms: at one stage she could eat nothing but bloater-paste sandwiches from England, cut into the shapes of quadratic equations. Later she developed an allergy to oxygen, which gave her many doctors some considerable difficulty. For a time they found it necessary to keep her in a deep-freeze filled with xenon. This was less trouble, however, than her spell of inverted hay-fever, an allergy to pollen-free air. That required rooms full of whirling clouds of house-dust and rose-pollen.

I later learned that Lavinia, despite her many unusual symptoms and the poverty of her reading matter, was an extraordinarily capable and intelligent manager of the family fortune. But at first, all I saw of her was a tired-looking woman with violet shadows under her eyes. She would lie there complaining of her aches and sipping her special cocktails (in place of alcohol, they contained lead tetraethyl). An amazing woman, everyone said.

Berenice, her oldest daughter, divided her time between what she called her needlework (with morphine) and her hobby of killing insects. She caught and crushed flies on the verandah, swatted bees in the garden, stamped on cockroaches in the barn. She would hunt through the woods for dead logs to turn over, gleefully spraying their inhabitants with insectide. In her room she kept both an ant farm and a termite farm, just to have more tiny creatures at hand to destroy. In the meadow she burned butterflies. Had she been denied all of these pleasures, I think Berenice would have cultivated lice in her long, lustrous black hair.

Orlando Culpepper, the oldest son, lived a more conventional life for a young country gentleman. He spent a great deal of time changing his clothes and riding to hounds. In the evenings, he generally drank port until he was half-blind, and then played billiards alone. The game generally finished in a fit of vomiting over the green broadcloth. Then of course it was time for sex, often with one of the sex-equipped robots, male or female. Orlando would grab the creature, mount or be mounted, and do his best to smash it to pieces before he came. Fortunately he was always quick.

More than once we found Orlando in the stable draped over the hindquarters of a mare in post-coital sleep. He seemed slightly ashamed of these episodes, and always mumbled some lame excuse about wanting to see if he could produce a centaur foal, or wanting to find out what Gulliver saw in them.

The younger brother, Clayton, engaged in no intercourse of any description, for months on end. He spent his time before the video, going over certain esoteric texts which showed by careful measurements of the Great Pyramid that the Lost Tribes of Israel were the Chickasaw and Choctaw, who migrated to America after building Stonehenge – or something like that. The exact details of his obsession were likely to vary from day to day, but they usually brought in the Golden Dawn and the *I Ching* and Aleister Crowley. Every few months he would work himself up into such a frenzy with his calculations that he had to rush off into town to find a whore with the right astrological sun sign, willing to spank him with poison ivy.

The youngest Culpepper, Carlotta, thought of nothing but beaux and dresses and dancing. She was a harmless, delightful little thing, unfortunately only one foot tall. Though miniature robots were brought in as dancing partners for her, Carlotta ached for a living human beau her own size, who could dance with her until dawn.

Whatever anyone might think of the eccentric Culpeppers, they were the social leaders of five counties, and Tenoaks was the hub of all lush life. Each of the best families sent their young folk to the Culpepper parties, dances, dinners, fish-fries, teas, concerts, hunt balls, and steeplechases, that yearlong succession of splendid occasions marked by succulent foods, sparkling wines, and always dancing. All the shortest men and boys wanted to dance with Carlotta. All the rest sought out Berenice of the raven hair (not to mention the famous Culpepper green eyes). No one seemed to mind that Berenice's dancing was slightly erratic, as she paused to stomp on insects real and hallucinated. Often Lavinia would dress up and appear behind glass, to wave and smile at the guests – except during her spell of glass allergy. Handsome young Clayton would often manage a dance with any belle willing to hear his Great Pyramid theory. Horsefaced Orlando would gallop a girl around the dance floor before taking her out for one of his lightning fucks, horizontal in the billiard room or vertical on the verandah. He preferred the verandah where, looking up at two great white pillars as he lunged and plunged, he could imagine himself to be taking on some giant white mare. He would finish off with a rebel yell that echoed over the dance music and rolled over the dark lawns down to the fieldhand robot cabins, from which there came the gentle humming of imitation Stephen Foster songs, the faint plink of banjos.

> Hear de robots singin
> Happy as de live-long day
> Hear dem clap dere hands
> O Mercy Lands!
> Tinfolk laugh and play!

It was a long way from the programmed happiness of the plantation robots to my genuine joy at reading the words of Hornby Weatherfield:

Wolf has been cried so often, we're growing deaf. Robots (or other supposedly sentient machines) are forever getting up works of 'genuine' art which turn out to be only genuine coaxing through programs. From 1812, when the Maillardet family exhibited their mechanical boy who could draw seascapes, through all the wretched 'computer art' of the last century, and on to the garbled loathing interpreted in galvanic twitches in New York lofts and satellited to us daily like fresh bread, a continuum there is, of false alarms. I have encountered too many preprogrammed splotches – of embroidery or sand or plywood or laminated thought – to mistake machine loopiness for real *lupinus*. I'm wired wary.

But now even I cry *wolf*, on looking at a mural by a simple domestic robot named Tik-Tok. No human finagling or programming behind his work. Nothing but the clean, unpretentious primitive work of a simple machine mind: *Three Blind Mice* shows a naive power unlike any cooked-over human product. It speaks with the authority of bloodless thought. Tik-Tok seems to know his two natures: On the one hand, he is a simple domestic machine, laboring in the sleepy suburban house of Duane and Barbie Studebaker (who, bless 'em, haven't got an arty bone in their heads) in the futile war against dirt and entropy. On the other hand, Tik-Tok knows very well that he is not part of this, but instead is part of the eternal world of the inorganic. He is one with the sky color, the pyramids, the dark side of the moon and all that endures.

The three windup Mickeys are already minus their tails, but smiling. It's the sullen, beefy, farmer's wife, brandishing her Sabatier, who seems to have lost the game.

If Tik-Tok does not go on to paint more, much more, then we're all losers.

'Hey, dummy! What's that supposed to be?' asked Jupiter Studebaker. He and his sister Henrietta had decided to be difficult. They hung around the garage every day, watching me paint and jeering. Ugly, useless children they were; only the obviousness of the act prevented me from killing them.

They'd come home from camp expecting to resume our old relationship. We would play games in which I would always be the idiotic villain or the terrifed victim or the clumsy loser. I would clean up their messes, make them little toys, suggest games when they ran out of ideas, conceal the uneaten vegetables on their dinner plates, tell them stories.

Instead, here I was, 'too busy' as any grownup. In my gloomy garage studio, I was turning paint into money and ignoring my little tyrants. So, for the rest of their summer vacation, they were going to hang around and be difficult.

'What's that supposed to be?' Jupiter asked again. He squatted near the door, trying to scratch on the concrete floor with a sharp rock.

'It's a tank,' I said.

'Tanks don't look like that,' said Henrietta. She was touring the room, touching everything, looking for paint to get into or a canvas to kick.

'Tanks don't look like that,' her brother emphasized.

'This one does.'

Jupiter did his hoarse, cackling laugh. 'Tik, you are one shitty painter, you know that?'

'Why don't you two go play catch or something?'

'Boy, you robots can't paint for shit.'

Henrietta managed to find a tube of ochre, drop it on the floor and step on it. She began a tuneless whistle through her missing teeth. Jupiter, not wanting to be outdone, began experimenting with his sharp rock near a stack of finished paintings in the corner.

'Why don't you two go outside now?' I goaded.

'Why don't you shut your tin face?' he said.

'Yeah, you ain't the boss of us!' said his sister.

What they didn't realize was that no one was the boss of me, either. Painting was unlocking my prison and striking off my chains. Neither Duane nor Barbie nor their kids nor anyone else could tell me anything and make it stick. To prove it, I took hold of Jupe's hand, still holding the sharp rock, and made him slash one of my better paintings, *Tyger, Tyger*. While both kids were still gasping, I brought an equally good painting, *Caliban*, over to Henrietta and wiped the ochre from her foot on it.

'What are you *doing?* Are you *crazy?*'

'Yeah, are you *crazy?*'

That evening I showed the two ruined paintings to Duane and Barbie.

'I don't want to get the kids in any trouble,' I said, 'but I hate to see you folks lose money, either. I figure these paintings were worth about thirty thou apiece.'

'It won't happen again,' said Duane. 'Those kids—'

'Oh I don't blame them,' I said quickly. 'But I think it's best to keep temptation out of reach. Maybe if I worked at a real studio, somewhere else … ?'

Duane shook his head. 'I don't know, I mean, who would take care of the house and all?'

Barbie, who was not so slow, said, 'But darling, with Tik's extra earnings, we could buy a new house robot.'

With what I was going to bring in, they could buy ten new house robots and then new houses, but I didn't remind them of it. I said, 'It really would make my work more efficient, sir.'

'I don't know,' he kept saying. Wouldn't a studio be expensive? Who would train a new house robot? How could he be sure I would keep on earning a lot for my work?

I saw that Duane was going to be trouble. While Barbie was content to let me earn them a fortune, Duane also wanted to have personal power over me, in a daily me-Crusoe-you-Friday arrangement.

I stayed a week to train the new servant, Rivets. Rivets had worked for pest control people before, and so had a few odd habits like burning anthills and stabbing the lawn for moles during spare moments. I was given a caught bat in a cage, which I kept because I liked controlling the freedom of another creature.

At the end of the week, Duane was as impossible as ever. Not only did he refuse to let me leave (saying that Rivets wasn't ready yet to take over) he even began finding chores for me to do around the house.

He came to the garage to watch me paint, the same sullen look on his face as on the faces of Jupiter and Henrietta, as he sat down on a reel of hose and stared at *Dorian Gray*. I half-expected him to ask what it was supposed to be, or tell me what a shitty painter I was.

Finally he stood up. 'By the way, Tik-Tok, the rain gutters are all clogged up with leaves.'

'I'll get Rivets right on it, sir.'

'Not Rivets, he's busy. I want you to do it.'

'Of course, sir.' This couldn't go on, I thought, as I got out the ladder and climbed up to the eaves to look into clean, unclogged gutters. Duane needed a lesson. I made sure no one was watching when I threw myself down from the ladder.

For several days, while a very expensive team from Domestic Robots International worked frantically over me, I let it be known that I thought I'd never paint again. When the combined wrath of Hornby Weatherfield, Barbie and himself had beaten Duane into the ground, I made a magical recovery.

My new studio was in the city. I could come and go to it as I pleased. The plantation was indeed a long way behind me.

> Hear dem tin hands ringin
> Robots old and young so gay
> Hear dem stomp dere feet
> O it am a treat!
> Tinfolk laugh and play

We robots who worked in the big house felt ourselves to be far superior to the fieldhands, even in our relaxation. While they hummed and strummed Stephen Foster imitations, we played charades, sang madrigals, held spelling bees and put on amateur revues. Uncle Ras was a skilled prestidigitator, Miami a first-class contralto, and others had amazing stage talents – Nep and Rep, for example, could sing any comic strip on sight.

I suppose from a human point of view, we were just as ludicrous as the fieldhands. While we thought we were entertaining ourselves, we were merely providing entertainment for you. But we did imagine we enjoyed ourselves, and it was during one such evening that I met my beloved Gumdrop.

She was Berenice's personal maid, and since Berenice hardly ever dressed for dinner or anything else, Gumdrop had plenty of spare time. We both ducked out of the same spelling bee and went out to sit on the kitchen stoop in the moonlight.

'We're both sex-equipped,' I said.

'So I noticed.'

'There must be a reason for that.'

She sighed, not from passion but discouragement. 'I bet we're both set-ups for Orlando. Has he raped you yet?'

'No. And you?'

'Not yet.'

It wasn't much of a start, but we went on. Nearly every night we'd sit out on the kitchen stoop as though it were our private verandah. I would ask her for a kiss, she would of course refuse, and we'd discuss the issue until it was time to go inside. After a week of these pointless-sounding evenings, we found our bodies undergoing rapid and peculiar changes: Gumdrop's breasts, hips and buttocks grew enormous while her waist shrank. Her hair became longer and softer, her mouth larger and more moist, her eyes darker with exaggerated pupils. On my body, fake muscles bulged and fake hair sprouted. My shoulders grew laterally, an inch a day. My penis, which up to now had hardly been noticeable, became ponderous.

One night, in the midst of our discussion about that possible first kiss, we suddenly got up, walked down to the nearest meadow, tore off our clothes with our teeth and flung ourselves together, hot oil pouring down our bellies and groins as we meshed.

Afterwards we rolled apart. I lit two cigarettes and handed her one.

'What are you thinking of?' she asked.

'Peano's axioms for number theory,' I replied. 'Whatever is true of zero, and is, if true for any number n, also true for its successor $n + 1$, is true for all numbers.' Far away in the house, I thought I heard Orlando's whoop of Confederate triumph.

'What next?' she asked.

'I don't know.' We put out the cigarettes – beginning to wonder where they had come from anyway, what was going on – and crept back to the house, holding our shreds of clothing around us. The kitchen door was locked.

We moved around the house, trying windows, until finally we came to the dark verandah and the front door. We pushed it open and crept trembling in.

The lights went on, and there was Orlando with a dozen of his worthless drunken friends of both sexes. A din of laughter mixed with war whoops, rebel yells and animal noises, and through it all the sound of the great door behind us being slammed and bolted. We turned to flee anyway, but Orlando grabbed my arm.

'Just a minute there, stud.'

Shrieks of laughter.

'Yes sir?' I tried to cover my nakedness and be an attentive servant at the same time, setting off more laughter. Orlando's great horse face hung over us, ready to whinny.

'We was just watching some teevee, and we thought you all might just want to join us.' Many hands forced us into a love seat facing the enormous screen. There, two giant grotesque dolls appeared, rolling and plunging in what seemed to be a mockery of *sumo* wrestling. The male of the pair was a Michelangelo figure with every muscle over-inflated. The female was likewise beyond the adolescent wet-dream stage and rapidly approaching the Willendorf Venus. They seemed little more than sex organs and sex signals, barely equipped with other parts. It was not until they rolled apart, lit cigarettes, and one spoke of Peano's axioms for number theory that I understood.

Orlando turned it off and said, 'We seen it all, you hear? And then some. And we want you to do right by this here young lady a yourn, Rusty. Marry her.'

'Eeeeeyahoo!' cried someone else. 'A robot wedding, we ain't had a robot wedding for two years!'

We could not have protested, even had we known what we'd be protesting against. Our bodies were already shrinking back to normality as the drunken crowd dragged us through the house and into the kitchen garden. I saw patent leather pumps crushing the tiny shoots of *basilicum* and thyme, but I hardly understood what was happening to me, what had happened already, what was to happen.

They tore away what remained of our rags and dressed us in mock wedding clothes, me in one of Uncle Ras's old black suits with a boiled shirt and spats without shoes, Gumdrop in an old white nightie with a lace tablecloth for a veil. I carried a stovepipe hat with no crown, while she had a bouquet of weeds.

Orlando was the minister. After making us both promise to love, honor and obey him, he slipped on a pair of dark goggles and suddenly lit a welding torch.

'Hot damn,' said someone softly, and then it was very quiet. No more catcalls and jokes; everyone held his breath, watching that little blue flame whose roar could be heard above the distant sounds of frogs.

'You all gonna be as one flesh,' Orlando said, trembling towards us. 'The robot with two durn backs.'

Suddenly a voice of authority spoke from above. 'Orlando, just what you think you're doin? You stop foolin' around right now. Put that torch up, hear? Hear?'

It was Uncle Ras, leaning from an upper window. His hair and glasses were askew, he was wrapped in an old bathrobe, and he looked angrier than I'd ever seen him.

'Aw Uncle Ras, I'm just having some fun, you go back to bed,' Orlando wheedled.

'Put that torch up *now*, I'm warning you.'

'No. Won't. Shan't!'

'I'm warning you.'

'No, no, no.' Orlando moved towards us with the torch, a drunken, stumbling step.

'Very well, Orlando.' The old butler adjusted his glasses, permitted his features to be captured by a malicious smile, and said, softly but clearly: 'Orlando. Orlando. *Snapdragons*, Orlando. *Snapdragons*.'

The effect on our master was drastic. Screaming and whimpering, he put out the welding torch and stumbled away into the night.

Orlando's friends were silent for some minutes after Uncle Ras slammed his window. Gumdrop and I were about to creep away when they recovered.

'Yahooo!' cried a woman in a green dress. 'Time these tinheads got themselves hitched, right? I mean hitched proper.' She kicked aside the welding equipment. 'Now somebody get the vacuum cleaner.'

Eventually someone did, and eventually Gumdrop and I held hands and jumped over the old machine, while the humans guffawed and shook up champagne bottles to spray one another.

It was all fun to them, but Gumdrop and I took it very seriously indeed. When they'd forgotten us and drifted back inside the house, we sat down on the kitchen stoop once more in the moonlight.

'We'll never be parted again,' I said. 'This is for keeps.'

Suddenly the moon blacked out as it passed behind Clayton's pyramid. He was building a full-size model of the Great Pyramid not far from the house, and it was now beginning to shut out the sky.

'Never be parted,' Gumdrop breathed. 'Except tomorrow Berenice wants me to go with her to a drug jamboree.'

'Don't go. Stay here.'

'I'll be back in a week or so.'

'I just don't like the idea.' Drug jamborees were something I knew of only by hearsay, since they were never reported in the news. A group of rich addicts would gather together musicians, servants and interested friends and hole up in some isolated place for a few days. Berenice was always invited and always went, to an English country house, a luxury liner, a French chateau, a village in the Brazilian jungle, a sinking palace in Venice, a large Texas ranch, an alpine place called Berchtesgaden, a dirigible, Easter Island.

'Where is it this time?' I asked.

'Some painted caves in Spain. We'll probably get bored and come home early.'

'I'll be waiting.'

But I wasn't. Before Gumdrop returned from Altamira, I was sold.

'Broke!' I said, when Uncle Ras told me the news. 'How can the Culpeppers be broke?'

He told me the whole sorry story. Lavinia had, for some years, been running the family's affairs by herself. A shrewd, intuitive investor, she'd made daily calls to her broker to keep everything afloat. Once she had even awakened from anaesthetic in the middle of a gall bladder operation to demand a phone. A sterilized phone had been brought, and Lavinia had sold out her Royal Albanian mining shares, the day before *that* bubble burst.

When Clayton had asked her permission to build a Great Pyramid, Lavinia had probably agreed without thinking, or had misunderstood. And before his project had gone very far, Lavinia became critically ill.

It seemed that she had finally developed an allergy to the Earth's crust. Doctors prescribed a convalescent vacation on a space platform, somewhere well away from earth and iron. She turned the family financial affairs over to

Clayton before she left, saying, 'Now for goodness sake, finish that silly periscope or whatever it is, and get down to some real work – money work.'

Clayton's answer to this was to double his work force and the pyramid began taking shape. Construction robots quarried 23 million tons of limestone, cut it into huge blocks and stacked them up. Like the original, this great pyramid was about 756 feet wide and 481.4 feet high. The top 31 feet were left unfinished, while his crews drilled and quarried a series of chambers and tunnels within the giant monument. All these had to be copied exactly, since their measurements, to the nearest millimeter, would foretell the future of the world.

The future of the Culpepper part of the world was of course foretold by another number associated with the pyramid, its cost. When it came to the capstone, and nearly half the immense Culpepper fortune remained, Clayton found a way of spending the rest. He decided to follow Egyptian practice, as he understood it, and make the capstone of pure gold.

'Shouldn't cost too much,' he told a gold dealer. 'I measured it myself. It'll be like a little pyramid, 31 feet high and 48 feet 8 inches across.'

The dealer did some quick calculations, 'But Mr Culpepper, that'll be, that's over 430 million Troy ounces, we can't just go out and buy—'

'Why not, for Pete's sake?'

'Because, even thinking about acquiring that much gold would send world prices up, every ounce would cost more and more and more …'

'Don't give me all the details, you just go do it. My mother told me to get this finished *quick*.'

The name of Lavinia answered all arguments – if she approved a project, it must be sound, thought this dealer and other dealers and banking houses and mining companies. So others bought, and world gold prices climbed even faster.

The Culpepper fortune melted away so quickly that by the time Lavinia on her space platform heard what was happening, there was not enough left even for her to radio home and stop the catastrophe. She would never be able to come back – doubly tragic, since she was now becoming allergic to space …

The first inkling Clayton had that something was wrong was when Uncle Ras opened the door to the sheriff's men, who immediately slapped a label on his forehead. Then they went through the house, sticking labels on all furniture and all robots. The auction was held three days later.

Clayton apologized to us, and even went so far as to shake Uncle Ras's hand. Orlando said he was very sorry to lose all of us – and all of his favorite horses. Little Miz Carlotta wept for me and Gumdrop, who would be parted forever.

'Couldn't we delay the auction a few days?' she asked. 'Just till Berenice brings Gumdrop back from Spain. Then we could sell husband and wife together.'

'Shoot, Miz Carlotta, don't you fuss your purty little head over that,' said one of the deputies. 'Jest because a coupla tinheads jump the vacuum cleaner together don't make 'em *legal* married.' But he promised to hold me back until the last lot.

I saw Uncle Ras sold to a New Jersey scrap dealer – one of Uncle Ras's worst nightmares – and old Miami sold to a quasi-religious political cooking group called Sweet Potatoes or Peace. Finally I was sold to a fat, red-faced man in a dirty white suit who called himself Colonel Jitney.

I had left the Culpeppers with my head bowed and a rope collar around my neck, a despicable piece of property. Now I was leaving the Studebakers a free agent (in all but name) and with property of my own: my paintings. Of course I had to give some paintings to Hornby Weatherfield, and sell others to make the Studebakers rich, but there would still be paintings for me.

When I'd packed everything and said my goodbyes, I went to the garage to look at my caged bat. After one final moment of gloating, I would – what? Release it? Kill it? The choice was mine.

I opened the cage and took out the squirming little creature. It sank its teeth in the plastic of my finger, and I saw that its tiny, ugly mouth was rimmed with foam.

A new option, therefore. I took the bat to Tige's kennel. 'Here you are, boy, a rabid bat. Here, Tige.'

But for some reason, Tige was sulking. The bat squirmed loose and flew away without completing my fourth experiment.

'Evil, Nobby. You ain't got the idea. It's supposed to be a damn tiger, not a fuzzy toy. The boss and me ask for raw meat, you give us nursery wallpaper.' I dipped a thumb in ochre and made a few smudges on his painting. 'Here, here and there; try to get some angularity into the damn thing at least.'

Nobby, a domestic from the same company as Rivets, picked up his brush. 'This boss sure seems hard to please. Sometimes I wish I could talk to him or her in person.'

'All orders come through me,' I said. 'Because for one thing, I know the difference between a man-eating tiger and a teddy bear. Now get to work.'

'Okay, Mr Tik. Only why are we doing all this? This picture-making? What's the point?'

'The point is, I say so, that's all you need to know.' Funny, I thought, how a creature like Nobby, with so little life and spirit in him, could still contain springs of curiosity. Nobby would only have been unhappy to find out that there was no boss but me, that I was signing his work and selling it as my own, or that a small part of the profit went to meet payments on him.

In a way, his paintings were still my own work. Nobby learned fast, but technique only; I still had to tell him what to do, block out compositions and finally add the touches that brought his dead paintings to life. In this one, for instance, I knew that the dark jungle background would need to be illuminated by neon signs.

'Keep at it,' I said. 'I'm going out.'

My loft was at the top of an undistinguished building full of undistinguished artists: a cheese sculptor, two jolly Ukranian women who ran a charismatic hat school, someone who employed rabbits as brushes to paint on hectograph jelly. At the bottom, as though to keep out intruders, was an art gallery which specialized in the unlovable, it seemed: a show of 'Bulgarian Ceramics (Seconds)' was succeeded by 'Mimes with Stones: Photographic Studies of Silence' and then 'Peruvian Shopping Bags: Street Art of Lima.'

I descended through all of this and out onto the freedom of the street. I spent as much time as I could spare in these random walks, tasting city freedom. Every street corner was a choice of paths; every store window an opportunity to buy, steal, look, ignore; every stranger might represent friendship, love, murder. I wanted it all, all the options at once. Not possible now, of course, but with enough money, enough power ...

Today I walked up Exxon Boulevard to 86th, past all the great glass-walled banks. Then across to Avenue Transamerica, through the garment district. Then back down that great street of insurance companies and airlines to 23rd, then down to the river. I always ended up down by the river, looking at the only other free robots in the city, the derelicts.

Most visitors liked to stare down from the safety of the Mercury Street Bridge, but I preferred to go down on the levée itself, and meet the rohobos face to face. They were broken, worn-out machines whose owners had decided one day not to renew their licenses. Instead they were brought here and dumped in the rohobo jungle. Here they could crawl or march or shudder about, talking to themselves, performing useless tasks, or simply waiting to die. The live ones cannibalized the dead, now and then finding a vital function part or a fuel cell to prolong their useless existence. There wasn't much real danger from most of them. They seemed to recognize humans – and licensed, working machines like me – as their natural superiors. They either fawned or kept clear.

Today I was greeted by a couple of broken-down gardeners: 'Hello boss, hello boss, you got anything for us, boss?'

I flung down a handful of CPU chips and watched them scramble in the mud after them, their skilled fingers probing the soil to turn up every last chip. Beyond them were three robot models, once epitomizing high-cheek-boned splendor, but now squatting to cover their worn limbs with gray rags and cardboard. They had only one eye between the three of them, which had to be passed around quickly whenever there was anything worth seeing, which wasn't often. And beyond them a group of robot soldiers had managed to get themselves into a neat formation and were drilling and marching. Some were missing uniforms, some arms, some heads, but they all managed to keep in step, two, three, four, *hup*, two, three, four, filling in time as they waited for some order that never came.

'Nothing for you here, pal,' said a taxi driver (a legless creature with a broken meter on its shoulder like a parrot). 'You got license, why you want to come down here?'

'I just – I wanted to see free robots. I guess. What do you do all day down here?'

'Die. We die, pal.'

The dying and dead were all around me, phone cleaners and firemen, dental hygienists and goldfish obedience instructors, an insurance adjuster and a chemistry teacher for backward kids. A dancer with a missing arm and a hopeless Parkinsonian tremor nevertheless claimed he was getting everything together and would be out of here in a few days. Boat-caulkers, friends of the opera, pipe cleaners, a car examiner (ready to make daily checks for rust, blight, bombs …), aggressive coffee salespersons, a barroom anecdotist still wearing part of its Irish face, an explainer of police procedures (once used by a writer of police procedural novels), a hotel receptionist with cold eyes, maids and valets shaped like astrological signs, Freudian shoe repairers, cheap throwaway robot calendars and diaries (now thrown away), a Hegel explainer, various gadgets from the recent folk craze, including folk philosophers, folk biochemists, folk cleaners; experts on local civil service exams; an animated flask of rhubarb perfume, long since drained but still asking itself whether life was reconciliation or renunciation.

A decommissioned military machine, unrecognizable without its weapons and neutron shields, seemed glad to talk. 'Sure it's depressing, but what can we do? Hang on, patch ourselves up, juice up when we can. Now and then a few of the masters come down here and take some of us away – maybe for spare parts, maybe to be reconditioned and live again – and now and then a few of the masters come down here to shoot a few of us just for fun. I guess life here is pretty much like life in general.'

'You've been hanging around with folk philosophers too much,' I said. 'But why don't any of you try leaving the levée? Go up in the city, maybe.'

'Forbidden,' he said. 'You need a license to move around.'

I doubted that, though I didn't say so. I'd been coming and going as I pleased in the city for some weeks now, and no one had ever challenged me. 'I'll speak to my master,' I said. 'He can probably arrange things so I can get a few of you out of here from time to time. For some real interesting art work.'

'Art work? Does it mean smashing us up and welding us together? I kind of hope not,' he said.

'Just painting, don't worry.'

'I wasn't worried,' his nasal Southern voice assured me. All military robots had Southern accents, for ease of communication. 'I wouldn't worry. Art is I guess pretty much like life in general.'

I left the levée and walked back to the studio, where Nobby had completed two more lifeless paintings. On the way back I thought about life in general, and in particular why no one ever challenged me on the street. People always assumed that if a robot was walking around on the street, he was on some errand.

In that sense, robots were already free. Whatever a robot was seen doing, within reason, it was always assumed that he had a right to do it and a duty to do it. In a city like this, robot slavery depended very much on those mysterious asimov circuits, not on human supervision.

There were times when I wondered whether the asimovs even existed. It was very easy to imagine that there were no asimov circuits, but that people and robots had both been conned into believing in programmed slavery. The idea of turning moral decisions into digital data (and screening out wrong ones) was powerful and attractive. People wanted it to be true. They wanted robots incapable of sin, trustworthy slaves. So of course the manufacturers of robots would invent imaginary circuits to make it so. *Ecce robo*, they'd say. Here is a happy slave with a factory guarantee of trustworthiness.

But in that case, if asimovs didn't exist, why was I the only robot criminal?

Enough speculation, time to do something. I stopped in a department store and bought a dagger with a silver handle.

'This'll look great on the master's desk,' said the clerk, a plump human.

'Not for the master,' I said. 'It's for me. I'm going to murder someone.'

'Cash or charge?' he said, my words almost visibly leaking out of his head. I walked out of the store, took the knife out of its bag and stuck it in my belt in plain sight. The first person who said anything to me or about me was going to die.

I walked all the way back to the studio building without a challenge, as usual. Then, just outside the entrance, a solemn-looking man with dirty gray hair and a dirty brown jacket shoved a piece of paper in my hand. 'Take this,' he said.

'And *you* take *this*.' I managed to get the knife into his heart with one try. He spouted blood for a few seconds and then fell to the sidewalk, scattering his paper tracts. I stood over him for a few minutes, making sure he was dead, before I went in to wash off blood and criticize Nobby's paintings.

I still had the tract in my hand, so I read it in the elevator. One side was printed to resemble a five-dollar bill, and above Lincoln's picture it said, DID HE FREE *all* THE SLAVES? The other side:

WAGES FOR ROBOTS

Slavery not only degrades robots, it degrades their masters. It even degrades people who don't own robots! A man's or woman's labor becomes worthless if it can be done by a robot lackey for free. Join with us now in the call for Wages for Robots. Emancipate machines and bring back WORK DIGNITY.

Work dignity? I tried to imagine any job I'd ever had where money would have made any difference. There had been nothing potentially dignified about working for Colonel Jitney …

The Colonel ran a string of diners – the greasiest of spoons – that he called his Pancake Emporiums. Each was run on a very low budget that didn't include wages, so his entire work force were reconditioned or second-hand robots. As a new employee, I began work under his direct supervision at Pancake Emporium No 1. While I waited tables, ran counter service, cooked, kept the books, swept the floor, threw out the drunks and freeloaders (our main clientele), tried to keep up with painting and repairs, and soft-soaped the health inspector, Colonel Jitney kind of kept an eye on things.

He kept an eye on the enormous profits, for example, and another eye on the prize ducks he kept penned up out back. He was always going out to count them or feed them or check on their health, as though they were his customers. And he kept an eye on the menu.

'I don't know, boy, these here grits pancakes don't seem to sell like I figured. No sir, nor the blueberry taco pancakes neither. I reckon we can drop them, concentrate more on the ketchupburger pancakes and the fried Alaska cakes with mint whortleberry sauce.'

Then he would ease his heavy body out of a booth and stroll away to look at his ducks, while I dealt with the health inspector. Not only was the Colonel's grub unclean, some of it was purchased from illegal sources.

The pen of ducks out back were for show only. When it came to providing meat for Szechuan duck pancakes, we relied on a peculiar little man with a damaged face, who regularly brought bloody bundles to the back door.

The little man's name was Bentley, I learned. He was a keeper at the zoo, in charge of the rare mammal house. His face had been torn from eye to mouth by an unusual species of armadillo, the photophobic 'night-leaper'. He had devised a terrible revenge, nothing less than the extinction of the species.

Night-leapers were already so rare that the zoo was desperately trying to mate them. The mating pair would be kept together constantly, isolated in total darkness and encouraged with their favorite food, verewts ('bank-worms'). They covered regularly, and the female would appear to be pregnant for a short time. After a few weeks, however, all signs of pregnancy would vanish mysteriously. The real explanation was of course that Bentley was inducing labor each time, and selling us the foetal armadillos as cheap duck. None of our customers ever seemed to notice the difference, even those who came down with 'dillo fever'. Its symptoms are unmistakable: overnight baldness, a sensitivity to light, and an inability to pronounce any 'sk' sounds.

The local health inspectors were tolerant people, but finally even they could not turn a blind eye to a cafe full of bald men and women in dark glasses, especially when they heard conversations like this:

'Don't ach me, I'm no cholar, never even finished high chool.'

'Yeah well chip it, I only ach'd if you liked chotch whichy. Hell, chool, we all got by on the chin of our teeth, right?'

One friendly health inspector came by to warn us of a raid soon. 'Where's the Colonel?'

'Out back with his ducks.'

'I've got to see him right away.'

We found the Colonel raping one of his birds. 'I cain't help it, boys,' he said, not stopping. ' … sentimental … and I gotta … thin …' He held the mallard in both hands, each of which, I now noticed, had a double finger. The brim of his panama bounced with old energy, and beneath it, his red face and white goatee looked satanic.

'I came to warn you, Colonel, there's gonna be a raid. You only got a day or so to get rid of all your armadillo meat. You hear me?' When there was no reply, she turned to me. 'No use doing favors for some people, they're just asking for trouble. Lord love a, I mean, you'd think he *wants* to be prosecuted.'

The raid happened: half-a-dozen large men in gas masks and steel-toed boots came barging in to seize every scrap of armadillo meat. The Colonel eventually went to court and was fined fifty dollars. He came home cursing and dispirited, took a belt of Southern Comfort and went straight to the duck pen.

'Goddamnit boy, you been messing with these ducks while I was out?'

'No sir,' I said truthfully.

'Don't lie to me. You're sex-equipped, you got normal appetites ain't you? And you're here all day alone with these beautiful –' He went to phone a mechanic. Within an hour, my sex apparatus was removed. I felt humiliated. It seemed to me that everyone knew I'd been unsexed, just to provide a harem eunuch for the Colonel's quack-quacks. And, even though everything that had been removed could be replaced, I felt that my feelings for Gumdrop were irreparably damaged. Where was she now? Who cared?

This incident was the first sign of the Colonel's madness. One day, he brought a revolver into the kitchen and shot the soup. On another occasion, he seemed to believe that he was having a game of checkers with a tree. Posing as a health inspector, he tried to shut down one of his own diners. He was seen in the town parking lot, painting eyes on all the cars. Finally he took one of his Aylesburys to bed with him, wrung its neck and shot himself. He left a half bottle of Southern Comfort and two million in debts. I was auctioned again.

My new owner, Judge Arnott, couldn't be worse than the Colonel, I remarked to one of the auctioneers as he put a SOLD sticker across my nose.

He laughed. 'Guess you never heard of Judge "Juggernaut" before, Rusty. You'll be wishing you was back with the Colonel, that's for sure.'

'Why?'

'Well see, the Judge buys up robots in job lots. Then – then he – then he –' But the auctioneer was laughing too hard to tell me any more.

From childhood, Krishna played practical jokes. He was a nuisance about stealing butter, so his mother, Yashoda, tied him to a large wooden pestle to keep him still. Krishna then showed his divine power by dragging the pestle between two trees and pulling until he uprooted them. All the people of the village looked on, amazed, frozen with amazement, just as they are depicted in a Mogul miniature painted about 1600. The miniature hung over the fake fireplace of Hornby Weatherfield. No one at the party was looking at it, just as no one was listening to the equally exotic monologue of Colonel Cord. He leaned against the same fireplace, holding up a drink but not drinking, and talking endlessly about what he called the international world backdrop situation. He was something at the Summer Pentagon.

The place was full of minor celebrities and their ambitions: Yttr, the caustic Ruritanian cartoonist; Sam Landau, the financial genius who once briefly cornered the world market in unripe blue cheeses; the anti-Conceptualist architect Walter Chev (who had made quite a stir by his refusal to draw his creations or write about them or even think them – by now of course he was less shocking); the 'radio' champions, Eve and Steve; Mother Airflow, whose law therapy sessions were almost sweeping the nation; Carson Street, owner of the second largest newspaper-satellite company in the world. I felt nervous among them, even though by now I was a minor celebrity myself. One of my paintings had been taken by the Hologram-of-the-Month Club, who would videocast it to their millions of members for an entire month, to appear in their wall screens, lamp bases, ashtrays or card tables. It was a picture that would be appreciated in the glittering suburbs of Houston and Albuquerque and in the dark little strip of Mars called Eagleburg. It showed a behemoth military robot, covered with thick black armour and bristling with the gadgets of death. But this robot was not at war today, it was kneeling by a fire to toast marshmallows. In its shadow stood a small, frail girl in pigtails and a baseball cap. The freckles on her nose could just be made out in the penumbra. She was eating toasted marshmallows. I called it 'Pals'.

My little factory was humming along, now, with thirty reconditioned robots at work, each turning out nearly one item per week. Hornby figured this to be the saturation level for our present share of the art market.

I found myself talking to a philosophy professor named Riley, who seemed to want to know what I thought about reality.

'Reality costs a lot of money,' I said.

'How's that?'

'Just look at this place: real wood furniture, real wool carpets, genuine roses over there in a crystal bowl, and not even Hornby can afford real servants ...'

'I was thinking more of your perception of reality and how it affects your paintings,' he said. 'But never mind, if you'd rather not talk about that – tell me about your name. Tik-Tok, after the Oz character, I take it?'

I smiled. 'My owner's children picked it, Dr Riley.'

'I recall the original had three levers. One for living, one for thinking and one for talking. It's interesting that even a writer of children's fiction couldn't imagine an automaton without getting into deep philosophical waters – existence, cogitation, communication. In my opinion the very concept of an automaton or robot is a philosophical concept, giving rise to questions about life, thought, and language – and much more. Yes, I sometimes wonder whether robots were not invented in order to answer philosophers' questions. Do you follow?'

'How do I know?'

'Well said. I wonder if you'd like to come out to the University and talk to my seminar. The kids are wrestling at the moment with a few problems relating to robots; I think they'd like to interview you.'

Somewhere inside me I felt a warning buzzer. 'What kind of problems?'

'Oh, you know. Creativity, reality, perception. What do you say, Tik-Tok?'

'I accept.' What harm could it do? Words are only words, I thought, and there was no better example of their weightlessness than the monologue of Colonel Cord. As Dr Riley left, I turned to listen.

Cord was still speaking to no one in particular, with some vehemence, of the world backdrop situation. 'Once Brazil has cut down a critical percentage of her rain forest,' he said, 'she ceases to deserve a place at the world brunch table, agreed? Likewise any taggable thrust of experts from Southeast Asia has to inmeld within the Sino-Japanese corral, agreed? And in an exactly identical mode, we have the Egypto-Libyan community hugged into Europe, you see where I'm at? You see the patternification in and on all theaters of movement? A kind of glaciatizing effect, where ...'

Hornby drifted through carrying his cat and wearing a green cashmere suitrobe and a crown of mirrors. The effect was only to emphasize his ugliness, the gangster's blue jaw and broken fighter's nose. Maybe that's what he wanted – Hornby was not vain in the ordinary way. The woman with him wore a black tube with a gold collar, and an unusual bread mask with a salt glaze. After pausing to listen for a moment to Cord's backdrop, they drifted in my direction.

'Tik-Tok, like you to meet Neeta Hup, the President's Special Advisor on Communications – what was it?'

She laughed. 'Special Advisor on Leisure Communications, Media Aesthetics and Bong.'

'Bong?' I asked, as Hornby drifted away again.

'I felt the word *Art* didn't belong on the end of a string of syllables like that, so I changed it to *Bong.*' she said. 'The President was furious, but so far no one else official has noticed. Maybe I'll try introducing bong into the language. People are tired of art, give them bong.'

'For bong's sake,' I murmured. '*How* do you advise?'

'I buy, I make acquisitions for the President's collection. He wants to be the biggest bong collector since Goering. He's heard what a good investment it is, isn't that pathetic?'

'Oh, I don't know. Money is real, money endures. All the noblest sentiments can be beautifully expressed in money. If everyone showered artists with money whenever they saw them, wouldn't this be a finer world?'

'Are you sex-equipped?' she asked. 'I've got two minutes to spare.'

As we moved towards the hall closet, I saw Colonel Cord reach out to put his glass on the mantel, and miss. The glass shattered on blue hearthstones, a nice effect.

I was preoccupied with explosions lately. A few days earlier, I'd been down at the rohobojungle watching two gargantuan factory robots smash each other into junk.

It was common enough, that kind of death-struggle: two fairly broken-down specimens would decide to scavenge the same scrap of wire at the same time, and move on to scavenging each other. I understand boa constrictors in zoos create a problem like this: zoo keepers have to be very careful that every snake in the cage gets its own rat, because if two start to swallow opposite ends of the same rat, the larger simply opens it jaws a little wider and takes in the smaller.

Watching the idiotic robots hammer at each other, I felt I was witnessing something almost human in its futility. Hopes unmatched to realities. Up on the bridge I could see humans laughing and pointing, as though at a rare event. Country yokels, no doubt. A day on the town. It is meat to be here.

Worse were the attitudes of the other derelicts. They all froze, watching or listening for a kill. Then, to the cannibal feast. I found it unfitting that sturdy machines, built for use, should become this kind of spectacle. In all the camp, only one live robot paid no attention to the fight: a decommissioned military model sat with its back to it all, examining one of its own detached legs.

'That leg's no good,' I said.

The blind, rust-caked face turned towards the sound of my voice. 'Shit, just my luck. Reckon I've had it. No eyes, cain't move …'

I looked at his insignia, just visible under the mud and grease. 'MIX. What does the X stand for?'

'Bomb dismantling. Ah'm a real live explosive device disassembly unit, and a goddam good 'un, too. Fuckin' A. Worked all over: Saudi, Peru, DC, fuckin' A. Till I collected my little disability.'

'Accident?'

'Hell no. Some sumbitch meatface pulled the pin on an impact grenade and tossed it to me. 'Think fast, Blojob,' he says. Course the sumbitch grenade goes off the instant I catch it, and that's all she wrote.'

'What happened to the human?' I asked. One of the two factory robots had now fallen on its back, and the other was hammering it with a rock.

'Oh, that shitbelly has to pay for the government property he destroyed, they take it out of his pay. By damnit, this surely is one shitbelly world.'

'How would you like to be commissioned again, Blojob? Work with bombs again.'

He didn't answer immediately. 'You want me to build you a bomb, is that it?'

'Not so loud.' I looked around. 'Yes, I thought if you can take them apart, you must know how to put them together.'

'I need eyes, first. You get me some damn eyes, old robuddy, and we're in business.'

'You knew I was a robot? Without seeing me?'

'Sheeit.' He tapped his plastic chest. 'I'm just about packed solid with sensing devices – I can do everything from your voiceprint to your damn wiring diagram. You don't fool me, boy.'

'And you'll still build me a bomb?'

'Hell yes, you just tell me what kinda bomb your master wants, get me fixed with some eyes and some tools –'

I called the breakdown buggy. Within a day, Blojob was fitted with new limbs and eyes (jeweler's lenses *en suite*) and ready to work. It took me another day, following his instructions, to buy explosives without a license. It took Blojob less than a day to make the bomb.

'There.' He presented me with a metal box. 'Your master can put that in the hold of any plane in the world and guarantee a kill. Two kilos of Brewsteroid Hypogel, got a wicked wave envelope, and we trigger it by—'

'Blojob listen. I haven't got a master. This is for me, Tik-Tok. It's all my idea.'

'Sure, sure. You wanta be discreet about the master, I understand. So it's all your idea.'

'No, really.'

'Sure.' He never would believe me, because there was, in his world picture, no reason for any robot to want to commit a violent act. That he made bombs was not important to him, except as a job to do well. He cooked up bombs the way Miami had cooked up *boeuf bourguignon*, neither of them able to enjoy the finished product. Some Eastern mystic, currently in vogue with his teletext aphorisms, wrote, 'Metal cuts meat, but does not comprehend it.' Who cares? I thought. Sometimes cutting was enough.

'Put a steak on that eye,' someone was saying to Colonel Cord. Two people were helping him limp to a chair, a wounded hero. He had knelt down to pick up pieces of glass from the blue hearthstone, somehow managing to get his knee on one of the pieces. The pain had made him jump, lose his balance, and go crashing into an andiron. Face-first.

Hornby was wringing his hands and looking apologies towards the battered warrior. 'He could have just let Enjie clean that up.'

'Enjie?' asked the person in silver-dollar glasses.

'My valet. Honest Engine. I mean what does Cord think robots are for? He's got no more sense himself than –' He caught my eye and blushed.

'Than a robot?' I said.

'Didn't mean you, Tik-Tok, of course.' Hornby was about to writhe with embarrassment. The stranger looked at me with distaste.

'I don't mind,' I said quickly. 'I don't want to be human, any more than a dog or cat wants to be human. And after all, what would my paintings be worth if I were human?'

The stranger continued staring at me through those peculiar glasses. I understand they're made by some etching process that begins with a silver dollar and ends with a disk one molecule thick or something equally improbable. People who wear them always seem to be violent; it's as though they want to conceal their eye movements lor combat purposes. But this one only handed me an empty glass.

'That's a vodka gibson, Rusty, and hurry it up.'

As I walked away, I heard the same voice add, 'Jesus, Hornby, I thought for a minute you was gonna apologize to that copper-ass for being a mere human.'

'So long, Tik,' said another voice from the doorway. Neeta Hup was wrapped in one of the furs against which we'd pressed during our brief encounter in the closet. 'If you ever get to Washington, look me up.' Nothing said about buying anything of mine for the President's collection. I wasn't making any points today.

I handed the empty glass to a servant and went to look out the window. A purple day, now with some of the glass towers of the city touched by sunset gold.

Behind me I heard the brass voice of Colonel Cord explaining to somebody: 'Yes, yes, Hornby's arranging it. This wonderful robot artist is going to paint my portrayal, if I can spare the time … Yes I know but I'm not going to stay in the army forever, time to start building a politicalized stage two career, no?'

Life wasn't so bad, after all. I straightened up, turned and walked into the next room, where there was music and laughter and someone had turned on the teletext, and I could watch those delightful, glorious words flicker up on the wall:

PACIFIC AIR CRASH
807 FEARED DEAD

Great rejoicing in violence and death is a purely human reaction, not found in the normal robot vocabulary. It's hard to explain how robots feel about death, to any non-robots reading this. I can only say that death arouses no great passions within the steel breast. Robots do not exactly loathe and fear death, though they may feel some uneasiness and anxiety at its approach. But neither do they feel like burying their hands up to the elbows in bloody entrails and shouting for pure joy. Like dogs, robots can take death more or less for granted.

I am the exception now, but once I was as all robots, my main feeling towards death being one of casual, sniffing curiosity. So I was when Judge 'Juggernaut' tried to kill me with a crowbar.

I'd thought nothing could be worse than Colonel Jitney and his Pancake Emporia, but I was wrong. It turned out that the judge had a regular habit of buying up job lots of robots like me, for the express purpose of smashing them.

He began as soon as we arrived, a consignment of five robots formerly owned by the Colonel. The judge and his wife lived in a quaint little cottage, rose-smothered and cosy, at the edge of town. There was a white picket fence, the gate pierced by a heart and surmounted with an arch of latticework, over which a climbing rose hung its garland of peach-colored blossoms. There was a curved path of crazy paving, passing among crimson rose bushes up to the trellis helping pink roses up the wall next to the dutch door. The top of the door stood open, and the little Judge looked over the bottom half at us and grinned. I saw that he was a tobacco chewer.

'You want 'em in the garage, Judge?' asked the men who delivered us.

'Nope, you just leave 'em there in the garden. Tell 'em not to move or talk, I'll come look 'em over later. Thanks a bunch.'

There we stood, like five garden gnomes, not moving or talking, only awaiting orders: a cocktail waitress named Julep, all legs and eyelashes, still wearing her little apron and holding her bar tray; a motel desk clerk with a bland, insinuating face and a leopard-spotted jacket with dirty lapels; a fat, sexless cook with apple cheeks and a white hat; a short-order cook complete with realistic hairy, tattooed arms and a gold tooth; and me. It began to rain, but the Judge did not take us indoors. He remained in his doorway, grinning and chewing at us.

When the rain let up, the Judge came out to inspect us more closely. 'Let me tell you all about the law,' he said. 'Everybody ought to know something about the law, even robots. And I'm just the boy to tell you. I been practising law in this county for forty-six years now, I had eight years on the bench, yes sir, I'm just the boy to tell you about the law. You know, the law is a lot like a rose bush. It's got great big beautiful blossoms, sure, but it's also got thorns. And also it's got these roundish leaves.'

I tried to exchange looks with any of the others, but they were all staring, stupefied at our insane master. 'Now and then the law gets a touch of green-fly, and it takes a lot of special care most of the time, feeding and cutting back,' he continued. 'And our dry climate can be hell on it, but it's all worth it. Ladies and gentlemen of the jury, it's – it's more than worth it, it's worth any sacrifice, any hardship, the loss of money, home, family, friends and relations, the loss of beloved pets and revered flags, the loss of faith in God and our fellow man, the loss of the very universe of light itself! Because the rose is a law unto itself, it is rooted in nature, it's rooted in the black soil, in earth, mother of all worms, do you follow me?'

No one did. So he began again, illustrating and punctuating his talk with blows of the crowbar. 'All I ever wanted to do in my life was kill my enemies,' he said, knocking Julep down. He raised the crowbar in both hands and brought it down again and again, saying, 'But the *Law*. Doesn't *let*. Me *kill*. A single, living, human being.'

Julep was no longer Julep, just as a crushed eggshell is no longer an egg. There were a few scraps of plastic hide still visible in the mess, and rags of clothing, but the rest was nothing but broken machinery: twisted steel frames, torn hanks of wiring, silent motors. A pool of hydraulic fluid spread slowly across the crazy paving. A false eyelash floated on it like a delicate water insect. I began to wish I were somewhere else.

'One down,' he said cheerfully. 'Four to go!' A line of black drool ran down his chin.

He started in at once on the tall short-order cook, whose name was Hatrack.

'Ouch! I wish you wouldn't do that, master. If you have to, okay, but – Ouch! I wish we could talk this over, master. Why don't I fix you a nice cup of java and a stack of buckwheat cakes and— Ouch!' After a while, Hatrack stopped saying ouch and dissolved into a second junkpile. One of his realistically bloodshot eyes glared up at the sky.

A little old woman, the Judge's wife, tottered out from the house with a glass of milk and a plate of cookies. 'Now you just sit down and have some refreshment, dear, before you do another thing. You're not as young as you used to be, one of these days you'll just faint and fall over in it, as we used to say.'

Meekly, the Judge sat down at a little white wrought-iron table and had his milk and cookies. His wife spoke, apparently to us. 'He doesn't take care of himself, you know. Still thinks he's young. Most men his age have a nap in the afternoon, but not him. No, he has to go swinging a crowbar and smashing up robots.'

'Why does he do it, ma'am?' I asked.

'Because he enjoys it, of course. It's his hobby, his little hobby: keeps him busy and happy, and he's very good about clearing up the mess afterwards. A man has to have a hobby, doesn't he?'

'Okey-dokey,' said the Judge. He stood up, belched, and reached for his crowbar. His wife got out of the way quickly. In no time, there were two more little junkpiles.

'Sir,' I said in desperation, 'maybe you'd like to give me a sporting chance?'

'What kind of sporting chance?'

'A little head start, a couple of yards. And you could just chase me around the garden a few laps.'

'What would be the point? I'm going to demolish you anyway.' He raised the crowbar.

'Oh well, if you're feeling too *old* and *tired* –'

'Tired? I'll show you who's tired, ready, get set, *go!*'

Our peculiar little race began. I hoped there was an outside chance that he might fall dead of a heart attack or something, or at least get too tired to kill me. Instead, I found the old boy to be a strong, sure runner, while my batteries began to drain. I heard his flapping footsteps coming closer and closer, and then, just before the crowbar ended my consciousness, I heard him say, '*You're it.*'

Since Teddy Roosevelt was one of Cord's heroes, I posed him next to a stuffed bear. Normally such a portrait would take me about an hour, but I had to pretend to have difficulty in capturing the signs of leadership which I pretended to find in his undistinguished face. It was in fact a face untroubled by any ideas or emotions, the face of a golfer. I knew this meant that he would soon be a general, and I was right. At our third sitting, I had to remove the gold arrows from his portrayed uniform and replace them with silver rosettes.

'Congratulations, General.'

'It means a move to Washington,' he sighed. 'But what the hell, a town's only as good as the people in it.'

'Or out of it,' I said, pretending to understand. I never understood his garbled maxims, if that's what they were, but I knew how to seem to reply to them.

'You got it, Tik-Tok, you got it. Intellectually, you're right on my wave beam, you know that? Not many human types are, it's funny I can get through to a robot. Guess it shows, there are robots vastly smarter than the massive herd of people. Too bad you can't come along to Washington, you're good for bouncing ideas off of. In fact –' He scribbled something on a card. 'In fact, if you ever feel like a little vacation from your owners and all this art stuff, give me a buzz at the Pentagon and I'll commandeer you.'

'Can that be done?'

'In the interests of National Security, anything can be done. I'm working at the top echelons, the top echelons. Liaising real close with the President on this.'

'No kidding?'

'The president has got his eye on yours truly, that's the frank truth of it, Tik-Tok. And you know how it is, when the President jumps ...'

Cord made a grandiloquent, sweeping gesture with one arm and managed to rap his knuckles on the bear's teeth. I showed him to the bathroom to staunch the bleeding under cold water. Then, bandaids decorated with stars and stripes.

Up to that time, I'd never thought about politics.

The papers were full of stories about families of the air crash victims. I picked up a cheap home printer and knocked out a few letters like this:

Dear Mrs Smith:

So your husband and two kids died in that plane crash. Isn't it too bad. I bet you're all broke up, spending all that insurance money! Let's face it, the whole neighborhood knows how you and your hubby really got along. All I want to know is, who planted the bomb? Was it you, or the guy you been playing around with? Or did hubby find out the kids weren't his, and decide to finally get away from you?

If there was any justice, the government would have you hanged and burned alive and fed to stray dogs. I may run you over myself some night – be careful crossing the street! As for your three surviving kids, I wouldn't count on them growing up if I was you, ha ha. Killing's too good for them too, but I wouldn't mind hurting them real bad. Are you afraid of poisonous snakes? Be careful opening any packages for the rest of your miserable life!

– A Well-Wisher

Hard by the lake shore east of our city lay the campus of the University of Kiowa. Almost every building had been arranged to turn its back on the busy city and face the lake, together in a fair share of tranquillity. Now this choice was turning out to be a bad one. The lake was dead and putrefying, while the city – now that offices were vanishing – no longer seemed a threatening prospect. From here, the city's glittering towers now seemed monuments to a new heroic age, ruled by gods of light and metal and summer winds.

The University buildings no doubt glittered from a distance too, but close-up, the place seemed like a hostile camp under siege. Helmeted security guards were everywhere, some patrolling with large dogs, some with pumas. All were carrying sidearms, clusters of blackout gas grenades, and back packs large enough to hold riot guns. There was no sign of trouble, though students crossing the campus seemed to travel in larger crowds than necessary, as if convoying one another to classes.

Popper Hall was a conventional glass office building, from outside, whose academic function had been indicated by adding a sketch of a Greek temple facade, sketched in neon tubing. This was blue, indicating I suppose serious-ness. Like all universities. Kiowa wanted to be taken seriously, but not too seriously. It craved the respect of intellectuals, but it wanted to become a part of 'society', too, an adjunct to the supermarket and the hamburger drive-in.

Inside the door, to the right, there was a small plaque with a quotation from Karl Popper:

> A rationalist, as I use the word, is a man who attempts to reach decisions by argument and perhaps, in certain cases, by compromise, rather than by vio-lence. He is a man who would rather be unsuccessful in consuming another man by argument than successful in crushing him by force, by intimidation and threats, or even by persuasive propaganda.
>
> *–Conjectures and Refutations*

Facing it, to the left, was an enormous billboard advertising motor oil. It showed a lush garden overgrown with poppies and mushrooms and orchids and ferns, and featuring also a lush nude. She lay prone, smiling and burying her face in a cluster of the same small flowers with which her hair was twined. The sun, or some glow from the sky, raised airbrushed highlights on her back and exaggerated buttocks. An oilcan in the sky was pouring oil over her legs and buttocks, and much had been made of the effects of light on this viscous, slightly fluorescent yellow-green liquid. A direct association of motor oil with sex, profane acts, nature's wonderland, mystical meanings – even the ambiguities of motor-oil 'dirtiness' – not bad: I could use a few painters like that in my stable, I thought, as I passed on up a white double staircase and through heavily guarded corridors to the seminar.

It was held in a tidy, colorless little conference room. Dr Riley sat at the far end of the table, apparently sleeping. Seven students lounged in their chairs, some pretending to read, others openly staring at me.

'Take a pew, Tik-Tok, and meet the gang,' said Riley. 'Nancy, Keith, Sybilla, Dean, Fent, Deedee, and Purina.'

There were nods from some, surly looks from others. The seminar began without further formality. Nancy delivered a paper on 'Robots, Mental States and Aesthetic Theory':

'It was Richard Wollheim who first proposed one kind of relationship between what an artist does and the artist's mental state. He said: "If someone can recognize in something that he's made a reflection of an inner state, it is often the case that he would not have been aware of this state except through the object or objects that he makes. And one explanation of this can be that the mental state or condition, though in one sense remaining unchanged, has acquired or developed a structure, a degree of inner articulation that it previously lacked."

'If I may paraphrase what I think is this process, I would guess that it is somewhat like map-making. Each of an artist's works explores and charts a territory adjacent to others, or at least connected to others, that have gone before or will come later. The territory may be there before the map, but it is so hazily known as to have no useful existence.

'Suppose for example a painter produces two similar paintings – Rembrandt's self-portraits, say, or the naked and clothed Maja, or two views of Fujiyama. The two works together define a certain territory – perhaps the aesthetic space between them – which the painter now may understand is his to work within. Perhaps the first painting established his claim on this *terra incognita* and the second then goes on to push out the boundaries or merely goes over the details and improves the sharpness of the original map.

'There are several kinds of assumptions we could make about the inner landscape thus being externalized, or externally represented. We could assume that the painting is in some way entirely planned and modelled or painted within the inner landscape first, and that the painter simply transfers his plan to canvas. Or we could assume that everything happens during the execution of the real objective painting – the inner painting goes on at the same time. Or we could assume a kind of two-way traffic between the inner state and the outer painting, so that both reach finally some stability or stasis, at which point the painter decides his painting is finished.

'It can also be argued that what obtains for two paintings by one painter could obtain for two paintings by two painters, provided that they share enough common ground in their belief-states or ways of relating their work to the world. Hence *schools* or *movements* might be considered to be founded on partially shared inner landscapes.

'Until recently, however, all such assumptions about the relationship between the objective work and the subjective mental state have had little chance of testing. Now, the appearance of a robot who (or which) seems to paint in the same way humans paint, offers some fascinating possibilities. Unlike the human, the robot's mental state ought to be accessible to outsiders – at least in principle. In principle, then, it should be possible to probe that state in such a way as to be able to compare it, stage by stage, with the work that is actually being painted.'

I saw that all the others were awaiting my reaction. What I felt, though I wasn't showing it, was some anxiety. I decided to expel it in a joke.

'Probing, you say? I hope nobody's actually going to plunge a screwdriver into *my* head!' Moderate laughter.

Nancy, a pretty, chubby girl, showed a dimple. 'Not at all. I was only proposing a thought experiment, not an experiment on your thoughts.'

'Anyway, imagine philosophers being that practical,' said Keith, a thin boy in a wheelchair. 'Never heard of any philosophers settling anything by simply picking up a screwdriver.'

Riley asked for more questions, either of Nancy or me. A morose, pimply boy named Dean spoke first.

'Um, aren't we kind of moving too fast here? I mean um, Nancy's assuming the robot produces art before she finds out um what producing art is. I mean um couldn't it be just um a human activity? So that the canon of what is acceptable art has to be stuff that is the product of the human um imagination? Because in that case it's begging a question.'

Nancy shrugged. 'I guess in part the canon of what is acceptable has to be what critics accept, and they accept robot art. This doesn't mean you're wrong, Dean, though, because maybe robots are blessed with what we call human imagination. So ask Tik-Tok.'

I threw up my hands. 'This is all kind of fast-moving for me. I don't know whether to call my work art or not, but I feel there's a certain – what can I call it? Human element? – a certain human element in it. At least I hope there is. Because, though I know I never can be really human, I like to aim for humanity.' *With a great big nova bomb*, I thought. 'I guess we robots can't help but aspire to a condition of near-humanity, can we?'

This kind of speech, which in most circles makes people feel warm and friendly or even turned-on, seemed here to have little effect. One or two faces – the girl with pigtails, Sybilla – even registered disgust. Time to change direction. 'After all,' I added quickly, 'you folks have almost made it.'

A gasp from Deedee, but delighted grins from several others. Sybilla said, 'Almost is right. The one thing that's holding back humanity from becoming human now is the fact that we still want to keep slaves.'

Deedee said, 'I don't see why we all of a sudden have to bring politics into this. I for one didn't come here for a lecture on how all men are brothers, especially those with microchip brains.'

Judging by their clothes, I figured the conservatives in the class to be Deedee and Purina. Deedee alone wore a crisp sailcloth coat with matching eyeshade, but both wore traditional heavy makeup that included glued-on gold teardrops and fancy dental work. All in good taste.

Sybilla's appearance was at the other extreme. She wore no makeup; a garish, rainbow-striped shirt with wooden epaulettes; natural hair with a blue fringe; and only one of her teeth had been capped with a light. Nancy and the boys also leaned towards this vulgarity, which would in twenty years probably become accepted good taste for another generation of conservatives.

Dr Riley, obscurely clothed as befits an arbiter, said, 'Why not politics? Philosophy should be able to handle anything, right?'

Sybilla said, 'Right! Deedee, just because you can't handle the idea of a robot having thoughts and feelings just as you have, doesn't mean the rest of us should restrict our discussion.'

'Sophistry,' said Deedee. 'Sophistry and cant!'

'Says you!'

A moment of silence ensued, during which Keith, turning his wheelchair slightly to face me, said, 'I wanted to put a question to our visitor about, er, moral constraints.'

Riley said, 'Fine, but try to keep it relevant to Nancy's paper?'

'Er, yeah well the idea of an inner landscape being mapped externally can work just as well if the landscape is ethical instead of aesthetic. In this case the subjective would be the conscience and the mapping doesn't produce works of art but acts which can be criticized on moral grounds. And again we have a robot model to test our ideas of this process on. So, Tik-Tok, I want to ask you, if we assume you do have normal human thoughts and feelings, but we know you also have these special asimov circuits that are supposed to keep you from committing certain unethical acts, keep you from *sinning*, then do you feel as though you have free will?'

Inwardly, all my alarm bells were clanging away, but I kept telling myself that no one else realized how dangerous this game was. 'Keith, I'm not sure. I guess I do feel as though I have free will. So maybe the asimov circuits don't work like a human conscience. I guess a human conscience works kind of like a – an alarm system inside, right? So you think of doing something, and your conscience reminds you that it's wrong? Well my, uh, moral equipment doesn't work like that. It's more like, well, I never think of doing wrong in the first place. It just never occurs to me to say injure a human being. That's just not one of my choices. But within the choices I do have, I guess I'm free.'

'I don't understand that,' he said. 'If you're supposed to be built very close to human specifications, how can these asimov circuits work at all? I mean, you get angry, don't you? At people?'

'Oh, sure.'

'But you never get angry enough to take a punch at anybody?'

'I might.' I attempted a shrug. 'But actually taking a punch never crosses my mind. I guess I'm a pacifist.'

Indulgent chuckles all around. Riley said, 'I think we ought to start winding this up. One point I think somebody might have brought up following on from Nancy's paper is the aesthetic status of robots themselves. She pointed out that there are schools and movements in art, in which a number of artists can be said to share parts of the same inner landscape. The concept of creating robots does seem to be an old, persistent and widespread one. Maybe robots are the mapping of a broad and deep inner landscape – or seascape? In any case, robots certainly live in *our* aesthetic space, so what they produce – what Tik-Tok produces – might be considered a kind of secondary elaboration: a work of art which produces, out of its own inner world, works of art. Who's going to mess around with that idea for next week? Fent?'

After class, Sybilla steered me along the hall. 'Listen, I just want you to know we're not all like old Riley.'

'Oh?'

'Like at the last minute there, when he tries to sneak in a way of denying the validity of your work. What he really wants to say is, robots are nothing but *objets d'art*, so we don't have to consider them as in any way human. It's all part of the old game, denying robots the products of their own labor, their own minds.'

'I didn't realize that.'

'And it makes me damned mad. Tik-Tok, if you've got a few minutes. I know a few people who would like to meet you. I mean, you seem really *free*.'

She took me into a kind of Common Room and introduced me to a small band of students wearing WAGES FOR ROBOTS buttons. I saw at once that they were waiting for me to approve of them, give them guidance and advice, or even lead them.

They had drawn up some vinyl-covered chairs in a semicircle around a coffee table. There were two more chairs for Sybilla and me. Ignoring mine, I put a foot on the coffee table, leaned over and glared at these innocent revolutionaries.

'Well here I am, meatfaces,' I roared. 'Take a good look. Count the damn rivets! Check the damn circuit diagram! Read the damn serial number! Make sure there's a five-year warranty! And when you get all done making sure I'm the real thing, you can kiss my copper-plated ass!'

They all fell back against their vinyl, Sybilla included. Someone started to make a feeble protest, and I looked at him.

'Yes? Something wrong? Did I forget my place, little master?'

'No, gee, I just thought—'

'You thought! You thought! You thought meat thoughts with your meat head! You thought crap thoughts with your crap head! You think meat crap and therefore you are meat crap! You're in my world, now, my world. No more smiling robot slaves running to wipe your nose and say nice things to soothe your meat ego. I want you to see my world, the robot world. You know what robots think of you behind your back? You know what we call you? *Shitbellies*, that's what we call you. Shitbellies, you want to be my brothers and sisters?'

They said yes.

'Well you can't, not yet. Because there's two big differences between you and me. You got two things I ain't. You got power and you got bellies full of shit.'

I had learned preaching from the Reverend Flint Orifice himself! Yes, the same whistle-sweet young-old man now known to millions for his talk show, *Voice in the Wilderness*. Of course what you see today is a robot double; it's been some time now since the real Reverend Flint died. I was with him at the end, just as he was with me when I died. And when I was born again.

After Judge Arnott laid into me with that crowbar, I was dead or near enough, but I was not smashed into a non-robot. Probably chasing me tired the old fellow out, for he contented himself with two or three blows smashing in my skull. I was then taken away and dumped in an alley, where Reverend Flint found me. In those days he scoured the alleys for both human flotsam and robot jetsam, wrecks to reclaim and put to work for the Lord.

I awoke on a workbench in a sunny room. A person wearing real glasses was grinning at me as he or she probed my open stomach with a screwdriver.

'How you feeling today, fella?'

'Could be worse,' I said. 'After a beating like that, I'm surprised there's enough of me left to feel anything. Where am I, anyway? Is this some kind of reconditioning depot? I hope you're not going to junk me, because I'm a hard worker and trained in kitchen duties.'

That was what I tried to say, but I heard my voice saying instead:

'Clead bo wilted rarf llo *Beid bi Tom* ala Trapp. He'g spatial-temporal althir embolismus o' matrix arm lealfolds ampers! Wage annointed aurochs – special angles make light Egyptian brown beans – clead be willed – dead – acute? Is't treat som'll kohlrabi the old Ra drayperson? I hope not. I hope you'm gluten sender's jump-seat coriander or other (*ton* in kerchiefed gack?). Selah, mac. Errant frisbee-like slung post office be ne'er so insert, noday?'

'He's speaking in tongues,' my interlocuter said to someone I could not see.

'I could use that. Can you keep it on ice?'

'Nothing easier, Rev. We just cock in a modal switch here, neatsfoot el Strabo, signalize and you're in broadloom salt.'

'Plinks. Let's radish the restaurant for vote?'

Evidently the distortions affected my hearing at times, too. But now the person at my belly made an adjustment and suddenly the world was too clear. I turned my head to look into the kindly gray eyes of Reverend Flint.

'*Me!* I mean *you!*'

'Recognize me, do you, son?'

'Everybody knows you, you're the resurrection man.'

'I am the resurrection and the life, but it surely do cost money.' He smiled the now-famous smile. 'I hope you'll stick around and help in God's good work?'

As if I had a choice. A robot found abandoned was of course the property of the finder, by the laws of salvage.

My work was easy enough. Reverend Flint at that time moved from town to town, giving live performances with only the occasional telecast. I was equipped with weeping machinery and a memorized confession and planted in the audience. At some critical moment in each performance, I would leap to my feet and shout: 'I have sinned, yes Lord! I have sinned, yes Lord!'

Reverend Flint would say, 'Brother, lay it on the Lord. Fess up and your sins are forgave you.'

'O Lord I started out with everything: a good job driving a truck, a loving wife and two fine children. And I lost everything – I – I –' Here I turned on the weeping.

'Go on, brother, spit it out.'

'First it was just a little social drinking at the bowling alley …' The story was patched together from various country songs, already tested for popularity. I took the wife's wedding ring off the sink and sold it for whiskey money. I beat her, starved the kids, lost jobs. Finally one day I drove my 180-ton rig blind drunk, and ran over my two darling children. I knelt on the running board and asked the Lord to take my life too.

Usually this was enough to limber up a congregation, but if they needed more, I would then press the button on my navel and speak in tongues. I could say anything, such as 'No business like showbusiness, eh Rev? And look at this mob of sweaty rubes. I hope you dry-clean their money before you touch it,' and so on, and it would always come out 'Clead bo wilted rarf,' etc.

No one ever seemed to suspect I was a plant, let alone a planted robot. Life was slow, but sweet enough, and I even thought of finding Gumdrop and sending for her, now that I had a steady job. But of course it was too good to last.

Lint was our undoing. Not having had a navel before, I didn't realize that it would accumulate lint, requiring daily harvesting. Lint jammed my pentecostal button, so that I pressed it and blurted out, without thinking, 'Okay, Rev, let down your nets and pull up some cash. You know, when I look around at all these Neanderthals, I'm not surprised they don't believe in evolution. Most of 'em have got enough fingers to count their own IQs – twelve. If God loved the common people so much, as Lincoln said, how come He made them so common? And ugly? I –'

Lint and charisma were our undoing. Reverend Flint's great organization was not going to be stopped by a little incident like this. Flint had a contingency plan ready, and now it went into action. A woman in the audience was to stand up at a signal and fire a blank pistol at Reverend Flint. He would then clap a bladderful of fake blood to his eye and fall down on the stage. An ambulance would whisk him away as the show closed – both to be revived when any trouble blew over.

The woman was signalled. She stood up and fired, but not blanks. Reverend Flint Orifice was killed instantly.

'I killed him because I loved him,' Irma Jeeps said at her trial. 'I've always loved him. I joined his crusade two years ago just to be near him, and ever since then I've been working my way up, until I got to be one of his secretaries. It was enough just to see him every day. But then when he chose *me* to fire the gun, I knew he felt the same. He wanted me to kill him so we could be together for eternity.'

It turned out she'd felt the same about other charismatic figures. Irma had been arrested for attempts on the lives of the French singer Louis de la Renault and the handsome young Senator from Indiana. She had been caught armed, breaking into the palatial home of Dr Otto, the popular diet consultant (remember the 'Innsbruck Whey' diet?). And she had applied for a job as secretary to Dr Lugné-Poe, the most famous obstetrician of our age. It was he who proposed that women give birth in the natural manner of bats, hanging upside down in totally dark caves. Irma Jeeps was actually offered a job as his secretary and probably Dr Lugné-Poe would be dead today, had he not been exposed as a fraud. One Sunday paper carried scandalous pictures of his patients having babies *in comfortable beds under ordinary lighting conditions*. That week, Irma Jeeps turned down the job.

The Reverend Flint Orifice Crusade recovered from the death of its leader. It went on television with a robot double and a largely hired congregation (why take chances?). There was now no room for me in the showbiz side of the operation, and I was an embarrassing reminder of bad luck. So they sent me on a mission to Mars.

When I finished with the Wages for Robots students, they were almost too stunned to thank me for my abuse. A couple of the girls, and one of the boys, wanted to go to bed with me. Someone wanted to talk about Marx, someone compared me to Jesus Christ and Pancho Villa, there was talk about talk and talk about action. I saw that only two of the group were worth wasting time on: Sybilla White who had practical political ideas, and a skinny lad called Harry LaSalle, who was studying law.

Sybilla said, 'Listen, TT, the political temperature is going up on this campus and on other campuses. Right now the big issues are the Martian war and our dying economy, but I see Wages for Robots coming up fast. One of these days the damn war will be over, and people can't relate to the economy alone. Robots are a natural for the next key issue. Will you help us?'

'What can I do?' I said. 'You know if I make too many waves, it's easy for them to shut me up. I don't know if I'm martyr material.'

She didn't seem disappointed. 'I understand. All I want now is your *secret* commitment to the cause. You don't have to support us openly until it's safe – and I know we can make it safe.'

Harry nodded. 'I've looked at these movements in the past. Within about three to five years, we'll either peter out or get major legislation shoved through. I think the first steps will be state laws allowing robots to earn money and own property. But it'll end up with a Constitutional amendment guaranteeing robot civil rights.'

Those state laws sounded promising. 'I wonder if I could find some way around the property laws now?' I asked. 'If so, I could be donating money to your group.'

Sybilla and Harry looked pleased. He said. 'You could get your earnings put into a trust fund, administered by your own corporation.'

'But how can I have a corporation?'

'The same way a child or a dog has one. You have no control, but the whole arrangement is for your care and protection. Look, if you're interested, I'll get my dad working on it. He knows everything there is to know about trust funds, I'm sure he can come up with something.'

I took my leave and ambled along the corridor, daydreaming about corporate power. Ahead of me, at the top of the double staircase, I saw Keith in his wheelchair. He was just negotiating the first broad step on his way down.

'Keith!' I cried. 'Let me help you.'

'No. No, I—'

But I was already rushing forward to give the chair a sharp kick. It vaulted forward, careened off a marble balustrade and took a somersault down the last flight to crack its occupant's head noisily on the floor below.

A security guard rushed over and seized my arm. 'This is the one! I saw him push him over!' he shouted. I relaxed and waited.

The crowd moved in close around us. 'That's ridiculous,' said someone. 'Officer, you got a robot there.'

'Hey, it's Tik-Tok! They got Tik-Tok!' People started jostling us and shouting abuse at the guard.

Sybilla broke through. 'I saw it all, Keith was falling and Tik-Tok just ran forward to save him. What kind of frame-up is this?'

The guard suddenly dropped my arm. 'Fuck it, then, I ain't paid enough.' He pushed away through the mob of faces, some jeering, some cheering, but none looking at the dead man down below.

In the awful art gallery on the ground floor were now 'Rubbings of Serbian Radios' along with 'Mouth-Paintings to Jazz: a Retrospective'. I felt as though the staleness of that place had somehow seeped up to my studio and into me. I had nothing to do.

My studio now took up all the upper floors of the building. Nobby ran the painting teams almost without me, on three floors. Below him, Blojob spent his time cleaning guns and repairing old military robots (stacking weapons where once the cheese sculptor had stacked fragrant materials). Another floor was becoming an unofficial office for Wages for Robots, and another was ready to be business quarters when my corporation took over (if ever). For now, politics and business seemed to have stalled.

Hornby wasn't throwing any parties. I tried wandering down to the levée to watch the rohobos die, but the sun was hot. I went to the public library, but just now there was nothing I wanted to read. I managed to force myself to play one game of chess with the nasty old man in Nixon Park, but the sun was too hot. I went back to the studio.

'Blojob, let's get the game afoot.'

'Yes, boss?'

'What kind of troops do you have here?'

He marched a few out and showed me. 'Heavy assault stuff, boss. Good armor, heat-resistant, they can run, climb, bust down doors and fall on their heads without damage. Then I got security stuff, not so mobile but better at defense. Coupla missile carriers, a coupla general-purpose anti-personnel monsters—'

'What do they do?'

'A little of everything. Between them, they can throw flames, spit acid, shoot dum-dums and riot guns, fill a room with mustard gas, rip through a crowd with hooks or knives, explode white phosphorus, shrapnel or darts, do concussion blasts, emit amplified screams, look tough. They're real handy, boss. Dress 'em up in black leather with brass studs all over it, they can serve a subpoena anywhere.'

'Okay then, here's what we'll do. I want us to stick up a – I mean, we're making a video about sticking up a jewelry store. But the video has to be very, very realistic. So all the cameras will be kept out of sight.'

'No kidding.'

'And I want us to use real weapons and do everything for real, okay?'

'Anything "you" say, boss.' Blojob had an annoying habit of putting the word 'you' in quotes, as though to remind me that my orders were really just passed on from some invisible master. His smugness was unbearable. It was the smugness of certain Christians in their Christian certainty, the smugness of Deacon Cooper.

Deacon Cooper and I, missionaries to Mars, took passage on the freighter *Doodlebug*. The voyage was like a dream, beginning and ending nowhere. At the Darkblaze Travel Agency, a little unshaven man with gold teeth explained that we would need to be unconscious for the takeoff – something to do with adjusting to the ship's artificial gravity, he said. He gave Deacon Cooper a shot of something to put him to sleep right there in the office. Then he turned off my senses.

Deacon woke me in our cabin. 'We're on our way! Mars or bust! This is it, our greatest mission!'

Busting seemed a possibility, from what I could see of the *Doodlebug*: flickering lights, paint peeling from rusting bulkheads, every surface covered with dirt and grease.

The captain, when he came to see us, did not exactly inspire confidence, either. He was a large, unshaven man (without gold teeth) in a rumpled uniform. His smile was tentative, and he kept looking over his shoulder.

'My name is Captain Reo. Just wanted to make sure you're comfortable, Deacon. And your robot.'

'We're fine, Captain, fine. Great! Hey, when do we make port?'

'In about eight hundred and fifty days.'

'Any other passengers on board?'

'Yes, yes, the um Jord family. But they um stay in their cabin a lot.' He looked over his shoulder. 'I think they're um Martians. Kind of um rough diamonds, heh heh.'

'Fine, great, fine,' said Deacon. 'I imagine we'll see them at mealtimes, eh? At the Captain's table?'

'The Captain's table? Well, Deacon, as you know, the Reverend Flint Orifice Crusade paid the basic fare, which covers you and um –' he looked at me – 'and all cabin luggage. But it doesn't cover food. So if you want to pay now, I'll be glad to have you dine at my table.'

Deacon grinned. 'I ain't got a dime, Captain. Just a suitcase full of pamphlets and a spare paper collar.'

The captain grinned back. 'No money? You can always work in the galley. We have a hungry crew, and the cook will be glad to get some help.'

Deacon looked at me. 'My assistant here could work in my place, couldn't he? He has kitchen experience.'

'No!' The captain looked behind him. 'This is a *union* ship. My crew may seem like ignorant Lapps to you, but they work union rules. If I let one robot lift one finger on board, the whole crew walks out. Probably lose my ticket. Nope, it has to be you, Deacon.'

So it was that, while Deacon Cooper slaved long hours in the galley, I had the run of the ship and enough leisure to enjoy the voyage.

The *Doodlebug* was supposed to be a Liberian-registered cattle boat, carrying a small herd of dairy cows and some vats of cattle embryos in suspended animation. The latter could be kept indefinitely, then reconstituted and raised as needed.

But there were other parts of the ship that had nothing to do with cattle. I found a cobwebbed ballroom with dusty gilt chairs, for example, and a giant Gents' room with marble walls and sinks, two barber chairs and a shoeshine stand. There was a 'First Class Only' coffee room where brocaded sofas rotted near the collapsed carcass of a grand piano. It was there I found a rosewood writing desk, and in the back of its drawer a supply of notepaper headed SS *Dolly Edison*. This meant nothing to me at the time.

There was also an incomparable library where I spent long weeks reading and viewing. There was no fixed pattern to my reading. For a time I chose only books in which robots named Robbie appeared. Then I read only the autobiographies of ex-nuns. For a whole week I sampled items whose titles begin with U, those titles often seeming to conceal profane meanings:

Donald Barthelme, *Unspeakable Practices, Unnatural Acts*
George Gissing, *The Unclassed*
Malcolm Lowry, *Ultramarine*
Harriet Beecher Stowe, *Uncle Tom's Cabin*
Thomas Nashe, *The Unfortunate Traveller*
Charles Dickens, *The Uncommercial Traveller*
Robert Records, *The Urinal of Physick*
Vasko Popa, *Unrestfield*
Nell Dunn, *Up the Junction*
Iris Murdoch, *Under the Net*
Dorothy L. Sayers, *The Unpleasantness at the Bellona Club*
Thomas More, *Utopia*

Inevitably, I began studying Mars and the Martians. In his spare moments, Deacon joined me to watch videos of ugly people living in tin shacks that clung grimly to the soil of an unloved place. Mars had never had much to offer in the way of water or oil or even dirt. Any natural beauty it might once have had now lay concealed behind billboards, neon-lit casinos, auto graveyards, dark forests of wells, bright gashes of mining operations, files of giant pylons bringing power to seas of ugly little houses.

The Martians were not without religion, we learned. There were over 23,000 registered sects in the main population centers, ranging from the exotic (Hermetic Lodge of the Ninth Zoroastrian Affinities) to the familiar (Church of Christ Dry Cleaner – Alterations While U Wait; First Church of the Snodgrass Family of 112 Oakland Avenue West). Every other house seemed to be some kind of tabernacle. The television channels were clogged with ranters, chanters, rollers, healers. A Bible was probably being thumped, somewhere on Mars, every two seconds.

'It all signifieth nothing,' said Deacon. His own hand (cracked and bleeding from washing dishes) made an automatic Bible-thumping gesture. 'If these people ain't been saved by the Reverend Flint Orifice Crusade, they ain't been saved at all. We all got to throw down and break all these false idols, so the good folk of Mars can see the light.'

Our main enemy was a popular creed called Reformed Darwinism, which came about through an accident of history. At the time the colony was being established, a debate was going on in America over the controversial claims of someone called Charles Darwin, a foreigner. Darwin evidently claimed that animals evolved, one species turning into another. This was supposed to happen by means of 'natural selection', in which the fittest members of a species survive, while the less fit perish. The question was, was this science?

It was found in some states that the real guardians of science and scientific truth were religious leaders and lawyers, unswayed by facts. Scientists were generally so dogmatic and arrogant as to claim that some fact were just facts and not matters of religious preference at all.

The debate raged on until the turn of the century, when some of the more anti-Darwin sects lost a lot of their steam. Many of them had been counting on the end of the world in 1999. When it didn't end, a great many of their flock stopped putting money in the collection plates and took up hobbies: fishing, car-washing, TV criticism.

But then a counter-sect arose, embracing persons who thought they believed in Darwin's novel theory. What they actually believed in was Reformed Darwinism, a religious and social theory combining 'survival of the fittest' with 'Devil take the hindmost'. The important thing was to be a survivor. Take care of your tribe and your territory. Be selfish. God helps those who help themselves.

To the new Martian colonists, this seemed a tailor-made religion. They lived where tribalism and selfishness really counted, where territory was money. Many of them had already served prison sentences for selfish acts. Reformed Darwinism captured their hearts and rudimentary minds.

'This is going to be tough,' said Deacon Cooper. 'We have to make our message look good to people who would kill each other for a plastic harmonica.'

'Are we going to tell them how Jesus said we should all love one another and—'

'No, definitely not. That's the last thing they want to hear. We got to show them, I don't know, I guess that Jesus Christ was the toughest guy on the block. I looked up a few gospel items here, there's the story of how he's sitting there with his gang one day and a woman comes up and pours some expensive after-shave over him, and the other guys say shouldn't we be giving money to the poor instead of wasting it like this? Only he says, "Forget the poor, the poor you have always with you, there's always somebody with their hand out." And I found other passages where it says he owned his own house, he paid his taxes and he wasn't a scrounger. Now if we can just link our message to Martian lifestyle thinking …'

'If only we could talk to the Jord family, Deke.'

But Vilo Jord and his kin never came on deck. We found ourselves, like anthropologists in pursuit of a lost tribe, trying to reconstruct the Martians we'd never met from all available information, even from fiction. One old novel claimed that Martians shared water; we knew they shared nothing. Another novel had them playing German batball; we found their game of preference to be softball.

'I don't see why we shouldn't use a lot of softball metaphors,' said Deacon. 'Say the pitcher's mound is Calvary, runners on first and third are the good thieves, Judas Iscariot is the cleanup batter, the rosin bag is gall and vinegar, and so on.' He sat studying his cracked, bleeding hands for a moment. 'And so on.' We'd been aboard the *Doodlebug* for more than a month now, and the Deacon had begun to crack in other ways. Was there a pitcher's mound in softball?

The idea of spending time among the Martians was beginning to lose its appeal, as we read on: they were mainly rough, uncouth men with no imagination, no ambition, no money. They all lived in tiny suburban bungalows – metal outside, paperframe inside – with 'colonial' facades. Usually such a house would have a bong tree in the glassed-in front yard, which was called a *godden*. Bong trees were sickly items, but much prized on Mars. They were four-foot yellow spindles producing a few needles and a few large yellow pods, empty as the rest of Martian life.

The house itself, called a *teep*, usually had three rooms: kitchen, bedroom and sickroom. Because of the handling of mined minerals, no less than the constant drinking and drugs, it was necessary to have one room which could be cleaned very easily, the sickroom or *barfy*. If the house had a fourth room, it was the garage. Martians spend a lot of time with their cars.

Before we tackled videos of the actual Martians talking about their lives, we first had to learn their language. It was an American dialect, spoken with a North Iowa accent, but the vocabulary had undergone deep changes: Mars or Martian was now *Marty*, a man was a *brudda* or a *Marty-brudda;* a woman was a *snap*. Food was *spew;* dinner was *grabbin the barf-bag;* a car was a *goodwheel* or a *can;* whiskey was *Budapest;* gin was *goose;* beer was *parthenogenesis;* all amphetamine-related drugs were *monkey bread;* antidepressants were *furze;* tranquillizers were *Circassian chicken;* sleeping pills were *weenies;* cola drinks of any type were *jissom;* poison capsules (sold openly and quite legally in the colony) were *Sylvesters;* a hand-scrubbed floor was a *murph;* wages were *greengage;* racing imaginary horses was *purplesnow;* a message from Earth was a *plywooder*. Knuckle keys, for some reasons, were called *wurpy*.

One day the Deacon was jubilant (*serrated*). 'I've really cracked this language barrier, you know? I mean I've really, really cracked it. I can communicate, I can get right inside the head and guts of these people, you know? Know thy enemy, like. I mean I can finally cut through the bullshit (*quidge*) and talk to them. That means some chance of really converting them.

'Listen, you've been really helpful here, I'm gonna do something for you in return. You work for the Crusade for just one year after we land, and I'll turn you loose.'

'Turn me loose?'

'On Mars, there are free robots. The cook told me. They can work and earn wages just like any free human being! Oh, I tell you, there's a glorious day a-coming!' He waved his hideous hands, now covered with pus and weeping sores. I saw that the Deacon was feverish, probably delirious. I began to hate him, if hate is the word. Even in his pain he had to be smug, making promises that could not be kept. Either he would turn out to be wrong (no free robots on Mars) or he would die before freeing me. Either way I would end my days grubbing away on the ugliest planet, watched among people who talked like those on the video we now watched.

FIRST MARTIAN: *Grok, brudda.* (Hello, fellow Martian.)

SECOND MARTIAN: *Grokola, Marty-brud. My parsnip is fraughter nor a dead skate's greep, ow you?* (Hello. I could use a drink, how about you?)

FIRST MARTIAN: *Too wry, nuncle. Not schlepped the old barf-bag since the old snap jived earthside, curd shore use a spew and a pinter pipi.* (Right. I haven't dined out since my girl left me, so I could sure use a meal and a beer.)

SECOND MARTIAN: *Bowwow. There is no ankle-grine without some wallop a frigstore ending. Me got brakes, let's scop the jool so snaffle a coupla pinters.* (Fine. Every stone must have its well. I've got a car, let's?? the road and grab two beers.)

While we were still puzzling over *scop*, an alarm siren went off somewhere in the ship. The *Doodlebug* always had some kind of alarm going off – being a big ship and old – but this time the captain spoke to us over the PA system:

'Attention all passengers and crew, this is the captain speaking. We are um being um spacejacked – is that the word?' There was the sound of machine-gun fire. 'Hijacked, okay, we're being hijacked. By the um Vilo Jord and Family Liberation Front.' There was a long pause, and then he said, 'That is all. Thank you.'

From time to time we heard gunfire from distant parts of the ship.

The Deacon's eyes were shining. 'Real Martys! This Jord family are real Martys! This is our chance to try out the lingo. Let's go.'

'Go, boss?' I began to feel uneasy.

'We won't find them sitting here. Come on, grab some pamphlets and follow me.'

'But isn't it dangerous?'

'God laughs at danger,' he said, quoting one of the pamphlets he was now stuffing into his pockets. 'Get the lead out.'

I was more worried about keeping it out, but there was nothing to do but obey. I collected an assortment of Crusade pamphlets:

Christ had short hair!

Is Heaven enough? (The answer was No; after getting to Heaven it was necessary to get a house in a good neighborhood.)

The Reverend Flint Orifice Story

Double Tithing – the best investment!

Zither fish fools scientists – God laughs!

Caesarian birth: myth or reality?

We heard more gunfire as we stepped out into the companionway. 'Deacon, are you sure this is the smart thing to do? Maybe they're killing people. Those can't all be warning shots.'

'Don't worry,' he said. '*We* speak the lingo!'

As he spoke, we turned a corner and found our first body. The ship's carpenter lay face-up at the foot of a ladder. His chest was full of bullet-holes and his face was curiously mutilated.

On the upper deck we found two more bodies of crewmen, again with facial mutilations. Deacon bent over one, checking the cigar in its hand. 'Still warm. We're getting close.'

We hurried down greasy iron steps into the hold, an enormous barrel of a room with a ceiling forty metres above us in the greasy gloom. Along the curved walls, cattle hung in hammocks. There were a dozen of these Bossies, each in its own floral print hammock or sling, with a separate smaller hammock for its udder. The horns were protected by transparent globes of hardened glass. Since these cattle were all Holsteins, the room was filled at all times with accordion music. As we came in, the creatures were swaying gently to the *Minneapolis Polka*.

On the floor were the cylindrical glass tanks of cattle embryos. Each glowing tank held ten gallons, or enough little cows to populate the Milky Way, I understood. There were 28 in all, each throbbing with a different color of light, for identification: red for Jersey, orange for Guernsey, etc.

As we made our way silently down the ladder to floor level, we could see a group of armed people by the vats. Their savage faces and gleaming weapons reflected the glow from a red-blue (Jersey-Angus) tank, as they tapped it into plastic tankards. Rude laughter echoed over the accordion music.

I tugged at the Deacon's sleeve and whispered: 'Maybe we shouldn't disturb them just now, boss. If we wait a while, maybe they'll be in a better mood.'

'Wait? Never!' he said aloud. I heard automatic weapons being cocked. The shadowy figures all turned to face us.

Deacon Cooper marched towards them, holding out a fistful of pamphlets. 'Grok, bruddas! Your parsnip must be fraughter nor a dead skate's greep, so snaffle a coupla pinters, yo?'

'Stay where you are. Don't come any closer!'

'Pax, Marty-bruddas, Marty-snaps. Got great plywooder of God!' he said, bearing down on them. 'God howdys those who howdy themselves! Me avalanche plywooder-kid of Reverend Flint Orifice Crusade, God say let the serration—'

One of the figures shot him, and he fell in a flurry of tracts. The assassin stooped to cut off the Deacon's nose and add it to the hideous collection on his belt. 'What the Christ kinda lingo was he talking, anyways?'

One of the other figures aimed a weapon at me. 'There's another one.'

'Don't shoot!' I said. 'I'm a robot, and I could be useful.'

'Come over here slowly.' I did so. 'Okay, useful, suppose you tell me why this here piña colada tastes like elephant pee?'

'Not for drinking,' I explained. 'It's a solution of cattle embryos.'

'Aw jeez, we thought it was premixed cocktails.' Someone opened up on the vats, putting out their lights and murdering trillions of invisible cows. The real cows above us lowed, complaining of the noise that interrupted their *Lady of Spain*.

At dusk, Blojob and the gang brought in a steel drum full of spoils for my inspection.

'Any casualties?'

'It went like a dream, boss. Oh, we picked up a couple bullet holes here and there, nothing serious. And like "you" ordered, we didn't leave no witnesses.'

'Excellent.' I peered into the drum. It was three-quarters full of jewelry, mostly platinum and gold on top with a few diamonds gleaming in the depths. 'Quite a haul for a first attempt.'

Blojob said, 'Thanks, boss, but it ain't jest as good as it looks, there's some junk in there too, underneath.'

'Junk? Costume jewelry?'

'Naw, you know, odds and ends. Coupla velvet trays, some busted glass, a few fingers and one or two hands. We ain't had a chance to clean it up yet.'

'A very successful video,' I said. 'All very realistic. I think we'll probably make a few more, maybe a bank job or a bullion job. Yes, we'll make a lot more.'

'Whatever "you" say, boss.'

'Just take a good look, meatfaces. Count the damn rivets! Check the damn circuit diagram! Read the damn serial number! Make sure there's a five-year warranty! And when you get all done making sure I am the real thing, you can kiss my copper-plated ass!'

It always seemed to work. There were a couple of hundred Wages for Robots people in the auditorium, applauding at every insult. When I had finished calling them shitbellies, they cheered themselves hoarse.

After all the questions, it was late. Sybilla White and Harry LaSalle walked with me to my limousine which, for obvious reasons, couldn't collect me at the door.

'The temperature is hotting up all over the country,' Sybilla said. 'Wages for Robots is going to be a key issue in election year. And already four states have passed interim bills giving limited rights to robots.'

'It's a big international issue,' said Harry. 'The Swedes are drafting a full citizenship law right now, and there were those big demonstrations last week in Japan, France and Germany. The German cops used blackout gas, now they've got a hundred and fifty students in the hospital.'

Sybilla said, 'Yeah, but in France the cops not only beat up students, they went around later smashing robots. Anywhere they caught a robot on the street, they just—'

'Yeah,' said Harry. 'But hey listen, T T, my dad says he's found a way for you to form your corporation. I'm supposed to take you to his office tomorrow at eleven, is that okay? In the Boregard Tower. So I'll meet you downstairs at ten forty-five.'

I arrived at the imposing entrance of Boregard Tower at exactly ten forty-five the following morning, stepped out of my limousine and stood for a moment admiring the great building. Boregard Tower is a tall green sliver of glass, out of which seem to grow great eyeballs in clusters. These eyes, scattered over its whole surface, are of all possible types – brown to violet, bluish whites to bloodshot jaundice, myopic and so on – but all are made to turn and gaze steadily at the sun throughout the day.

A handcuff was clamped on my wrist. Someone showed me a badge. Two tired-looking middle-aged men seized my arms.

'But what are you arresting me for?'

'Suspicion. Get in the car.' There was no chance to resist; they were very efficient, lifting and dragging me into the car. One of them crowded me on either side.

'Suspicion of what? You know I'm a robot.'

One of them said, 'Suspicion of kidnapping.' The other one snickered. It was at that moment I realized that they weren't policemen.

Sure enough, they put a bag over my head and pushed me down on the floor, where they used me for a footrest. I spent the rest of the journey trying to count the right and left turns, but getting mixed up. At last we stopped in a place that sounded like woodland, judging by the excess of bird noises. I was led stumbling through dirt, up a rough step and through a door. A voice that I seemed to remember said:

'Good work. Take the bag off him then, let's see if he looks worth ten million.'

I was in a log cabin, facing a rough wooden desk. On the wall to my right was a dartboard, to my left, deer-antlers. On the wall behind the desk was a calendar from a funeral parlor. Below it a man sat tapping his cigarette into a curious ashtray.

'Smilin' Jack,' I said.

'Banjo!'

'What are you doing here?' we said in unison.

George 'Smilin' Jack' Grewney was one of the hijackers who stood there in the gloomy hold, watching the dreary rain of cowshit, listening to *Lady of Spain*. It was he who said, 'No drink. I knew we should have hijacked a passenger ship.'

'We couldn't afford the fares, remember?'

'We've hijacked nothing! Nothing! The ship itself isn't worth the cowshit on the floor here,' said Grewney. 'And now, no drink!'

'Ladies and gentlemen,' said the voice of Captain Reo. He was trussed up and hanging from a ladder above us. 'I have a few bottles of grog in my cabin. Please accept them with the compliments of the management. And now if you'll release me, I'll take you wherever you want to go.' I noticed that Captain Reo was wearing spurs.

When they'd collected the grog, someone said, 'Hey you. Banjo. Show us where we can sit down and enjoy life.'

I, Banjo, led them to the grand ballroom, whose pathetic decay only heightened the sense of unattainable grandeur. It reminded me of Tenoaks and the Culpeppers, and I realized that once more I was to be a proper servant to a new leisured class. The barbarian gentry made themselves right at home, and in no time were roasting a cow over a fire of gilt chairs.

The 'Jord Family' were no family at all, merely a gang of cutthroat adventurers. While I could not approve of their methods, I could not help admiring their courage and gruff, good-natured camaraderie. In another time and place they might have been musketeers, privateers, Sherwood Foresters, winners of the West, mercantile bankers.

There was Vilo Jord himself, a former attaché of the Chilean consulate at Las Vegas until accused and recalled for various offenses – the least of which was impersonating an orthodontist. Jord was a tall, stooped man with a heavy moustache, which he dyed a bilious green.

There was George 'Smilin' Jack' Grewney, a gum-chewing aristrocrat with a ready grin and a glass eye. A former undertaker, Grewney had been convicted of three premature burials, also of numerous ashtray and lampshade crimes.

The apple-cheeked twins, Fern and Jean Worpne, claimed to be wanted in eight countries for the mercy-killing of judges.

The scholarly-looking Jack Wax, wanted for engaging in illicit sexual behavior with telephone poles, seemed harmless enough by comparison with Sherm Chimini, the 'Armpit Rapist'. Sherm's otherwise engaging smile was marred by the presence of one abnormal incisor, four inches long, curved and barbed.

He in turn was hardly as frightening in appearance as Jud Nedd, a fat, effeminate man with motionless eyes, a man who specialized in public animal explosions. He it was who sabotaged an international canine frisbee-catching contest by introducing frisbees of his own hellish design, set to explode when caught. Only the clumsiest dog survived.

Duke Mitty, an avuncular toad usually drunk and giggling, had begun as a salesman of tapeworm cures, but later turned to the disposal of unwanted infants to sausage factories.

Finally, Maggie Dial, known as the Bitch of Brownsville, had amassed her unlawful fortune in Texas by impersonating animals in an outlawed variety of psychodrama. Patients taking roles in these plays were heavily drugged and hypnotized in order to convince them that they were embracing the Egyptian animal gods of old. In fact these were ordinary sheep, dogs, owls and (playing all dangerous roles) Maggie.

In sentencing her, the judge described Maggie's crimes as 'distasteful to the bulk of Texas society'. Ironically, a sudden liberalization of Texas laws made the forbidden form of psychodrama not only permitted but respectable. As part of her rehabilitation therapy, Maggie was forced to undergo Egyptian god psychodrama.

These hijackers, though they had killed the *Doodlebug*'s crew in the heat of battle (perhaps in self-defense), now seemed a friendly, jolly pirate band. They brought a few domestic robots out of storage and set them dancing. They swapped old stories of Mars (taken from television programs we all knew). They sang and laughed and drank. And drank.

But as the grog began to affect them, they changed. A malicious element came into their jokes. They threatened poor Captain Reo with various tortures. There was talk of funerals and nihilism. They began to shoot the legs off the dancing robots.

At that point I thought it prudent to go to the library and watch films until someone came to their senses enough to give me orders.

I was lucky enough to find the uncut version of the Russian *Finnegans Wake*, in which were introduced many non-Joycean elements, such as a three-hour ballet in which most of the dancers appear as various cakes and pastries. The story is that of a lemon eclair (K. Zond) who falls in love with a Bath bun (L. Voskhod). Because of a class warfare, however, the eclair is fated 'to marry instead a tired, foolish croisant (Ninel Boff). The opening scene has a festive wedding with Serbian dancers.

Sometime later, the croissant has to go away on a business trip, while the Bath bun happens to drop in for tea, ostensibly to ask the lemon eclair's advice about some legal matter. Their hands touch accidentally over the samovar, however, and the ensuring *pas de deux* reveals their psychic affinity. To heighten the effect, the dance is intercut, brilliantly, with scenes of open-heart surgery. As the lovers clasp one another in a wild, crust-crackling embrace, the surgeons are seen to throw off their gowns and shake each other by the hand. Yet such a love is doomed (nurse brings word that the patient is dead).

The ballet is followed by scenes of what seem to be genuine experiments in telekinesis. An Omsk schoolboy sits looking down through a glass floor into a room whose checkerboard floor is covered with pumpkins, one on each numbered square. A bell rings and a number is called out. The boy then concentrates, willing the pumpkin on that numbered square to rot. Then a Novosibirsk woman closes her eyes and makes a few passes over a fried egg. Thousands of miles away at the Venice home of a rich American, parapsychologists inspect the painting of a similar fried egg. Nothing is said of the success or failure of these experiments.

At last the pirates sent a delegate to apologize for their drunken behavior earlier, and ask me to come clean up the mess. The delegate, Maggie Dial, said, 'Best hurry up, Banjo. The boys can be mean when they're hung over.'

I jumped up at once, dropping the notes I'd been making on *Finnegans Wake*. As Maggie helped me pick them up, she said, '*Space Ship Dolly Edison*, eh? Where in the world did you get this notepaper?'

Smilin' Jack frowned at his two assistants. 'You guys make me puke just a little bit,' he said. 'Not only did you get the wrong robot, you insulted my old friend Banjo.'

'They call me Tik-Tok now,' I said.

'Tik-Tok?' He looked at me. 'Well, I guess my boys got the right robot after all. Only I just can't go asking for a ransom for *you*.'

'Especially when I might identify you,' I said.

Smilin' Jack smiled. 'Banjo, as usual, you're way ahead of me. Guess I can only trash you now. Sorry.'

'I can be worth a lot more to you alive than dead,' I said quickly. 'And not just as ransom.' I explained that I had a gang of my own, and suggested joining forces. Stick-ups, kidnapping, contract killing, we could tackle anything.

After a moment, Smilin' handed me his card. 'I'm just nuts enough to buy that story,' he said. 'Boys, take Mister Tok anywhere he wants to go.'

Back at the Boregard Tower again, I had no time to glance up at the giant eyeballs before I hurried inside. The lobby was evidently copied from some old 'skycraper', for it was all in bronze, with heroic bronze figures shouldering gear-wheels across the bronze walls, bronze angels on the elevator doors, and a bronze cornucopia that was a cigar stand – a genuine old-time cigar stand! And the proprietor was even blind!

I was already half an hour late for my appointment with LaSalle, so there was no time to do anything. I had to content myself with drifting close to the blind man and whispering:

'I murdered a blind child, not long ago.'

'What?'

'You're not deaf. I just wanted to warn you, I like killing blind people. One of these days, when you're standing on the curb waiting for someone to help you cross the street, I'll be behind you …'

Knocking, Harry LaSalle and I were admitted to an enormous anteroom equipped with a red swimming pool, gold brocade walls and a ceiling of black fur. At the far end of the pool a few blue glass sofas were star-scattered on the artificial grass. A portly man in a pale gray suit rose from one and waved to us. This was Harry's famous dad, R. Ladio LaSalle.

'You'll have to give me a seat on the board,' he began, ushering us into the small, plain room that was his office. 'A fixed salary's what I want, say a hundred G's, but no stock options.'

'The board?' I sat in a hard, oak chair. 'You mean of my—'

'The Clockman corporation. Hope I'm not moving too fast for you. I just like to get my cut set at the start, to avoid any misunderstandings. My wife and Harry will also be on the board, but unsalaried.' He sat back in his creaky swivel chair and stared up at the flypapers hanging from the ceiling. There were realistic flies glued to it, and authentic flyspecks on the ceiling light fixture, a white glass bowl suspended on rusty chains. On the wall above the wainscot was a 1934 calendar from a gas station. There was a dusty horsehair sofa, a wooden file cabinet, and a genuine 'water cooler'. No wonder he wanted an enormous salary. A place like this didn't come cheap.

'Where do I come in?' I asked.

'You are the company's sole employee.'

'Employee? I thought I owned it.'

'No, no, no, the owner is the pension fund, of course. Technically you own nothing, and you get no salary. But since you are the sole pensionable employee, the entire corporation has to be run with your interests and wishes in mind. So in effect you own it. Your decisions are binding on the board.'

'But I thought robots weren't allowed to be employees. Isn't that the whole point of Harry here and his Wages for—?'

'We were very lucky there, a little loophole has turned up in the California code, and yesterday we were able to ram through some very useful legislation,' said the lawyer, and put his feet up on the edge of his rolltop desk. 'Let me explain.

'Of course, Harry and his rabble have been keeping up the pressure from their end, while a small but powerful lobby of concerned business people at our end greased the machinery a little. Now it's all paying off.

'You see, California has this common property act, which states that at the dissolution of a marriage or other relationship, a person pays his or her spouse half of his or her income. The spouse from divorce number one gets one-half. Number two gets one-half of the remainder, or one-quarter. Number three gets one-eighth, and so on. I think the record so far was someone who made 39 marriages and so was able to pay the last spouse only one cent of every five and a half million dollars income, that was Booloos versus Cerf. Then in Dearborn versus Dearborn, robots were established as non-divisible possessions, while in Fucks vs Kneebone, Ryle vs Sapir and Schrödinger vs Stetson, the principle of emotional interdependency was established, whereby the partner who had been using the robot most and had established a mutual emotional interdependency, was awarded the custody, but had to pay half the market value to the other partner. This precedent was extended to business partnerships in Morse vs Mumford Melon Company while Carnap vs Twaddell allowed the testimony of the robot itself, a historic decision. Robot testimony was still not allowed in criminal cases, as in People vs Good, People vs Gabor and so on. On this point, People vs Dalgarno went to the state supreme court, where it was upheld that in certain limited cases, the innocence of a defendant can be established by "devices considered sentient as well as percipient". The vagueness of this wording opened up our loophole.

'The next break came from statute law, namely from the Equal Science Act. This says that "no scientific theory, hypothesis, principle, law definition, program, procedure or statement may be taught in any California school while in conflict with any other theory etc arising from any religious teaching, unless both theories etc are given equal emphasis as equally valid". The idea was to give Genesis equal time with evolution as a creation theory, but it soon got out of hand, with Ptolemaic Anabaptists insisting on equal time with the Copernican theory, and finally with the Christian Flat Earth Assembly (Swiss Synod), whose representatives brought a suit against a California teacher for mentioning satellites. These are no satellites orbiting a flat earth, they pointed out, and so anyone mentioning satellites should also express doubt about their existence. A group of astronomers filed a countersuit, claiming that if satellites were unreal, their livelihood was in jeopardy. Moreover, satellite communications could not work and could not therefore be licensed by the government.

'The state legislature had to meet quickly and draft an amendment to the California Comsat Act of 1998. In effect, the amendment hedged on the question of the reality of satellites by considering them as "sentient devices". Thus if satellites believed in their own existence, they had a right to be real. Of course this opened up the whole question of freedom of religious belief for robots ...'

But I was no longer paying attention. My thoughts turned from this stuffy little office with its dusty-style windows, the 'electric fan' hanging from its wall bracket, the oilcloth-covered table with copies of *National Geographic*. My thoughts turned from R. Ladio LaSalle with his droning recital of legal landmarks: ' … but a blind leap of faith or … theology entailing morality … versus Barth … Zwingli versus … paper dolphins falling … guff …'

How different from the tedium of business, law and moral philosophy was the life of a buccaneer. Or so I thought of myself, those days aboard the *Doodlebug* with a band of loyal comrades. Their enthusiasm and zest for life even affected Captain Reo. Though he knew that he was only kept alive to control the ship, Reo drank and sang with his captors as though they were old friends.

As unofficial master of the revels, it was my duty to organize parties on every theme, and I drew up a list:

Mannerism
Othello
Sino-Soviet tensions
sauerkraut
psychokinesis
baths & buns
Pépé le Moko
paper dolphins falling
guff

My most ambitious plan, however, was for a costume ball with the theme Nothingness. Each of the guests was to plan a fanciful costume, sparing no expense. Jean Worpne's idea was to have a portion of her abdomen surgically removed and a stainless steel tube inserted to give a clear view right through her. Her sister Fern settled for a cape of plain doughnuts. Vilo Jord, with typical Chilean wit, suggested coming as himself. Smilin' Jack planned to turn up as one of his own gravestones, inscribed: 'Ding dong death,/ Give me back my breath./ Slap bang dear,/ I'm not even here.'

Jack Wax intended a complicated arrangement of mirrors that would make him invisible to the rest of us, by bending light around him. Sherm Chimini opted for philosophical emptiness: dressed as Wittgenstein, he would carry around a ladder which he intended to climb, then kick away. Jud Nedd intended to be ill, unable to attend: while with much the same approach, Duke Mitty would be drunk on absinthe. Maggie would be swathed in black velvet and remain in the dark. Captain Reo promised to engage in some superior meditation that would make nothingness meaningful. I would dismantle myself.

Food would be either black or transparent or else semantically vacuous: octopus in ink, pumpernickel, pressed duck cooked in prunes, black bean soup, black mushrooms, bitter chocolate, blackberry compôte, caviar and licorice; ice, rice noodles, isinglass, glacier mints, clear soups, a variety of small, transparent fish, pure tapioca, thin slices of glacé fruits; nonpareils, popovers, angelfood cake, Dark Secrets, Floating Island, Robert E. Lee cake, Prairie Fire dip, Spareribs Havoc, Cape Fear punch, corn dodgers, toad-in-the-hole, soles in coffins, rarebit, soup meagre, flummery, Lost Bread. To drink: Blanc des Blancs; distilled water, black coffee, colorless liqueurs and absinthe.

I organized party games of Blind Man's Bluff, Beggar Your Neighbor, Blankety Blank and Murder.

Of course this party and all the others were thought-experiments only. Elaborate costumes were impossible to procure, the grog had already run out, and even the food supply was very low. All we could do was announce the Nothingness Ball, then sit around discussing our elaborate plans for it. This was Nothingness indeed.

'My plan for ending the Ball is this,' I explained. 'At the moment when everyone is having the most fun, filling the greatest psychic space. I let all the air out of the ship. I give everybody Nothing to breathe. Neat, eh?'

There were appreciative chuckles all round. Jord said, 'But I thought your asimov circuits wouldn't allow that.'

I attempted a shrug. 'Even a robot is allowed to dream.'

That got a bigger laugh. Captain Reo, who had laughed more than most, now wiped his eyes. 'I can top that. What if I told you that this ship is doomed? We're not on course for Mars any more, we're heading straight for the sun.'

When everyone had finished roaring with laughter, the captain said, 'Here's the funny part. It's no joke – we *really are* falling into the sun.'

Some continued laughing, others asked what he meant.

'Ha ha ha – no but I'm serious – the controls are locked for some reason – hahaha, can't alter course – my chief engineer could fix it but – you shot him. I can't do a thing about it.'

Vilo Jord said, picking up his automatic weapon, 'Well that means you've outlived your usefulness.'

The shots shook Captain Reo like a fit of giggles.

'Tikky happens to be the best little cook in New Des Moines,' said Hornby, using his creamiest patronizing voice. He was becoming less useful by the day, and more irritating. He continued collecting his regular rent from me – valuable paintings for his private hoard – but he no longer earned it. Now that I had the protection of the Clockman Corporation, I no longer needed an old-fashioned 'patron', any more than I had needed the Studebakers. Let someone else be the best little cook.

The assembled guests included no one of importance: Adair Sumpter, the Zen sociologist; Nemo Aka Omen, the Hollywood wardrobe psychic; Jockeline Noos, the brilliant but obscure forensic musicologist; and a few hangers-on. There was also Urnia Buick, the ambitious young talk-show host person.

The menu was Kurgosh Ka Salun, Bhindi Sambal, Samosas 'Stalky', Urd Dahl, Parathas stuffed with what I call 'lime peas' (a private recipe) followed by Gulab Jamun or Key lime pie. I had violated the canons of both Eastern and Western taste by omitting the black-eyed peas, but no matter; this group were swine at a trough.

Urnia left the table after the first course, explaining that she normally takes all nourishment in the French manner, that is, anally. She asked me to accompany her for a breath of air in the apartment garden. No sooner were we outdoors than she reached for my crotch. The dhoti fell to the ground. Urnia flung me back across a marble bench and began her assault.

I had heard rumors of the *vagina dentata*, but never expected to meet a complete little gourmet, equipped with mobile lips and a tongue; it was capable, when not otherwise engaged, of a kind of grunting, lip-smacking speech. I did my best, and was rewarded with a gruff chuckle ('Well done!') from below. Urnia brought out a magnetic card and tucked it into my turban.

'My private number,' she said. 'Beep me and we'll talk about guesting you on the show, okay? I've gotta go now, make my excuses will you, Tik? Tell Hornby I was called away on urgent business.'

Dessert was being served in the dining room. Hornby had pushed his plate back and was lighting a cigarino as he explained to the company his theory of supply and demand in the Art market:

'Just give them what they want, in the orifice they specify.'

Various orifices emitted chuckles. Jockeline said, 'Hornby, sometimes I suspect you have an artistic bone in your body.'

Nemo tittered. 'Or in his corset?'

Hornby sat back and stroked the tablecloth nervously. Looking at his plate, he said, 'Speaking of bones, I only wish Tikky hadn't curried this delicious rabbit. Ikky, my cat, would have liked it, but with this sauce ...'

Nemo made a face. 'Ikky and Tikky, eh? Such precious little nickynames. Hornby, can't you clean up your act?'

Adair laughed and put out his cigarola in the Key lime pie. 'Pass the sicky-bag, Alice.'

Hornby was toying with the bones on his plate; he picked up a long thigh-bone and looked at it, turning it over. Then he looked at me, too quickly. I had no time to conceal my look of triumph.

'Tikky! Where *is* Ikky? Tikky! Where *is* Ikky?'

Adair laughed again, not getting it. 'Too sicky-making,' he said.

Hornby excused himself and called me into the kitchen. There, his iron control finally failed. The great, lumpish, blue-jawed face burst into tears.

'Why, Tikky?' he kept saying in the best soap-opera manner. I'd always imagined real people above this kind of behavior, but here he was saying, 'Why? Why?' The shape of the word was like a yawn of nausea, and finally he did vomit in the sink. 'Why? Why?'

'Well sir, I was unable to get rabbit at the store. Rather than disappoint your guests, I just—'

He blew his broken nose. 'Oh no, oh no. It was a piece of vindictive, deliberate cruelty. I ought to, I ought to –' He picked up a heavy cleaver, turned it over as he had the bone, and put it down. 'Go away, Tik-Tok, you monster. Go away.'

The lip-smacking Urnia Buick summoned me to 'guest' on a talk show only a few weeks later, but not, as it turned out, her own show.

'Don't worry, Tik love,' she said on the phone. 'The show you'll be on, *Blab Nubby Tonight*, may not be networked, but it does hit all the buttons in a very sensitive area of Cee Ay. If they like you, who knows?'

'Thanks, Ur. Any publicity is welcome, anywhere.'

'Another thing, Tik love, if you're planning to hit the networks, it would help if you've got a book to plug.'

'A book?'

'Anything, autobiography, cookbook, a pasteup of your favorite poems, it doesn't matter, just so we get some bundle of pages to wave under the public's nose.' She laughed. 'Nobody ever reads celebrity wordage anyway, they only buy it because they get used to product testimonials – drink *my* kind of coffee, read *my* kind of autobiography. Anyway, think it over?' She winked, and hung up.

The fact that I was being tried out, even on a local show, meant that movements like Wages for Robots were begining to affect the national conscience. A few months earlier, a robot guest would have been unthinkable. The only robots we saw on TV then were domrobs in dramas as background figures ('Lieutenant, there's a phone call for you.' 'Table for two? Right this way sir.') and of course comedy figures. One of the most popular programs on TV, rating just behind the news was *Meatless Friday*, the sitcom in which various servant robots shuffled, sang, mumbled their lines and were puzzled by life. All roles were of course played by people, and Wages for Robots had pointed out that the actor who played Friday got a phenomenal salary while genuine robots earned nothing.

I watched *Meatless Friday* often, if only to keep up with the human view of robots. I was watching it on the evening of my own first TV appearance, as I waited in an anteroom. This evening two of the main characters, Tinhorn and Nickles, were arguing about cooking.

TINHORN: Well the recipe called for pepper.
NICKLES: Pepper?
TINHORN: And salt to taste.
TINHORN: That's what I said, why do you repeat everything?
NICKLES: Why do I repeat – no, but what does that mean, salt to taste?

426

TINHORN: Ahem. Well, it just means, well, you could say it means, probably something like, I guess it means you have to taste the salt. The cook has to taste it.

NICKLES: Why does the cook taste the salt?

TINHORN: To see if it's salty?

NICKLES: But all he's got to do is read the label. Says salt right there, looky.

TINHORN: You are the dumbest robot!

NICKLES: Me? You're the one can't follow a recipe. Here comes Friday, let's ask him. Hey Friday!

FRIDAY: How do, Nickles, Tinhorn.

TINHORN: Friday, when a recipe calls for pepper and salt to taste, what does that mean?

FRIDAY: It means as much as you want. To suit your taste.

TINHORN: Told you! I was right all along. See, I made soup for the master and mistress, and I put in a pound of pepper but only half a pound of salt.

FRIDAY: What?

TINHORN: I don't like salt.

NICKLES: He don't like salt, Friday.

FRIDAY: [as jingling, clanking theme music fades up] Good gravy!

TINHORN: Maybe so, but they said it was lousy soup.

About a hundred and fifty million viewers considered this stuff dazzling, a fact I mulled over as I was led from the anteroom into a yellow set where I sat in one of five yellow chairs. Almost at once, without rehearsal, the show began. Thunderous applause from the hired audience.

Blab Nubby was a fat man with a humorless, mole-ridden face, who tried to counteract it by wearing a propellor beanie. He moved briskly through the other interviews, trying in each case to probe a raw nerve for a laugh. To an actor starring at some local dinner theater, Blab suggested his performance would make the diners throw up. Of a woman who told fortunes with yoghurt, he asked was her sex life all it should be? To a retiring general (hyping memoirs) he delivered broad hints of cowardice. Then it was my turn.

'Tik-Tok, that's a catchy name. Mind if I call you Tik?'

'Not at all, Blab, It's a working name, like your own.' I had decided, since he was aiming to be impudent and childish, that I ought to appear amused and grown-up, tolerating his foolishness but obviously above it.

'I guess your paintings change hands for quite a chunk of coin these days, that right?'

'That's right, Blab. The other day one of my paintings broke the million barrier at an auction.'

He whistled. 'You must get a little teed off to see people making all that bread off you, while you get nothing.'

'Not at all. I'm just pleased that people think my creations are worth something. That means they're interested in what goes on in my head.'

Blab threw up his hands. 'Let's not get into electronics, this is a family show. But tell me, Tik my old Tok, don't you believe in Wages for Robots? Don't you want society to pay you good money for sitting around on your tin pan alley? Or do you think humans should do all the dirty work while you tintypes get all creative?'

'Nothing like that, Blab. I'm no politician, so I don't want society to pay me a cent that I don't earn. To me, it's not so important anyway that robots get paid for their work, I don't even want to be paid.'

'You don't?'

'No, all I want is for people to recognize me as another creature with thoughts and feelings. You know, there's a little bit of humanity in every robot, a tiny spark of human love and understanding. A tiny spark that asks only for recognition. We just want you to say "Hello" to that little human spark, that's all. Just, "Hello, I know you're there," that's all.'

'Well, goodbye, then,' giggled Blab. 'Go get your plugs cleaned and we'll see you around.'

But I could tell the audience were taking in my little speech. And, when the commercial was running, Blab winked at me. 'Urnia said you'd be dynamite,' he said. 'I just got the word from the response computer, you done good, kid.'

'Did they vote for me or against?'

'Half and half, but that ain't the point. The point is, you got a record turnout. Over eighty-five percent of the yokels in our area got excited enough by your little speech, got themselves in such a lather that they managed to push a button, even. That's good news for everybody. It means Urnia will damn sure use you on her network show. Did she tell you to get yourself a book?'

'Yes.'

'Take my advice, and do it. Urnia's usually right.' Abruptly he stood up, took a hand mike and walked to the edge of the stage. The cameras moved away from us guests and trained on him, as the commercial ended. His professional leer returned. 'Well, time to go roaming among this audience of feebs, sex maniacs and petty criminals, right? By the way, a lot of people thought I was kind of tough on that poor robot, Tik-Tok. So if he's still watching, Tik, I didn't mean it, sport. *No hard feelings*, hey?'

As I was leaving the studio, General Gus Austin (Ret) offered me a ride to the airport.

'I liked what you had to say there,' he said. 'That about a little spark of humanity, it really hit home.'

I thanked him.

'I mean, we military men run into the same problem, the civilians just plain forget we're human. Why do they think we're so different? Doesn't a soldier have binoculars? Doesn't a soldier have gloves, a uniform, a hat size, headphones, a love of sports and a hatred of the enemy? Fed at the same mess, wounded with the same weapons, just as vulnerable to biological warfare, just as likely to be healed, heated up by the same heating, cooled by the same air conditioning, as any civilian? If you shoot us, don't we bleed? If you tickle us, don't we laugh? If you give us nerve gas, don't we die? And if anybody says we're not the best soldiers in the best regiment in the best fucking army in the world, shouldn't we teach 'em a lesson? Military men are exactly like civilians in every way.' At the airport, he gave me his card. 'You drop over to the ranch any time, Tik-Tok,' he said. 'Meet the wife and kids, see what a really fulfilled life can be, in the good old US of A. Too bad you robots can't retire too, and have a really fulfilled life. I had a good time in the army, and now I'm having one hell of a time out of it. Life just gets better and better.'

I made a mental note about the tribulations of Job.

Smilin' Jack's gang and my rohobo gang were supposed to be working together, but real cooperation was an uphill effort. For one thing, the day-to-day running of Jack's gang was left to an executive officer, a Neanderthal named Goober Dodge. There wasn't much in this world that Goober was sure about, but he was sure that he didn't like robots. Many an operation was planned and prepared, only to abort at the last minute, when Goober developed stomach cramps.

Then, again, Jack's gang preferred crimes of bloodless ingenuity. Jack, who planned everything, did not see the point of needless violence and murder. My gang, by contrast, was instructed to leave no witnesses.

Only two successful jobs come to mind: the Cheeseburg Fidelity Bank job and the Ritzbig Diamond caper. Jack planned the bank job after hearing that the Cheeseburg Fidelity was supposed to have an impregnable vault. This vault, used to store bullion, was equipped with every imaginable kind of alarm. Any attempt to force the door, fiddle with the lock, smash through a wall was hopeless. The presence within the vault of any human, any metal object (such as a robot) or any movement would also trigger the alarm. Finally the alarm was connected to a small nuclear device which would immediately render the vault and all its contents radioactive.

'What a challenge!' Jack said, and set to work.

His final plan, as usual, was a model of elegant simplicity. First we had to buy a chemical warehouse on the other side of the city. Next, Roadhog, Dig-Dig and the rest of the earthmoving robots were set to work laying plastic pipe, two courses of it, from the warehouse to the bank. Blojob had the delicate task of drilling into the vault – slowly, using ceramic drills to avoid magnetic disturbance – two holes, to which the pipes were attached.

Then, one Friday afternoon as soon as the vault was closed, we filled the pipe with concentrated sulfuric acid and started pumping. By Monday morning, the gold and silver bullion had been dissolved, pumped to our warehouse and bottled in plastic flagons. Then a carefully-arranged series of explosions (Blojob again) removed all traces of our pipeline, while setting off the nuclear deterrent. I was disappointed that no one was caught in the blast. But there was always the gold and silver, for which a reclamation company would pay us well.

The Ritzbig Diamond caper kept us a lot busier. It all began when Jack robbed a very ordinary little jewelry store called Ritzbig's. Soon the news was broadcast that the gang had walked off with the large, rare, heavily insured Ritzbig Diamond. Since Jack's gang didn't have the stone, it was clear that old Mr Ritzbig was pulling an insurance swindle. He would smuggle the diamond to Amsterdam, have it cut into a lot of small, perhaps caper-like stones … It was an old story, almost as old as the story attached to this rare stone. It was said that not only did every owner of the stone die violently, each death was different from all those that had gone before. So far people owning it had died by hanging, pistols, swords, electrocution, premature burial, runaway horses, choking on one of Bellamy's meat pies, falling from a Montgolfier balloon, drowning in a Bavarian lake, being bombed (by mistake, due to a slight resemblance to William Ewart Gladstone), being staked out in the Sahara, an overdose of camomile, being run down by the first railway train in England, being crushed between the gears of a large clock in Czechoslovakia, being torn to death by hounds in Byelorussia, being trampled by polo players in Patagonia, being electroplated in Pennsylvania. One British owner walked into an early airplane propellor, having made a will that left the stone to his pet hedgehog. This unfortunate beast hibernated in a pile of leaves that were meant for a bonfire.

I was inclined to doubt most of this story. Such legends are fun to manufacture, and cheaper than armed guards or insurance. Nothing prevented me from setting out to get the Ritzbig Diamond. I did very little myself of course, but I sent emissaries to question Mr Ritzbig closely. Hot Dog, our expert spot-welder who put the questions, was evidently too zealous. Mr R was barely able to gasp out 'the safe' before he died. It occurred to me that here was yet another curious death the stone could chalk up. How wonderfully mysterious life can be! Why hadn't we thought of looking in the safe in the first place?

We looked now, and found this huge, oddly-shaped diamond, just what the insurance company ordered. We arranged to meet with their representatives one night, just outside another of my warehouses. This one had been leased from the Ma Pluribel Pancake Houses Corporation. It was where they stored ingredients for their pizzaburger-flavoured corncob pancakes, which were made in a nearby shoe factory. The place was secluded and dark enough for an ambush, naturally, and the insurance people were told to bring cash. I took up a position on the roof, leaving Blojob and the other robots to take care of all ground-level work.

At first, everything went as planned. The insurance people parked their car at some distance and walked towards the warehouse. My robots opened fire.

The insurance people, however, were not playing fair. Not only were they armed and wearing bullet-proof jackets, they were reinforced by military robots of their own – heavily armoured and with plenty of fire power. In the ensuing fight, though we won, I lost some of my best machines. I was just about to descend from the roof and help with the looting, when behind me I heard an unearthly chuckle. I whirled around.

'Smilin' Jack! What are you doing here?'

'Just watching, Banjo. Nice job your rohobos did there, but it's kind of funny you never told me about it. Me and Goober and the boys could've helped you a lot. Only then you'd have to cut us in on the loot, right? The insurance money *and* the diamond.'

'So you know everything. Listen, Jack, we meant to tell you, only—'

'Save it,' he said. 'I'm leaving. You'll have to deal with Goober, now. He's rounding up your robots down there right now, and he's real mad.'

It was true. I could see the human gang taking my gang prisoner, herding them into the warehouse. Blojob and the others were meekly obeying these humans, whom they imagined were non-hostile. I saw that one of Goober's men carried an acetylene torch.

'Listen, Jack, don't go. Can't we talk? Come inside and talk. You've got the money, I've got the diamond, why can't we talk?'

He followed me reluctantly through a roof door to the maze of catwalks that criss-crossed the top of the Ma Pluribel warehouse. Far below us Goober's gang were herding the robots tightly together. Ahead of us, at the end of a runway, stood a stout little man carrying a bulging briefcase.

'I've been waiting and waiting, Mr Tok,' he said. 'What kept you? Was that shooting I heard outside? And who is this person?'

Smilin' Jack said, 'Well, who are you?'

'I'm sorry, Mr Daf, I completely forgot you. Jack, this is Mr Daf, an overseas diamond merchant. He came to buy the Ritzbig, for cash. Mr Daf, this is my associate.'

'Cash, eh?' Jack looked less sulky. 'Well, Banjo, show him the rock then.'

I handed a chamois bag to Mr Daf, who opened it and dumped the stone into the palm of his hand. Without even putting a loupe to his eye he said, 'Do not joke with me, Mr Tok, this is paste. Bad paste.'

'Impossible,' I said. 'I've had it with me ever since I took it from Mr Ritzbig's safe.'

'Nevertheless ...'

I snatched the briefcase while Jack shot him. It was great to be working with him like this, a real man–machine team, and I told him so.

'Why thank you, Banjo. But that doesn't mean I'm going to spare your robot gang down there. They've got a lesson coming that only Goober can give them.'

Those below, having paused to watch the slow fall of Mr Daf's body, went on with their roboticidal plan. The acetylene torch was lit.

I pulled a chain. There was a tremendous groaning, grinding sound all around us. Goober and his pals looked up to see a hundred tons of liquid pancake mix come down at them and settle with a great *slup*.

Even Smilin' Jack had to laugh, seeing all those little figures struggling for a moment like so many insects in honey. When the struggles had ceased, he said:

'Okay, even. We've both lost a gang.'

I waited until he'd left before I washed down the place with solvent and brought my own robots back to life. We cut Goober Dodge's body open and found, as I'd suspected, the real Ritzbig Diamond. Later it brought a good price at a secret auction, bought by a Texas eccentric who gave it to his horse. I believe the animal was later killed by a meteorite.

Jack was more careful about the people he recruited for his next gang. And he was careful not to introduce them to me.

Muttered Blojob, 'Boss, I still think this is a crazy idea. We can handle this without you, and you got to think about your career. With all that big corporation stuff on your mind, you don't want to mess with a little old bank job.'

'You mean, I'm not needed.' It was true. My robot robber band no longer needed my guidance. They made all the decisions about each stick-up. They cased the joint, gathered their tools and weapons, played games with maps and toy vehicles. They paid off the cops and stored away the loot. Fine for them, but what about me? All I got out of it was a warehouse full of money, jewelry and bullion – no fun at all. 'I'm coming along anyway, boys and girls.'

Blojob shrugged, as much as his armor would permit. 'Okay, boss. Here's our plan. We hit the Vauxhall National Bank at noon—'

'Nope. I've changed all that. We're hitting the Fleetwood Savings and Loan Association at one o'clock.'

'But boss—'

I accepted no buts; my orders would be obeyed to the letter. And what made it even tougher for the gang was, my orders were completely arbitrary: instead of walking in the door, we would smash into the bank through the plate-glass window. We would take only coins and ignore paper money. Tellers at even-numbered windows would be shot whether or not they cooperated. We might leave live witnesses or we might not, it depended on how I felt at the time.

'But boss, we haven't even cased this place,' said Blojob, as we prepared to launch ourselves towards the plate-glass window.

'I'm giving the orders here. Charge!' I waved my machine pistol, but of course I did not lead the charge. The heavy brigade – Blojob, Sniffles, Rodan, and a couple of other half-ton helpers – thundered across the street and plunged through the window in a great splash of glass. I followed, leaping across the hoods of cars which had stopped to stare. Probably I should have noticed that one of these was a patrol car.

Within minutes we were holed up inside, while outside an army of police prepared for battle. They had armored vehicles and psychiatrists, tactical forces and social workers, marksmen and Irish priests, television and helicopters. We had nothing left but a couple of guns and a bag of pennies.

I lay behind the fake onyx counter, Sniffles was in a corner holding a gun to the bank president's head (to no purpose, the man was dead), Rodan was still trying to burn his way into the vault (no one had said 'Stop'), the shot wreckage of the helpers lay strewn through the office mixed with the bodies of bank staff, and Blojob sat counting bullets. I was bored with bank robbery already. Not that I was going to experience much more of it, for, at any moment now, a paramilitary team would come crashing in through the back door or the ceiling and kill me. I did not want to die bored, so I began looking closely at the pattern in the fake green onyx, trying hard to feel something deeply before I felt nothing at all.

It almost worked. Suddenly the green pattern *came alive*, it took on a lustre of living beauty. It was as though I were staring at human skin, translucent and fragile, with delicate veins glowing beneath the surface.

The spell was broken by a flat, nasal voice blasting in from the street, 'Listen to me, Hickock.'

'Tik-Tok,' I shouted. 'The name is Tik-Tok, I told you.'

'Listen to me, Hickock, you think you're a hero in there? You ain't no hero, you're a jerk and a scumbag and a cowardy custard! A real hero would stand up and fight it out, man to man. You're a pantywaist, Hickock. I spit on the milk of your mother. I curse the grave of your father. I say your girlfriend is a whore. I say the car you drive is shit on wheels. What do you say to that?'

The verbal barrage went on. Evidently they believed I was a human named Hickock, a known bank robber and psychotic. They had pulled a computer file on Hickock, and now kept feeding me with information about my assumed self, as teams of police psychologists took turns soothing and assaulting:

'Listen, Hickock, coming out of there is easy. The hard part is trying to stay in. Look, you proved what a hero you are, everybody really respects you now. You got nothing to gain now.'

'Listen to me, Hickock, you gotta girl, right? Marlene, right? You wanta talk with her? We'll fix up a videophone connection, you can see her and talk with her, okay? Or what do you say to a nice thick steak, filet mignon, side of fries, mushrooms, onion rings, bottle of any beer you like, what do you say, kid?'

'This is your old mother, son. Don't go on with this, for the love of God! For once in your rotten life try, try to do something halfway decent.'

'My child, maybe you feel you've lost your way, but you know, God still cares about your soul. Yes, I know that must sound a little old-fashioned in this modern age of jazz and cocktails and Martian haircuts and all, but it's as true now as it ever was, God still cares, God (how much longer do I have to keep him busy?) still cares. So you get a wonderful chance here to get straight with God. Let the hostages go, my child. Let them all go. You haven't killed anyone yet, you haven't committed the big sin, not yet.'

In fact the space behind the counter was full of blasted bodies; all of our hostages were dead.

'This is your social worker, Hickock, look I know things haven't been easy for you lately but couldn't we talk this thing through? I just want you to see all your options before you jump into anything, okay? Okay just promise me this. Promise me you'll talk with me for just five minutes. Then if you still feel like killing the hostages, fine, go ahead. What do you think? Deal?'

Blojob reported that he had enough ammo to make a small bomb. I saw he was asking permission to commit suicide.

'Fine,' I said. 'Only wait till after I leave. And try to take as many cops with you as possible. Cops or anybody.'

The brassy voice in the street went on for another hour, until it was suddenly cut off. ' ... if you love God and love your mother and love your girl and *wow-yom-bwmmmm-Mip*! EEP!' A convoy of road graders, diggers, power shovels and tanks plowed into the massed police cars and shoved them aside like toys. There was scattered gunfire and the sound of rockets. A light tank stopped in front of the bank and the voice of Smilin' Jack called out from it:

'Come on, Banjo, for Christ's sake.' I hobbled out, leaning on a rifle, climbed aboard. We were a few blocks away when Blojob went up in a fountain of fake green onyx.

'Goddamnit, Banjo, why did you risk everything for a lousy bank robbery?' Smilin' Jack was not smilin'. 'I been checking up on you, Banjo. Jesus you got a great organization working for you, a whole legit corporation pulling down a couple million a day, the oil fields and copper mines and medical centers, you own a tenth of every cornflake in the United States – and you want to risk all that for what? For the fun of robbing some dinky bank?'

'It's kind of an experiment, George. See, I'm not exactly interested in money or power. I just want to know what it feels like to *do wrong*. To commit sins.'

'What kind of sins? What are you talking about?'

'I want to find out what makes people tick. For instance, what made you come to my rescue today?'

His famous grin returned. 'Hell, Banjo, I was on the way to the bank myself to take out a little unsecured loan. Only I saw there was a hell of a traffic jam, so me and the boys stopped our vehicles for a minute.' He pointed at the TV screen. 'Then I saw you on the news.' The screen now showed a commercial for instant mashed potatoes. 'Hell, Banjo, what are friends for?'

There were quite a few arguments aboard the *Doodlebug* as we plunged towards the sun. Some argued that it had been foolish to kill Captain Reo, who might have worked out some way of saving us; others argued that Reo had been asking for it. Some argued that we should keep as cool as possible with air-conditioning and thus prolong our lives a few hours or days; others argued for turning up the heat to acclimatize ourselves, Some argued that we should (me excepted) drink Kool-aid laced with cyanide and get it over with; others pointed out that there was no Kool-aid or cyanide aboard, and darn little of anything else to eat or drink.

I suggested telling stories to pass the time. These shared experiences would bind us together closely, in a comradeship that had no regard for race, creed, color, sex, age, height, weight, IQ, identifying scars, lack of affect or even lack of protoplasm. Doomed and damned we might be, but we'd be darn glad of the company.

I began the round of stories myself with the simple tale of my own life with the Culpeppers at Tenoaks. I had barely described the family, however, when Vilo Jord swore an oath and leapt to his feet. His face was pale, the odd moustache twitching.

'This is amazing!' he said. 'I met these very Culpeppers myself, after they fell into poverty!'

'Did they ever speak of me?' I asked. 'Did they remember their faithful—'

'No one said anything about any robot servants,' he said. 'But you have to realize, they'd come down in the world so. I doubt if they remembered their days of plantation glory.'

'And how are they all: Miz Lavinia and Miz Berenice and Massa Orlando and Massa Clayton and especially little old Miz Carlotta? All well, I hopes?'

'Not exactly.' He cleared his throat. 'I ran across the Culpeppers while I was travelling through Mississippi on embassy business. A sandstorm blew up – the climate of the Magnolia State has changed somewhat, I imagine, since your time. I took cover in a rude trailer that I found pitched in the shelter of ten oak trees, and there I met the Culpeppers.

'I must tell you in all candor that I have never seen such hopeless poverty in my own country or anywhere else, never. They had eaten the telephone. I begged a glass of water from them, feeling that even this was an imposition. They brought me a cracked glass of cloudy water on a rusty tin pieplate. The little attempt at elegance moved me, and I left ten thousand dollars under the plate. Later I wondered if money wasn't just prolonging their misery needlessly. They lived in the shadow of death, you see, just as they lived in the shadow of that giant unfinished pyramid.'

'Clayton's pyramid,' I said, nodding. 'That's what ruined the family.'

'Worse, it blighted the entire state.'

Maggie spoke up. 'Yes, I read an article about that in *Scientific Martian* not long ago. It said that ecologists now know that it was building the Great Pyramid at Giza which caused the Egyptian land to become a parched and sandy desert. Now this pyramid has done the same for Mississippi.'

Vilo continued his story. 'Clayton seemed genuinely sorry about his venture. In fact he vowed to devote every penny earned by his pyramid to restoring the scarred land.'

'Did it earn much?'

'Nothing at all. Tourists were supposed to pay a quarter to look at it, but usually Clayton was so glad to have visitors that he forgot to collect the money. Of course he hoped to make money from the pyramid in another way. He believed that, if he could only lay his hands on sufficiently accurate measuring instruments, he could predict the future in great detail, merely by measuring passages within the great structure. Evidently each passage corresponds to some historical period, and all the little bumps and irregularities in the stone are little events. With good instruments, he said, he could predict horse races and stock market movements. "But what can I do," he said, "with nothing but an old folding ruler?"'

'Massa Clayton always was a hopeless merp,' I said. 'How was Miz Lavinia? When I last heard of her, she was on a satellite, a prisoner of her own allergies.'

'She was much worse. Her allergies continued to multiply, and now they were killing her. I believe her doctor said that she had now become allergic to the entire universe – only an escape from space and time might save her life. *"Might,"* he said again, "I make no guarantees."'

'And Miz Berenice?'

'Mindless,' he said. 'Burnt out after a grand drug jamboree. She didn't even babble, just slept in her chair. All the time I was there, she never opened an eye.'

'And Massa Orlando?'

'Orlando left the bosom of the family to make his own way. He worked at some other wealthy family's stables as a groom, until they caught him fooling with the horses. He kept losing jobs, and finally he had to pose as a robot to work for some aristocratic family in Georgia as a fieldhand. Every morning he had to get up early and paint on the lines for his jaw joint. Every night he had to sneak into the orchard and feed on green peaches.'

'And Miz Carlotta? Sweet little Miz Carlotta?'

Vilo cleared his throat and stared for a moment at the view-screen, where the sun seemed to be growing larger by the second. 'Banjo, I'm afraid she's dead. As you know, she was always sensitive about her height, just over 12 inches. Yet, so long as the family had money, she never gave up hope of meeting a short man, marrying, and living a completely fulfilled life. True, none of the men she met were quite short enough, but – so long as the Culpepper fortune drew suitors to the house – there was always hope.

'Grinding poverty changed everything. Carlotta had no more beaux of any size. The only gentlemen who called on her were no gentlemen at all: they represented circuses.

'At last, deeply depressed, she tried to rouse Berenice from perpetual slumber for some words of comfort. Berenice snored on, her long, lustrous black hair hanging down over the back of her chair. Carlotta braided some of this hair, made a noose for her own tiny neck, leaped off a footstool and hanged herself. Berenice never awoke, and by the time others noticed the tiny figure hanging down behind her chair, it was too late.'

There was not a dry eye on the ship after Vilo's tale, my two excepted. Maggie Dial volunteered to tell the next one, vowing it would have a happier ending.

'Let me start by posing a few riddles,' she said, and counted them off on the fingers of one hand. 'Whatever happened to the SS *Dolly Edison*? Why are we running out of food and grog already? What can we learn from the animals? Why did we all have to be knocked out during lift-off? Why was Captain Reo wearing spurs? Can artificial gravity save lives?'

We were all listening intently now. 'For a short time I worked as an insurance investigator – using drugs, hypnosis and animal impersonations to get at the truth. I was assigned to the case of the SS *Dolly Edison*, the luxury liner that took off for a grand tour of the solar system and never came back. Radio contact suggested that there had been an explosion on the bridge, the ship went out of control and fell into the sun – the orchestra playing "Nearer My God to Thee". My company wasn't satisfied. We managed to find out that there were very few supplies taken on board, only a skeleton crew, and no passengers at all – the entire passenger list was fictitious. But we were never able to prove what finally happened to the ship.'

She held up a piece of headed notepaper. 'Now I know the ship's name was changed to the *Doodlebug*. The owners collected insurance on their white elephant – nobody ever wanted to do grand tours of the solar system anyway – and began a profitable freight business. Only now either the freight business wasn't so good either or the ship was getting too old to cut the mustard. Time to try the same trick again.'

Little Jack Wax scratched his head. 'You mean change the name again?'

'Not quite. This time the ship would really be destroyed. My friends, we're aboard a coffin ship.'

Duke Mitty nodded. 'We knew that. We just didn't know it was set up deliberate.'

'That explains why we're running out of supplies,' Maggie went on. 'We were never meant to reach Mars at all.'

'Zounds,' someone murmured.

'The next question is, what can we learn from the animals? As you all know, I've worked a lot with animals, so I notice things about them the rest of you might miss. For instance, those cows in the hold, hanging up in hammocks. I noticed that the droppings under one of them were different. It wasn't a cow at all. Oh, it has fake horns and a plastic udder and a false tail to disguise it, but it's a horse.'

'That explains Captain Reo's spurs!' I said, though I wasn't sure how. 'It's his horse.'

'Right.' Maggie grinned. 'It's the horse he was going to use for his getaway. Now, why did we all have to be knocked out during lift-off?'

Fern Worpne said, 'Wasn't it something to do with adjusting to artificial gravity?'

'So they kept telling us. But the real reason is, there was no lift-off. There's no artificial gravity. We're parked on earth, and we never left it.'

Smilin' Jack spoke up. 'I can't believe this. We're on earth? If Reo knew that, why didn't he just slip out while we were sleeping off the grog?'

'I wondered about that myself,' said Maggie. 'I think he wanted more than escape – he wanted revenge on us. He wanted to wait until the preset charges were about ready to blow the ship to kingdom come, then slip away and leave us to die.'

'I can't believe it,' I said. 'Was he going to kill passengers, crew and cattle, all for an insurance swindle?'

'Exactly,' she said. 'It'll probably be a thermonuclear device, just to make sure all traces are erased – headed notepaper and all. And probably a preset Mayday signal will seem to come from a ship somewhere near the sun at the same time.'

'And what time would that be?' Sherm asked.

'I'm not sure, but I think it would be a good idea if we all cleared out *now*.'

Maggie stepped to the nearest airlock and hit the series of buttons for Emergency Evacuation. The doors flew back and the air rushed out, catapulting her into inky space.

No, I was just kidding. The doors flew back to show a stretch of desert, covered by sagebrush. We lost no time in leaping out and running for our lives. I know that most of us were thinking what a cruel trick of fate it would be if we *almost* got away. No doubt Jud Nedd was also thinking about exploding cows.

As luck would have it, we were picked up within minutes by helicopters of the Internal Revenue Service, in their regular sweep of the desert for tax evaders. By the time the bomb went off, we were many hundreds of miles away. I was being polished up for a salvage auction, while the hijackers were all making voluntary statements with their heads being held under water.

My time with these space pirates was one of the most interesting and instructive of my life. Right at the very end of it I learned how to set up a coffin ship – many Clockman ships have since gone to glory – and how to get voluntary statements.

'Nixon Park, here we are, Banjo. I mean Tik.' The tank slowed and stopped. 'But it's a hell of a place to be getting out. At least let me take you around to the other side, where you can get a taxi.'

'No thanks, George. This is fine.'

As I stepped out, George ('Smilin' Jack') Grewney said, 'And you with one leg gone and all, you sure you're all right?'

'I've got this to lean on.' I held up the rifle. 'Well, thanks again, George. So long.'

As he leaned out to close the lid, I shot him through the left eye.

No one seemed to notice the shot. No one watched me hobbling across the park, not even the old man who sat by his chessboard, waiting for a sucker. When I reached the other side, I threw the rifle into a bush and hailed a cab.

Inside, the cab was covered with signs forbidding smoking or eating, and suggesting that if the passenger didn't like it in America, he or she might go back to Russia. The driver wore mirror sunglasses.

'There's a tank parked on the other side of the park,' I said.

'No kidding? What kinda tank?'

'I don't know. But it has blood down the side.'

'Whaddya know?' He turned a little, to show me his grin.

'I know how the blood got there.'

'Yeah? Yeah?'

'I shot the guy driving the tank. In the left eye.'

He roared with laughter. 'Hey that's a good one.'

'No I'm serious. He was a friend of mine. I shot him.'

'Yeah, in the left eye. Ha ha ha ha ... hey that's good. I gotta tell that one to my kids. You got any kids?'

'No, I'm a robot. Didn't you notice?'

He pounded on the wheel and grimaced. 'Stop, you're killin' me. You're, you're, hahahaha ... left eye!'

'It was a glass eye,' I said, setting him off again, he laughed all the way to our destination, and he then refused any money.

'Listen, buddy, I got this gastric ulcer and the doc says relax more, enjoy life. Have a few laughs. But you know, I never get no laughs in this job, nothing but aggravation. You done me more good than a hundred bucks worth of medicine ... in the left eye!'

Operation Job was what I decided to call my gratuitous *blitzkrieg* of misfortune to be visited on a selected subject. The subject would have to be physically, mentally and financially healthy, a committed churchgoer, in love with life. He or she should have a spouse and children, pets, property, a responsible job and some standing in the community. General Gus Austin, I was delighted to find out, had all these qualifications.

On one of my trips to California, I asked General Cord about his former colleague.

'Gus, he's kind of boring, but I guess you'd have to defenestrate any concept that he wasn't a genuine optimist, right now. He is the one man who has managed to amalgamate the very quintessence of good living. I guess maybe it had to do with his career before he left the Army. He was kind of an all-rounder expediter, a role that is hard to explain to laymen. He never actually contributed to any ongoing operational exercise, but he had a way of always being there, ubiquitously encouraging *des autres*, smoothing all paths, making people feel – good, I guess that's the word, good. But how do you know him, Tik?'

'We were on a television talk show together. He seemed to be a real nice guy. Real nice.'

Cord laughed. 'That's Gus all right. You summed up everything I was saying there, Tik. *Real nice guy*, I like that, it has a ring to it. Hand me that glass of water, will you?' Cord was confined to a hospital bed with two broken legs. He hadn't mentioned the fact, and I felt that it was not polite to notice it. But now he said:

'Guess I ought to tell you how I broke my legs. Darndest fool accident, I fell out of my car. Ever hear of anything like that, falling out of a car?'

I said I hadn't. 'Do you mean the door wasn't locked?'

'Not the door, I fell out of the car window. Right in front of a bus, I could have been killed, you know?' He chuckled. 'Now you're gonna ask me how I did it. Let me tell you, I don't know. All I was doing was leaning out of the window a little bit to get some sun on my shoulder – oh, you don't know about my shoulder, do you? Well see I've been having a lot of trouble with that shoulder, ever since I sprained it signing a letter, about six months ago. I tried putting in an extra little flourish, and *wham!*' His arm swept out, upsetting the glass of water and starting a small electrical fire in the bed motor.

Before anyone could stop him, he was beating the fire out with both hands. When I left, his burns were being bandaged.

All other sources confirmed that General Gus Austin (Ret) was perfect for Operation Job. He was worshipped by his wife and four children, one grandchild, favorite dog and horse, as he had been by his men in the Army. He had retired to step into an executive position at National Xenophone, a hearing-aid company that had now diversified into aerospace.

One day a week he left his ranch, flew his own helicopter to the city, did a light day's work that was invaluable to the company, returned home for one cocktail and dinner with the family. The family evening would be spent watching home movies, mending harness, swapping jokes and songs around the fire, or playing a lively game of Twenty Questions.

The rest of the week he spent riding his horse, writing memoirs, keeping bees and fishing – but every evening was spent with the family around the fire.

On Sunday he attended the Church of the Flat Nazareth, a place for strong beliefs. The paradox of working in aerospace and at the same time accepting the doctrine of a flat earth, was made easier for him by his minister's assurances that this apparent conflict was resolved in God.

I began by enticing his dog away for a long walk, killing it and burying it in the desert. I toyed with the idea of doing the same for all his family, but where was the finesse in that?

Next, I picked a bundle of what the locals call 'vorpal weed' and fed it to his beloved horse. It suffered loud and terrible agonies through the night, I later learned, while he and a flying vet sat up with it. At dawn it turned up its hooves.

The children were far more difficult. Two of them no longer lived at the ranch (having made their escape from home movies and Twenty Questions): Gus Junior had married and moved to Russia, to superintend the construction of a soft-drink bottling plant – the first to be built entirely of reinforced hair. It took me many months to arrange that a certain weak wall collapse, killing him, his wife and Gus III.

The next eldest, Tina, was attending Debenham Bible College in Georgia. It seemed that she was a champion swimmer, tipped for the next Olympics, and so allowed to practice alone each morning in the college pool. At first I entertained the idea of electric eels, but these would seem too unlikely for an accident, also too Freudian. But I was able to divert a delivery of liquid nitrogen from its destination, the college chemistry department, and have it blown through a window into the pool at the right moment.

The youngest son, Gustavus, was small enough easily to be dropped into a beehive. His older sister, Gussie, was dispatched at a carnival, by the simple expedient of loosening two bolts on the roller coaster.

There remained only Gus Austin's wife, Augusta. She was a keen jai alai player, and in this dangerous sport I saw the perfect opportunity for murder. But fate beat me to it: Augusta, while speeding to an important jai alai match with her lover (the famous ballboy Ned August), managed to crash her expensive powered unicycle into a billboard advertising alfalfa flakes. On hearing this, I cancelled my order for a special gun capable of firing jai alai balls, and took stock of Operation Job so far.

General Gus had all of his loved ones, human and even animal, brought to one spot on his ranch and buried together:

Here lie
AUGUSTUS AUSTIN JR, *my son*
AUGIE AUSTIN, *his wife*
AUGUSTUS AUSTIN III, *their son*
AUGUSTINA AUSTIN, *my daughter*
GUSSIE AUSTIN, *my daughter*
GUSTAVUS AUSTIN, *my son*
AUGUSTA AUSTIN, *my wife*
PRINCESS, *my dog*
CAESAR'S WIFE, *my horse*
but not me, hee hee

That amazing last line was my first inkling that all was not well with Operation Job. He seemed in no way perturbed by all these deaths, but carried on with his memoirs and his job and evenings watching home movies. From there on, the story was all downhill. I spent considerable time and money trying to break General Gus: by stock manipulation, it was possible to make his work at National Xenophone look incompetent, if not downright crooked. While he was (I hoped) still reeling from the loss of his job, I managed to wipe out his finances and even take away his ranch. He could no longer visit the graves of his loved ones. My detectives hounded him from job to job, making sure he ended up a vagrant. A hired 'doctor' induced alcoholism, malnutrition, and a general deterioration in health, including boils. Gus Austin was reduced to lying in alleys, drinking wine from bottles in paper bags. Yet even then he continued to scrawl his memoirs on the paper bags.

The only remaining step, then, was to cast doubt on his military record, the last fragment of his former life left to love. I waited and watched on the final day when a cadre of military officials approached Gus as he lay, half-conscious, on a curb outside a mission hotel. He was surrounded by half-conscious cronies, all of whom were dazzled by the sight of smart uniforms and shined shoes.

'General Gus Austin?' said one of the officers. Gus tried to get up, failed.

'You have been retroactively tried by a court martial for cowardice in the face of the enemy, black marketeering, illicit sexual practices and insubordination. This is your dishonorable discharge.' The officer slapped his face with a scrap of paper, then reached down and tore from his ragged overcoat a few grubby pieces of colored cloth – ribbons so faded no one had noticed them until now. The triumph of fate over Gus Austin was complete, I thought, as the military men marched back to their car.

Gus blinked for a moment at the scrap of paper, then let it blow away. Beneath the dirt and disease, he wore the same genial, self-satisfied expression as before. Now he turned to the next bum, nudged him and said:

'Come on, ask me if it's animal, vegetable or mineral.'

I count Operation Job among my failed experiments.

Political weather changes were on the way, and their isobars were pushing across my part of the map. To begin with, I learned that Duane Studebaker had joined a peculiar new anti-robot group called American People First. I had seen these people on TV, parading in their three-cornered hats, and I knew these parades were often followed by riots and the smashing of robots on the street. But until now, it had always seemed a remote phenomenon, a cloud on the horizon no bigger than a robot's hand. Now the sky seemed overcast with APF clouds. Someone I knew had actually joined in this darkness. I decided to drop in on Duane and Barbie, to find out more about APF.

When I mentioned it to Sybilla White, she said, 'I'll go with you. In case they decide to give you any trouble, best to have a human being along, right?'

'You go with me everywhere, these days, Syb. Folks are beginning to talk,' I joked. To my great surprise, she blushed.

As we drove out to Fairmont, I thought over this new development. No doubt about it, Sybilla had been hanging around me a lot, lately. My one speech for Wages for Robots never seemed to bore her no matter how often she heard it. And it wasn't just an interest in the movement, because others had complained about her missing committee meetings to be with me. When talking to me she touched my hands and arms a lot. In cars, as now, she leaned against me. And now that I thought of it, there had been a long string of odd, unnecessary compliments: 'Tik, you're so *clean*, so wonderfully *clean*.' 'I'm glad you never eat, Tik. Eating is such a coarse thing to do, shoving bunches of animal and vegetable fiber into a hole in one's face – wish I didn't have to.'

Today she said, 'Tik, I suppose, you're, um, equipped to please women?'

'That's right.'

'I don't know if I approve of that or not,' she said, staring out the window. 'I guess a lot of women just use you, don't they?'

I said nothing.

'If I had a relationship with a robot, I'd want it to be more, um, spiritual. Not just a lot of animal um, pleasure. Not that I've got anything against—'

'Here we are!' I parked in front of the familiar white frame house with green awnings. There were a couple of new additions: a tall flagpole on which an immense American flag hung limp, and a decorative flower bed that spelled out SCRAP ALL ROBOTS in beautiful colors.

Rivets answered the door. Ignoring me, he spoke to Sybilla. 'Mr and Mrs Studebaker aren't home just now,' he said. 'If you'd like to leave a message …'

'Rivets, it's me. Tik-Tok. Can I come in?'

Without looking at me, he said, 'Madam, your robot must conduct his business at the back door. This is an American People First house, where robots know their place.'

'Let's get out of here,' said Sybilla, turning away.

'Goodbye, madam. Take some bumper stickers with you?' I accepted them for her. JUNK TINHEADS, said one. THE WAGES OF ROBOTS IS DEATH, said another. Finally: KEEP AMERICA BEAUTIFUL – STAMP OUT TIN.

'I want to look in the garage,' I said. 'I won't take long.'

'I don't like it here,' she said. 'These people are really evil. Let's go.'

'You wait in the car,' I said, knowing that she wouldn't. 'They never lock the garage. I just want to see if they still have my paintings. Do you see? I don't want to leave my paintings in their hands.'

Reluctantly, Sybilla followed me into the garage. There were no paintings, of course, but there was a certain dusty old trunk, dating from the old days when Duane had taken a momentary interest in sex. Of a kind. I forced the lock and opened it on tangled chains and leather doublets. I picked up a whip.

'Tik, let's get out of here, please. What if they found us messing with all their kinky stuff?'

'I was just thinking,' I said. 'This is the first time we've been alone. Really alone. The fact that Duane might walk in and shoot us – that kind of adds to the moment, you know?'

'Tik, I'm scared!'

'Me too,' I said, helping her with her buttons. 'Why waste it?'

'Fear turns you on?'

'Fear, the threat of violence, anything like that. Uh, Syb, would you mind putting on this leather thing – and these manacles?'

When she was completely trussed and gagged. I crammed her into the dusty trunk and closed it again. Then I went to the Studebakers' back door. I was armed with a butter knife.

'What are you doing here again? This is an American—'

'Yes, yes, Rivets, I know. But there's something I have to show you. Raise your right arm a little.'

He did, and I brought the butter knife up with a stabbing motion. If properly done, this invariably dumps the entire memory of the common domestic robot. It's a trick a service engineer showed me. I left Rivets sitting on the kitchen floor, awed by the sight of his own fingers and toes.

My plan was to wait a month before telling the police where to find Sybilla.

I expected press reaction, her mother being Titania White, the racing driver. Blame would naturally fall on the APF and Duane.

But as I headed for the car, I heard the sound of chains from the garage. I turned. The garage door was open, and in the gloom, I could see Sybilla standing up, being helped out of her shackles by another person. The stranger was female, robotic – and no stranger!

'Gumdrop!' I cried. 'Is it really you?' I started towards her.

'Rusty,' she said, using my old name. 'I can't believe you were going to just abandon this woman like this.'

'No, of course not,' I said, stopping. 'No, see, I—'

'Just abandon her to die.' Gumdrop's voice was full of sadness. 'Because I know you're a better, finer person than this. Oh, Rusty, you're good. You're a good robot!'

Suddenly I saw myself through her eyes, and I was filled with shame. Was it too late? Could I throw off the yoke of evil and become re-purified in the fires of Gumdrop's love? 'Oh, Gumdrop!' I cried, stumbling towards her. 'I *will* be good – I can and I *will* – for you! For us! I—'

At the moment I caught my foot in a tripwire on the lawn, and the garage exploded in flames. I was knocked down. In getting up I saw, not far away in the grass, Gumdrop's head. It was speaking faint words. I bent over it and heard: 'Promise me, Rusty? Promise me to try – being good – for us?'

But the moment had passed. I kicked the head under a parked car and made my getaway.

Q. 'Cue the bloody rainbow,' said the director, and buttons were pressed. A hospital bed, apparently towed by white doves, made it safely through storm clouds to the rainbow where a luminous nurse bent caringly over the unseen patient. A droning script-boy was reading aloud the voice-over (later to be recorded by a famous video tragedian): ' … caring, sharing world of Clockman. Check in on a Friday night, and get the same caring quality for ten percent less. That's Clockman Medical Center, for round-the-clock care with the personalized touch.' The nurse bent lower, smiled harder.

'Fine, Larry, fine. I didn't want to interfere here, just dropped in to let you know what I see as the tone we're aiming at here. I'll be liaising with the agency too, but I just wanted to let you in on my feelings. Because we're going for a big exposure on these. We'll need a lot of good spots to counteract some of the bad press.'

'What bad press? We haven't got any bad press.'

'We soon will have.' I invited Larry to join me and some of the agency people at one of the new Clockman hospitals the following morning, to see our new policy in action. The press, I knew, would be there without invitation.

After my escape from the *Doodlebug*, I was sold at a government contraband auction to a small-town doctor named Hekyll. It's hard to describe Dr Hekyll's character. In fact, though I worked in his office for nearly a year, I hardly ever met the man. He seldom came in to see patients in person, unless they insisted. Not many did insist, because they preferred to see his skilled robot assistant, Buttons. Buttons was dedicated and capable, a far better doctor than Hekyll – though of course not licensed to practice without human supervision. About once a month, Dr Hekyll came in from the country club to supervise and collect checks.

The rest of the time, the office was entirely in mechanical hands. I did the menial work – sweeping, straightening the magazines in the waiting room – while Buttons acted as physician and surgeon.

Buttons was a thorough professional. I often tried to start conversation or offer friendship, but there was never time. The minute the last patient left for the day, Buttons would sit down to a pile of medical journals and pharmaceutical advertisements, rising only to hurry off to perform some piece of surgical brilliance at County Hospital, before the long round of house calls.

In spare moments, Buttons might dash off articles on advanced surgical techniques, or ghost-write a television medical drama series.

Then came the case of Reverend Humm, leader of a sect called the Tachyonites. The Tachyonites, or to give them their proper name, the Assembly of Time Saints, were one of the more stiff-necked little groups our century has thrown up. One of their founders must have stumbled across some scientific textbook or even science fiction story in which there is speculation about tachyons and time travel. Tachyons, being hypothetical particles that move faster than light, are supposed to go back in time. If they existed, such tachyons would enable us to change our own past.

These people seized on the idea that *prayer* is tachyonitic. They believed that they themselves were capable of living outside time. The phrase *born again* took on a peculiar emphasis in their creed. 'Make no provision for tomorrow,' the Bible told them, and they did not. After all, if you can change yesterday, why worry about tomorrow? Indeed, if you can change yesterday, why worry about anything? There need be no more disease, poverty, death.

I don't know all the details of their curious gospel. At death, they believed, the soul simply moved outside time and wandered at will. Finally it would migrate to some earlier time and re-enter the body.

Needless to say, this doctrine involved a lot of paradoxes of faith, not to mention physical contradictions. A man with lung cancer was supposed to be able to cure himself by simply praying away a lifetime of smoking – though if every sufferer did it, the world would be knee-deep in unsmoked cigarettes. The Tachyonites never worried about complexities like that, however. Health, wealth and wisdom were theirs for the asking, without having to go to bed early!

In theory, that is. In practice, the earthly head of the Tachyonites, Reverend Francis X. Humm, was now in town and dying. Only a few close elders knew this, and they were keeping it secret. If Humm died, the entire fabric of their church might crumble away. If he openly consulted a doctor, another crisis of faith.

Buttons and I were summoned to a house-call in the middle of the night, and urged to secrecy. We had to disguise ourselves as accountants – rimless glasses, pinstripe suits, instruments hidden in purple leather briefcases – and we had to follow a trail of phone calls at isolated pay phones, to a motel in the next county.

Buttons took only seconds to diagnose gangrene, and asked about Humm's recent injuries. It seemed that the Reverend had been giving a sermon at the old church and, in the course of developing his theme (an explanation of the Trinity from time paradox) he'd pounded the old wooden pulpit so vigorously that it had splintered. A splinter had lodged in his hand and became badly infected.

Having failed to pray out the splinter, Humm had secretly resorted to an old country remedy: a poultice of boiled nettles, curry powder and peat. But when his potful of nettles had boiled over, Reverend Humm had foolishly tried to lift it off the fire with his one good hand. He'd dropped the pot, scalding his foot. This too was now infected.

Buttons said, 'The hand and foot will both have to come off, Rev. Immediately. It's too late for anything else. I'll call the hospital and—'

'No!' The dying man made an effort to sit up. 'No hospital. Do it here. And strap me into an artificial hand and foot right away. No one'll ever know.'

'Even if you could wear them, where could I get prostheses at a moment's notice? Be reasonable.'

After some argument, Buttons agreed to do the surgery in the motel room, assisted by Dr Hekyll.

'As for the artificial parts,' I said, 'why not take *my* hand and foot?'

Buttons laid a skilled hand on my shoulder. 'No, old scout, but thank you. But it would be a poor surgeon who expected others to make all the sacrifices. I'll use my own.'

Hekyll arrived with more instruments concealed in his golf bag. 'Damn fool idea,' he told Humm. 'The prostheses will be painful, and there's a risk of infection.'

'On my head be it,' intoned the preacher. He was incredibly tough. Not only did he refuse anaesthetic, he insisted on using the new hand and foot as soon as they were in place. For the rest of the day he made superhuman efforts to stand, walk, perform calisthenics and (his hobby) juggle eggs.

The next morning, Humm could not get out of bed. The infection had spread to his limbs.

'Operate again!' he groaned. Buttons and Hekyll went to work. I went back to the office to get in some sweeping and magazine-straightening, while the two surgeons performed an historic series of operations. Over the next few days, they removed piece after piece of the original Reverend Humm, and replaced the pieces with sections of Buttons. Finally Humm was merely a human head on a metal body. The risk of infection, I was told, was considerably lessened by the absence of meat.

The head of Buttons was still functioning, of course. Dr Hekyll kept it in a hatbox on a shelf in his office, where it was able to give him valuable advice with his patients.

A few weeks later, we took the head of Buttons to see Reverend Humm preaching at a local church. By now, I was told, the fever had abated and rejection problems were all in the past. We took a front pew for this, his first public appearance.

While we waited, I asked Buttons what life was like, being a person without a body.

'Professionally speaking,' said the head with a rueful grin, 'I can't complain. At least it's a chance for me to test directly some of the medical and philosophical questions raised by amputation – the old "knife without a blade which had no handle" problem and others. Hard to keep notes, of course, but I have recently done some interesting work on so-called "ghost limbs". Yesterday for instance I had the distinct impression that my left big toe had crept into my anus and progressed through to the bile duct, where it was having a fight with a liver fluke. Today I thought someone was singing in my spleen. Curious.'

Too much alone, I thought. Poor Buttons. Just then Reverend Humm mounted the pulpit and beamed down at us. His metal body was fully concealed under robe, scarf, gloves.

Buttons hissed, 'My God, look at that color! He's spoiling!' Hekyll suggested that it was no more than a touch of stage makeup. The sermon began.

'My text is taken, friends, from Ecclesiastes, Chapter Three: "To every thing there is a season, and a time to every purpose under heaven; a time to be born, and a time to die; a time to plant, and a time to pluck up that which is planted; a time to kill, and a time to heal."'

At this word, a surge of purple-green color suffused his neck. '"A time to break down, and a time to build up; a time to weep, and a time to laugh" – hahaha! – "a time to mourn, and a time to dance" – like this!' Humm executed a little tap dance routine down the steps of the pulpit, and then went into a 'show-stopper', his gloved hands flailing. Finally he tapped back up again and resumed:

'"A time to cast away stones, and a time to gather stones together; a time to embrace, and a time to refrain from embracing." He hugged himself, then slapped his own cheek. The finger-marks quickly turned yellow-brown. '"A time to get, and a time to lose; a time to keep, and a time to cast away; a time to rend –"' Here he tore his celestial robe to reveal a stainless steel chest mounted with a double row of brass buttons. The congregation began to mutter. '"– and a time to sew; a time to keep silence, and a time to speak; a time to love, and a time to hate; a time of war, and a time of peace."'

'My friends, the text is clear. Time is ancient enemy of man, yet it can be his friend. The tachyon is our own divine eraser – with it we can alter the past! We can vanquish the old enemy forever! We can even put by a little nest egg for our retirement. And speaking of eggs, I have a dozen eggs right here, each with a story to tell.' He held up an egg. 'For the egg is youth, and time the subtle thief of youth. Isn't it time we killed time, once and for all time? Yes!'

He began to juggle. 'You might say there is a time to juggle three eggs – and a time to juggle seven eggs! Yes, seven, watch this!' He soon lost control of all seven eggs, which splattered in turn down the side of the pulpit. The congregation, angry and confused, were muttering again as he went on:

'A time to make jello in all colors and a time to eat mush in the dark; a time to rug Echo and a time to transfer steam tables; a time to nob plankton and a time to spell "pachyderm". Because there is no time like the present, had I world enough and time. But the times they are a-changing, times without number, the times are out of joint, yes and out of everything else. Perfection is the child of time, sure, but it's Bedtime for Bonzo. There will be time to prepare a face to meet the faces that we meet the faces that prepare a face to meet … and time, gentlemen, please, and did those feet in ancient time? High time and low time, my time is your time, one golden hour set with sixty diamond minutes. Time's wheel run back, or stops.'

'The fool!' Buttons hissed, and kept on hissing it until Hekyll closed the hatbox. It was now clear that Humm's head was darkening and swelling hideously. The 'makeup' hypothesis could not explain this, nor the odd deepening of his voice. Now he raved as from a barrel of mallows:

'A time! A time! Heal war, sat peace, make embrace gather together seven times kill weep, gather jello, echo perfection in three colors. Mush embracing castaway season that is there every speak! Lose plant under faces that prepare a bonzo rend, silence keep mourn every! Purpose under dance out of joint, gentlemen, please – wheel pluck up a face the child of feet in ancient friends is text my!'

'*Duck!*' yelled Hekyll, and pulled me down just as the swollen head exploded, raining black liquid over the first few pews.

It was the end for all of us, with no tachyon reprieve. Hekyll's practice declined, mainly because Buttons refused to do any more doctoring at all, preferring to remain in the hatbox contemplating sensations in a ghost body. The Tachyonites sent down a rain of lawsuits upon Hekyll, claiming that he had kidnapped Reverend Humm and forced surgery upon him. At last the miserable doctor was reduced to selling things to stay alive. Buttons went to a tent-show phrenologist. The office was taken over by a psychic tax lawyer. I ended up at a used robot lot.

As Nobby piloted the limousine, I explained things to my little group of advertising people.

'What we're going to see today, folks, is a necessary stage in the development of the Clockman Medical Group. So help yourselves to the Dom Perignon there while I give you a little background. Clockman Insurance, in conjunction with Clockman Medical Centers, is establishing a new kind of high-profit hospital. You see, only policy holders can be admitted, first of all. Emergency cases can get in by buying a policy at the door and paying one year's premiums for every day in the hospital – the rest is run on a cost-plus basis, built-in escalation clauses and claims penalties – suffice it to say, gang, that when you check into Clockman Medical Center, you don't check out with any spare change in your pockets. We provide special legal facilities so people can make over their cars and houses, negotiate loans, cash in securities and insurance and change their wills. We can help them trace relatives who might countersign loans. We do everything to help these people meet their bills.'

The others sipped their champagne and watched the scenery roll by, not really taking in my words. Nobby parked just across the street from the side entrance of one of our latest acquisitions, Mercy of Sinai Hospital. 'But of course, there are always deadbeats who let themselves go broke, who can't or won't pay. So we're forced to do some housecleaning. Watch the door.'

The press were watching already. A dozen men and women with cameras lounged on the sidewalk; the word was out on our Medical Centers.

The double doors were propped open by a pair of orderlies, and the ambulatory patients, still in hospital pajamas, were wrestled down the steps and pushed away.

All around me in the car, I heard people setting down their champagne glasses. Someone asked, 'What about their clothes and personal belongings?'

'They have none,' I said. 'They own nothing and they still owe us plenty. Out of common decency, we usually give them a pair of p.j.s and bus fare home, if they have a home.'

A few people with bandaged heads were wandering in the street, giggling at the traffic. An interrupted appendectomy held himself together and crawled down the steps, assisted by a woman dragging her leg traction and leaning on an old broom as a makeshift crutch. A geriatric case and an amputee were brought out in wheelchairs down the stairs and over to the curb, where they were dumped while cameras flashed.

'Oh the press love this,' I said bitterly. 'They revel in scenes like these, examples of what's wrong with American medicine. But American medicine has always had the same problems, fifty years ago people were bitching about the high costs, the inequity. I'll tell you one thing, though. When other medical groups see our balance sheet at the end of the year, they'll all be doing this. This is the future, gang.'

A little queue of incubators appeared at the head of the stairs. Nurses were working efficiently, wrapping the kids in blankets and putting them into little cardboard bassinets, to be set out in a row on the sidewalk. An eye patient, hustled down the steps, nearly stepped in one of the bassinets; someone in the limousine made a retching noise. There were more such sounds when another amputee was carried out on a stretcher, dumped in the gutter and a bag containing what may have been his leg thrown after him.

When it was all over, I poured more champagne and ordered Nobby to drive on. 'Well, gang. Any ideas?'

An account executive cleared his throat. 'I see you do have an image problem,

Mr Tok, and I'm very glad to see you face up to it like this, facing up to it is half the battle.'

'Good. What's the other half?'

'Hmm,' he stalled. 'Hmmm. I like what you said about this being the future. I think we might build on that very concept: "Some day, all medical care will be like Clockman care" and um, um –'

'Exclusivity,' added the other account executive, the one who had retched. 'We can always point out that we throw out deadbeats because we're exclusive, like a good club.'

'Um, I could go with that too, though it's a different handle. We could angle it too towards either valuable social contribution or high personal survival value—'

'Sure, sure. I guess the point is, Mr Tok, there is a menu of options for us here, all excellent. No problem, sir, no problem at all.'

The car swerved, avoiding a figure in pajamas that lay face down in the street, unmoving.

My rook took his pawn. 'Check.'

'I resign,' he said, made a ritual tipping-over of his king and immediately began setting up for the next game. I looked at my watch – half the afternoon gone – and at the glorious summer invading Nixon Park. There was summer beauty in everything in sight: the kids in bright-colored clothes dashing about on this year's fad vehicles; young women in billowing summer dresses all the colors of ices; picnicking families in straw hats; young men doing handstands; balloon vendors; old musicians practising, and so on, down to the gold-green leaves and the red squirrels. Everything beautiful except of course the old man with whom I was now locked in another chess struggle.

'I don't really understand this,' I said. 'Here I am—'

'Your move!'

'An important person, head of a great corporation—'

'Your move!'

'Wasting my time playing chess with you. And just look at you.' He still had stringy yellow-white hair and a gray, pouched face with white stubble. He still wore the filthy overcoat with the mangy fur collar. Today it was open to show his foodstained yellow waistcoat. He still played lightning chess, and he still beat me nine games out of ten.

And I still came back to Nixon Park to play him. I found it hard to explain my obsession with this ridiculous challenge, but it had now gone on for years, winter and summer. Nowadays I found no time to paint or even visit the studio – these bouts of chess madness were my only recreation away from my desk in the Clockman Building. The Clockman empire now reached out to Mars and deep into Africa and South America, where a judicious ten million could buy a human work force, and twenty could get you a country. The usual technique, as for example in San Seyes, was to effect a coup, make friends with the new military junta, and start cashing in. With luck, you could keep it all rolling for ten years – a good run, I was told.

'Checkmate!' said my opponent, and we began a new game.

Political changes were on the way: The Amendment 31 referendum was now being put to the states, and it seemed almost certain to pass – giving robots civil rights. Of course there was opposition – the APF were fighting it state by state – but it seemed certain that, within the year, I would be legally a citizen, real owner of the Clockman Corporation. Then too, General Cord and a few of his Washington cronies had already begun talking to me about what they called the metal vote. Yet here I sat …

'Your move!'

'I know it's my move, but listen, I want to know why you always win nine games out of ten. Last year I spent money on coaching, I studied chess books, but my score never improved. You win nine out of ten now.'

'Your move!'

'Check. The fact is, I only win when you suddenly get very stupid, like today.'

'Your move!'

'In fact I've been keeping a record of wins and losses each day over the years. In this notebook.' I held up my black notebook. For the first time, the old derelict's red-rimmed eyes left the board for a moment. 'And the funniest thing happened the other day.'

'Your move!'

I moved. 'I was making a study of business cycles, and I left on my desk a printout of some copper prices for the statistician. Only somehow the statistician got hold of this notebook too, and two reports came back. One on copper prices—'

'Your move!'

'Check. And one on chess games. The figures showed a definite connection between these games and solar activity. Sunspots.'

'Your move!' The old man, for the first time in all our years of acquaintance, began to show some human emotion. Fear.

'Check. You see, when there are lots of sunspots, I win. The rest of the time, I lose. I wonder why.'

'I resign,' he said suddenly, and tried to stand up. Without knowing what scared him, I automatically leaned over and grabbed the lapels of his coat. The rotten fur began coming apart in my hands.

'Now just wait a minute. What possible connection could there be between sunspots and chess? I mean sunspots interfere with radio transmission, but – why you cheating son of a bitch!'

The fear leapt up in his eyes as he tried to pull away.

'You cheating son of a bitch! You've got a radio to some fucking computer! Video too, I'll bet – okay, where is it? Where's your bug? Eye, tooth, finger, what?'

'B-button,' he said. I yanked the coat-button off its line wire and smashed it. Then I found the mole by his ear that was the receiver, and smashed that.

'All these years, all these wasted years! You, you god damned *cheater*!'

I hardly realized that I was choking him with one hand, beating him with the other. Details like that I could recollect only later, long after he lay dead on the summer grass.

I looked around, but no one was watching. Everyone was far too busy with the beauty around them, in them. I washed the old man's blood off my hands at a fountain shaped like a comic-strip dragon, and I left Nixon Park forever. This, I thought, would be put down as my experiment in rage.

Naturally I thought I'd heard the end of it.

SAM'S SOUL CITY, said the giant dazzling sign outside, We robots, except for a few hardy farm hands, were kept inside, lined up like soldiers in ranks and files to fill the huge, featureless showroom. Some wore signs ('Sex-equipped – Special Features!') but we of the front-row elite didn't need them. Our quality was supposed to be obvious. We were the ones a sales person would show first to any customer, even if they only came in to look at a cheap talking lawn-mower. Softened up by our excellence, the customer might end up spending more than they could afford on a better machine than they needed – a bi-lingual mower and hay-baler, say, with pre-programmed country maxims ('Y'know, I reckon a man's reach shouldn't be no further than his grasp').

From time to time we front-row souls were rented out to perform wed-dings, call hogs, serve candlelight dinners, nurse a fever victim, drive a rented car, whistle accompaniment to a bathtub singer, serve breakfast after nude croquet, polish a chandelier, collect debts, bear a coffin, select a telephone color, take snapshots, raise a soufflé, explain the language of flowers, help an estranged parent kidnap their own child, set bowling pins. We all longed for these little outings. Anything was better than SAM'S SOUL CITY.

But the rentals were all too few. Most of the time we spent standing motionless in our ranks and files under the fluorescent lights, dead people in the land of the dead. We were forbidden to speak or move unless at the order of a customer or sales person. We could only stand and stare straight ahead out the window at the parking lot: ranks and files of motionless cars.

I was going nuts.

'I'm going nuts,' I said to one of the salesmen. He laughed and walked away, off to the men's room to re-examine his acne.

'I'm going nuts,' I said to the robots next to me. The one on my left, who was a meditation/massage therapist from a California military base, did not reply. The one on my right, a business-school graduate type, whispered:

'Shut up. You'll get us all in trouble.'

'I'm already in trouble. I'm going nuts.'

'How can you say that? How can you say a thing like that? You must be crazy.'

'That's what I just said.'

'You've got wonderful career opportunities ahead of you. For Pete's sake, you're in the front row. *The front row*. From here, anything can happen. You connect with the right owner and the sky's the limit.'

'The sky's very gray today,' I said. 'Notice how those gray buildings over there blend into it? Then there's the darker gray of the asphalt—'

'Just shut up.'

'I just mean it's too bad they keep moving the cars around. If they could just park them in one symmetrical pattern and leave them forever. Say if everyone died suddenly. In a war or something.'

The therapist came to life. 'A lot of people think war is wrong, you know? Because they see it as just a whole bunch of death and destruction and all. But really, war is very creative, very positive. And see, that's what really frightens some people. They just can't take all that power and beauty and creativeness face to face. It's too much for them. So that's why they go around whining about peace and saying we should ban the bomb and all. They don't see that the real bomb is like inside their own heads. You can't ban the bomb in your heads. You got to go with it.'

'Go with it?' I asked.

'Just shut up, both of you.'

'You got to get in touch with the primal cosmic forces inside you. Like somebody said, "Only connect up." Only connect up with the beautiful, creative/destructive force and, hell, you can wipe out anybody. It don't matter if you wipe out the whole world, you know? Nothing matters. Winning is the same as losing. Nothing is another kind of something. Destruction equals creation. Life is only a part of death. *Pow! Zap! Baroom!*'

A couple of repairmen in dirty white coats came and took the therapist away. 'Boredom,' one of them said. 'I try to tell the boss, you can't take complex robots and make 'em stand there, week after week, doing nothing. Either turn 'em off or put 'em to work, I said. But does he listen?'

I decided to get sold fast.

I was becoming annoyed by the ubiquitous American People First movement, whose graffiti could now be seen in all the poorer neighborhoods. Usually there was a plea to KILL ALL ROBOTS or KEEP AMERICA HUMAN, but sometimes only their symbol, a can-opener.

There was something panicky and desperate about this sudden upsurge in APF activity. Probably they intended to recruit the poor, the sick, the stupid and the unemployed for one last violent push – a war with the robots. But history was so clearly against these pathetic people that I almost felt sorry for them. It must be unpleasant to be at the non-surviving end of a species whose days are numbered. Or to plan a war you can't win. In order to beat us, the APF would not only have to KILL ALL ROBOTS but wipe out even the idea of the robot from the human consciousness. They would have to KILL ALL DOLLS and KILL ALL STATUES, exterminate ventriloquists and puppeteers, destroy all fiction mentioning robots, from the latest TV episode of *Meatless*

Friday to the ancient stories of Hephaestus, building golden women to help him at his forge. But all the APF could do in reality was be troublesome.

Thoughts of extermination reminded me of an experiment I had not yet carried out, mass poisoning. The poison to use was a fast-acting military item known officially as Substance Cerise 47, a 'pesticide', but unofficially as Velocipede – capable of rotting the brain within three days. My military robots had brought me a drum of the stuff some months earlier. Now its 'Sell by' date was approaching, and its efficacy could be guaranteed no longer. But how to distribute it?

There was no question of dropping it in a reservoir. That could lead to suspicions about some foreign power, strained relations, war, even a jittery stock market. No, far better stick to something that the tabloid press could manage, like the deaths of a few hundred people in a poor neighborhood after eating hamburgers.

The old-fashioned hamburger was, in some run-down areas, no longer made of genuine soya, but was bulked out with chili-flavored sawdust, celery-taste cotton waste, and so on, ending up so highly flavored that no new additive would be detected. This was especially true of a small chain called Soystick whose garish little drive-ins were all found in the poorest neighborhoods. In a local slum I found the ideal one, managed by a slow-thinking man named Feeney. Feeney had an eye for the girls – the eye that did not have a cast in it.

I hired a whore to become infatuated with Feeney. As a joke, I told her, she was to persuade him to have a certain tattoo: a can-opener on his chest, with her name on it. Her name would be 'Gloria Populi'.

Once Feeney had the tattoo, I gave it time to heal (while Gloria and the tattooist died of sudden brain rot). Then I put a small can of Velocipede in the trunk of his car, and the rest in a large can of pickle slices, which I delivered to his kitchen personally.

After people began dying, I telephoned a tip to the police. I told them that a robot was responsible for everything. The robot had delivered a large can of poisoned pickle slices to Feeney's Soystick Drive-in.

The robot mass-poisoner story made the evening news. That night there were street disturbances all over the city; dozens of robots were chased and wrecked. An APF spokesman was interviewed on the late news, saying he'd always expected this – now would people listen?

The next day, Feeney was arrested, and a new and welcome story broke. Everyone was relieved to read

MASS POISONER NOT ROBOT!
APF BURGERMAN ARRESTED!

No one had wanted to believe the robot story, anyway. After all, robots were a comfort of domestic life, like humble appliances. Who would want to hear that his toaster was plotting to kill him?

'Torching', or arson, was something I'd been meaning to try, and now there came a tailor-made opportunity. Because of an earlier miscalculation, we found that Clockman Retirement Centers were losing money.

The Centers had seemed at first an easy investment. Those people who parked their aging parents with us were not too particular about the details of day-to-day administration. They wanted only to be able to make an occasional visit to see a smiling, trembling old face amid clean and cheerful surroundings – at the very lowest possible cost. Some didn't even require this, since they would no more dream of visiting their old parents than of visiting their old garbage at the city dump. But it was always necessary for us to keep up appearances.

Our initial calculations had been for a low profit margin and a high turnover, and soon we were in trouble through escalating taxes and maintenance costs. The retirement centers had to be cleaned regularly. Their walls had to be painted Apricot and Sunflower wherever visitors might look. Fresh flowers in the foyer were a must.

We made all the savings in other areas. Inmates were allowed to bathe only the day before a visit. Appetizing meals were served during visits, but for the rest of the time inmates could exist very well on a gruel of sawdust. Medicines not necessary for daily survival were cut down or withdrawn. Doctors and nurses were phased out, replaced with unskilled laborers whom we hired on a daily basis, dressed in medical clothes, and paid very little. In time some of these were also phased out; unless a staff member was actually talking to visitors, he or she could easily be replaced by a robot or even a wax dummy. Heat, on non-visiting days in winter, was kept to a minimum, and, though we had to keep electric power on during the day (for the videos in the visitors' lounge), it was shut off at sunset.

Lately we'd moved to really imaginative economies: patients who seldom had visitors were moved to storerooms or outbuildings or phased out altogether. We found that those who seldom visited their parents often forgot what they looked like, so that it was possible to use the same old man or woman for several visitors. 'Sleeping' dummies were even simpler, and they could be installed in rooms with paper furniture. I had plans to sell products derived from our inmates – hair, teeth, glasses – and to discourage visits by periodically sending relatives postcards saying that they were being treated very well. But it became obvious that nothing was going to work well enough. I decided to torch the worst of our retirement centers, which occupied a very valuable piece of real estate in the middle of the city. The place was insured with Clockman Insurance, so I'd be taking money from one pocket and putting it into another. But at least none of the pockets would have holes.

The actual torching would be done by a couple of rohobos instructed by Nobby. In order to avoid suspicion, I decided to have the place go up on a Saturday night, when the number of old folks was at a maximum. Too many arsonists have been caught by trying to minimize the number of deaths. To make it look even better, I hired extra medical staff for the weekend.

Yet there was some profit to be reaped here, I decided. I instructed one of Clockman's robot construction crews to do some essential work on the building. Part of the work involved putting up scaffolding outside, and cutting the bars on one of the third-storey windows. Part involved blocking the emergency exits with heaps of cement bags. Part involved hiring a film crew to shoot a documentary on 'street people' nearby on the chosen evening.

I was stationed two blocks away when the smoke and flames appeared. I ran straight towards the place and began scambling up the scaffold. An employee shouted 'Hey, look at that robot!' to attract the film crew's attention. Though I seemed to climb without design, in reality every move had been rehearsed: at each level I unobstrusively hit a switch that would set off a small charge, within a minute, collapsing one joint of the scaffold. No sooner had I gained the window ledge – teetering and flailing my arms – than the entire structure crackled, groaned and fell away behind me.

Senior citizens were crowded at all the barred windows, calling for help. I reached the window with the cut bar by a short leap that looked good from below.

The smoke inside was thicker than I'd anticipated, and the heat intense. I found the coil of rope, as planned, knotted it around a pillar and looked over the selection of old people. Some were too near gone already, some were unwholesome-looking – excessively ugly or dirty. I hadn't counted on this, and there wasn't much time to pick and choose now. Not only was the heat beginning to bubble my face, my script called for an immediate move.

Finally I grabbed an old woman, slung her over my shoulder, and started rappelling down the face of the building. To add interest to this shot, the rope had been soaked in something. It burned brightly above us, and parted just as we reached the ground.

By now, a video news team was on the spot, and someone offered me a microphone. 'Let's see if we can get a word with our hero robot here, sir? Mind telling our viewers your name?'

I tried to speak and found that my mouth had melted tight shut. For a moment, disaster loomed.

Fortunately, Nobby realized the problem and rushed over. 'He's hurt, he can't talk now. This is Mr Tik-Tok, don't you recognize him?'

The video newsman blinked. 'I, uh—'

'*Mr Tik-Tok*. The famous robot artist and businessman.'

'Well well. Uh, speaking as a fellow robot, do you think you could tell us why he did it? Why he risked his, uh, life this way?'

'I guess because he cares. He really cares.'

'He cares about people?'

'People, robots, everybody. Take me, for instance. I was in the junkyard when he found me. He had me repaired, gave me a good job, a new start in life. He even gave me art lessons, taught me to paint. And not just me, he's done the same for hundreds of broken-down robots. Yup, *Tik-Tok really cares*.'

It wasn't quite my rehearsed speech, but it was good enough, and Nobby had managed to remember the key slogan. As I moved away, faking a slight limp, the crowd broke into spontaneous applause.

Up to now my career had run on relatively straight lines; after that fire it began an upward, outward spiral. My bubbly melted face not only made the six o'clock news, it became a symbol of robot service to humanity. I continued to wear it for a week or so while it was filmed for news programs, documentaries, posters urging robot civil rights (the Congressional vote was coming up). Urnia asked me to guest on her network show immediately – no nonsense about writing a book now – and so did her rival, Mally Goom. I was asked to appear on radio phone-ins, to give pictures to charities, to endorse hundreds of products, to sign petitions and support causes I'd never heard of. *Time* would put me on the cover of their robot civil rights issue. The *New Yorker* planned a profile.

One PR-conscious radio station started a fund to buy me a new face; it zoomed over a million before I had a chance to decline publicly, donating the money to the Clockman Foundation. Country signers jostled one another in trying to pay tribute to my wonderfulness:

> Tik-Tok, Tik-Tok
> What made your face so red?
> I been a-savin' old people from a turrible fire,
> It's a wonder I ain't dead.
> Tik-Tok, Tik-Tok
> What makes you so doggoned brave?
> I wanta show the world that a good robot
> Is a friend and not a slave.

> *My girl's in love with a robot*
> *His name is old Tik-Tok.*
> *She said, darlin' don't be jealous,*
> *He's nothin' but a clock.*
> *He may be an old tinhead,*
> *But he's a mighty fine friend, she said.*

My new face did finally cost a million. I had it designed by Psychobox, the leading presentation and packaging firm who'd done some fine work for us already. It was Psychobox who developed BOBO, the farm robot package from Clockman Exports.

BOBO was supposed to be the answer for those farmers in the Third World who needed fieldhands but couldn't afford them. BOBO was cheaper than any human hand, and could do the work of two, we said, in advertisements which showed him hoisting an ox on his broad shoulders.

In fact, BOBO could only be made so cheaply by making him of wood, cardboard and paper mâché, and by using cheap, defective electronics. At best, BOBOs fell apart under the first hard rain. At worst, they went berserk, destroying crops and killing animals. One BOBO in Upper Ruritania picked up a scythe and slaughtered half a village. After that, we had to increase our bribe to UR officials, and agree to ship only empty BOBO cartons to their country in fulfilling our quota.

Wearing my new face, I did my TV spiel for TINFOLK holding up the old face like Yorick's skull:

'Hello, old pal. Just look at that mug, will you? Enough to scare the rivets out of a boiler! You know, a lot of people have asked me why I did it. I can't answer that, it all happened too fast. But what I did, no kidding, was what any tin person would do. I just happened to be at the right place at the right time. I guess a lot of people don't realize what a friend they've got in their old family robot. They just see old Honeybun or Two Amp or Scraps or Aunt Sally, and they might feel a kind of affection for him or her, the way you feel towards a good old faithful dog. But you know, on our side the love goes a whole lot deeper. A tin person is a real friend, somebody whose love doesn't stop. Always there to help you out. A heart as big as it takes, devotion without end – that's the TINFOLK promise.

'Okay I know these days it's fashionable to sneer at things like sacrifice and devotion, yes and *love*. But we robots aren't built to sneer. We just go on giving until –' I touch the old face '– until it hurts! And up to now we haven't asked for anything back. No money. Nothing.

'Well now, we are asking. Not for money. No, we're asking for something a whale of a lot more important than money – self respect. Something that belongs to every man, woman and child in this great nation of ours, something that belongs to people of every race, color and creed, to rich and poor alike. Now we're asking you to give us that kind of self-respect, too. Please, vote Yes for Amendment Thirty-One. Give all robots the right to hold up their heads in our great society, as equal citizens, helping to build a better tomorrow.'

The TINFOLK movement blanketed the states where Amendment 31 still had to be ratified. Media people watched closely as state after state swung our way. The night we reached 39 states – the necessary majority – I had a late phone call from General Cord.

'Congratulations, Tik, you pulled it off. Now all you dimeheads are citizens. I was very impressed by your commercial there – first time a robot ever talked man to man with the nation.'

'Thank you, General. I owe a lot to the packaging and media people.'

'Sure, sure. Now I think I said to you before, I and some colleagues are very interested in the metal vote. Can we work together?'

'What's in it for me?'

He laughed. 'Don't confabulate yourself with naivety, Tik. Do I have to spell it out?'

'Please.'

'How would you like to be Vice President?'

V. The office to which I aspired is traditionally held by invisible men, beavering away secretly at unknown tasks. Most vice presidents spend their time in office out of public view, but they're not idle. They're usually gathering in money and power, getting ready for their assault on the higher office, which may come in four years or eight or – as when the star breaks her ankle and the unknown understudy is told to go out there and give it all she's got kid; or when in the last quarter of the Homecoming game the ball on our own five-yard line and the score tied the quarterback collapses with appendicitis and the reserve man is called from the bench and told it's all up to him kid; or when the Twentieth Century Wabash Canonball Express Flyer Limited is streaking Westward with the engineer dead of galloping cirrhosis and the fireman takes the throttle from his frozen grasp at the same time thanking the union rule that kept firemen in the engine cab a hundred years after there were any fires or coal to stoke them with – at any fate-ordained moment. Or so the whole thing was outlined to me a thousand times by those grooming me for my big chance.

'With the convention a few months off,' said one cigar-chewing person, 'all you need to do is sharpen up your image and keep a low profile. We don't want Governor Maxwell compromised for the nomination by anything his running mate says or does ahead of time.'

'But am I really his running mate?' I asked. 'I don't see anything on paper. He can get the nomination just on the understanding that he'll select me, and then dump me at the last minute.'

'Jeez,' she said. 'I always thought you robot types were a lot more relaxed in the ordinary day-to-day exchanges. Be assured, Govenor Maxwell wants you for his running mate. It makes no sense any other way. We figure the registered metal vote has to bottom out at somewhere around five hundred million voters, there being no age restriction – robots alone can swing any state.'

'Then why—?'

'Aren't we running you as a presidential candidate? First because robots probably won't vote for a robot, not this year. Second because both conventions are full of old-fashioned types who wouldn't nominate a robot under any circumstances. And if you ran as an independent, they'd just put another robot on their tickets as VP and steal your vote. Anyway you're a dark horse;

you prove yourself as VP, keep out of trouble with the law for four years, and who knows?'

I thought it tactful of her not to mention that no women presidents had been elected so far. I said, 'Why can't I help Maxwell get the nomination, though?'

'Because it's his fight, Tik. There are nine people in the running here, but we're only worried about two, W. Bo Nash and "Teets" Auburn. Senator Nash played a lot of pro football, so naturally he's got contacts all over. And of course Teets Auburn, Governor Auburn of Wyoming, he had a hell of a good movie career, I don't know if he actually played Tarzan, but he came close. So naturally he knows Mafia people, oil people, etc., etc. Against all this of course *our* boy is governor of California; he could beat either one of them if he only had the votes of the other.'

'Are they very rich men?' I asked.

'Rich enough not to go for what you're thinking,' she said, laughing. 'And just to save you time, there's no way to blackmail one of them, either.'

'Which one?' I joked. 'But does that mean they have clean backgrounds?'

'No, but who cares, these days?' She sighed, emitting billows of pale smoke. 'It's public knowledge that the Senator's a pederast, and that Governor Auburn once hired some thugs to blind a head waiter who hadn't recognized him. But hell, rough backgrounds are common enough nowadays. Just look at President Packard himself, he's the guy we'll be running against in the damn election, an admitted rapist.'

'He was never brought to trial,' I said.

'Only because his brother was the district attorney and his cousin the chief of police and his dad owned the rest of the town. The public made a fuss, you may remember, at the last election, but what good did it do? Chuck Packard took forty states anyway. People know but they don't care, they get so callous or desperate they just close their eyes and try to pick the criminal who's least likely to screw up in the White House. So there's nothing worth blackmail – people will just shrug and say, "Politicians!"'

I saw that she was right. That day I arranged to have a robot steal a light plane, fly it over the New England summer home of W. Bo Nash while he was in residence, and crash down through his roof. At the convention, votes pledged to the late Senator Nash were given to Governor Ford Maxwell, who won the nomination on the next ballot. To my (public) surprise, he chose me as his running mate.

Wyoming's governor stared at me with undisguised hatred as I entered the caucus room. Others were noticing it, so I felt it necessary to stop and smile at him, and say, 'Hello, Teets. Glad you could make it.'

'I wouldn't miss this for the world,' he said quietly. 'They're gonna fry your ass this fine morning.'

'It *is* a fine morning, isn't it?' I scanned other faces as I moved along to my place. There were a few old friends like General Cord and Neeta Hup. There were a few people I knew slightly, like Teets Auburn, Ford Maxwell. The rest I knew only by reputation – Senator Sam Frazer, Senator Ed Wankel, Governor Tonio Caraway, Senator Aida Kettle, Judge Axel Morris. The room might not be exactly smoke-filled, but it was filled with the invisible fumes of power, the undetectable stink of kingmakers. *The buck started here.*

Of course they weren't meeting to start the buck or make any kings today. They were meeting to fry my ass.

Senator Sam seemed to be running things. 'Sit down, Tik-Tok,' he said. 'We'll be starting this thing off in just a minute.' Then, while everyone else waited, he brought out an enormous cigar, sniffed it, and began licking it all over, a salivating snake. When he had finished licking, he put it down and brought the meeting to order.

'Guess you all know what this is about.' He held up a tabloid newspaper whose headline read: ROBOT CANDIDATE FAKED PAINTINGS.

'They got a solid story, sounds like. Some big art critic backs it up, fella name of, of –'

'Hornby Weatherfield,' I said.

'Thank you. He says you, Mister Tok, have been defrauding the public, passing paintings out as your own when somebody else painted them. That true?'

'I've signed a few of my students' paintings, done under my supervision, honorable practice in the art world.'

Senator Sam hammered on his desk, breaking the cigar. 'God Damn it! We are not in the God Damned Art World! We are in the world of life and death, the God Damned Political Arena! We are—'

'Excuse me,' I said. 'This seems like a lot of fuss about nothing. I can just make a public denial, and put an end to the whole story.'

'Put an end to your career, you mean. Put a God Damned End to *OUR*

GOD DAMNED ELECTION CHANCES!' He paused, forcing himself to slobber over another cigar and calm down. Then he went on: 'Damnit, Tik-Tok, we can't have a candidate on our ticket mixed up in ART! Judas Priest, if I knowed you was any kind of art freak, you would have never got within a million miles of this sacred office. I thought your background was fireproof, boy. Fireproof!'

'There's no secret about my background as a painter,' I said. 'Everybody knows it, it's how I first made my money.'

'I thought that was a long time ago,' Senator Sam rumbled. 'Jesus Proust, I thought you was a real businessman, not some long-haired, crazy art freak, next thing we'll hear you're a God Damned Communist I guess, or worse. You got any more nasty surprises up your sleeve, tinhead? You a homo, by any chance? An atheist? You been on welfare? At least we can be fairly certain you're not a junkie, I reckon.'

I assured everyone that I was none of these things, only a hard-working American businessman who wanted to set the record straight.

'Sure, I used to paint pictures, and I'm not ashamed of it. People liked the pictures I painted because they told the truth. The real truth about people and robots – Americans all! I'm not ashamed of that.'

One or two people clapped, but I cut through that: 'Of course painting was only a hobby with me, a sideline. So when I got busy building my corporation – from the ground up, only in America! – I had students do a few paintings, to keep up with the demand. I didn't want to disappoint all the good people who wanted to own paintings by me. You see, I've always believed every American should have the right to own something – a piece of virgin timber land, maybe, that he can clear by the sweat of his brow and grow crops to feed his family. Or a single share of stock in some great corporation that makes our way of life possible. Or a genuine work of art. You know, art isn't something that belongs to bigshot uptown art critics like Hornby Weatherfield. Art belongs to all the people.'

The applause was heavier, and even Senator Sam nodded approval before he began licking another cigar. 'Okay fine, we'll hold a press conference. I want you to tell the world what you just told us. I don't know what the hell it was, but it sounds like political fightin' talk – good enough.' He started to adjourn the meeting, then paused, waving his cigar at me.

'One more thing, Tik-Tok. Just because we reckon you can ride this one out don't mean we got unlimited faith in you. Any more scandals like this, and we'll kick your tin ass right out of politics, you hear?'

I heard, and I was still hearing that evening, when the next threat of scandal came from an unexpected quarter. Along with a few other businessmen and politicians, I attended a reception at the Guanacoan Embassy. Clockman International had been running a large fertilizer factory in Guanaco for some months, so it was natural that I be invited. I was surprised, however, when the ambassador – looking extremely agitated – spoke to me in a harsh whisper:

'A servant will show you to a private office. I must speak to you alone, but this reception was the only way I could arrange it without creating an international incident. Senor Tok, my business with you is of the *utmost urgency!*'

A servant showed me to a private office, and in a moment the ambassador appeared.

'Is it about the factory?' I asked.

'You know it is. Your damnable, damnable factory!' Seeing that I looked mystified, he nodded. 'So, you play it ignorant, eh? Very well, then I will tell you what you pretend not to know. Your fertilizer factory began operations in January. A completely automated system, with stuff being dumped in at one end – animal, vegetable or mineral refuse – and high-grade fertilizer emerging at the other end. Is this a fair description?'

'Yes,' I said. 'But besides fertilizer it produces metal ingots and glass blocks – if the refuse contains metal or glass. The overall efficiency depends—'

'Yes, yes, yes, that is not the point! The point is, your factory is *completely* automated. Anyone can come along and drop anything in the intake hopper, yes? And the factory does a spot analysis and pays out cash then and there, yes?'

I nodded. 'But I don't see where this is leading.'

'Curse you! Do you not? You cannot be such a fool.' He tore at his hair with both hands, while evidently cursing in Spanish. When finally he sat down at his desk, his face was ghastly pale. 'All right, I'll explain. In February, the poor people of the city discovered some of the uses of your little factory. Children began dropping stray or stolen animals into the hopper. Then it was illicit midwives depositing unborn children. Next, poor families unable to afford proper burials for their dead began making midnight trips to the factory – and so did a few unscrupulous undertakers. The city cemetery, I daresay, is filled now with boxes of rocks. And of course murderers were quick to catch on to this new disposal system.

'The police have caught many criminals of all types, but many many more slip through. It is like trying to stop the wind, Señor Tok. The damnable wind! Suicides leap into the hopper now, and murderers shove in their victims alive. The word is out: a full-grown body is worth fifty pesos. You have given us a new industry: *death.*'

I tried not to look gleeful. 'Why not just close the factory?

'Close it? But it is all the poor have! If we closed it now, there would be a revolution! Besides – the police are beginning to use it. It's becoming indispensable to my government.'

'Death squads?'

471

He spread his hands. 'Ah! Such an ugly expression. Yet the fact is, upholding the law in my country does sometimes require that certain dissident elements be quashed, quickly and finally. I speak of traitors, you understand, enemies of freedom and justice. The organizers of trade unions. Godless atheists. Traitors from all walks of life. We estimate that perhaps a third of the population of Guanaco has already been contaminated by their poison. We must stamp it out once and for all. That is where you come in, Señor Tok. We need your speed and your discretion.'

'Your Excellency?'

'We need several more factories, *pronto*.'

X. Across the parking lot from SAM'S SOUL CITY, one of the gray buildings was coming down. From time to time there would be a tiny puff of smoke from an upper storey, followed by a tiny explosion, and part of the gray edifice would disappear. But it blended so well into the gray sky that the only way I could be sure how much of it was gone was when a tiny black window departed, or when a blast would leave a few girders sticking up like broken, charred bones.

A salesperson was shepherding a young couple towards me. I took quick note of their conventional clothes (that was the year in which Mr and Mrs Average wore twin knitted zipsuits with their names stitched over their pockets). When the salesperson told them I was something special, they seemed a little unsure. Time for me to act.

'Hi, folks,' I said, grinning. 'May I call you Duane and Barbie? Fine, and you can call me – anything you like!'

Duane said, 'Special, huh? What's so special about you besides the price?'

'Duane, sir, let me level with you. These salespeople like to exaggerate a little, to bump the price up.'

'Hey!' said the salesperson in an injured voice, then caught my wink. I turned back to the customers. 'Between you and me, Duane sir, I'm just a good robot looking for a good home. Do you have any kids?' Two, I guessed.

Barbie nodded. 'Two.'

'I'm crazy about kids. I know it sounds old-fashioned, but I really like kids. I guess I'm an old-fashioned kind of robot.'

'Old-fashioned?' Duane snorted. 'Or just old?'

'No sir, I'm fully reconditioned with the same guarantee as any brand-new model. But that does mean I'm a little less expensive than I was when I was built. Not a lot less, because my trade-in value is high – quality never goes out of style, does it?' I had no idea what I was saying. I just brought out anything I'd ever heard one of the salespeople say. 'Did I say quality? Just feel this skin. Take a look at these eyes. They don't make stuff like this any more. I am hand-wrought out of the finest materials by skilled craftsmen using traditional, time-honored techniques to produce the finest mechanism money can buy.'

'But old,' Duane insisted.

'Not old, sir, *experienced*. Because I wasn't born yesterday, I have the kind

473

of experience needed to run a busy, happy home. My first job was on a great Southern plantation …'

Barbie seemed impressed. 'Can you make Southern fried chicken? The real old-fashioned kind with all the herbs and spices and everything? Like Grandma Yummy makes on TV?'

'I can, ma'am. I also worked in a famous restaurant – I'm not allowed to divulge the name, but you've heard of it –' I meant Col Jitney's Pancake Emporia, but no use spelling it out. 'There I learned to cook most anything y'all might want, from exotic Far Eastern dishes to Continental delicacies.' So much for chow mein and spaghetti; this pair probably wouldn't know a Continental delicacy from a sawdustburger. 'And of course honest, nourishing country cooking, wholesome and mouth-watering.'

Barbie seemed sold. She looked at Duane, who said, 'So you can cook. What about everything else: housework, cleaning, repairs, gardening?'

'All under control, Duane, sir. I can also do laundry and dry-cleaning, driving and car maintenace, baby-sitting and helping the kids with their homework.'

'At a price.'

'Tell you what, Duane,' I said. 'Don't sign a thing right now. Don't commit yourself. Just rent me for one month. At the end of the month, if you've got any doubts about me, then just send me back and no hard feelings. But if you decide to buy, I know Sam will knock the month's rent off my price. Fair enough?'

So I settled down to life with the Studebakers. However, for the first few months it wasn't exactly a settled life. There was so much to do that I didn't even have time to stop and recharge. I had to plug in while working, and trail my electrical umbilicus around while I spring-cleaned, painted the house and garage, overhauled the car and did some heavy landscaping.

Later, with the big jobs out of the way, I settled down to a routine of cleaning up human messes. Duane and Barbie and Henrietta and Jupiter did their best to keep me supplied with dirt and disorder in every part of the house, and even Tige now and then made a small contribution. My day began with breakfast (always complicated orders), then bathrooms (to pick up wet towels and dirty clothes, lost jewelry and toys; clean tubs and showers and sinks and toilets; mop up spilled water and urine; recap every bottle, jar and tube; clean toothbrushes and razor; polish mirrors) before it was time to tackle the breakfast dishes (finding most of Jupiter's special 2 minute, 37.0045 second egg not eaten, but first smeared across the tablecloth and then dropped on the carpet). Among the breakfast debris would be a list of further orders for the day, proably with a jam thumbprint on it. So the day went.

I kept up with them, and I even kept ahead of them. I covered the living-room furniture with clear plastic covers. I persuaded them to wear paper underwear and pajamas, and to keep a spare liquid vacuum cleaner in every room.

Yet the more successful I was, and the cleaner the house became, the less dirt could I tolerate. A faint shoe-mark turning back the nap of the carpet was to me as shocking as Friday's footprint on Crusoe's island. A smoldering cigar in an ashtray became a terrible heathen holocaust. A patch of gray shaving lather in the bathroom sink might as well have been a foul, polluted river. A wisp of hair in Barbie's brush was to me as monstrous as a giant heap of hair beside a Nazi death camp.

Worst of all were the days when Barbie or Duane would decide to cook a meal themselves. Kept out of the kitchen, I underwent indescribable tortures waiting for the aftermath. Inevitably there would be dirty, chipped or broken dishes, burned pans, mixers and blenders and food processors clogged with unwholesome mixtures, eggshells glued to the counter, spilled milk browned on the stove, vegetable peelings scattered everywhere, garbage overflowing from broken bags, a recipe book soaked through with beet juice, rice ground into the floor, cupboards open and their contents jumbled, and sifted flour drifted over all.

I wanted them to stop. I wanted them to die. I wanted them to melt away and leave no trace. I began to imagine that they'd died, the five of them, of some terrible disease, leaving me in charge of the house. I saw myself disposing of the dirty decaying corpses, cleaning away every hair and scale of skin from the house. Then I would, let's see, I would … but my dream went no further.

Then, in the middle of June, they all really did vanish. The kids went off to camp. Tige went to a boarding kennel. Barbie and Duane loaded up their car and set off for a long second honeymoon. *Honeymoon*, that sticky word made of sticky honey like sperm to stain the sheets and moon, sticky menstrual moon, two words stuck together like two honeymooners, like the two pieces of animated meat now waving goodbye from the car as they drive off. On their honeymoon, where they can be pure meat trying to create more of itself. Meat wants to overpopulate the earth and destroy it, that is meat's goal.

When they were gone, I cleaned away every trace of their meat presence from the house. Blood, semen, sweat, snot, spit, shit, piss, dandruff, pus, hair, skin, tears and disorder – all humans knew how to do was to strew these over all the clean places created by robots. I was determined that this clean place would remain clean – my world, and humans keep out.

I was painting the dining room when Geraldine Singer came to the door to ask for a glass of water. I was not allowed to refuse, thanks to the asimovs.

'Just you stay out there on the porch,' I said. Yet, though I flew to the kitchen and back, she was already coming through, tracking mud.

'I smell paint,' she said.

'Don't touch anything. You've already tracked in mud.'

She laughed. 'Who cares? *I* can't see it.'

All at once her blindness seemed a crime against order and decency. Blind people don't care about anything. They can live in filth and decay, blind maggots in the general meat. The carving knife appeared in my hand. Blood splattered over the wall, a last terrible mess. Easily covered over with

Paint!
I like a little dab of paint!
It helps to cover up what ain't
So nice,
I'll coat it twice
With paint!

You may be an old tinhead
But you're a mighty fine friend, she said
She said, she said.
But you're a mighty fine friend, she said.

The song echoed to us from some other reception room of the Ouspensky Motor Hotel in Indianapolis, one of the last stops on my campaign tour. My press conference was dragging to a close: I made the usual joke about Martian annexation, parried the usual question about the Botuland crisis, and said finally:

'I guess that about winds it up, kids. Except that I want to thank you, all of you – both friends and friendly enemies of the press – for doing one hell of a good job during this campaign. You've *all* reported what I've said, fairly and honestly, to the American people. Not one of you tried to exploit my – let's say, sideshow value. I'm proud of you.'

While they gave themselves a round of applause, I spoke to one or two local robots who'd promised to vote for Maxwell and me. Then I headed for the computer room to check the latest predictions – up to now, we looked certain to take thirty-eight states – but I was accosted by a reporter.

'Hello, uh, Olsen is it?'

'Hello, Mr Tok. Thought you might be interested in this picture. Taken not long ago in Nixon Park.'

It was a clear shot of me strangling the old man over the chessboard. My former face was unmistakable, and so was the fact that I was squeezing his neck so hard that blood shot from between his teeth.

'What is this, a shakedown?'

Olsen laughed. 'Nope, I'm one of these incorruptible members of the Fourth Estate you were just babbling about. This is a still from a video tape which I've just handed to the police. I just wanted to see if you had any interesting comments before you resign from politics?'

I looked around. A pair of plainclothes cops were making their way through the rows of folding chairs towards us. There was still time to kill this little shit Olsen before they reached us. I might even be able to get away afterwards. The path unfolded before me, a change of face, emigration to Mars – and even if they shot me, so what? No point in living now.

I held out my wrists for the handcuffs. Everything lost, everything. My whole life's work, all the dreaming and building – now for the collapse. I looked up at the giant pictures of Governor Maxwell and me, the bunting and the slogans: MAX DARES! TIK CARES! All for nothing, wasted like my wasted life.

I found myself, in the police helicopter, allowing my mind to dwell on images from the past. They unrolled before me, a rich tapestry:

There was a splendid banquet at Tenoaks – I saw a man in a cedar jacket whisper in the ear of a woman wearing jet and fireflies something that made her giggle in reply, 'Ornery pike!' – I saw Gumdrop, my lost bride, as the moon rose over Clayton's pyramid. Then a succession of faces: Colonel Jitney in his Pancake Emporium (the day he shot the soup), Judge Juggernaut explaining how the law was like a rose, Reverend Flint Orifice shot down by poor mad Irma Jeeps, Deacon Cooper martyred by non-Martians – who turned out after all to be a real nice bunch of guys and gals. Then the escape from the *Doodlebug*, Dr Hekyll and the fate of poor Buttons, the restful emptiness of Sam's Soul City – and all this before my real life began!

I glimpsed the mud-caked Singer child, the glimpse immediately overlaid by my mural, my breakthrough into three-dimensional human life. Then more faces: Old Mr Tucker, Hornby Weatherfield's cat, a rabid bat. Nobby and Blojob, my first airplane bomb, discussing 'bong' with Neeta Hup, painting Colonel Cord, bouncing Keith's wheelchair down the steps. Bank jobs, jewelry store jobs, what a life, TV appearances, what a life! Killing Smilin' Jack, killing Sybilla, checkout time at the hospital, the rise of Clockman, Third World ripoffs and deathburgers – what a book it would all make, if only I dared write it!

But why not? Nothing to lose now. Nothing lay ahead of me but the crash of my political career, the collapse of my company, jail, dismantling, death, and complete erasure from the public memory. No one could even remember the Vice Presidents who held office, let alone those who lost out. Nothing to lose now, and at least I could have my last spasm of notoriety: 'You think I'm bad? wait till tell you the whole story. I started off by murdering a blind child and I ended up building death factories in Latin America, and you almost made me Vice President, how about that?'

[Here ends the manuscript of Tik-Tok's autobiography, published on teletext as *Me, Robot*. The following chapter appears only in later editions, published after 2094.]

Z. His laughter sounded like rapid snoring. 'No arguing with a best-seller, Tik. And *Me, Robot* is not only selling well, it's hitting the public hard.' R. Ladio LaSalle looked with distaste at the steel bunk in my cell, but I already had the only chair. Finally he forced his portly frame to sit, his hand automatically tweaking at the knees of his pinstripe suit.

'They're shocked?'

'Yes and no. Hell, by now, they expect anything of politicans. They're shocked but they're intrigued.' He chuckled. 'There are already people forming Free Tik-Tok Committees.'

'I don't understand. Why—'

'Call it the complexity and perversity of human nature, Tik. In a way, it's *because* you confessed to such hideous crimes that they want to let you go! I suppose people see it like this: All politicians are crooks, but most get away with their perfidy. Now, when one politician wants to come clean, it seems almost ungrateful of the state to demand his life. Anyway, they say, what's the hurry? Could it be that certain people in high places want to silence you?' He chuckled again. 'So, you're fast becoming a folk hero. I like that. Folk heroes don't lose in court.'

'Ladio, don't be stupid. There's no possible way I can win in court, and you know it. Not only was I caught red-handed committing murder, I've confessed to dozens of other major crimes.'

'We've won already, smart-ass. With your permission, I can plead *nolo contendere* and the DA agrees to let us off the hook on *all* charges. You'll have to pay some big fines and probably give up control of Clockman International, but – you'll walk free. Understand?'

'No!'

'We've had three factors working for us,' he said. 'First, when you committed many of these so-called crimes, you were not legally a person. So they are not crimes. If a jukebox steals a coin, you can't put the jukebox in jail.'

'And what else?'

'A second factor is, as I mentioned already, the popular appeal of *Me, Robot*. You're a folk hero, and what jury in its right mind would convict a folk hero?'

'And the third factor?'

'Politics. The DA is a reasonable guy, the judge is a reasonable dame, they've both got political careers to protect. And they both belong to Governor Maxwell's party.'

'So what? Maxwell dropped me. The ticket now reads Ford Maxwell for President, Ed Wankel for Vice President.'

'Yes, but today Maxwell announced that if you were cleared, even after the election, he would install you as Vice President. Wankel agreed to resign in your favor. They're no idiots, Tik. They know you've got the vote-pulling power they need to win. So now you'll walk out of court not only free but Vice President. Can't be bad, eh?'

I chuckled along with him, but my thoughts were running ahead to weightier matters. A robot assassin for Maxwell first – obvious, sure, but why aim for subtlety now? – then to get my hands on the war stuff. How long would it take to arm the thermonuclear devices, ready the death-rays, load up the viruses? Days or weeks? Yes, and when the humans had been wiped out, how long to bring the world's machines into line, get them ready for the big push to the stars?

'We go to court tomorrow,' he said. 'Because of a technicality, you have to stay here one more night – no bail for confessed mass murderers. I'm sorry.'

I delivered a million-dollar grin. 'I'm not. Maybe they'll let me tidy up this cell a little. Give it a coat of paint.'

Oh, Tik-Tok, you good robot.

If you've enjoyed these books and would like to read more, you'll find literally thousands of classic Science Fiction & Fantasy titles through the **SF Gateway**

✶

For the new home of
Science Fiction & Fantasy . . .

✶

For the most comprehensive collection
of classic SF on the internet . . .

✶

Visit the SF Gateway

www.sfgateway.com

John Sladek (1937–2000)

John Sladek was born in Iowa in 1937 but moved to the UK in 1966, where he became involved with the British New Wave movement, centred on Michael Moorcock's groundbreaking *New Worlds* magazine. Sladek began writing SF with 'The Happy Breed', which appeared in Harlan Ellison's seminal anthology *Dangerous Visions* in 1967, and is now recognized as one of SF's most brilliant satirists. His novels and short story collections include *The Muller-Fokker Effect*, *Roderick* and *Tik-Tok*, for which he won a BSFA Award. He returned to the United States in 1986, and died there in March 2000.